0706 8 ill 85

Also from Futura by Alan Stratton:

THE EMPIRE BUILDERS
THE HUNTERS
THE PEDDLERS

ALAN STRATTON

THE LADY

Futura

A Futura Book

ISBN 0 7088 3158 3

Reproduced, printed and bound in Great Britain by
Hazell Watson & Viney Limited,
Member of the BPCC Group,
Aylesbury, Bucks

Futura Publications
A Division of
Macdonald & Co (Publishers) Ltd.
Greater London House
Hampstead Road
London NW1 7QX
A BPCC plc Company

PART ONE

The time before

1936-1937

1

The parade must have been over two miles long. Gina had been watching for fifteen minutes and still she couldn't see the end of the column of marching children where it wound up the sweeping rise of Via Veneto to disappear around the curve. Her eyes searched the ranks of faces; but none returned her gaze. Despite the noon heat of the July sun the youngsters, all boys between eight and fourteen, stoically kept their chins up and their eyes fixed as the bravura tattoo of their boots beat up a cloud of dust which filmed their grey shorts, black shirts, blue neckerchiefs and tasselled black caps.

Stepping from the kerb Gina peered into the oncoming troop, and her face lit with pleasure as she recognized the figure for which she'd been waiting. 'Hey, Filipo!' she yelled above the din of the stamping feet, and waved exuberantly at the small boy in the marchers' midst.

The child didn't respond, but Gina continued to shout and gesticulate knowing her eight-year-old brother would hear her, glimpse her, take strength from the affection she threw to him.

She waited until Filipo had passed before turning from the spectacle to slip away through the sparse crowd. Few people watching today. But, then, the citizens of Rome had seen it all before; countless times before. For as many of her twenty years as she could remember, Gina had been surrounded by constant marches, pageants and festivals. And once, like everyone else, she had loved them. But that was a long time ago – before cheering became compulsory.

As she hurried along Via Ludovisi she frowned briefly at the vexation of this latest dictate from a nonsensical list which included women being banned from wearing trousers and men being forbidden to use a handshake as a form of greeting. 'Our whole way of eating, dressing, waking and sleeping, all our everyday habits will be changed,' the Leader had declared.

'The hell they will!' Gina's father had riposted, with an anger that was echoed throughout Italy. Yet few of the voices dared dissent through open doors, and those that did were never heard again.

Several clocks struck the quarter hour and Gina quickened her pace through the narrow streets. She was late, customers would be arriving, her father would need her. At the summit of the Spanish Steps she called, 'Hi, fellers!' to the trinket-sellers and laughed good-naturedly at their cheerful risqué replies as she rattled down the wide stone cataract, her thick mane of tawny golden hair flouncing on the shoulders of her white blouse, blue skirt swishing around her long, tanned legs.

Strangers turned to the tall, striking figure. Few would have thought her Italian from her height and colouring, though her strong, finely-sculpted features and wide, upcurving lips echoed the Roman half of her ancestry. And while her aura of self-confidence and vivacity would have identified her, wrongly, as a woman of the New World, there was a dark depth in her eyes, a restrained sensuality which was unmistakably Latin.

From the bottom of the steps she dodged crowds and traffic across the square and into Via Condotti. Ristorante Rossi stood midway on the thronged street. Gina pushed the half-glass door and entered.

The restaurant was long and narrow with ornate but old gilt wall lamps and rich but faded frescoes. The patina of two centuries glowed on the leathered side booths which once had vied with the nearby Caffè Greco for the patronage of Gogol, Goethe, Chopin, Byron and Stendhal. A few feet inside Gina was confronted by a huge man in a red wool shirt and, despite the heat, a sleeveless sheepskin jerkin. His magnificent moustachios bristled with pleasure as he hailed, 'Greetings, Principessa.' Max Barzini, Tuscan, patriot, inveterate card-player, and Gina's godfather, was helping out during this hectic tourist season as part-time cashier. Before Max gleamed an equally outsize brass and mahogany cash register which he played like a Mighty Wurlitzer whenever customers presented their bills. The machine was fronted by a hand-printed card declaring, 'We wish all our friends luck.' This sentiment was sincere, but the sign's true purpose was to mask the words 'NCR Made in USA', for, though the majority of the clientele would have welcomed with open hands a supply of Coca Cola or Lucky Strikes, it wouldn't have been wise to advertise publicly the use of anything non-Italian.

Gina returned a warm, 'It's good to see you, Max,' to the beaming giant and headed between the booths and two bustling waiters. Lunch was already under way and the place was filling with working men, businessmen and a few soldiers. All but the latter called friendly greetings as Gina passed.

The man who came through the rear door was of medium height. His dark velvet jacket and green silk bow tie were comfortably rumpled and worn with casual elegance. His silver hair was thick from a straight brow above features which were handsome though their once-carved lines had been softened by fifty-eight years. In spite of his age however the humour of his brown eyes and sensitivity of his full mouth were unmistakably mirrored in the face of his daughter.

Gina kissed him and grinned, 'Coffee, Poppa? How many cups is that today? I hope the Leader's spies aren't watching from across the street.'

'Bah!' exclaimed Alfredo Rossi as he raised the cup he was carrying. 'Drink less coffee. Another of the man's ridiculous edicts. Probably because his pal Adolf has told him it isn't Aryan.' Inhaling the vapour from the black liquid he sighed appreciatively. 'Anyhow, this is worth getting arrested for. The real thing. Not that *surrogato* poison made from burnt peanuts.' To the question in Gina's eyes as she caught the aroma Alfredo Rossi answered, 'From the Foreign Press Club.' Smiling he added, 'Yes. Fallon's back.'

Gina gasped with delight and her questions came tumbling out. When? Where? How did he look? What did he say? Was he staying?

'Take it easy, young lady.' Her father held up his hand against the barrage. 'Fallon was only here a moment. He had to get to the Press Ministry. News about Mussolini's meeting with Hitler. The setting up of something called the Rome-Berlin Axis. Little Benny has pretensions to be joint ruler of Europe.'

Gina's pleasure at the English Reuters correspondent's return faded abruptly and she glanced anxiously toward the customers, warning, 'Be careful, Poppa. You know how dangerous it is to use such nicknames for the Leader. His secret police are everywhere. You might end up in court. Be fined. Or worse, have the restaurant confiscated.' Forcing a smile in an attempt to add some levity and detour the conversation from what was truly a dangerous route, she joked, 'Then where would I get a job?'

Setting aside his coffee Alfredo Rossi reached out and gently gripped his daughter's shoulders. Sadness had veiled his eyes but his voice was firm. 'I've told you, you must forget about working here. The time is fast approaching when you must leave Italy. And take Paola and Filipo with you. Soon. Before it is too late.'

'But, Poppa,' Gina protested, 'you've listened to our customers, to people in the street. They don't want war. They're sick of war. Most of them are sick of a leader who has led them into one conflict after another for the past sixteen years. They won't follow him further. There'll be a revolution. Uncle Max is sure of it.'

'Max is an old storm-horse. Full of snorting and stamping. But it will take more than battle-cries to get Italians running to the barricades.' Alfredo Rossi sighed and his arms sagged. He said quietly, as if to himself, 'How in God's name did we allow it to go so far?' For a long moment he stared unseeing down the crowded room, then, shaking off the distress, he declared, 'Work to do. Come along, miss. Our customers need feeding.' Extracting his order pad from his jacket he stepped away; but, pausing, he looked back and said reassuringly, 'Don't worry. Everything will be fine. I promise.' He turned briskly toward the nearest booth of expectant lunchers.

Gina watched, and, for now, the shadows retreated. Donning a navy apron from a peg on the wall, she followed her father.

They worked ceaselessly for two hours while the restaurant turmoiled with men, women, some children, amid a thickening atmosphere heavy with the aroma of tobacco, wine and olive oil. Above the heat a pair of soughing ceiling fans laboured in vain, and only the Tuscan giant at the cash register remained unfilmed by swea. ๑" ก.s stool by the freque.๒t'y openɪɪ.g door.

But this was the period of the day Gina loved. Pleasure spurred her as she dashed back and forth with armloads of dishes and a head full of orders. Satisfaction filled her as she memorized with practised ease the sequence of customer arrivals, intuitively recognized those who were in a hurry, those who didn't wish to be rushed, the ones who would eat heartily and leave a good tip, the ones who were as stingy with their stomachs as they were with the waiters. She fielded requests and demands, complaints and compliments, traded news and gossip, jokes and the occasional insult. And through it all she smiled. 'Remember,' her father had tutored. 'Always. Smile. When you're throwing a bad-tempered client out of the door, smile.' Since Gina was first permitted at nine years old to wait on table during the mid-morning lull, she had followed the advice; confronted with the most refractory diners she had kept her smile stitched in place. As she did now; though when the fray quietened her enjoyment slid away with the departing customers, and she strove to counterfeit her good humour for the last lingerers.

Wiping the wooden tables she recalled the brief exchange with her father. It had been a reprise of the discussion which lately had invaded all their conversations, smothering brighter but frailer subjects like a persistent weed. Yet it wasn't newly seeded. Gina now knew that it had always lain beneath the surface; she had merely been too young, too contented, too protected to notice. But then, until five years ago she had been blind to so many things – including the true face behind the glistering façade of her beloved Rome.

To Gina, born in 1916, five years before the Blackshirts' take-over of Parliament, Fascism was a way of life. Amid the pomp and gaiety manufactured in the capital for the benefit of foreign tourists and journalists by the Ministry of Popular Culture, it was difficult to believe in the brutalities rumoured to take place in the suburbs and country towns. Shielded from anti-Government talk by her father and Uncle Max who understood the danger in a youngster's innocent gossip, Gina had led a normal, happy youth, developing from a bright, attractive child into a beautiful teenager with her mother's disarmingly open face and flashing eyes, and her father's generosity and easy laughter.

Throughout her formative years she had been particularly close to Alfredo Rossi, sharing his love of life and literature, eagerly absorbing all he taught about running the business; and following her mother's death the father-daughter bond had strengthened into a deep and understanding friendship. The two worked together, relaxed together. Most of all, they planned together. During the heat of the afternoon when the restaurant was closed they sat on the tiny, third-storey balcony

11

looking across tangled ochre roofs towards the sun-reflecting ruins of a Rome that was two thousand years past, and they planned the future. By the time Gina reached twenty-one there would be enough money saved to open a second Ristorante Rossi where the tourists flocked beyond those distant ruins. Later they would add a third eating house, among the swish set's favourite watering holes in Piazza Navona. Eventually their family name would be gilt-lettered above the entrances of restaurants in Naples, Florence, Milan.

The infinite finances and details of these schemes filled Gina's every waking moment. Then at night the possible realities were supplanted by incredible dreams as the Rossi empire took root across Europe, and, the greatest triumph of all, blossomed in her mother's legendary birthplace – America. And Gina had believed she could attain the goal. As she partnered her father's hopes her horizon had been clear.

The clouds began to gather the afternoon of her fifteenth birthday.

She had been returning from school. In brilliant sunlight on the busy street the two soldiers had beaten the man's body with their Manganello clubs until he crumpled to the cobbles like a broken marionette. Passers-by hurried on. But Gina stood frozen while the soldiers dragged their victim upright and rammed a bottle between his lips. She cried out as the man vomited the force-fed liquid and she recognized the stink of turpentine. A lifetime's illusions were shattered in the moment and she fled homeward to spend the remainder of the afternoon huddled on her bed in a fever of fear and confusion.

It was a day before she was able to recount the incident to her father. It was six months before she learned to live with the truth. But by then she also had come to realize that her witnessing of the so-called 'baptism' of the anti-Fascist had unshackled Alfredo Rossi from a torment of indecision: having rarely discussed politics in front of his daughter, now he could talk freely about the realities of their country's regime and how it had been before the rise of Mussolini. The sympathy between the two gained a new strength; and while Gina once more took the day in her stride, her cheerfulness was tempered by a growing maturity. The arrival of Fallon in her life added a further dimension, and she faced the future with optimism and resolve. Her ambitions were again clearly defined.

They had remained so until this spring when the restaurant's

12

after-hours debates between Alfredo Rossi, Fallon and Max Barzini began to turn with increasing frequency to speculation of war. As the Englishman brought news omitted from Government-censored Italian media, Gina's father and uncle grew daily more troubled. And during the afternoons, sitting with Gina on the balcony, Alfredo no longer indulged their fantasies; his laughter became shorter, his brooding silences longer, and when he talked of an uncertain future it was with a co-mingling of sadness and anger. A month ago he had broached the subject of Gina, her sister and brother leaving the country, had suggested they should sail for America. During the last week there had been added urgency in his words.

It had left Gina feeling beleaguered. All her life she had respected and obeyed her father. But she also had been raised in a society whose members were profoundly aware of belonging to a family. To desert her father was inconceivable. America was a dream, and dreams, she told herself, were for the very young.

Now, the frenetic lunch period over, Max and the waiters had left. As Gina came out of the kitchen, the restaurant was empty except for an obese man in a too-tight linen jacket talking to her father. She shuddered with distaste when she recognized the lardy face with its obsequious smile.

Gina had disliked Ugo Balbo since she was a child. In those days he frequented the restaurant, and others in the fashionable districts, attempting to insinuate himself into the business and social community, currying favour, always with an eye for the main chance. He had styled himself an hotelier, a title derived from his ownership of a seedy saloon with three bedrooms in an alley off the Porta Portese flea market. His customers were the low life from both sides of the criminal tracks, and his income was boosted by the titbits of information he gleaned and sold and bartered amid this clientele. And his profits were fat. By the time Gina had reached her teens Balbo's saloon had spawned half-a-dozen offspring, each larger and more garish than its predecessor; and Balbo had graduated from catering to the lower ranks of Rome's underworld to hosting exclusive entertainments for the upper echelons of the law as well as the lawless. Respectable business folks still shunned him, but they dare not ignore him: over the years, in this capital where bribery and corruption had become common currency. Balbo had bought himself the locations of the skeletons in a thousand closets, and, word was, these days he had not only a grip on a fistful of city councillors but also carried a clutch of Government officials in his back pocket. He was a man to treat with caution.

As he spoke to Alfredo Rossi, Balbo's several chins strained over his sweaty collar and he mopped his bald skull with a grubby handkerchief. His voice was as soapy as his expression. 'But it is a very good offer. I'm being most generous. Especially for these unstable times. I hope you will reconsider. You could be making a mistake. A serious mistake.'

Alfredo Rossi was tight-lipped as he replied, 'I've given you my answer. And it's final.' He opened the door and issued the gross man out to the street.

Gina had halted midway down the restaurant. She watched her father close the door, turn and walk towards her. And beyond his shoulders she saw Balbo's smile dissolve as he stared at Alfredo Rossi's back with eyes that were as cold and as hard as washed pebbles. Momentarily an inexplicable thread of fear tightened on her heart, but it was gone as abruptly as the man, and her father was standing before her saying, 'Damned snake-in-the-grass! If he comes around one more time I'll wring his oily neck.'

'The usual offer?' asked Gina.

'A few thousand more than last time. Still ridiculous, though he talks as if he's doing me a favour. And even if I was thinking of selling out, it wouldn't be to that bloated crook. Not in a million years. I'd rather set fire to the place than see it turned into a chrome-plated hangout for his cronies.' Alfredo exhaled angrily. 'I know. You've heard it all before. Ever since Balbo first started waving his cheque book. I'm sorry. I shouldn't let the lout fire my temper that way.' His annoyance held a moment longer than he quelled it with a faint smile.

Gina said gently, 'No need to apologize. I understand. The man makes my hackles rise too. But there's nothing to worry about. He can't force you to sell. And when he eventually gets fed up with being turned down he'll clear off to pester some other unfortunate restaurant owner.' She reached for her father's hand, squeezed it, then declared brightly, 'So, I still haven't had time for a cup of that fantastic real coffee. Come on, let's be utterly corrupt and make a whole fresh potful.' She tugged him toward the counter.

14

The front door rattled open.

Filipo rushed in. The tassel of his black cap bouncing, he ran the length of the restaurant to clasp his sister's waist, then pulling away greeted, 'Hello, Poppa.'

Alfredo reached for him. 'Hey! Don't I get a hug?' But Filipo hurried around the counter answering, 'Cohort Leader Carnera says touching isn't manly. Isn't Italian.' As his father and Gina exchanged concerned glances the youngster went on, 'We marched all the way from Villa Borghese to Constantine's Arch. I never missed a step. Didn't feel tired. Truly.'

'That's fine, Filipo,' his father said tightly.

Filipo, pouring himself a glass of milk from a jug beneath the counter, asked innocently, 'Poppa, is it true that the Leader is the Voice of God? Cohort Leader Carnera said so.'

Alfredo caught his breath and the colour sped from his cheeks. Before Gina could intervene he snapped, 'No, it is not true. And don't let me ever hear you repeat such a thing.'

Filipo's small face broke from its usual cheeriness and he glanced anxiously between his father and sister.

Alfredo ordered, 'Now go upstairs and take off that damned uniform.'

Filipo hesitated only a moment, then, his lower lip beginning to tremble, he set down his milk and hurried for the rear doorway. As his footfalls diminished along the hall Alfredo Rossi clasped the edge of the counter with both hands, breathing hard, gripping until his knuckles turned white. 'This mad Fascist idolatry,' he said bitterly. 'Poisoning a child's mind.' He inhaled deeply, his chest shuddering with anger. When he at last turned to his daughter his face was scarred by sadness, his voice hoarse. 'I shouldn't have spoken to Filipo so harshly. He doesn't understand.'

'He'll get over it,' assured Gina. 'He's a resilient little chap.' She prompted, 'Hey, how about that cup of coffee? Why don't you get it started while I talk to Filipo? I'll tell him you'll be up later.'

Filipo was sitting on the edge of his bed in the room he shared with one Bible picture of the Madonna and umpteen magazine portraits of foreign movie stars. His shiny black curls were tumbled forward, accentuating the dejection of his slumped shoulders. Misery was etched on his cheeks.

Gina sat beside him, put her arm around him.

Turning to her he snuffled, 'I'm sorry. I didn't mean any

harm. It's just that . . . Oh, Gina, I'm so . . . mixed up. Why does Poppa think Cohort Leader Carnera is so bad? Is it wrong to want to be manly, to become a good Italian? The headmaster as school says . . . '

'Shh.' Gina stroked his hair off his brow. How could she explain to a small boy the difference between propaganda and truth? She sighed, feeling so helpless, impotent to translate her concern for her brother into the answers he desperately needed for the questions crowding his life. She said gently, 'Remember only one thing. Your Poppa is the wisest man in the world. Whatever others may tell you, never forget what he has taught. Though don't argue with Cohort Leader Carnera. Just listen and keep silent and always think about Poppa's words. Sometimes you'll be confused. But one day you'll understand. I promise. Trust me.' She kissed his cheek.

For a while Filipo stared perplexedly. Then wiping the back of his hand beneath his eyes he said, 'I love you, Gina.'

She swallowed hard, gathering him to her chest, fought back the sudden swell of tears, held him until her emotions subsided. At last releasing him, donning her brightest face she said, 'Shall I tell you about Momma in New York?' And his features glowed. It was his favourite treat. Gina, though herself a voracious consumer of everything from her father's library of leather-bound Greek classics to her mother's dog-eared collection of Edgar Rice Burroughs, rarely told Filipo fairy stories. Since he had been old enough to sit up and take notice she had related the tales which never ceased to light his imagination, just as they had illuminated her own childhood – the adventures and misadventures of their mother, Doris Strunksy, who in the decade following her fourteenth birthday had high-kicked her way from the travelling tent shows of America's south-west to the stages of Manhattan's Broadway.

Alfredo Rossi had been thirty-three when he met Doris. He wasn't rich but was able to afford comfortably the trip to America, the first holiday he had taken in the three years since he inherited the running of the family business following his father's death. It was a week after he arrived in New York that he managed to obtain a ticket for *La Belle Paree*, the opening show at the city's new Winter Garden theatre. From his seat in the stalls Alfredo was stunned by the extravaganza; but neither Jolson nor the other feature players captivated his attention more than the long-legged blonde of the chorus, and after her front spot solo routine in the second act wild horses couldn't have kept him from his vigil at the stage door.

Years later Gina would ask her mother, 'Why did you choose Poppa from all the other men waiting that night?' To which her mother would reply, 'I don't know. But sometimes, once in a lifetime maybe, something passes between a man and a woman. And they know, they just know, they will be right together. One day you'll understand.'

Doris and Alfredo were married in Rome's Trinità dei Monti on June 1st, 1912, and from that day Doris never again set foot on a stage. All her energies were devoted to her husband, their business and their daughters – Gina, and Paola, six years younger.

Gina recalled her mother as an elegant, laughing woman, always striding, never merely walking, vibrant, rarely resting, sitting only to eat or perch her girls on her knee to regale them with exciting tales of her life as a dancer in the U.S.A.

Thus the sisters grew up knowing almost as much about the country three thousand miles away as they did about their homeland. They also matured into being bilingual, for while Doris's Italian always remained sketchy, Alfredo's English was excellent. ('A skill,' he'd smile waggishly at his wife, 'acquired while serving our American and English visitors who expect the entire world to address them in their own language or not at all.') As the daughters shared their parents' native tongues, so they inherited their generosity and love of life. Gina however was more of her mother – decisive, vivacious, inches taller than her schoolmates, and with a tumult of blonde hair which was the wonder of all who met her. Paola, on the other hand, was her father's child – sensitive though tenacious, dark-complexioned, wearing her raven hair plaited and pinned in a coil on the back of her head. What the sisters had in common was a natural beauty, the wellspring of which was their mother's smile.

Gina would never forget the smile; a lighting of Doris's face which seemed to cause a glow amongst all around her. It was the last image Gina had of her mother, the way she had smiled that day when Gina, twelve years old, had been ushered into the hushed bedroom, treading so quietly because everyone had said she must not disturb the new baby. But she knew that wasn't the true reason. Over the past nine months she had begun to understand the whispers about Doris's age, the medical reasons for the long delays between the children's births. Even so, as she entered the room she wasn't prepared for the unfamiliarity of her mother's face; her skin was waxen, her lips translucent, even her eyes had faded. Only her hair, scattered like gold on the pillow, retained the vibrancy which was the essence of the woman.

Gina glanced at her father standing beside the cot of his new-born son, his features crumpled by grief. She stepped to the bed, lifted her mother's hand, felt the last dregs of strength leaking from it. She was overwhelmed by helplessness, felt there must be something she could do; where the doctor's ministrations had failed surely her vast love could succeed. But as her eyes burned with tears she knew that the truth was in the agony of her father's face.

Swiftly she bent and kissed her mother's mouth, and jolted involuntarily at the coldness. As she dropped the limp wrist she felt Max Barzini's big hands on her shoulders. She allowed herself to be led to the door. Then she turned and looked a final time at the woman who had lighted all her years. And she saw the smile, a faint glimmer of the brilliance that once had been, yet Gina knew all that was behind it, understood the massive effort that had willed it to appear.

Max led her from the room, and at last her defences tumbled, her grief flowed as she buried her face against his chest.

It was later when, above the closed restaurant, all the apartment's windows had been shuttered, Gina sat with Max at the kitchen table and he said softly, 'You must think of Paola and Filipo. You must be more than their sister now.'

Eight years on, beside her brother on the bed, she ended her tale of Doris Strunsky on Broadway, saying, 'That's enough for today. I have to go help Poppa with the account books.'

'Aw, Sis,' Filipo groaned in English.

'Don't call me Sis,' Gina chided good-naturedly. It was his latest Americanism, picked up from one of the innumerable Hollywood movies banned by the Government but regularly invading the country via divers routes to be viewed with clandestine avidity by a populace sick of the Fascist-approved Italian productions supposed to enrich minds as well as the native film industry but which, reduced to pap by the Censor's Office, were capable of neither. Gina wasn't sure how Filipo found his way into the private screenings, though she had a shrewd suspicion that when he and Fallon exchanged knowing nods and eye signals it was on behalf of more than the British and American comics (also banned) which the Reuters correspondent received in his London press pouch. She said, 'How about you change out of this uniform now?' adding the clincher for his returning happiness, 'Then you can come down and have a cup of real coffee.'

'Can I?' His eyes popped. 'Wow!' And he leaped from the bed, cried, 'Shazam!' and attacked the buttons of his shirt.

Gina went out of the room. But as she walked along the hall the smile she had shared with her brother faded, and a strange feeling of disquiet shadowed her down the stairs.

2

Since she entered her teens Gina had had her share of suitors – maybe more than her share – all handsome boys who plied her with love tokens, led her on endless walks amid the magnolias and ilex trees of the Borghese Gardens (marvelling that her father allowed her out without a chaperon), constantly related their sporting and romantic prowess, and took every opportunity to remove their shirts and display their hard, young bodies. And Gina loved this time, revelled in this age of growing and learning, developing from a striking child into a beautiful young woman, heading toward adulthood with ease and cheerfulness, without conceit or pretensions yet always enjoying the effect she could wreak on the opposite sex, good-naturedly bewitching her beaux during her waking hours while captivating them with more explicit magic in her unbridled dreams. She loved them all. Yet she was in love with none of them. She was unable to imagine herself ever falling into that groggy-eyed daze that caused her girlfriends to moon around as if they'd lost their senses. She couldn't believe there was any man capable of captivating her so completely, able to send her self-control sailing out the window.

That was before she met Robert Fallon.

He had walked into her life a couple of months after she

turned seventeen. He sat with three other men in one of the restaurant's side booths and talked animatedly about the disarmament conference in Geneva, the international economic assembly in London, and the widening rift between left and right in the two-year-old Spanish Republic.

Gina had never heard such a loudly concerned Englishman. Heated debates were a way of life among Romans (news-papers, magazines and books were rare in most homes, 'Not,' Alfredo Rossi once had pointed out, 'because Italians are illit-erate, but because they'd rather discuss life than read about it.') Other Europeans too gave public vent to their emotions. But the British Gina had encountered were always so reserved. And neat. At ninety degrees in the middle of St Peter's Square, male and female appeared as spit-and-polished as children on their first day of school. Unlike the expressive newcomer.

In battered brown tweed jacket, baggy green corduroy trousers and open-necked navy blue shirt, with a notepad protruding from a side pocket, pipe and pens sprouting from the chest, he looked like Gina's idea of Mark Twain. She guessed he was in his thirties. He had a squarish face and a solid jaw, a look of hard strength emanating from the broad cheekbones beneath impenetrable grey eyes with which he occasionally scanned the restaurant to examine people causing them to glance away as if he were trying to stare them out. He wasn't classically handsome and maybe his ears were too big (his brown hair falling in all directions was certainly too long), but when at last he turned and looked directly at Gina she tumbled head over heels in love with him.

She was convinced it wasn't infatuation – that happened only to immature teenagers and she was a sophisticated adult – it was love all right, that indefinable something her mother had said she felt when she first met Gina's father. The only problem was, in Gina's case the traffic was all one-way. Robert Fallon (among the foreign correspondents he was called simply Fallon, which Gina wrote upon a piece of paper and carried in her purse) didn't seem even to be aware that she possessed female features (some of which, though she did say so herself, were very noticeable indeed); during the entire three years of their acquaintanceship the only time he had touched her was when he took her arm to cross the street.

As he did now negotiating the frenetic evening traffic around Aurelius's Column in Piazza Colonna. Once having attained the safety of the narrow sidewalk however, he returned his left hand to its customary position in his trouser pocket while the right tapped his pipe against his teeth.

This latter implement - a knotty, black briar affair - Gina never had seen lit; though at the early, whimsical stage of her romancing she'd imagined he secretly puffed opium through it while working on his novel. 'Every journalist in the world is working on a novel,' he had said. 'But ninety-nine per cent of them are either too slothful, too drunk, or too busy keeping body and soul together to ever finish. Which am I? The original Idle Jack.' Gina doubted this. Since Fallon had introduced himself on that first visit to the restaurant she hadn't known a day when he wasn't researching some project. As well as his regular Reuters reports he churned out countless features for any newspaper or magazine that would run them. 'Trouble is,' he observed, 'the citizens of Ipswich, Nebraska don't give a hoot if some Italian proconsul is indiscriminately massacring prisoners in Majorca; the good folk of St Malls, Cornwall think that half a million murdered Abyssinians are no concern of theirs. When they all eventually wake up it will be too late.'

Happily, this evening his mood wasn't so gloomy. It was a month since the day of Filipo's march. Rome was bursting at the seams with pilgrims and vacationers. Ristorante Rossi was hard pressed to cope with the deluge of customers. This was Gina's first free time for a week; she had spent it at Fallon's apartment with one of his holidaying pals who ran a small London hotel, and a female correspondent from New York's *Associated Press*. Lubricated by a couple of litres of *verduzzo* the conversation had slipped from its customary politics to more frivolous matters and Gina had been delighted by the hotelier's hilarious stories of catering to the English middle class, and the newspaperwoman's glamorous tales of partying with Manhattan's beau monde.

Gina remained pleasurably intoxicated by the wine and gossip as Fallon now walked her home. Beside him she had a powerful urge to lay her head on his shoulder. Damn it, why could he always make her feel this way? During the past three years as he marched in and out of her life - going off for weeks at a time to file his bloodied reports from Abyssinia, Greece, Spain - while her emotion for him had ripened from besotted yearning to a deeper, mature affection, there were still times when his nearness filled her stomach with a million whirling butterflies.

Her present enchantment was interrupted when they passed the entrance to a courtyard where a small crowd was dancing, singing and laughing around a young woman garlanded with blue poppies. The house behind them was likewise decked with gentians and cornflowers and blue ribbons. Pausing to watch, Gina said, 'A boy child born.'

Fallon examined his pipe. 'Lot of fuss.'

'You know how important it is for Italian families to have a son. How special for a woman.' She fondly observed the celebration, said quietly, 'It must be wonderful.'

'I thought you wanted to be a restaurateur.'

'Of course. But that doesn't mean I can't be a wife and mother as well. Just as soon as somebody asks me.' The statement came spontaneously, but as it hung on the air Gina blushed to her toes. In all the time she had known Fallon she had never revealed her feelings toward him. She'd often wished she was one of those emancipated American movie ladies who growled at their favourites, 'Come up and see me sometime,' but, for all her outward assuredness, her instincts were innately Italian; a girl might flirt outrageously with a male if their ardour was mutual, but to express her attraction to a man before he had declared his interest was unthinkable. She murmured, 'He'll turn up some day, I suppose.'

Fallon stared at her. His eyes travelled her face, flickered across her figure.

Did they? Or was it her imagination? Had he for a fleeting instant been looking at her as a woman? The experience was past in the blink of an eye, leaving Gina feeling disconcertingly unsure and unbalanced. But she couldn't let the moment pass, she had to know, had to make her bid here and now. Levelly holding his gaze, she began, 'Fallon . . . '

The cry cracked along the street: 'Gina!'

She swung around. Her sister was running across the traffic. Of all the times to choose! Gina muttered a vexed oath at her blighted hopes, rummaged hurriedly for an excuse to scoot Paola on her way. But then she saw the approaching fourteen-year-old more clearly; the tail of her usually perfect plait was swinging loose, a lock of hair was plastered to her sweaty brow, her features were blotched and her eyes bloodshot, as she ran forward she was snatching ragged gulps of air. Alarm pierced

22

Gina. 'What on earth's the matter?' she called.

Paola halted, panting, 'Gina . . . thank goodness . . . I looked . . . and looked . . .' Her voice was broken by more than breathlessness and Gina now saw the wet smudges of anguish on her cheeks as Paola choked, 'I went to Fallon's. I couldn't . . . couldn't find you . . . Oh, Gina . . . It's Poppa.' Tears burst forth and her control splintered, 'He's been arrested.'

A shroud of silence fell on the street. Gina could see her sister's chest heaving but she was as deaf to the youngster's distress as she was to the joy of the celebrations in the blue-beribboned house. The paralysis lasted several moments. Then she was running. Oblivious to vehicles and pedestrians, reck-less of her own safety she barged through the astonishment and indignation of the night crowds, raced down alleys and across tiny squares, fear pursuing her like a demon, until only the sudden lancing stitch in her side was able to halt the headlong flight, cause her to double over clutching her ribs.

When at last the pain subsided, Fallon and Paola had reached her. The Englishman gripped Gina's arm. There were no words between them, but they went on together.

Via Condotti was as thronged as the rest of the city, and it wasn't until they were within a few yards of Ristorante Rossi that they saw the two Blackshirt troopers, one hammering a sign to the window frame, the second standing across the entrance, a rifle with fixed bayonet cradled in his arms.

Gina's heart was suddenly leaden, and when she looked at Fallon the knowledge she read on his face intensified her dread. She hurried through the knot of curious onlookers causing the trooper in the doorway to swing toward her, his rifle jumping to his shoulder. The second Blackshirt, dropping his hand to his hip holster commanded, 'Halt!' Gina numbly obeyed and in response to his curt, 'Papers,' fumbled in her purse for her identity card. As the man examined the document then turned his attention to Paola and Fallon, Gina stared at the door's smashed lock and broken glass, beside it the nailed sign: CLOSED BY GOVERNMENT ORDER. But it was the scene inside the building which shattered her caution, sent her pushing past the trooper to dash into the restaurant.

Beyond a booth where a grey-suited man glanced up from interrogating three terrified-looking waiters, Max Barzini was leaning against the counter dabbing a bloody cloth at the pulped flesh of his cheek. 'Principessa!' he exclaimed, endeavouring to conceal the wound with his big hand as Gina ran and reached toward his face. 'I'm all right. Your father too. He was taken but not harmed.' Pulling her to his chest he held her close, clumsily stroking her hair as Fallon and Paola advanced along the aisle.

Clinging to Max, Gina fought the turmoil of her emotions. There was so much within her; a multitude of questions, and answers she dare not contemplate. A wave of dizziness swept her and she remembered the wine she had drunk at Fallon's apartment. Where was Fallon? She couldn't recall seeing him since they stood outside a courtyard where a boy child had been born; the time between was a blank. Panic raced upon her, but in that instant her head cleared and the fearfulness of the situation glared starkly real; yet, as she felt Max Barzini's arm round her, heard Fallon's reassurances to Paola, Gina sensed a kernel of strength beginning to form. She held it, gathered it to herself until she was as calm in her acceptance of the inevitable as she had been that day eight years ago listening to the priest intoning, *'in nomine patris et filii et spiritus sancti . . . '* while she whispered goodbye to her mother for the last time. Now, stepping back from the big man she asked dispassionately, 'Where is Filipo?'

Surprise at her tone registered on Fallon's and Max's faces before the Tuscan answered, 'He's safe with Cousin Letti. He wasn't here when . . . '

'Fine. I'll go to him later.' Gina turned to her sister, wiped the youngster's tear-streaked face with her handkerchief. 'Are you all right? Of course you are. There's nothing to worry about. I'm going to see Poppa. I want you to stay with Uncle Max and take care of your brother.' She kissed Paola's cheek, briefly held her then strode down the restaurant to the staring grey-suited interrogator. She demanded stonily, 'Where have they taken my father?'

Villa Fiorito was thus named for the imitation blooms which garlanded every pillar, wall and ceiling. It had been built early in the seventeenth century by a cardinal for a secret lover; unable to walk openly with his mistress in any of the city's glades, he had instructed masons and artists to create a garden from plaster and paint. Legend had it that when, as an old man, the cardinal confessed, Pope Alexander VII visited the villa and was so bewitched by its beauty that he instantly forgave the transgressor's sin. Thereafter it was said the house was enchanted and that couples holding hands beneath the atrium's camellia-wreathed portico would be forever lovers. For three hundred years the villa's promise was as treasured as the blessing of the Trevi Fountain.

In May 1933 Rome's gaols could no longer contain the ever-increasing number of detainees awaiting examination by the Special Tribunals personally set up by The Leader to prosecute those he labelled 'insidious intellectuals'. The Government began commandeering properties to serve as holding centres. Among them was Villa Fiorito.

Gina stood beside Fallon in a beautiful but empty room which was a bower of Carracci roses. A sign on the wall warned, VISITORS MUST STAND ONE METRE FROM THE LINE; this referred to the yellow band crudely painted across the marble floor. She caught her breath as her father was led in by a trooper. As far as she could see he was unharmed.

Striding purposefully to the line Alfredo breathed, 'Thank God you're all right. Paola and Filipo, are they safe? And Max? That crazy man, he tried to prevent them taking me. They hit him with a rifle butt.'

'Everyone's fine,' assured Gina. She reached out, and as her father's hand automatically responded the guard's Manganello club flicked at their touching fingers. Gina's anger flared but her father's grim frown and brief headshake stilled her protest, and the smirking guard slouched back, his stance almost negligent save for the black heavy wooden cudgel swinging threateningly at his side. Gina was reminded of her encounter five years ago with the street 'baptism' of the anti-Fascist. She fought to contain her anguish as she asked her father, 'Did they hurt you?' and knew instinctively that his quiet 'No,' was an untruth.

'Alfredo,' interjected Fallon. 'Why did they arrest you? Have you been charged?'

'Not yet,' replied the restaurant owner. 'But the troopers who came for me were bleating their usual hysterical nonsense. Called me a Communist, an enemy of the state. Even accused me of trafficking in pornography. They took away copies of Maupassant, Jack London and *Life* magazine.' He smiled bitterly. 'However, there isn't time to discuss politics. I don't know how long they'll hold me here, or when you'll be permitted another visit. So, Gina, listen to me. And please, don't interrupt. I've never commanded you to do anything in your life, but I have to order you now. Take your sister and brother and get out of Italy. Even when I'm released from here there'll be a bleak future for us in Rome under the present regime. Besides, I can no longer bear to see my children being corrupted in this land. Fallon, you know the friends who will help, please ask them on my behalf.'

'Don't worry, I'll personally see the youngsters to safety,' responded the Englishman. 'In the meantime, I'll contact your lawyer, have him protest immediately against your detention. And I'll see what I can stir up with the foreign press. We'll have you back home in no time.'

The guard laughed, and it was the most chilling sound Gina had ever heard. Her head was spinning again. Everything had happened so fast. Less than two hours ago she'd been partying with Fallon and their friends, playing at life in her ivory tower. Now it seemed she had been catapulted into another dimension. She clung to the core of strength that had formed within her at the restaurant, organized her resolve, determined not to let Alfredo see her desolation.

The guard rapped, 'Time.'

'Damn it!' protested Fallon. 'Another minute.'

The guard brandished his Manganello, his eyes at once challenging and contemptuous.

Alfredo said, 'It's all right, Fallon. Thank you for coming. Gina, please try to explain to Paola and Filipo. I'm sorry you have to . . . ' He was cut off as the guard seized his arm and pushed him toward the door. He threw a look back at Gina, holding her gaze as he was hustled out of sight.

Gina felt an almost physical agony, as if a part of her had been torn away. What in God's name had her family done to deserve this? She wanted suddenly to lash out at something or somebody, not only to inflict pain in retaliation against the savage wrong that was being done, but also to hurt herself, for she felt she was somehow responsible, that since she was fifteen she had known what was happening in her country but had chosen to veil the truth, had not permitted the shadows to darken her carefree and elegant lifestyle. She shuddered, was hardly aware that Fallon had taken her hand, walked her out beneath the camellia-adorned portico and along the evening street. When she eventually came to her senses she looked around to discover they were in Via Barberini. There were youngsters laughing and shouting as they cavorted precariously on the low wall around the Trevi Fountain; tourists wandering in their summer clothes, chattering in English, German, French as they tossed wishful coins into the water; two tonsured monks smiling indulgently as they strolled amid the noisy goings-on. Gina breathed raggedly, 'Fallon, please take me home.'

The restaurant was eerily quiet, shuttered for the first time on a weekday night since Alfredo Rossi's great-grandfather had founded the business.

Gina had parted quickly from Fallon, grateful for his caring but also for his understanding of her deep need to be alone. She lay on her bed and stared at the bright stars through the window, the same stars that had shone there all her life. She listened to the familiar sounds of the still-busy street, all the intimate activity which had been the background to her dreams for twenty years. She breathed the scent of the room – ancient timber, lavender, the herbs and wines of the kitchen below – the fragrance of her nights since the day she was born. And in the darkness, as the clock on the mantle ticked away the hours, these were the sensations which finally lulled her to fitful sleep, these and the touch of tears which slowly coursed across her cheeks.

Throughout the following days Gina gathered the fragments of her shattered life. She was thankful for the nearness of Fallon, Max Barzini and their many friends, but she increasingly had a sense of isolation, felt that she alone was shouldering the adversity which had beset her family.

The morning after Alfredo's arrest she walked with her sister and brother along the Tiber, sat on the grass beside the summer-shallow river and told the youngsters that a terrible mistake had been made, that their father would soon be home. Every day thereafter she visited Villa Fiorito, but always was refused admission, was told access to detainees was not permitted until after their appearance before the Special Tribunal. All her requests for the date of the hearing, her pleas to send Alfredo food, books, even fresh clothes, her enquiries about his health were ignored. She had contacted her father's long-time friend and lawyer Cesare Fermi, but although he at once went to work on the case, his applications to the courts for information also were repelled. His reassurances to Gina were, she realized after a fortnight of futile effort, as well-intentioned but as empty as her own false optimism with which she sought to encourage Paola and Filipo.

Still she refused to abandon hope. When Fallon brought news of the progress he'd made toward obtaining false emigration documents, she thanked him but wouldn't be drawn into discussing further the prospect of leaving the country. Alone in the shuttered restaurant the plans she formulated as she daily reviewed her worsening financial situation, were for the future of the whole Rossi family; she never could accept that this would not include her father.

It was four weeks after the arrest, with early September sunlight warm across the kitchen table where Gina was studying the account books, when she was interrupted by unfamiliar footfalls across the courtyard. A shadow filled the open doorway and she squinted to distinguish the man who had entered: sweat-patched linen suit tight over his belly, the fleshy folds of his neck overlapping his collar. Ugo Balbo waddled forward wearing the same soapy expression Gina had seen two months ago when the devious hotelier had been here offering to buy Ristorante Rossi. She shuddered with distaste as she rose and said with cool courtesy, 'Signor Balbo. What can I do for you?'

'My dear.' The gross man effused intimacy, seized her hands, pulled them to his red lips. 'Such news. Such dreadful news. I was away on business when I heard, but returned as soon as I was able. Alfredo, your father, was a good friend. We'd known each other so many years. Brothers, you might say, in our noble trade, since you were a child.' His face was varnished with a transparent smile. Pulling out a soiled handkerchief he mopped his bald head, glanced toward the water carafe. 'So hot today.'

Ignoring the hint, Gina remained standing.

Annoyance flickered behind Balbo's eyes but his obsequious mask held firm as he continued, 'If there is anything I can do, my dear girl, don't hesitate to let me know. Help with your affairs, assurances to your suppliers, administration of your accounts. Consider me at your disposal. In the meantime I shall appeal to the highest authorities. I am not without influence, you understand. I know your father is completely innocent of these malicious charges, and I shall do everything in my power to secure his release.' Stuffing his handkerchief into his chest pocket he wrung his pudgy hands. 'Of course, one must speak with the right people, have the best advisers acting on one's behalf. And this, I am afraid, costs money. A good deal of money. But, then, what is a few thousand lire for the well-being of a colleague? I will expend whatever is necessary to help my old friend, and return him to his family.'

Suppressing the temptation to tell the odious creature he was the last person in the world from whom she would accept help, Gina replied levelly, 'That won't be necessary. We have a lawyer. Signor Fermi is most capable. And we can afford his fees.'

'Certainly you can, dear girl. But every little helps, does it not? And besides,' Balbo's eyes narrowed, 'it isn't wise to turn aside a good deed. Nor polite. I'm sure your mother taught you that, didn't she?'

Gina's hackles rose. The mere mention of her mother in this man's mouth seemed obscene. Her self-control fracturing, she retorted, 'I'm extremely busy, Signor Balbo. I'd be grateful if you left now.'

The fat man's smile was immovable. 'I understand. The strain you are under. So much on your mind. So much to do. Your brother and sister to care for. Your home to look after. And, of course, the business. A great responsibility for one so young. But, you see, that is the reason I am here.' He delved his inside pocket to extract a folded sheaf of papers. 'Before your father's . . . present trouble . . . he and I had been engaged in negotiations. We were on the brink of finalizing our transaction. I don't suppose he told you, wouldn't confide complicated business matters to his children, but the fact is for some time he'd been prompting me to purchase Ristorante Rossi.' Seeing the shock leap to Gina's face, Balbo hurried on, 'I understand your surprise. However, you're an intelligent girl, you must try to comprehend your father's motives. He was – and he would be the first to admit it – no longer a young man. The pressures of commerce were beginning to weigh on him. And he was mindful of his family's future. A substantial cash sum would mean security for you all. That was the reason he came to me. As you know, my business interests are far-reaching. Expanding. Highly profitable. Alfredo felt he could best serve his restaurant by ensuring that it joined my organization, was placed in my care as it were.'

Gina seethed with indignation. The man took her to be a complete fool. Before she could retaliate, however, he was brandishing the sheaf of papers saying:

'The documents were drawn up some time ago. Alfredo was to have signed this week. If it hadn't been for these unfortunate circumstances . . . ' He shook his head with mock grief. 'But all is not lost. Although your father is being held incommunicado, his lawyer can act on his behalf. If you, my dear, take him the papers, assure him of Alfredo's acceptance of my offer – and you will see from the figures I am not being ungenerous – then the contract can be signed, sealed, delivered within the week. And all your problems will be over.' Condescension was moulded onto the man's loam face as he extended the document.

But, standing firm, Gina suddenly was aware that his confidence had faltered. He was searching her eyes, struggling to comprehend what he found there. And as she saw his hesitation she was fired by a sense of reckless triumph, was goaded to strike out, to retaliate against everything Balbo represented. All the desperate anger which had tortured her these past weeks was now concentrated on the man. The last image she had of her father being bullied toward his cell reared across her mind, and unable to contain her grief she shouted, 'Get out of our home!'

Balbo jolted, almost dropping his contract. His smile fled as his jowls trembled with shock. 'My child,' he blustered. 'You don't know what you're saying. You're upset. Distraught. I understand.' He reached out. 'But you must be calm. Rational. Listen, dear girl . . . '

'Don't touch me.' Gina's voice was a hiss. 'You leech! You lying crook! My father wouldn't sell his business to you if you were the last man on earth. He despises you. And all your kind.' Her despair flooded forth. 'You aren't fit to stand on the same street as him, let alone call yourself a colleague. Your whore-houses and gambling dens are cancers in our city. You and your stinking Government cronies have turned Rome into a cesspit. You and the pig who calls himself our Leader . . . '

'Gina!' Robert Fallon strode across the room. Seizing her arm he pressed her down onto a chair. His voice was knife-edged as he turned on the fat man. 'Signor Balbo, please leave. Miss Rossi is in no condition to receive visitors.' Glancing at the contract which Balbo still clutched before him he added,

'Whatever matters of business you have to discuss must await Alfredo Rossi's return.'

Balbo's cheeks had become ashen during Gina's assault, and all vestige of his previous *bonhomie* was gone when he snarled, 'Return? Traitors don't return.' He swung to Gina. 'I gave you your chance. You've thrown it away. And you'll be sorry, young woman. You'll rue the day . . .'

'Get out!' ordered Fallon.

The fat man's face quivered, then with a parting venomous glare he lumbered out through the doorway.

Gina stared at Fallon and the breath went out of her. As the Englishman sat beside her holding her hands on the tabletop, she whispered brokenly, 'Do you think . . . ? What he said about traitors . . . Might it be so?'

'Of course not. He was trying to frighten you into submission. Everything will be all right. Just have faith and patience.' Fallon smiled. It was the smile that once had set Gina's pulse racing, filled her head with romantic visions. Now such fancies were dead. As she looked at Fallon's rugged features, his compelling grey eyes, she consciously tried to recapture the emotion she had felt toward him every day for three years. But she could not: though she told herself her love for him was as deep as ever, she was unable to bring it to the surface, was incapable of feeling anything save the hopelessness which had been growing within her since that fateful night two months ago. She said bleakly, 'I'm glad you came. Thank you.'

Fallon again assured her of the future. Later he accompanied her when she visited Paola and Filipo at their cousin's house. He laughed with the youngsters, entertained them with tales of London and New York. In the evening he took Gina and Max to a press party at the Grand Hotel. When he walked her home and stood in the entrance while she unlocked the door, Gina briefly considered inviting him upstairs, was gripped by a harsh need to be in his strong arms, to lie with him, hold close to him until all her terrors faded. She said, 'Goodnight, Fallon.'

He answered, 'I'll see you tomorrow.'

There were so many tomorrows.

As the year dwindled, the city emptied of tourists. Gina scarcely noticed. The shell she had erected around herself

31

became ever more impervious to the outside world. She didn't know whether the days or the nights were worse: during the day she could at least keep busy, though these were the hours when she most ached awaiting news from Signor Fermi; each night she lay staring at the darkness, planning the family's future, until toward dawn she fell into semi-consciousness taunted by a voice which retorted, What future? Christmas came and went despairingly. What deeply pained her was to see the pleasure on the faces of her sister and brother. Nowadays they asked less frequently about their father. How long, she wondered, before they completely ceased to think of him? The year turned, and she found herself having to concentrate to recall his face. They won't keep him for ever, she repeated over and over. There is still justice. We will be together again. I shall see him soon.

She saw him in March.

When Signor Fermi brought the date of the hearing Gina's heart soared. But her joy was short-lived as he explained the forthcoming proceedings. Witnesses would be called on behalf of the prosecution, but none would be permitted for the defence. Alfredo Rossi would not be allowed to speak: a statement on his behalf would be read in court by Signor Fermi. Gina couldn't believe it. The attorney said helplessly, 'It's what has become of the law in our country.'

A week later they went to the courthouse.

Fallon stood with them in the vast marble lobby amid hordes of lawyers, police, judges, detainees' families. He held Gina's hands, squeezed them as if willing strength into her. Signor Fermi already had explained that the Englishman must remain here; only one family member would be admitted to the hearing. Also he warned Gina against speaking. 'Not a word. No matter how you feel. Any interruptions will go against Alfredo.'

Gina held to Fallon a moment more, before following the lawyer down a long, teeming corridor.

She had assumed they were entering the main Hall of Justice; the door however opened into a small antechamber, a stark room with one high window across which a metal grille had been fixed, its new-bright metal in hard contrast to the dingy once-cream walls. The only people present were three men sitting behind a scarred wooden table, unremarkable men in grey suits, their sole insignia of authority the Party badges in their lapels. A fourth man, cadaverous in a black jacket, stood beside a desk holding an open file.

None of the quartet gave Gina more than a cursory glance as she sat on one of the dozen straight-back chairs ranged in front of the table. She felt Signor Fermi's hand on her shoulder where he positioned himself at her side. She had promised herself she would be acute to everything which happened here today, yet now her mind seemed numbed, her only awareness was of the chill which clung to the room, and she physically jolted when the standing man suddenly rapped, 'Examination ninety-two. Alfredo Rossi.'

A corner door instantly swung open, a Blackshirt trooper stamped in, followed by two more flanking Gina's father.

Gina's throat burned as the heartrending impulse to cry 'Poppa' welled within her, and she jammed her knuckles to her teeth, bit down hard to prevent the type of outburst the lawyer had warned against. Then, pulling her hand from her mouth she met Alfredo's gaze and gave him a smile which contained the very essence of her soul. But her father did not respond. His eyes flickered briefly across his daughter's face, then he dropped his gaze to his handcuffed wrists. He looked, Gina thought despairingly, not merely haggard, but shrunken some-how, his clothes hanging more wretchedly on him than they had six months ago, his once-splendid silver hair, roughly cut during his incarceration, too long and straggly now around his emaciated face.

'Charges,' snapped the standing man, flicking through his file. 'Sedition. Revolutionary activity. Housing corrupt litera-ture. Treachery to the Fatherland. Banditry. Conspiracy. Bribery. Defilement of the name of the Leader.

Gina's breath was sucked away as the monstrosity of the declaration slashed her like physical blows, and only the tight-ening of Signor Fermi's grip on her shoulder prevented her from crying in retaliation.

The man at the centre of the table triumvirate demanded, 'Are the charges refuted?'

'Yes, sir,' Signor Fermi answered. 'My client, the defendant Alfredo Rossi, refutes all charges submitted here. He further begs the Special Judges' indulgence in presenting a statement of denial.' The lawyer paused, then read from a yellow sheet of paper: 'I, Alfredo Rossi, do hereby solemnly affirm on oath before this Tribunal that the accusations made against me are wholly unfounded and that I am innocent of all crimes against the State. I am not a Communist. I am not a Socialist. I have never been a member of the Communist or Socialist Parties. I do not uphold the views of any enemies of the Fatherland. I do not support the actions of any subversions within the Fatherland. I have always upheld the Italian law. I have always upheld the will of the Leader. I have always . . .'

Gina was no longer hearing the catalogue of submission. She shut her ears to the self-abasement of the man who had instilled in her the necessity for personal pride in one's own beliefs. Now she could not look at her father, dared not meet his gaze. She scanned the others in the room: the troopers, staring boredly at the blank wall; the skeletal man who had read the charges, leafing disinterestedly through his file; the three judges, examining documents on their table. And she realized with mounting horror the sham that was taking place here. This wasn't a court of law, this was a show, a speaking of parts by players who knew the ending before they began. Even Signor Fermi was an actor in the deception; he had known all along how it would be; he had placated her with false promises; filled her with useless hope.

She felt a scream rising within her, like a huge bird trying to tear itself from her chest, and the pain was so real she was sure her heart would literally burst. Until this moment she had not realized that her previous existence had come to an end. During the direst moments since her father's arrest she had never conceived that an entire way of life, a family, all its joys, its plans, its loves could be snuffed out in an instant. Now the truth fell on her with absolute finality. And it crushed her. She thought its weight would kill her. She could not see, hear or speak. She couldn't even think.

It was long minutes before the voice penetrated the recesses of her brain: 'Sworn statements on behalf of the prosecution?'

'Yes, sir,' affirmed the cadaverous man. 'Witnesses to all the charges.' He began to read from a list.

The string of names burned Gina back to her senses. Yet they too were part of the nightmare. She recognized none of them, was certain her father was likewise ignorant. But, as the man closed his file, she understood that protest would be useless. The room was silent now and she could hear the hum of the surrounding building. How many more chambers like this? How many innocent men and women being tormented? How many lives hanging in the balance on this sunny spring day? She felt Signor Fermi's hand urging her to rise. The man at the centre of the table was speaking.

' . . . have been accused of heinous crimes against the State, our Leader, the very fabric of Italian democracy. Having heard the evidence of respected witnesses, this Tribunal's verdict is unanimous. The penalty for treason is execution by firing squad.'

Ice filled Gina's veins and her legs began to shake. She clutched at the lawyer for support.

'Alfredo Rossi,' intoned the judge, 'in your case we are prepared to accept your plea for clemency. Your sentence is hereby commuted. In recompense for your crime, all your property will be confiscated. And, until such time as the court decides you are a fit and proper citizen to return to society, you will be banished. Hearing closed.'

The guards seized Alfredo's arms, swung him around and frogmarched him out of the door.

Gina was stunned. She hadn't had a chance to snatch a parting glimpse of her father's face. The words of the sentence were ringing in her ears. Banished? Through a haze of nausea she struggled to remember what she knew of exile. 'It's a means of eliminating political opponents,' Fallon once had said, 'without too much fuss or expense. But it's also being used by crooked judges and their cronies to work off grudges or get rid of their own personal enemies. The decisions are absolute. There is no court of appeal. The victims are transported to some remote spot – a village or island – where they have to fend for themselves or perform menial labour. They aren't locked up but their location is secret, and so isolated that escape is virtually impossible – and futile, because there's nowhere for them to go. I've seen the effect of banishment. It's worse than solitary confinement.'

Now he said, 'We'll get Alfredo away. I promise.'

Gina had been led numbly from the courtroom. Fallon and Signor Fermi were facing her in the thronged corridor. She stared blankly at the Englishman as he continued, 'In the meantime, remember Paola and Filipo. They'll need you more than ever now.'

He went on, with the lawyer adding sympathetic assurances. But as Gina watched, their voices faded, became an incoherent drone. She was utterly incapable of concentration, as if her brain couldn't cope with the enormity of what had happened. Her life had ended, yet here life rushed on around her: so many people hurrying to and fro, faces hopeful, defeated, confused. They were the faces of crowds in the street below. Gina was sitting with her father on the balcony looking across the rooftops to the sun-bright ruins of ancient Rome; they were talking and laughing and planning, planning a future when the Rossi name would be gilt-lettered above the entrances of restaurants in Naples, Florence, Milan. But she wasn't happy. Why couldn't she capture the pleasure this gossip usually brought? She was filled with an overwhelming sadness. She turned to her father, but his features were indistinct. He was several yards away talking to another man. She knew that man. A judge. She'd seen him somewhere recently. And that wasn't Alfredo. That was . . .

Reality returned in the rush and din of the courthouse corridor, and Gina stared as the man who had passed sentence on her father shook hands with Ugo Balbo.

The gross hotelier glanced toward her.

And she was lacerated by his triumph. She understood everything. He held his spite on her for a long moment before he turned to shoulder his way through the crowd. But as Gina stared at his retreating back, something began to happen inside her. The agony receded. Distant thunder tolled in her head, rising to a roar, a mounting crescendo of hate. She could feel nothing, only the hate, and the acid of vengeance burning away all else. At that moment she knew she would survive; whatever happened she would survive to meet Balbo again. She was dedicated to survival – and destruction.

Somewhere a door banged shut. And as she walked away from that place, a door closed in Gina Rossi's soul.

3

She said, 'I'm going with him.'

Fallon could only gasp, 'You can't!'

'I can,' insisted Gina. 'Families are permitted to accompany exiles. The Government doesn't care. They're glad to see the back of anybody related to potential troublemakers. I won't allow my father to go alone.' The determination of her voice belied the doubts which had plagued her since she made the decision.

When the idea had first presented itself, the day after the court hearing, Gina had shied from it, had then withheld it from her mind by concentrating on the financial priorities. The tribunal's confiscation verdict had been applied to all Alfredo Rossi's assets. Under the scrutiny of two Blackshirt troopers, Gina had been authorized to pack her own clothes, plus those of her sister and brother, along with a few personal items. All furniture, household equipment, even paintings and ornaments, were deemed subject to the dispossession order. The restaurant was padlocked and officially sealed as she stood and watched amid morning shoppers busying themselves about their everyday rounds. That afternoon she had closed her own bank account; and by the end of the week had converted her few pieces of jewellery to cash (excepting her mother's wedding ring and emerald necklace – Alfredo's first gift to Doris when she arrived in Italy). Only then did Gina reconsider the possibility of accompanying her father.

It took a further week to reach her decision.

She said to Fallon, 'Please don't try to dissuade me. My mind's made up.' She was at his apartment window, standing with her back to him, looking across the orange and ochre rooftops. It was one of those golden Roman evenings, quiet and still before the hubbub of the night, that time of sharp sunlight and shadow when the city truly seemed eternal. Could she really leave it? For some unspecified place? To face an unknown future?

Fallon asked, 'Paola and Filipo?'

'They'll have Cousin Letti, and Max, and you. They'll have so many to give them affection.'

He scraped his pipe against his teeth; said eventually, 'You have little idea what exile is like. Gina, I've seen what it can do to people, to strong, intelligent men and women.'

She turned to face him. 'Which is why I must go with Poppa. To cook for him, care for him. To do whatever I can to make his existence bearable. It isn't in return for all he has given me, Fallon. It's simply the way it has to be. You understand?'

The Englishman sighed. At last he nodded and smiled slowly.

When his lips curved from his teeth, a warmth and gentle understanding lit his usually brooding features. Yet still there was a strength about him, an inner strength which seemed indestructible, causing Gina to falter, undermining her resolve, planting the impulse to sink against him, let him envelop her with his strength. As he stepped toward her she said quietly, 'Don't touch me. Not now. Please.' Then she added, 'But sit with me a while. I'd like that.'

Later he walked with her to her Cousin Letti's house. There, on the street, he asked when Alfredo was due to leave. She told him Friday. It was a lie.

In her room she laid her cash, passport and Alfredo's conviction decree in the bottom of a small suitcase, covered it with sheets of newspaper before packing the one change of shirt, pants and socks her father was permitted, plus, for herself, two skirts, blouses and underwear. She added Alfredo's razor, a comb, her sewing kit and a tablet (courtesy of Fallon) of English Pear's soap. As an afterthought she packed two fine mosquito nets, recalling the time long ago when the family, holidaying in Campania, had stayed over-night in a village tavern and had been bitten almost to death due to lack of mosquito nets, whereafter Alfredo had always insisted on taking their own nets, even when visiting the insectless ski fields of the Dolomites.

With a mixture of grief and affection at the memory, Gina closed the suitcase. She then lay on the bed.

Soon after dawn she was crossing the street, her heels clacking in the sunny emptiness. She did not look back, dared not look back, just as she had dared not to look into the rooms where her sister and brother were sleeping. Since rising and dressing in her bright, flowered summer frock she had concentrated only on each passing minute, fearing to let her mind move into either the future or the past. She hesitated only once when, passing beneath Constantine's Arch, she checked her wrist for the time and discovered she had forgotten her watch – the small, gold timepiece, her eleventh birthday present from her mother. She automatically began to turn, but stopped herself, re-faced ahead and went on.

Alfredo was waiting in the courtyard of the Villa Fiorito, flanked by two troopers. He was dressed in the dark velvet jacket and white shirt he'd been wearing the evening of his arrest; and even though the clothes had become creased and soiled, still they were a defiantly civilized contrast to the coarse, black uniforms of his captors. His haggard face however, held no such daring. The eyes that had once sparked with vitality now watched the approach of his daughter with a lacklustre stare.

Gina strode purposefully forward. This was her first meeting with her father since she and Fallon had come to him here that fateful night last August. Her speech was prepared, all the things she had been longing to say, and the defence she would insist upon when he told her she must not join him. In her brightest, most positive voice she greeted, 'Hello, Poppa. They've given me permission. I'm coming with you.'

The glazed veil across his eyes briefly lifted. Then it closed again and he murmured, 'Thank you.'

They had travelled south from Rome in the rear of a covered truck, side by side on a slatted bench facing two guards, their only view the world behind retreating through a cloud of dust. As the enclosed space in the rattling, jouncing wagon became ever more sweltering, the land in their wake grew increasingly wild. The rich villas and bright villages along the recently repaved Via Appia gave way to crumbling farmsteads and hungry-looking settlements; the lush cypresses and vineyards above Lake Albano were replaced by seared broom and arid plains. And as the sun climbed toward a blazing noon the entire land shimmered like a mirage beyond a curtain of liquid heat.

Gina had scant idea where they were, could judge their direction only by the vehicle's shadow jolting along behind. When she had asked the guards their destination she had been met with stony silence. The men, she guessed, were not Fascist fanatics, more likely two conscripts resentful of their lot and the pair of condemned troublemakers who were the cause of this miserable, uncomfortable detail. They offered to share neither their conversation nor the oranges from their packs, and Gina damned herself for having dismissed the need to bring anything but bread and meat. When the men swigged from their canteens she turned bitterly from the sight and sound, though her concern was more for her father's thirst than her own. The agony she had felt when she first saw him outside the prison had dulled to a grinding ache as she sat here watching him stare trance-like at the swaying board floor never once returning her gaze or looking back whence they had come.

Without her watch Gina could only guess the time, and reckoned they'd been travelling almost three hours when the truck eventually trundled to a halt at the barren roadside.

The cab door slammed, the driver's slovenly footfalls crunched along the side of the vehicle and as he appeared at the open rear the two guards jumped down to join him. For one sickening moment Gina thought she and Alfredo were to be left inside the stifling wagon, but then one of the soldiers brandished his rifle in a gesture to exit. Inwardly gasping with relief Gina stood, clutching her small food parcel, extended her hand to her father, and together they climbed out to the simmering but fresh air. She flexed her cramped muscles, scanned the landscape.

The rocky, parched hills stretched as far as she could see on three sides, while to the west the featureless plain ran flat to meet the metallic azure dome of the sky. Nothing moved in the burning wilderness; not a breath of breeze stirred the dead, spiky grasses; not even the cry of a bird broke the incandescent silence.

Returning to their situation, Gina realized they were being ignored by their captors. The three men had moved off the dusty track and were relieving themselves in a dry creekbed. For a crazy instant she had the idea that she might bundle her father back into the truck before rushing to the cab and racing to freedom. Then the hope died still-born as reality confirmed the futility of attempting escape. She reached out and squeezed her father's hand, and as he looked at her she saw a flicker of his old strength in his tired eyes. He walked away from her, across the road to follow the example of the soldiers. Gina too realized the necessity, looked around for cover and seeing none moved beyond the side of the wagon. A couple of minutes later when she stood and turned she met the grinning faces of the three men. Her anger flared, but before she could voice her contempt the trio had strolled away chuckling. It was then she began to comprehend the impotence of her position, understand what Fallon and Max had tried to explain about banishment, the effect on a human being when it loses not merely material possessions but is also denied the dignity of self-will.

She returned to the rear of the truck.

Her father was sitting on the road, back against the cab in its thin wedge of shade. The soldiers were squatting, chatting and laughing, sharing cheese and a bottle of wine in the greater slice of shadow at the vehicle's side. As Gina skirted them they leered up her legs and one made a crude motion with his fist. Gritting her teeth she strode on by. And heard the call: 'Hey!' She froze; saw that her father had been prompted by the yell. Her mind raced with fear, not only at what they might do to her, but at what would happen to Alfredo if he attempted to intervene. Unable to still an onslaught of shaking, she turned – and stared into the three red, glistening faces. Sweat poured across her vision, burning her eyelids, mingling with unbidden tears of defeat and anger and hopelessness.

'Well, do you want it or not?'

It was moments before Gina realized the soldier had spoken, a second more before she saw his outstretched fist was holding the water canteen. Slowly, cautiously she reached for the offering. As she took the tin container the man returned to the gossip of his companions, grunted disinterestedly when Gina whispered, 'Thank you.' She carried the cool can, with the bread and meat, to her father.

They were back in the wagon within an hour, and when the hot, swaying journey resumed Gina was weighted by the oppression of the atmosphere, lulled by the motion of the vehicle. The guards slumped back, dozed; and though Gina fought to stay awake she too at last succumbed. Her broken dreams were of soldiers spilling cans of glittering water, Paola and Filipo hand in hand eating oranges on a deserted street, Fallon and Max sharing cheese and wine in a crowded, sweltering restaurant, she and her father beside a rocky road planning their future.

'Let's go. We haven't got all day. Out.'

Gina awoke with a start. One of the guards was prodding her with a rifle butt. Alfredo was on his feet being hustled to the rear of the truck. Gina stood, swallowing, trying to bring moisture to her parched throat. She lifted the small case and followed her father.

The unpaved village square was carpeted with chalky dust. A beaten earth road entered from north and south between flaking stuccoed houses whose outside stone staircases climbed to doors as sun-leached as desert bones. A shabby church stood at one side. In the centre were a roofless well and a gnarled fig tree. Beneath the tree a yellow dog was the sole visible inhabitant. But Gina could sense the others. She shuddered involuntarily as she felt their eyes watching from behind furtive shutters, and was abruptly conscious of her bright summer dress and Alfredo's rumpled but elegant clothes, feeling damned by their expensive sophistication in the midst of this primitive meanness.

A man marched from a drab, squat building. He was tall and muscular in tight-fitting black uniform, beribboned and medalled with the insignia of district leader on his shoulder. The hard shine of his cap peak and jackboots seemed to defy the dust which filmed the village. His pocked features were heavy, with a broad nose and fat lower lip. Appraising Gina and Alfredo as he halted before them he rapped at the truck driver, 'Papers,' and snatched the copy of the conviction decree when the man sullenly produced it.

Gina had seen the escort soldiers' open animosity toward the Blackshirt and it was with a pang of regret that she watched the trio climb into the wagon's cab. She couldn't see beyond the sun's glare on the windscreen, and it was as if the men had disappeared. Her last human link with Rome was snuffed out. And the isolation which, these past weeks, she'd tried unsuccessfully to imagine, now seized her with a chill grip.

Ignoring Gina, the Blackshirt barked, 'Move!' at Alfredo, and as her father obeyed, Gina followed toward the squat building.

The small office contained only a littered desk and a chair behind which a two-foot square photograph of The Leader hung alongside a poster commanding WAGE WAR AGAINST FLIES. A few months ago Gina would have appreciated the humour of this insect-spotted remnant of one of Mussolini's more preposterous decrees, but facing it now she bitterly recalled Fallon warning, 'One day people will realize that being ruled by a lunatic isn't funny.'

Sitting at the desk the Blackshirt scanned Alfredo Rossi's exile orders then looked up and rasped, 'I am Commander Galeazzo Sturzo. The raj of this district. My duty is to administer the law of the Fatherland. And I do it with pride. Do you understand that, Rossi? Pride. Of course you don't. Your kind don't know the meaning of the word.' He smacked his palm on the table top causing Gina to flinch as he rapped, 'But you will. You're going to learn. You're going to learn a lot during the coming years. Including how to work. Yes, you've been granted the privilege to work. To harden your lily-white hands in the service of your Leader. You must have clever lawyers, Rossi, to earn you that favour, as well as exemption from daily flogging. But,' his voice became knife-edged, 'don't imagine you can take advantage of the Tribunal's leniency. Don't think your expensive legal traitors have bought you a life of ease. Or that their word counts for anything here. I am the law here. I am justice. And you will obey me. Every second of your existence you will obey me absolutely. Do you understand?' He glared across the desk, his face grotesque with malice. 'I said do you understand?'

Alfredo Rossi nodded, murmured, 'Yes.'

'Yes, what?' yelled Sturzo, jumping to his feet, crashing his fist amid the litter. 'Yes, sir. Sir. You call me sir. You're not the boss of a fancy restaurant now, Rossi. Oh, yes, I know all about you. You and your rich friends. Intellectual filth. Communists. You're the ones who would bring our great nation to its knees. Would have us kowtowing to the English and Americans and stinking French. But our Leader will put an end to you. Our Leader will rout out the cancer in our midst. Your day is ended, Rossi. You high-and-mighty snobs with your inherited wealth are finished. Finished. Do you hear me?' Small flecks of foam bubbled at the corners of the raj's mouth as he bawled, 'Say it! Say you're finished. Say it before I thrash it out of you.'

Gina had shrunk from the maniacal outburst. This ranting paranoia wasn't new to her. She had heard it at Fascist rallies in Rome. But there she had always been able to walk away from it, leave it on someone else's doorstep. Now, in the confines of this seedy room she was paralysed by its vehemence; and she suddenly knew that this was what her father had been forced to endure throughout his months of imprisonment. Worse, she thought, than any physical beating. What mind could survive such terrible violence? And though she screamed mental defiance, she yielded to relief when she heard Alfredo breathe, 'We're finished.'

'Again!' roared Sturzo. 'I can't hear you.'

And the restaurateur answered, 'We're finished.' Staring at the floor, repeated loudly, 'We're finished. Sir.'

'Right,' spat Sturzo, thrusting his reddened face forward. 'And don't ever forget it.' His shoulders heaved and a shudder, of almost sexual release, shook his chest. He sat heavily, stared at Gina. It was the first time he had looked at her since entering the office, though he glanced swiftly away and snapped at her father, 'Your quarters are behind the church. Report here tomorrow morning. Six o'clock.' He flicked a dismissive finger and began to examine papers on the desk.

Without raising his head Alfredo turned and walked to the daylight. Gina watched the raj, but he refused to acknowledge her, and she went out through the doorway. As she took her father's arm and headed toward the church the full import of her situation, the reason for Sturzo's disregard, gradually dawned. Her exile was self-imposed, and – though it was meagre consolation – the raj had no punitive power over her, she was free to come and go as she chose, to communicate with civilization, and, so long as she abided by the civil law, was unchallengeable. Her spirits began to climb.

Moments later they crashed.

Behind the church was a crumbling-walled empty animal pen and a single-storey, stone-built hut. Beyond was only scorched desolation. Gina bit her lip to still her anguish, went slowly with Alfredo into the crude dwelling. Its interior, lighted by one tiny window, was stone-floored. It contained a rough wooden table and two wooden chairs; at one wall stood a single-door low cupboard, at the other a three-drawer dresser; in a rear corner a bed was covered with grey blankets. The lime-washed walls were smoke-yellowed; matted cobwebs nested in the angles of the tiled roof, and a thick layer of dust lay everywhere. Despite the heat, the air was heavy with the dank must of abandonment.

Gina's heart was thudding. This must be a mistake. No one could be expected to live here. Her impulse to dash back to the daylight was snapped as her father slumped onto one of the chairs. Quickly stepping to him she whispered, 'Are you all right, Poppa?'

His gaunt face was raised. 'Tired,' he murmured.

'Of course. Just let me shake out the blankets. Then you can rest.' Her hand faltered to stroke his hair but she snatched it away and turned abruptly. Bunching her fists, she fought to subdue her harsh breathing, to blot out all thoughts except the practicalities of survival. Regaining self-control she carried the bedding to the yard, beat it against the animal pen wall. She decided against further interior cleaning for fear of disturbing

44

so much filth. A rapid search of the cupboard and drawers revealed a thick pot mug, two tin plates, an earthenware bowl, a rusty oil lamp and a leather bucket. The latter she carried to the well in the still-deserted square, returned with it slopping water. Filling the mug for Alfredo she encouraged, 'We have a little food left.'

He shook his head. 'Sleep is all I need.' He shuffled to the bed, sat and dragged off his shoes. Then, looking up at his daughter, he said flatly, 'I'm sorry,' and he sank back with his eyes closed.

Gina remained watching him for a long time.

It was footfalls and voices which eventually broke her trance. She went to the door to see two men prodding two scrawny pigs into the animal pen. 'Hello,' she called, donning her brightest welcome, waving as the men turned. Then her arm dropped, for the instant the pair saw her they hurried away, not even throwing a backward glance as they disappeared around the church. A yell leapt to Gina's mouth but it died unvoiced and she sagged against the doorframe.

Soon others came, until there were ten pigs in the pen, but all the men shunned Gina, gave the hut a wide berth. She was past caring as she stared across the miserable landscape. The sun was dying behind the hills, and although its warmth still soaked the earth, the sight of it sinking into a blood-red pit chilled Gina, filled her with a cold that seemed to penetrate her very bones.

She returned inside, closing the door. In the deepening gloom she removed the mosquito netting from the suitcase, rigged one section over her sleeping father, took the other to the table where she placed a folded skirt on top of the suitcase, then, sitting, she lay her face on this makeshift pillow and draped the net about her head and arms. Exhaustion claimed her. Yet she couldn't sleep. In the black, dank void mosquitoes constantly droned around her; moths, sounding as large as birds, rustled in the roof, fluttered against the flimsy net; earthbound creatures whispered across the floor. From beyond the window came desolate sounds: the chittering of bats, the grunts of the hogs, the bark of wild dogs, thin unidentifiable cries.

It was the longest night she had ever spent.

Sturzo was waiting outside his office. Beside him stood a two-wheeled, box-sided handcart. Inside this, a bucket of rusty

45

nails, rough timber, a few tools, a bulky roll of paper, a lidded stone crock its sides glazed with congealed paste. As Sturzo pulled out the paper roll, Gina realized it was a sheaf of posters. Detaching one, tossing the remainder back into the cart, the raj uncurled it, held it rigid to display the face of the Leader. He snapped at Alfredo, 'Forty posters. You'll erect them at half-kilometre intervals.' He re-rolled the portrait, pointed it down the southbound road. 'On rocks, trees, walls. If there isn't a suitable surface available you'll make one.' He nodded at the timber. 'And you'll do it perfectly. Every one of those posters will be square, immaculate when I inspect your handiwork tonight. Yes, all forty of them. Don't even contemplate returning until you've finished. Do I make myself clear?'

Alfredo Rossi replied dully, 'Yes, sir.'

'You're learning,' the raj rasped maliciously. 'And you're going to learn more. Respect. Respect for the Leader, for the Fatherland, and for the Party which has spared your traitorous life.' He began to turn toward the door, but halted and warned, 'And you do your job alone. Without help.' He shot a deadly look at Gina.

Her anger flared. Torn between defiance of this bully and care that she didn't bring his wrath on Alfredo, she said levelly, 'I am free to come and go where I choose.'

Sturzo's face blazed. Through tight, white lips he hissed, 'But the prisoner isn't free to move anywhere except on my orders. And while he is carrying out the work of The Leader he is forbidden to communicate with, receive aid from, even to stand within five hundred paces of another human being. Defiance of any of these rules will earn him a public flogging.' His nostrils flared as he sucked in air, and his eyes narrowed. 'Don't think you can get clever with me. Your high-class education is worthless here. Your wealth and your intellectual airs count for nothing. And you're going to understand it. You're going to rue the day you left Rome. Before the summer is out you'll be willing to sell your soul to get out of here.' He held his hatred on Gina a moment longer before stamping into the building.

Gina dug her nails into her palms, ground her teeth against the scream of rage which filled her chest. It was seconds until, regaining control, she was able to face her father. And it was as if she looked at him across an abyss. When he had woken this morning he had seemed revived. He had talked haltingly of how they must cope with the situation, said that once he was stronger Gina must leave. It was a ghost of his old self speaking; nevertheless it had raised Gina's confidence. Now, imagining the toil he must endure today, her optimism sank. With a glance toward the office door, she kissed him, a swift but deeply affectionate touch of her lips. Then she watched, her eyes blinded by caring, as he pushed the cart across the square and down the long, stony road. She waited until he had halted at a distant lightning-blasted tree trunk, nailed up one of the posters and continued toward the featureless horizon.

Only as she walked back toward the church did she become aware of the sun's glare, its increasing fierceness beating upon her head. The realization that Alfredo had no hat drove the dejection from her mind, refired her purpose.

In the hut, before tackling any other task, Gina tore the skirt from her summer dress and fashioned a beret. She damned her lack of needlecraft but the resultant headgear (patterned side inward), though crude, would protect her father from the solar heat. Satisfied with her meagre effort, she faced the morning with renewed resolve.

It took her three hours to sweep and scrub and dust the tiny room. When she was done she was streaked with sweat-runnelled grime. Worst of all, her hair was clogged with filth. Never before had she felt such a need to plunge into a tub, to douse her itching scalp. Better not to dwell on such fantasies, she told herself as she lugged the bucket from the well. With a chair to guard the closed door, she stripped and washed – using another piece of her vandalized dress – standing with the bowl of water beside her on the table. Then she lathered her head with the tablet of scented soap, closing her senses to the memories raised by the perfume. No memories – she made the resolution there and then – no recall of a past which was gone forever, for there lay only pain, perhaps more than she could bear. Afterwards, she carefully wrapped the soap, stored it like a precious jewel in the suitcase.

Revitalized, dressed in fresh plain blue blouse and skirt, her hair tied back with yet another strip from the dress, she went forth to seek supplies.

Climbing the outside stone staircase of the first house she reached, Gina knocked. Allowing a pause she rapped again. Another moment and the door squinted an inch to reveal a frightened child's eye in a sliver of face. Smiling, Gina was about to speak when a woman's voice called sharply and the door slammed. Gina contemplated knocking once more, but even as she raised her fist she sensed it would be futile. And, descending the steps, she was pursued by the trepidation that she would receive the same rejection wherever else she tried.

Fifteen minutes on, her suspicions had been confirmed. None of the village doors had opened to her. The half-dozen black-swathed women she'd seen in the square had hurried from her approach. Her initial reaction had been anger, but when she defiantly confronted a man as he exited from a barn, it wasn't resentment or hostility she saw in his eyes – it was fear. The naked emotion caused her to step aside; and her anger withered as she slowly grasped the extent of her isolation, the totality of Alfredo's exile.

Striding into Sturzo's office she demanded, 'Are we expected to starve to death?' Briefly afraid as the raj's head jerked up, she stood her ground until he at last said, 'The prisoner is granted a food ration. From the farm at the eastern boundary. The wages he receives for his labour will cover the cost.'

Gina knew there was no hope in argument. Facing the Blackshirt she felt his hatred like hands at her throat. Suddenly felt something more. His eyes remained as cold as glass beads, yet they flickered, almost imperceptibly, across her breasts. The sensation caused Gina to catch her breath. Men had touched her with their fantasies before, young and old, some shyly, some passionately, but she had never been troubled by what – Cousin Letti had told her – was the way of the world. Here, however, the look from Sturzo left her feeling violated. He had immediately returned to the papers on his desk, but as Gina turned and went out of the door she knew he again was watching. The back of her neck crawled and she shuddered as she walked away.

The sky was molten lead by the time she found the farm. The man there wordlessly handed over Alfredo's paltry ration of bread, goat's cheese and dried chickpeas. Gina had brought money from the base of the suitcase, but she dared not overspend for she had no idea how long the cash must last. In any case, the man grunted refusal to her request for meat and eggs and all she received was more of the staple supplies plus a litre of olive oil and a string of shrivelled herbs.

Back at the hut she vowed she would not cry.

Night was closing in before Alfredo returned. Gina had waited for him outside the village, thrown caution aside and run to aid him when he came shufflingly out of the darkening desert. As he sank onto a chair she was relieved to see that her worst imaginings of the sun's assault had proved false. Later he told her he had spent the hottest hours of the day beneath the upturned handcart; Sturzo had checked his progress late in the afternoon, given him forty more posters to erect on the north road tomorrow. Gina had made herb-flavoured dumplings from crushed bread and ground chickpeas, a sauce from the cheese, oil and water. Alfredo ate ravenously then, without bothering to undress, collapsed onto the bed and was instantly asleep. Gina remained seated at the table.

A week passed before she slept on a cot she constructed from ancient timber, sacking and straw.

The farmer who'd provided the food ration was her source. At first he ignored her approaches. One morning, however, when she proffered payment for the holey meal bags in the rear of his barn, he stared hard at the money before waving it aside, nodding at the discarded sacks and leaving her to help herself.

Over the following days Gina came to realize that the man would grant her requests on those occasions when Sturzo was out of the village. Thereafter she only called for supplies when the raj was away touring the other communities of his official district. The farmer, as poor as his neighbours, could part with little; nevertheless he furnished Gina with tarnished cooking utensils, lamp oil, a mirror, candles, and a candlestick; he also eventually permitted her to purchase a few vegetables, dried fruits and, sometimes, a slice of sausage. With these scant ingredients, mustering all her culinary skills, Gina did her utmost to provide a varied diet, not only for her father's sake, but also to remind herself of her individuality in the grinding monotony of this alien world.

The colours of this world were the dead, dusty black of the villagers' clothes, the harsh white of the houses and earth. Its sound was the unceasing, day and night chirring of a million insects. Its pulse was the throb of lizards' throats as they basked on the rocks of the parched creek bed.

During the mornings, before the veils of heat shimmering on the scorched landscape climbed from their lowest ebb of seventy degrees to their afternoon high of a hundred and ten, the inhabitants of the village went about their silent routine of survival. The women, some with infants on their hips, others as withered and sapless as the starved trees, trudged to the well with leather buckets and earthenware gourds. The men plodded out to the arid fields and olive grove, some leading weary donkeys, others with the scrawny pigs which were tethered to stakes in the wilderness where they would forage ceaselessly amid the rocks, scrub and their own excrement.

Each noon, when the men returned, doors were closed, windows shuttered. Nothing stirred again until the time before evening when the sun slid toward the smoking horizon and the land's glare burned down to shades of brass and copper. Then the people came forth once more, venturing out as if in awe at the passing of another day; the women to stand in cowled silence, the men to squat in desultory conversation.

It was, Gina observed, an existence devoid of all gladness. The poverty here was no worse than in the slums of Rome, yet there, even in the direst tenements there was laughter. But then, laughter was the sound of hope, and in this place hope died still-born.

Most of the time the land was airless, but occasionally the wind would come, raising dust and grit in smothering clouds; the sun was blotted out and the sky became an ochreous dome. The dust blew beneath the door of the hut, between the cracks around the window-frame, and even when Gina stuffed these gaps with rags, still the insidious particles found their way through, seeming to penetrate the very walls to film everything within.

Yet these invasions Gina found perversely welcome, a break in the endless tedium. All her life not a single moment had been unfilled; now her days were a pattern of unrelenting loneliness. Her initial expectation of being able to come and go as she pleased had been dashed. No vehicles passed through the village and to request transportation from any of the half-dozen inhabitants who owned carts would have been futile. Thinking she might walk to a town she had asked the farmer this location. He produced a yellowed map and indicated a spot named Baremo. Gina's flimsy hope perished when she saw that the next settlement – and it was smaller than Baremo – was twenty kilometres distant; the nearest town was twice as far. She recalled Sturzo's words: 'You'll be willing to sell your soul to get out of here.'

She rarely saw the raj, but on those days and nights – two or three a week – which he spent in the village, whenever she went to the well she knew instinctively he was watching from behind his office window.

Her greatest privation was the lack of conversation. After the first week in the village, Alfredo had seemed to adapt to his daily toil, and in the evenings Gina would encourage him with bright talk during their meal. But, she came to realize, he spoke only of mundane matters, avoided all those subjects – literature, politics, art – which once had enriched their lives. And then, as May turned into June, his attempts to initiate even meagre gossip gradually diminished. Gina knew, heart-breakingly, that he never had truly brought any hope to this place, that all his dreams had been destroyed months ago in the Villa Fiorito. By July he was consuming his suppers in silence, staring through the open door, frowning, as if trying to recognize the landscape or remember why he was here. Gina began to fear for his sanity.

She feared also for her own resolve, wondered how long she could resist retreat. She felt immeasurably older (was surprised when looking in the mirror to see a face which, apart from its darkened skin, was unchanged), but each day she willed herself to survive, refused to listen to the voice which, with increasing insistence, whispered that her self-sacrifice had been futile.

Through the emptiness of the afternoon, when the temptation to brood was strongest, Gina escaped into her notebooks. She had realized from her earliest days in Baremo the need for purpose, that her mind must have a constructive project on which to concentrate. At first she merely assembled her journals' jottings into logical order. Gradually, however, she evolved a grander scheme. In tiny writing and minuscule drawings (to conserve the precious paper) she conceived and began to build a new Ristorante Rossi, describing in precise detail furnishings and décor, listing to exact quantities crockery and cutlery, preparing with consummate care menus and wine lists. It was a restaurant of which her father would be proud. Before long it was filling her every waking hour.

And never once did she permit herself to believe it would not become reality. When that thought threatened – usually in the stifling stillness of the hour before dawn – when her defences were at their weakest, when her nerves seemed stretched to breaking point, then she would go out to stand in the pewter light where, forcibly pushing aside the images of defeat, she would tell herself all the good things that would soon happen; soon, in a few days, a very few days' time.

The blistering summer wore on.

In early September Gina found a newspaper in the farmer's barn. September 4th 1937 – the date beside the *Popolo d'Italia* masthead seemed unreal. Was it the beginning of autumn? Had it really been five months since she read or heard a single item of news?

A front page photograph showed General von Blomberg, the German Minister of War, observing Italian military man-oeuvres. The caption reported that the general was greatly impressed, and that Mussolini, later in the year, would pay a reciprocal visit to Berlin. On page two, in a personal interview, the Leader stated that female emancipation must be reversed; so-called 'intellectual' women were mental abnormalities; girls in higher education were wasting the country's money, and henceforth their schooling would be restricted to those subjects with which a female's brain could cope, i.e. household management and child rearing. Elsewhere in the paper Gina read that experts had proved that Shakespeare had been the pseudonym of an Italian poet, that twelve million Italian soldiers were now equipped with the world's most advanced weapons, that Italian fashions had taken the Paris shows by storm, and that Italy's air force was now ten times greater than Britain's.

She left the newspaper where she'd found it. The hotchpotch of half-truths and nationalistic nonsense neither amused nor angered her; nothing had moved her.

In the hut she cupped her hands into the water bucket, doused her face, held her palms to her temples thinking she might pierce some feeling to her brain. But there was no response, no emotion within her. She went and stood at the doorway, watched a raven methodically picking to pieces the carcass of a fat white mouse, wondered if anything would move her, ever again.

4

Gypsies.

The goatboy had carried the word; and though the houses were afternoon-shuttered Gina sensed the expectation rustle through the village like the October breeze amid the coppering olive trees. She ran across the yard and climbed to tiptoe on the pig pen wall, shielding her eyes against the desert glare until she distinguished the two horse-drawn wagons far off on the white ribbon of road. They came closer, swaying, throwing off bright flashes as the sun touched their metal bolts and bands. The first was canvas-covered, tall and long like the prairie schooners Gina had seen in her father's American history books; the second was square-sided of timber, green with gaily painted circus scenes.

She watched as they approached, past the first dwellings, temporarily out of sight, then she hurried back across the yard, around the hut and the barn to the square.

The wagons trundled to a halt. The lead driver jumped down, strode along the side of his vehicle swiftly unknotting the ropes which secured the canvas. He tugged loose the final fastening and as if by magic the cover flew up and backward over the bow ribs of the roof to expose the interior. On a raised platform, the length of the wagon, a second man and two women were lifting and slotting a six-foot high backdrop into position. Even from her distant vantage point Gina could recognize clearly amid the brightly painted montage the dome of St Peters, the Colosseum, the Leaning Tower of Pisa, gondolas on a Venetian lagoon. Memories, imprisoned for these past desolate months, suddenly broke free, and her throat filled as she devoured the theatrical scene. Bereft of self-control she started forward.

The wagon's occupants had stationed themselves each end of the platform, and a further half-dozen men and women had jumped from the second vehicle, chattering and laughing, forming an arc in front of the stage. Clad in reds, blues, yellows and greens they were a vibrant splash of colour in the sun-bleached arena. Now the driver who had led the arrival was striding to the centre of the stage, rattling a tambourine above his head, yelling, 'Roll up! Roll up! Good people of Baremo, come out of your homes. Greet the greatest travelling show in Italy. Roll up! Roll Up!'

Exhortations, however, were unnecessary. As Gina had advanced, doors had sprung open and black-dressed women, wide-eyed children and siesta-befuddled men had exited cautiously, stared briefly then hurried forward to form a silent, inquisitive crowd. Gina, overtaken, had halted some fifty paces from the wagon though she could see over the villagers' heads to the man who continued to rattle his tambourine, gathering his audience. The sun was at his back and Gina bridged her eyes to study him.

He was tall in mustard cord trousers and a purple moleskin waistcoat open across a bronzed chest. His deeply sunburned face was framed by thick chestnut hair, almost hidden by a bushy beard. Rallying the slower stragglers he shouted, 'Thank you, citizens. Thank you for answering my call. We are the Troupe Bobini. The most splendid, the most acrobatic, the most incredible, the most daring entertainers ever to appear before the King of Trogland. Yes, we are the world-famous company you have all read about in your newspapers. We are the extraordinary performers who . . . '

As he forged on, punctuating his tub-thumping with rattles of his tambourine, Gina was tugged further into the past. She hadn't heard such ballyhoo in a long time, not since the fairs and markets of her childhood where she had been fascinated by the songs of the troubadours and antics of the players. In later years she had realized that the barkers' proclamations needed to be taken with a large pinch of salt, though she had come to appreciate how cleverly they played on an audience's emotions, converting the most dour-faced sceptic into an enchanted follower. Like this character, quoting newspapers to folk who barely could write their own names, beguiling them with references to the imaginary land of Trog when most didn't even know the direction of Milan. Gina's dejectedness deepened. The thought of La Scala's city recalled her own isolation, a bitter reminder that her feelings of affinity with the man on the stage was a one-way sentiment, that to him she was just another gawker in the crowd.

'Tonight,' he cried. 'Seven o'clock tonight. Yes, by torchlight you'll see the great Troupe Bobini. Come one, come all. Don't be late for the most sensational show on earth.' With a final flourish he bounded from the platform and led his waving companions into the wooden wagon.

The villagers remained mesmerized for several moments before they began to babble excitedly and drift back to their homes.

But Gina scarcely could pull herself from the deserted stage. The painted landmarks of the backdrop tethered her with vivid reminiscences she was now powerless to suppress. When she eventually walked away the heart-rending images pursued her; and back in the gloom of the hut they glared with an intensity that refused to be driven from her mind's eye. All the desperation, all the pent-up grief of the past months rushed down on her in an avalanche which she felt would crush her very soul. Crying out she collapsed onto the chair, crashed her fists on the table top then ground them into her eyes until the pain drove knives into her brain and the mental pictures were blinded by a curtain of red. Her arms slumped and her shoulders sagged. And in the shadows, quietly with deep aching sobs, at last she cried. She cried for a long time.

The rap on the door was faint.

Gina straightened. Her chest heaved as she dragged breath into a throat swollen with despair. She didn't know how long she'd abandoned herself to the misery, but as she wiped her face with her palms and looked around she realized that the sun had retreated from the cracks of the door. When the knock was repeated more insistently she willed herself back to rationality. No one had ever come to this door. No one would dare. Unless . . . Her thoughts sprang to her father. Someone had brought a message. He was ill. Or injured. Or worse. Sturzo had done something terrible to him. She started out of the chair as the door opened.

The figure was a black silhouette against the light.

On her feet Gina squinted, her nerves mauled by fear as she tried to distinguish the intruder. With false courage she demanded, 'What do you want?' and as the form stepped forward shutting the door she cried, 'Who are you?' her voice rising to the edge of a scream in the moment she discerned the bearded face.

The man from the stage-wagon stared, his eyes examining her from head to toe and back again with a shock rising to mirror Gina's own. At last, as his gaze explored her features, he whispered, 'My God!'

And in the same instant Gina's stunned mind recognized the impossible. The word trembled from her lips like a moth: 'Fallon.' Then she was flinging herself into his startled arms, all caution, fear, reserve gone, holding him, sobbing, gasping, laughing, touching his hair, his cheeks, his lips, repeating, 'Fallon, oh, Fallon!' over and over, her reeling senses unable to form any other coherent sentence until she finally sagged against him, too shattered even to cry, clinging to him, not daring to release him lest she wake and discover it had been a mocking dream.

His hands moved to her shoulders, gently pushed to hold her at arms' length. He said, 'What a fantastic tan!'

She replied automatically, 'I must look awful.' And her heart went out to him for prompting the response with his remark which, though absurd, was the most perfect introduction he could have chosen to avert her barrage of emotion. Reading his face she now saw the strain with which he was reining his own feelings, and she heard it in his voice when he said, 'Take it easy. I realize this must have come as a shock.' He smiled faintly. 'But sending a postcard to let you know we were on our way didn't seem like such a good idea.'

'We?'

'Paola and Filipo are hidden in the wagon.'

Gina was unable to restrain a cry, but before her flood of questions could burst forth Fallon was pressing her onto a chair, sitting in front of her and commanding, 'Please, don't interrupt. I have only fifteen minutes until Sturzo returns. Yes, we know all about him, where he is at the moment, had to learn his routine before we dare approach you. Now, listen carefully.'

He rapidly unfolded how it had taken weeks to discover Alfredo's whereabouts followed by further bribery of officials to obtain the travel and work permits to join Max's old card-playing friend Bobini whose troupe of players was one of the few surviving under the Fascists' ever-harsher anti-migration laws introduced to control what the Leader condemned as 'The Gypsy Menace'. 'It was the only way we could arrive here without arousing suspicion,' explained Fallon, going on to recount their reconnaissance of the village and – to Gina's amazement – their meeting yesterday with Sturzo to present their credentials and arrange the forthcoming show. 'There are a hundred details I don't have time to relate,' he said. 'Suffice to say we're getting you out of here tonight.'

Gina could only gasp, 'Where to?'

'America. There's already a network of good families helping so-called dissidents across the border in the north. But that's too far from here, whereas the south coast port of Taranto is less than a hundred kilometres away. Passage has been arranged on a freighter bound for New York via Malta and Marseilles. You'll be at sea by dawn tomorrow. With Paola and Filipo, of course. Max also. He's in Taranto now making sure everything is okay. He insists on taking care of you until you're on the other side of the Atlantic. Besides, it would be too dangerous for him to return to Rome after your escape.'

Gina's mind was spinning and it was taking every iota of her concentration to follow what Fallon was saying as he sketched in details of the getaway plan which had been arranged with the aid of the sympathetic ship's captain. Though she wanted desperately to interrupt, to abandon practicalities for just a moment to sit and talk, she nodded mutely when he asked if she still had her passport.

'Good. One genuine document will help when you arrive in the United States. The others are forgeries – the time it's taken to obtain them is another reason why we've been so long in coming for you.' He checked his watch. 'After our show finishes at nine o'clock tonight we have to move the wagons a couple of miles down the road – Sturzo's orders. You'll have to wait here when we leave. I'll return for you thirty minutes later.'

Suddenly Gina was thinking rationally again. 'No, you mustn't take the risk. You must remain with Paola and Filipo, just in case anything goes wrong. But it won't. Don't worry. Poppa and I are perfectly capable of making our way to a rendezvous. Where shall we meet?'

Fallon looked doubtful, then he conceded, 'All right. We're taking the disused Roman track through the hills. Less chance that way of encountering someone who might question why we're travelling at night. We'll wait for you beside the twin rocks off the village road. You know the spot?'

Gina nodded. 'Keep the coffee hot.'

Fallon reached out, touched his hand to her cheek. 'I know you've been through a tough time. And I'm sorry I couldn't come for you sooner. But it will be all over within twenty-four hours.' He scanned her face, adding with gruff gentleness, 'By the way, you look marvellous.' Then he stood swiftly and strode to open the door.

Recovering from his remark, Gina followed and waited behind him while he checked the yard and the land beyond the pig pen. As he glanced around at her she said softly, 'Thank you for being here, Fallon. And for . . .'

'Sure,' he said. 'All in a day's work.' And he ducked and ran out along the wall of the hut and in a moment was gone.

Gina stared toward the corner where he had disappeared and the strange co-mingling of exhilaration and bewilderment which had held her these past minutes quickly evaporated. She fell back against the doorframe as if abruptly unstrung. The entire episode now seemed unreal and she was prompted to pursue Fallon to assure herself that he and the wagons truly existed. Of course they did! She banged her fist against the wall, driving out the doubts, mustering her wits. Closing and bolting the door, she pulled the suitcase from under the bed and began to pack, all the while concentrating on the job in hand, not permitting herself to speculate for an instant on what was to come lest fear weaken her resolve. When she was done she concealed the suitcase in the cupboard. Then she busied herself around the two rooms, fiercely holding her self-control as she awaited her father's return.

When he arrived home, haggard with exhaustion, Gina hestiated to broach the subject of Fallon's visit, fearing that her father might be too mentally numbed to understand the situation. But, deciding she couldn't risk him falling asleep and becoming more befuddled, she sat before him at the table and broke the news. Alfredo stared with tenuous comprehension as Gina spoke, and at the end of each sentence she anticipated his interruption. But none came; as she carefully explained the plan, her father said not a word. When she was finished his silence continued and she felt a rising panic, wishing she had told Fallon the truth about Alfredo's uncertain sanity.

Then he said, 'Thank God for the finest friends a man could wish for!' And as he smiled faintly Gina saw the returning will of the man who once had guided all her years. She was even more convinced of his building strength when he went on, 'We must not discuss it further in case we talk ourselves into a reason for staying. Let me say only this, whatever happens tonight you must think of the people who have risked their lives to help us. If I should falter don't sacrifice them for my sake. Promise?'

Gina bit her lip. 'I promise,' she answered.

'That's settled then,' Alfredo declared firmly. 'Now how about some supper? Then I'll rest during the show. And with a full belly and revived legs I'll be able to race you from here to Fallon's rendezvous.' The tiredness ran away from his face, and at last Gina could see the end of this long, cruel road.

The stage-wagon was an oasis of ochreous light in the blackness, its backdrop illuminated by half-a-dozen blazing torches which threw weaving flares and shadows across the faces of the crowd. The entire population, even the babes in arms, were there, milling and pushing, craning to witness the promised spectacle.

Gina stood to one side, and in spite of the trauma of today's events plus the prospect of what she must do later, she couldn't discard the thrill of expectation, the tingle of the blood which had presaged every curtain-up since her first infant introduction to the murderous comedy of *Punch and Judy*, the romantic tragedy of *Pierrot and Columbine*. Even the presence of Sturzo on the opposite side of the square was inadequate to quell her excitement, and she was gripped by an unwary rashness, an urge to shout with joy at this celebration of her impending freedom. She impatiently tapped her foot, as eager for the entertainment as she was for the moment of escape. Illogical, she warned herself. Be calm. And she made a concerted effort to steady her breathing, mindful that her mounting euphoria must not be allowed to cloud her judgment, that tonight she needed her reasoning as never before.

'Citizens of Baremo!' The disembodied voice cracked from the darkness, silencing the crowd as abruptly as a gunshot. 'Welcome! Behold the most fantastic show on earth!'

And without more ado, to an accompanying barrage of tambourines and drums, a half-naked man leapt onto the stage flourishing two flaming brands with which he flagrantly swaled his arms and torso before tipping one to his lips, lapping the spilling fire into his mouth then blowing it in a roaring jet above the heads of his audience.

Cries of delighted fear greeted the magic, and Gina joined

the applause as the man bounded to the percussion beat, bathing himself in fiery liquid, his muscles glistening with smoking streams, his face sweating droplets of burning yellow while he spat tongues of incandescence up into the night.

The crowd responded, emboldened now, shouting and waving, inciting the performance to greater pyrotechnic heights. Gina had never before seen such a sudden, total change in people. The women's faces were alight for the first time since her arrival here. Their menfolk were seizing them, jostling them, frightening them with good-natured shouts as each gout of flame spouted overhead. The children had been lofted to shoulders where, yelling rapturously, they were joggled to the rattling rhthym. Even the crippled ancients, brought forth on rickety chairs, shuffled their feet and cackled deliriously.

And Gina's heart went out to them. At last she saw this as a village of people. They weren't zombies, they were warm, emotional human beings capable of the same loves and fears and griefs as she or anybody else; and, she understood, it wasn't just the merciless daily grind that deadened their sensibilities, it was something more, the want for fellow feeling, the need to know that someone somewhere cared whether they lived or died, the simple desire to be acknowledged. Gina shook off the brief sadness, avoided being drawn along that path, pulled herself back to the pleasure of the moment as the fire-eater sprang from the platform to be replaced by a girl in purple bodice and basque throwing spinning golden clubs into the air, catching them, bouncing them, whirling and dancing as a fiddle joined the cacophony.

The extravaganza dashed on. Acrobats, a ropewalker, a buffoon, a tumbling midget cavorted before the painted montage. And then they were among the crowd, clowning and tantalizing, handing out coloured feathers and small candies and goblets of wine.

Gina knew instinctively it was wine the instant she saw Fallon laughing and bowing to present a flagon to Sturzo. She had forgotten the raj during the captivation of the show, now she saw that he was as incensed as the villagers; his black shirt was unbuttoned, his face lit by excitement. Watching, Gina saw him snatch the flagon from Fallon and guffaw as he tipped back his head to pour a spout of liquid down his throat. Choking and spewing the wine onto his chest he clapped

Fallon's shoulder with extravagant camaraderie and bawled, 'Bring on the gypsies. Let's see the dancers.' And as if in immediate response a black-haired girl with flaring scarlet skirts appeared on the wagon and began a swirling tarantella. Sturzo roared approval, gulping from the flagon as Fallon encouraged him with flattery and applause.

Gina smiled, discerning the plot. Robert Fallon, you're a rogue and a genius! She felt suddenly light-headed. The night, the music, the stamping of the throng closed in on her. The comprehension that this was not a dream, that this was truly the end of her months of exile, rushed upon her like a wave of drunkenness. Swaying, she reached forward for support, clutched at an outstretched hand.

'Gina. Are you all right?'

She blinked, stared into the thickly whiskered face, reassembled her senses. 'Fallon. Yes. I'm fine.'

'Where's Alfredo?'

'He's resting. But he'll be ready.'

'We'll end the show in half an hour. By then that Fascist glutton will be on his second flagon. Give him a further thirty minutes after the troupe has left. Time for him to swallow enough to floor an ox. The villagers ought to be out for the count also. You remember where to come? The meeting place. Beside the twin rocks on the old Roman road. Are you sure you can make it with your father? Shall I return here for you? I think perhaps I should.'

'Of course you mustn't,' insisted Gina. 'It would be too great a risk.' She gripped his hand, wanted so much to press herself into his arms, wished they were already away, hundreds of miles away where she could sink down with him onto cool, fresh grass beneath moonlit trees, tell him all the things she had waited so long to say.

Fallon stepped back. 'Sturzo's watching.' Laughing theatrically he cried, 'Good fortune, beautiful lady! All the luck in the world will be yours.' Then he was striding into the crowd, waving to his companions and calling, 'On with the show.' And with leaps and bounds and cartwheels the troupe returned to the stage amid delighted applause.

The second half of the show was a carousel of lights, music and dance, but though Gina was still whirled with exhilaration she was calmer now. She could still feel Fallon's grip of her hand, a tangible reminder of his closeness; and she took strength from it, gaining confidence minute by minute until, when the troupe's extravagant finale was ended, she was nerveless, almost audacious in her eagerness to be away.

As the performers lowered the backdrop montage and secured the canvas roof over the stage-wagon, the villagers began to drift back to their homes. Sturzo had reeled away with his second flagon, and only a small group of young couples remained in the square prancing in imitation of the acts they'd seen. Gina stood in the shadow of a gable observing the troupe's preparations to leave. She saw Fallon harnessing the horses before turning to survey the village. As he walked to the painted wagon she remembered that Paola and Filipo were in there and it was all she could do to prevent herself from rushing to them.

At last the vehicles moved, creaking and rumbling as they rolled toward the road between the houses. Gina stepped from the darkness to stand and watch them trundle away. They were clearly visible in the moonlight and she remained there a long time until she could discern only two grey shapes diminishing in the distance. Less than thirty minutes, she thought suddenly, and then I'll be following.

She strode swiftly across the now-deserted square, around into the blackness behind the barn.

She entered the hut, glancing around the gloomy, lamplit room, this shabby cell where she had been imprisoned for what now seemed a lifetime. It looked smaller and poorer than ever; the few pieces of crockery, the mirror, the candlestick, these items which she once had cossetted as treasured possessions, appeared pathetic now, and she experienced a pang of regret at leaving them, felt irrationally guilty at their abandonment, as if she were deserting old friends. Sadness clutched her, a brief temptation to remain here. Closing the door she renounced the sentimentality, mobilized her fixity of purpose. She stepped forward; saw the dark bundle in the corner of the floor. Her stomach lurched, but the cry of alarm caught in her throat as she distinguished the shape – recognized her father.

She was on her knees beside him, her arm around his shoulders, raising him, cradling him, exhorting, 'Poppa. Please, Poppa! Wake up!' Only then did she see the blood on his mouth, the ruptured flesh of his cheek and brow. She whimpered with shock and fear, clutched at her father's chest, her own heart standing still as she prayed for his pulse and choked, 'Please don't let him be dead. Don't let it end here. Not now.' And she realized there was a muted thump beneath her palm. She breathed, 'Thank God,' regaining her mental balance as she strained to reach a blanket on the bed, drag it to bunch under her father's head. Laying him back, she lifted his hand, rubbed it, patted it, urged, 'Poppa. You must wake up.'

For long, aching seconds the only movement was the infinitesimal rise and fall of his chest, until at last with a moan he shifted, his eyelids fluttered and opened and he stared blankly at his daughter.

Gina whispered, 'Poppa, can you hear me?' She scanned his eyes, searching for recognition, and exhaled a sigh of relief when she finally saw it.

Alfredo's mouth opened and the movement contorted his features with pain. Gina touched trembling fingers to his lips to still the effort but he turned his head to one side and croaked, 'Let me . . . speak . . . I . . . ' The words died to a rattle; his eyes faded and rolled and he hovered on the brink of sensibility, his bone-white fingers clawing at his daughter's wrists as if to hold himself from the pit of unconsciousness.

Perceiving his massive exertion, Gina appealed, 'Don't try to say anything. Lie still. I'll fetch help. I'll bring someone. They must come.'

'No.' Desperation strengthened Alfredo's voice. 'He'll be back. He'll kill you.'

Even as Gina gasped, 'Who?' she knew the answer.

'Sturzo. He was here. Drunk . . . Crazy drunk. He was looking for you. Wanted you. He saw . . . saw the suitcase.' As Gina shot a look across the room to see that the case had been taken from the cupboard, Alfredo continued brokenly, 'Yes. He knows. I . . . I told him. He beat me. Though it wasn't that. I could stand that. But . . . he threatened. The . . . meat hook. My . . . eyes. Oh God, I'm sorry. So sorry.' He fell back on the blanket, tears streaming over his bloodied cheeks, shoulders shaking uncontrollably as he sobbed a final, 'I'm sorry.'

Fighting down her own anguish, Gina said thickly, 'It's all right, Poppa. It doesn't matter. We can still get away. There's still time.' She knew it was a lie. There, kneeling on the stone floor in the shadows, she knew that all chance had gone, all hope had flown. Their dream had crashed; the flimsy, childish plot had been nothing more than a scrap from a fairy tale, it had no basis in reality. Reality was this place. Reality was exile. For ever. And there was no escape. She murmured, 'I love you, Poppa.' Then she gathered his face in her hands, held it and kissed it, watched the eyes glaze and close, felt it become a dead weight as her father again blacked out.

The door flew open, smashed back against the wall splintering shards of timber from the frame. Sturzo stood framed before the moonlight, legs apart, fists knotted at his sides. He was panting; sweat bathed his features, ran down his throat and rivuletted the matted hair of his chest, soaking his gaping shirt.

Gina had jolted to her feet at the violent entry. She glanced desperately left and right. But there was no way past the looming man. No place to run.

He snarled, 'That's right. You're going nowhere. You're staying here. With me. Understand? And now it'll be on my terms.' He lurched into the room wrenching at his trouser belt. His belly heaved as he tottered and swayed sideways to bash against the chest of drawers, his hand jerking out for support, sending the mirror and cups flying, shattering on the stone floor. He swore, regaining his balance, lumbered forward, flinging a chair out of his path, rasping, 'Now. Now you'll kneel, rich whore.'

Gina feinted to one side, swinging then in the opposite direction. But he was fast for his size. Too fast. As Gina dodged in an attempt to outflank him, he lunged, his fingernails raking her neck, grabbing her hair, yanking her almost off her feet. She cried out at the lancing pain as her hair tore from its roots and she fell sideways thumping against his bulk.

His arm encircled her, lifted her, carried her back and slammed her down on the cot, driving the air from her lungs so that she was momentarily paralysed, sucking desperately for breath. And in that instant Sturzo fell on her, his great bulk atop her, legs straddling her thighs. One hand tore into her blouse, grabbing roughly for her breast, the other rammed downward between their bodies, dragging at her skirt, tugging it to her waist. Panting, grunting he thrust his face into Gina's, coarse tongue and teeth raking her lips, alcohol-sodden breath filling her mouth.

She gagged on the stink, rolled her head to escape but then felt his knee driving between her legs. She strove against him. Hopelessly. As he pinioned her she thought her ribs would crack. He was clawing her stomach, fingers digging into her flesh, tearing at her underwear. Gina knew she must scream, through the pounding waves of horror she understood that she must summon the strength to scream. But she could not. Only an agonized thread of sound escaped her throat.

Thunder roared in her head. Warm, salty liquid stung her broken lips. Sturzo's face was only inches from her own, and she saw in minute detail the bristles of his jaw, the pits in his cheeks, red veins in the whites of his eyes, striations on his teeth as he moaned, 'Beautiful. Beautiful.' The words she once had dreamed Fallon would whisper.

Sturzo was jamming himself against her, gasping and mumbling. But she felt nothing. Gina had ceased to feel as she stopped struggling. She was motionless, physically and mentally, willing herself into a void, shutting out all sensation. Briefly there was a sharp pain within her, but it was remote, as if it were merely the memory of a pain. Then there was only oblivion. How long it endured she didn't know; would never know that the assault lasted less than three minutes.

Her return to sensation came as a dull roaring in her ears, like waves pounding on a distant shore. She was rushing toward the sound, her breath pumping in harsh gasps, increasing until she was snatching deep gulps of air as the boom of the surf towered to a titanic roar. Her eyes snapped open and she was abruptly aware of the heaving of her chest, the deafening pulse of the blood in her temples. And she saw Sturzo, recognized the satiated features of the man above her. Never had she felt such intensity of emotion. Her hate was a living beast, a monster with a will and strength of its own. It screamed, wrenched itself free, slashed upward then gouged downward through the man's brow, eyes and cheeks, raked livid channels from which sprang fat crimson seeds, welling and running, threading the stubbled jaw to fall and splash like opening buds across Gina's naked chest.

Sturzo reared back. His hands groped at the wounds as he bellowed like a lanced bull.

Gina lunged to the side, part scrambling, part falling from the bed, stumbling to her feet. But Sturzo blindly hurled himself in pursuit, powering off his knees and smashing into her from behind, his momentum driving them both forward to crash against the wall. As they rebounded and he reeled to wrap her in his savage arms they collided with the table. Gina heard his roaring obscenities; heard too her own cry as his fist flailed a glancing blow across her forehead. She tottered. A second swing clubbed her. Gina's legs buckled. And then she was falling. She glimpsed the looming bulk of Sturzo, the blood-streaked rage of his lacerated features. The ceiling seemed to fly away. The walls toppled backward.

Thumping into the chest of drawers she hung there, arms outflung, clutching for support as the blackness began to descend. Her fingers floundered amid the shattered crockery. Touched something smooth and hard. Closed around it. Through the miasma of advancing oblivion she understood what it was; and she knew that she must raise it or she would die.

Summoning a final surging effort she swung her arm upward; slammed it down with every ounce of her draining strength; felt the weapon strike with cracking force.

She didn't see what happened next. The earth turned giddily and she was pitched spinning into an inky whirlpool. When she came up from the vortex it was moments before she comprehended she was still on her feet. Her father was standing in front of her. She dazedly stared at him, then followed his gaze to the floor where Galeazzo Sturzo was lying, his eyes and mouth pinned open in a gape of surprise while the spring of blood from the side of his head pumped into a pool of widening red. Gina stood frozen in horrified fascination as a rasping breath creaked from the raj's throat and like a deflating balloon his chest slowly collapsed. Then he was utterly still.

The long ensuing silence was broken when Alfredo Rossi took the candlestick from his daughter's hand and threw it into the corner. The alien clang snapped Gina to her senses. She gasped, 'Oh, Poppa!', but as she stepped to gather him into her arms he slumped onto a chair. His shoulders sagged and his head swayed, and Gina, fearing he would topple, seized his arms, entreating, 'Let me help you to the bed. Please. You must lie down.'

'No!' The strength of his tone startled Gina. Pushing her hands aside he seemed to shake himself to sensibility. He licked his lips, moved his tongue inside his battered cheek, winced thickly, 'The pig broke my teeth.' He swayed again and hung on to the table for support, but when he spoke once more his voice, though taut with pain, held a determination Gina had not heard in many months. 'Get the suitcase.'

It was then she realized he hadn't witnessed what had happened, must have woken only after Sturzo's attack in time to see her deal the final blow. Thankful, pleased he didn't know the truth, she tightened her torn blouse into her waistband and obeyed his instructions. When his fluttering hand indicated the tabletop, she lugged the case up there.

Alfredo snapped open the lid, seized his few remnants of clothing and tossed them onto the floor. As Gina blurted, 'Poppa . . . ?' he slammed shut the bag and commanded, 'Now go.' The words were delivered with imperative force and before Gina could recover from her stunned reaction he added, 'You've never disobeyed me in your life. Please, no arguments now.' He coughed, a harsh, racking spasm which doubled him forward, but he fought it and extended a halting palm as Gina started toward him. 'You've remained here long enough,' he rasped. 'These endless, dreadful months. I should never have let you stay. I allowed my own misery to cloud my judgment. Perhaps also I was being selfish. But it is always difficult to release that which we treasure most in all the world.' He smiled and Gina saw the pain the effort ignited.

She was drowning in a deluge of emotion. She must reach out, gather this man, this dearly beloved man, into her arms, lift him and carry him from this place. To safety. To freedom. To all the years they had left together. But as her heart filled, she knew the grief of reality. Still she couldn't move.

'You must go,' persisted her father. 'You must go without delay. Fallon will be waiting.'

'I can help you.'

'Not far enough,' Alfredo replied grimly. 'I might make it to the yard before I pass out. Then what will you do? Drag me? On my backside?' He forced another grin. 'What an indignity to mete out to your poor old father.'

Gina said desperately, 'I'll send some of the men back for you. I'll run for them. I'll run now.'

'Damn it, no!' Alfredo's clenched fist bashed the table. 'Do you think the villagers didn't hear all that happened tonight? Of course they did. And as soon as they gather their pathetic grains of courage they'll come to investigate. They might be as pleased as you and I to see the end of Sturzo, but they'll have no choice but to raise the hue and cry. Not a single man must come back for me. It would cost his life. And your life. And the lives of Paola and Filipo. Had you forgotten them? They're out there waiting. Waiting to be away from this God-forsaken land. And you, with every minute you waste are risking their freedom. Is that what you want? To condemn them forever.' A spasm wracked his chest, twisting his features. When it was past his face was ashen, his eyes more deeply sunken, and his lips pulled thin as wire across his teeth. He hissed, 'In Christ's name, Gina, save them! Save your sister and brother. Save yourself.' And then the strength appeared to rush out of him, the exertion of his final plea throwing him back on the chair where he hung like a broken scarecrow. His eyes held his daughter with aching appeal before their lids flickered and closed and his breathing sighed to a shallow murmur.

Gina choked back a cry, her own resolve draining. He couldn't leave her now; not when she needed him more than ever before. He couldn't abandon her to shoulder so much alone; not after all she had endured. It was unfair. Unjust. How could she go on?

Pain lanced her and she stumbled back clutching her stomach. The harsh reminder of what had gone before recharged her objectivity. She must reach Fallon and the troupe, they would know how to aid her father. Swiftly but gently she eased Alfredo's limp form onto the floor, covered him with the blanket. In spite of his frailness she was sweating when she was done. Kissing his brow she whispered, 'I'll save you, Poppa.' Then she rose, lifted the suitcase and, suppressing a shudder as she stepped around the blood-haloed head of the raj, hurried to the door.

She hadn't gone half a mile before the delayed after-shock of the savagery struck. Wave after wave of nausea hit her like hammer blows. Sturzo's face reared before her and she recoiled from the brutal stink of him, so distinctly feeling the rake of his teeth it hurt her lips. She came out of the agony squinting, blinded momentarily by the sickness. For a while she was disoriented, fear a rake of talons on her flesh; then the events of the night rushed upon her once more and she fled.

She ran. She didn't know how long she ran; wasn't even sure where she ran. She was running in a dream. Overhead the night was deepest purple frosted by stars, with a full moon which poured liquid silver over the countryside, transforming rocks and grass and trees to gleaming metallic sculptures, creating a landscape without distance, without end. Gina tried to focus on the ground, but the eerie light confused her sense of depth and she could only stumble blindly, lurching onward across rises and hollows unable to distinguish one from the other in the eldritch luminosity.

Stones stabbed through the soles of her shoes. Branches raked her legs. Boulders seemed to spring to life, stepping into her path, shouldering her aside.

Sweat burned her eyes. Blood fouled her mouth. Her breath was sawing in harsh gasps now, scouring her raw throat. She knew she couldn't go on, couldn't possibly run further. What was the point? For where was she going? She was lost, hopelessly and completely lost in this hostile no man's land. She tottered on, dulled by fatigue, no longer sure whether her flight was reality or a nightmare.

When at last she fell, sprawling in ragged underbrush, the suitcase went flying from her hand, slithering down an invisible slope. Sobbing with frustration and defeat, Gina crawled in pursuit. The ground shifted and she slid on an incline of sliding scree, a slow-swishing ride downward until she bumped to a halt, arm flung forward on the stalled case.

She remained lying there, her cheek pressed to the cool, familiar leather, her last link with actuality. She could sleep here, couldn't she? She must sleep. Just for a few minutes, enough seconds to regain her strength, then she would go on; that would be the sensible thing to do. Mental exhaustion erased her thoughts. Closing her eyes she drifted toward marvellous oblivion, her muscles melting like wax as she rolled sideways to be gathered into the arms of sleep. Her cheek dropped onto the coarse ground and as the sudden jolt caused her to gasp, dust sucked into her mouth and nostrils. In a fit of coughing and retching she scrabbled to a sitting position, hunched there until she was able to stagger to her feet. Mindlessly hefting the suitcase she cradled it like a precious doll as she shambled forward.

How often she fell she never knew. After a while she was beyond the point of knowing or caring. Her legs moved with the inexorable tread of an automaton. She was no longer aware of where she was heading, only that she must not sleep. You must never stop; must never look back. The warning echoed and re-echoed in her head, a mumbling drone which obliterated all other sensations. She didn't feel the flints puncture her feet; didn't hear her own moans of pain; didn't taste the bile in her throat; didn't see the dark figures loom from the shadows.

Fists seized her. She whirled to flee but there was something large and heavy in her arms. She tried to cast it aside but her hands wouldn't obey and as her ankle twisted she tumbled under the obstinate weight. As Gina went down she saw faces and lights, but they were spinning away, high into infinity as she toppled over the edge of consciousness.

Voices pulled her back.

She wondered what they were saying; wondered who the people were, gathered in a semi-circle above her, men and women staring down with awe-filled eyes. She wondered why they were lifting her. She didn't mind being lifted; it was better than what had gone before, although now that was a waning memory of something that had happened long ago. She didn't mind being carried, but she wished they'd be more gentle, that they wouldn't hurry so. There was no need to hurry. Her father had always told her: never hurry, look where you're going, you'll get there in the end. Was this man her father? His face was familiar. Why was he crying? Why couldn't she move her legs? Why was there a pain in her stomach? What was the warm, sticky liquid on her thighs? She didn't care. Not any more. A softness was beginning to settle around her; down feathers kissing her body with endless gentleness. She gathered them to herself. Lay cocooned in them. All sensation faded and the man's face dissolved. Darkness came.

5

Gina was suddenly awake. At first she didn't realize it, thought she was still unconscious, dreaming, for the room was like nothing she had seen before – and it was riding up and down. It was tiny, with space only for the cot upon which she lay. The wall beside her face was grey-painted metal, scabrous with rust, studded with huge rivet heads, and from beyond it issued the din which she assumed had wakened her – a dull, steady roar punctuated by a series of rasping scrapes.

She pulled herself upright, clutching feebly at the blanket for support as she yawed with the motion of the room, was pitched in the opposite direction and banged her head against the wall. White light exploded behind her eyes but the pain brought some sort of clarity. She understood that she was conscious. And it took only a few more moments of fierce concentration for her to realize that she was on board a ship.

Questions tumbled through her brain but the struggling answers were swamped by a sudden wave of sickness and she fell back. Her skull was aching, tortured by the rhythmic rasping as the groundswell of nausea rose in her belly. She reached up and gripped her head as if to squeeze out the pain but the effort sent her reeling and spinning so that she felt boilingly, savagely ill and her arms fell at their sides and she lay panting, puny and beaten.

She drifted then, too sick to move, to turn her head, even to attempt to think rationally. She was pulled down a black tunnel. Into the past. Into a hut in the middle of a burning plain. A man was sitting slumped at a table; another was lying on the floor, his head in the mouth of a livid scarlet flower. Agony lanced her insides and she jacknifed as the spasm drove the image from her mind. She wrapped her arms about herself, pulled her knees to her chin, huddled there drenched in sweat, shivering uncontrollably, falling, falling into a deep nightmare-filled sleep.

When she came to again the visions were gone.

She stared up at the rusty metal ceiling for a long time praying that the biliousness wouldn't return, and when she finally felt that the worst might be past she risked turning her head. There was a couple of feet of space between her cot and the wall and she was prevented from rolling into this by a metal bar. There was also a door. It opened and Max Barzini entered wearing his red wool shirt and sleeveless sheepskin jerkin. Gina cried, 'Max! Thank God! Where are we? What happened?' She was swinging her legs from the bed, lurching to her feet before the big moustachioed man was able to move, and only his closeness prevented her from braining herself on the bulkhead as her muscles collapsed. He seized her and lifted her back onto the cot as she gasped, 'Oh, Max, I can't stand. What's the matter with me?'

'Nothing.' He held her down, touched her brow with his wide fingers. 'The fever has broken. You're fine. Just weak from lack of food. Two weeks is a long time.'

'Two weeks!'

He nodded calmly. 'Since we sailed from Taranto. We're on

our way to Marseilles.' He stilled her interruption. 'No talking now. You need rest. Time to rebuild your strength. I'll bring you some soup. If you drink it without saying a word, this time tomorrow I'll let you put your feet on the floor. For two minutes.' He regarded her with mock severity. 'A deal?'

Gina sighed, and when the wan smile she mustered took an awesome effort she granted that Max was right. She whispered, 'Just one question. Please. Paola and Filipo?' As the Tuscan reassuringly squeezed her hand, gently confirming, 'They're perfect. You'll see them tomorrow,' Gina felt her strength ebb. She closed her eyes, gave herself to the motion of the ship. Slipping back towards sleep she murmured, 'And Fallon?' And the last thing she heard before she drifted was Max's: 'No need to worry about your Englishman.'

Blessedly, she slept without nightmares, was surprised by how much better she felt when she woke. So deeply had she slumbered, she was unable to gauge how long it was since Max's visit, but sensed it must be a long while, for she was hungry and impatient to be up. With nothing to occupy her mind, her thoughts wandered. And she remembered. In vivid detail she remembered everything. At first she cut off the visions, afraid she would be unable to face them, but, she told herself, she couldn't shut out that last night in Baremo for ever. As she had as a child when tentatively venturing into a forbidding alley, she clenched her teeth and looked straight ahead. Then she ran forward. Across a phosphorescent, moonlit landscape she rushed and stumbled toward the scene of her fevered dreams. And there she forced herself to watch, not a jumble of subconscious images, but the precise portrayal of reality.

When it was over Gina was shaking, as if physically battered by the violence. Nevertheless she had survived. The shell which had begun to form within her the day of her father's arrest was stronger than ever, a rock upon which she would build her future – and the future of her sister and brother.

'Where are they?' she asked when Max eventually appeared with a bowl of chicken broth to be briefly huffed by her resistance to spoon-feeding but then to watch with paternal pride as she proved her ability to take care of herself.

'Drink the last drop, then they can visit with you,' the big man promised.

The reunion was joy and sorrow, hugging and kissing,

whispering and shouting. Paola and Filipo drenched Gina with their emotion. She in return swathed them with her love. It wasn't until several minutes had been consumed by jubilant, unintelligible gabble that the youngsters released their sister, Paola to sit on the edge of the bed, Filipo to stand at the wall, and Gina was able to ask them with measured calm how they were, had they been all right in Rome, did they understand where they were going. As Paola answered in her bright, sensible manner, with Filipo throwing in his enthusiastic contribution, it became increasingly apparent to Gina that the pair were not unhappy, nor was their sunniness an act put on at the behest of Max. They were genuinely lighthearted, almost excited at the prospect of what lay ahead. Listening to their optimism she was wounded by sadness, felt they should be exhibiting more grief at the execution of their previous lives. Had they forgotten everything? Including their father? Why shouldn't they be told right now all that had happened? Why should she carry the burden of knowledge alone?

Gina stilled her thoughts there. For perhaps this was the root of her resentment: self-pity. And that was an emotion she had promised herself she would never indulge again. Although, as she shared the youngsters' affection during the following hour, it took all her will to maintain this resolve. Because, as the time wore on, she knew with mounting certainty the answer to the two questions she would put to Max on his return.

When he arrived to shoo the youngsters out and was about to follow, she said, 'Is Poppa dead?'

The big man's face cracked like a suddenly struck mirror, and Gina saw her own heartbreak reflected there. But her voice held steady as she requested, 'Please tell me, Max. Now. Before I lose the courage to listen.'

A great shudder shook the Tuscan's chest and Gina feared he was about to weep, but he took a ragged breath, sat at the end of the cot, and haltingly recalled what had happened.

After Fallon and the Bobini men had found Gina on the hillside track and carried her to the wagons, the Englishman had waited until he was assured she would live and had then retraced the route to Baremo in search of Alfredo. By the time he reached the village, however, the place was in pandemonium: women were standing wailing in the square – 'Doubtless,' said Max, 'because they were terrified of being implicated in the raj's killing' – and men were rushing aimlessly back and forth. Torchlights had been set up in front of the Rossis' hut and a crowd was milling around the door. Fallon, unable to approach the scene, had watched as long as he dared before returning to the wagons knowing that further delay would endanger the entire troupe. They had reached Taranto the following morning to find Max and the freighter waiting to sail.

(Here Max faltered in his story, swallowed hard, and then, staring at the floor, continued.)

The radio bulletin had been broadcast while the ship was still in port. In a village to the north, Commander Galeazzo Sturzo, the respected and admired district leader, had been brutally murdered. The perpetrator of the atrocity was named as Alfredo Rossi, an exiled Communist to whom the raj had given accommodation and employment. Several eyewitnesses stated that the Commander had been strolling in the village square when Rossi attacked him from behind. Vigilant officers of the militia had captured the assassin as he attempted to escape. Under the recent amendment to the Constitution, a Contingent Tribunal had been held immediately and in view of the overwhelming evidence against Rossi – whose criminal record included treason and sabotage – the judges had no alternative to a sentence of guilty and the penalty as prescribed by law. Alfredo Rossi had been executed at the scene of his crime.

Gina felt as if she were teetering on the edge of a titanic cliff, poised to plummet and shatter on the rocks below. She closed her eyes and held her breath – until the vertigo gradually subsided and she was pulled back from the abyss. When she looked up at Max, she asked quietly, 'Fallon returned to Rome, didn't he?'

The Tuscan nodded.

Lying back, Gina said, 'Please leave me a while.'

She walked on deck twenty-four hours later. She had discovered her case under the cot and, contrary to Max's breakfast-time orders, dressed and swayingly made her way through a maze of corridors and companionways to emerge into the sunlight. She was at the starboard rail and along the horizon she could discern the long sepia smudge of land. 'France,' she said aloud, and it was as if the single word sealed her sense of freedom. Gulls called overhead, white kites sailing on invisible threads. Gina turned her face to the prow, breathed deep, tasted the freshness, opened her lips to let it spill between her teeth, across her tongue, as clean and cool as champagne, clearing her brain, re-invigorating her blood. Hearing footfalls, she looked around at Max. Before he could speak she said, 'I'm all right. Truly. Don't worry, my friend, it's all behind me now.' Minutes later she was sitting in the metal chair which he brought to a spot in the stern, blankets around her knees, the Tuscan's big knuckly hands on her shoulders where he stood at her back. Later Paola and Filipo came, and the four of them remained there – sometimes talking, sometimes not – as the freighter chugged on toward the west.

Gina told her sister and brother about their father's death while they were docked at Marseilles. They had only – she learned from Max – a vague idea of where she and Alfredo had been during the past six months, so she simply said that he had passed away in his sleep. With the faint confusion and embarrassment of all youngsters faced with such news, they exhibited no more and no less grief than Gina had anticipated, although, the following morning, Paola came to her with their mother's gold watch offered on her outstretched palm. Kissing her, Gina refused the return of the gift.

They were at sea for many weeks as the freighter discharged and took on cargoes at Algiers, Gibraltar, Lisbon. Gina felt no boredom at the endless seascape and coastlines. She was calmed by the sameness, and the further they sailed the stronger she became. By the time they set the Portuguese coast at their back to plough the Atlantic on the last leg of their journey, November had passed and she was filling her days with adding to her notebooks (recipes from the ship's Madagascan cook), extending the plans of her restaurant (now more splendid than the Paris Ritz), instructing Filipo in mathematics (on the rare occasions she was able to drag him away from the boiler room, or wheelhouse, or wherever else he was playing Clark Gable in *China Seas*), and coaching him and Paola in English (Max too, although he growled like a bear parted from a honeypot each time he was separated from the crew's never-ending poker game).

In the second week of December the news came that in Rome, after a two-minute meeting of the Grand Council, Mussolini had announced Italy's withdrawal from the League of Nations. Gina felt neither surprised nor perturbed; her homeland already seemed a very long way away.

Christmas came and they all agreed it was the best they had ever spent. With the captain's permission, Gina mixed a traditional English pudding from a recipe she'd learned years ago. The Madagascan watched with mild amazement as she added chopped carrots to her sultanas, raisins, cherries and dates, but he, and all his shipmates, after consuming the final crumbs, declared they would raise their ban on female crew members if Gina would take over the galley.

It was the first appreciation of her skills she'd received in a long time, and on her bed that night she allowed herself the luxury of self-satisfaction. She also permitted herself to look back – something she'd avoided since the day she woke to find herself on board. Now she recalled incidents from her childhood, life at Ristorante Rossi, shopping expeditions with her mother, theatre visits with her father. The experience left her caught between grief and pleasure. Before dawn she rose and walked on deck, turned toward the lighting horizon in their wake. Then, her back to the image of her loved ones, she summoned the features which for months she had kept behind the shades of her mind. Also she raised, slowly, the stone of vengeance which had lain hidden in the darkest corner of her soul. And there, Gina stood alone, gripping the imaginary scarab – as she stared into the face of Ugo Balbo.

Six nights later the ship echoed to the strains of 'Auld Lang Syne'. When the celebrations were done, leaving Max to deal his first hand of the first morning of 1938, Gina and Paola and Filipo went up to the fresh air. Far off on the horizon a yellow aurora arced across the black backdrop of the sky.

'Land ho!' exclaimed Filipo.

'New York,' murmured Paola.

Journey's end, thought Gina. She put her arms around her sister and brother. One journey's end, yes; but how many more lying ahead?

PART TWO

Arrival and Departure
1938-1943

6

Like a Byzantine fortress, thought Gina. Her arms around
Paola and Filipo, she was staring across the blunt prow of the
ferry as it ploughed its way across the oily-dark water of Upper
New York Bay toward the bulbous-towered buildings of Ellis
Island. Although it was only early afternoon the sky was
darkened by a mantle of freezing fog, and tendrils of mist
coiled on the marbled surface of the sea. Ahead to starboard,
derricks and warehouses and rusting ships loomed in the murk.
To port, the saturated haze shifted and swirled allowing
ghostly glimpses of the Statue of Liberty. Beside Gina, legs
astride his kitbag and her suitcase, Max blew on his fingers,
condensation shining on his whiskers, filming his throat at his
open-necked shirt. His huge sheepskin jerkin was draped
around the youngsters, burying them beneath its fleecy
warmth.

Gina shivered in her cotton dress and thin jacket, wondered
if they could survive such biting cold. The joyous New Year
celebrations of two nights ago on board the freighter seemed
like a long-past dream. Now the day was utterly still; not a
breath of breeze stirred the boat's limp, wet pennants; no
sound, save the dull throb of the engines, the slosh of swell and
an infrequent cry from an unseen bird.

They had disembarked at six a.m. eager and inquisitive.
During the following hours their spirits, systematically, had
been crumpled.

In Gina's mind the morning had merged to an oppressive
confusion of waiting in dank, bare rooms; being directed along
endless, windowless passages; searching for and at last finding
grimy, cold-water washrooms; completing reams of yellow
official questionnaires; being asked repeatedly, Country of
origin? Place of birth? Name of parents? The relentless
inquisition had hammered and hammered until Gina's head
seemed as if it would burst; but through it all she hung on to

her smile for the sake of her sister and brother, joshed and chivvied them, buttressed their confidence with her own courage. Still she thanked God for Max, at her side, holding her arm, glowering menacingly at the slightest approach from any shifty-looking male immigrants.

It was seven hours after their arrival when they were escorted to the ferry for Ellis Island carrying the khaki cards they had been issued bearing the words FURTHER EXAMINATION; and it took all Gina's will to summon a convincing laugh and answer, 'Of course not,' to Filipo's 'Are they sending us back to Italy?'

When they reached the island, to be shepherded through more buildings, across fog-wet yards, and abandoned at last in a vast dining-room, even the mugs of steaming black coffee around which they wrapped their numbed fingers did nothing to dispel Gina's sense of foreboding, only accentuating her gloom when she sipped the liquid and the rich flavour recalled Alfredo Rossi's voice: 'The real thing. Not that *surrogato* poison made from burnt peanuts.'

They sat in silence for an hour until they were summoned through more passages to a cavernous room where lines of bewildered adults and children, babbling in a confusion of languages, progressed slowly to a long wooden counter where uniformed men interrogated them in English, while examining and re-examining their passports and visas.

As Gina joined one of the lines, she recalled the awful tales she'd heard of this notorious island. In its peak year, 1907, it had processed a million and a half aliens (including over three hundred thousand Italians). It was the place of the 'one-minute doctor' where a chalk mark on a person's back denoted immigration acceptance or rejection: 'H' for suspected heart disease would be chalked on an old man with purplish lips; 'L' for 'lame' on a limping child who might have rickets; 'E' for 'eye disorder' if trachoma was diagnosed after the examinee's eyelid had been lifted swiftly with a buttonhook; and – the guarantee of immediate deportation – 'F' for 'feeble-minded' on anyone too stupefied to give their name.

Gina knew that these practices, necessitated by the overwhelming flood of refugees, had long since been replaced by humane methods and conventional exams; nevertheless she was aware of the 1924 law imposing drastic restrictions on immigration, with a strong bias against Southern Europeans.

Her heart was in her mouth when she reached the head of the line and waited while the officer behind the counter leafed through her passport and the false documents obtained by Fallon; and a wave of panic hit her as he set all the papers aside, nodded at a row of benches at the rear of the room and ordered bluntly, 'Wait over there.'

Gina hardly knew what she was doing as she obeyed; scarcely heard her own voice as she assured Paola and Filipo, 'Everything's fine. Just a little longer, then we'll be on our way.'

Sitting, she watched dazedly as the lines shuffled forward. Some of the immigrants were sent on their way, their faces glowing with gratitude and relief; others were led out, protesting and weeping; a few were instructed to sit on the benches.

Max walked toward them. A uniformed man was close behind him. Gina stood abruptly, took a rapid pace to meet the big man, knowing what he was going to say before he reached for her shoulders and declared, 'I have to stay awhile.' The brief warning look he flicked toward the youngsters stilled Gina's gasp of anguish and she felt the pressure of his fingers on her arms. Smiling broadly, Max stepped to Filipo and tousled his hair then gently touched Paola's cheek. 'You two take care, you hear. Of yourselves, and your sister. And behave. I'll be seeing you in a few days' time, and if I learn you've been up to no good . . . ' He growled with mock menace, and the youngsters laughed and stood and he gathered them against his chest, kissed their heads, held tight before releasing them.

Gina said hoarsely, 'If we're allowed through I'll get word to you.'

'Of course you'll be allowed through,' assured the Tuscan. 'So will I. Keep a place for me at the table, Principessa.' He swiftly kissed her before being led out by the uniformed officer.

Several minutes later Gina was still staring at the door where Max had exited when a voice beside her announced, 'You're free to go now.' She looked around at the grey-haired, uniformed man, then down to his extended hand and the documents he was holding. She wordlessly reached out, but was halted as the man said unemotionally:

'Do you know how many of your countrymen there are in the one square mile of Italian Harlem? One hundred and fifty thousand. Throughout the city of New York, over a million.

Foreign white residents in the city number five and a half million. Poles, Spaniards, Irish, Slavs, Lithuanians, Germans, Russians, Persians. All with different languages, religions, customs. But they all have one thing in common. Poverty. Half the families have no regular income.' He looked long and hard at Gina, glanced toward Paola and Filipo. He gave a single shake of his head, returned to Gina and said, 'You should be warned. So many come, but more return than stay. They decide it is better to be poor in their own country than starve in a foreign land.' Sighing, he handed over the false passport and papers. 'I hope the friend in Rome who got you these never regrets what he has done.' He walked away.

The fog-wet streets teemed. Gina was awed. She had never seen such jammed traffic, nor so many people. Automobiles, buses, trucks and trolley cars poured back and forth. Women picked amid the pushcarts which clustered at every corner; businessmen rushed to hail taxis; vagrants combed the gutters; policemen waved batons, blew whistles; children ran and yelled, played tag, leapfrog, football, jump-rope and potsy. The air was solid with din: the roar of the crowd, the rumble of the elevated railway, the yap-yap of distant tugboats, the wham of steam shovels, the racket of music from every window.

Filipo enthused, 'Isn't it fantastic?'

From the frantic harbourside – where Gina had kept tight hold of her sister and brother while fending off the importunings of would-be guides, self-appointed greeters, moneylenders, beggars, priests and relief-aid agents – on the advice of a news vendor, they had taken a bus to the intersection of Broadway and Broome Street to seek the President Hotel. Alighting into the pandemonium of the darkening afternoon, Gina had been prompted to ride immediately out again. But to where? She had no idea which way to turn. As she shivered in the chill dampness, she decided her prime concern must be to find a place to sleep. She led the youngsters along the street, past brightly lit shops and restaurants, skirting alleys and yards of grimy warehouses, sooty factories and endless façades of brownstone tenements spiderwebbed with fire-escapes, festooned with lines of limp washing.

The President Hotel was four stories of flaking brickwork with worn stone steps up to a glass door and a handwritten hanging sign – CHEAP CLEAN ROOMS.

Gina's heart sank. She hesitated as her sister and brother stared at the decrepit building. Maybe it wasn't as bad as it looked. 'Wait here,' she instructed and went up the steps, pushed the creaking door to enter a ten-foot square lobby. The stench assaulted her like a physical blow – a stomach-turning miasma of dishwater, urine and sweat. She clamped a hand to her mouth, paused only an instant longer to survey the filthy walls, a lank-haired woman behind a scarred desk, before hurrying out to the cold, fresh air. She gasped for breath as she descended the steps.

Paola asked, 'Are we staying here?'

'No,' Gina answered quickly. 'It was too . . . ' She regarded the youngsters' perplexed faces. 'We don't have to settle for the first place we see. I'm sure there's plenty of accommodation. Let's try along here.' She turned down a side street.

She was right. There were plenty of buildings with vacancies. But Gina had investigated half a dozen before she found one that didn't stink as badly as the President Hotel. The despair which was beginning to claim her abated slightly in a foyer which though bare was at least clean. Her spirits rose further when the thin-faced male clerk said this week there was a discount on the rent. He added, 'Of course, that only applies to married couples. We don't take no single women with kids. Still . . . ' he grinned with big, yellow teeth, 'I reckon you and me can work that out, Beautiful. Know what I mean? And,' he peered through the window to Paola on the sidewalk, 'I'll be real happy to baby-sit for you.'

Gina's blood ran cold. Too shocked to speak she stared at the man's leering face, then spun around and almost ran from the building. Seizing Filipo's hand she tugged him along, snapped at her sister, 'Don't dawdle. We haven't time to spare.' Her nerves were raw. She knew she was losing control. Halting, she took several deep breaths. You must keep your grip, she warned herself. Though a dreadful helplessness was rising within her, she smiled at her sister and brother, at their faces which had lost all their earlier adventuresome eagerness. 'I'm sorry I was abrupt,' she said with feigned levity. 'I thought it was later than it is. Hasn't it turned dark quickly?'

Filipo said, 'I'm tired, Gina.'

She bit her lip, held on to her smile. Looking around she realized they had come a long way from the main thorough-fare. Not a sensible thing to have done, she thought. I'm becoming overtired too. She suppressed a shiver as tenatacles of chill mist drifted around her legs. 'Well,' she said brightly, 'can't stand here all day. We'll just investigate a couple more places then we'll make our decision. Okay?' As the youngsters nodded she set off, retracing their route.

Back on Broome Street, huddled people hurried by the parading muddle of shops, apartment blocks, eateries and bars; cars and trucks tracked the wet paving. South's Rooming House was well-lit, smelled fresh. 'Sorry,' they told Gina. 'No unmarried mothers.' She didn't bother to argue. Nor did she at the next establishment that gave her the same dismissal. She had trudged across several despairing intersections before she came to the small grocery store whose upper storey had recently-painted windows. Amid the display of sausages, cheeses, bread, fruit and vegetables, a card declared, APT. TO LET. White letters on the glass stated, ITALIAN & AMERICAN PROVISIONS – ENRICO PONTI.

Gina faltered. Should she bother? Waste more time? Would she be better employed seeking a public hostel, even a charity home, at least a place that would provide a roof over the youngsters' heads. This has to be our last chance, she told herself, shepherding Paola and Filipo beneath the jangling doorbell.

She breathed deeply, almost tasted the heavy aroma of the meats and spices. A shudder of pleasure shook her and she stood, momentarily appreciating the atmosphere which once had been such an integral part of her life. The cloak of despond which increasingly had weighted her through this dark afternoon, slipped a fraction from her shoulders as she stepped toward the counter and the aproned, plump woman with greying black hair who was beaming at the youngsters. Before Gina could speak the woman greeted her:

'Nah then, ducks, don't tell me, pahnd to a penny it's me rooms yer after.'

The Italian on Gina's lips slipped back down her throat as the woman continued in an English dialect she didn't recognize:

'Knew it soon as you come through the door. Yer clothes. You ain't exactly kitted fer New York in January. Still, be thankful the weather's as good as it is. We're often up to our plums in snow this time of year. Worse'n ever I remember it in London. Now then, the apartment. It's on the side. Only two rooms. But spotless. I take particular particularization abaht that. My husband, the late Mister Ponti, God rest him, was a stickler fer particularization.' She quickly lifted a flap in the counter, beckoned Paola and Filipo through, was issuing them into a rear corridor while Gina was still gathering her thoughts. 'Come on along then,' called Mrs Ponti. 'See fer yourself. Ready and waiting it is. Complete with pots and pans. And bed linen. A gas fire. Meter of course. Bathroom dahn the hall. Abaht the rent . . . ' She'd disappeared around a corner, her voice diminishing behind the clatter of the youngsters' feet on the stairs.

Gina glanced back through the window. On the bustling sidewalk people's faces glistened with the wet cold; above, the streetlamps were curtained by the thickening fog; the sky was now inky black.

She followed Mrs Ponti.

The room was as fussy as its owner. Pink hollyhocks climbed the wallpaper; yellow roses covered the rugs on the blue linoleum floor; tasselled cushions jostled on the rexine sofa ('Just pull the lever, ducks, and you've got a double comfy enough fer Snow White'); at one wall stood a massive Victorian sideboard with a vine-draped mirror, at the other a small circular dining table and four chairs; in the curtain-enclosed corner was a porcelain sink and a small stove. The adjacent room contained a wardrobe, dresser and twin beds separated by a black-and-red-dragoned Chinese screen.

After a tour of inspection Gina thought this wasn't quite how she'd fantasized her settlement of the glamorous Manhattan of her mother's long-ago stories; however, it was a whole lot better than the bowels of an Atlantic freighter or a hut in the Italian desert. She re-crossed the living-room to peer out of the window, across to a blank brick wall, down to a narrow bare alley.

Mrs Ponti said, 'Ain't much of a view, ducks, but it's quiet dahn there. Clean too. I don't allow for no slinging of washing water aht the window. Not like some of the places you'll see. Lord love us, you'd wonder where some of these foreigners was dragged up! No offence, dearie. Present company excepted. I could tell as soon as I saw you, you wasn't one of them Neopolitans. A terrible lot they are and no mistake. My husband, the late Mister Ponti, God rest him, was from Florence, you know. Wouldn't have nothing to do with Neopolitans he wouldn't.'

'We're from Rome,' said Gina. Her instincts told her the apartment was all right. Its neatness, its cleanness, above all its lack of the awful stench which had pervaded the previous buildings, testified to Mrs Ponti's 'particularization'. And the woman herself, though garrulous, had an open face; she could be trusted, Gina decided, to keep an eye on Paola and Filipo when necessary. Besides, the plump comfort of the sofa was looking more inviting every second. She said, 'This seems most acceptable, Mrs Ponti. May we move in right away? I'll be happy to pay you a week in advance.' She opened her purse.

'Course you can, love. I can see as how these two young 'uns could do with a sit down. You too, I shouldn't wonder. No,' she waved away the proffered money, 'that's not necessary. You get yerself settled in. Come dahn and arrange yer rent-book and everything in the morning. Love us, we've got to have a bit of trust in life, haven't we? Anyways, I could tell right off you wasn't Neopolitans.' She beamed widely and exited closing the door behind her.

As the landlady's footfalls diminished down the hall, silence settled on the room like a deep sigh, and Gina was flooded with a feeling of relief. All the travails of the past months seemed suddenly ended as she stood here at last with no pursuers, all adversaries and adversities left behind. She was once more in a home of her own. The sofa was beckoning more insistently. But as she was about to succumb to its charm, she became aware of Paola and Filipo standing in the middle of the room. Like lost souls. Quickly quelling that sentimental image, and the urge to sit, she mustered her strength and in her best no-nonsense tone ordered, 'Come along, you two. There's a lot to do here. Paola, you and Filipo will share the bedroom. Turn the sheets back to air them. Boil the kettle and fill the hot water bottles. Filipo, unpack the case, help your sister stow our things in the dresser.'

She stepped to the gas fire and the adjacent meter on the hearth. After twice reading the instructions, she gratefully found she had – amongst the cash she'd converted to dollars and cents at the docks – the requisite coins, and was doubly thankful that the contraption ignited without blowing up. The elements burned orange and the warmth soaked Gina's face. Holding her hands to the grill she luxuriated in the glow for a moment before rising and saying, 'Well, don't stand there all day. Hop to it. I'm going downstairs to the grocery, then to the butcher's shop we passed. I'll be but a few minutes. No fooling around when I'm gone. Open the door to no one but Mrs Ponti.' She started across the room. But halted as she met her sister's and brother's eyes. Striding swiftly to them she gathered them into her arms, Paola's cheek against her own, Filipo's head pressed against her breast. She held them that way for several moments; then she hurried out and down the stairs.

When she returned a quarter of an hour later with two large brown paper sacks of supplies, the youngsters had completed their chores. Gina then got them busy washing the pots and cutlery from the cupboard and laying the table while she prepared salad and boiled tripe in a thick tomato sauce. The traditional Tuscan dish wasn't exactly *haute cuisine*, but it was nourishing, filling and cheap.

The latter attribute was the most important. As they had trudged the street this afternoon Gina had noted the prices of goods in all the store windows. Mentally reviewing their finances, she had reckoned they could survive for a month before they became destitute. Of course, she assured herself, that could never happen; with her experience of the restaurant trade she would land a job by the end of this week. Nevertheless, her inner voice had urged caution, and the budget she planned allowed for few luxuries. She did, however, fund for a café meal twice a week, having noted that many of the neighbourhood establishments offered items called 'Blue-Plate Specials' and 'Deluxe Half-Dinners' at little more than it would cost to eat at home. And, she was sure, it was important that Paola and Filipo return as soon as possible to some semblance of their previous existence. Raised in the gregariousness of Italian life, and the security of a close community, they must not now become introverted by being cooped up in the apartment, with only their schoolmates for camaraderie.

School! The thought jolted Gina as she watched her sister and brother heaping Parmesan on their *trippa alla fiorentina*. That was an item which must be given priority – along with the hundred others on her lengthening list. But, for now, everything could wait. Nothing should impinge on this meal, their first together in this new home in this new country. What a massive fact that was, she thought. And yet here they sat, Paola and Filipo digging into their dinner, chatting, laughing, as if all the preceding journey had been a mere walk to reach this picnic spot. Thank God for the adaptability of youth.

Later, after she'd managed finally to get them to bed and had opened up the sofa for herself, she glanced at the mantle clock to discover it was only eight-thirty. Yet she was tired: not achingly, killingly exhausted as she had been so many times these past months, but deeply, pleasurably heavy-eyed. Outside the street echoed busily. Familiar sounds – voices, footfalls, automobile engines – all the intimate activity which was the lifeflow of the city. Gina realized she hadn't heard it since she slept in her room above the restaurant in Via Condotti; and she switched off the light she half-expected to see through the window the rooftops of Rome.

She stepped softly to the door of the youngsters' room. They were still whispering – a mixture of English and Italian – reviewing the adventure of the day. At last their gossip began to tail off until they both yawned and murmured, 'Goodnight.' Gina was about to turn away when she heard Paola ask quietly:

'Are you frightened, Filipo?'

'Of course not,' he replied. 'Gina's with us.'

The morning dawned bright and clear. On the street everything looked more sharply defined than it had yesterday. Above the city the sky was a polished blue, the sun low but incandescent throwing long shadows across Broadway.

Paola and Filipo had risen with the bubbling expectancy of children on Christmas Day. Gina had considered reminding them that they were respectively sixteen and ten, but, having woken greatly refreshed, she too was slightly intoxicated by the spirit of anticipation. She agreed that she would delay until tomorrow her visits to the School Board, Immigration Department and other government offices: today would be devoted entirely to shopping and exploration. Having concluded her business with Mrs Ponti she had pursued her sister and brother who were already halfway along Broome Street, Paola peering into a pawn shop, Filipo on the running-board of a battered Plymouth Roadster scrutinizing the car's interior. As Gina approached the pair, Filipo called, '*Voglio andare al Empire State Building. Voorei vedere King Kong.*'

About to respond in Italian, Gina checked herself. She must be firm on this matter. 'English, please, young man.'

'American,' returned Filipo.

She threw him her steely look.

He implored, '*Se non fosse* . . . but can we? Can we visit the Empire State Building? *Per favore*. Please, Sis.'

'Don't call me Sis. All right. Providing we get all our chores done first.' Feigning indifference to his whoop of joy Gina turned to the window beneath the three brass balls where Paola was standing. The place was an Aladdin's cave. She had seen some heaped conglomerations of merchandise on the stalls in the Porta Portese flea market, but this outpiled them all. At a glance she took in an accordion, a fur coat, a top hat, a stuffed owl, tin soldiers, a leather-bound set of encyclopaedias, a set of false teeth, a doll with one eye, a radio. She hardly heard Paola say. 'It all looks so . . . *triste* . . . sad.' Gina resurveyed the window's cornucopia. After a moment she ordered, 'Wait here,' and purposefully entered the shop.

Five minutes later she emerged packageless but wearing a look of satisfaction which prompted considerable interrogation all the way to Broadway. She refused to be drawn, however, and the youngsters abandoned their efforts when they reached the bustling, swaddled crowds on the main thoroughfare.

Though the sun was bright, the air was keen from the north, stinging their faces as they turned toward the heart of the city, a sharp reminder of their need for more suitable apparel. There was, however, no shortage of good, inexpensive clothes. The ravages of the past six years were apparent in the abundance of second-hand stores and the quality of the garments they offered; and silk and astrakhan rubbing shoulders with huckaback and denim evidenced the Depression's commitment to the Constitution in treating all men as equals.

Reviewing her budget, Gina led the way through the door lettered BEST PRICES PAID on the corner of Bond Street.

When they exited Paola and Filipo were muffled in serge overcoats (Paola's with a velvet collar), scarves, woollen gloves and lined boots, she in a rabbit-skin hat, he in a Sherlock Holmes deerstalker with ear-flaps, his insistence upon which Gina had indulged since in spite of its eccentric appearance it seemed eminently practical and came with an additional attribute of having once belonged, according to the storekeeper, to a P-kip-see Vasser drama student. Gina, with no idea what that was, guessed she was being kidded as 'fresh off the boat', but the man appeared good-natured enough and his prices compared favourably with those of his numerous competitors, so Gina accepted the joshing and added to her purchases several blouses, shirts and sweaters. She kitted herself in similiar fashion to her sister and brother, though her hat was knitted red wool and her coat tailored cloth, flimsier than it should be for the weather but chosen, with a grain of vanity, for its greater degree of style than its heavier, more shapeless railmates.

Thus garbed, toting their parcels tied with hairy string, the trio proceeded northward toward the object of Filipo's fascination, with even Gina succumbing to the thrill of expectation as she beheld the height of the distant Empire State Building.

It took them two hours to reach it.

In 1931, Italy, like every other country in the world, had been stormed by front-page headlines when the title of 'the tallest building on Earth' was wrested from the famed Chrysler tower. Skyscraperless Romans had marvelled at the photographs of the 102-storey monolith, while some Fascist architects had contended that the images were faked as part of a US Government propaganda campaign. Three years later however the Ministry of Popular Culture permitted an RKO Radio Pictures movie to be shown in selected cinemas and awestruck Italians saw that the Empire State Building truly overlooked the whole of New York. There were, of course, those cynics who suggested that if the edifice was real so too then must be the gorilla who scaled it. Nevertheless, all who viewed the adventure, believers and detractors alike, retained the astounding vision of the soaring landmark.

Gina's enthusiasm took a backward step when she discovered the entrance fee was a dollar, fifty cents for herself plus a quarter for each of the youngsters, but, after an elevator ride which seemed to be heading for the moon, when she exited to the daylight all thought of the expense fled as suddenly as her heartbeat leapt. Astonishment pinioned her before she was able to follow the youngsters to the parapet.

All around, the city seemed to be reaching up for them: the tiered skyscrapers like elongated wedding cakes, and the thousand-windowed towers, so high that some were haloed by wisps of cloud. Far, far below was a park, a postage stamp of green amid a latticework of canyons; way beyond, the sky was watery blue, the sea a motionless silver, shimmering in the white light.

Gina gazed across the vista, found it impossible to equate it with any city she had ever seen. She wasn't afraid, but nor did she feel welcome; she wasn't homesick, but nor did she feel akin to this incredible place. She looked around at Paola and Filipo – they were tiptoeing and pointing and 'Oohing' and 'Ahing' – and in their faces she saw all the emotion which was eluding her. When they took her hands to pull her along the walkway, gesticulating as ever more extraordinary sights came into view, she went with them, smiling but not knowing whether she felt happy or sad.

It was much later before her uncertainties were submerged by the further wonders of the day.

They had returned to the streaming crowds, to be caught in the inexorable flow northward, past increasingly extravagant stores, overflowing bazaars, bars, dime-a-dance halls, cabarets, more restaurants than Gina could count, until at last they reached the four-block-long intersection at Seventh Avenue which was Times Square. In its way it was as overwhelming as the view from the Empire State Building. The jumble of new skyscrapers and older, lower buildings were topped by the ramshackle tangles of metal which were the skeletons of the world's largest accumulation of electric signs, and were fronted by a galaxy of billboards exhorting the onlookers to drink cola, eat peanuts, chew gum, buy a new automobile, visit the race track, see the country's most beautiful girls, attend a movie première.

For the time being Gina settled for the first, Paola for the second, Filipo for the third.

They then continued: passing the Knickerbocker Building (formerly the Knickerbocker Hotel, Gina informed the youngsters, where their countryman the great Enrico Caruso – a Neopolitan, Mrs Ponti might be interested to know – had entertained and lived); buying a newspaper from the corner stand outside the Times Building; collecting maps and fact sheets from the nearby Police Department information booth; pausing to watch the hurly-burly in the lobby of the Astor Hotel; peeping through the window of the startlingly painted red, black and yellow Lindy's Restaurant; stepping aside for a laughing group of fur-coated females and elegantly-suited males exiting from Jack Dempsey's Broadway Bar; and standing finally beneath the marquee of the Winter Garden.

'Where Poppa first saw Momma,' said Gina.

They remained there several silent moments. Gina hoped her sister and brother felt the same lump in their throats she did, but, not wishing to cloud the day with memories, she led them onward into the sunshine.

By three p.m. she was feeling mildly exhausted, but checking the faces of Paola and Filipo she found they looked fresher than daisies, still scanning the world with eager anticipation, as bright-eyed and bushy-tailed as they had been when they dashed from the apartment over seven hours ago. I must be getting old, she thought. Donning her best get-up-and-go, she said breezily, 'It will be dark soon. So, before we start for home, to celebrate today you may have one treat each. So long as it doesn't cost more than . . . ' she swiftly reviewed the family finances, decided that today was too special for over-thriftiness ' . . . two dollars. Anything you choose.'

'Anything?' Filipo's eyes gleamed.

'Well . . . ' Gina wondered if she would regret her offer.

Paola declared, '*Vorrei la permanente.*'

'What?' Gina was nonplussed.

'A permanent wave,' said Paola. 'And my hair cut. *Corti e ricci. Con la frangia.* A proper American style. *E moderno.* At a real . . . *parrucchiere.*'

She wants to look like Cleopatra,' teased Filipo. 'With a ruby in her . . . *ombelico.* Like in the movie.'

While Paola made stabbing motions at her grinning brother, Gina fleetingly wondered how he had managed to see a restricted adults-only, foreign motion picture. Deciding it was best not to pursue the question, she gave herself to the more immediate problem posed by her sister's request. Her initial reaction was a quick rejection of the idea. Paola's luxuriant hair was beautiful. Her plait when unwound reached almost to her waist. It had been brushed, a hundred strokes a night, since she was four years old, and now shone like ebony silk. Everyone had admired it. Alfredo Rossi had loved it. Yet Paola, Gina knew, had never truly liked it, had, since she turned thirteen, considered it unfashionable, continuing to wear it only to please her father. Gina thought, she's a contrary combination of the old and the new ways. But she has, too, a quiet determination. She'll always get what she wants; not, like me, and Momma, by knocking down doors, rather by persistent pushing, until whatever barrier she's up against eventually surrenders. Dwelling for several moments on this unassailable fact, Gina at last asked, 'Are you sure?'

'*Sì,*' assured Paola. 'And you promised.'

'Very well,' agreed Gina. 'Be it on your own head.' She smiled at her small witticism, though it fell short of the youngsters, then surveyed the surrounding pageant of shop fascias, signs and windows until she espied, silver-scripted on a pink hanging board, HOLLYWOOD BEAUTY PARLOUR. She led the way across the street.

Ten minutes later she was on the sidewalk with Filipo, having left Paola to the ministrations of a pink-clad girl with platinum curls and Cupid's bow lips who had assured Gina she wouldn't know her sister following the expenditure of 'a dollar seventy-five for the works'. While Paola had glowed with enthusiasm at this promise, Gina had fretted with uncertainty. Yet at the same time, in the pink-walled, pink-carpeted foyer of the salon, she had been unable to resist the speculation of how she herself might look if her blonde mane was permed into one of the chic styles posing on the parade of shiny showcards; and it was with a co-mingling of disappointment and relief at being unable to satisfy this curiosity that she returned to the street to fulfil Filipo's treat.

'A double feature,' he declared.

She should have known.

Movie houses were as numerous as live theatres, but a twenty-minute search was necessary until a programme acceptable to Filipo was found. As it was now mid-afternoon they had missed the Early Bird Matinée cheap rate and had to pay a quarter. Gina would have preferred to visit the Paramount which boasted an orchestra and speciality acts along with the film, but it was Filipo's excursion, so they ended up in the Bijou watching a cowboy wearing an enormous white stetson and white buckskin shooting innumerable characters wearing black stetsons and black suits, followed by James Cagney on the right side of the law in *G-Men*. The western, Gina thought, was ludicrous, but the anti-gangster movie terrific, with the added poignancy of fictional slums disturbingly like the real places she had seen yesterday on the bus ride from the harbour. And when she and Filipo exited to the oncoming night, Gina still recalled – would for a long time – Cagney saying, 'I seen too many back alleys to want to go back to them.'

Filipo, however, had been unconcerned with the film's social, political or moral passages; he had simply, thoroughly, enjoyed himself, bouncing on his seat along with the action, ducking bullets, and consuming (Where does he put it all? Gina wondered) popcorn, two Hershey bars and ice cream. Firing an imaginary pistol at passing traffic, he asked, 'Will we visit Hollywood tomorrow?'

Gina regarded him with great fondness. Not wishing to baffle or disappoint him with the geography of New York's distance from the movie capital being the same as that to Rome, she replied, 'Some other day. Right now we have to get to the Hollywood where your sister is being turned into a star.' Taking his hand she headed for the beauty parlour.

A young brunette and an older blonde were reading magazines on chairs in the foyer. Smiling 'Good evening' then instructing Filipo to wait, Gina went through to the salon, searching the faces beneath the driers for her sister. When none of the females was familiar she continued to a rear room where half-a-dozen customers were in various stages of shampooing and perming. Beckoning a pink-overalled girl and enquiring the whereabouts of Paola, Gina learned that the youngster had been 'finished' fifteen minutes ago. Stabbed by sudden panic she hurriedly checked the powder room before running back past the driers to the foyer, calling, 'Come along, quickly,' to Filipo who was chatting with the brunette.

'What's the rush?' he asked.

Gina pulled up in mid-stride. Stared at the girl. And slowly her eyebrows climbed and her jaw sank. Claudette Colbert! The unmistakable apple cheeks, saucer eyes and pencilled, arching brows, the tweaked bangs and short-cut cirls. But why on earth was she wearing Paola's velvet-collared coat?

She was still shell-shocked when they returned to the now neon-bathed Great White Way.

The bus was packed, but they managed to get a seat, Filipo jammed in by the window. All the way during the long ride home to Broome Street, Gina cast covert glances at her sister. Paola's transformation was incredible. She had changed, in less than four hours, from a pretty but child-faced teenager, to a beautiful young woman. The cosmetics were part responsible, but the dramatic metamorphosis had been wrought chiefly by the new hairstyle. And Paola revelled in it, unashamedly studying herself whenever possible in the reflecting bus windows, constantly touching the waves at her ears as if to make sure they were really there.

Gina, relieved that the shearing hadn't been a disaster, was happy for her sister. Yet it wasn't without sadness that she rode away from the bright lights. For back there she felt they had left something more than Paola's tresses. It was as if the two youngsters had renounced a part of their previous selves, had become, if not quite American, certainly less Italian. And both seemed content in their new skins, exhibiting no regret at the shedding of the old. Gina appreciated that she ought to be pleased, rather than downhearted, at their rapid acclimatization, and, she guessed, her disappointment was not so much due to her sister's and brother's apparent kinship to this city as to her own inability to feel the same.

When they alighted from the bus, Gina announced, 'We'll eat in a restaurant.' It would be the finishing touch to their day; and, she'd decided, it might dispel her despondency.

Casting caution to the wind she chose what seemed to be the most expensive establishment on Broome Street, the Grotta Azzurra Inn, and gave Paola and Filipo the run of the menu. That the place could justify its prices was proved by the excellence of the food, the cheerful attentiveness of the proprietor and his staff, and the fact that the crush of clientele was wholly Italian. As wine, song and conversation flowed from table to table, Gina began to fade in and out of the past. She exchanged jokes and badinage with waiters and customers, drank the best part of a bottle of Chianti, accepted several more drinks from she knew not who, passed from happy to elated to maudlin and back again, overlooked the fact that her brother and sister, like everyone else in the room, were chattering in their native tongue, and eventually shepherded the youngsters into the night, oblivious to how much the celebration had cost.

She sobered fifteen minutes later when the restaurant check fluttered from her pocket to the living-room floor and she realized she had parted with six dollars. Still, she told herself as she sank to the sofa, they wouldn't have another day like this for quite some time; and, as Max used to say, 'Better to spend one roaring night a week than seven with stingy groans.' The old villain's maxim was related to rather more intimate matters than dining out, but Gina was sure its sentiments suited tonight's extravagance very well.

This self-assurance was vindicated when Filipo squeezed his arms around her neck and – in English – yawned, 'It was a wonderful day. I love you.'

Gina hugged him, kissed him, held him a long moment before promising, 'I'll come and tuck you in later.'

As Filipo left the room, Paola joined her sister on the sofa. With her make-up faded and tiredness softening her veneer of sophistication, she looked more like the girl who had accompanied Gina during the first half of the day. She asked quietly, 'Is it all right? *Mia permanente*. Do you hate it?'

Gina pulled her close. '*Mi piace*. It's beautiful. You're beautiful. The boys at school will love you.' She smiled. 'Yes, you do have to go. I'll arrange it tomorrow.'

The first thing she did in the morning, however, was return to the pawnshop to collect the item she'd bought and left there the previous day. As she lugged it through the door, Paola exclaimed, '*Una radio!*' Filip cried, 'Wow! Can we hear *Amos 'n Andy*?' Gina setting the mahogany-boxed receiver on the sideboard, plugging it into the wall socket, declared, 'It's to help us learn our new language. When I get back I'll expect you to tell me all the news – in English.' She exited as four hands flew toward the knobs.

She spent the following seven hours visiting Government departments, the library, the post office, the Visitor and Convention Bureau, untangling red tape, collecting information, gleaning all she could to enable her to regulate the existence of herself and her family. For that is what Paola and Filipo now were. Her family. Her responsibility. She was pledged not to fail them. And by the end of this third day in their new country she felt considerably more assured in her vow.

She took home wool, needles and a sweater pattern for her sister, a jigsaw depicting the liner *Nieuw Amsterdam* in the Hudson for her brother. In the lamplit sitting-room, Paola commencing her knitting on the sofa, Filipo sorting his puzzle on the table, to the radio background of Woody Herman in 'Mood Indigo', Gina stood at the sink washing their dinner pots. She looked around at the engrossed pair; permitted herself a sigh of relaxation; knew they were going to survive. Just one more step, and their roots in American soil would be secure. Just one small step. She'd take it tomorrow.

Tomorrow she'd find a job.

7

She began by aiming at the top. Primed with determination, armed with a lifetime's expertise (plus a potential employers list compiled from the *New York Guide*), Gina set out to offer her executive services to the upper echelons of Manhattan's restaurateurs.

During the first hour she didn't even get to give her name to a hat-check girl. Wherever she called, as soon as she mentioned employment she was dismissed with a curt headshake at the door. In the next half-dozen places, reinforcing her persistence, she at least got to talk to an assistant manager or *maitre d'*, but was always cut off with the same response: 'We've got all the secretarial help we need. Nobody uses females for serving *haute cuisine*. There's a part-time spot for a cocktail waitress.'

In the biting wind of Lexington Avenue she gritted her teeth. It wasn't so much the rejection that pained her, but the inhospitality with which it was delivered. In Rome, family tradition in the catering trade could be traced over centuries. From the finest establishments of the Via Veneto to the smallest trattorias of the Trastevere, a grapevine of information and reputation linked owners, management and employees. Newcomers to this community were rare – Fascist laws severely restricting cross-country migration – thus an itinerant worker, even if no job was available, would be welcomed with interest and courtesy.

As Gina plodded on, the vast difference between her home and New York became increasingly apparent.

It wasn't until late afternoon that the cellarman in the side alley of the Lobster House, busy inventorying a beer delivery, waved her toward a door with the information, 'The boss is in the bar.' Gina, confidence recharged, resolute now to present her credentials come what may, strode along a narrow passage which led to a small, dimly-lit and elegant room. Amid potted palms glass-topped, chromium-framed tables with green velvet-shaded lamps curved in front of a plush-upholstered bar. A large, balding man in shirt sleeves and open waistcoat perched incongruously on a tall stool was watching a girl in a sailor suit tap dancing a frenetic hornpipe in a space between the chairs. The girl whirled into a big finish, did the splits, and posed, arms aloft, face almost rupturing with forced enthusiasm.

The man proclaimed flatly, 'Not bad. Tell 'em in the front office you got two spots Saturday night,' and as the girl backed out exuding profuse gratitude he swung around to Gina and said, 'If you can't hoof as good as that, don't waste my time – or yours.'

Gina hurriedly explained, 'No, I'm not a dancer.' Then, giving what she knew was her best winning smile, she launched rapidly into her presentation, determined to say her piece, not permitting the man to get a word in edgewise as she related all her experience, threw in considerable proof of her abilities including the correct way to lay cutlery, which wines to serve with various dishes, the vintage years for champagne, how (with the aid of her handkerchief) to fold a serviette into a water lily, and finally, with a shrewd recollection of the establishment's name, the authentic Sicilian recipe for *aragosta allo spiedo*. She concluded by beaming more brightly than the successful tap-dancer, then waited, heart in mouth, as the man stared into a stunned silence.

At last he said, 'You're wasting your time.'

Gina inhaled sharply. As she groped for something more to say, some extra scrap of persuasion, the man went on, 'Don't get me wrong. Your routine was impressive. And I believed it. If you've got any more lobster recipes I'll be glad to pay you a couple of dollars.'

Gina's patience began to fracture. 'I don't want charity,' she retorted. 'I came here for a job. A skilled job. I can do anything you ask. As well as anybody. Better than most. I'd heard that America was the land of decency and equal opportunity. But it seems I was told wrong. And now that I've seen the truth, the way people are treated, I'm beginning to think I should never have come here, never brought my family to such a heartless place.' She began to turn.

'Hold it.' The man slid quickly from his stool, caught her arm. Facing Gina's simmering anger he said frankly, 'You'd better understand the way it is.' He released her and began, 'You know how many fellers I had looking for work this week? At least three dozen. And I said fellers. Men with wives and kids to support. Not all dishwashers either. Experienced waiters, chefs, bartenders. Sure, I know you said you used to have your own place, but so did a thousand others in New

York. Once-successful restaurateurs, night club owners, hoteliers. Wiped out by the Crash. They come here from all over the country, thinking this is the only place they stand a chance of starting over.' He sighed. 'They got about as many prospects as a snowball in hell.'

Gina mentally flinched.

The man continued, 'I'm sorry I cut you down before. No offence intended. But it's been one of those mornings. Three hundred over lunch. An idiot who kicks up because his turbot doesn't taste like tuna. A dame who thinks the Fresno jug-wine should be better than imported Chablis. A yappy-mouthed lapdog that pees – excuse me – all over the carpet.' He smiled. 'You know how it goes.'

It was the first acknowledgement of fellowship Gina had received all day. Relaxing slightly, she nodded.

The man regarded her. 'Before you wear down any more shoe leather let me give you some advice. If you trek a few hundred miles around the Village or Little Italy you eventually might land a job. But tramping the streets this end of town will earn you nothing but blisters. Up here the guys who hire and fire have enough on their plate without also having to interview every busboy and kitchen hand. You only got to see me because Ed out back figured you were here to audition. Entertainers I got to check out personally. All other staff, from the sommelier to the cigarette girl, come with proven references. From an agency.' To Gina's stare he asked, 'You don't have them back home? I should've figured.' He checked his watch. 'I got a quarter hour before the next would-be Ruby Keeler arrives. Pull up a stool.' He walked around the bar. 'I think you could use a drink.'

That night Gina took her potential employers list and threw it in the trash can.

When she'd left the Lobster House she'd felt as limp as a wet rag – and considerably older and wiser. She now knew the facts of life: there wasn't the remotest chance of climbing the ladder of her ambitions from any place except the bottom rung, and even a foothold on that was going to be hard-won. But travelling back to Broome Street she rebuilt her resolve, prepared for the struggle ahead.

The following morning she was outside the Madison Catering & Hotel Bureau fifteen minutes before it opened; still she was twentieth in the rush through the door. In an oak-panelled tiny cubicle she sat before a morning-suited, fish-eyed character and re-ran the presentation she had given the previous afternoon, but with greater care and practised enunciation, pausing politely when her interrogator asked a question, answering firmly but modestly. When she was done, all the details noted in the man's ledger and he said, 'And your references, Miss Rossi?' she unhesitatingly opened her purse and handed over the envelope. She smiled guilelessly as the man extracted the letter and read. But it was with overwhelming relief that she accepted its return. The proprietor of the Lobster House had said, 'Without a reference you might as well not waste your time coming north of Forty-Second. I can't say you worked here. All the reputable employment agencies would know it was a lie. You'd never get a job. I'd never get another decent pastrycook. What I can do is give you a letter of introduction; vouch for your credentials. Why should I? In exchange for the recipe, what else.' Gina had mentally pledged her heart to the man.

She did so again as her Madison Bureau interviewer said condescendingly, 'That seems quite satisfactory.' He handed her a small printed card on which he had written a number, and pronounced, 'You may now sit in the waiting room. When we receive notification of a vacancy, if you are suitable you will be sent to fill it. May I remind you, staff from this bureau are of the highest calibre. Conscientious in their work and morals. Should we receive any complaint from an employer, the misdemeanant is stricken from our register, and, of course, is recommended to be blacklisted at every other agency in the city. That will be two dollars for your enrolment fee.'

Gina paid; returned to the outer office and waited.

It was some time before she understood that the number on her card meant there were six hundred and seventy prospective workers ahead of her on the employment allocation list. When the counter clerk explained the system it seemed superficially fair. The following morning Gina discovered it was less than perfect.

Enrolees were issued assignments according to their length of registration. But only if they were on hand when a vacancy occurred. Therefore, as about a dozen jobs were available first thing each morning, the twelve hopeful workers at the head of the list had to be at the bureau when it opened at seven-thirty. So did the next twelve, in case any of those with precedence didn't show up. A further twenty to thirty needed to be on hand for the positions which invariably came on the market during the first hour of the working day. Thus there was always an initial stampede to the counter followed by a nerve-racked milling around the room while telephones rang and numbers were called. By mid-morning the majority were still without jobs; they then would run to a second agency, later a third and fourth, before returning to the Madison. Their life was a desperate waiting game – waiting for, somewhere in the city, a chambermaid, a head waiter, a desk clerk to fall ill, get fired, drop dead.

By the end of her first week in New York Gina was a hardened player in the game.

After she had enrolled Paola and Filipo in school, established their daily routines, the only time she took out from touring employment agencies was to make enquiries about Max Barzini. She'd phoned the Immigration Department several times without success, so one drizzling afternoon she took the bus to the harbour depot. Hundreds of people swarmed around the building, filled the corridors, jammed the enquiries office to petition the four hard-pressed counter clerks. It took Gina the best part of two hours to get to put her question. After an age of anxiously watching the clerk check registers, she almost cried with relief when told the Tuscan was still detained on Ellis Island but that no deportation order had been made against him. No one, she was informed, was permitted to visit the island, but letters could be sent.

She hurried home with the news for Paola and Filipo, and after dinner sat at the table to write to Max, sent him their exploits, their address and all their love. He was going to be all right, she told her sister and brother. When the youngsters were in bed she repeated the assurance to herself. Max must survive. He had given so much, so unselfishly – he and Robert Fallon.

Gina mentally paused, recalling the Englishman. He had been at the boundaries of her mind for many days, but in the turmoil of her new existence had not reached her innermost thoughts. Now she evoked, tentatively, his image.

She remained at the table for a long time reliving her moments with the Reuters correspondent before it occurred to her to write to him. Should she? Her inability to arrive at an instant positive decision confused her. As did her reaction to her reminiscences. She felt none of the old romantic longing.

Or was it that she purposely shied from it? Gina shrugged aside that speculation, returned to the prospect of writing to Fallon. How could she? She didn't have his address. A letter to his office might cause him embarrassment. These were the excuses she gave herself. Perhaps it would be better to contact him via a third party. Certainly. Convinced this was the correct course, she took the assurance to bed, along with the question, Who?

It was Saturday afternoon – the employment bureau was closed, the youngsters were helping Mrs Ponti stack provisions – when Gina thought of David Lowell. She remembered the English hotelier, Fallon's friend whom she'd met in Rome, and recalled his good-humoured tales about catering to British holidaymakers at his Richmond hostelry named The Grange. Odd, mused Gina, how some encounters return to mind so vividly. Perhaps that was because it had been the day her father was arrested. Resisting being drawn into that sad recollection, she concentrated on composing a letter to David Lowell. How do you write to a person you met only once? Particularly if your motive is to enquire about someone else?

She took up her pen. 'Dear Mr Lowell, you probably won't remember me, but . . .'

An hour later she'd filled eight pages with a synopsis of the past two years and had all but overlooked to mention Robert Fallon. The committing to paper of her experiences seemed to distance them in reality, and as she scribbled her signature Gina felt a rising sense of well-being. Accomplishment too. Such was her happy satisfaction she went immediately to the Post Office and mailed the letter. She barely thought of receiving a reply. That the task was fulfilled was sufficient. She resolved not to think of Fallon again. All her energies, mental and physical, must be devoted to her family. And that meant landing a job.

She was at the Madison Bureau each morning when it opened, and while she waited for her number to come up she listened and she learned. From the gossip, the complaints, the laments of her fellow hopefuls, she learned the workaday details of the city's restaurant and hotel trade: that the Board of Health had declared the cleanest eateries to be in Chinatown; that the Waldorf-Astoria had raised its single-room-with-bath rate to seven dollars a night; that an upcoming ordinance would banish fourteen thousand pushcart food peddlers from the streets; that there were now over forty hotels in Manhattan with television in their rooms; that three people had died after eating stuffed krishes in a Cherry Street café; that a recent debutante supper for five hundred at the Ritz cost five thousand dollars; that there was plenty of dishwasher work downtown paying twenty cents an hour.

Gina thought about the latter each evening as she paid Mrs Ponti for the supper groceries. But she remembered the advice of her Lobster House benefactor: 'If you apply for a job in one of our la-di-da hotel teashops and tell them you've been serving for twenty years in a greasy spoon on the Bowery, they'll inform you the job's taken. On the other hand, if you let them know you once filled a glass of water for the Duke of Windsor, they'll have you pouring the Earl Grey before you've had time to button your uniform. Never forget, in this trade, in this city, it isn't what you do that counts, but where you did it.'

As the weather grew daily more bitter, and the Rossis' cash reserves sank rapidly lower, it took all Gina's will to heed the warning and hold fast to her course. Her determination to survive became all-consuming. While to her sister and brother, Mrs Ponti, all those she met at the bureau, she was outwardly her normal caring and interested self, within her was a chill, hard core of insentience that permitted no emotions to lessen her resolve. Even at mass (establishing the youngsters at the Church of St Andrew had been as essential as their schooling) though she joined in the service, she didn't truly listen. Her belief in the church's moral teachings was immovable, but her faith in the aid of an unseen Deity had been replaced by an iron-cast conviction that she alone would shape the family's future.

She would not give up, she told herself every night, repeating the promise until it became an oath; and when, during the fourth week of January, her money ran out, she didn't think twice about entering beneath the sign BROKE? – CALL ON UNCLE which overhung the door of the pawnshop where she had purchased the radio.

The broker gave her a hundred dollars against her mother's emerald necklace. A tenth of its value. She didn't argue. She'd reclaim it within a month. Within a month she'd have work. Gina swore it to herself as she pocketed the cash, leaned into the winter, and headed for the employment bureau.

Everybody called it the Howard. And everybody who was anybody stayed there when they were in New York. Its full title was the Howard West, and most visitors guessed that it was thus named for its location, facing the sun dawning behind the Metropolitan Museum across the oasis of Central Park. Those in the know, however, were aware that the palatial six-hundred-room hostelry was a memorial, erected by Alicia Cornell who, when she heard in 1901 that John Jacob Astor IV was to build the Astor Hotel as 'a temporary home for those who are used to the best of everything', had paid double-time to architects and construction crews to complete the baroque monolith ahead of her rival's mock-Renaissance edifice.

The year the Howard West opened was the year Alicia Cornell became a widow. Not that her new status, even though it came only eighteen months after marriage, bothered her too much. Alicia had not married Earl for his love, but because his name was Cornell.

The Cornells, their English forebears' wealth and titles granted in return for propping up a succession of shaky monarchs, had been among the upper echelons of New York's original Four Hundred; and while in recent years their capital in crumbling investments had dimished, their stock in society remained gilt-edged – the self-appointed elite of the city being unwilling to cold-shoulder anyone who claimed a bloodline to British Royals. Prestige however didn't pay mortgages. Earl had not married Alicia for her beauty, but because her name was West.

It had been sixty years earlier that a squat, heavy-shouldered teenaged Slav, Walthe Vestric, had jumped ship in Boston. Walthe's cabin-boy life at sea had taught him one important fact: comfort-starved travellers will pay any price for whatever salve they need to ease their aches. His chance to profit from this knowledge came six years after his arrival in America.

Gold was discovered at Sutters Mill in 1848; and within eighteen months forty-thousand hopefuls had rushed to California. Among them was Walthe Vestric. But he didn't bring a pick and shovel. He brought four ex-Army twenty-foot-long tents – all he could afford to buy and freight – and at Angels Camp he charged two dollars a night to sleep beneath canvas. Six months on, with tent-hotel saloons in a dozen shanty towns, while prospectors panned a hundred dollars a day Walthe made ten times as much supplying shelter, food, liquor, women and any other commodities which the newly-albeit-briefly-rich considered essentials of their lives.

Fifteen years later, Walthe Vestric returned east. He settled in New York with three million dollars, a pale wife and a new identity. It was Walter West who died an hour into the new century leaving behind a string of brick and timber saloons, hotels and restaurants scattered coast to coast. On his deathbed he confided to his daughter he had only one regret: none of the properties bore his name.

Alicia rectified the omission four years later (three months before the Astor opened). The Howard West was given the Christian name of her son, the surname of her father.

The afternoon was bitter; the wind knifing down the Hudson, carrying the smell of snow from the deep-buried Catskills. The maroon-coated and capped doorman of the Howard banged his hands together, stamped his feet, his breath pluming in white clouds as he forced his chattering teeth to smile when he opened and shut limousine doors, blew his whistle for cabs and cursed the weather which kept people's hands in their pockets and might reduce his tips for this shift to less than fifteen dollars.

In the hotel's basement Gina felt no warmer despite her several layers of clothes, woollen hat, socks and boots, and was making a concerted effort to prevent her entire body from shaking where she sat straight-backed on the rickety Bentwood chair before the woman who had just caused her heart to leap with joy.

Mrs MacDonald was small and round, floral collar of her frock peeping over the top of her grey wraparound apron, face as polished as an apple with bluebonnet eyes, white hair in a neat bun on top of her head. Her hands, which fluttered about her paper-littered desk while she talked, and her forearms were redder and shinier than her cheeks – a legacy, Gina would learn, from the first twenty years of her working life spent in the Howard's laundry where, since she was twelve, her skin had been flayed by scalding steam, lye soap and raw soda.

Now fifty-four, Mrs MacDonald was the hotel's head cleaner, responsible for the three hundred girls who maintained the pristine condition of the Howard's bedrooms, suites, public rooms, restaurants, offices and eight miles of corridors. She was facing Gina in her unheated, eight-foot-square, subterranean headquarters surrounded by tottering cartons of cleaning materials, addressing her in the burr she had brought from Edinburgh at eleven years of age. 'You'll work sixty-six

105

hours a week,' she said, 'with two half-days off, plus an extra hour on Sundays to attend mass or whatever other service you follow. Mrs Cornell,' as she uttered the name her voice became almost reverent, 'unlike many employers, permits her workers freedom of religious choice.'

Gina, her reserves of strength as depleted as her cash after five weeks of waiting, hoping, tramping around the agencies, would have agreed to worship a totem pole if it had guaranteed a job. Such abasement however had not been necessary. That morning one of the hotel housemaids had reported sick; measles was diagnosed, and her position would not be held open for the week's quarantine the disease necessitated. Gina, at last heading the line at the Madison Bureau, had run all the way here after being handed the job introduction card, her ticket to work for fourteen dollars a week.

'A uniform will be provided,' Mrs MacDonald sing-songed. 'Its cost will be deducted from your wages at fifty cents a week. You'll be expected to wash, starch and iron it regularly. If you don't have washing facilities at home, you may use a sink in the staff toilets. There'll be a charge for the soap you use, of course. Its price, along with a list of other items you may purchase, including lunch or supper, is posted in the locker-room. Employees are not allowed liquor on the premises. When they are working they must not smoke, talk or sing. You will be a housemaid. You will work in corridors and public rooms. You will not be permitted to enter bedrooms until you have proved satisfactory in your work and trust-worthy in your personal conduct. Then, in a year or two, if you're fortunate, you'll be promoted to chambermaid. If when on duty you encounter guests you will step aside. You will not look them directly in the eye, nor, of course, will you speak. If a guest greets you, you will curtsy briefly with the requisite reply and the title sir or madam. If a guest asks you a question you will apologize for not knowing the answer.'

But what if I do know the answer? The question voiced itself in Gina's head, although she realized by now that to ask it would be futile Housemaids weren't supposed to know anything: like children and animals they should be seen and not heard, and in common with those two species should be unswervingly grateful to the hand that fed them.

Listening to the smiling Mrs MacDonald continuing her rules for successful employment, Gina's initial happiness at landing the job began to wane. The chill of the cramped room crawled up her legs, and the sense of triumph was overlaid by a feeling of defeat. She shivered involuntarily, but tensed her muscles against a further spasm lest this woman think she was a weakling or had some disease like Gina's unfortunate predecessor. Because, although the degradation of the position was now apparent, Gina needed the work. And, she told herself, here she would be indoors, secure from the freezing New York winter. Besides, no matter how heavy the labour, it could never be half as bad as the toil her father had endured in Baremo. Nor would it be for ever. Even as she watched her name being scribbled in Mrs MacDonald's register, she vowed she would move on from this place within twelve months with the experience and prestige of a job at the Howard West banked as collateral against her future – and the future of Paola and Filipo.

'We're all one big happy family at the Howard,' smiled Mrs MacDonald. 'Now, off you go . . . ' she squinted at her register, checking the name she had entered, ' . . . Jeanie.'

Five minutes later Gina had retraced her route from the bowels of the building, through a maze of passages and stairways to recognize the distant rear entrance via which she had arrived. About to head toward this escape she was halted by the red-lettered warning NO UNAUTHORIZED PERSONNEL on a door by her left. Drawn to the small glass panel above the sign, she peeked through – and caught her breath. For a full minute she stared in fascination at the scene beyond the window, like Alice, lured by, yet hesitant to cross into that alien world. Then, reminding herself that she didn't become officially 'personnel' until five-thirty tomorrow morning, she strode through.

The marble-floored, mirror-walled lobby of the Howard had been created for women to parade their jewels and for men to flaunt the money that paid for them. Gina was transfixed by the pageant of opulence, the confidence of the immaculate denizens of this gilded land as they loitered, greeted each other, switched on smiles with practised ease, moved purposefully yet unhurriedly toward their destinations, maroon-jacketed bellboys buzzing amongst them like horseflies attendant on a pedigree herd. Angrily Gina snuffed out that derisory image, chastising herself for giving way to the pang of envy which had evoked it. 'Jealousy is the most wasted of all emotions,' Alfredo

Rossi had tutored. She swallowed against the lump in her throat, obliterated the memory of the foyers of Rome's Excelsior, Majestic and Grand where she would visit with her mother to take tea, so English, yet served with that dash of *evviva la vita* which so essentially was the heart of her beloved Eternal City.

She watched the spectacle for several minutes before she realized she was being observed with suspicion by a bellboy. Then she raised her chin, squared her shoulders and strode forth wearing her dignity and her second-hand cloth coat with an air of total assurance; across the elegant expense, her huge gold eyes scanning the guests, her lips curving a greeting. As she exited she faltered briefly when the doorman sprang to her service, cab-hailing whistle rising to his lips, but she forged ahead saying radiantly, 'Thank you, but I shall walk. It's such a splendid day. So bracing,' and she swung down the avenue, doing her best to maintain her poise in the clumping boots, promising herself that the next time the man touched his cap to her she'd leave him wide-eyed with appreciation, not open-mouthed with shock.

Striding, she was seized by the desire to laugh out loud. A swelling thrill of freedom was filling her. The job at the Howard West might be a far cry from her original expectations, but for now it was security. And that meant emancipation; release from the major worry which had chained her these past weeks.

So numbed was she by the emotion, she had walked the length of Central Park before she was brought to her senses, and a halt, by the millrace of traffic surging past a statue atop a granite column. Checking the street signs Gina discovered she was facing Columbus Circle. So that must mean the character on the monument was . . . .

Quickly crossing Broadway she stood beneath the pillar and for several moments gazed up at her marble compatriot. Then she turned, and as she surveyed the sweep of activity in front of the General Motors tower, around the arc of the Park Theatre, for the first time since her arrival in New York, she didn't compare the scene with Rome. She knew she still couldn't – wouldn't for a long time – regard this as home, but at last she sensed a kinship, the feeling of belonging which had eluded her for so long. At this moment she realized too that, if only for today, she had absolutely nothing to do, no employment bureau to visit, no doors to knock upon. She exclaimed aloud, *'Fantastico!'* and when the lad sitting on his shoe-shine box glanced around with surprise, she threw him a smile which lit up the rest of his day.

Gina spent the remainder of her day in an orgy of self-indulgence. Window shopping. ◄

She toured every glittering display along Central Park South, down Fifth Avenue, amid the construction din of the still-growing Rockefeller Centre, pausing only once for a cup of coffee, aware of neither her hunger nor fatigue as she revelled in choosing ensembles from Bonwit-Teller, Bergdorf Goodman, Russeks, Saks, not succumbing to homesickness even when Tiffany's façade conjured memories of Venice's Palazzo Vendramini. That her spending spree was imaginary did not matter; the joy of pretending, and being free to do so, was enough. And it wasn't until the street suddenly filled with homeward bound office workers that she realized the day had flown and she reluctantly ended her fantasy.

It was dark by the time she returned to Broome Street. As she turned the key in the lock, frantic whisperings came from within the apartment, muffled shufflings, the thump of something falling. Gina entered, closed the door, surveyed the room.

Paola, slipping a stitch of her knitting, smiled around from the sofa. 'Hi, Gina. Had a good day?'

Filipo, belly down in front of the heater, chin on his knuckles, glanced up from his book. 'Hey, Sis!'

'Don't call me Sis.' Gina watched the pair of them return nonchalantly to their occupations. Frowning, she searched the room for signs of hastily hidden breakages or spillages. Seeing nothing apparent she enquired carefully, 'What have you two been doing?'

'Nothing,' they chorused.

As innocent as Hansel and Gretel, Gina thought. But, she wondered, who have you pushed into the oven? Tugging off her hat, shaking out her hair, she decided that whatever mayhem they'd committed would eventually come to light, and, anyhow, everything was forgivable today because nothing must overshadow her great news or the celebration she had planned. 'I've got a job,' she declared triumphantly.

Filipo continued to stare at his book (which, Gina vaguely noted, was upside down), muttering, 'Uh huh.'

Paola murmured, 'That's nice.'

Gina's cheeks filled with indignation. 'Nice!' she exclaimed. 'Is that all you can say? Don't you understand? Did you hear me? I said – I've got a job.'

'So have I,' boomed the voice from the kitchen.

Gina spun, simultaneously almost jumping out of her boots, her mouth springing open but the shock freezing on her lips as the side door bounced wide and the huge figure loomed over the threshold. She reflexively jolted back, hands snapping up to her mouth. Then Paola and Filipo were leaping to their feet, bounding across the room, bleating with laughter, dashing to the giant, sheepskin-clad man to be gathered into his arms as he hailed, 'Principessa. Don't you recognize an old warhorse?'

Gina's hands fell at her sides, all lingering thoughts of her future at the Howard West evaporated and a great surge of joy filled her as she started forward, tears bursting from her eyes, flowing down her cheeks as she ran and buried her face in Max Barzini's chest.

'So,' he said, 'now you can tell me about the job.' He set down his glass, the entire contents of which he had quaffed in one gulp, and recharged it from the bottle of Barolo delivered by the waiter to their corner table in the Grotta Azzurra. In the apartment Max hadn't given Gina time even to brush her hair, insisting as he shooed the youngsters into their coats that they must celebrate immediately. Little more had been said as they hurried along the evening street, Gina's arm linked with Max's, Paola clutching his hand, Filipo running ahead from one pool of lamplight to the next. And for the first time since she had left Rome over two years ago, Gina felt a strengthening surge of confidence. An exhilaration, almost a lightheadedness, was upon her, and the stinging wind no longer chilled her, but sent the blood racing through her veins, singing in her ears.

The sensation persisted here in the restaurant as she sipped the red wine and replied to Max, 'There isn't much to tell. They haven't explained my duties yet. But the work will be easy. There'll be plenty of breaks. And the person in charge, Mrs MacDonald, seemed very fair. I'm looking forward to it.' She smiled widely at her three companions. The lie however was only for the sake of Paola and Filipo, for she knew that no matter how inpenetrable her expression Max could read her face like an open book. She continued casually to her sister,

'I'll be on shifts. We'll have to make some arrangement with Mrs Ponti to look in on you the nights I'm working. And to make sure you're up in time for school.'

'There'll be no need,' rejoined Paola. 'I can cope. I'm not a child, you know. I'm seventeen.' She glanced at Max. 'Almost.'

He grinned appreciatively, twirled his moustache in fingers and thumbs. 'It shows. In America a few weeks and already you're a sophisticated lady.' He cast an eye over her new, fringed hairstyle and the lick of lipstick she had surreptitiously applied, Gina now noticed, somewhere between the apartment and here. 'You're going to be as beautiful as your sister,' he said. 'Your poppa would have been so proud.'

The statement came naturally, but it fell hard into the circle around the table, and the big man's eyes filled with self-reproach as he ground shut his jaws.

Gina interjected quickly, 'He would indeed. Of Filipo too. Isn't he handsome?' She stroked her brother's hair, flushing the blood to his cheeks. 'And so clever. Already he speaks American better than me. And his teacher says he's one of the fastest learners in his grade. We're going to have a professional man in the family. A doctor. A lawyer. A banker even.'

'I'd rather be a movie star,' declared Filipo.

'Yes, well, you'll grow out of that,' returned Gina, then, seeing the small hurt in her brother's eyes, added, 'Didn't you marvel when you visited the Empire State Building? Wouldn't you want to be a big businessman sitting way up there? On top of the world. Higher than everybody.' She reached for his hand, squeezed it, and, as it always did, his face lit with her contagious enthusiasm. Gina went on, 'And, of course, Paola will be married to someone just as important. Max, these two are going to be so successful, you and I will probably get gold-engraved invitations to Sunday lunch.'

The youngsters smiled embarrassedly and the big man chuckled. At that moment, to Gina's relief, forestalling any speculation on her own future, the waiter arrived with steaming platefuls of *gnocchi alla romana*, and conversation was suspended as forks dug rapidly into the cheese-smothered semolina dumplings.

For a while there was only the sound of appreciative munching, until Max, dabbing his whiskers with his red-checkered napkin, pronounced, *'Questo e molto buono!'*

Gina agreed. 'Yes. This is an excellent trattoria. Owned by a family from Fiesole. But I've found that not all the so-called Italian places are as good. Some of them have Americanized the traditional recipes, cut down on the oil and herbs, diluted the flavours. Which is foolish. I'm sure there are plenty of non-Italians who'd appreciate genuine Umbrian or Florentine cuisine.'

'Maybe you should open a Ristorante Rossi,' joked Max.

Gina glanced at her brother and sister, intent on their food. Sipping her wine she said thoughtfully, 'Maybe I should.'

The remainder of the meal passed in happy conversation, the commerce of the café bustling around them as if to underline the fact that their lives were returning, if not to how it had been, at least to some semblance of order. Max explained how, having appealed to, argued with and railed against the battalions of bureaucrats who had attempted to strangle him with red tape, he had eventually been released this afternoon with a temporary visa and the promise, 'or the threat,' he laughed, that his case was to be 'taken into consideration'. 'From what I heard on Ellis Island,' he said, 'the wheels of American *autorita* – officialdom – turn as slowly as their Italian cousins. The false papers I handed in say I'm Max Barzini, Albanian fisherman.' He winked at Paola. 'By the time my case comes up for consideration, our megalomaniac Leader will have carried out his threat to invade the country of old King Zog – my bogus homeland – and I'll be a displaced person. The U.S. Immigration Department will be politically – how do you say? – – *mettere in ceppi.*'

Filipo provided, 'Hog-tied.'

As Max laughed approvingly at the expression, Gina smiled, 'This is the American he learns.' More seriously she asked, 'Do you think it will come to that, Max? An invasion of Albania? And the consequences?'

The Tuscan shrugged. 'I wouldn't be surprised. I heard a lot of tales on the island. From fresh arrivals. News we missed when we were crossing the Atlantic. It seems Little Benny has been flexing his muscles, growing more confident every day. The sentence the Special Tribunal passed on your . . . ' He cast an eye at the two youngsters, but they were busy with their zabaglione and he went on, 'That's happening more every day. One rumour had it that five hundred men and women were taken by boat to Sicily and left on the beach without food or shelter. They won't get any help from the island's villagers. Chances are most of them will die from exposure and starvation. The Fascists are determined to stamp out anyone who ever spoke a word in opposition.' He shook his head. 'But they'll overstep themselves. Somebody will stand up to them. It has to happen. Though when it does, God help our country.'

As Paola and Filipo looked up at Max, their faces clouding with uncertainty at his hard words, an uneasy silence fell across the table.

Gina swiftly broke it by saying brightly, 'Hey, that's enough politics. This is a celebration. Come on, family, here's to our reunion.' And she raised her glass, coaxing cheerily, pulling her companions back to the party.

They spent the following two hours in pleasurable gossip. Max told them he'd already discovered that due to his size he'd have no problem getting work as a 'dock-walloper' humping cargo; and anyhow, he said, he reckoned he could supplement his income from poker, pinocle and craps ('I took fifty dollars off the island officers. These Americans are gambling crazy. I'd make a fortune it it was legal.') He'd rented a room a few blocks from Mrs Ponti's store, and insisted he'd help out keeping an eye on Paola and Filipo when necessary.

Everything's going to be all right, Gina thought contentedly. She with a job ; Max free; the youngsters thriving. She smiled as the big man began to sing an Italian song, joined in as the other customers also happily chorused along, ignored the clock on the wall as it threatened ten p.m., called the waiter and ordered another bottle of wine.

8

By eleven-thirty the following morning she was wishing she hadn't drunk so much and had been in bed considerably earlier.

As she agonizingly rose from her kneeling position in a rear corridor of the Howard West, Gina heard her spine crack and almost cried out when she straightened her back. She had never thought this simple labour could inflict such torture.

Every muscle in her body had its own separate, distinct ache; even her fingers, from their constant clutching of the polishing rags, spasmed with pain.

Since her arrival at the hotel six hours earlier, there had been no respite from the toil, and no variation to its grinding monotony. Gina had spent the entire morning polishing the board floor of the stark, unheated corridors flanking the Howard's offices. One square foot per twelve seconds. That was the allotted time for the task, a fact repeated three times by Mrs MacDonald as she recited to Gina the correct method, the only method, for the application, removal and buffing of beeswax. The round, apple-faced Scot had fluffed around the swarming, basement locker-room like a mother hen cherishing her chicks, and Gina had been about to shake off the misgivings that had stalked her, when the head cleaner's plump, red hand suddenly flashed out to slash across the face of one of the girls. 'One more time I hear smutty talk like that,' the woman snapped, 'ye'll be back on the bread line.' Then, smiling benignly, she had concluded her inspection of the lockers and exited.

The sound of the cracking blow had remained in Gina's head as she sweated to maintain the polishing routine by keeping pace with Cassie, the girl sharing the duty, and the hardship of working life in this bastion of luxury began to impress itself on her every fibre.

'Get a natural rhythm going, Hon,' Cassie had advised. 'It'll hurt like hell for the first couple of days, but you'll get used to it.' She smiled warmly. 'And you got to be grateful for small mercies. We could be on toilet-cleaning detail.' She pinched her nose. 'Ugh! You wouldn't believe some of the stuff gets dumped down those pans.'

Cassie had short waved hair as shiny as spun copper. Her eyes were laughing emerald in a dimple-chinned face which was at once elfin innocent while seeming to contain the wisdom of the world. She had been partnered with Gina on this shift by the team supervisor. None of the other girls in the cavernous, overcrowded, smelly staff locker-room-cum-cafeteria had offered Gina any warmth, but as she'd struggled hurriedly into her uniform – shapeless brown smock and mob cap – she'd been welcomed with instant friendship by Cassie. 'Take no notice of the rest of them, Hon,' the redhead encouraged around her gum. 'You're too good-looking is all. That scares them. You're competition. They figure you'll pull the cutest hops – bellhops, you know. And when it comes to promotion, you'll be head of the line.'

'But that's foolish,' returned Gina. 'People don't get promoted because of their looks.'

'You sure don't know a lot about the hotel business, do you, Hon? Climbing the ladder means getting ever nearer the great white gods. The Guests. Housemaid to chambermaid, maybe someday to waitress. Take a squint in the tearoom. You see any dogs working in there? You mustn't look like Jean Harlow – that wouldn't be no good for the ego of the old broads you're serving. On the other hand, it don't exactly whet folks' appetites to have the cake stand hauled in by Bela Lugosi.'

Gina had laughed, and some of her apprehension had retreated. It was her first sample of Cassie's good humour and sound advice, and she'd be forever grateful for the brightness they brought to the severe world of the one-thousand employee warren.

Pushing their cans of beeswax and boxes of cleaning rags, the pair had progressed – each at one square foot per twelve seconds – along the endless floor. Occasionally one of the office doors would open and someone would exit. At first Gina had looked up each time this happened, smiling and about to exchange a greeting with the fellow employee. No one, however, had even looked at her: male and female, young and old, the office workers hurried back and forth oblivious to the two lesser mortals shuffling along beneath them. Eventually Gina had paid no attention to the activity between the doors, but she could not subjugate the harshness in her throat as she glimpsed the highly-shined shoes, neat trouser cuffs and silk-stockinged ankles swishing imperiously by.

'At least we get lunch before that gang,' Cassie said, standing and lifting her cleaning materials when her small gold watch announced eleven-thirty. 'Course, we start two hours earlier than they do. But who's counting?'

Beside her Gina stretched, luxuriating in the pumping of blood through her cramped muscles, but feeling slightly nauseous after the long bout of kneeling, bent foward, head bowed. As the sickness subsided she followed Cassie who was off at a trot down the corridor.

They clattered down the stairs, along the tortuous stone passages to the subterranean locker room which was swarming with laughing, chattering females. Here, early this morning, Gina had been too wrapped up in her own trepidations and speculations to pay much attention to her sister-toilers. Now, as she surveyed individual faces, she realized the age range ran from a girl who looked no more than twelve, to a woman whose raddled features couldn't have been less than eighty. Would the young one, Gina wondered, labour here until she was as wizened as the crone? And, the question crept menacingly into her head, where would she herself be by then?

Cassie, rapidly accentuating her eyes and lips with mascara and lipstick, broke the depressing thought. 'We get thirty minutes, Hon. Sorry I can't eat with you. But I got to run. A date, you know.' She winked, buttoned her red coat, tugged down the brim of her hat. 'By the way, don't lay your purse nowhere. There are characters work hotels one day only, lift what they can, never show again. See you later.' And she was gone, leaving Gina feeling more alone than she had at dawn.

This half of the vaulted, windowless cavern was packed with the employees' lockers – ranks of piled eighteen-inch-square wire cages reminding Gina of rusty prisons wherein squawking fowls awaited their fate in Rome's Campo dei Fiori market. The other end of the room was the cafeteria – its only right to this title being owed to the vast, motley collection of tables and benches crammed into the area, where the babbling horde was rapidly gathering.

Taking her cloth-wrapped salami and bread (her budget not allowing for the purchase of a lunch pail), Gina edged amid the throng until she found a vacant spot at which to sit and slowly consume her first meal as a member of the Howard's 'one big happy family'.

The afternoon was a repeat performance of the morning. By three p.m. the multitude of pains throughout Gina's body had merged to one all-pervading ache. Her knees were blistered in spite of cushioning them with polishing rags; her fingernails were packed with wax and grit; her eyes burned from the continual draught which blew through the chill labyrinth. A small consolation came from Cassie who whispered, 'Chin up, Hon. You only get this detail for one week in every couple of months. Unless you're new. Or on fatigues. Like me.' She grinned in reply to Gina's quizzical stare. 'I was three minutes late yesterday morning. Worth it though. A heavy date the night before. And it earned me this.' She waggled the wrist with the gold leather-strapped watch.

Gina admired the tiny timepiece. 'Your boyfriend?'

'Well, kinda. This week anyhow.' Cassie flicked her eyebrows up and down. She studied Gina, seemingly pondering whether to explain further, but her decision was forestalled by the sudden appearance of Mrs MacDonald trundling around a corner. The head cleaner halted, pudgy fingers laced as if in prayer, shot a suspicious look at Cassie, swiftly surveyed Gina's handiwork, declared, 'Very good, Rosa,' and waddled off along the gleaming testimony to the girls' efforts.

Cassie hissed, 'Old fart,' causing Gina to almost choke on a gulp of laughter.

Together they polished onward; and before the end of their shift they had become firm friends.

As they talked – hushedly but more confidently now that Old MacDonald had done her rounds – Gina volunteered little of her past, settling for admitting she was a recent immigrant, and relating a few details of her arrival and establishment in New York with Paola and Filipo. Cassie, however, had no qualms about laying bare her entire history. Born in Brooklyn, she'd scrubbed her way from Central to Battery Park and back in the ten years since she'd fled from drunken parents at the age of thirteen. Her easy come, easy go philosophy, bolstered by an innate belief that some day a movie star would discover her buffing door-knobs and whisk her away to Beverly Hills, had ensured she never rose above housemaid. But, despite her apparent disinterest in anything other than the contents of *Photoplay* and *Screen Romances*, she knew, Gina came to realize, more about running hotels than Conrad Hilton.

'You know,' the redhead remarked, 'there's supposed to be a Depression in this country. Bankers jumping out of windows. Fifteen million unemployed. But take a look at this place. Can't grab reservations fast enough. I'm telling you, Hon, there's a bundle to be made out of the hotel business. A fortune.' She shifted her gum, waxed another square foot, concluded, ''Course, you got to be a millionaire to build a joint like this in the first place.'

They worked until five-thirty.

Then Cassie was rising, stretching, saying, 'That's it, Hon. End of another cheery day in the employ of lovely Alicia Cornell.' Before Gina could query the identity of the owner of the name, Cassie was adding, 'Let's go. We'll celebrate with chestnuts in the park. My treat.' As Gina hurried with her once more to the lockers to join the horde of girls furiously stowing their smocks and caps, donning coats and hats, dabbing on make-up and dashing for the exit.

The girls flooded along the stone-floored corridor, twittering and laughing, their din rattling against the bare, green-painted brick walls. Gina and Cassie were caught in the flow, caught up also by the contagious euphoria of freedom, escape from the drudgery of their labour. Chill, fresh February air blew from the far exit, heightening Gina's exhilaration, quickening the blood through her aching muscles. But as she lengthened her stride, the outrace of bodies slowed. She bumped into the girl ahead; was jostled from behind. Shoulders closed around her. The rush decreased to a walk; to a shuffle; to a tight-packed, impatient crowd. Hemmed in, Gina peered over the heads of the crocodiling girls to the bottle-neck at the distant doorway. She glanced questioningly at Cassie.

The redhead shrugged. 'Search. Management don't trust us. Friskers on duty twenty-four hours a day. You can't leave without being checked out, head to toe.'

'Is it always like this?' Gina asked.

'Sure. Not just the Howard, though. Most big hotels, factories, stores, also got security checks.' She grinned around her gum. 'And I can't say I really blame them. Hell, if they didn't keep both eyes open, half the furniture in the place would walk. Mind you, there's still plenty of items come down this corridor every week. Mostly things folks need. Soap. Linen. Polish. Towels. Food, of course. Takes a little ingenuity is all. Like taping a pound of cheese under each armpit. Or a steak inside your thigh. Wearing a wig to hide stuff under. Replacing your underskirt with an unstitched pillow-case. Sewing a couple of table napkins together, going home in them instead of your knickers.' She edged forward with the crush. 'We had a girl did that. No kidding. Got away with two dozen. Until the day they did a strip-down search. Her name was Ruby Rivers. She had to explain how come she'd got HW embroidered – twice – on her butt.' Cassie laughed aloud, and several nearby girls took up the humour.

The queue slowly advanced.

'Course,' Cassie continued, 'you don't always got to be so devious. One old biddy, day she retired, walked out with two new buckets on one arm, a carton of cleaning materials under the other, a couple of brooms and a mop over her shoulder. The dummies on the floor didn't give her a second look.' She shook her head with admiration at the memory; went on, 'On the other hand, some girls conceal stuff in the rarest places.' She craned above the heads, called, 'Hey, Moll! Tell my new buddy Gina how you got a dozen silver teaspoons out of here.' The brunette beamed luridly and Cassie said to Gina, 'But remember, Hon, if you try that, you first got to practise walking with your legs real close.'

The coarse merriment which followed this advice carried the girls to the door and a small lobby where two women in green smocks, one thin and sere, the other husky and florid, stood beside a narrow trestle table.

Beside Gina, Cassie breathed, 'Damn! The Bull.' To Gina's puzzled look she whispered, 'The big one. Grade A bitch. Takes her work seriously. And enjoys it. Too damn much. You know, gets a thrill out of frisking girls.' She looked into Gina's face, studied her mouth, eyes, the blonde halo. 'Heck, Hon, can't you look less attractive. Buck your teeth out, cross your peepers. Pick your nose when you reach the Bull. Otherwise . . .' She worriedly shook her head.

'I understand,' said Gina, smiling. 'But I can't help the way I am. Besides, I haven't stolen anything. I've nothing to hide, so nothing to fear.' She turned from Cassie's apprehension, faced ahead to the girls filing past the search table. All knew the routine, opening their purses and baskets ready for inspection. The two green-clad women glanced into the bags. Sometimes they rummaged through the contents. Occasionally they ordered a girl to tip her belongings onto the table and to empty her pockets.

Six bodies ahead of Gina the husky searcher suddenly demanded that a slim, fair youngster open her coat and raise her arms. As the pale victim silently obeyed, the woman ran her hands inside the coat, around the girl's waist, up her sides, over her breasts. She smirked, lingering at her task. Then she tugged apart the blouse, thrust her fist into the brassière; and, her face flushing from amusement to triumph, she yanked from between the girl's breasts a small crystal fish – a table decoration from the luncheon room.

Cassie muttered, 'That lousy bull. She's perverted, but she's nobody's fool. It's the eyes. She sees it in their eyes.' Watching

119

the tearful girl being hustled away, she added, 'But that was dumb, stealing a crummy ornament. Useless. Not worth getting canned for.'

'Will she be prosecuted?' asked Gina.

'No. She'll just be on the street. Without references. No chance of a job at any of the decent hotels. She'll end up in some fleapit flophouse. Her whole future down the tubes for the sake of a stupid piece of glass.'

The ripple of conversation caused by the incident had died away as the big searcher returned and without more ado ordered the next girl forward – rapidly followed by four more. Then Gina.

The woman's practised gaze flickered automatically over Gina's close-fitting coat, and among the contents of her purse. She nodded, satisfied; looked up at Gina's face. And her eyes widened. For seconds it was as if she couldn't believe what she saw, until at last she drawled, 'Mother, what have we got here? This is new. And tasty. Eh, Jess?' She prodded her withered partner but, not awaiting a response, leered at Gina, 'And what do we call you, Sweetie?'

Gina's palms were sweating. Until a moment ago she'd been in control, quelling the disquiet, cloaking the memories, assuring herself it would be all right, there was nothing to fear, this was free America, not Fascist Italy. The search routine was humiliating, but it wasn't the end of the world. And if this female got some sort of sick pleasure from her degrading job, perhaps she should be pitied rather than condemned. She was, after all, a great slab of a woman, with her flat oxlike features and cropped iron hair, unattractive, Gina guessed, to either sex. She had told herself all these things as she approached her inquisitor. But that was before she faced the creature. Now she was driving her nails into her hands to stop them shaking. She answered firmly, 'Gina. My name is Gina Rossi.'

The woman's hard grin widened. 'So. An Eyetalian. A gypsy. But a blondie. A real blondie?' She flicked at Gina's hair. 'That real, Sweetie, or courtesy of Clairol? You trying to fool us? And what other secrets you got? Maybe we should take a closer look.' She sneered mockingly. 'Find out at the same time whether you're a natural blonde, eh?'

Cassie shot, 'She's got nothing. It's her first day.'

The woman's face blazed. 'Who asked you? Button your mouth if you want to be working here tomorrow. Get out.

You're holding up this line.' As if in response, the girls jostled forward, forcing Cassie past the cursory inspection of the shrivelled second searcher and through the exit.

The big woman returned to Gina. 'That's right, Sweetie? You're hiding nothin'?' Her eyes travelled Gina's figure, lingered insolently on her breasts before she looked into her face and taunted, 'Well, reckon we ought to make sure. Wouldn't want you to get the idea that thieving from here is easy as lifting from the five-and-dime. Arms up, Sweetie.' And as Gina slowly complied, the woman reached forward seizing her hips, pressing, feeling, sliding her hands down to Gina's thighs, returning to her lower ribcage, moving upward . . .

Gina flinched and involuntarily stepped back, an audible hiss escaping from her throat.

'What?' the woman flashed venomously. 'Scared, are we? Something to hide? Like all you crafty Eyetalians. Right, we'll soon find out just what you've got tucked away. We'll . . . ' Her voice trailed away and her leer crumpled as she stared into Gina's face.

Gina's teeth were clenched, her breath sucking hard into her nostrils. She repeated, 'I have nothing.' The declaration was flat, almost inaudible. Her features were expressionless; but the dark fire in the depths of her eyes was murderous.

The woman knew it, and though her fury wreathed like smoke in the towering silence, she at last rasped, 'Move on.'

Gina was bathed in cold sweat as she wordlessly walked away, and her mind still frozen when she left the building and in the evening blackness of the alley almost bumped into Cassie who blurted, 'What happened? What'd she do? Are you okay?' Before Gina could reply, the redhead declared, 'One of these days that bitch will get the high jump from Brooklyn Bridge – wearing concrete shoes.'

It was the first time Gina had heard the expression, and as she realized its meaning, the humour of it extinguished the dark memories which had been kindled by her encounter with the searcher. She smiled, making a mental note to recall the joke-line for Filipo. Shedding the remnants of her fears she said brightly, 'How about these chestnuts you promised?'

'What?' Cassie's brow remained furrowed; then her cheeriness relit as she answered, 'Oh, sure. There's a guy with a cart down the street. Across by the park. Let's go.'

They hurried down the alley, around huge garbage bins, out

to the street-lamp brightness and the crowds bustling beneath the ornate façade of the hotel. As they passed the colonnaded entrance Gina wondered if the busy, maroon-uniformed doorman was the one she had seen yesterday morning. To the man's surprise she gave him a broad wink before following Cassie from the sidewalk to cross the traffic-streaming avenue. Reaching the perimeter of the park they slowed their pace. Gina noticed the wind had dropped and it was a few degrees warmer. Looking up she saw no stars, only an umbrous mantle tinged by the lights of the city.

'Snow by morning,' stated Cassie, sniffing the air. 'Smell it. Probably already a foot deep in Vermont.'

'My sister and brother will love it,' replied Gina. 'It rarely freezes in Rome. The snow in the mountains was a special treat when we took winter vacations.'

'Well it's no treat in this town, believe me, Hon. It lies around, piled up for a couple of days before it gets churned up to the filthiest brown muck you ever saw. And when that gets tracked into the hotel, it melts all over the place. Guests don't care where they stomp it. Gives Old MacDonald the vapours. She has us sponging and scrubbing twenty-four hours a day, terrified in case the lovely Alicia swoops out of her eyrie and spots a speck of grit on her precious carpets – though that's less likely than a visit from God.'

Again hearing the name Cassie had mentioned earlier, Gina was about to query its ownership when they arrived at the chestnut-seller's cart. Cassie handed over ten cents for two heaped brown paper cones, passed one to Gina. Breathing the sharp aroma of the scorched shell, Gina juggled the cone while snapping the piping hot husk from the kernel. Biting the nut she sucked in air when the heat stung her tongue. 'It's good,' she declared, her eyes watering.

Smiling happily at the approval, Cassie strolled across the bridle path. People hurried by, children running and jumping over the grass, a man in a cream overcoat and svelte fedora being towed by three scuttling Pekingese. Cassie said, 'This time of day the park's safe. But in a couple of hours' time it'll be best to keep to the main tracks. Too many screwballs in here at night. I guess you ought to know, Hon, Manhattan isn't much like the Busby Berkeley version. Over two hundred murders in the borough last year; almost three hundred felonious assaults; more than seventy cases of rape. They print the figures in the newspaper. Like the baseball scores. You got to watch out on the streets. Tell those two young ones at home – Poll and Phil – to take care. This isn't Rome.' She chewed a chestnut. 'I reckon that's some sort of beautiful place, right? The Soul of Civilization. Nils Asther said so in *Wild Orchids*. Or it might have been Paul Muni in . . . ' She cut off abruptly when she saw Gina wince as they descended three stone steps. 'Hey, Hon. You okay?'

'I'm fine,' assured Gina. 'Just my knees. A little sore.'

'Let me take a look.' Before Gina could step aside, Cassie had bent to lift her coat hem. 'Moses!' the redhead exclaimed. 'Oh, Hon, I'm sorry. I shouldn't have suggested we walk. I forgot how you'd be on your first day.' She bit her lip as she squinted at the dark patches of dried blood gluing Gina's rubbed-through stockings to her knees. 'You got to get home. Bathe those. Treat them with boracic powder.'

'They aren't too bad,' answered Gina. Seeing the deep concern in her new-found friend's eyes she added lightly, 'Though I don't know how I'm going to bend to take my knickers off.'

Cassie's brows rose; then her anxiety was dispelled with an appreciative laugh. 'You're as wacky as I am! Shall we take the subway? I can ride with you as far as Jackson Square.'

'I'd like that,' smiled Gina. 'Come on,' and she took Cassie's arm and they headed toward the park exit.

Home-going crowds swarmed into the station. Gina and Cassie jostled their way to the ticket booth, then waited fifteen minutes on the milling, draughty platform until their train arrived.

Over the past fortnight, Gina, using the subways and elevated lines in her quest for work, had learned the rules of survival during the city's frenetic rush-hours. Now, when the express squealed in, regardless of her pain-stiff knees, with shoulders, elbows and grim determination she battled to a vacant seat. With Cassie jammed in beside her, packed bodies hanging two-to-a-strap above her, as the train pulled out she asked, 'Who's Alicia Cornell?'

Cassie returned surprise. 'You don't know? Proves you haven't lived long in the good ol' US of A. The lady has her name stamped on large chunks of it. She's the hermit, the tycoon, the slave-hirer, the multi-millionairess who's your boss, is all.'

'The owner of the Howard.'

'Along with heck knows how many other rich folk's bunk-houses from here to the Pacific Ocean. Inherited a fortune from her old man. He was an immigrant, from Transylvania or some place. Made his pile chiselling Forty-niners out of their gold dust. Thought it would buy respectability. But things were no different those days than they are now. The gentry who'd done their plundering a hundred years earlier didn't take kindly to crafty foreigners coming along snapping up the bits of Manhattan they themselves had neglected to steal. The avenue nobs wouldn't cross the street to talk to the likes of Vestric the saloon-keeper. Alicia settled their hash though. Married her way into their exclusive club. A Cornell. Genuine blue-blood. Smart old dame, that Alicia. Nailed her place in society, then set about quadrupling her fortune. Sold or demolished her daddy's ramshackle fleet of booze-and-broad joints, built herself a whole new line. The Howard is the flagship.'

'Have you ever met her?' asked Gina.

Cassie laughed. 'You're kidding, Hon. The likes of you and me don't even get to meet the head housekeeper.She's the one who keeps Old MacDonald on the trot. No, I've never seen Alicia Cornell. But then, few folks have. Not many know what she looks like. Phantom of the Opera probably. Over sixty years old. But she's still got all her marbles. Oversees her empire from a penthouse on top of the hotel. Rules with a rod of iron. Everybody. Including her son, Howard. Yes, the place is named after him. He's the old girl's only offspring. His father was killed in an automobile smash not long after marrying Alicia. Now he, Howard, lives with his mother. Spends his time sailing, skiing, swimming through the society pages. Chasing girls. Catches plenty too. Though the old girl makes sure none ever catches him. Rumour is he's been engaged half-a-dozen times, but Alicia always headed him off before he made it to the altar.'

'Protecting him from – *il civetti* – gold-diggers.'

'Of course. Plenty around with an eye open for a rich, good-looking guy. Well, we all got to watch out for the main chance, don't we?' Cassie grinned and winked. 'But not all Howard's fiancées were after his dough. A couple were better heeled than the Cornells.' Her forehead puckered. 'Can't figure it. You'd've thought old Alicia would be doing her best to mate her young stud with a thoroughbred filly. That's how the aristocracy expand their kingdoms, isn't it? And Howard is her only chance. Last of the line.'

'Perhaps that's why she won't let him go,' suggested Gina. 'Without him she'd be alone.'

'Maybe,' mused Cassie. 'But I don't think Alicia Cornell has that sort of heart. Doesn't have a heart at all. She's the one personally makes the rules for the Howard's slaves. Pays starvation wages. Won't let organized labour anywhere near the place. She's reckoned to have a secret file on everyone in her employ, even down to such as us. If she heard we'd so much as walked past the door of the Hotel and Restaurant Workers' Union, we'd be out faster'n that dumb kid who stole the glass fish.' She peered through the window, checking the station as the train sped out of the 23rd Street platform. 'Not that I'm interested in unions,' she went on. 'Nor any other oufit that wants me to pay dues. I've belonged to nothing and nobody in my life. And I intend to keep it that way.'

Gina asked, 'How about a husband?'

Cassie shrugged. 'Sure, I'll get hitched one day. But not until the right candidate waves his ticket. You know, a guy with the looks of Clark Gable and the bankroll of John Rockefeller.'

Gina smiled. 'Don't you believe in love?'

'Of course. At least three times a week.'

Two nearby strap-hanging girls laughed aloud. Gina also appreciated the humour; and yet the lightness of the moment was followed by a swift shadow. Two years ago she'd have treated Cassie's remarks as a joke, never for one moment translated it into a cynical truth. Now she saw fleetingly a new side to her own face, an expression which shocked her with its hardness. She quickly shut out the image in time to hear Cassie say, 'I'm truly glad you came to the Howard, Hon. We're going to be pals, I know it. Next time we go out it'll be for more than chestnuts. We'll have a real slapping two-dollar dinner at Delmonico's. A date, okay? Hey, this is my stop.' She jumped up as the car doors slid apart, and was swept in the surge of bodies toward the opening.

Gina didn't even have time to say goodbye, just saw her friend's hand waving above the jostling heads, heard her voice call, 'See you tomorrow.' Then incoming passengers piled aboard and the train accelerated away.

Gina travelled on.

During the downtown ride the wounds on her knees tightened. They then cracked again when she stood to exit at Delancey Street. And by the time she'd hobbled the four blocks home, she didn't know whether to laugh or cry as she climbed the stairs like a crippled cockroach.

Entering the apartment she put on her happy face, not wishing to raise the concern of her sister or the morbid fascination of her brother, and retired to the bathroom to tend secretly her raw flesh. She spent the following two hours taking infinite care to keep her legs concealed as she related to Paola and Filipo her day at the Howard West, embroidering the tale with such golden threads she almost convinced herself of the hotel's flawlessness.

When the youngsters were at last in bed, Gina sewed a pair of rag pads with elastic garters to tie them to her knees. She managed to hold her concentration until the final stitch was knotted, then, laying aside her handiwork, she leaned back, and her body turned to marshmallow. Her muscles sighed with relief, and her brain abandoned any further effort to keep her awake. Without realizing it she sank sideways on the sofa, drew up her legs, tucked her hands beneath her cheek. And dreamed of wire cages packed with squawking housemaids, and bloodied knees crawling endlessly across deserts of polished floorboards, and an ancient bejewelled woman sitting atop a golden tower. A voice asked, 'Where is her family? Who are her friends? What does she have up there all alone?' A second voice answered, 'She has money and power. What else does she need?' The old woman's face shifted, changed; its wrinkles faded; the hair melted from grey to gold. Gina peered, concentrated, striving to distinguish the features. But they hovered beyond a veil of mist, and as she reached out to sweep aside the curtain something fell with a thump.

She awoke abruptly, disoriented, misplaced in time and space. Then as her senses returned she saw her sewing kit and the two knee pads where they had slipped to the floor. She bent to retrieve the items, carried them to the sideboard, switched off the light and returned to the sofa.

But it was a long while before she again slept.

9

The snow came the following morning. It emptied out of a sky the colour and texture of old sacks, burying streets, filling doorways, bringing traffic to a standstill.

Paola and Filipo thought heaven had arrived right here on earth. Muffled in scarves, hats, mittens and umpteen layers of clothes they rushed out to the wonderland to spend the next three days rolling in it, sledding on it (on teatrays and cardboard cartons), piling it, throwing it, eating it and behaving more idiotically than Gina had ever known (though when, on her free Sunday, she accompanied them to Sara Roosevelt Park, she couldn't resist the temptation to fling a few handfuls herself and then take a surreptitious taste which brought instant recall of her happy childhood vacations in the Tyrol).

All this, however, was before the wind rose.

The blizzard tore amongst the buildings, thrashing the inhabitants, blinding and deafening them as they struggled about their daily existence. Then followed the snowploughs, piling the gutters, mixing the virgin whiteness with grime and debris until it resembled frozen stew. By day it melted, trickled grittily across the sidewalks. At night it refroze into iron-hard chunks and icy sheets. Storekeepers, so their customers wouldn't break a leg on their way to part with cash, scattered salt and ash and sawdust onto the glacial muckiness while huge dray- and wagon-horses urinated mighty steaming streams into it.

Within a fortnight even Filipo was suggesting escape to California, where, he assured his sisters, the sun shone twenty-four hours a day and everybody was a movie star living on free oranges.

Gina was tempted to take his advice. Cassie had been right about the weather's effect on the Howard West. Winter trailed its feet all over the hotel, and Mrs MacDonald rushed around like a red frenzy to keep the girls scrubbing in its wake. Still, Gina toiled on . . . pushing her polishing rags out of February and into March. She was then drafted to door-brass duty: hinges, finger-plates, room-numbers, plus over eighteen hundred knobs all to be buffed until Mrs MacDonald could see her plump face in them. Thence to carpets: a sprinkling of water to settle the dust before vigorous brushing (the use of noisy vacuum cleaners not being permitted in public corridors). Toilets: marble by the acre, chromium and brass taps and pipes, porcelain sinks and lavatories (ugh! as disgusting as Cassie had predicted). Furniture: a return to the polish and Mrs MacDonald's eagle eye inspecting every chair leg, spindle, ladder back and Chippendale fretwork. Mirrors: ten thousand square feet of glass to be cleaned with crumpled newspaper before burnishing with old towels. Woodwork: doors, skirtings, panelling, shelves, sills, banisters. Stone floors (the most hated duty): miles of granite flags in the subterranean passages to be scrubbed and cold-water-washed, scores of steps to be pumiced and whitened. There were also separate work details for drapes, ornaments, lamps and upholstery (three thousand feather cushions to be turned and plumped twice a day, toted to the yard and beaten once a week).

It was treadmill labour of unremitting tedium. Yet Gina felt no resentment. Unlike her fellow toilers who regarded this as a way of life, she banked every experience as collateral against her future, for as the weeks wore on she thought increasingly of Max's joking remark about opening a restaurant of her own.

She tentatively mentioned the idea to Cassie during a lunchtime stroll. The redhead responded, 'You gotta be kidding, Hon. Nobody can save that amount of dough. And a female has got about as much chance of borrowing it as she has of being elected mayor.'

Gina didn't bring up the subject again. Though she continued to value Cassie's friendship.

So did Paola and Filipo. The youngsters had taken to Cassie with instant affection the first evening she visited their apartment. Paola eagerly listened to hair-care and make-up tips, while Filipo was enthralled by the redhead's reportage of the goriest scenes of the gangster movies which had never been shown in Italy. By the end of the evening their accepted nick-names were Poll and Phil. Gina flinched slightly at the diminutives, but didn't wish to play killjoy after a supper which had given so much pleasure to them all. As Cassie had left she'd patted her stomach, exclaiming, 'Best meal I've eaten in a blue moon, Hon. What was it?'

'*Lepre agrodolce.* Sweet and sour hare.' Gina had been unable to resist a flush of pride at the compliment.

'Sounds terrible,' said Cassie. 'But if you ever win on the numbers and open that restaurant, I guarantee folks'll beat a path to your door.'

And so life fell into a pattern. And Gina was almost content. After the cataclysmic events of the past two years she was happy to be finally in a secure routine with the opportunity to recuperate from her mental wounds and rebuild her strength. She was scarcely aware of the passing of the months, hardly noticed the city changing out of its dark winter overcoat into its green spring suit; did not appreciate fully the passing of the seasons until her sister insisted on discarding her woollen stockings in favour of 'real imitation silk', and Filipo pleaded for a trip to Coney Island.

The youngsters had thrived, seeming to grow healthier and happier by the day. Quick to learn, they coped easily with their schoolwork. Eager to explore, they were soon as familiar with their environment as native Manhattanites. Their ability to speak the language was a tremendous advantage, and Gina constantly reminded them of the lack of prospects for the immigrant children whose parents were too ignorant or insular to give up their native tongue. Paola retained a more pronounced Italian accent than Filipo, who – needless to say – developed a slang-peppered twang barely distinguishable from that of the Bronx-born newsvendor on the corner of Grand Street and Third Avenue, who permitted the boy free perusal ('as long as youse mitts is clean') of his vast stock of movie magazines. Gina, daily exposed to the hundreds of languages and dialects of her co-workers, made a conscious effort to speak modulated English – based on her memories of Robert Fallon.

His voice was what she remembered most clearly. But, then, since writing months ago to his Richmond hotelier friend David Lowell (she had not received a reply), she had avoided recalling anything else about him, or any of the time they had spent together. The feelings she'd had for Fallon, she'd told herself, had been schoolgirl infatuation, an impressionable girl's crush on an older, wordly man which was all part of the painful pleasure of growing up. Fallon had been an essential but transient ingredient of her life. He must be allowed to fade from her memories, as she surely had melted from his.

'Principessa,' Max ventured one evening in late August,

sitting beside her, sharing one of the forty bottles of Marsala he'd taken in lieu of cash from a blackjack-playing wine importer. 'Don't you ever . . . well . . . at the hotel . . . meet any men?'

Gina faced him. 'What could I possibly want with a man?' She swiftly raised a palm. 'Don't tell me.' Seeing his genuine concern, she smiled. 'Don't worry about me, old friend. What happened in Baremo didn't turn me into a male-hater, or anything odd. I'm perfectly normal. I just haven't had the time. Truly.' She laid her head on his shoulder. 'So, who were those two blonde pastries I saw you nibbling when I passed Zucca's Café last night?'

Max coughed and almost choked on his Marsala. But Gina's humour was shortlived as she wondered if any of her assurances to him had been true.

The man's voice said, 'Hi. You're new around here.'

Gina looked up from where she was polishing the mahogany skirting-board of the tenth-floor hallway. And she caught her breath.

He was tall, slim but muscular in an immaculate white tuxedo. His hair was black, a colour seemingly reflected in his deep eyes beneath which his features and wide mouth were sharply defined. Handsome. But, Gina thought, vaguely foreign-looking, though this impression was belied by his voice; the perfectly modulated Harvard accent was as assured as his smile. He observed, 'That shine will last for ever.'

Coming abruptly back to her senses, Gina realized her arm was still automatically polishing as she stared up at the stranger. With a flush of unsettling distraction and annoyance she shifted her kneeling cloth and concentrated on the next yard of burnished wood.

Since her first days at the Howard she'd understood that passes from male (and occasionally female) guests came with the job. Housemaids were the lowliest of the low; as essential as ashtrays, but more easily replaced. 'So when one of our high and mighty guests gropes you in the hall,' Cassie had advised, 'you either stand still and enjoy it, or you run like hell. What you don't do, what you never do, what there is no point in the world in doing, is complain. Believe me, I've known girls raped. When they reported it they found themselves outside the rear door. Remember, Hon, it's the guests who pay the piper.

And that gives them the right to call any damn tune they please.' Cassie had shifted her gum from one cheek to the other, patted her shiny copper curls and ended in her best Mae West, ''Course, if you ever fancy making a little music with the characters in silk shorts . . .' she'd rubbed her thumb and forefinger together, ' . . . there aren't any withholding taxes on the wages of sin.'

Gina recalled the remark as the stranger in the white dinner jacket commented good-naturedly, 'I'd heard the Howard's staff were famous for their politeness. You could at least say, Good afternoon.'

Gina looked up at him, considered gathering her boxes and rags and walking away, even contemplated telling him to take a running jump. She knew what retribution the latter course would bring if it got back to old MacD, but as she stared into the almost violet eyes it wasn't just discretion which caused her to say quietly, 'Good afternoon.'

'Italy,' he said.

'Pardon? Oh, yes. Is my accent so obvious?'

'It's most attractive. So are you.'

Gina's eyelids automatically dropped. She snapped them open again. What on earth was she thinking of? She'd been about to act the coquette. Here, with a total stranger! Yet, even as she reminded herself of who she was and where she was, she couldn't help but glance over his long legs, up his thighs, thence to the width of his chest in the immaculately tailored jacket. As her eyes once more met his she felt an acute embarrassment, mingled with a sensation she hadn't experienced since she was seventeen. The tempo of her heart had increased and she was sure her face had turned bright pink.

He said, 'We could talk more comfortably, and agreeably, if you stood up.'

'I don't have time. Besides, I doubt we'd have anything to talk about.' The rejoinder was bold – what Cassie would have called 'a come on'. Gina knew she must stop this before she made an utter fool of herself.

'I'm sure we would,' he countered. 'I knew it the first time I saw you.' To Gina's stare he explained, 'A couple of weeks ago. And several occasions since. But you've always been with one of the other girls. Busy keeping this mausoleum immaculate. I've been hoping to get you alone. No, please don't take that the way it sounded. I only meant we could be more intimate.' He smiled wryly. 'That isn't the right word either. Not making a very good job of this, am I?'

'Perhaps you should save your breath.'

'Now that wasn't kind. And you didn't mean it. You know I'm not a rogue. Do I look like one? Careful, Miss, don't say anything you'll regret. In fact, say only one word – Yes. To my invitation. For cocktails.' He assured, 'In a public place. Everything above board. Just grant me fifteen minutes and I'll guarantee you'll discover I'm a very decent fellow. Please.' His eyes appealed with all the innocence of a schoolboy pleading a special treat. There was nothing immature, however, about the curve of his lips and the hard line of his jaw, set with extraordinary strength and persuasiveness. Standing there above Gina, his presence seemed to dominate the wide, richly carpeted hallway. He asked, 'How about the Stork? Or El Morocco? Somewhere quieter if you'd prefer.'

Gina tore her gaze from his mouth. Quickly rising with her polishing gear she declared, 'I'd prefer to be left alone to get on with my work. But as you are obviously fortunate enough to be able to stand around here all day, it seems I shall have to be the one to leave. Thank you for your offer, but, contrary to popular belief, all housemaids are not dim-witted fillies champing at the bit to gallop off with the first stallion who flares his nostrils.' There, she thought – particularly self-satisfied with her translation of the metaphor – put that in your pipe and smoke it. She added, 'Though I'm sure, if you prowl around the corridors long enough, you'll find what you're looking for. Good afternoon.' And with her chin up, shoulders squared (and, she thought, a great deal of poise considering she had rag pads elasticated to her knees), she marched off toward the stairs.

She'd gone six paces when she heard him chuckle.

Two hours later, as she hurried to the subway, the rich sound was still echoing in her head.

Beside her, Cassie observed, 'You're kinda quiet, Hon. You okay? Anything bothering you?'

'Nothing,' replied Gina. 'Nothing whatsoever.'

Which, of course, was absolutely untrue.

She prepared the evening meal without realizing what she was doing; sat and swallowed it without knowing what she was eating. Paola sat beside her and chatted about school. Filipo interrupted with his own revolutionary views on the educational system. Gina heard little of it; she smiled and answered and interjected a comment here and there and was hardly aware that the youngsters had gone to bed. She made herself hot milk and read the newspaper, a special report on the city's soon-to-open World's Fair, but the drawing and descriptions of the fifty-eight nations' exhibits failed to capture her imagination; not even the Italian Pavilion, which was to feature a marble statue of Mussolini, could arouse her interest. When she finally laid the paper aside to reach for her milk she discovered the cup was stone cold. She'd daydreamed for two hours.

This was ridiculous. She knew it. This was girlish whimsy: the fantasy of the tall, dark stranger. Yet she couldn't dispel it, she was powerless to switch her thoughts to other subjects, no effort of will could keep her mind from tracking back to the encounter in the Howard's hallway.

She tried to rationalize, told herself it was the excitement of a new person introducing himself into the sameness of her daily round, that her response would have been the same no matter what the would-be Valentino had looked like. Not true, her inner voice countered, there had been something special about him, and there certainly had been something extraordinary about her reaction to his eyes and his voice, a reaction which repeated itself now as she slipped into her nightgown and lay on the bed. She'd never felt this way since the day she met Robert Fallon.

Gina sat up abruptly at the thought of the Englishman. It was her first memory of him in months. She stared at the night-grey oblong of the window, expecting to frame Fallon's features there. But they didn't materialize. Try as she might she was unable to picture the man who once had filled her every waking moment, the man to whom she owed her life. The only face she could see in the darkness was the one with the sharply-defined cheekbones and the mesmeric smile. Falling back on the pillow she declared, 'This is ridiculous!'

The following lunchtime Cassie countered, 'Of course it isn't. It's marvellous.'

Gina had decided to abandon her earlier decision to keep the encounter to herself; she was hexed and perhaps the only way of exorcizing the haunting stranger was openly to discuss him.

Cassie urged, 'What did you say his name was? You didn't ask him! Aw, Hon, now we can't check the hotel register to

133

find out whether he's in a room or a suite. Guys with rooms are okay, I mean they aren't likely to be on their uppers if they can afford just to set foot inside this joint, but it's the fellers in the suites who have got a pipeline to the mint. They're the prime ribs to stick your tag on. Your mysterious admirer might be one. We have to find out.' A light bulb winked behind her eyes. 'Tell you what, we'll stake out the lobby as soon as we're off duty. He's bound to show up there sooner or later. One of the hops will I.D. him for us.'

'Cassie, hold it.' Gina smiled at her friend's runaway enthusiasm. 'I don't have time for that. Besides, I'm not sure I want to know who he is. What good would it do? I'm not about to accept his invitation.'

'Are you off your trolley?'

'No, I'm not!' laughed Gina. 'It's just that I've never done anything like that before – gone out with a total stranger. That doesn't happen in Italy. Even the most flirtatious Roman boys would never stop an unknown girl in the street – or a hotel corridor – and ask her out, they'd know she couldn't possibly agree. You have to realize how different the customs are in New York. It takes time to get used to them.'

She declaimed in similar vein for the next twenty minutes with Cassie constantly interrupting to bemoan 'the waste of a prime prospect', but when their break was over and Gina went alone on a different work detail she realized the talk-it-through-and-it-will-go-away theory had proved completely false. She was as bewitched as ever, spent the remainder of her mirror-burnishing shift staring into her work in the hope that he would appear behind her. Yes – in the hope. No use denying it, she was aching to see him again. All through the following day too, and the night – especially the night – she was locked in the fantasy of a besotted teenager. For three days she lived a dream of how it would be at their next encounter.

The dream shattered on Friday morning.

Six a.m. Gina was polishing the marble floor of the lobby. He entered through the front doors. He was resplendent in evening dress. So was the brunette on his arm.

Gina shrank when she saw them. Her pulse pounded with embarrassment. On her first encounter with the stranger, alone with him, she had been emboldened rather than disconcerted by his interest; she had temporarily forgotten the huge social gulf which separated them. But crouching here now, dwarfed by the pillared grandeur of the lobby, she was crushingly aware of her shapeless smock, mobcap and grubby knee pads, the sense of shabbiness heightened by the sophisticated glamour of the dark-haired female at the man's side.

She cringed. They were striding, laughing, toward her. He was looking toward her. She snatched up her equipment, turned, stumbled, banged into a chair, toppled it, didn't stop to right it, couldn't flee fast enough from her humiliation and misery and bitterness.

She spoke to no one during the remainder of the day; said little to Paola and Filipo over the evening meal. Later she sat at the table, forced herself to review her notebooks; but after turning every page, when she closed the cover she hadn't seen a word. She hadn't seen anything except the svelte brunette in the hotel lobby – her perfectly coiffed hair, her elegantly gowned figure, her jewelled throat and wrists. Gina had re-run the dawn encounter a hundred times. Like a self-pitying hag!

'Like a self-pitying hag.' She said it aloud. Stood abruptly, repeated it, then, from midnight to two in the morning, washed and scoured and polished the room (scooting her sister and brother back to bed when they arose to investigate) from top to bottom. Twice. When she at last sank onto the sofa, the demons had retreated.

By noon the next day they'd been left far behind. So had all notions of romantic dalliance. With anyone.

Like all the girls, unable to indulge in the expense of magazines, Gina had learned to make the most of the reading matter found in guests' bedrooms – often in their waste baskets. The minutes she saved by reducing the cleaning time allotment for each room she spent in rapidly absorbing the contents of everything from *Saturday Evening Post* and *Atlantic Monthly* to *True Proposals* and *Nick Carter Weekly*.

It was a fortnight since her encounter with the stranger, a week since her unexpected promotion to chambermaid, two minutes left of her afternoon shift, when she flicked through a magazine and discovered a feature on London's Savoy Hotel, how it had become a centre of American life in England during the World War. There was a photograph of the Mirror Room where the United States' entry into the war had been celebrated in 1917, with an adjacent picture, taken six years later, of Lord Curzon, the British Foreign Secretary, unveiling a bust of Abraham Lincoln when the room was renamed to honour the sixteenth President.

This was the page of the feature which first claimed Gina's attention. The World War was mentioned several times, and it focused her mind on the recent news from Europe. An agreement had been signed last week in Munich permitting Germany to annex the Czechoslovak Sudetenland; the conference had taken place under the German threat of invasion. Max Barzini had said angrily, 'Giving in to bullying thugs,' an echo of Winston Churchill's condemnation of the appeasement: 'We have sustained a defeat without a war.' Max had gone on to say that now Hitler had proved intimidation could pay off, 'His buddy Musso will think he can get away with it too. There's going to be an explosion over there, Principessa. I can smell it coming. And then, by God, that pig who drove us from our home will get his just deserts. When they beat him to death with a Manganello I'd like to be there to see it.'

Gina had been shocked by the vehemence of Max's emotion. She had tried not to dwell on what he had said, had concentrated on more mundane topics. As she did now, turning the magazine's page to a photograph of the Savoy's famous Grill with its elegantly attired diners. She was starting to read a tale about the hotel's cat Kaspar when Cassie's head popped around the doorjamb with:

'Hey, we should've knocked off two minutes ago.'

'Oh, yes. Coming.' Gina swiftly gathered her cleaning kit, stuffing the magazine into her smock pouch and following Cassie out to the service stairs.

The rush through the passage maze and the routine of changing to her street clothes in the locker room bedlam, was now so habitual Gina had almost reached the exit lobby and was holding her purse open for inspection when she realized she had automatically transferred the magazine to her coat pocket.

A flicker of panic coursed through her, but she snuffed it as quickly as it had ignited, annoyed with herself for the irrational reaction to the magazine's presence. But it was at that moment she entered the lobby and recognized who was on security detail. She burned with the abruptly rekindled anxiety as, six girls ahead, the big, ox-faced searcher prodded the pockets of an elderly cleaner.

Cassie whispered, 'What on earth's the matter? You're as white as a sheet. Are you sick, Hon?'

Gina, unable to find her voice, shook her head. She was in a fever of indecision. She wasn't afraid of another confrontation with the searcher, but she did fear the dismissal it might bring. When she left this job – as she had recently been contemplating – it must be for better-paid, pre-arranged employment.

The line advanced. And Gina's nerves gradually quietened. She was being absurd, she told herself. Many of the girls brought magazines, comics, newspapers, in and out every day. They were never challenged. Were they? Cassie had already exited when Gina halted at the table, waited while the big searcher rummaged through her purse, scanned her figure as she opened her coat, grunted and beckoned the next girl. Gina couldn't prevent an exhalation of relief. Snapping shut her purse she began to turn away.

'Hold it!'

Gina froze.

The searcher rasped, 'What's that?'

As Gina slowly refaced the table she met the woman's penetrating gaze. 'It's the eyes,' Cassie had said the first time they were here together. 'She sees it in their eyes.' Gina's hand moved toward her pocket. 'This? A magazine.' As casually as possible, in response to the searcher's outstretched palm, she handed over the rolled copy of *Collier's*.

The woman's brow rose. 'Pretty fancy. And expensive.' Her voice was suddenly deadly. 'Since when could chambermaids afford Fifth Avenue magazines? Where'd you get the dough for this? Where'd you buy it?'

'I forget,' shrugged Gina.

'Liar!' The yell hit Gina like a physical blow, flushing the blood to her cheeks, causing her to flinch involuntarily. 'What?' the woman flashed venomously. 'Scared are we? Scared 'cause we're stealing guests' belongings? And more? More to hide? Like all you crafty Eyetalians. Right, we'll soon find out what you've got tucked away. Strip search.'

A gasp went up from the surrounding throng, a couple of expletives were muttered, but eyes glanced nervously away as Gina looked desperately around for support. She thought briefly of fleeing; she could escape in a moment, down the alley, onto the avenue, lost in the crowd. Regathering her confidence she said, 'I took the magazine by mistake. I don't want it. And

I have nothing else to hide.'

'We'll see about that,' growled the woman. Grabbing Gina's arm, she propelled her toward a corner door, thrust her through into a bare, windowless cubicle. Flicking a switch to illuminate a high, stark yellow bulb, she commanded, 'Get your clothes off. All of them. Now.'

Gina began slowly to unbutton her coat. As she slipped it from her shoulders, she instinctively looked around for a chair or hanger. Realizing there was none, she carefully folded the garment and laid it on the dusty, paved floor. Her mouth tasted like ash as she took off her blouse, placed it on top of the coat; stepped out of her skirt. She shivered as the dankness of the cubicle crept across her naked shoulders and back. She removed her slip. Hesitated.

'I haven't got all night,' rasped the woman.

Gritting her teeth, Gina unhooked and slipped off her brassière. Her blood was now ice. She was trembling from head to foot, unable to control her muscles. There was a rising sickness in her, and as she looked into the face of the woman, the hard, flat features began to dissolve and flow, shifting and changing; the hair darkened; the mouth fattened. And she was no longer looking at the searcher. She could see only Galeazzo Sturzo. She didn't hear the searcher's command, only saw the lips move, the eyes burn. Her chest was full of drums, their reverberation hammering in her head as she squeezed shut her lids, hooked her thumbs into the waist of her panties.

Sturzo stepped toward her. She watched his tongue travel his lips; smelled the alcohol on his breath; felt his hands slither over her flesh, cup her breasts, slide wetly through the sweat that was rivuleting her body. She heard: 'Beautiful. Beautiful.' Sensed the coarse fingers scour her belly, exploring downward. It didn't matter, her inner voice assured; this was meaningless, a fleeting moment. She stood, unmoving, uncaring, feeling nothing. Until the perspiration stung her eyelids. She blinked hard, driving out the salty liquid. Looked down. And saw the red, ox-like face. But it was not the face that had haunted her nightmares since she fled from the horror of that night in Baremo. The shock of recognition, the sharp knife of reality, sent her jolting backward.

'What the . . . ?' exclaimed the woman.

Gina's arm arced round, driven by sudden fury. Her open palm slashed across the tyrant's cheek, snapping her head sideways, causing her to stumble and thump against the wall. The blood sped from the woman's gross features in an instant and her hand snapped up reflexively against a further blow. She stood, stunned, the air sucking thickly into her nostrils. Then the rage began to flow from her eyes as her lips drew back in a vicious, silent snarl and her ashen face bloomed with the flaming weal of Gina's fingermarks. She started forward.

The door snapped open.

Mrs MacDonald demanded, 'What's happening here?' Before either Gina or the searcher could reply, she snapped, 'Get dressed, girl,' then turning to the red-faced woman ordered sharply, 'Leave us alone.'

Retaliation burned on the searcher's face, but there had been something in Mrs MacDonald's tone, a warning which caused the woman to glare defiance only briefly before stamping across the cubicle. Though before exiting she flung back at Gina, 'You won't get away with this.' She bashed shut the door behind her.

Gina was still standing naked. Then, when the head cleaner instructed, 'Hurry now,' she swiftly gathered her clothes. As she pulled them on she bridled her anger, prepared to explain the magazine.

Mrs MacDonald said, 'This was unfortunate, most unfortunate. It won't happen again. She'll no' trouble you again.' For a moment she bit her lip, then, regathering her customary briskness she said, 'Your work has proved quite satisfactory. You'll no' be working the bedrooms tomorrow. You'll be on special duty. Mind you come with spotless hair and fingernails. Mrs Alicia Cornell is most particular about the girls who clean her apartment.'

10

The room was huge. The hotel's suites Gina had peeked into were large, but none compared with this. The wall she faced was sixty feet long with a walk-in marble fireplace, logs burning, above which hung an enormous, ornately-framed painting of a heavy-set, swarthy-faced man with white hair, wearing a frock coat and a diamond-pinned cravat. Though there were a score more pictures on the walls, this was the only portrait. The furniture was as rich and solid as the man: tapestried and brocaded antique sofas; sideboards and tables patinaed with age; lamps and vases and ornaments. The atmosphere of wealth was almost tangible. So was the smell of power.

Gina set down her can of beeswax and box of rags, surveyed the four-foot perimeter of board floor around the Persian carpets. No different from the hundred miles of timber she'd polished during the last nine months; except this glowed with a deeper intensity, clearly reflecting the treasures of the Cornell apartment.

Gina knelt. She worked for over an hour.

The apartment was utterly still; no sound save the rustle of Gina's skirt and the hissing of the burning logs. Once, a girl in a grey smock entered via a side door and replenished the diminishing fire but, her task completed, she exited without glancing in Gina's direction.

'Even the slaves up there figure they're several cuts above us,' Cassie had said. Gina stood, recalling the remark, and a brief bitterness stabbed her. She flinched from the sensation. She hadn't felt it in a long time, had thought it had been left, dead and buried, the other side of an ocean. Since her arrival at the Howard she had appreciated, with a professional eye, the hotel's perfection; never once had it caused her resentment or envy. But now, for an instant, the imperious silence of this room cloaked her with despondency.

She abruptly stretched her arms above her head, sending the blood pulsing through her cramped muscles, quashing the invidious emotion as swiftly as it had arisen. Relaxing the tension she looked up to meet the dark eyes of the portrait. There was a vague familiarity about the face. But she let that thought go, held the gaze a moment longer, then gave the old boy a bump and a grind that might have made him jump out of his frame, and with a wink and a cheerful laugh bent once more for her wax can. A voice in the adjoining room froze her in position.

The double doors at the end of the room had been half-open since Gina arrived, but the room beyond was in semi-gloom, and she had thought better of investigating. Now, as she stared toward the opening, a figure moved into view. The woman was very old. She wasn't tall, but was broad-shouldered in a floor-length, wide-skirted black dress. In profile her nose and mouth were large on a time-etched face the colour of parchment, and her hair, pulled severely from her forehead into a tight chignon, was iron-grey. But despite her age there was a strength about the woman, a contained force in her stance and the low, gravelly voice in which she was giving orders to someone within the room.

Gina straightened but remained transfixed. Then the woman turned, looking directly at her from eyes that were as black as jet; and Gina felt the stare penetrated to her very soul. In that instant she recognized the likeness to the portrait on the wall. But even as she realized she was facing Alicia Cornell, the door swung shut and the woman was gone.

As silence again settled on the room, Gina had the brief feeling that the incident had been a figment of her imagination. A fragment of a dream. Or a nightmare. The thought came unbidden, and she was gripped by a momentary chill; a warning voice whispered, and an inexplicable sense of caution held her.

She returned to her task.

The sense of unease faded as she worked her way around the floor. Twelve seconds per square foot. She wondered if she ought to allow longer for this privileged timber, but the time allowance Mrs MacDonald had dinned into her was now a natural rhythm. Besides, she decided, she was giving her best and no one was entitled to more.

The gold-cased carriage clock on a side-table read ten-forty-five when she reached the final corner. Dusting her hands with satisfaction, she turned to survey the results of her toil. And met his smile across the room – the smile that had caused such havoc to her senses three weeks ago.

No tuxedo this morning: a double-breasted navy blazer, white silk shirt, maroon tie. His hands were casually in his trouser pockets as he leaned against the doorframe. 'Good morning,' he said. 'You're even more beautiful in the daylight. Women must envy you. Or hate you. Most of them prefer the subtle safety of electric light.'

Recovering from the shock, Gina fought to gather, and control, her stability. Reflexively she stood, pulling off her mob cap, shaking out her halo of hair. Her mouth had gone dry and her pulse had accelerated, but she presented a calm she did not feel as he halted in front of her and, holding his easy smile, chided with mock hurt, 'You've been avoiding me.'

Gina hardly heard the words. She felt unnerved and off balance, on a tightrope between indignation at being cornered and – in spite of how she'd felt when she saw him with the brunette – an unquenchable excitement at being so close to him again. Although his eyes still held their humour he was looking at her intently. She asked abruptly, 'What are you doing in here?'

He laughed. 'You don't know? You really don't, do you? How long have you been in New York?'

'If it's any concern of yours, ten months.'

'Don't you read the newspapers?'

'If you mean do I look at the society pictures, no, I don't. I have better things to do.' The terse remark had vocalized itself before Gina could prevent it. The statement was true, but not in the denigratory way it had sounded. Her sense of confusion and annoyance at being flustered out of her customary self-assurance caused her to take a deep breath. She was aware of what was happening, understood her feelings. But she had no intention of making a fool of herself. She said briskly, 'Please, excuse me. I have work to do.'

'You can spare me a few minutes.'

'I can't spare a second.'

'Nobody is that busy.'

'You don't know Mrs MacDonald.'

Again his laugh, and although there was no malice in it, it flushed Gina with a sudden anger. She truly was wasting time. There'd be the devil to pay if she wasn't out of here and on to her next duty double quick. And, the thought stabbed her, if those double doors opened and Alicia Cornell . . .

'Don't worry,' he said as if reading her mind. 'The old girl is closeted with her accountants. Her favourite occupation. She won't show up again until sherry at noon. Believe me, I know.' He shrugged. 'She's my mother.'

The words fell like a bomb, seeming to Gina to boom from far off then hang, suspended in the air until they faded away and the silence became opaque. At last Howard broke it with, 'It isn't that terrible, is it?'

Thoughts were battling around in Gina's head like deranged butterflies, but maintaining her outward composure she replied, 'No. I should have realized. Foolish of me. I'm sorry . . . Mister Cornell.'

'No need to be. It's I who should apologize. Playing adolescent games. I ought to have owned up from the beginning. But I really did assume you'd know me. Everybody in New York . . . ' He cut off the sentence with a laugh. 'There I go again. Look, before I make any more blots, how about we erase everything that's gone before, and start over with a clean sheet?' He raised questioning eyebrows. 'Please?' And before Gina could decide on a suitable rebuttal he was holding out his hand and saying, 'Hello. I'm Howard Cornell. I think you're a very attractive girl, and I'd consider it an honour if you'd take tea with me.' He remained standing stiffly, arm extended, his face a statement of contrition.

Gina hesitated, searching his eyes, studying the strong lines and planes of his features, but she saw no mockery there. She reached for his proffered fist, and as his firm, sure grip closed, she felt the involuntary flutter in the pit of her stomach. Quickly releasing his hand, glad he couldn't read her mind, she said, 'I'm pleased to have met you. Now, I must get back to my duties. Good morning, Mister Cornell.'

'Please, it's Howard. And you can't rush away. Not after the trouble I went to to get you up here.' To Gina's dropped jaw and the exclamation she was about to utter, he assured, 'No, there won't be any gossip. Mrs MacDonald is very discreet. Besides, I merely passed a message via our personal housekeeper that the corridors you'd polished were especially excellent, and that we'd like you for our apartment.' He held up a defensive palm. 'I know, it sounds like the lord of the manor ordering his vassals to be brought forth. But, you were playing hard to get, and I can't help the fact that we own the place. And anyhow,' he gave her that boyish-but-oh-so-mature smile, 'it seemed like a good idea at the time.'

Gina hesitated. All her common sense told her to run from this scene. No matter how charming, how genuine Howard Cornell seemed, what could he possibly want with her except a swift sexual adventure? No doubt the kind he had with every chambermaid who took his fancy. Yet despite all the warning voices, she could not move. It was impossible not to be drawn to this man. There was a strength about him, but a vulnerability also. The spark he had ignited that first time they met in the tenth floor hallway had now been fanned to a glow which was threatening to burst into flame. Gina knew she must extinguish it. Now. She declared decisively, 'No. Thank you, Mister Cornell. Tea with you is absolutely out of the question.'

'You aren't giving me a chance.'

'What chance do you give to female employees who daren't say no?' Gina was jolted by the curtness of her reply, but it was too late now, the words hung between them like a red flag.

Howard's face tightened and Gina saw the muscles of his jaw spasm. Then the tension slid away and he conceded softly, 'Very well, Gina. You'd better go.' He bent, lifted her wax can and rag box, held them toward her. 'Don't worry, I won't bother you again.'

Gina's mind was repeating fervently that she'd be insane not to get out of here. She formed the sentence, Goodbye, Mister Cornell. She heard herself say, 'A stroll, perhaps?'

'Pardon?'

'That's what we do in Rome. My home. A man and a woman. The first time. Stroll together.'

His surprise gave way to a smile, and there was an honesty and warmth in his response. 'Then that's what it shall be? Your free afternoon. Tomorrow, isn't it? The park. I'll meet you by the zoo entrance at one p.m.' He seemed about to say something more when voices came from beyond the double doors and he said, 'I must go now.' He shrugged, boyishly, still holding the box and can.

'Yes.' Gina reached and took the polishing equipment, fumbling with the mobcap in her hand, stuffing it into her pocket rather than stick the frightful thing back on her head. 'Well . . . ' she said lamely. 'I'll see you tomorrow.' And she walked swiftly across the silence of the Persian carpet, out through the door, along the hall, and didn't stop until she was on the service staircase, where she sagged back against the wall and spent the next ten minutes convincing herself that she hadn't been the victim of an hallucination.

During the remainder of the day she listed the thousand reasons why she couldn't indulge this madness; why she should phone the Cornell apartment and tell him, Howard (she kept repeating his name aloud whenever she was alone), that she had made a mistake, wasn't free to see him tomorrow, or any other day; why she had to regain her sanity; why she must stop feeling as if she'd drunk a whole bottle of champagne.

Naturally, she accomplished none of this.

* * *

144

She rose with the dawn. Whistling and humming she was showered and dressed, had dusted and polished and hung washing in the yard before she roused her sister and brother from their slumber with the cheerful threat of 'A wet washcloth down the neck for the last one out,' which provoked, 'How childish' from Paola and, 'By you and whose army?' from Filipo but which brought them both forth to breakfast where she confettied them with blithe spirit for a further thirty minutes before departing, with extra hugs and kisses, for the Howard.

The very name caused her heart to thud.

Before heading down the side alley to the employees' entrance, she stood across the street from the hotel and stared at the carved letters – HOWARD – of the portico (oblivious to the ones which spelt WEST) until they were imprinted on the retinas of her eyes so that when she eventually looked up the face of the building to the topmost storey she could still see them hovering in front of the curtained windows. The windows behind which he must be standing. Or sitting. Or still lying in bed. In his pyjamas. Or just pyjama pants. Or . . .

Gina cut off that speculation as a dark memory shifted in the recesses of her mind. She would not permit it to surface, would not allow it to shadow today's brightness with doubts or confusion. Jingling her happiness like a pocketful of loose change, she ran across the traffic lanes and in to her labours.

The morning flew.

The meeting was as she had dreamed it would be.

She was at the park entrance at ten minutes to one, pacing, her breath puffing whitely in the cold air; autumn was retreating in the face of an early advancing winter; this first week of November there had been sharp nightly frosts, and today the pale sun hadn't the strength to thaw the crystal riming of the deepest shaded grass or warm the hard edge from the chilled air. Gina however was untouched by the weather; she was oblivious to everything but the presence of Howard Cornell. She had taken particular care with her hair and make-up. The topcoat she had bought in January really didn't look too unfashionable, and she'd added a long red wool scarf which she thought gave her quite a jaunty air. When she'd checked herself out in the mirror she had been pleased with what she saw. Hoped he would be too.

He was. He said so as he strode up to her, dressed in a

double-breasted grey overcoat with a black and white spotted silk muffler, reached out and held her face in his leather-gloved hands. 'You're lovely.' For a heart-stopping minute Gina thought he was going to kiss her, but then he released her and said, 'Have you seen the Bethesda Fountain? We'll walk that way.' And he took her hand, slipped it under his arm as casually as if they'd known each other for years, and led her toward the track where half-a-dozen children were riding Shetland ponies.

Gina was captivated. She told herself it was because this was the first time she'd strolled with a man since she was twenty – and now she was twenty-three. Nonetheless, there was a thrill to being beside Howard (she had ceased utterly to think of him as Mister Cornell) which was inescapable. As he talked and joked, his charm and laughter seemed to spill out and touch even the strangers who passed. His easy manner infected Gina. And she returned it. They talked about their intentions for the coming Christmas: next month's celebrations at the hotel when Howard would, by tradition, supervise the decoration of the twenty-foot high pine tree which would stand in the lobby; Gina's plans for a genuine Italian-style party with her sister and brother, Max and Cassie. It was the everyday gossip of intimate friends.

But they were total strangers.

That thought touched Gina with a warning finger as Howard pointed along the wide, tree-lined Mall and said, 'In the gas-light era this was a playground for children. For a dime they could ride the length of the walk in barouches drawn by goats. I remember. I was very small. I used to watch.'

Gina set aside her momentary apprehension and asked, 'Did you take such a ride?'

Howard frowned. 'No . . . My mother wouldn't permit it.' His casualness briefly retreated and there was a strange darkness in his eyes. Then it was past and he shrugged and said, 'I guess mother always knows best.'

They continued along the Mall, Howard describing the surrounding sights (Gina exclaiming interestedly, not wishing to disappoint him with the revelation that she'd spent almost every lunch break of the summer here); around the concert ground with its orchestra shell facing the stern bust of Beethóven brooding over a female figure rising at the foot of his pedestal; beside a roped-off roadway with bicyclists swishing by; down broad steps through an arched underpass and onto a wide brick terrace fronting the lake. In the centre of the terrace the bronze angel Bethesda, wings outspread, poised above her fountain and pool. The worn stone of the terrace's balustrade, the gurgle of the water, and the misty wooded hillside across the lake were a sudden, vivid reminder to Gina of the gardens of the Villa d'Este at Tivoli where she had once strolled, sixteen years old, in romantic quietude with a boy cousin of the same age.

She looked around at Howard. He was no boy. Even as he stared toward the far trees, his face in repose, there was an intense masculinity about him, not merely the strength of his features, but a vitality charging the air around him, filling Gina with a co-mingling of unease and exhilaration. This had all happened too quickly, she cautioned herself. Her affection-starved emotions had caught up with her, sent her rationality reeling. And she didn't want any romantic involvements (least of all as the passing fancy of a wealthy playboy): she hadn't the time; had work to do; money to save toward her goal – a restaurant with her name above the door, which, though it seemed as remote as ever, she was determined she would achieve.

Howard said, 'Dinner with me tomorrow?'

Gina hesitated. 'Let me think about it.'

The next hour drifted by on charmed wings. Having walked the entire length of the park and exited opposite an unpretentious apartment block which Howard pointed out as 'The home of your compatriot, Mayor LaGuardia,' Gina realized she could recall little of the afternoon's conversation. Her preoccupation had been with the man at her side. Pausing on the sidewalk she consciously tried to remember what they had discussed. Very little. It all had been inconsequential (immature?) chat. They had exchanged scant information about themselves: each time Gina had attempted to inject a more personal note into the gossip, Howard had sidetracked with another joke or anecdote. But, she chided herself, what do you expect? Unlike you, he hasn't spent the past twelve months avoiding dreams of the opposite sex. To him this is just another easy-going date; nothing special about it, and nothing serious. So stop reading it like a romantic novel, accept it as everyday reality.

He asked, 'Well? Have you decided?'

'What?' She read again that boyish plea in his eyes. 'Dinner tomorrow? I don't know . . . '

'I understand. You prefer to take it a step at a time. Very well. Lunch on your next half-day. Friday. Or shall I arrange to have your free afternoon brought forward? Yes, I will, I'll have a quiet word . . . '

'No. You mustn't. Thank you, but . . . '

'Okay. Friday then. I'll just have to be patient.' He grinned. 'I'll meet you at twelve-thirty. The same place as today. That shall be our special spot. Our lucky rendezvous. You will be there? Won't you? Please.'

Gina spent the next two days in an agony of impatience, working without knowing what she was doing, holding conversations without knowing what she was saying, spending the evenings visualizing the hotel and its penthouse apartment where she imagined Howard would be wrapped in similar dreams of their next afternoon together. The only time she took off from the reverie was to purchase a new outfit – persuading herself it was about time she stopped wearing secondhand clothes, ignoring the admonishing voice that said the French-blue silk blouse, cream cotton skirt and peep-toed, ankle-strapped high heels were hardly suitable for the oncoming winter.

On Friday morning she was thankful Cassie was on a different shift, and didn't have to explain to her friend why, at the end of her detail, she rushed to change, apply her make-up, then spent fifteen minutes combing and tweaking and perfecting her coiffure. Though the temperature had plummeted last night, barely risen since, she eschewed the prudence of a sweater, left the top two buttons of her blouse unfastened beneath her coat.

By the time she was satisfied with her perfection the other girls had long gone. It was twelve-fifteen!

She flew from the locker room, sharp heels rattling excitation along the empty corridor. Slowing at the lobby she snapped open her purse for inspection, said a silent prayer of thanks that the Bull wasn't on duty, held her breath during the cursory surveillance, then raced into the winter-raw afternoon.

She ran the length of the alley, bursting from its mouth onto the teeming avenue like a long-imprisoned bee zooming from the hive. Traffic flowed back and forth before her, a rushing, booming river of metal separating her from the frost-canopied island of the park.

On the kerb she prowled left and right, advanced impatiently into the gutter. Though no break in the streaming barrier was visible, after only a second's pause she plunged ahead. Horns howled, brakes squealed, drivers' heads popped out of windows, wide mouths yelling expletives which were drowned in the din. Gina ran, dodging and weaving, eyes calculating, pinpointing with hair's-breadth accuracy the route between the rushing fenders and radiators. A surge of exhilaration spurred her; a dozen years of daily duels with Roman motorists had honed her reflexes to a razor edge, and with her skill pitted against the relatively limping pace of Manhattan traffic there was no contest. She skipped onto the sidewalk, threw a pretty wave at a distant, dumbfounded traffic cop, and headed into the park.

Her breath came in short, hard gasps as she half-walked, half-ran, shortcutting across the white-rimed grass, aware of the draining minutes but mindful also of the threat to the precious shoes and the damage to her coiffure. She hurried on, reprimanding herself for agreeing to meet at the zoo entrance – so far away on the other side of the oasis – as she skirted the iced ponds and fountains, statues and monuments, workers sharing their lunches with pigeons and squirrels, nannies vigilant to their Park Avenue charges, lovers oblivious to everything but each other.

The sight of the young couple, hand-in-hand, slowed Gina to a walk. What was she doing? Where on earth did she think she was going? Rushing toward she knew not what, like some giddy schoolgirl on her first date. The voice she had first heard when she faced Howard in the Cornell apartment whispered again: she would be insane to pursue this man. And yet the euphoric feeling would not loose its grip. A brick wall could not have halted her advance toward the rendezvous.

There were few people around the zoo entrance, a scarcity of pedestrians on the sidewalk. An ancient Chinese, hands deep in the pockets of his frayed, floor-length overcoat, guarded a rusty, tin-sided, smoking handcart offering CHEAP LUNCH, FRANKS & KRAUT 5c. He glanced around hopefully as Gina arrived, but returned to staring at his shuffling feet when she halted, peered north and south, checked her watch.

She was one minute early. She stared at the tiny gold hand,

watched it creep minutely toward twelve-thirty. She was so still, so utterly aware of the time she thought she could feel the very earth turning beneath her. On the half-hour she looked up. The scene seemed unaltered from sixty seconds earlier. No sign of Howard. But, then, he had an hotel to oversee. Didn't he? Had important things to do; couldn't be expected to leap out of his office in the middle of a vital meeting to rush to a tryst like an over-eager adolescent. The way Gina had! The thought scalded her. She smiled faintly at the Chinese, suddenly feeling slightly ridiculous; mentally avoiding speculation of what her sister and brother might think if they could see her now. The Oriental remained inscrutable, heightening Gina's sense of foolishness.

She paced, affecting an air of nonchalance, refusing to recheck the time. The resultant heat of the run had swiftly faded, and the frost now exploited her vanity of shunned woollies, easily penetrating her coat, chilling the film of perspiration beneath her blouse. Her feet too began to freeze in the pretty but flimsy shoes. People and traffic passed; a carriage from its base down near the Plaza, the bedecked horse panting great feathers of condensation, a young couple behind the driver, swaddled in rugs, wrapped in their dreams. Gina's eyes smarted in the wind. She was sure that the sense of elapsed time was an illusion, knew that mere moments had ticked by.

When she rechecked her watch it was twelve-forty-five.

Her heart hammered as the hand raced around the face. She poised on the kerb, searching the distance. Waited and waited. She knew he'd been delayed on business, or by an encounter with a friend. Or had been taken ill. That was it. That was why he had been unable to relay a message to her. Relief flooded her.

But it drained in an instant, and the cold that suddenly lanced her was more bitter than the icy air. Her fantasy crumbled. The past days fell in an explosion of shattered hopes, splintering to reveal the cruel glare of reality. In a moment the magnitude of her stupidity had towered before her. How could she ever have been so puerile? What on earth had possessed her so fatuously to believe that Howard Cornell might have the slightest interest in Gina Rossi? Somehow, she realized, she had suffered the delusion that he was attracted to Gina Rossi, daughter of a wealthy Rome restaurateur. But, of course, that was someone who had died a long time ago, a girl

Howard Cornell had never known. The Gina Rossi he had met was a housemaid, the lowest of his low employees, a female in a shapeless brown smock who wore rags around her knees and smelled of beeswax and dirt and who wasn't permitted even to look into the eyes of one of his guests. A girl as forgettable as the date he had made with her.

A man in a camel coat and derby hurried past, scanned Gina with casual interest, smirked approval and continued along the avenue. The Chinese was selling steaming frankfurters to a woman in a fur hat.

Gina walked away; and ended the dream.

Cassie enthused, 'You should take a look at him. My date last night. Shoulders like Johnny Weissmuller. They got that way from swinging polo sticks and golf clubs, and carrying dough to the bank. He's loaded. Inherited his old man's corned beef plant in Chicago. And his company sponsors the Miss Wholesome Meat Beauty Pageant. He says I should enter. Says I got what it takes. And he should know, he's seen hundreds, maybe thousands of contestants. Plenty of them have wound up in Hollywood . . . ' she pulled on her coat ' . . . I shouldn't wonder.'

Gina looked into the redhead's bubbling enthusiasm. It was the end of their working week, thirty hours since Gina walked numbly away from the zoo entrance of the park. She hadn't mentioned the incident to a soul. She had placed her new blouse, skirt and shoes in the wardrobe, closed the door on them as firmly as she had shut her mind to further thoughts of Howard Cornell – and her own naïveté. The aberration had been temporary; it wouldn't happen again; never again would she permit her emotions to rule her head; in future she'd take Cassie's advice: 'Lock your heart in your purse, Hon. Don't ever take it out. That way it'll never get broke. Always keep a feller waiting and wanting . . . ' she'd flicked up an eyebrow ' . . . but not too long.'

That memory rekindled Gina's smile as she joined the line leading toward the locker room door where a woman was distributing pay envelopes.

Cassie was continuing, 'He said all I had to do was send my picture – full-length, in a swimsuit, you know – and my measurements, to the selection committee, and they'll return me an official application form. Not every female who sends her photo gets chosen, of course. But he says I'm a cinch.' She winked broadly, elbowed Gina in the ribs. ''Specially as he's chairman of the committee.'

Gina couldn't resist Cassie's cheerfulness. She reached the head of the line, took her pay envelope and walked into the passage with her friend following. Distractedly dipping into the envelope she nearly overlooked the slip of yellow paper among the dollar bills. Curiosity knitted her brow as she extracted the note from the money and unfolded it.

Sickness seized her as she read the brief words, and she halted abruptly amid the hurrying girls.

Cassie, stuffing her wages into her purse as she walked, glanced around, saw what had happened and retraced four rapid strides to where Gina was standing. 'Hon, what's up? Those crooks paid you short again? I tell you . . . ' she recognized the paper in Gina's fingers. 'My God! They canned you. Oh, Hon . . . ' She reached out both hands to grip Gina's shoulders. 'I'm sorry. I . . . ' Her usual bluffness was lost as she stared helplessly at her friend.

For a long moment Gina didn't see Cassie, her gaze was fixed on the distant end of the corridor. Then the light suddenly returned to her eyes. Understanding, she exclaimed, 'That damn magazine! That sadist who searched me. She reported me. Branded me as a thief. For a worthless sheaf of paper.' The anger flushed in her cheeks, the Italian rose in her voice. '*La cagna!* She isn't going to get away with it. I won't be treated like a piece of dirt. And I'm not going to crawl away without a whisper.'

Cassie said helplessly, 'Hon, you can't do any good. You . . . ' But Gina was already striding away.

She marched along the corridor, her heels cracking angrily on the stone floor. When she reached the door lettered HEAD CLEANER she yanked the handle and strode into the carton-jammed cubby-hole office, causing Mrs MacDonald to jerk back on her chair like a startled rabbit. Tossing the crumpled dismissal notice onto the desk Gina snapped, 'That came from you I believe. No, don't tell me you were only following orders. You know the injustices that are going on in this place. You know what that searcher does to the girls. You saw what she was doing to me.' She stabbed a finger at the scrap of yellow paper. 'Yet you'll still be a party to that. You're despicable. As guilty as that pervert. And that's all I came here to say. Not to apologize for taking a pathetic magazine. Or to plead for my job. You can keep it. I came to tell you what I think of you, and this hateful hotel, and the Fascists who own it.' She snatched a breath, the bile rising in her throat as she glared into the elderly woman's caring blue eyes.

Caring? Gina was taken aback by what she thought she saw. She attempted to thrust the impression aside. But there was no mistaking the emotion. Her anger faltered. Something was wrong here. This wasn't how she had imagined it would be. Mrs MacDonald was not on her feet screeching in retaliatory rage, nor was she shrinking with fear. On her face there was only a sadness and quiet understanding. Gina struggled to bolster her collapsing indignation, searching for the remainder of the aggressive phrases which an instant ago had been in her head. They were gone.

Mrs MacDonald said quietly, 'I'm sorry.'

Gina stared.

The head cleaner went on, 'Perhaps you're right. Perhaps someone should speak their mind. But . . . ' she sighed ' . . . it won't be me. I learned a long time ago to keep my thoughts to myself. And what was my reward? Work. When people were dying from starvation – yes, girl, here in this so-called golden city – I had a job, a regular wage to take home to my family. I'm not making excuses, just hoping you'll see that we all must eventually learn to take orders. That power dictates to every-one. Including you.'

Gina breathed, 'I'll never be a lackey again.'

Mrs MacDonald shook her head. 'You don't understand what I'm trying to say.' Her eyes now held only pity. 'Firstly, that the gulf between Broome Street and Central Park West is a million miles wide. Secondly – though I'll always deny I ever told you this – that Mrs Alicia Cornell is not about to let a chambermaid cross that gulf on the arm of her son.'

Filipo asked eagerly, 'May I have the stamp?'

Gina, hunched on the edge of the sofa, looked up at him, unseeing. She had been sitting here for the past hour, since arriving home from the Howard. Cassie had wanted to accompany her, but Gina had refused; grateful though she was for her friend's sympathy, she wanted only to be alone. After leaving the hotel she'd walked all the way to Broome Street, almost five miles, oblivious to the biting wind, her senses deadened by shock. In the apartment, thankful Paolo and Filipo were still in school, she'd remained in limbo, too stunned to feel either anguish for her predicament, or anger against its injustice.

The trance had continued even as the youngsters entered, called 'Hello,' noisily discarded their overcoats and boots. It at last was broken by Filipo's voice.

Gina looked at the envelope he was holding.

'You forgot to collect the mail from Mrs Ponti,' he said. 'The stamp,' he repeated. 'May I steam it off?'

Gina struggled for comprehension. She stared at the airmail sticker and the postage stamp portrait of Britain's George VI. Pulling herself together she replied, 'Of course,' to her brother, taking the envelope, removing the contents and returning it to him. As he enthused, 'Thanks, Sis,' and headed for the kettle, Gina unfolded the two thin blue sheets and read: 'Dear Gina, sorry to have taken so long to reply, but I was away on business . . .'

David Lowell went on to say how pleased he was to have heard from her, recounted his efforts to keep his Richmond hotel, the Grange, on a financial even keel, included a couple of anecdotes about eccentric guests, and ended by reporting that Robert Fallon was assigned to Sydney, Australia. He added, 'P.S. If ever you fancy a holiday away from the bright lights of Manhattan, you and your family are always welcome here.'

Gina set the letter aside. A holiday! She'd be hard pressed to pay the rent for more than the next fortnight if she didn't find another job. That, she affirmed, must be her absolute priority. She did not re-read the Englishman's letter, did not give another thought to Fallon. Nor to Howard Cornell. Nothing must be permitted to loosen the vice of her determination.

She turned, smiling, to her sister and brother.

11

Fourteenth Street had changed its mood more often than anyone could remember. Carved from the wilderness in 1811, it had first been home to Manhattan's nobility; later, when the mansion owners moved north, the theatre transformed the street into the city's Rialto; after the turn of the century giant retail stores made it an exclusive shopping mall; and when these businesses followed their wealthy clientele, it was reduced to a commercial vein for the needle trades which had flowed into Union Square. Nowadays it was garbed in its tawdriest colours. The windows of its once-stately homes fronted warrens of peddlers and panderers; its sidewalks were lined with cheap clothing shops, flashy burlesque spots, hole-in-the-wall lunchrooms and taxi-dance halls. Along this garish promenade billowed a daily flood of bargain hunters, a nightly torrent of pleasure seekers; and always moving in the tide were the beggars, blind, armless, legless on wheeled trolleys, playing tin whistles and banjoes, rattling coins in cans and cigar boxes, knowing the poor give unto their own.

Beside the scarred reception desk in the linoleum-floored lobby of the Mayfair Hotel, the manager's door opened and two men came out.

One was bald, middle-aged, the quality of his off-the-peg suit reflecting that of the lobby furnishings. The younger character however wore a double breasted chalk-stripe that nothing less than a hundred dollars' worth of hand-stitching could have created. The blue polka-dot handkerchief in his breast pocket matched the tie snugged under his button-down cream collar. The fedora he carried was grey and svelte. Beneath thick, black wavy hair his face was sharply handsome, olive complexioned with a dark shadow around his jaw.

A confident smile curved his full lips as he met Gina's eyes where she was standing at the desk; but before he could utter whatever cute remark she was sure he would make, the other man was saying, 'Okay. You can put two machines in next week. But you'd better make sure they're serviced regular or they'll be out with the garbage.'

The dark character held his smile on Gina a moment longer before replying, '*Va bene* Don't worry. I keep my promises. My word is my bond. Ask anybody. Johnny Sabato never welched on a bet or a deal in his life. And believe me, you won't regret this. Vending machines mean profits the easy way. A couple of months you'll be begging me to put in six more. I guarantee.'

They walked to stand at the street door discussing percentages, but Gina lost the conversation as she was tugged back to her confrontation with the rheumy-eyed character behind the desk with 'Assistant Manager' pinned to his creased lapel, as he said archly, 'I told you. We aren't hiring. I don't intend to argue about it. I certainly don't intend to discuss this hotel's policy with . . . ' he looked down his acned nose, ' . . . people off the street. Now, move along.' With a dismissive flick of his head he returned to his ledger.

Gina burned with anger and despair. Clenching her fists she glared at the dome of the bent head, to the mottled scalp beneath the thin hair. Her impulse was to snatch up the large brass ashtray and bash it down on the skull. Frustration seethed through her. But there was something more – a dreadful fear that this was how it was going to be wherever she went; that her worst suspicions were true, Alicia Cornell had put out her omnipotent word that Gina Rossi was a pariah to be forever banned not only from the upper echelon hotels but from the lesser ranks also.

It was a week, seven desperate days since her dismissal from the Howard. In that time she'd been refused acceptance by all the major employment agencies, and turned away from every door she had knocked upon. Now, here in this two-dollar-a-night Fourteenth Street hostelry she bitterly recalled her first day of work in New York, waiting on the search line, and the girls who'd been caught stealing the crystal fish; Cassie's words: 'She'll finish up in some fleapit flophouse.' The memory chilled Gina. And a plea rose in her throat; her mind formed the words of submission, the self-prostration which would cause this creature who held her life in his hands to pluck her from the brink. But even as her lips parted, her teeth remained clenched. Her jaw was rigid as she bit down on the dirt she was about to eat; and the corner of her mind that was the essence of her will refused to yield. Damn it, she wasn't beaten yet!

She turned and carried that thought across the lobby, past the two men, out to the street. Beneath the marquee she halted. The rain had quickened, slicking the sidewalk to a wet shine which reflected the depression of the buildings – and the way Gina felt.

She didn't hear him exit behind her, was jolted physically and mentally by his voice: '*E una bella giornata, vero?*' Recovering quickly Gina appraised the immaculate character who'd peddled two vending machines to the hotel manager. He was now wearing the fedora, its brim tilted sideways and forwards, accentuating the roguish quirk of his mouth. Seen too many Warner Brothers gangster movies, she decided, replying coolly, 'The weather is no joke,' but giving way to a grain of curiosity with, 'And what makes you think I speak Italian?'

'You understood what I said, didn't you?' He laughed. 'Plus, I haven't seen eyes like that since my momma went to heaven. Deep as the pools of the Borghese Gardens.'

Full of it, thought Gina. And, judging from his Mulberry Street Italian accent, the nearest he likely had been to Rome was Nero's Clam Bar across from Grand Central. The wind gusted, knifing through her thin coat. The last thing she needed right now was a come-on from a counterfeit Little Caesar. She peered through the approaching traffic for a bus.

He said, 'I heard what was happening in there. You're looking for a job. That skinny creep gave you the cold shoulder. So, who needs a spot in a dump like that anyhow? You ought to be uptown. What do you do? You a typist? Receptionist?' He measured her. 'Sure. Maybe a secretary even.'

'I'm a chambermaid,' Gina replied flatly.

His surprise bloomed. 'You gotta be kidding. I don't believe it. What's a beautiful . . .'

Gina's glare cut him off. All the frustration, disappointment of the past week rushed in on her, whipped her anger. But the tongue-lashing she was about to deliver died unvoiced. It was something in his face, an innocence lurking behind the urbane façade; and when he continued, 'Honest, I didn't figure you for shoving a broom. You in some sort of bind?' she saw the genuine solicitude in his eyes. Lowering her hostility she replied, 'It's a long story.' But before he could pick on it, added, 'Though I don't have the time or the inclination for the telling. Let's just say there doesn't seem to be much chance of me getting a hotel job in this city.'

He pursed his lips, frowing. Then his sun reappeared and he said, 'So the hospitality business ain't the only game in town. You shouldn't oughta waste your time on that anyhow. With your looks . . . ' He unsalaciously surveyed her figure and legs, continued, 'And your shape, you could model maybe.' Seeing her sharp reaction to that he rubbed his jaw, pondered, then asked, 'Can you dance? No, not on a burly line. I mean foxtrot, waltz, stuff like that.'

Gina nodded, cautiously.

'Take a walk four blocks down. Mention my name at the Starlight. Reckon Harry'll be able to use you.' He extracted an engraved white card from his fob pocket, handed it to Gina. As she noted he had an address in the dock area and the title IMPORTER, a long black limousine, its years preserved beneath a mirror glaze, swished to the curb. While she was still searching for something to say, the man named Johnny Sabato climbed in, chunked shut the door, wound down the window.

Gina finally managed, 'Thank you.'

'Sure. No problem.' He winked and smiled, touched the rim of his fedora. *'Arriverderci.'*

The limousine pulled out into the streaming traffic. Gina watched until it was lost in the throng. She looked again at the business card, thought to drop it in a trash can, but as none was nearby slipped it into her purse. Raising her umbrella she crossed the street to enter the Hotel Riviera.

Three hours later she was home at the apartment – still without a job. Preparing vegetables at the sink she was wrapped in apprehension, was deaf to Paola and Filipo laughing at a radio show. Her mind now kept returning uncontrollably to the past, to the harsh days she had spent tramping the sidewalks between employment agencies. 'Stop thinking about that,' she said aloud and banged her peeling knife down on the drainer. The sound jolted her, and turning she faced the startled stares of the youngsters. 'Sorry,' she said lightly, raising a pale smile.

Paola shrugged to her brother. 'Going a bit nutty.'

'Old age,' he said and instantly deranged his features and figure into a hideous and hunched semblance of antiquity.

Paola recoiled, squealed with mock horror then seized him and tickled him until he cried, 'Mercy! Mercy!' and they returned to *Fibber McGee and Molly*.

Gina watched them, wrenched by affection and concern. She continued quickly with the preparation of their dinner. When all was under way she took a notebook to the table, sat and stared at the figures she'd scribbled earlier. But there was really no point in reviewing them again; they stated, irrevocably, that the Rossis would be penniless by the end of the week. Gina knew, of course, that she could always borrow from

Max. But that would be a last resort. It also would entail confessing that since being fired she had been living a lie: rather than distress her sister and brother or Max she had not told them what had happened; she hadn't actually lied to them, had merely let them think that each day when she went out she was going to her job at the Howard West as usual. But the deception's lifetime was fast expiring. If she didn't find work soon . . .

Quelling her doubts Gina went out and along the hall to the bathroom to wash her face. There, opening her purse for her comb she saw the white business card. Extracting it she again read the name, J. Sabato, and recalled his suggestion to use the card as an introduction at the Starlight Room.

But Gina knew what the Starlight Room was. A taxi-dance hall. A place where men paid to dance with 'hostesses'. The thought made her flinch. Though Gina, after ten months amid the bawdy exploits of Cassie and the other hotel girls, nowadays accepted a moral standard a hundred times broader than she'd known in Italy, she still couldn't shed fully a Catholic upbringing which threatened the fires of eternal damnation for a woman who accepted payment from a man.

Even for a dance?

Gina wrestled with her conscience. Reminded herself that ten days ago she had considered – in spite of her religious conditioning, in spite even of the dark memories of Baremo – the possibility of sexual intercourse with Howard Cornell. In the small, chill bathroom she smothered that thought. She washed her face in cold water, combed her hair. When she returned to the apartment Paola was tending the simmering pans, Filipo was setting the table. A regular routine in a regular lifestyle. A security which was essential to their survival as a family. An existence which was Gina's responsibility.

And which must not be destroyed, she avowed.

The doorway huddled between a double-feature movie theatre and Schimmel's Delicatessen. A tiny lobby, red overhead bulb illuminating the crumpled cigarette packs blown in off the street, fronted a narrow staircase. On the second floor, in the eight-by-six foyer, the flaking gilt price of tickets on the window of the booth was ten cents. The photographs on the opposite wall were the flashy smiles of a score of welcoming girls, underlined with the promise 'They'll make you want to dance.'

Above the door facing the stairs a hand-painted gold-on-purple sign announced HARRY DIX'S STARLIGHT ROOM.

'Oh, a friend of Johnny Sabato.' Harry Dix was gaunt to the point of emaciation; oiled hair widow's peaked above mournful eyes in a long horse-like face. Allowing mild interest to supplant his glumness, he said, 'Sure, we can always use another girl. Specially if she comes with Johnny's recommendation.' He scanned Gina head to toe with brief professionalism then without further discussion invited, 'Come and meet the others,' and led the way out of his photograph-smothered cubby-hole office.

The dance hall was dimly lit, pink-painted walls faded and scuffed, stuck with silver paper stars. Overhead a slow-revolving mosaic-mirrored globe sent endless butterflies of light reeling around the room. In one of the farthest corners, above an archway small electric bulbs spelled BAR; beside it on a tiny platform a five-piece band played an indifferent 'I Get Along Without You Very Well'. A handful of couples drifted with the music. The bare board floor on which they moved was uneven, unpolished, with wide dark patches. These, Gina would learn later, were machine oil stains from the days when the place was a garment sweatshop where girls toiled through twelve-hour shifts to keep body and soul together.

This afternoon the employees weren't so overworked. They were grouped at two of the small circular tables which lined the room's perimeter. Four blondes, a brunette and a redhead, their counterfeit hair shades as garish as the rhinestones on their throats and fingers. They slouched like unstrung dolls, staring unseeing at the dance floor, a couple of them smoking, one orange-boarding her nails. Gina's first impression was that they were sisters, they looked so alike. But it was an illusion, she realized, conjured by the sameness of boredom which masked their faces, the similarity of the satins that sheathed their curvy figures. When Harry Dix tiredly announced, 'This is Gina,' the girls looked up and their eyes focused, but their disinterest remained manifest as the dance hall owner murmured, 'Show her around,' and retreated.

Gina, smiling, greeted, 'Hi.'

The girls nodded, turned away. The brunette, twin weals of rouge as livid as her crimson dress, nodded perfunctorily at a chair and before Gina had begun to sit, recited in a monotone, 'Customers get a ticket at the booth. Joe punches the ticket at the door. One ticket buys one dance. No ticket no dance. No more'n four dances in a row with the same guy. Keep your hands away from the customers' pockets. Keep their hands away from you, period. A guy won't take no for an answer, call Joe. When you're offered a drink, order a Manhattan. Any personal arrangements you make with customers, keep off the premises. And don't let Dix know. If he gets vinegar on his ulcers from griping dupes, their wives, girl friends or the Law, you'll be out so fast your feet won't touch.' Her gaze closed from the middle distance and fastened on Gina; and there were suddenly hard points glinting beneath her spiky lashes. She warned coldly, 'Stay away from other girls' regulars.'

Gina considered contesting the abrupt, unprovoked belligerence but shelved the temptation when the brunette looked away and lit a cigarette. As the band ended its number half the dancers remained standing, the rest wandered back to the tables. Feeling somewhat marooned, with no further communication apparently forthcoming from the girls, Gina stood, deciding to retrace Harry Dix to ask when she should report for work. Turning, she almost walked into the fist clutching the ticket.

He didn't say anything, just loomed there, holding up the pink tab, shyness hiding behind the expectancy in his big brown eyes. He was tall and thin as a pole, raw-boned in a USAAF uniform that fit where it touched; his long red neck supported a lantern-jawed head cropped to the point of baldness. He looked, it occurred to Gina, like an outsize fourteen-year-old. That thought, and the silent supplication in his face, halted her as she was about to step past him. She was rooted, clutching amid her options which had scattered like loose change.

Other men were moving around her, girls rising from the tables, pairs heading on to the floor. The band went into 'Isn't This a Lovely Day', and when the gangly Air Force lad declared, 'I can do this one pretty good,' Gina's indecision lasted only a moment longer. She stepped toward him and took his ham-like hands, but before she could introduce herself was whisked away into the swirling flecks of light.

At first a thin thread of fear tightened around her as she was stabbed by the idea that this entire project had been a dreadful mistake because she had forgotten how to dance. But even as the supposition was raised and considered in her head, she realized she had travelled the length of the room and was passing the bandstand, her feet gliding backward with smooth precision, keeping perfect step with the boots of the boy who had looked so ungainly when stationary but who now moved with surprising grace. He was staring off into some middle distance, eyelids half-closed, an expression of sheer joy on his young face.

At that moment Gina had the impulse to cry. The years rolled back and she was dancing at her nineteenth birthday party, in her father's arms in the grand ballroom of the Gritti Palace in Venice. She was wearing the new red taffeta dress with the daring neckline, Alfredo Rossi was handsomely resplendent in tailed evening suit. They were a million miles from Blackshirt marches, rumours of beatings, whispered plans for revolt; the night was a velvet dream, and Gina had pretended it would last for ever.

'You dance real fine.' The voice brought her back to reality. The boy was smiling at her. Pushing aside the memories she returned his appreciation, gave herself to the moment, moved closer to him as he expertly steered her around the tinselly hall, over the bare, oil-stained boards.

The magic was over as abruptly as it had begun, and the boy was back to being a big gangly creature standing before her saying, 'Thank you, miss. That was just beautiful. I've never danced in no fancy city place before. We don't have nothing like this down home. And . . . ' He looked at Gina, his features flushing but his eyes level and candid ' . . . no ladies as pretty as you neither. Do I give you my ticket now?'

The tears sprang to Gina's eyes, burning the lids. She answered hoarsely, 'No. That's all right. Use it again. I have to leave.' And she strode swiftly away, across to the door, out to the lobby and the chill air from the narrow stairway. Gathering herself she stepped to Harry Dix's office, knocked, waited for his, 'It's open,' and entered.

Dolefully looking up from the ledger on his desk the horse-faced dance hall owner acknowledged, 'Oh, sure, the new girl. You meet the others? Good. You'll get along with them just fine. We open noon til two a.m. It's pretty quiet this time of day, but nights it picks up. And Fridays and Saturdays we pack 'em in. You do a seven-hour shift. Work it out with the girls. I don't care who comes in when so long as I get the hours covered. You'll make around twenty a week. Take any tips you like from the customers, but no hanky-panky. This is a straight place, and I intend for it to stay that way.' He stared at Gina, seeming to see her for the first time, observing at last, 'That's a funny kind of hairstyle. But different. I guess I like it. Yeah. It'll be okay. You don't have to change it. But a little more rouge, eh? Lipstick too. The movie-star look, you know. The guys who come here, they like it that way. And you got the right kind of dress, don't you? Sure, of course you do. See you tomorrow then. Give my regards to Johnny.' He returned to his ledger.

'That's great,' enthused Cassie. 'It must be a lucky day for both of us. You getting a job, me being accepted for the beauty pageant.' To Gina's surprised stare she forged on, 'You know. Miss Wholesome Meat. In Chicago. I told you I mailed my picture. To the address my corned beef millionaire gave me. Well, they wrote back. Sent me an official entry form and everything. Isn't it fantastic? It's true what they say, Hon – real talent will out. If you've got it, it'll get you to where you want to be. And don't worry, you'll make it too. This job at the Starlight is just the beginning. Heck, another month you'll be doing your Ginger Rogers' 'Cheek to Cheek' in one of those ritzy joints on Fifth. Then you and me both – with Poll and Phil naturally – will beat it out west.' She patted her red curls. 'Course, that's if I don't marry the canning king. Stockyard City isn't exactly Beverly Hills, but when you've got the dough you never see the gruesome side of town anyhow.' She tipped generous measures of bourbon into two shot glasses, brought them across the room.

Gina had come directly here to Cassie's apartment after being hired by Harry Dix. The dance hall might not be the most salubrious place in the city, but as she'd exited past the photographic parade of hostesses, briefly imagining her own portrait amongst them, she had been unable to resist the surge of pleasure at having landed the job, and had been spurred to share the news with her friend. Now, however, taken aback by Cassie's announcement, she asked with surprise, 'You've definitely decided? You're going up to Chicago?'

'I already made the reservation on the Twentieth Century. Leaving in a couple of weeks. That'll give me time to buy some new outfits.' Cassie winked. 'Maybe find a feller to pay for them.'

'You're incorrigible,' smiled Gina.

'Like I told you, Hon. You got to make the most of what you got, while you can. Anyhow, if I do bring a little pep into the life of one of the Howard West's super dupes, it'll be my swansong. Once I've won the pageant I won't need a man to pick up my tabs ever again.' She tossed down half her liquor. 'Cheers. Here's to us, Hon. And a big nothing to all fellers. Chumps the lot of them.' She swallowed the remainder of the bourbon.

Gina returned the toast, sipping her drink. She smiled; but the happiness that had brought her here had now faded. A sadness pervaded her as she watched her friend refilling her glass. For the first time since she'd met Cassie she sensed a bitterness in her, a caustic edge to her usually lighthearted banter.

She said, 'I hope everything will work out just fine.' She leaned forward, kissed Cassie on the cheek, pulled a veil over her doubts and fears.

Gina had considered concealing from Paola and Filipo the dress she'd bought *en route* home from Cassie; but realizing that sooner or later the purple, satin sheath would have to be brought to light, she decided to reveal it, and the reason for its purchase, as soon as she arrived at the apartment.

She sat the youngsters before her on the sofa, told them the white lie of having had to leave the Howard West because of staff cutbacks. She explained, without drama, the need to maintain their income, the necessity of her job at the dance hall. To her relief the only questions they asked were practical ones such as what hours she would work, would she still accompany them to mass on Sunday, would they be able to afford new valves for the radio. Gina assured them everything was going to be fine. 'I'm so pleased you understand,' she said. 'Now all that remains is for you to approve my new dress. Wait here.'

She went quickly to the bedroom, changed into the purple sheath. Returning to the living room, with a mannequin twirl she posed, arms upstretched and fanfared, 'Taran-tara! The Starlight Dance Hall Special.'

A stunned silence followed. Then Filipo gave a high, appreciative whistle and pronounced, 'You look like a vomp.'

'Vamp,' corrected Gina. 'And you're supposed to be too young to know what that is.' She gave him her steely look, tempered with a wry smile, believing that the best way to treat this situation was with a varnish of humour. She was grateful her brother was taking the situation in his chipper stride. As she turned toward Paola, however, her hopes faltered when she saw the frown marring her sister's brow. Maintaining her feigned brightness she quipped, 'Well, I know it isn't Schiaparelli, but you must admit it has a certain *je ne sais quoi*.' She flicked her hips, winked exaggeratedly at Filipo. But the seeds of cheeriness cast for her sister's benefit fell on stony ground.

Paola murmured, 'I suppose it's all right. If you've got to work at that place.' She took up her knitting from beside her on the sofa and began resolutely to work the needles.

Gina's heart shuddered. She glanced anxiously toward Filipo and was flooded with relief when he returned an understanding nod saying, 'I have something to read,' and went through to the bedroom, closing the door.

Gina took a deep breath, walked to the sofa and sat beside her sister. She said softly but firmly, 'You're not a child, Paola. I shouldn't have to explain again why I took this Starlight job. Nor should there be any reason to apologize for this dress. So, please, don't give me a hard time . . . ' she lightened her tone ' . . . as your brother would say in Americanese.'

For several moments Paola continued to stare fixedly at her clicking knitting needles, then her hands were still. Facing Gina she said numbly, 'You don't understand. I love the dress. It's . . . glamorous. You're glamorous. You'll be out every night now at that dance hall. Having fun. I'll be stuck here, taking care of Filipo. It's not fair. You're right, I'm not a child. I'm a woman. If we'd stayed in Italy I might be betrothed by now. I'd have a boy – a man – of my own. I'd be the one going dancing. Instead of sitting here with this damn knitting.' She thumped the wool and needles into the corner of the sofa, stared ahead, her lower lip defiantly refusing to tremble.

Gina studied the profile of her sister. A strong profile. The face of a young woman, But behind it she saw the features of a small girl. And saw the confusion and hurt in her. She hadn't seen it so clearly, she realized, since the morning over two years ago when she'd sat beside the youngsters on the bank of the Tiber, as she was sitting now, and explained to them that their father must go away, and that life as they had known it until then must come to an end. Thereafter had she, Gina asked herself, taken her sister for granted? Or had she been over-protective? Or had she been selfish? That unwelcome question chilled her. Would it have been better for Paola and Filipo to return to Rome to live with Cousin Letti? Paola, in particular, was not politically-minded. She was a normal, healthy Italian girl, whose inherent drive was to marry a handsome man, produce several babies, and be queen of her household. These past months she had presented a bright face to the world. But how deeply was she pining to follow those natural instincts?

Gina sagged under the weight of the inquisition. Even during the first dark days in this city, living with the immigration officer's words, 'More return to Europe than stay; better to be poor in their own country than starve in a strange land,' she had not doubted her motives, had been certain that the three of them must remain together. They were a family. A whole. They had been fragmented once. But that must never be permitted to happen again.

The assurance straightened her spine, jolted her into the present. The uncertainties ceased kaleidoscoping and she focused on what she knew to be fact – that she was unequivocally right. There must be no deviation in that belief. And she must never permit sentiment to cloud her judgment, nor lessen her resolve.

She said briskly, 'Well, once I've settled in at the Starlight, we'll have a rethink on our schedules. I'm going to make sure I take a full day off each week. And we'll spend it together, doing only what you and Filipo want. I promise.' She slipped her arm around her sister's shoulders, pulled her close. 'I'll even take you dancing. Truly.'

Paola turned, and the warmth slowly returned to her eyes. 'And I can have a dress like this?'

Gina swallowed. Hard. Crossing the fingers of her free hand behind her back she smiled, 'Yes. Why not?' She kissed Paola's cheek. No point in negotiating difficult bridges until she reached them.

Within a couple of days Gina had realized that not all her dance hall partners would be as pleasant, or as skilled, as the gangly USAAF boy; and her initial cheerful expectations were as bruised as her ribs and feet.

The Starlight's girls had a self-concocted, make-do shift

schedule which they constantly bickered over, fighting for prime off-duty hours with the tired old weapons of sick grannies, dying pets, dentists, sprained ankles and periods. As new girls always got the tacky end of the stick from this mess, Gina was drafted onto the seven p.m. to two a.m. stint. The toughest of these hours were the four spanning midnight, when the fellers who genuinely wanted to dance had gone home, to be replaced by a motley collection of celebrants who, having already painted the town red, were looking to gloss it an even more lurid shade. Dancing with this crew consisted less of keeping close to their meandering feet, more of avoiding their wandering hands. Like a wrestling match, Gina thought; but there were no breaks between rounds, for no sooner had the band ended one number, bringing her momentary release from some mauler's bear hug, than it was into its next and another combatant was brandishing his ticket.

By the end of her second night, however, Gina had learned most of the tricks of the trade: from exhaling garlic breath into the face of minor offenders, to grinding her spike heel onto the instep of the hardest cases. And if some bully-boy attempted retribution for this treatment, there was always Joe, built like a beer truck, employed to punch tickets and anybody who chanced entry without one.

But Gina was determined to fight her own battles. She was confident she could – her upbringing in a turmoiling restaurant in the heart of Rome had taught her how to size up a situation, the way to distinguish between a disgruntled client and an ugly customer, whether to pull her punches or hit hard. Above all, she was intent on making this job a success. The work was exhausting, but the money wasn't bad, and even better when, on her third day she asked an amazed Harry Dix, and received his permission, to work additional hours. Replanning her precise budget, she reckoned the family would now live with an extra degree of comfort, and she'd even be able to save a few dollars a week. The obstacles on the path into her future still appeared formidable, but now they only seemed cliff-like, rather than mountains.

After three days at the Starlight Gina had established a routine: rising at six-thirty (after less than four hours' sleep) to see Paola and Filipo off to school, then, after their departure, snatching an extra couple of hours on her bed before returning it to its sofa-state. The remainder of the morning and early afternoon she spent rapidly cleaning the apartment, shopping, scanning the newspapers (always checking the 'Businesses for Sale' columns), and chatting briefly with Mrs Ponti who now not only looked in on the youngsters when they returned from school, but also checked them during the evening if Max Barzini was otherwise engaged relieving the local cardsharps of their ill-gotten gains.

Gina arrived at the Starlight at four p.m., worked through for ten hours. The dance-hall girls didn't pillory her efforts, merely regarded her as slightly crazy. But then, since her arrival, none had offered either friendship or enmity, with the exception of the brunette who, on Gina's second evening, confronted her in the washroom and repeated the caution about staying away from other girls' regulars. Later, Gina guessed that the warning shot had been fired because she had danced twice with a tall, black-haired character who partnered the brunette for most of the evening. Under other circumstances Gina would have ignored the girl's protest, danced with whomsoever she chose. The matter, however, seemed too trivial to fight over. And, besides, she had no desire to cause waves; not so much for her own sake, but for Harry Dix's.

From her first day, though she had realized she wouldn't become close to any of her fellow hostesses, she had felt an instinctive friendliness toward the sad-faced dance-hall owner. The afternoon she asked his permission to work extra hours, sitting before his desk in the cramped, photograph-plastered office, she had sensed a desire to talk hesitating behind his natural reticence. Understanding he wouldn't initiate a conversation, doubtless because of the lack of communication from the other girls, Gina sought an opening. As she glanced at the cavalcade of wall photographs, she recognized many of the world-famous faces – bandleaders, musicians, singers – and noting that many bore scribbled autographs and good wishes, she asked Harry if he knew all these celebrities.

That had been like pulling the bung out of a pent-up geyser. Harry had talked soldily for over an hour, ceasing only with reluctance when Joe came to say Gina was needed in the hall.

Each day thereafter, Gina would spend some time chatting with the dance hall owner, exchanging small pieces of her experience for large slices of his, fascinated by his tales of life as a musician during the Roaring Twenties. Harry had, as they said in the Tin Pan Alley papers, played a mean horn. Six years ago he'd headed his own combo, cut a promisingly successful phonograph record for RCA, guest-spotted on the *Fleischmann Hour*, and was tipped for a big future. But all that was before the raid on the Sag Harbor speakeasy where an over-zealous prohibition enforcer laid his baton on everything in sight, including Harry Dix's ribs. The surgeons had said his punctured lung wasn't so serious – he just wouldn't find it too easy to blow those long, high notes in future.

'Which,' shrugged Harry, 'is like telling Joe Louis he can take a crack at the title, but with only one fist.' He smiled wanly. 'So, I bought this place. And I'm still wondering if it was a bigger mistake than playing the one-nighter at Sag Harbor.'

Gina wondered too. It hadn't taken her long to conclude that as a businessman Harry, even with one lung, made a great trumpet player. She wouldn't profess to know a lot about running a taxi-dance hall, but there was little she didn't understand of a restaurant's working and financial routines, and she was sure their basic principles should apply equally to the Starlight. Before the end of her first week she realized the place's organization was a shambles: she'd seen beer stocks covered with the dust of ages in the storeroom; noted that Joe's ticket-punching was severely hit and miss; discovered that the girls who worked afternoons had little to do, whereas those on the night shift were danced off their feet; and had chanced upon Freddie the bartender 'liberating', under cover of his overcoat, a two-gallon can of maraschino cherries.

The more she saw, the more she felt the subject ought to be broached with Harry. Yet her opposing judgment suggested caution: the dance-hall owner shouldn't have any further dents inflicted on his confidence; and Gina musn't lose his friendship by appearing to be a know-it-all.

She spent a long time on the horns of the dilemma.

12

Paola's hair shone like black silk. A single pendant pearl nestled at the cleavage of her breasts which swelled from the neckline of her blue dress. Her figure flared in all the right places, and her legs were made longer by high heels.

Gina felt she was looking at a stranger, a beautiful stranger; and that only increased her trepidation as a vision of the Starlight's clientele flashed in her head. To her sister's reminders of the promise that they would go dancing, Gina had come up with one put-off after another for the past fortnight. Two days ago her evasions were running as thin as Paola's patience. Tonight she was entering the dance hall lobby – Paola at her side.

As Gina exchanged pleasantries with the elderly woman who worked the ticket booth, Paola asked, 'Where's yours?' She was surveying the photographic parade of hostesses. Gina shrugged, answering, 'They haven't got round to taking it yet.' She hoped her sister wouldn't question why none of the portraits matched the girls in the dance hall, not wishing to admit Harry's secret that all the pictures came from a model agency three thousand miles away in Los Angeles.

Fortunately, further discussion was stalled by Joe, who lumbered through the door and greeted, 'Hey, Gina, how ya doing? Who's this? Another new one?' He shook his massive head. 'Dames come and go so fast I can't keep track. Still,' he grinned at Paola like a big kid appreciating a kitten, 'she's kinda cute. Young too. I hope she stays.' He playfully snapped his ticket punch in the direction of Paola's navel causing her to step quickly sideways.

Gina, recognizing the pleasure behind her sister's brief uncertainty, bid Joe a swift, 'See you later,' and strode through the doorway.

Entering the dance hall Paola halted, drew in breath and stared like an enraptured child at the thirty-odd couples dancing the Continental beneath the flashing mirror-globe. Her eyes remained riveted to the scene when Gina took her elbow and steered her to a vacant table. As they sat she whispered, 'It's beautiful.'

Resisting the instinct to dampen Paola's enthusiasm, Gina poised poker-backed on the edge of her chair, nerves taut as piano wires. Stop being irrational, she reprimanded herself, your sister's perfectly safe. Relax. Nevertheless she almost jumped out of the seat when from behind her Harry Dix's voice said, 'So, this is Paola. It's good to see you at last. Gina talks about you all the time. Some big sister you've got. How're you liking

New York? Don't tell me. The most fantastic city in the world - - with maybe the exception of Rome. Of course it is.'

As Paola smiled brightly in response, Gina introduced the dance-hall owner who then excused himself saying there was someone waiting for him in the office.

Watching him retreat, Paola said, 'He's nice. You said he was sad-looking. He isn't at all.'

This declaration surprised Gina. Upon reflection, though, maybe Harry was happier these days; she'd been too busy to notice – or to indulge any self-congratulation of her own efforts which had wrought the change in the previously harassed man. Now a glow of satisfaction warmed her and she settled back on the chair and accepted without thinking the two unordered cocktails which the waiter delivered with the explanation, 'Courtesy of the guy in the grey flannel.' Before she could gather her wits, her sister was sipping the drink to exclaim, '*Zenzero!* Ginger Beer.' Bewilderment briefly faltered across her eyes, then understanding dawned and her face lit with mischievous humour as she laughed, 'Wait until I tell Filipo. He'll be delighted. The Starlight is a clip joint.'

'It's no such thing,' retorted Gina. Deciding that truth was the best policy, she explained, 'The girls are offered a hundred drinks a night. They can't always refuse. Nor can they keep ordering Coca Cola. Men expect them to be sociable. But if they constantly drank liquor, they'd be pie-eyed within an hour. So . . . ' she nodded at Paola's glass. 'Though that doesn't make this a clip joint. The customers get genuine alcohol, unwatered. But before you ask, no you can't try it. Poppa didn't give me my first taste of whisky until I was eighteen. You can wait that long too.' For a moment she thought the schoolmarmish remark might bring a frown to her sister's brow, but Paola was too enchanted by the evening to permit such a minor prohibition to dull the magic as she smiled happily, watching the dancers, sipping her innocuous drink.

The man said, 'It's in return for this dance.'

Gina, these days inured to the Starlight's activities, hadn't noticed the music cease and the ensuing flurry of bodies around the tables. Now she realized the comment aimed at her sister came from a middle-aged man dressed in three-piece grey flannel. Taken unawares, she hadn't time to contest his approach before the band was into 'Muchacha', Paola was throwing perplexed eye signals as the man reached for her hand, and a burly tuxedoed character was tanking forward brandishing a ticket. Gina began to speak but Paola was already hesitantly rising, the flannelled business type was telling her she looked like Claudette Colbert, and the moose in the tux was arriving with, 'Come on, Blondie. Let's you and me show 'em how.' Reflexively Gina stood, took the pink tab, and still grasping for a straw in the tide of confusion was whisked into the whirl of couples, losing sight of Paola as she too was borne away.

The music thumped and the dancers jumped, sliding and jerking to the rumba rhythm. Gina glanced left and right, searching for her sister but snatching only glimpses of the scene as her hulking partner threw her this way and that, grinning affably and chanting, 'Muchacha, I gotcha, and I'm hotcha for you.' Stumbling to match a pace which bore no relation to the music, she caught fleeting sight of Paola and was relieved to see that the grey-flannel character had his hands where they should be and was laughing good-naturedly as he guided his young companion through the unfamiliar steps. Gina relaxed a fraction and gave an iota more concentration to preventing her arms being wrenched off.

The number seemed to last forever.

When it was over, Gina made her way back to the table, sat regathering her breath and her composure. It was a couple of minutes before she realized Paola hadn't returned. She was on her feet in an instant, frantically scanning the room. About to run for the door, she halted, gasped with relief as she saw the familiar dark hair and the profile of her sister where she was sitting the other side of the hall. With a man!

Anger shot up Gina's spine like mercury in a boiling thermo-meter. She stalked across the floor, her head already foaming with the invective she was about to fire at the chalk-stripe-suited character who was baring gleaming white teeth at Paola as optimistically as a wolf entertaining a plump, young lamb.

Reaching the table she commanded her sister, 'Back over there please, Miss.' She swung to the man. 'This girl doesn't work here. She . . . ' Her words trailed away as his dark left eyebrow rose with the same smiling quirk as his full lips. Her mind flashbacked, searching for the memory then suddenly recalling the encounter on Fourteenth Street as he grinned,

172

'*Bunoa sera*,' and he surveyed her gown saying, 'Chambermaids certainly don't dress the way they used to. *Come sta?*' To Gina's stunned silence he added with mock hurt, 'Forgotten me already? And I thought we'd meant so much to each other, that day in the rain.' Glancing to Paola he said, 'You see, I'm a failure with all women. Rejected. Take pity on a poor Italian boy and grant me one dance. Just one. *Per favore.*'

Gina cut in sharply, 'She doesn't dance.' But she was caught mentally in the conflict between her protectiveness of Paola and her gratitude at having a job here on the strength of this man's name. While remaining on the defensive she smoothed her tone. 'Mister Sabato, isn't it? I believe I'm in your debt. Your business card opened the Starlight's door to me. Thank you. I shall return the favour as soon as I am able.'

'Forget it.' Johnny Sabato waved away the appreciation. 'We all got to lend a hand occasionally, don't we. Besides,' both his eyebrows rose and he winked, 'it was worth it just to see you in that dress.'

Gina flushed, but quickly realized there was no salacity in his face, only a warm humour and admiration. Relaxing, she returned his smile. 'It is rather loud, isn't it? But it's what the customers expect. They enjoy it. It gives them something to remember; a little glamour to hang on to.' She stopped, aware that she was voicing an opinion she'd shared with no one; a presumption that would have been slated by the other girls as sentimental eyewash. But, to her surprise, she thought she recognized a genuine understanding in this unlikely man. Pushing aside the thought, she said, 'If you'll excuse us, we have to leave now.' To his questioning glance at Paola who had sat silently and wonderingly throughout the exchange, Gina explained, 'This is my sister. Young sister. She was only here for a brief visit. We're leaving now, for somewhere less . . . noisy. Paola, please fetch our coats.'

Paola's eyes fired small darts. She briefly resisted, then, sighing resignation, she began to rise.

Johnny Sabato said, 'Sisters?' His stare flickered between the girls until he nodded and said, 'Of course. I see the resemblance. *La bellezza. La figura.*' His hands made a swift hourglass. 'But so different. One dark. One blonde. Ah, you had an Italian poppa and an American momma. Yes?'

'Yes, Gina returned quickly. 'Now . . . '

'Me too,' he enthused. 'We should drink to that. To our parents. Three Manhattans, okay?' He winked. 'But I'll make sure Ed squirts in some rye.' He pulled out a chair, held it for Gina as he shot the drinks order at a waiter with the rider, 'McCoys.' The man raised an understanding thumb and wheeled away. Johnny Sabato observed, 'We're going to have to quit saying it. McCoys. Joe Public is starting to use it too. Heard a guy at a news stand the other day. ''The real McCoy,'' he said. How about that? The old bootlegger getting his name famous. Hey, maybe folks'll remember me like that someday. Wouldn't it be something? Then you'll be able to say you knew me when.' He beamed, adjusted the knot of his perfect blue silk tie, held his gaze on Paola.

Gina cautiously watched him, but again sensed a candour that was free of conceit. So, there was no harm in one drink. Was there? She sat beside Paola – who suddenly asked, 'Were you a bootlegger, Mister Sabato?'

He laughed aloud as he took his seat. 'Not exactly. Though I drove a few trucks now and then. But that was back when I was sixteen. Fourteen years ago. Which makes me thirty, right? Though I look older, right?' He smiled. 'Not such a bad thing. Helps you get respect. Guys think twice when they look at my face. The sort of face that makes peaceful women feel restless, and restless women feel peace. A lady magazine writer I knew once told me that. Cute, huh?'

Paola's throat, Gina noticed, had flushed, and she was locked on to the ingenuous storyteller with the eyes of a besotted fawn. She interjected, 'We haven't been properly introduced. My name is Gina Rossi. My sister is Paola.' The announcement, she was pleased to note, broke the moment, and Johnny Sabato half-rose, reached across the table and shook their hands in turn. As he reseated himself, the waiter arrived with the drinks, saying, 'Compliments of the house.' Johnny tipped him five dollars.

Gina enquired, 'Now you rent vending machines?'

'And I import. You name it. Whatever folks need. Whatever's going cheap in Cuba, South America, Europe. Fire-damaged goods. Bankrupt stock. Some feller's misfortune has to be some other guy's good luck, right?' He raised his glass. '*Salute.*' Downed half his liquor. 'Of course, I only supply places like the Starlight. Places that aren't nailed down by the Syndicate.'

'Gangsters!' Paola exclaimed.

Johnny glanced left and right. 'Well, I wouldn't go around shouting that too loud. And anyhow, who's to say who's a gangster in this town? A guy with cardboard in his shoes on a street corner selling apples he lifted from a warehouse? A health inspector getting free lunches at a Park Avenue hotel for keeping quiet about the rats in the basement? A banker fore-closing a mortgage on a storekeeper having a tough time? An official in City Hall passing confidential highway plans to his brother-in-law in the construction business?' He shrugged, swallowed the remainder of his drink.

Gina raised a mental eyebrow. The brief speech had been delivered with ease and sincerity. And, she had to admit, there was a nugget of truth in the generalization. But, observing the rapt expression on Paola's face, she decided the acuteness of the crackerbarrel philosophy should be blunted. She said, 'Yes, you could say perhaps all those characters are criminals. However, you hardly can suggest they are in the same league as Bugsy Siegel.'

Johnny Sabato sharply lowered his glass, his relaxed humour blinking off like an extingished light. 'Don't ever let him hear you use that nickname. He hates it. Call him Benny. Always.' His eyes stressed the caution.

Paola asked, 'Do you know Mister Siegel?'

'Of course. But, then, so do most of the hoteliers and restaurateurs in town. Remember, half the fancy joints in Manhattan were once speakeasies. Guys like Benny kept them supplied. And some of them are still tied in with the Syndicate. In spite of our new D.A. Tom Dewey attempting to screw the lid on the rackets, there's still plenty of gambling, loanshark-ing, numbers-running taking place in broad daylight. Of course,' he looked at Paola with honest emphasis, 'I never get involved in anything like that.' Then he exclaimed, 'Hey, neither of you is drinking. Come on. It's good liquor.' He laughed. 'The real McCoy.'

Gina glanced at her sister, saw her hand hover hesitantly toward her glass, recognized the supplication in the young eyes, a plea not to be lessened in this man's presence. She thought, well, Miss, whatever ideas you've got about playing Lady Sophistication in front of this semi-Italian, semi-literate, semi-hoodlum, you can forget; you're not getting mixed up with his type; or any other type for that matter; you'll have your first drink with a man, a respectable, educated man, when I decide and not before.

What she said was, 'Cheers.' Raising her glass she sipped, seeing the flood of relief in Paola's face.

It was the end of the second week of December when Gina popped her head around Harry's door to say 'Goodnight' and he muttered distractedly, that she stepped into the office and bantered, 'Hey, if you stare at those ledgers much longer your eyes will drop out.'

Glancing up, Harry responded blearily, 'What? What's that? Oh, Gina.' A tired smile leaked down his long, horse face. 'I guess you're right. These books are the bane of my life. I'm a bandleader, a horn player, leastways a dance-hall owner – not a darned accountant.' He tossed aside his pen. 'I was always hopeless at figures, but the shoestring I'm on here doesn't allow for paying a book-keeper. So,' he sighed, 'I have to do it. Otherwise I get the IRS, Department of Labour, City Hall, a whole army of bureaucrats beating my brains out with affidavits. Sometimes I think I'd be better off driving a hack. Still, I reckon even those guys got to file their tax returns.'

Gina took the couple of paces to Harry's desk, looked down at the ledgers, and swallowed the chuckle which rose in her throat as she scrutinized the hodgepodge of figures, blots, erasures, crossings out. Keeping a straight face she remarked, 'It looks as if you could use a little help. How about letting me have a go at getting these sorted out?' To his mournful but quizzical stare she explained, 'I used to take care of the accounts for my father. It's not so difficult when you have the hang of it. Just In and Out columns, and knowing which items are allowable against tax. I'll bet the rules here are pretty much the same as in Italy. Anyhow, I could get whatever information I need from the library, maybe even some advice from the Internal Revenue office.'

A flicker of optimism had lighted Harry's eyes, but it swiftly dimmed as he shook his head. 'Believe me, you'd be welcome to take a shot at the job. Lord knows, you couldn't be any worse at it than me. But, I told you, I can't afford to pay for the book-keeping.'

Gina considered for a moment, recalling the can of cherries she'd seen the barman stealing, and the ancient beer bottles in the store. She said decisively, 'It won't cost you a cent. Let me take care of the books, and, most importantly, your stock control.' Ignoring his incomprehension of this expression, she insisted, 'I'm certain there's money you could be saving here by keeping a tighter check on your supplies. That's one of the essentials of . . . ' she searched for the translation of her father's accountant's phrase ' . . . optimum profitability.' She repeated it in her head, savouring its impressive ring. It certainly had an effect on Harry, she noticed; he was watching her with new interest. She concluded, 'You can pay me out of whatever I save you. If I was mistaken and there's nothing to be gained, you won't owe me a dime. You've got nothing to lose.'

Harry stared at her, looked down at the ink-tracked pages of his ledger, back to Gina. 'And I thought I was crazy.'

'Do we have a deal?' Gina asked.

Slowly he nodded. 'But don't blame me if you end up in the bat house.' He added, 'Though when the heck you're going to find time for all this I don't know. You're already doing the extra hours here. Don't you ever feel tired?'

Gina smiled, trying to remember the last time she didn't feel tired. It must have been a very long time ago. 'Harry,' she confided, 'I'll tell you a secret. I made myself a promise. When I've got one thousand dollars in my savings account, I'm going to rent the best suite at the Plaza, hang the 'Do Not Disturb' sign on the door, and sleep for a week.'

At last Harry's face folded into an elongated grin. 'Now that's what I call a worthwhile ambition. I wish you luck.'

There's no such thing, Gina thought. Still, she was grateful for the dance hall owner's sincerity, and for giving her the opportunity via his book-keeping to add a few dollars toward that target thousand. She said briskly, 'I'll fetch a carton from the bar to carry the ledger and all your dockets and invoices.'

'You're going to start tonight?'

Lifting the book, inspecting the numeric chaos, she grinned. 'If I leave it until tomorrow, I might change my mind.'

Never had she said a truer word.

When she sat at the cleared dining table that evening and made her first sortie into the jungle of the Starlight's finances, she seriously considered abandoning the attempt. However, buckling on her resolve, armed with pencils, scratch-pads and Harry's much-thumbed ready-reckoner, she attacked the tangle of figures.

It was two a.m. when she leaned back on her chair, no longer able to ignore the protestations of her over-worked eyes. Beside her the waste basket overflowed with pencil sharpenings and crumpled, calculation-covered scratch-pad sheets. A great deal of detritus for such minor results. Nevertheless, she had made some progress into Harry's anarchic yet imaginative accounts; and as she closed her eyes and the ledger, she had the first inkling that her original supposition had been correct - the Starlight ought to be producing several extra dollars profit each week.

She determined to pursue the project tomorrow night. And that was a sad reminder of the appointment she must keep in sixteen hours' time.

Red-capped porters, travellers, well-wishers swirled around the hummocky islands of baggage on the platforms at Grand Central. The Twentieth Century Limited stood huffing impatiently, steam and smoke pluming to the night blackness beneath the arcing station roof.

Gina rubbed the inside of the misted compartment window, peered out through the streaked condensation, searching for a clock. 'It must be almost six,' she said.

Cassie, sitting opposite, returned, 'Don't worry. You'll hear them yell "All aboard." You won't be stuck on here, with me all the way to Chicago.' Her voice softened. 'Though I wish you were coming, Hon. You and me would take the Windy City by storm. Then, soon as I'd won the Pageant, we could be on the Chief to paradise. Holl-ee-wood. And with our looks, and . . . ' she squared her shoulders, inhaled (to the considerable appreciation of the two sporty-coated fellers across the aisle) 'with our other currency, we'd buy ourselves a spot on old Sam Goldfish's chorus line before you could say knife. From there it's no more'n a short stride - showing the dimples in our knees - to the front of the marquee.' She shifted her gum from one cheek to the other, winked cheerfully.

Gina returned the humour. Though she didn't feel it. Cassie's proposed departure had, during the past fortnight, seemed unreal. Had that, Gina wondered, been because she just didn't believe her friend would go off on this hare-brained trip? Or was it because she subconsciously could not accept that yet another person whom she loved was being taken from her? Everyone she had ever cared for, it seemed, had visited her life for but a brief moment, as if the Fates had decided she must never be permitted to form any lasting bonds, as if . . .

Nonsense! Gina quashed the thought, mentally shook herself. She didn't believe in fate, luck, pre-destiny or any other excuses; she'd left any such childish superstitions three thousand miles, two years and a lifetime away on a rocky hillside in southern Italy. Since then she'd dinned it into Paola and Filipo: 'Everybody alibis their failures. Blames circumstance. Calls it misfortune. There's no such thing. You build your own destiny. Paint it the colour you choose. And if it turns out a hideous mess, that's nobody's fault but your own.'

In the Twentieth Century's compartment she looked at Cassie: her figure-hugging, Peter-Pan-collared green velvet coat; tiny, cockeyed hat of feathers and fluff perched on the side of her red-curled head like a humming bird about to nibble her ear. The outfit, plus the dress and silk lingerie beneath it, Gina knew, had cost all her friend had, and then some. 'So, I hocked a few things.' Cassie had admitted when Gina visited a couple of nights ago. 'Okay, all my darn things. But what the heck! I can't turn up at the corned beef mansion in that old cloth hand-me-down. And if . . . well . . . you know, if my undies get . . . seen . . . they can't be those burlap sacks from last year's S-R catalogue.' Cassie had paraded around her apartment wearing the lace-edged emerald pants and brassière, and Gina had been unable to prevent the brief pang of envy as she recalled her long-ago fantasies of how she had planned to dress when she met the right man at the right moment of her life.

In the railroad car Gina said affectionately, 'Take care of yourself up there in Al Caponeville. Don't get in too many scrapes.' The emotion began to well in her. Forcing a laugh, she warned, 'Keep him waiting and wanting. But not too long.' She stood quickly and Cassie followed and they swept into each others arms, clung together.

Cassie whispered hoarsely, 'You watch out too, you hear. Don't let none of those Saturday night dancers step on your toes. Give my love to Poll and Phil. Send me a wire if the goddamn Howard West burns down, I can always use a laugh.'

Gina held her friend a second longer, shocked by the intensity of her own feelings as her eyes stung with unshed tears. She stepped back, running her knuckles beneath her welling lower lids at the moment the voice hollered above the outside racket, ' . . . board!'

'Go on, get out of here!' ordered Cassie, dabbing at her mascaraed lashes with a minuscule hanky.

And Gina swiftly turned, hurried along the aisle, down the steps to retrace the distance to the compartment window where Cassie was standing, peering out through the wet glass. Gina waved. Cassie blew kisses, mouthed, 'Don't forget to write.' Gina thought, write where? Then up at the head of the platform the massive gold and green locomotive snorted and groaned and the coaches jerked and Cassie jolted, clutching at her hat. Bodies surged around Gina, shouting and waving, some beginning to walk with the moving train. She was caught in the flow, carried along, into the past, with a stream of girls, giggling and chattering down a stone-paved corridor, the chill February air burning her blood as she ran from her first day of toil at the hotel, Cassie beside her, face shining with enthusiasm and laughter.

The face now was borne away, breaking up, becoming a fracturing mask as the loco's gathering speed sent water streaming horizontally across the interior of the windows.

Gina halted. No longer able to see her friend, she stood, holding that tattered image as the train whistle screamed and the coaches thundered away into the night. She remained there a long time, long after the caboose lights had winked out, until she slowly turned and walked back along the cold, hard platform.

Twenty nights, two visits to the library, one to the IRS, and considerable quantities of paper later, Gina strode into Harry Dix's office. Laying three pages of neatly-written figures in front of the dance hall owner, she announced, 'Four thousand dollars a year.'

Harry stared incomprehendingly, then as he transferred his gaze to the sheets of paper, his jaw slowly sank to his chest.

'Give or take a couple of hundred,' said Gina, 'that's what you're losing.' She smiled at his incredulous gaze. 'Yes, I found it difficult to believe too. But I've checked the figures several times. There's no mistake. Look.' She pointed to a column of her calculations. 'There's a whole list of items you haven't set against tax. Cab fares, washroom materials, stationery, a percentage of your home phone. You didn't even claim for *Metronome* magazine. It's a trade paper; you're entitled. All these small allowances add up.'

Harry looked mournful.

Gina continued, 'The biggest loss is on the girls. There are just too many for the afternoons. Whereas on your busiest nights you've got customers standing in line for partners. Also the girls come and go as they please and are perpetually fighting amongst themselves for free time.' She shook her head. 'You've got to have a more practical system. Three less girls and a proper rota for the rest. The same goes for the janitor of this building. He's charging you for twice as many hours as it should take to handle the cleaning here.' She smiled ruefully. 'That's a subject I'm expert on. Finally, there's your supplies situation.' She chose her words with care. 'With better control you wouldn't be . . . wasting so much. On that second sheet you'll see I've outlined a simple stock control schedule. It wouldn't be difficult to implement. Like taking care of the accounts, just a matter of getting started then keeping to a routine.' She shrugged, her brief speech over sooner than she had anticipated. 'Well, that's about it.'

Harry slowly ran his finger down the columns of numerals, his expression struggling for comprehension as his lips moved soundlessly. And Gina felt a flush of pride; a confidence she hadn't experienced in a long time. During the past week, untangling Harry's book-keeping, she had become deeply engrossed in the challenge. Even the sadness of Cassie's departure had temporarily faded. The Starlight's accounts, she realized, had been the tonic she needed to cure her depression, the answer to her need for a greater sense of accomplishment once the basic needs of survival had been moderately exceeded by her dance hall wages. Now, in Harry's office, she was aware of a fresh sense of purpose. Her old assuredness was burning; and she had to admit – with a degree of shame – that she felt she should be the one sitting behind the desk. She quashed that vanity as Harry said:

'I'm glad I don't work for you.' He held up his hand against her flush of hurt. 'Just kidding. Although . . . ' he re-appraised the figures, 'you do expect the girls – the ones we'd have left if your plan was implemented – to keep on their toes. And the janitor certainly wouldn't have time spare for leaning on his broom.'

'There are girls in this town scrubbing floors twelve hours

. . . ' Gina cut off the sharp rejoinder, aware of the understanding in the dance-hall owner's eyes. She said quietly, 'I just don't approve of people cheating their employers; any more than I condone bosses paying starvation wages.' She inwardly sighed, suddenly embarrassed by the apparent sanctimoniousness of the remark. The elation which had built during the previous days began rapidly to crumble. This had all been a mistake. She'd allowed herself to become intoxicated by her own accomplishments. And it had fuddled her senses. But now, as her last dregs of self-congratulation drained, she was left coldly sober, feeling painfully like a smart-aleck.

She took a backward step, shrugging. 'I just thought . . . Well . . . maybe I shouldn't have become so involved.' She turned toward the door.

'Where are you going?'

Gina smiled faintly. 'To put on my dancing shoes.'

'The hell you are. And leave me to take care of all this?' Harry brandished the stock sheets and work schedules. 'I told you, I'm no businessman. This is going to take organization. By someone who knows what they're doing.' To Gina's stare he confirmed, 'Sure. Who else would I get to do it? So, don't just stand there. Pull up a chair. You're elected.'

A moment of uncertainty held Gina, then all her elation came flooding back. She reached out and took her sheaf of statistics. 'Thanks, Harry. You won't regret it. I promise.'

'How could I regret saving forty dollars a week?'

Gina stepped to the desk. 'The first thing we must do . . . ' Her voice trailed. She frowned; then corrected, 'No, Harry. Not forty. Eighty. That's how much . . . '

'I said forty,' the dance hall owner declared. 'I'm not that dumb. I can do simple division, you know. Four thousand a year equals approximately eighty a week. Right. Forty for me, and forty for you.' Before Gina could even open her mouth, he warned, 'Any arguments, and the deal's off. If you hadn't come up with your calculations and proposals I'd have had nothing. So, forty is a whole lot better than that. The other half of the extra profit will be yours. You've earned it. Or, you will. I reckon by the time you've got this operation in some sort of order, you'll need that week at the Plaza.' He smiled. 'So, are we going to stand here all day like a pair of daisies? Let's go, we've got a fortune to make.'

13

It wasn't a fortune. But it was better than even Gina had reckoned. She worked and she calculated and she saved. She daily reviewed the Starlight's finances as painstakingly as she had once ordered her family's budget. She maintained strict stock control, cut down on wastage, made it plain to Freddie the barkeep that if so much as a pack of cocktail sticks walked so would he. When she pinned the new work rota on the washroom wall, the girls ranted and raved, swore they'd all leave at the end of the week. A fortnight later they were still there, still moaning and groaning, but not complaining about the extra dollars they were taking home, or the free sandwiches Gina had delivered from the delicatessen downstairs. 'Napoleon said an army marches on its stomach,' Gina told Harry. 'And, anyhow, I also made a deal with the deli to make up a supply of stuffed bagels which we'll sell to customers over the bar – I told the band to play six fast numbers in a row every night around nine o'clock, that will give the customers a hunger as well as a thirst. The discount I negotiated for a guaranteed regular order of bagels means the sandwiches won't cost us a cent, and we'll still come out ahead on profit.' She smiled. 'Plus, the salt beef and the lox . . . .' 'You don't need to tell me,' cut in Harry. 'It'll make the customers want to drink more.' He gazed down at the handsome pages of his new ledger, shook his head. 'When shall I expect us to put in the takeover bid for Twenty-One?' Gina replied casually, 'Better give me till April.'

She didn't quite make it by then, but she did reach the Plaza Hotel. The promise she'd made herself to sleep there for a week when she had a thousand dollars in her savings account became grantable sooner than she'd expected.

As conditions at the Starlight had been polished, efficiency honed, profits raised and the walls painted, so business had flourished. The regular clientele had doubled when word went around about the dance hall's new peppy image and its happy girls. And Gina's financial prophecy to Harry was coming true, twofold.

On April 2nd, 1939, an hour after making her deposit at the bank, she checked into the Plaza.

She didn't stay for a week, just one night, but it was enough. She'd offered to bring Paola and Filipo, but both declined, saying they couldn't see what fun there'd be in staying at a stuffy old hotel. Although it didn't seem quite like the youngsters to turn up such an opportunity, Gina shrugged off any speculation of their motives and luxuriated in following the bellhop who led the way across the hotel's opulent lobby to the bank of elevators.

Three hours later she was lying amid eiderdown pillows and silken sheets in the largest bed in the most gorgeous bedroom she had seen in her entire life. The sensation was incredible; at once calming but euphoric, pure but erotic. She just remained there, unmoving, floating, wallowing unashamedly in the sybaritic abandonment. She didn't, of course, sleep a wink. Who on earth wouldn't stay awake to appreciate such incredible pricelessness – when it was costing a staggering ten dollars for the night?

She rose with the dawn, hurried to pull aside the curtains and greet the sun. Warm. It was moments before she realized it; there was so much warmth filtering through the glass. She snapped open the catch and yanked up the sash-cord window, breathed as deep as a hibernating animal breaking out of its winter prison. She could smell it, spring's sharp edge in the air, could see it in the freshness of the sky's blue, in the bright eyes of the pigeons perched on the adjacent sills staring out, like Gina, as if too surprised to attend to the usual business of the day. She shouted, 'Hi, fellers!' sending the birds batting toward the rooftops as she swung around to stride for the bathroom.

While she showered, as usual she calculated. Another three thousand dollars, she reckoned, and she'd have enough, with a bank loan, to be truly the mistress of her own destiny. Yes, she thought, just one more year and all the past backache and heartache will have been worthwhile. I'll make the dream come true. I'll see a restaurant with my own name above the door.

Whistling cheerfully, Gina dressed.

She carried the sunny mood downstairs to the busy restaurant. She usually wouldn't eat so early, but today she wanted to hold on to this luxury a while longer. Having been issued to a white-linened table laid with cutlery for one, decorated with spring flowers in a slim crystal vase, she ordered hot chocolate, warm rolls and fruit preserves, the traditional breakfast she always served to Paola and Filipo but which she hadn't consumed since she was sixteen years old.

The waiter retreated. Gina leaned back and observed the seemingly effortless efficiency with which guests were seated, served, brought newspapers and packs of cigarettes on silver trays. With a practised eye she identified the businessmen, the celebrities, the tourists, the regulars; she knew intuitively those who were relaxed, those in a hurry, those who were slightly overawed by the elegance, those whose bombast was a pretentious mask for their commonality. She smiled inwardly, unashamedly savouring her own expertise, as self-assured as the *maitre d'hôtel* over there who regulated the unfaltering pace of the service while coping with the hundred tribulations of his staff, the thousand whims of his customers.

Content, she re-surveyed the scene.

And looked directly into the eyes of Howard Cornell.

For one lurching moment she thought she'd made a mistake, but then Howard's expression was lighting with recognition and Gina's confidence of seconds ago disintegrated. All at once her hands began to shake, a tremor that rapidly ran up her arms, increasing until she felt her entire body might spasm out of control. He's moving out of his chair, was all she could think. I have to get away.

Pushing out from the table she rose swiftly, started toward the doorway, negotiated between the seated diners, vaguely hearing a waiter's concerned, 'Madam?' but not daring to look back, nor to hesitate as she felt a wave of dizziness rock her senses. Coward, a corner of her mind admonished. But no amount of self-control could slow her escape, could lessen the fear of feeling Howard's hand upon her shoulder, and she almost was running by the time she reached the lobby.

Unthinkingly, she strode for the elevator, a creature of prey heading for a bolt hole. The floor was two miles wide. Gina crossed it on legs turning to lead. The elevator doors opened. The uniformed operator looked out. Gina lengthened her stride. People hurried all around – guests, pageboys, porters with luggage – obstructed her path. Voices. Greetings. Names being called. 'Gina.' She hadn't heard it, refused to believe she'd heard it. Her swinging arm collided with someone, something. The elevator door was closing. 'Wait,' she cried and dashed the final half-dozen paces, narrowly avoiding the sliding panel.

When she turned, the lobby had been shut off, the operator was smiling, asking, 'Floor, please?'

Gina heaved with relief, feeling at once successful and mildly foolish. That was a ridiculous thing to have done, she now conceded. A gross overreaction. It wasn't after all, as if she hadn't known it might happen some day. In fact, since being fired from the hotel, she hadn't merely accepted the possibility of encountering Howard Cornell, she had actually rehearsed the scene in her mind a hundred or more times. Of course, in the fantasy her confidence had been titanic, her poise supreme, and the disdain with which she withered Howard as caustic as vitriol. Should she return to face him? The question pricked her as the shame of her flight slowly bloomed.

'Which floor, madam?' the operator repeated.

'Seven, please,' Gina answered automatically, and then she was riding up and away from the necessity of decision, refusing to be drawn toward an inquest on her actions, rejecting all further thought of her inglorious retreat.

Back in her bedroom she packed the few items she'd brought here. It took only minutes. She cast a final look around the room, re-appreciating its handsomeness, touched again by the pleasure it had given her. 'I'll see you again,' she said aloud, determinedly. Gina was once more in full possession of her self-control. And she did not flinch when the knock came upon the door. Setting down her suitcase she walked across the room.

'Hello, Howard,' she said as she stepped back from the open threshold. 'Please, come in.'

He entered, hesitant, a boyish penitence behind the dark maturity of his eyes. 'The desk clerk gave me your room number. I told him I was a friend.'

'So you are,' Gina responded. As she'd packed, knowing Howard's arrival was inevitable, she'd gathered her nerves for the meeting. Now, she told herself, she was calm, commanding her emotions, her palms were sweating only as an after-effect of her earlier ferment.

Howard closed the door. 'Gina, I'm sorry.'

'For what?'

'Please, don't pretend. I must explain, try to explain. Also, I must know – why didn't you answer my note? I didn't know what to do. If only you'd . . . '

'Note?'

'The one I sent cancelling our rendezvous at the park. As I wrote, I had to go away. To our office in San Francisco. An important business deal to arrange. Mother said she would take care of it, but of course I couldn't allow her to travel so far. I tried to see you the following day but they said you'd walked out on your job. There's so much I want to say, Gina. Can't we sit a moment?'

Gina barely heard the request. She was trying to construct some sense from Howard's disjointed submission. Note? She'd received no note. Walking out on her job? None of it true. She mentally swept it all aside. There was no need to sort through it. Obviously, Alicia Cornell had arranged Gina Rossi's removal from her son's life with expedition and precision. And yet . . . Gina searched her logic . . . could Howard truly be so naïve as to swallow any of the fictions? Surely he knew his mother's attitude toward his girlfriends. It was common knowledge that Alicia had seen off dozens and had actually paid off at least four. Didn't he realize? Of course he did. That certainty now placed itself four-square before Gina. She heard his voice, from the day they'd strolled in Central Park, 'I guess Mother always knows best.' She called to mind too some of his conversation, recollected thinking it somewhat immature. And now she understood. Now she saw through Howard's manhood to the boy beyond.

He prompted, 'Gina, please let's talk,' and the deep resonance of his voice, the dark fire in his eyes that had unseated her senses the first time she'd met him, caused her pulse rate to accelerate.

As Gina's gaze held his, her emotions convulsed. There was nothing juvenile about the fullness of his lips, the hard line of his jaw, nothing boyish about the latent strength of his chest and arms. She wanted him. That truth struck her with sudden force. Spontaneously, she resisted. But there was no denying what was happening inside her. She instinctively understood it. This was not a teenage arousal, nor the uncertain evocation of dreams. This was a sensual, animal need; her climactic response to the emotional surges of the past sixteen hours. She was powerless to prevent it. She had no wish to prevent it. As all her religious conditioning reared a seawall before the tide of her passion, Gina drove it aside. She closed her ears to the threat of perdition, heard her own voice say:

187

'I don't want to talk, Howard.'

She stepped to him, and kissed him. And her senses soared. I'm twenty-four years old, she thought, and this is the first time I've kissed a man. Her entire body burned with the kiss as she experienced the moist movement of Howard's lips, the touch of his teeth, the scent of cologne on his throat, the faint aroma of coffee on his breath.

His hands gripped her shoulders, pushed her back a pace. Catching his breath, he stared in surprise. But his hesitation lasted only a moment. He pulled her toward him, and this time their kiss was deep, fierce. Gina's pulse pounded in her temples as her head bent back under the pressure of Howard's desire. She melded herself to him, feeling her nipples erupting almost to the point of pain as she kneaded her breasts against his chest. Then she realized his male hardness was grinding against her lower belly.

In that freezing instant she thought of the monster Sturzo. The terror of his assault flared across her mind and all the doubts and fears she had carried since that night rushed forward. Gina gasped, recoiled from them. Stricken by the memory she stood facing Howard, seeing his perplexity at her abrupt disengagement. Yet even as the spectre of Baremo pinioned her, the insentient core that Gina had forged within herself strove against it. Every atom of her determination resisted. I will not be beaten, she asserted. I will not.

Howard said uncertainly, 'Gina?'

Move, she commanded her hands. And, slowly, they rose to the top button of her dress. They halted there, trapped like the breath in Gina's lungs. Then they twisted and pushed. The dress parted at Gina's throat. She released the next button. And the next. One more, and the dress was open to the waist. She reached up to its collar.

Howard said, 'Please, let me.' Gently, he eased the dress from her shoulders, slipped it down her arms to her hips, and let it drop to the floor. He repeated the operation with her slip. Then, moving half a pace closer, he released her brassière. With a sharp intake of breath, he stared at Gina's breasts. After a long moment he breathed, 'You're very lovely.' His knuckles tilting her chin, he leaned forward and his lips brushed her cheek as his hand descended her throat, between her cleavage, to lightly cup her breast.

Gina tensed; but with ruthless self-will she seized and

squeezed Howard's hand, roughly guiding it down her stomach, into the waist of her panties.

And now the fire came. The chill that had fettered her loosened its hold as Howard's fingers moved, carefully but firmly, caressing, exploring, opening. The fever in Gina rose. She concentrated on it, gave herself to its slow smouldering, locked her mind on the feral reponses of her body. For one more heartbeat her head was stormed by the words of the catechism as well as by the drunken roar of Galeazzo Sturzo, then Howard was lifting her, kissing her brow, her eyes, her mouth as he carried her to the bed, and deep inside Gina the barriers she had long ago erected were consumed by the flames of her carnal heat.

That their subsequent lovemaking was brief was of no account. As Gina arched up to Howard, it was enough just to be here, at last with a man, confidently taking him, giving of herself, sure in the knowledge of her instincts.

When Howard ultimately gasped, 'Gina, Gina!' spasmed and slumped beside her, she intuitively knew that this was not how it truly should be. Nevertheless she lay back, content, luxuriating in the satisfaction of the moment. A wave of relaxation rolled over her. There were no anxieties, doubts or self-recrimination, just a deep glow of fulfilment, a warming thrill of accomplishment. She smiled at that. For why deny it? She had pleased Howard, excited him, proved to herself she could, and that filled her not only with pride but also with an enormous sense of relief. Her fears about being sexually aberrant had been erased. She was not frigid. She was normal. As normal as Cassie or any of the girls at the Starlight. With that thought Gina arose from the bed.

Howard reached for her. 'Hey . . . ' He surveyed her figure with deep appreciation, smiled and said huskily, 'It isn't over yet. We've the whole day ahead of us.'

Gina swiftly gathered her clothes from the floor. Standing before Howard where he had propped himself on one elbow, she answered frankly, 'No we don't, Howard. It is over. For ever. Please,' she stepped back a pace as he sat upright, 'I don't want a scene. No overtures. No reproaches. What we just did was fine. I'm please it happened. I'm glad you've been a part of my life. I won't go into reasons, but I'd like you to know I'll always be grateful to you. Also, I'll always care for you. However, we won't see each other, by design, ever again.'

'Gina, I don't understand.' Howard began to swing his legs from the bed, reached a sitting position on its edge.

Gina halted him there with the strength in her eyes; and the fact that she was capable of doing so was sufficient to convince her that she was right. Thus, when she scanned again the muscularity of his shoulders, the strength of his jaw, and the maturity in his eyes, she wasn't surprised that none of this sent her heart racing. Howard Cornell the man had given her all she needed. Howard Cornell the boy had nothing more she wanted.

She walked with her clothes to the bathroom. Pausing at the door, looking back she said, 'Perhaps, after all, Howard, your mother does know what is for the best.'

The next time Gina saw Howard was in a magazine photograph taken at the Rhode Island Independence Gala. He was with a svelte and beautiful blonde. Gina wondered how long it would be before Alicia scooted that rabbit on her way.

Spring flowered in the city. When Gina had taken over Harry Dix's administration, the work had given her a fresh impulse of motivation; now, its increasing success gave her a renewed sense of well-being. She was briefly saddened that Cassie hadn't written, but expecting the redhead to sit down for a whole five minutes and actually compose a letter did require a stretch of the imagination. Besides, whether or not she'd won the beauty pageant, Cassie would make out, one way or another; she'd show up again some day. And though Gina missed her friend she knew she needn't worry about her as the year ticked off its seasons.

Some weekends Max took Paola and Filipo to the race track at Belmont Park; in July Mrs Ponti took them to the street celebrations for Our Lady of Mount Carmel in Italian Harlem; Johnny Sabato (who, somewhere along the line – Gina couldn't quite recall where or when – had become a friend of the family) took the youngsters ice-skating, roller-skating, bowling and swimming. Filipo grew. Paola left school and enrolled at secretarial college. Gina worked and saved.

They were all happy.

The only cloud to cross their lives came in September when Europe went to war. For a time a sort of hush seemed to settle on the city, while the bigots, the idealists and the political profiteers had their say. But, apart from a few isolated incidents, the great mass of ordinary New Yorkers – French, German, Polish, Italian – continued to work, travel and watch Movietone News together; and by Christmas the headline reports from London, Rome, Berlin were being read with no more and no less enthusiasm than the sports pages. An important event was taking place. But it was taking place three thousand miles away.

Even Gina experienced this sense of distancing. She wondered what she felt. Just a numbness. A paralysis seemed to have negated her emotions. But, then, perhaps there was no longer anything she could feel for the country which had launched itself toward the abyss. For that was not her country, her Italy. The Italy she had known and loved was a different place, a romantic city of youthful illusion. And that had disappeared, for all time, the day her father was arrested.

The only event which gave the far-off war an edge of reality was the receipt of a brief note from David Lowell. Gina had not replied to the letter she'd received from him the day of her dismissal from the Howard West, hadn't thought he'd wish to start a regular correspondence. That, she decided now, was still perhaps the case, but she understood his need to communicate at a time when his life – as her own had been – was torn by inexorable events. He reported he'd enlisted in the Navy, mentioned that Robert Fallon was a war correspondent. Gina kept her reply light but not over-cheery. A week after mailing it she read in the newspaper about the torpedoing by Italian aircraft of several British convoy ships en route for Malta. She did her best to put that from her mind.

Her life continued along its level, busy course. Each week she added to her savings; reviewed her commercial plans; detailed her financial blueprint.

In March 1940 she calculated she'd be ready to make her move in three months' time.

She did so considerably sooner.

Having spent all this Thursday afternoon in the Starlight's office, she decided to return to the apartment in the early evening. When she walked into the living-room Paola stared with surprise and said abruptly, 'What are you doing here? We weren't expecting you. Aren't you working?'

'Not tonight,' replied Gina. 'I'm staying home tonight.' She took her coat through to the bedroom. Sitting on the edge of the bed to change her shoes she frowned. Now what sort of a greeting was that? And, had it been a trick of the light in the room, or her imagination, or had there been, momentarily, a glint of dismay in her sister's eyes?

Returning to the living-room, Gina sat on the sofa, watched Paola knitting, her small hands working delicately at their task. Funny, she mused vaguely, I thought she was fed up with that occupation. She couldn't remember seeing her sister thus engaged since the time last year when she'd asked to be taken to the Starlight. Gina pushed the thought aside, retracked her concentration to the mental plans she'd been making. It was some while before she focused on the clock and realized where the hands were pointing. She exclaimed, 'It's eight-thirty. Where on earth is Filipo?'

'Pardon?' Paola looked up from her needles. 'Oh, I suppose he's . . . playing with his pals.'

'At this time of night?'

'It isn't so late.' Paola casually counted her stitches. 'He'll be all right. Don't worry.'

Gina stared at her sister, knew instinctively Paola was hiding something. She asked, 'What time does he usually come home?'

Paola shrugged.

'Late?' Gina stood. 'This late? Put that knitting down.' The sharpness of her command snapped Paola's head up, flushing her cheeks; but Gina was uncaring of the reaction, she was now fiercely worried, certain that Filipo was up to no good and that his sister knew it. Newspaper reports of juvenile delinquency flashed through her head as she ordered, 'Answer me.'

Paola winced but replied, 'Yes, he's usually this late.'

'Usually?'

'Every night this week.'

'My God!' Gina sat with a thump, gathering her scattered thoughts. Filipo out on the streets – these awful streets – for how many hours? Every night? And with whom? Doing what? Gina swallowed. Her mouth was bone-dry; and yet her body was suddenly wringing wet: perspiration had popped in her armpits when Paola had made her admission, was now rivuletting her sides. The younger girl was watching Gina with a mixture of contrition and fear, her mouth slightly open as if about to speak, but with words unwilling to voice themselves. Gina told herself she must think rationally. Paola had said Filipo had been out every night this week, so tonight was no exception, and he had come to no harm thus far; therefore it was fair to assume that at this moment he was in no danger. Thoughts of murder and kidnapping retreated and she said levelly, 'Do you know where he goes?'

Paola nodded mutely, her face pale.

'Well?'

'He goes . . . to the movie house.'

'Every night?' To Paola's repeated nod Gina said angrily, 'Don't be ridiculous. He can't afford it. You've never lied to me in your life. Now, please, tell the truth.'

'I am,' insisted Paola. She dropped her gaze, picked distractedly at her knitting, nibbled her lips in turn. When she looked up her colour had returned and her eyes were truthful. She said, 'He works there.'

Works? Where? What are you talking about? Gina's mind shot the rapid-fire questions; but the sentences remained in her throat as she sat staring dumbly at her sister.

Then Paola told her. She'd told it all by the time Filipo returned home at nine-thirty.

As he entered and closed the door a small jolt ran through him when he saw Gina. His gaze flicked anxiously to Paola's face and the expression he saw there halted him in his tracks. After a pregnant pause he smiled blithely and sauntered forward greeting, 'Hi, Sis. You're early.'

Ten out of ten for nerve, thought Gina. She said, 'Don't call me Sis. Where have you been?'

Filipo's smile struggled for survival. 'Around.'

'Around is a very large place. Do you think you could be a little more specific?' They traded a long silence, and no words were necessary for each to realize what the other knew.

Paola said abruptly, 'I think I'll go to bed.' Quickly gathering her knitting, kissing her sister then Filipo – avoiding the supplication in his eyes – she said, 'Goodnight,' and left the room.

Gina regarded her small brother. Not so small really; and thirteen last month. She frowned as she measured him. She hadn't realized how much he'd shot up lately. But, then, there were a lot of things she had overlooked in recent months. For the past sixty minutes, as she'd sat here listening to her sister, her initial shock at Paola's revelation had burgeoned into anger, but had then given way to deep self-recrimination. She needed no long inquest, no arguments for or against her own case. Quite simply, she had neglected her family. Superficially with the best intentions; but, she knew, the long hours she put in at the dance hall plus those she donated to Harry Dix's ledgers, were not relinquished grudgingly. She enjoyed the arduous work, even at times gained a masochistic sort of pleasure from the mental exhaustion. Once (it seemed so long ago) in Baremo, each morning she had willed herself to survive. Now that survival had become a way of life; the striving for success had overcome all else.

She patted the sofa. 'Would you like to explain?'

Filipo, his smile flown, his face pinched with consternation, came and sat beside her. He stared down, chin on an apprehensive chest. Slowly he turned. Shifting his eyes to his sister's face he replied, 'I don't think I can.'

Gina stroked his hair from his brow. 'If you're old enough to work, you're old enough to explain.' She smiled. 'And perhaps I'm old enough to understand.'

She said to Max, 'Quite simply, he thought we were broke. He even had some mixed-up ideas about what I was doing with the male customers at the Starlight.' She smiled. 'He'd seen so many fallen angels in the movies he figured that's how I was having to keep a roof over our heads. He hadn't yet worked a week, was going to present me with the grand sum of five dollars on Saturday – which was what the child-exploiting crook at the movie house was paying him to slave four hours a night collecting and hauling trash from under the seats, picking cigarette butts out of the lavatory stalls, and sweeping the lobby. Of course – though I didn't say as much to Filipo – I know his labours to supplement the family budget, and save me from white slavery, weren't entirely altruistic. He did, after all, get to see three double-features a week, albeit as he crawled around the aisles collecting candy wrappers.'

Across the apartment's empty table, Max, hands clasped remorsefully before him, said, 'I'm so sorry, Principessa. I should have been around more often. I should have taken more care of you all. But . . . ' His big shoulders heaved ' . . . I've been – how do you say – bumming around. Playing cards. Shooting craps. Only working when I needed to. It's no good. I've got to stop this. I must get a proper job, settle down.'

Gina laid her hand on the Tuscan's knuckly fists. 'No, old friend, it wasn't your fault. It was mine. I should have been more aware of how the youngsters felt, and what they were up to. I dread to think of all the things that could have happened to Paola. I should have realized the time I took her to the dance hall that she's no longer a child. One day, very soon, she's going to want to start seeing boys. Well, that can't be so long as we're living here. We must have a proper home. A place where Filipo can bring his pals, and Paola can entertain a young man. And, most importantly, where I can keep an eye on both of them. I must find such a place, Max. Within the week.'

'But, Principessa, that won't be so easy. And even if you succeed, how will you be able to stay home nights with your present job? Will you find another?' He shook his head pessimistically.

Gina said, 'There's only one answer. To live the way we did in Rome. That's right, above the store, as they say in America. I'll do what you suggested the first night you were here. Remember? I'll open a Ristorante Rossi.' As the Tuscan's jaw slowly dropped, Gina added, 'And it will keep you out of mischief. You said it's about time you had regular employment. Right, you're hereby hired. As general manager.'

'But I don't know a thing about . . . '

'You helped Poppa often enough.'

'I only operated the cash register.'

'That's the most important job. And you're brilliant at it. You can check the figures on a till faster than I. It's what comes from having to calculate in a second the gambling odds on the turn of a card.' Gina stood suddenly. 'That's settled then.' She strode to the sideboard, returned with scratch pads, ready-reckoner and pencils, reseated herself and started making rapid notes. 'Now, we're going to need a list of catering suppliers . . . There'll be a liquor licence to obtain . . . I'll talk to Johnny Sabato about furniture and equipment . . . I must think about staff . . . And finding premises.'

Max sat and watched. Once or twice he said this and that, and Gina replied. Later he brought coffee, then sandwiches, and she thanked him. Of course, none of these times did she look up. For the next three hours she didn't look at anything except the words and figures where they flowed onto the sheets of paper. Not until Paola and Filipo came rattling in did she finally lean back on her chair, flexing her neck muscles, to greet them with kisses and declare, 'We'll be moving out at the end of the month.'

If anyone had ever doubted it they didn't know Gina Rossi too well. Within two days she'd found premises.

Johnny Sabato exclaimed, 'West Forty-Seventh! You must be kidding. You know the rents on that street?'

'Certainly,' replied Gina. 'I also know what the local restaurants charge for a salad. Yes, their expenses are high, but so are their profits. I can make *scaloppa milanese* for the same price wherever I operate, but I can sell it on Forty-Seventh Street for four times as much as I could on Broome. And there's a ready-made clientele up there. At night, of course, the society crowd and the well-heeled tourists who want a change from their hotel menus. But – even more importantly – in the middle of the day, all the ladies who are swanning up and down Fifth Avenue with time and money to spare. Plus the thousands of businessmen who pour out of the Rockefeller Centre and all the other office buildings. Not all of them want to eat and run. Plenty have clients, associates, girl-friends to entertain. And while they're doing it they drink. In the right atmosphere with good cuisine and excellent service, they need little encouragement to drink like fish. Which, for the restaurateur, can be ten times as lucrative as providing them with food. You know as well as I, the mark-up on imported wine is often more than a hundred and fifty per cent.'

She added, 'I have a family to support, Johnny. Their future to secure. I need money to do it. The only way to make money – real money – in the catering trade is from either a fast turn-around, low-cost operation or a high-class, high profit establishment. For myself the choice is immaterial. But for Paola and Filipo, I intend to have the best. The very best.' Looking hard at the real estate agent's photograph of the slim, elegant brownstone building, she declared emphatically, 'I shall open on Forty-Seventh Street.'

By the following evening she wasn't so sure.

At eight-thirty a.m. as she'd exited from the subway beside Trinity Church, crossed Broadway and faced the narrow canyon which ran to the East River, she had been prompted to glance up at the corner street sign to assure herself that she had alighted at the correct station. During the past months her self-imposed regimen of newspaper and magazine consumption had included – whenever she could obtain a free copy – the *Wall Street Journal*. But because there always had been too few hours in her days, she had never visited the famous thoroughfare from which the financial daily took its masthead. Thus in her mind's eye it was as glittering as the family names of Belmont, Kuhn, Loeb and Morgan which shone on the façades of its private banks. The reality of the gloomy chasm in which she stood was a stark contrast to her imaginings. The towering buildings seemed featureless, their eyes blind. Not a soul was alive in the grey desolation; and the chill which pierced Gina came not merely from the bitter air whining high in the ravine walls.

Habit had driven her from the apartment considerably earlier than necessary. Tugging up her collar she began to walk, awaiting the banks' opening. She recalled something her father had said: 'The characters who build empires are those with a one-track mind. Determination and persistence are their tools. No matter how tough a barrier, the man – or the woman – with the unshakable resolve to overcome it, will eventually succeed. It's the stuff that makes millionaires. And dictators.'

It was ten minutes to nine when the rattle of footsteps echoed in the canyon; at first like distant gunfire, but rapidly swelling to a cannonade. And then they came. Pouring from both ends of the street, from the intersections and alleys: the tellers, stenographers, clerks and secretaries, rushing from buses, trains and ferries to start the wheels of commerce turning. And close behind, the managers, directors, brokers and accountants, arriving by limousine, taxi and private seaplanes which wallowed in to the pierside at the foot of the street.

So relentless was the flood, Gina was forced back against a wall, remaining pinioned until the onrush ceased as suddenly as it had started. A clock struck nine, and she regained the sidewalk, once again alone in the bitter emptiness.

A quarter-hour later she was warmer and surrounded by the hum of hushed voices; but she felt no less alone where she sat before the leather-inlaid desk of the silver-haired, bespectacled man who turned a tortoiseshell pen between his fingers as he listened to her lay her soul on the line. Having entered the massive bronze doors of the City Bank & Trust Company, Gina had been ushered to this spot beyond the long row of gilded tellers' cages by a cadaverous, grey-clad woman who, when she commanded, 'Follow me,' had pursed her lips as if tasting the name Gina had given but finding it too sour to either swallow or spit out.

The woman's attitude was now mirrored behind the man's gold-rimmed eyeglasses as he peered at the loan application which Gina had completed at the sub-branch where she had her three thousand-plus dollars on deposit. She had considered handing in her application there, but had decided to save time, and create a favourable personal impression, by coming to the head office. She needn't have bothered.

The man shook his head. 'No, Miss . . . Rossi. We couldn't possibly consider granting the finance for this venture. Not without collateral.' He glanced dismissively at the papers Gina had laid before him.

The four pages of neatly typed (painstakingly on Harry Dix's ancient Remington) facts and figures had been, fifteen minutes ago, Gina's reasoned blueprint for the future. Now, after their cursory evaluation by this parsimonious money-lender, they were nothing but yesterday's absurd scribble. Gina felt crushed; not only by the man's attitude but also by the titanic weight of marble and mahogany and brass which pressed in from all sides. She had never before been intimidated by grandeur, and this place was no more august than the Rome banks she had visited with her father, but here the atmosphere seemed overcharged with pomp, and though she fought to maintain her confidence, still her coat felt two sizes too small, her work-reddened hands two sizes too large, and she was sure that the hair escaping from beneath her specially-purchased snap-brimmed hat was the most outrageous shade seen here since the bank was founded.

She declared decisively, 'But the restaurant will show a profit.' At his cool reaction to this retaliation she softened her voice, did her utmost to subjugate her Italian accent, and added compliantly, 'I know you think me young. Perhaps I am. But I have more experience than many twice my age. I understand the finances as well as the practicalities of running a business. I know I can succeed.'

'As you've already stated, Miss. And so has everyone else who has sat in that chair. Every Tom, Dick and Harry,' he smiled superciliously, 'and Polly, who comes here thinks that the few years they have worked at their trade makes them an expert. Bricklayers believe they are builders; newspaper vendors, publishers; bellboys, hoteliers; counter-clerks, storekeepers.' He stressed, 'And waiters, restaurateurs.' Before Gina could protest he went on, 'You people really must learn.

Banks do not have money to throw away on schemes which amount to nothing more than wishful thinking. Our country has been through a difficult period. A harsh struggle. And in spite of whatever that man in the White House and his so-called Brains Trust might say to the contrary, we are a long way from the end of the tunnel. The nation must exercise caution. All of us must keep our belts pulled in. And you immigrants, you newcomers to our country, must be grateful that you are here, and respectful of what you have been given.'

He stared at Gina, and his expression became sugared with paternalism. 'For your own sake, you must understand that what I'm telling you is right. I am much older than you. And wiser. Take my advice, my dear, don't venture into realms which are outside your comprehension. You're an attractive girl. I'm sure you'll soon have a husband.' He smiled thinly. 'And then you won't need to worry.'

Gina looked at him coldly. The blood was thumping in her temples. She wanted so much to lean forward and smack the presumption off his face. But her instincts reined her anger. This was her first port of call, there were others she could visit, and she didn't want this Shylock's retribution preceding her along the old-buddy line.

She stood abruptly, reached out to the desk and retrieved her typewritten sheets. Carefully slipping them into the document case she said, 'Thank you for your time. I shall always remember what you said. Good morning.' And she turned and strode past the customers at the tellers' cages, out beneath the grandiose portico to the street. Without pausing she continued along the sidewalk, knowing that if she faltered now her will would drain.

Within minutes she was sitting before the leather-inlaid desk of a silver-haired man whose mahogany desk calendar was gold-scripted 'First National Bank'. The man's appearance was as similar to that of the previous character as his environment. So was his attitude. Years later when Gina tried to recall details of this black morning, all she could see was a succession of identical faces, identical mouths rejecting her with identical words. As she toured the street, the names on the burnished plaques – Bank of Manhattan, Bank of New York, National City Bank, Chase National Bank – passed before her until she was uncaring of whose headquarters she was entering, was barely aware that she had detoured from Wall Street and had pursued her quest into the adjoining byways. And it wasn't until the homegoing hordes once more surrounded her, that she finally turned away – carrying the words:

'Collateral. By law, you must show collateral.'

She said, 'Harry, you'll have no problems. You can afford a professional book-keeper now. You won't miss me.'

The dance-hall owner's long face wore its most doleful expression. 'Like I wouldn't miss an arm.'

Gina looked across his desk with great fondness, said softly, 'I love you too. You did so much for me by hiring me, letting me take charge of your accounts. I'll be forever grateful.' She bit both her lips in turn. 'But . . . I have to ask you for more. You're my only chance. I . . . '

'The shirt off my back? Take it.'

Gina returned Harry's smile, but her voice was serious as she carefully continued, 'If all the Starlight's debts were paid off, plus the mortgages you've got against equipment, I figure the business and the lease would be worth around fourteen thousand dollars. See,' she handed him a foolscap page, 'I've typed up a balance sheet and capital assets summary. All I have to do now is get a certified accountant to authorize the figures. There are plenty who'll do it by the end of the week if I pay them double time.' She drew a breath, aware that she had known this man but a few months, that he was, in his way, a satisfied man, not a craver of the high life, not a risk taker. She continued, 'The banks would accept the assets as collateral. They'd loan perhaps ten thousand dollars against them. If you could . . . It would need your . . . ' She faltered; her resolve and the prepared persuasion she'd worked up last night after her abortive sortie to Wall Street now leaked rapidly away. She couldn't do it. What had possessed her to contemplate such a course? How could she possibly take such advantage of her friendship with Harry? There had to be some other way . . .

He said, 'When shall I sign the papers?'

Gina stared; at last shook her head. 'No. You don't understand what I was going to ask.'

Harry returned, "I'm not that dumb. And stop fiddling with those paper clips. Heck, if you're going to be a bundle of nerves asking for a measly ten grand, how're you ever going to get to buy out Hilton? No arguments now. I've got nothing to lose. Even if you run off to Hawaii with the money, I'll be able to pay it back easily from the extra profits I'm making here – thanks to you. So, like I said, when shall I sign?'

Gina's throat was so full she could barely speak, but she was suddenly on her feet, around the desk, hugging the dance-hall owner, planting kisses all over his head. 'Harry, you won't regret it. I swear to God. And I won't run off any place. I'll be too busy. Building up the most successful restaurant business in New York. In the whole United States. I'm going to do it, Harry. I know it.' She stepped back. 'And you're going to have a part of it. I'd already decided. Ten per cent. Please, don't turn it down. I want you to have it. Besides, I need a partner who's a native New Yorker. There's so much I've still to learn. You'll be the one to teach me.' She held out her hand. 'Please?'

A long smile crawled, slowly, up Harry Dix's face. When his features were lit like a lantern, he took the proffered hand, said, 'Did I ever tell you I can't stand Italian food?'

Johnny Sabato exclaimed, 'Five per cent!'

'All I'm asking in return is six months' credit,' said Gina. 'On tables, chairs, lamps, ashtrays, carpets, drapes, anything on that list you can obtain. Don't tell me where it comes from. I'd rather not know. Just so long as the police don't turn up on opening night to take it all back. Well? Do we have a deal?'

In the building on Forty-Seventh Street, the lease for which Gina had signed an hour ago, Johnny Sabato surveyed the wide, empty room before bringing his gaze around to Gina's sister and brother who also were staring wide-eyed at their soon-to-be new home. He winked at Filipo, then turned to Paola and said, smiling, 'It looks like we're about to become partners.'

'It's only cutlery,' complained Max, staring at the knife sample left by one of the suppliers. (Gina had refused to visit any showrooms or warehouses, declaring that if manufacturers and wholesalers wanted her business they could come to her. Those close to her raised disquieted eyebrows at this insistence, but she didn't bother to reveal her vow never to retrace her steps on the sidewalks where she had trekked so many soul-destroying miles.)

She replied to Max, 'The design is very attractive. But those deep-etched curlicues will be a devil to clean. And the blade is fitted into the bone handle. It will eventually work loose and water will be trapped inside. We'll have the plain knives that are all one piece. Same with the forks. The type with three prongs, not four. Easier to wash. Speed and convenience, Max, have to be the prime considerations when purchasing equipment. A waiter, for instance, when he is clearing can't waste time running to the kitchen with only a fistful of dirty knives on each trip. Ten sets of knives and forks must be gathered together on one plate. Without falling off.' Gina picked up the cutlery design she had chosen. 'To do so successfully the knife blades are placed under the handles of the forks, thus . . . ' She demonstrated using the samples. 'And, when necessary, a fork handle must fit easily under a spoon arch, like this . . . so that the whole set interlocks at right angles. That modern shape with the flattened arches was produced for its looks, not for practicality. The designer should have spent a month in a busy restaurant before being turned loose at his drawing board.'

Max sighed silently. He had considered expressing approval of the green-patterned crockery but baulked at the uncertain hurdle and was glad he did when Gina dismissed it with:

'The outfit trying to palm that off are crooks. It's domestic weight. Wouldn't survive five minutes of banging around in a sink. This,' she declared, 'is what we need. See: a thick, rolled edge. Less vulnerable to chipping. Nine-inch size. Even a two-pound steak looks lost on eleven inches. We'll have the rectangular vegetable dishes. Easier to stack than the ovals and better for arranging food portions. Also, their lids are flat and have side handles not top knobs, so they can be inverted and used as serving dishes. Cups? The ones with the straight sides. They'll stack tightly thirty on a tray, and when they're clattered together – which is quite unavoidable – the point of impact will be the sides not the rims.' Noting her requirements in a ledger, muttering to herself as she made mental calculations, Gina moved along the array of samples which were laid out on edge-to-edge tables down the side of the room where she had done the deal with Johnny Sabato last week.

Following her, Max read the quantities she was listing. Frowning he ventured, 'That's a lot of teaspoons, Principessa.'

Gina answered, 'I'm afraid we can't purchase only enough items to cater for a full house. Customers come and go all night, so cutlery and crockery always has to outnumber them. Some of it will be in use, some being washed, some awaiting washing. And, inevitably, some of it will be in bits on the floor. Our crockery stocks must be twice the amount required in use. Cutlery stocks fifty per cent of the amount in use. But . . . ' she smiled at Max and tapped her list, 'the item you mentioned – teaspoons are a law unto themselves. They have a life of their own. They'll leap like lemmings into customers' pockets, down drains, under floorboards, amongst the leftovers. Of the hundreds who'll escape every month, the only ones we'll ever see again are those which return from the swill man. He has a special sieving tank that captures the fugitives before they become part of the pigs' diet.'

They moved on.

When Gina finally snapped shut her book she smiled, 'Thank you, Max. You were a great help. Oh, by the way, I've been meaning to give you this.'

Max took the sheet of paper, slowly read it. Frowning, he asked, '*Che cos e questo?*'

'It's a five per cent share of the business.' To his oncoming protestation she said, 'Please, old friend, it's how I want it to be. And it's how Poppa would have wanted it to be. So, let's go and drink on it, all right?' She took his arm, walked him across the room, said casually, 'There was just one thing, Max. About your first four months' salary. I wonder if you would mind if . . . '

14

Mauve is an old lady's colour – so went the fashion adage. And true, it could drain a complexion, could seemingly reflect added years in the shade of a woman's hair. But, Gina had decided, Johnny had been right that time when he'd spoken of his own face which belied his youth: 'Helps you get respect,' he had said. She had always known that it was the manner in which a person conducted himself, or herself, what he said, more importantly the things he had to say, which dictated how others saw him. On the other hand, she had thought with a wry smile as she'd viewed herself in the Saks' mirror, it didn't do any harm sometimes to add a layer of respectable maturity.

The gown had originally been high-necked, long-waisted, with short puffy sleeves and a rear train. The hauteur of the Saks' sales person had staggered visibly when Gina produced the sketch of the alterations she required. Nobody, it seemed, had ever dared suggest such a philistine assault on the Fifth Avenue, albeit off-the-peg, perfection. Gina, however, had neither the time nor the temper to explain that although the garment's basic cut and tailoring were faultless, it did not have her individual personality. But it hadn't been necessary to argue the point, the credo 'the customer is always right' being sufficient to send her sketch to the alteration hands for completion by the end of the week.

Now, surveying herself in the bedroom mirror in the Forty-Seventh Street apartment, she knew with unshakable self-assurance that her instincts had been right.

One upper quadrant of the gown's bodice had been slashed away leaving that area of Gina's shoulder and chest naked; the puffy sleeves had disappeared; the waist had been shortened; the train had been pleated; the muted violet silk now clung with a sensual vitality while avoiding emphasis of any particular curve or feature, thus maintaining, heightening, the gown's inherent elegance.

'You look like a million bucks,' approved Filipo.

Gina didn't doubt it. Still, she promised herself, one day she would no longer have to make do and mend with refashioned store-bought dresses. One day, like Garbo, she would be dressed exclusively by Adrian Gilbert; and the hard-earned dollars which had paid for this sham *haute couture* would be the loose change she spent on a new hat.

She said, 'You're kinda cute yourself, bud.'

Filipo reddened, shrugged, ran his hand through his shining jet curls, tugged at the gleaming white collar behind his black tie. 'I hope I'm not going to have to wear this monkey suit every night. I feel like a ventriloquist's dummy.'

'You're gorgeous. You'll be the most handsome man in the place. And I'll be so proud to have you escort me down the stairs.' She brushed a non-existent speck from his lapel. 'So, if you're ready, we'd better face our guests.' She squared her shoulders, raised her chin, and linked her hand through her brother's arm.

They exited from the bedroom, went down the hallway of their private apartment, through the door onto a wide ivory-carpeted landing with muted pink-shaded wall lights and urns cascading pink, luxuriant blooms. At the end of this foyer were ivory leather-padded doors to the ladies' powder room and the gentlemen's cloakroom; halfway along was the staircase which swept down to the restaurant, where laughter and conversation were bubbling against the background of 'Begin the Beguine'.

Gina and Filipo walked forward.

As Gina descended the stairs she felt she was floating into a dream. The restaurant spread beneath her, seemingly haloed by an aurora of gold. This afternoon on her final (thirtieth) tour of inspection it had looked beautiful. Now it appeared magical. The mirrored columns and walls reflected the pink velvet chairs, the ivory-linened circular tables with their settings of cutlery and crystal and misted ice-buckets of champagne. Around the room bowls of gardenias echoed the pastel shades. Overhead, Tiffany lamps shed a lambent glow. And amid it all stood the guests: the males dinner-suited in elegance, the females gowned to perfection. They fluttered their fingers to greet their fellows, laughed lightly, exchanged intimacies with casual ease.

Gina's heart raced. Perspiration had popped across her shoulders. She faltered, gripping Filipo's arm.

He hissed, 'You can't fade now, Sis.'

'Don't call me Sis.' And she continued down, smiling blithely, nodding and mouthing 'Hello' to she knew not whom, with an air of total authority and confidence – and praying she wouldn't fall flat on her face.

And then, as she reached the restaurant floor, feeling her pulse might now drop to only twice its normal rate, someone started to clap. Within an instant the whole assembly was doing it. The room was rocked by applause. Gina hadn't the foggiest what to do. So she just gave them her best nonchalant wave, like the photograph she'd once seen of Carole Lombard leaving the Beverly Hills Hotel, and strode forward as if she knew precisely where she was going. Which, of course, she didn't, but just as she thought she might be obliged to march right on through the lobby and out the front door, a hand was gripping hers, turning her, leading her toward a semi-circle of beaming faces.

She blinked; recognized them all:

Max, moustachios curling with delight; Harry, long features

lit up like the Fourth of July; Paola, raven-framed smile as beautiful as a Goya portrait; Mrs Ponti, coiffed hair and sequinned frock more sparkly than her Cockney accent. And beside Gina, now releasing her fingers, handing her a plastic light-switch on the end of a flex, Johnny, mouth grinning and saying, 'Some crowd, huh? The real McCoy.'

Gina numbly looked around. Last night she'd fretted back and forth, asking a thousand times, 'Do you think they'll come? Are you sure they'll come? What if they don't come?'

Harry has assured her, 'Believe me. They'll come. I sent your invites, then called every one, personal. I knew them all way back, when bootleg gin and Dixieland jazz was our nightly diet. And we all went a little crazy. Did a few things that wouldn't look so good in daylight. Don't worry. They're all in town, and this time tomorrow they'll all be here.'

This morning, as the past six weeks' war of nerves and tempers between the armies of electricians, painters, plumbers, carpenters and supplies had reached its Armageddon, Harry's promise had been the furthest thing from Gina's mind. And even when a miracle occurred and the battlefield was suddenly transformed, she'd still never once thought of the guests. Her senses were in a daze as she'd checked the staff, the food, the wine, and at last gone upstairs to change.

Not until this moment did Harry's words return.

Scanning the room, Gina caught her breath as amid the crowd she caught glimpses of familiar yet elusive features – a movie actress, a crooner, a bandleader, a politician, a boxer, a golfing personality – society column faces which were there one moment, then, as Gina blinked, were gone, like fleeting images in a dream. She turned toward her family, whispered hoarsely, 'Thanks, Harry.'

Johnny said, 'So, press the darn thing.'

'What?'

'The button. In your hand. Press it.'

She stared dumbly at him, then down to the switch she was holding. And rationality returned. Looking up into Johnny's dazzling grin, she thought, If balloons fall from the ceiling, I'll never speak to you again. She squeezed.

For a moment she thought nothing had happened, then a great cheer went up followed by a new burst of applause, and Gina peered at the surrounding sea of faces, stared at their eyes, swivelled slowly to follow the line of their mass gaze, looked down the length of the room, across the three steps rising to the bar, above the polished counter, to the ivory fascia and the slim, pink neon script which had just winked on:

– The Lady –

They'd discussed it, argued about it, fought over it for weeks. On the day the bank loan came through and Gina signed the lease on the building, when they all got together that night for a self-congratulatory celebration, the question on everybody's lips was, 'What are you going to call it?'

It was the one item Gina hadn't considered.

There was, naturally, no shortage of suggestions, running the edificial gamut from the Colosseum to Caesar's Palace, and the culinary scale from Il Delizioso to La Nosharia (Filipo had a new Jewish friend). Max insisted it should be Ristorante Rossi, and Harry thought it should be simply Gina's. She was tempted by both, but with a surge of nostalgia for the former and a grain of vanity for the latter. Yet, somehow, none seemed satisfactory, not quite what she was looking for. 'It has to be special,' she told them. 'Different. The city is full of "Casas" and "Trattorias", "Peppo's" and "Mama's". Good or bad, they've all labelled themselves as Italian restaurants. I don't want that.' To their wounded chauvinism she explained, 'Of course we'll serve Italian food. The best. But I don't want to be categorized. I want to be . . . unique.'

It was the first time the opinion had vocalized itself, and Gina felt a rush of embarrassment. But it was the truth. It was what she had decided the morning the real estate agent had driven her to Forty-Seventh Street.

As he had shown her around the three-storey house, once the home of a wealthy wine merchant, he had stressed that the acquisition of the building was a unique opportunity. Gina had not doubted it for a moment. Though the place had been neglected in recent years, its architectural pedigree was unquestionable. The rooms were perfectly proportioned, the walls dadoed and corniced, the doors porticoed. Above all it was the staircase which captured Gina, sweeping upward to the gallery with carved stone balusters and handrail; and she could see clearly Manhattan's café society ascending and descending there, pausing for a word or joke, the men puffing their majestic Havanas, the women brandishing their fashionable cigarette holders. Exiting with the agent, when the man had said, 'I hope you'll contact me in a few days' time, after you've had time to consider,' Gina had replied, 'I'd like to start moving in this afternoon.'

'It's going to be all right,' she'd assured her incredulous family. 'I know it.' That was all she could say; she couldn't explain that even when all she'd had before her was the brownstone's photograph, she'd been utterly positive that they were meant for each other. The way Momma once said a woman should feel about a man, she thought. So, she mentally shrugged, who's to say I shouldn't feel the same about a building?

Over the next four weeks (having interviewed and employed on Harry's behalf a book-keeper for the Starlight) she transformed the house into a restaurant which, though not as lavish as the establishment she'd planned in Baremo, was as coolly elegant as white ermine, with an underlying vivacity as subtle as moiré silk.

'Everything must be first-class,' she'd told Max. 'Including our staff.' When he'd asked should he call an agency, Gina had replied, 'The people we'd get wouldn't necessarily be the best; simply the ones at the head of the line the day you phone. I'll take care of it. The way I would in Rome.' That night she set up appointments with four dozen prospective employees – the weeks she'd spent in the waiting room of the Madison Bureau, chatting to and exchanging telephone numbers with her fellow hopefuls, had proved to be far from a waste of time. Several of the contacts didn't turn up, but those who did, sitting on wooden chairs amid the barrage of activity in the evolving restaurant, had been hooked within five minutes. Gina Rossi's enthusiasm and determination was infectious. By the late afternoon she had a full complement of staff – including a Chinese chef.

Max was aghast.

Gina laughed. 'Chang's credentials are excellent. He was unemployed through no fault of his own. And there's no reason why he shouldn't prepare ravioli just as well as he does subgum chow mein. Besides, according to the Board of Health, his countrymen run the cleanest kitchens in this town. And you judge a good cook not only by what he puts on his plates, but also by what he keeps off his floor.'

She had a growing sense of victory. Just one unresolved problem remained. It was scribbled on a hundred sheets of paper – all of which had been banished to the trashcan. 'Damn it!' she exclaimed aloud on the sidewalk as she watched the contractors erecting the marquee. 'It has to have a name!'

'How high above the door is this going?' one of the workmen called to his mate.

'I'm not sure,' the man replied, then nodding toward Gina, advised, 'Better ask the lady.'

As the applause died away and the chattering guests seated themselves to the accompaniment of popping champagne corks, Gina remained standing, staring at the pink neon script. It was the first time she'd seen it. Everyone had kept telling her there was a last-minute hitch with the wiring. Now, she realized, they'd been kidding, but she loved them for holding back this surprise, this simple yet so emotional moment. The same sign, she knew, also had been illuminated outside the building. It would be seen by hundreds of passers-by. As Gina sat she vowed silently that it would be seen tomorrow night too, and the night after, and all the nights to come. Until people no longer glanced around to read it; they'd just know it was there. Its shape and colour would be imprinted in their minds as indelibly as the famous logos of Sardi's or The Colony or The Caviar. The Lady had arrived. And the Lady was here to stay.

The remainder of the evening floated by.

Gina reckoned she must have been photographed a thousand times. Every time a celebrity came over to offer congratulations and assure her of future patronage, flash bulbs exploded like fresh bursts of applause. And, she had to admit, she loved it. So, she saw, did the family. Max laughed mightily, sharing an Italian joke with a baseball star. Mrs Ponti giggled girlishly, tickled by a whisper in her ear from a radio comedian. Paola blushed to her roots, tumbled by one sigh from a handsome singer. And Harry happily swapped old times with everybody who walked by. But it was surely Filipo who got the biggest thrill of the night when Johnny stood to introduce the dark-haired, sensuous-lipped man in his mid-thirties who stopped at the table and in nasal East Side-ese said:

'Miss Rossi. You got a class joint here.'

Johnny said, 'Gina, may I introduce Mister Siegel.'

Filipo audibly breathed, 'Wow!'

Gina shot him more than her steely look but when she rose to face the heavy-lidded man she saw only good humour in his open, handsome face. She said boldly, 'I'm very pleased to meet you, Mister Siegel. Or may I call you Benny?'

He took her hand, held it. 'You can call me any time. But in L.A., right? I'm based over there now. It's where the real action's at. You come out and visit. I'll introduce you around. Those Hollywoodites, they're all buddies of mine. Jean – Jean Harlow, you know, may she rest in peace – was godmother to my two daughters. You got daughters? No, excuse me, of course you don't. But someday, huh? Certainly you will. A woman has to have daughters, right?' He glanced around the table. 'Already you got a beautiful family here. One day you'll have daughters too.' He smiled, and at last released Gina's hand. 'Their father will be a lucky guy.'

'Thank you,' said Gina.

Siegel nodded. 'I better be going now.' With a glance toward Filipo, then a shielded wink to Gina he added in a stage aside, 'Still a few guys I gotta bump off tonight.'

When Gina sat, Filipo's jaw was on his chest.

Later, as the last of the guests were leaving, Johnny, pouring Gina a club soda at the bar said, 'Yes, he has a great deal of charm. But make no mistake, he works for the Syndicate, and if they tell him to bury somebody, he'll do it without batting an eye. So take care. You're going to make it – I've never had any doubts – but when there's the smell of success in the air it brings the vultures; from the ones who'll settle for any piece they can get their claws into, to those who won't be satisfied until they've picked your bones clean.'

Gina smiled. 'You have such a way with words.'

'I'm serious. And I don't want any harm to come to you.' He glanced toward the family chatting with the final stragglers. 'Any of you.'

He said goodnight fifteen minutes later.

Gina and Max surveyed the debris of the evening. Gina pulled off her shoes with a sigh of relief, leaned against the big man and said, 'We'll clear it in the morning. For once, old friend, all I want to do is sleep.'

The policeman entered from the lobby. When he saw Gina he walked between the tables, took off his cap as he came up to her and asked, 'Miss Rossi?'

The night sergeant behind the desk of the downtown precinct

house pushed the silver purse forward, scowled at Gina as he held out a pen and growled, 'Sign here.'

Cassie scribbled on the receipt, picked up her purse, faced Gina and attempted a smile – which became a wince as the facial effort pulled at the blueing bruise along her jaw and the yellowing eruption around her eye. A minute ago, when she'd been brought forth from the cells wearing a red sateen sheath with matching pillbox hat, her astonishment at seeing her friend had mirrored Gina's own emotion, and the two had stood staring wordlessly at each other while the sergeant rubber-stamped the bail notice Gina had just covered.

Still neither spoke as they went out to the street, and it wasn't until they were in a cab heading up Broadway that Cassie blurted, 'How the heck did you find me?'

Gina, locked in a confusion of surprise, anger and happiness at the abrupt reunion, replied flatly, 'The police came knocking on my door. It seems your purse was full of press clippings – the advertisements announcing the opening of the Lady, and a couple of society columnists' paragraphs with my picture. The good officers of the law thought you might be planning to burgle me, or kidnap me, or even do me in.' She looked Cassie straight in the eye. 'Which one was it to be?'

'Oh, Hon, you know I would never . . . '

'And what am I expected to think? You disappear for sixteen months. Never write. And when you show up again you're behind bars and dressed like . . . like Dillinger's moll.'

'Aw, Gina, that's unkind.'

'Well, I'm mad. Look. Can't you see I'm mad?'

For a long moment they traded turmoiling emotions. Then they were hugging each other, clinging together, part-laughing, part-crying, until at last they sat back, dabbing hankies at damp eyes, both too full to speak as the cab headed toward the lights of midtown. Cassie was the one to break the silence. Dropping her gaze to her purse she said quietly, 'Hon, about the way I got the shiner . . . I think you ought to know . . . '

'I don't want to know,' cut in Gina. 'Just tell me what happened in Chicago. The pageant?'

'Oh that.' Cassie looked up. 'No big secret. I was a dope, is all. Sure, I could've become Miss Wholesome Meat. Easy. The corned beef heir was going to fix it, no problem. I realized it was going to cost, of course – nothing's for nothing in this world – and I wouldn't've minded paying up. After all, you saw his shoulders, who'd've shoved them out of bed? But . . . well, I don't go a bundle on the family plan. I didn't mind too much when he asked his brother to join the party. But when it came to his sister . . . ' She stared at Gina with an expression straight as a plank, before adding with exaggerated indignation, 'Well, you gotta draw the line someplace.'

Gina held her gaze. Then they both laughed aloud.

After a while, as their humour subsided, Cassie said, 'Heck, Hon, those characters with dough, they think they can buy anything and anybody.' She chewed her lip. 'And I guess they can. I confess the only reason I ran out of there was on account of I figured they'd make it worth my while to stay. Eventually, you know, they could have. Because everybody has their price. All of us. That's the way of the world.' As she drew in her breath her chest shuddered and her face again clouded.

But then the cab was pulling in at the curb. They were climbing out. Cassie was admiring the marquee; following Gina inside, to greet an astonished Max who had waited up; entering the restaurant with, 'Holy smoke! Jeepers! What a joint!' staring as if she couldn't believe her eyes.

With quiet thanks to Max, saying he should go to bed now, Gina led Cassie to the restaurant's white-tiled and stainless steel kitchen where she swiftly made coffee while replying to Cassie's rapid-fire inquisition on how the Lady had come about. When she'd filled two mugs, she pulled a stool to the drainer and said, 'Now answer me a question. Why didn't you write, contact me, come around to the Starlight?'

Cassie sighed, perched facing her friend. 'I did come by. One day last May. But the old girl in the booth said you were busy in the office, said as how you were running the place, were in partnership with Harry Dix now. I waited in a café across the street. But when you came out you were wearing a new wool two-piece, and a hat, you looked so classy you coulda had a date with William Powell. And I was in my old dress, clogging around in flatties. I seemed . . . well, you know . . . It was the first time I'd ever felt so . . . envious and small and . . . just plain crummy. That was why I never came around again. Can you understand that, Hon? Can you understand the way you made me feel?'

Gina gripped her mug, held it very tight. 'Yes,' she said. 'I can understand. Very well.'

Cassie smiled palely, then with a quick breath her shadow

passed and she said brightly, 'But heck, I don't blame you. I blame myself. I always knew you weren't cut out to be no chambermaid. I saw it the first day I met you, when you were hobbling around on bloody knees. Remember? How could anybody forget. Lousy job. Lousy hotel. Best thing that ever happened when they canned you, Hon. You'll never regret the day you walked out.'

'Neither will you,' returned Gina. The response was spontaneous, though now she realized the idea had been building since the moment she'd seen Cassie in the police station. She said, 'There's a job for you right here. No, don't argue. It isn't much. Sort of . . . ' Gina rapidly concocted a story. 'Assistant to the manager. Max. He's going to need someone to help with the female staff. You know what a hard time that can be, and I'll have my work cut out with buying supplies, helping Chang with the cooking, preparing new recipes. Believe me, Cassie, we need you.'

The redhead frowned. 'I don't know . . . '

'So what are you going to do? Go back to wherever you got that black eye?'

Cassie raised a self-conscious palm to the swelling. 'Hon, you've got to know. Please,' she insisted, 'I need to say it.' She took a deep breath. 'I'm not making excuses. Or apologies. It's how it's always been, since I was fourteen and some guy at the hotel I was working offered me a ride in his fancy foreign limo. We've all got to give up the old . . . you know . . . sometime, don't we? I got a brand new five-dollar bill for mine. The most cash I'd ever had in my hand at one time in my whole life. So I figured if I could get . . . tipped . . . for what I enjoyed anyhow, what the heck. And I never felt guilty, not through all the guys and all the years.' She paused. 'Until tonight.' Cassie shook her head as if with disbelief at that admission. Then she shrugged and her voice was matter-of-fact. 'Well, that's it. Full confession. I won't be surprised if you figure I'm not such a great character to have as a pal after all, the sort you'd rather keep away from Poll and Phil. But,' she smiled crookedly, 'at least you've heard the truth. I just wish I'd told it sooner, is all.'

A curtain of silence fell, and through it Gina read her friend's expression, and she knew, as she had the first morning she worked with Cassie, that there was no hidden side to the character behind her face. A face that was free of all pretence.

The face of the one person who had held out the hand of friendship when it had been needed most.

Now she reached out and took that hand, held it tight, feeling the warmth of it, returning its generosity. She slid suddenly from the stool, saying briskly, 'The first thing you need to realize when you're working here, is that we start at the crack of dawn. So it's a good idea to get to bed early. There's a spare room upstairs.' She strode to the door, looked around and prompted, 'Are you going to sit there all night?' And as her friend found her smile, set down her coffee and stepped toward her, Gina turned, throwing over her shoulder, 'You know, Cass, my big problem always was, I never could understand half of what you were talking about.'

15

The Lady was a success – all the way.

In less than a month word had flown to the four points of New York's compass and customers had come running, not just to sample 'the new place' but, more specifically, to savour recipes which one leading culinary columnist had described as, 'The most authentic Italian cuisine I've tasted this side of the Appian Way.' Gina didn't bother to inform the self-appointed expert that there was no such thing as Italian cuisine, only Tuscan, Romagnan, Venetian, Ligurian, Apulian, Umbrian, and that of a dozen other fiercely individualistic regions, but she did send the writer her prayer of thanks, plus a bottle of Dom Perignon '21. (Though she'd have defended unto death her belief that her country's food had done more for the world's palate than the rest of Europe put together – and despite George Auguste Escoffier – she had to admit that Italy's *vino spumante* had a long way to go before it reached the same league as France's champagne.)

The celebrities who'd attended the opening night at Harry's request didn't need a second bidding. They returned, towing their entourages, spreading largesse, vying with each other for the favoured tables, and always bringing in their train the reporters and photographers who, while publicizing the chosen few's revelries, never (after a couple of glasses of The Lady's hospitality) omitted to mention where they had been held.

By the time summer gave way to autumn, the slim, pink neon script on the marquee was a landmark which no self-respecting tourist wouldn't recognize, and which no one genuinely interested in the best 'Italian' food in town would fail to visit.

As the restaurant bloomed so did Gina.

Her beauty flowered into something more. She matured into an elegant, exquisite woman. Prompted more by her own curiosity than Paola's and Cassie's exhortations, she visited the National Beauty Parlor and came out with her hair no shorter but sleeker and wavier, layered into a frame around the subtle but dramatic make-up which the head beautician had suggested after Gina rejected the ounces of pancake and powder which were the current rage. She had never been much interested in her own figure since the curiosity of her early teenage years had waned, but now when she regarded her nude self in the mirror she wasn't too dissatisfied with what she saw: she flared in all the right places, and her thighs were long and firm; if anything, she admitted, her bust was too big, and, mindful of what invariably happened to the upper structure of most of her countrywomen when they approached middle age, she commenced a nightly regimen of hand presses which a feature in a library copy of *Physical Culture* assured her was what kept the WACs in shape.

It was the only planned exercise she ever did – or needed. Every muscle in her body was kept in a state of almost permanent movement as she daily rushed around from dawn to way past midnight.

At six a.m. each morning she was at the Gansevoort Market – popularly known as the Farmers' Market – where the growers from Staten Island, Long Island, New Jersey and Connecticut, in coveralls and muddied boots, stood on the flatbeds of their trucks yelling their wares and prices. Here, amid the mountained crates and baskets, Gina jostled with the mob of merchants, wholesalers, pushcart vendors and restaurant buyers, searching with unerring eyes, evaluating with infallible hands the fresh vegetables and fruit which would fill the day's menus, while around her legs urchins and derelicts scrambled for a stray apple or potato and to one side patient nuns awaited the unwanted remnants of the morning's trading.

Later she would visit her other suppliers: the fish and meat markets; the dairy; Zito's Bakery, where they still produced bread by the old-fashioned method in tins, which, Gina insisted, was the only way to achieve the real traditional flavour; thence down the street to Mandaro's to purchase mozzàrella, gorgonzola, scamorza, ricotta, provolone and other perfect examples from the store's four hundred varieties of the world's cheeses.

During the remainder of the day Gina would cook, create new recipes, check the accounts, encourage the staff, chat with customers, read the headlines, recheck the accounts, and snatch a bite to eat as she hurried through the kitchen en route from one involvement to the next.

In the hour before bed Gina would write in her notebooks. During the day nothing escaped her attention; just as she had from her earliest time at the Howard West she gathered information, gossip and ideas and each night transferred the miscellany to paper. She now had seven fat, bulging-edged, feint-ruled books stuffed with her jottings and was nearing completion of an eighth with recipes, menus, wine lists, ideas for improving service, kitchen routines and profitability.

PROFITABILITY was the heading on many of her pages. As she recalled the precise work schedules laid down by Mrs MacDonald, she adapted and applied the time-allocation techniques to the running of the Lady. She also recorded with minute precision how to earn an extra cent on every incoming dollar while maintaining the highest standards of cuisine and, most importantly, ensuring that none of her customers went home without their stomachs having been filled to the brim.

Another ever-extending section was devoted to COMPLI-MENTS & COMPLAINTS, pages which contained the gamut of customer comments from the faintest praise to the pettiest criticisms. The latter were rare, which was just as well because Gina did not adhere to the ill-founded credo that the customer is always right. She dealt fairly with all situations. If a client had a genuine grievance ('Which, with the best will in the world,' she reassured Max and Cassie, 'is unavoidable even in the most exactly managed establishments,') then he was sent home with a large Havana cigar (women with a bouquet hastily assembled from the lobby displays) and the invitation to return at any time for a complimentary meal.

Bogus complainants on the other hand received short shrift.

Gina could spot a crooked diner at a hundred paces before he'd even inspected his cutlery: the character who would make much ado about seating his family in the right spot, loudly recite the menu with explanations (most of them erroneous) of all the foreign terms, more loudly recount the lavish cost of the meal he ate elsewhere the previous week, scrutinize the wine label as if attempting to detect printer's errors, treat all the staff like his personal bonded slaves, then at the end of the evening complain stridently that the coffee was cold and when this was denied by a long-suffering waiter declare that he had been abused and that the outing (which invariably he would insist was his daughter's birthday treat) had been ruined. In many restaurants the oaf would usually get what he had been playing for all along – the cancellation of his bill. In the Lady however he got Max Barzini looming toward him like a volcano looking for some place to erupt – a sight guaranteed to inspire the most obdurate fraudster to reach speedily for his wallet.

Similar inclemency was meted out to loutish diners who fussed about their food but who, as Gina said, wouldn't know a truffle if they trod in one. Thus when a hatchet-faced harridan whose society accent was as phoney as her jewels protested that her lunch was unfresh, Gina personally sampled the bluefish, quickly explained that this species when served chilled was supposed to have a slightly bitter flavour and when the woman persisted with her indignation suggested politely that she transfer her custom down the street to Barney's Cod Bar.

All such incidents were entered in the notebooks, to be reviewed from time to time with humorous recall, but always with a mind to their worth in the scheme of Gina's ambitions.

One of the best moves she'd ever made was to ask Cassie to join her. The redhead had proved her worth a hundredfold. She treated the restaurant as if it was made of solid gold, busying about her tasks with a duster permanently in one hand, so that while she was checking cigarette stocks she'd be buffing the bar top, while she was mediating between two hassling hat-check girls she'd be polishing an ashtray. Whenever Cassie came hurrying into view, Gina stepped swiftly aside lest her friend gave her a quick shine as she passed by.

It was a cheerful ship.

Max was the only member of the crew who some days wore a frown. His unhappiness always followed his reading of the European headlines. More than any of his card-school compatriots, he was harrowed by what was happening to his homeland. Italy was, after only a few short months of war, reaping the whirlwind of Mussolini's megalomania and his lies about the country's strength and weaponry. While the army suffered humiliating defeats in Greece and North Africa, in Rome the Leader defended attacks on his infallibility by increasingly vicious anti-Fascist purges and, following Hitler's lead, fierce persecution of the Jews and gypsies. Max would mutter aloud, 'He has to be stopped. Someone must finish him.'

The Tuscan's dispiritedness was never long-lived however when Gina and Cassie joshed him about his latest *innamorata* causing him to suffuse tomato red as he attempted to escape from their innocent-eyed but oh-so-knowing enquiries.

The Lady's first Christmas Eve arrived and was a fitting close to the year. The lobby could hardly accommodate the huge tinselled tree; the restaurant groaned under the weight of streamers, holly and balloons; and Max (with not too much protestation) donned a Santa Claus outfit to distribute gifts to the customers and, at midnight, lead the singing of carols. What sentimental moonshine, thought Gina as, washed by the heart-swelling strains of 'Silent Night', with her arms around her sister and brother, she sang louder than anyone while the tears coursed down her cheeks.

It was the last Monday of February when the robbery occurred. Gina was wakened in the small hours by an unidentifiable noise. Swiftly donning her dressing gown she went out to the hall, switching on the lights, and entered her office to discover the desk drawers ransacked and the bureau broken open. The sash window had been forced. The burglar was gone. The following morning after she'd reported to the examining police sergeant that only a few dollars were missing from the petty cash tin she felt – deservedly, she supposed – like a recalcitrant schoolgirl rather than the victim of a crime as the officer (thank goodness they were alone) gave her a ticking-off for having such ancient window catches and door locks. Gina admitted it was a matter she'd postponed too long; there had

been so many priorities. Within two days she'd ensured the
building was as secure as Fort Knox.

A week later, seated at her desk an hour before the evening's
opening, Gina closed her ledger with a thud of satisfaction.
Profits were surpassing her most daring dreams. The bank loan
was being repaid regularly, and in three months' time, at the
end of the Lady's first financial year, Harry and Max and
Johnny would receive a dividend on their shares. And still
there'd be a respectable amount left in the kitty. What to do
with it? Gina mused. Money that wasn't working was wasting
its time. She shifted in her chair, feeling fidgety. She'd come
this far, and everything was fine. But she couldn't now sit still
and ride comfortably around on her carousel. There were new
horizons to reach; she could feel their calling with a quickening
of her blood. She'd succeeded with one restaurant . . . could
she double her success with two . . . ?

She opened her notebook, but as she was about to write Max
entered and said, 'Excuse me, Principessa. A problem. There's
someone who insists on seeing you. Wouldn't leave and
wouldn't give a name.'

'I haven't time for salesmen,' returned Gina. 'There's
something I just thought of and must get down on paper. If
whoever it is won't leave reasonably, it's someone I wouldn't
want to do business with anyhow, and you're free to get rid of
them in any way you see fit.'

The voice rasped from the hall, 'Now that just isn't friendly.
Is it, Sweetie?' The hulking figure stepped into view, sneered
at Max, 'And you can get lost, Primo, me and your boss don't
need no company while we're talking over old times.'

Gina stared as her emotions lurched. It was several seconds
before she could get her words to rise beyond her larynx.
When she at last spoke her voice was unnaturally flat. 'Never
mind, Max. Everything's all right. Thank you.'

The big man hesitated. 'You don't need anyone?'

'No,' Gina snapped. 'Just leave us.'

Max faltered between hurt and concern, but then, with a
backward glance at the visitor, retreated to the hall, closing the
door.

The woman with the slablike face and cropped iron hair,
wearing a heavy skirt and peajacket, smirked, 'Now, that's
better. Real cosy. Just you and me, Sweetie. Nice and private.
So that we can discuss the good old days. Those times we had

at the Howard.' Her tone hardened. 'Before you got to be Lady High and Mighty. With all this.' She swept the office with a virulent glare. 'When you was nothing but a two-bit housemaid. A floor scrubber. A rag-shover.' She sneered. 'Who stole five-cent magazines.'

Gina was snatching short breaths. At her sides her nails were digging into her palms. In an instant she had been hurled back across time, was now physically shaking from the dank cold of the cubicle in the Howard West where she stood naked as this creature's hands . . . Rising to her feet she said levelly, 'What do you want?'

'Boy, aren't we something these days!' mocked the woman. 'What do I want? What big favours can you dole out? A job? You think that's why I'm here? Figure I'm looking to be your dishwasher, or trash carrier, or kitchen gofer?' She scorned, 'Or body searcher?' Her malicious sneer raked Gina's figure. 'Well, forget it, Sweetie. I don't work for greaseballs. Don't take orders from lousy Eyetalians.'

Gina felt the vicious delivery of the derogatory name like a blow across her face. Her instinct was to retaliate, verbally to slap down this woman. Yet something stilled her voice as she regarded the coarse features, seeing in them not merely hatred but also a deadly look of triumph. Fighting to smooth her nerves, to remain in control, she said coldly, 'If you've come here to insult me you're wasting your time. If you have anything else to say, please do so. I have only fifteen minutes before I open the restaurant.'

'Sure you have,' rasped the woman. 'So you can play the fancy pants dame for the sucker customers. So you can queen it with your society buddies. So you can rake in another sackload of dollars.' She took a threatening pace forward, causing Gina involuntarily to step back. 'Well that's why I'm here, Sweetie. Not to bad mouth you. Not even to bash in your prissy face. I'm here for my slice of the action. A share of all the dough you're making. You'd like to share it with me, wouldn't you, Sweetie? Of course you would. And you're going to. You're going to give me plenty. A heap more than I got outta here last week.'

Gina stared, at first uncomprehending. Then she followed the woman's contemptuous gaze across the desk and to the bureau, and understanding assaulted her.

The woman rasped, 'Come to you, has it? Sure, it was me

220

broke into your crummy office. I told you you'd pay.' Her hand moved to her cheek as it had the day at the Howard West when Gina's fingers had left their livid weal. 'And you would've paid, with this dump in flames. Yeah, that's what was supposed to happen. The thirty bucks from the cash box was just by way of a bonus. No sense in burning good dough. I'd have bin counting it while I watched the flames light up the sky if you, or somebody, hadn't woke too soon. You had a lucky night, Rossi. Real lucky.' Her face hardened. 'But then, so did I.'

Though the words had no meaning for Gina, their tone chilled her. Still she felt she must make some move and she instinctively glanced toward the telephone.

'I wouldn't if I was you,' warned the woman. 'Not till you've taken a look in there.' She nodded toward the bureau.

Gina hesitated. An alarm was sounding far off in her head. As she strove for rationality the clangour grew louder. Take a look. For what?

'You haven't missed them, have you?' sneered the woman. 'Had nothing on your mind but the cash, right? But there was a couple of other items in there amongst all the dumb insurance papers and junk that it would've been a pity to let go up in smoke. Don't you know? Not so damned smart after all, are you?' She glared with aggressive superiority. 'Passports, dummy. And identity papers. They're worth good money in this city. I figured fifty bucks for yours and the kids'. Of course, that was before I found the piece of paper you'd squir- relled away inside one of them.'

Fear was enmeshing Gina. She said tensely, 'Paper?'

'You've gone kind of pale,' taunted the woman. 'You heard right enough – paper.'

Gina mentally berated herself. After the robbery she hadn't made a thorough check on the contents of the bureau; hadn't imagined anyone would steal more than cash. Now she knew exactly what her antagonist was talking about.

'A real important piece of paper, wasn't it?' the woman went on. 'And me at first almost tossing it out with the trash. But I didn't. Oh no. Because I saw the words on it. Sure, Italian words. Figure I wouldn't understand them? Wrong, smart bitch. I worked with you thieving Guineas forty years. I had to listen to your damned voices on our streets all my life. I know what you're whispering about. I know what you've got to hide.

Yeah, like your piece of paper. With the name Rossi in it. Alfredo Rossi. Other words too, like court, and criminal, and arrest, and condemned. I didn't have to be able to read them all to know what that piece of paper meant.' She leered spitefully. 'Who was he? Your old man? Brother? Maybe even husband? And what'd he do, this Alfredo of yours? He a thief? An arsonist? A mafioso? How about a murderer?'

Gina flinched.

The woman probed, 'That what he was?' She shrugged. 'No matter. All that's important is that you know I know he was a villain. But, don't worry, I ain't about to give away your secret. I won't throw you to the headline hounds. Don't want your fancy pants customers knowing they're being served by the relative of a jailbird, do we? That wouldn't be good for business. Might even wipe you out. And we can't have that happening, can we? We've got to keep that cash register ringing. Right, Sweetie? Right?'

Gina was too stunned to reply. Her head was spinning with the woman's words. Alfredo's conviction decree; Gina had kept it all these years, had almost forgotten it. Now this creature had it. But – Gina's thoughts turmoiled – did it really matter? What if the newspapers discovered her father had been exiled by the Fascists? Would that be so damning? Weren't the people of America aware of the cruel injustices of Mussolini's dictatorship? Should she fear the disclosure of Alfredo's so-called crime? No. Gina was sure she should not. This woman had put together a few words and translated them into common criminality; but she had been unable to read the full text of the decree, its political realities had eluded her. So her proposed blackmail weapon wasn't as sharp-edged as she believed.

And yet?

Gina's dilemma was not buried.

The woman barked, 'I said, right?'

Jolted by the demand Gina swiftly gathered the shards of her reason. She said tightly, 'How much?'

'Well, that's what I like,' smirked the woman. 'Straight down to cases. Not that you got an option, eh, miss big shot restaurant owner? You bet your life you don't.' She raised her fist, smacked it into her palm. 'Twenty-five thousand dollars.'

Gina gasped. 'You're crazy.'

'Don't bad mouth me,' snarled the woman. 'And don't waste breath bulling me you can't find the dough. Beg it, borrow it, steal it. I don't give a damn. But you'll find it, Rossi. All of it. Or you and your thieving, murdering family will wind up on every front page in the country. Understand?'

Gina inwardly shrank from the woman's vehemence. But she stood firm, traded her antagonist stare for stare and said, 'How can I be sure you still have the decree . . . the paper?'

'I got it, is all.'

'And the passports?'

'Them too. Why should I have bothered to sell them for fifty measly bucks when I knew you was about to make me rich? You'll get the whole wad back – soon as I see twenty-five thousand. Cash.'

'It will take time to raise so much.'

'Course it will,' shot the woman. 'You think I'm stupid? I don't expect you to come up with the dough tonight. Not even tomorrow. You got a week. A whole seven days before I come around to collect. And remember . . . ' she made a stabbing motion with her finger, 'don't get no cute ideas about calling the law. If I so much as see a traffic cop glance in my direction I'll start yelling your secret to the rooftops.' She glared for several threatening moments. Then her features crawled into a malignant grin. 'Well, it's been a real pleasure talking to you again, Sweetie. Quite a reminder of old times. All we shared together, eh? A pity I can't stick around a little longer, maybe take up where you and me left off. Still, why be impatient? Another week, when I pick up the twenty-five, we can wait that long, can't we? For what you might call, a more intimate reunion.' Her eyes idled crudely on Gina's mouth before she all at once swung around and stalked across the office. At the door she looked back, her face once more a slablike mask.

Seconds later Gina was staring into the empty hallway. The encounter had left her breathless, as if it had been a physical contest. Now, in the ensuing normality, the heaving of her lungs was the sole evidence that the confrontation had actually taken place. Against the familiar, reassuring hum of the restaurant readying itself for the evening, she relived the previous brutal minutes, heard again all the woman had said.

When she'd been over the words three times, though her nerves were scraped raw, her breathing was near-normal. She arose and went to the bureau where it took only a brief search to confirm the woman's claim. As she slumped back against the wall maimed by the unavoidable truth, Max entered, asked concernedly, 'Principessa, are you all right? Is anything wrong? That person, you knew her?'

Gina straightened. 'Yes, someone . . . just someone I worked with at the Howard West.' She raised a smile. 'I'm okay, thanks, Max. Perhaps a little tired. But, certainly, everything's fine.' She returned purposefully to her desk. 'I'll be along in a while to say hello to our early customers. First there are a couple of things I have to take care of. See you later.' Quickly opening a ledger she ran her finger down a column of figures, turned the page, reached for her pen. She heard Max murmur, '*Si*, Principessa. But don't work too hard.' Not until the door gently clicked shut did she look up, push the ledger aside and allow the thoughts to rush in.

As she'd already divined, the woman's belief that Alfredo's conviction order might be damaging to Gina and The Lady was misconceived. However, she had been unable to inveigh against the would-be blackmailer. For while the decree was harmless, the other stolen items were deadly. Paola and Filipo's identification documents, dismissed by the woman as worth only fifty dollars, were in fact beyond price. Because – the truth lacerated Gina – they were false. In the eyes of the law her sister and brother were illegal immigrants, and if their papers were revealed to the authorities they could be deported. This horrifying reality was all that had raged in Gina's head as she'd faced her tormentor. And although her demons of irrationality were now under control, still she could not drive out the grim memories of the weeping families who had been rejected at Ellis Island. How could she permit that to happen to Paola and Filipo? How could she let them be returned, alone, to the certain retribution of Mussolini's regime? But what was her alternative?

A knock on the door and Johnny Sabato entered. '*Buona sera, signorina. Come sta?* You look terrific. Me? *Sto bene. Molto bene.* I placed ten vending machines this afternoon. Figured a celebration is called for. Where? At my favourite restaurant, of course.' He walked forward adjusting the immaculate knot of his silk tie. 'Hey, I don't expect a twenty-one gun salute when I arrive. A burst of mild applause will do. Even a single shot like, hello.' He halted. 'Shall I go out and come in again?'

Gina focused on his handsome features, their slight frown as he sought her response. Her own face felt waxen with anxiety, as though if she spoke it surely would shatter into uncontrollable grief. She inhaled deeply, held the steadying breath. With rigid calm she said, 'It's good to see you, Johnny.'

How she got through the remainder of the evening she'd never know. As everyone laughed and drank champagne around Johnny's celebratory table, Gina kept her smile in place, said all the things expected of her while her mind remained trapped in her office reliving and reliving the confrontation with the blackmailer.

She was hugely relieved when Johnny called an early end to his party because he had an out-of-town trip at first light tomorrow. Her nerves remained on a rack however, and when Filipo cajoled, Aw, gee, couldn't he stay up to listen to the basketball match, she snapped at him, No, it was about time he started thinking about something other than games. Max, raising an eyebrow at this, accompanied Filipo upstairs, while Johnny had a parting drink with Paola in the bar. Gina, claiming a need to check the morning's shopping list, returned to her room. For the following three hours she remained straightbacked on her desk chair unable to form a logical thought. Not until the walls began to close in on her did she return downstairs to the dark, silent restaurant, and through to the lobby.

The sky was starless black as she went out to stand on the deserted street. Not a soul moved here; not a sound broke the stillness. Gina was utterly alone. Though she was dressed only in her wool suit she was oblivious to the frosted air as she walked slowly toward the intersection at Fifth Avenue. The sidewalks had been cleared of the snow which had blanketed the city for the past month, but ice waterfalls from frozen gutter overflows still clung to the faces of the buildings, and mounds of glacial muck straddled the kerbs. Gina shivered, not with cold but at the memory of her first winter in the city, those bitter weeks she'd spent searching for a job when her sole motivation had been the survival of her family. Had it all been for nothing? Would everything be cancelled out with the stroke of a bureaucratic pen at the discovery of Paola and Filipo's false papers?

She stood at the corner for a long time. Occasional cabs cruised past; sometimes a driver called to her and receiving no response drove on. A police car sirened across a distant intersection. Late-night revellers came and went from the hotels along the avenue. A derelict shuffled his way in the lee of the department stores' windows.

Gina saw none of this. But as the wind rose around her, the mist in her head cleared. When she at last retraced her steps to the Lady she was no less afraid, but in her clenched fist she was carrying a nugget of hope. Back at the apartment above the restaurant she paused outside her sister's then her brother's doors. She resisted, however, the temptation to look in on them; she couldn't risk her emotions being further torn. In her office she sat at her desk.

By the time the first sounds of morning were breaking into the streets, Gina had made her decision, had formulated her plan.

During the next seven days she held the plan in the recesses of her mind, dare not bring it to the surface lest its fragility break her resolve. Burying herself in the workload of the kitchen and the office, she didn't permit herself one free moment to dwell on what was to come.

The week crawled by.

On Friday morning Gina awaited the woman's arrival. At eleven a.m. she took a call on the lobby phone. The woman gave her a downtown address, ordered her to be there by noon. Before Gina could collect her shattered thoughts to protest she was holding a dead receiver. This wasn't how she had planned for it to be. A hundred different courses of action swarmed through her head. Thirty minutes later she was leaving the building. Because she knew there was truly no alternative.

The saloon was a hole in the wall; a long, narrow room squashed between a tattoo parlour and a barber school in the shadows of the elevated railroad at Bowery and Division Streets. A bar with wooden stools ran half the length of the left-hand wall; tables and chairs stood around the bare board floor. The walls were plastered with photographs and posters of boxers, illuminated by the yellow light from three dingy globes hanging from the ceiling. On the counter a showcard advertised next month's fights at Madison Square Garden. Behind this the yeasty-faced bartender was deep in a copy of *Ring* magazine. Gina was the sole customer.

This worried her. When she'd arrived a few minutes ago to

discover the place was empty she'd baulked on the threshold. She wanted the safety factor of other people, for she knew she would stand little chance, that her scheme would be torn apart, if her blackmailer became violent. Assuring herself that a saloon couldn't remain devoid of drinkers for too long she'd crossed toward a rear table, only to be halted by the bartender's gruff, 'Counter service only.' Gina had hesitated, then ordering a whiskey sour had taken it to sit by the wall.

Now the minute hand of the big clock above the door clicked into the afternoon.

Apprehension was a swirling cloud in Gina's head as she picked nervously at the string around the bulky brown paper parcel which she had carried here and set upon the table beside the untouched glass of liquor. The collar of her heavy herringbone coat was turned up almost to the brim of her hat and the nearby radiator was clanking with steam, but still she couldn't control the shivers which sporadically ran through her. What if the woman doesn't come? she agonized. What if she doesn't bring the passports? What if I can't persuade her to hand them over before she opens this parcel?

The clock stood at 12.10.

The bartender turned the pages of his magazine.

The door opened and a black figure stood silhouetted against the momentary oblong of sunlight. As the door creaked shut and the entrant's features became visible, Gina jolted reflexively to her feet.

The woman approached with an exaggerated swagger, hands stuck in the pockets of her peajacket. 'Well now, Sweetie. Here we are again. Getting to be a regular old buddy routine, eh? Maybe we should make it that. Once a week, say, you and me sharing a bottle and . . . ' She smirked suggestively as she halted before the table.

'Do you have the papers?' Gina said flatly.

The woman's face hardened. 'Watch your tone, Rossi. If you want what I'm holding you'd better think about how polite you're going to be.' She glanced around as if suddenly aware she was all the way into the saloon, and when she turned back to Gina the insolent bravado had been replaced by nervous tension in her eyes.

Gina's trepidation rose. There was danger in that look. How unstable was this creature? Had she come prepared for trouble? As that suggestion stabbed Gina she glanced anxiously to where the woman's fists were concealed in her pockets. A gun there? Don't be irrational, she warned herself.

'Twenty-five thousand,' the woman rasped, shifting her stance to aggressively plant her feet apart.

Gina hesitated on the brink of her next move. She'd lived through this scene a thousand times in her head. It had to work out in reality. It must not go wrong. Besides, there really was no other way to go, and she was too far along the road to retreat now. Reaching forward she pushed the brown paper parcel six inches toward her adversary, held it there on the tabletop and said, 'You'll get this when I see my documents.'

Flashing a look at the package, the woman retorted, 'What? Do you think I'm dumb? You figure I'm about to hand over that decree or whatever you call it, and then you're going to grab your bundle of dough and make a run for the street?' She gave a short, harsh laugh. 'Forget that, Miss Cutie Pie. You'll see the paper when I'm counting my money. Right?'

The distant door swung open and two men in scruffy overcoats and seamen's caps came in and walked to the bar. Gina gave a silent prayer of thanks. Their presence was her safety factor. Everything was fine. Her next move, however, was crucial. She said defiantly, 'I don't even know if you've brought the documents. You might be . . .'

'Quit stalling,' shot the woman. 'Here.' She jerked her fist from her jacket, brandished a slim wad of papers. 'What you think these are?'

Gina peered. 'They don't look like . . .'

'You're not blind. See.' The woman held up Alfredo's conviction order. 'And this other junk is what came out of your bureau.' Seizing the order with her free hand she tossed the remaining documents onto the table.

A massive flood of relief washed Gina and it was all she could do to prevent herself from snatching up what she clearly recognized as her passport plus Paola's and Filipo's identification papers. With aching calm she reached out, lifted them and slipped them into her pocket. Resisting a sudden sensation of weightlessness and the impulse to burst into either laughter or tears, she released the brown paper parcel and said casually, 'That's all yours.'

If there was unquenchable mockery in the words it obviously went unnoticed by the woman who grabbed the package, yanked at the string, tore apart the paper, all the while holding onto Alfredo's crumbling conviction decree. Her face was gleaming with anticipation, her lips working spasmodically as she slashed at the parcel's thick wrapping, rending it from side to side to violently invade the neatly aligned stacks of . . .

She recoiled as if she'd plunged her hands into carrion. Consternation deranged her features.

'Yes,' said Gina. 'It's newspaper. All of it. That's what you, and your blackmail weapon,' she flicked a contemptuous glance at the crushed decree in the woman's fist, 'are worth. Go ahead, take it to a newspaper. They'll translate it. Properly. They'll learn how my father was cruelly condemned by . . . ' She halted there, knew it would be pointless to explain more to the creature before her, understood also the danger in prolonging this moment of victory. Her adversary was swaying her shoulders from side to side like an animal that doesn't know which way to turn. Gina swiftly stepped out from behind the table, strode toward the door.

The saloon was a desert of bare floorboards. The urge to run was fire in her legs. With every step she expected the roar from behind, the thunder of pursuit. The two men at the bar looked toward her, exchanged grinning remarks. The bartender didn't shift from his magazine. Gina pulled open the door, stepped outside.

Sunlight, icy air and traffic din bombarded her. She strode across the sidewalk and the gutter, into the street, raising her arm to flag an approaching cab. Traffic swarmed around her. Swallowed her. Within minutes she was being borne homeward.

She couldn't believe it had been so easy. During the cab ride back to The Lady she had been too stunned to do anything but stare blindly ahead. But once within the warmth and security of the restaurant, thence her apartment, the full realization of her triumphant audacity poured upon her and she burst into laughter, fell onto the bed and sank into a cloud of euphoria.

She knew, of course, it was the elation of relief. Nevertheless she did nothing to dissuade it from pursuing her into the following week. As she sang and whistled her way across the days, Cassie tentatively asked if she was seeing a feller, Max perplexedly enquired several times if she was feeling all right, and her sister and brother wondered at, but didn't object to, the armloads of presents she daily brought (though Filipo seriously considered forgoing the gifts in order to avoid the hugs and kisses which were a compulsory accompaniment).

It was the Monday following her downtown meeting with the blackmailer by the time Gina began to settle back to earth. She decided to make one more celebratory purchase, for the only person who hadn't received one – herself. She spent the entire afternoon touring Fifth Avenue, eventually emerged from Bonwit-Teller into the neon-lit blackness, toting an exquisitely-wrapped package containing the most outrageous *décolleté* scarlet nightdress in the world. Ridiculous. But everyone was allowed to act a little crazy once in a while.

She strolled back south, pausing to survey the dazzling store windows, all of which she had already viewed as she walked north, and it wasn't until she'd travelled the entire eight blocks to Forty-Seventh Street that she realized how late it was – the restaurant would have been open an hour!

She strode the final block. Rounded the corner.

Stopped as if she'd hit a brick wall.

The Lady was on fire.

Smoke was billowing from the doorway, streaming up the face of the building like skeined serpents. The sidewalk and street in front of the restaurant had been cleared of people and traffic; wooden cordons corralled the crowd beyond a firetruck and two police cars around which uniformed men of the two forces hurried and shouted and gesticulated.

Gina's heart had leaped into her mouth. She dashed forward, but fifty yards from the restaurant was forced to slow her pace by the crush of people and vehicles.

The onlookers strained in a massed arc, faces alight with anticipation, arena spectators craning for the main event. Gina swallowed revulsion at the display of voyeurism but was relieved to realize that the evening-dressed couples were patrons of the Lady. She strode forward, swiftly picking her way between parked automobiles whose drivers and passengers were standing on running-boards and hoods. Reaching the barrier she peered toward the crowd, searching the faces, her pulse pounding, until she recognized Chang and his kitchen hands, beside them three waiters, Sam the bartender and Jenny the cigarette girl, and, way off across the open space, Cassie, her arm around Filipo.

A bang echoed from the building and the throng reflexively surged backward. Gina snapped toward the sound, hesitated only a moment before pushing between the cordons and starting across the open space. Firemen ran past, unravelling a hose; someone was bawling, 'Where's the hydrant?', and the rattling extension ladder began to climb the wall of smoke.

'Hold it, lady. You can't go in there.' A burly police sergeant cut in front of Gina, raising a paddle-like hand.

'Who's in charge?' demanded Gina, her tone halting the officer's advance. 'I rent that building. Are my people all right? Is everyone out of there?'

'Oh, good evening, ma'am,' the policeman responded deferentially as he surveyed the quality of Gina's coat, and touched the peak of his cap. 'I don't know. The place was already afire when I arrived. The lads'll be through to the back in a minute. They'll let us know if the place is empty.' He glanced in the direction of the team disappearing into the roiling greyness of the entrance.

Gina followed his gaze, but as she squinted into the fog another explosion blasted the night and the glass showered down causing her to duck before she shot a look upward to see flames belch from a shattered upper window, a tongue of crimson and gold licking outward, spitting sparks. An instant later yellow light flared behind the tall street level window, illuminating the interior to give a flash picture of chairs and tables, columns and mirrors, wreathed with writhing blue tendrils. Now Gina could hear the blaze, the crackling and roaring above a prolonged hiss, punctuated by sharp detonations.

The policeman, catching her arm, gently but firmly pulling her away, said, 'The liquor going up. You must keep back, ma'am. For your own safety, and so's the men can do their work.'

Reluctantly Gina allowed herself to be drawn aside as a second firetruck came racing down the street, horn blaring. Its crew was leaping to the ground before it veered to a halt, hauling forth their equipment, rapidly joining the battle lines.

Gina watched, shading her eyes, alone as the policeman strode away to join his men, and a numbness slowly pervaded her senses. After several minutes she was only vaguely aware of the surrounding activity: hoses shooting arcs of water over the adjacent buildings; an ambulance arriving spilling medics; a radio van and a man brandishing a microphone questioning the crowd; besmirched, choking firemen staggering from the restaurant, others running in to replace them.

'Gina. Thank God. Are you okay?'

Jolted from her reverie by the yell, Gina saw Paola shaking off restraining hands to spatter across the water-streaming street. She was wearing a white evening dress torn at the hem, smutted across the bodice. Relief surged through Gina as she ran to her sister, clung to her gasping, 'Are the others all right?'

'I think so,' answered Paola. 'All the customers got out. But I haven't seen . . . ' She cut off, scanning the scene. 'No, there he is,' and she pointed to a shirt-sleeved figure shouldering his way toward them behind the cordon. 'Where were you?' Paola called to the man as she hurried with Gina to the barrier. 'I haven't seen you since you brought me outside.'

When he reached them Johnny, his usually slick hair dishevelled, his eyes redly seeping, smiled wryly. 'I figured I'd go back for these.' He raised his arms to display the three green leathered ledgers. 'I know how much your sister enjoys book-keeping. Couldn't let all her handsome in-and-out columns go up in smoke.'

Gina shook her head, not knowing whether to kiss him or call him a crazy fool. She was forestalled from either by a roar from the crowd which swung her toward the building in time to see a fireman rush from the fuming doorway, batting at his burning arm. Two colleagues were on him in a moment, swaddling his flaming jacket, leading the man along the sidewalk thirty yards from Gina but near enough for her to hear the wounded man shout to his chief, 'In the basement! Couldn't get through. Somebody down there.'

Gina's mind gasped, Max? She involuntarily stepped forward, knuckles pressed to her teeth, but was held from advancing further by Paola. Every fibre of her being impelled her to pull from her sister's grip and rush to the building, but she knew it would be hopeless and her limbs sagged as she stared horror-struck at the gouts of orange heat bellying from the second storey, rising on rufous plumes, rolling over the rooftops to veil the distant lights.

For what seemed an age she remained there, visions of every fire she'd ever seen in the movies flaring across her mind: visions of crackling walls, towers of fire, and the charred remains of victims. Yet this reality was far worse. The din and the stink and the turmoil rained down upon her with the spray from the hoses. Her hair was sticking to her brow and her coat collar was wet around her face. No fictional excitement here; just dirt and disarray and danger. Even the massed onlookers had fallen mute, their earlier eager expectation replaced by a dumbstruck awe while the grimy, desperate battle was played out before them.

Suddenly the umbrous vapour thinned. The outline of the doorway became visible and beyond it steam and smoke swirling in tattered ribbons across the lobby. And through that murk staggered three figures, like apparitions in the fog which fumed around them, taking form as they advanced, then stumbling into the open. Two firemen supporting a third man, his clothes smoking, face indistinguishable behind a blackened mask. A big man.

'Max,' choked Gina, and before anyone could stop her she was dashing across the puddled street, tripping over a hose, holding her balance to rush to the Tuscan and throw her arms about him only to be pulled off by the police sergeant as she gasped again, 'Max! Oh, Max!' reaching tentatively, tremblingly to his scorched features, barely catching his rasping, 'Principessa,' before the medics were grasping his arms, leading him away and Gina was prevented from following by the sergeant's firm grip and his assurance, 'Nothing you can do. They'll take care of him.'

One of the fireman pulled off his helmet, wiped his forearm across his gleaming brow. 'He was lucky. The smoke hadn't got to him. That's the killer. The smoke. Probably what finished the other poor devil.'

The words seemed to hang on the air. Gina's lips formed a question but no words came and she felt suddenly as if she were trapped in a nightmare. She spun to search the faces of the crowd. Who? Who was missing? Her desperation was broken by the call, 'Make way there.' Turning, she saw the stretcher bearers exiting through the curtain of sluicing water. Police and medics converged on the pair as they carried their burden toward an ambulance. Gina ran behind hearing one of the crew ask, 'Dead?' To which came the reply, 'Afraid so. Not too badly burned, but must've been trapped by the fire. Choked to death.'

Gina urged, 'Please, let me through.'

The policeman, still at her side, responded, 'All right,

ma'am. No harm, I suppose. Someone has to make an identification sooner or later. If you've the stomach for it.' He ordered the stretcher men, 'Hold it, fellers. Let the lady take a look.'

'Thank you,' whispered Gina, stepping forward. Clenching her teeth she craned to view the body. The sickly smell of scorched flesh rose as the blanket was pulled back from the face. But it wasn't this which caused her stomach to heave. Gina let out a sharp cry as she jerked back from the cropped grey hair and the ox-like features of the woman blackmailer.

They gathered in the storeroom of the haberdashery across the street – Gina, Paola, Filipo, Cassie, Johnny, everyone from the Lady. Their friend the proprietor made them hot drinks while the police sergeant took brief statements from them all. Outside, the crowd had dispersed once the blaze was under control. The fire teams continued to work inside the building.

Gina's first priority had been to phone the hospital for news of Max, and all the preceding trauma had receded when she'd been assured his injuries were superficial. She'd then checked on every member of the restaurant's staff, shared her concern with each individual, promised they would all continue on full wages until they were back in business.

In ones and twos they left for home. Eventually only Gina, her sister and brother, Cassie and Johnny remained. It was nine p.m. Johnny was saying he'd take time off from his office tomorrow to help out where necessary when the police sergeant called Gina aside.

'A message from the lieutenant,' the uniformed man said. 'They've confirmed your identification of the dead woman. Located her apartment. The lieutenant would like for you to come over to the precinct house. He said it was important.'

He was a sandy-haired, middle-aged man at a cluttered desk in a glass-partitioned corner of the squad room. Gina sat before him and listened without interruption as he explained that his men had located the dead woman's apartment and brought him a few notebook pages she'd had there but which he'd decided were meaningless and had consigned to the incinerator. He said he had no idea how or why the woman had evaded Gina's kitchen staff to enter the restaurant's basement.

'Also,' he went on, 'there is no evidence to suggest she

started the fire. Nor am I in possession of anything which might offer a reason for her wanting to do so. And I am sure, Miss Rossi, you wouldn't wish to hazard an explanation for her presence on your premises, would you?'

Gina's mouth felt very dry, though she knew it was not an after-effect of the blaze. She responded to the lieutenant with a single shake of her head.

'Good,' he said. 'Then, with your consent, I shall not open a file on the incident. Believe me, I have far more important matters on my plate.' He opened one of his desk drawers. 'By the way. That big feller they took to the hospital. Along with that other crazy friend of yours, he was trying to rescue your office files and such. He was halfway down the stairs when the smoke got too much for him. The armload of stuff he was toting was taken by a fireman. It was dumped in a patrol car. Ended up here. The stack of journals and general correspondence you can collect from our property room any time. But these,' he reached into the drawer, 'I thought you might like to have tonight.' He laid a number of items on the desk in front of Gina.

She stared down at her insurance policies, bank statement folder, registration contract for the Lady, her passport and Paola and Filipo's identification papers.

The lieutenant said, 'They could so easily have gone up in smoke. Still, you could always have got copies, couldn't you? Even the immigration stuff. Once somebody's been accepted through Ellis Island, they're legal immigrants. They have the District Commissioner's stamp to prove it. So if they lose the foreign papers they came in with all they have to do is sign a form to say so and they're issued with new American docummentation. You know, some people don't realize that.'

He smiled and stood. 'Well, Miss Rossi. After the time you've had I guess you could use some sleep. I'll say goodnight.' He extended his hand across the desk.

Gina slowly arose.

She reached out and took the proffered fist; held it for a long moment.

235

16

When Gina walked out of the Fifth Avenue Hospital the afternoon following the fire, she was chuckling, feeling even happier than she had after her interview with the lieutenant.

Within minutes of leaving the police precinct house she'd been in a cab on her way to see Max Barzini. In the mêlée of the hospital's emergency department she had fired questions at every passing nurse, doctor and even a few patients, but it was half an hour before a young intern afforded her the half-minute it took to check his clipboard and shoot her a string of ward and floor numbers. By the time Gina had toured labyrinthine stairways and corridors, to discover a small becalmed lobby with a quietly writing duty nurse, it was long past midnight. The nurse smiled casually and said, 'Oh, he's okay. A bit toasted around the edges, but sleeping like a baby now.'

Gina spent the night on a straight-back wooden chair in the waiting room. Despite the nurse's assurances, she wouldn't leave without personally seeing the big Tuscan. Throughout the night her thoughts kept returning to the blackmailer. The whole deadly episode had taken place in the short space of a week; that was all it had been since the woman brought her demands to Gina's office. If only I'd known, she thought, about the immigration regulations. Or made an effort to find out. If I hadn't been so involved in business . . . Perhaps my personal relationships too are . . .

As the overhead lamp blinked off and dawn lighted the window, Gina thrust uncertainties and speculation aside. She shut the door on the recent past, concentrated on the immediate future.

Max went down for minor burns surgery in the morning, slept under further sedation until noon. Gina was permitted to visit his bedside along with his lunch. But as she strode toward him her pace suddenly staggered and her emotions lurched. She stared, tottering into shock, colliding with dismay; then, snapping her hand to her gaping mouth, she swayed between consternation and mirth.

Max glowered. 'Crazy doctors. Said it was too singed. Said I should start afresh.' He ran a huge, scandalized hand over his shaved dome, thence across his denuded upper lip, rumbled, 'I feel like a bloody turnip.'

It had been the relief Gina needed.

By the time she got back to the Lady her spirits were sailing. They dipped as she approached the building – the marquee had gone and the stonework was blackened – but rose again as she entered. It didn't look – or smell – good, but a whole lot better than she'd expected. Around men hauling barrowloads of debris, the lobby walls were foul with soot, but, apparently, undamaged. The restaurant, wet and filthy, seemed particularly desolate because the furniture and carpets had been removed; yet the staircase, even grimy and water-stained, still had the grace of a duchess rising from the ruins. As Gina looked up the sweeping flight, Johnny Sabato appeared on the landing, waved and descended two steps at a time. He was wearing old jeans and baggy brown sweater – the first time Gina had seen him anything but immaculate. Not at all like a wheeler-dealer, she mused, more like the respectable guy-next-door, any feller's pal, any woman's husband . . .

The observation was eliminated as Johnny strode toward her saying, 'I just called the hospital to find out where you were. They told me Big Max is fine.'

'Yes,' replied Gina. 'But if you want to take him a gift when you visit, better make it a fedora.' She smiled, 'I'll explain later. Where are Paola and Filipo?'

'Down the street on Madison. Checked into the Ritz-Carlton.' Forestalling her horrified expression, he assured, 'Don't worry about the expense. All gratis. The manager came personally this morning with the offer. And he wasn't the only one. Folks in the business take care of their own. They've been lining the sidewalk to help the Rossis. You've got promises of enough stock – all free – to open two dozen restaurants. Nor is it only the trade who've been around. Come take a look.' He led the way across the bare floor to a storeroom behind the lobby. When he opened the door the mountains of bouquets almost fell out. To Gina's amazed gaze he explained, 'From customers. Also in amongst that floral jungle is about a ton of candy, gallons of wine, perfume, more well-wishing wires and cards than you can count, and from the owner of the millinery store round the block the biggest, craziest hat I ever saw, she said she hopes you enjoy it as much as she enjoys the lunch she has here every Friday.' Johnny grinned. 'Cassie's upstairs praying we get a call from the manager who comes in from Bergdorf-Goodman.' Then his face clouded and he added concernedly, 'Hey, you look kinda tired. I think it's time you got some rest.'

Gina continued to stare at the roomful of gifts, murmured quietly, 'I never knew so many could be so kind.' Turning away she faced Johnny, seemed suddenly to realize what he had said, 'Rest!' Her arm swept the devastation. 'With all this to get straight? Time enough to rest after we've reopened. Next week.' She set off toward the stairs. 'Now, you'd better give me a run-down on the damage. Thank you for getting the cleaners in so quickly. But have you called the painters? Carpenters? Has the insurance assessor been? We'll have the kitchens refitted by Thursday . . . ' She continued forward, her voice a tickertape of schedules and finances trailing out behind.

Johnny, seizing the end of it, swiftly followed.

The fire chief's report came the next day.

The blaze had started in the basement. Cause unknown. It had climbed the rear stairs, inflicting more harm on that side of the building than on the front. A storeroom and two upper floor bedrooms had been gutted, but, thanks to the swift response of the fire teams, damage had been confined mainly to furnishings and equipment; the essential fabric of the three storeys was unimparied.

On Friday evening, four days after the conflagration, the refurbishing crews, after working – and being paid double time for – eighteen-hour shifts, had the lobby, cloakrooms and restaurant looking as brand, spanking new as they had before the Lady's pink neon sign first winked on eleven months ago. Tomorrow they'd be able to start on the private apartment.

Gina frowned as she walked with the crew boss to the door. She said thoughtfully, 'No . . . Leave it till Monday . . . I think, maybe . . . ' As she stared into the middle distance, the man shrugged, said, sure, his wife might appreciate him being home for more than two hours at a stretch, bade Gina good night and departed before she could change her mind.

Gina returned upstairs. She prowled the grimed apartment, the storerooms in the rear, then the empty top floor – which had been unused since she took over the building; and all the while her mind was ticking, ticking, running along lines of fantasy, but never losing touch with the reality of the idea which had been taking shape over the past forty-eight hours.

When she finally lay on the couch in her office she was still unable to switch off. The growing excitement in her would not permit sleep; and she was still wide awake when the first water-wagon trundled down the dawning street.

She made herself, hot, strong coffee, re-read all the wining-and-dining ads in her stack of New York guides, then when the daylight outshone the electric lamp she called Johnny Sabato, enquired – as he struggled from six a.m. oblivion – if he was free to escort her that night. 'But don't get any wrong ideas,' she warned. 'The only reason I'm asking is because there are still some medieval establishments in this so-called modern city that won't admit unaccompanied females.' She added something like a growl before thanking Johnny for his co-operation.

When he arrived twelve hours later, resplendent in tuxedo, ebony waved hair gleaming, Gina passed him eighty dollars with the explanation, 'Expenses. I wouldn't want to dent your reputation by being seen picking up the tabs.'

Johnny stared at the cash like a kid who'd been handed his first live frog. 'Say, come on, Gina, I can't take this. I never in my life – neither did any other guy I know – let a lady pay the dues.'

'Well, you'll have to get used to it,' Gina replied frankly. 'Please, don't get me wrong, I'm a firm believer in all the old-fashioned customs such as men duelling for a maiden's honour. But at the same time I like to pay my own way. Is that so weird? Anyhow, tonight is business, so,' she turned to Max (still a mite singed but otherwise his big healthy self after the brief sojourn in the hospital), 'we'll put the eighty dollars through the petty cash as Research and Development.' And with an appraising glance across the restored restaurant she slipped her sequinned black jacket about her shoulders and headed for the door, exiting before Johnny and Max had time to exchange bewilderment.

In the cab she consulted a list from her purse and instructed the driver, 'Café Latino, Barrow Street.' When Johnny, regathering his charm, said, 'You'll love my tango,' Gina replied, 'I won't have time.'

He understood the statement when they left the Latin-American nightspot after downing one cocktail while watching six brilliantined characters in tight red pants and frilly blouses blow tinny trumpets and shake their maracas. 'Mucho rhythmo,' Johnny had grinned while Gina pencilled notes on a pad and headed for the door. Catching her on the sidewalk as she hailed another cab he enquired, 'Are we in some sort of hurry?' 'Yes,' she answered as the Yellow slid up alongside. 'There are fourteen more spots on my list.' She was into the seat, poised impatiently while he was still cranking his jaw shut.

Next stop, Club Gaucho. They remained there watching the heel-banging mock Argentinian cowboys for less time than they had had the jiggling imitation Brazilians.

After that Johnny didn't say much, just concentrated on attempting to help Gina on and off bar stools, up and down stairs, and in and out of taxis. He didn't remember much either, just vague snatches of sights and sounds as they sped amid the streams of light from one splash of entertainment to the next: a lunatic comic running around on his hands at the Nut Club; a guy in a striped sweater and French beret throwing a similarly-clad girl across the stage at the Bal Tabarin; a Spaniard dancing on his hat at the Havana-Madrid; a girlie show at the Midnight Inn (where Gina lingered even less); a first-rate swing band at the Hickory House (where she stayed much longer); an extravagant floor show at the Paradise; an old-style song-and-dance man at Bill's Gay Nineties. Apart from these the evening was a blur, ending some time after one a.m. with a gang of revellers blowing squeakers down his ear outside Dickie Wells in Harlem.

When they eventually returned to the Lady and Max enquired, 'Where did you go?' Johnny replied, 'Better ask Gina. She kept the log.'

Gina simply said, 'Goodnight.'

She didn't appear again until four p.m. the following afternoon. Dressed in sweater and slacks, hair tied back with a ribbon, she walked in to the bar where Johnny and Max were installing two new cigarette machines. When they looked up and chorused, 'Sleep well?' she declared, 'We're going to open a night club.'

Several seconds elapsed before the men took their stunned eyes off each other to stare at Gina who had continued to the bar and was pouring herself a cream soda. They approached her with the caution of men in white coats. Max made a long noise as if having difficulty clearing his throat, but the silence wasn't otherwise broken until Johnny echoed, 'Night club?'

Gina set aside her drink, briskly opened her notebook. 'I've

240

sketched a rough layout – stage, bandstand, seating – based on what we saw last night. None of those places was big, nor over-plush, not in the aristocrat-watering league, but that's why I chose them. They're the ones we'll be competing with. No point in going bankrupt trying to steal the Rainbow's clientele. Not yet.' She took a sip of soda. 'Likewise, we can't start out with top headliners or a Gold Diggers spectacular. On the other hand I have no intention of presenting whirling dervishes or chimpanzees on unicycles. As Mister Siegel said, The Lady is a class joint. I intend for it to stay that way. We'll have an old-fashioned line-up. Seven dancing girls, female singer, male crooner, eight-piece band. Music that's easy on the ear. Entertainment the customers will want to come back to.' She tore several hand-written sheets from her pad. 'Max, here's a list of the additional glassware and so forth we'll need. You know the quality I want. Please call the suppliers, have them work out their best price.'

As Max took the paper in a dumbstruck hand, Gina smiled at Johnny, 'By the way, thanks for joining me last night. You were a great help.' She added, 'And I enjoyed it.'

Johnny shrugged, 'My pleasure.' He started to continue tentatively, 'Gina, there's something I've been meaning to say . . .'

'Principessa . . .' Max finally cleared his throat. '*Me scusi* . . .' He scratched his re-bristling dome. 'But where . . . where will we put the stage? We don't have room down here for no dance floor, not even a bandstand.'

Gina sighed, explained patiently, 'The night club won't be down here, Max. It will be on the next floor. With some of the internal walls removed, there'll be heaps of space. We'll move the apartment to the top of the building – we've been paying rent on those empty rooms for too long.' Her eyes probed Johnny's. 'It's only common sense. Isn't it?'

'Oh, sure,' Johnny answered quickly. Then added with caution, 'But it is rather a sudden, and a large step. Maybe it might be an idea to seek a little advice before jumping in at the deep end.'

'Well, of course.' Gina snapped shut her notebook. 'That's where I'm going now.' And the swing of her hips riveted two pairs of eyes until she was out of the bar.

The same photographic portraits paraded a welcome along the

wall of the Starlight's lobby. It seemed like yesterday that Gina was here, chill in her thin coat, pocketing her pride as she offered Johnny Sabato's business card as her passport to a much-needed job. Such a small favour Johnny had thought he was doing her. Yet without him would she have survived? Of course she would, she assured herself. Nevertheless, she'd be forever grateful to the man; although, she thought with an inner smile, perhaps she'd never fully shown her appreciation. (Though she'd never admit it – not even to Cassie – she had entertained a couple of fantasies featuring herself and Johnny, but had ended each with a cold shower and concentrated application to stock control before they could lure her onto any misguided routes to reality.)

Passing the ticket booth of the Starlight, she shelved all thoughts of romantic involvement with anybody as Joe lumbered through the door, squinted then blinked recognition and rumbled, 'Hey, Gina. Long time no see. You're lookin' good.'

'Thanks, Joe. How's business?'

'Slow, slow, quick, quick, slow.' The big man grinned happily as if his thousand-times-said rejoinder was freshly scripted, then added, 'Catch you later,' as he brandished his ticket punch at a pair of arriving sailors.

Gina stepped by him, into the dance hall. The mirror globe's petals of light swirled across the floor where a couple of dozen couples were shuffling a slow waltz. And in an instant Gina was cloaked by an unheralded sadness. Despite the fresh paintwork, the new chromium-frame tables and chairs, the gaudy dresses and make-up of the hostesses, still there was a drabness about the place, that feeling of fadedness – heightened now by unavoidable comparison to the Lady – to which Gina had closed her mind during her existence here.

She returned quickly to the lobby, knocked on the office door and entered to the dance-hall owner's: 'It's open.'

Harry looked up from his desk, and his long face lit like a lantern. He was out of his chair, effusive with greetings, before Gina had advanced two paces. He gibed good-naturedly about being honoured by a visit from such a famous restaurateur. 'In the *New York City Guide* even.' Bowing humbly, he pulled forth a chair. 'After you leave I'll have the seat framed.'

Sitting, Gina shared his humour, the sadness of the previous moments now swiftly evaporating. She refused a catalogue of drinks, and for the next quarter-hour exchanged news and views as if it was four months rather than four days since Harry visited the evening after the fire. At last capturing a gap in Harry's conviviality, Gina leaned toward the desk, announced, 'There's something I want to show you,' and took from her purse the sheets of paper with the night club sketches she had revealed to Max and Johnny an hour earlier. Laying them under Harry's quizzical eyes she said, 'This is what I want to do.' She then explained for the second time today the plans she had formulated in the small hours of this morning following her tour of the city's cabarets. For Harry however she was more explicit, detailing her intentions, expanding specific points, all the while emphasizing her presentation with vital and eloquent movements of her shoulders and hands.

Through it all Harry remained silent, his head sometimes nodding, lips pursing, brow knitting as his expression travelled from amused surprise to concerned interest.

It took twenty minutes. When it was done Gina's upper lip was filmed by perspiration. She took out a handkerchief, dabbed her face, wiped her hands realizing that her pulse had quickened and she was almost breathless with tensed excitement. Maintaining her air of composure she declared, 'That's it. Now all I need is the opinion of an expert. What do you think?'

Harry looked across the desk. 'I think you're crazy.'

'I know,' returned Gina. 'But how about the club?'

Harry smiled, though his eyes were guarded. 'Okay. You want it straight? The honest answer? This is is: you've got about as much chance of surviving in the night club jungle as Wendell Wilkie had of beating FDR out of the Presidency last year.' The last vestiges of his humour retreated. 'Always assuming you can borrow enough money to construct the place, and that your neighbours won't kick up a stink, and that City Hall will extend your liquor licence and that they'll grant you the necessary entertainment licence, assuming you clear all those obstacles you still have to run a course where some of the toughest characters in the business have fallen and broken their necks. Shall I go on?'

'Could I stop you?'

'Believe me,' assured Harry. 'I'd love for you to succeed. And if all it took was guts and heart and being the greatest book-keeper in the world, I know you'd make it. But it takes more. So much more. Let me tell you:

'You don't just have to worry about the price of onions and the chef's aching back. Turn the Lady into an entertainment spot and first off you'll have to figure what acts to book. Not that you'll have a short choice; the day word gets out, you'll need a club to beat off every vent, fire-eater, scat singer and hoochy-koo dancer east of the Mississippi, plus – to drive you completely round the bend – their agents. But that's the easy part. Suicide time arrives when you actually become an employer of a motley troupe of characters all of whom are convinced the only reason they don't have Bob Hope's contract is because their second cousin twice removed isn't married to the secretary to the head of Paramount. You have to know where to find an instant replacement when your female vocalist calls to say she's in bed with flu even though you know damn well she's under the sheets with her latest protégé. You have to be able to cope with a drummer who's the best in town – so long as he keeps taking the little white grains. You need a broad shoulder for broken-hearted chorines to cry on, but you also must have a big hand to swat their butts when you discover they've been conning you with crocodile tears. And while you're beating your brains out with all this you also have to understand orchestration, stage lighting, programme timing, choreography and how to rewire a busted microphone.' Harry took a breath. 'With me so far?'

'All the way,' answered Gina. 'You've now told me every-thing I wanted to know.'

'I only just started.'

'Of course, but you can give me all the other stuff later. Right now I'd like to discuss the most important point. Who I'm going to get to run the place.'

'Well, there are plenty of guys who'd . . . ' Harry's voice fell away, and, very slowly, his assuredness slid down the collar of his shirt. He moved back from his desk, regarding Gina as if she was something dangerous. 'Now hold on. I can see what you're thinking. And you can forget it. Much as I appreciate everything you did here. Much as I love you. I'd need to have my brains knocked out to take on what you're about to suggest. I told you, it can drive a person crazy. Oh, no, lady. Oh, no.' He shook his head as energetically as a refractory horse. 'It's been great knowing you. Goodbye. Don't bang the door on the way out.'

* * *

After Harry had sold the Starlight for fifteen thousand dollars, invested two-thirds of this in the soon-to-be-opened night club, and signed a contract to become vice-president of the new holding company which would control this venture plus the affairs of the restaurant ('I didn't know what I was doing,' he reiterated to Max and Cassie and Johnny at every opportunity. 'I must have had some sort of blackout'), he then took over the supervision of the club's construction and decoration, leaving Gina free to re-establish the Lady's business.

As she daily bent over her desk, scribbling notes on scraps of paper for transmission to the bar staff, Chang and his kitchen crew, even the powder-room attendant, her eyes burned with enthusiasm. Where before the restaurant had run along successfully enough, now Gina knew she could make it gallop. Within a month of re-opening after the fire, most evenings and the noon-to-two period were running at capacity. But, she fretted to herself, there are more hours in the day than those when folk are eating lunch and dinner.

At eight a.m. one morning she called a conference in her office. 'We stay open until after midnight,' she stated. 'But we sell very little food then; most of the late customers are just drinking. Chang, will the kitchen staff work extended shifts? On bonus rates, I'm sure they will. Max, how many movie houses are there in the vicinity which don't close until one in the morning? Twelve. We'll offer their late patrons a special menu. Table d'hôte. Four courses and coffee for a flat two dollars. The menu will be changed twice a week. We'll promote it with billboards in the movie theatre foyers in exchange for advertising those theatres' coming attractions in our rear lobby. The weekly sweetener for the movie-house managers will be a bottle of wine whenever they bring a partner for a meal.' She checked the figures on her pad. 'I can cover that cost with the extra discount I get from the wine shippers for an increased order, plus the tax allowance against promotional expenses. I'll still come out ahead on profit.'

'It's called productivity,' she said to Cassie a fortnight later when they surveyed a packed restaurant at one a.m. 'Just like a factory. You have to keep it running as many hours as possible. So long as it's standing still it's costing us money. Now, once the club is operational, this is what we'll do with the afternoons.'

At three p.m. the third Friday of the following month,

Cassie, in sage green suit and veiled hat, presided over The Lady's first thé dansant.

Meanwhile the club had opened and was progressing apace. It wasn't yet able to afford headliners to compete with Paul Whiteman at the Biltmore's Roof Garden or Tommy Dorsey at the Manhattan Room, but under Harry Dix's expert direction, giving opportunities to first-class musicians and singers who had yet to hit the big time, the Lady was rapidly establishing a reputation for introducing new talent. Harry, naturally, told everybody he was being driven round the bend, but there was no one who didn't comment that the ex-horn-player-cum-dance-hall-owner's long face had never looked happier as the customers clinked their cocktail glasses through the hot, care-free summer.

It was the summer of the year when Gina first wore stockings made of nylon; when the U.S. Army took into service a new-fangled vehicle called a Jeep; when Max tried to explain (to anyone who would listen) the system of parimutuel betting introduced at all New York race tracks; when Britain's 11th SAS battalion raided Italy's Tragino Aqueduct; when Filipo became old enough to pin a large blow-up of Betty Grable's legs above his bed (thought he was too young to mourn the retirement of Garbo at the age of thirty-six); when Congress passed the Lend-Lease Act but reconfirmed its determination not to commit its young men to the conflict in Europe; when Benjamin Siegel en route through the Nevada desert stopped for a coffee and pondered awhile in a roadside diner with a roulette wheel in the back; and when Cassie went eight times to see a low-budget movie *Las Vegas Nights* because it contained a couple of brief appearances by an up-and-coming singer named Frank Sinatra.

It was a summer they'd all remember.

Gina was working at her desk. To the sharp rap from across the room she called, 'Come in,' continuing calculating then glanced up, raising a surprised eyebrow as Paola came toward her. 'Since when did we start knocking on each others' doors?' Gina asked, returning to the ledger. 'Drink? Coffee? There's a thermos over there.'

'No thanks,' replied Paola.

'Uh huh,' muttered her elder sister.

For a while there was no sound in the room save the scratching of Gina's pen and the brisk swish of her turning

246

pages. Then Paola said abruptly, 'We have to talk.'

'Uh huh.' Scribble. 'Can't it wait?' Scribble. 'I'm rather busy. I think I've figured a way to make an extra . . . '

'You're always busy!'

'Of course,' Gina responded absently. 'I have to be.' She carried on writing. But then the tone of Paola's voice registered and she looked up. 'No need to be snappy, Miss. If I didn't do this,' she tapped the lists of figures, 'where do you suppose we'd be? The business doesn't run itself, you know. I sometimes wonder if you realize how much it costs to . . . ' She cut off the sentence. She'd been about to finish, 'keep you'. She snapped down her pen, angry with herself for the unheralded spark of emotion which had almost caused her to say words she would regret. Why? Was there, deep down, a grain of resentment at her sister, an invidious speck of envy at Paola's development into a self-assured, poised, beautiful woman? Absolute nonsense! What was her mind playing at? Besides, Paola wasn't really any of those things. She was still a teenager. Had barely left school. Hadn't she? Gina frowned, trying to remember her sister's age.

'Johnny and I want to get married.'

At Paola's words, Gina thought her heart had stopped. She was paralysed. She felt as if she was under water – that experience of weightlessness, the strange tactile numbness, and the sense of alien sounds coming from far away. Perhaps she was having a dream. That was it, she'd fallen asleep at her desk. She really must start getting to bed earlier.

'I hope you'll give us your blessing,' said Paola. 'Because our minds are made up. Johnny's told his parents and they're happy for us. We want you to be too.'

Gina's bemusement fractured like a coat of ice. 'What on earth are you talking about?' she demanded. 'Is this your idea of a joke?'

'Of course it isn't,' returned Paola, her voice as straight as a steel rule. 'I know this comes as a surprise . . . '

'Surprise! That's the understatement of the year, Miss. Married? What can possibly possess you to suggest such a thing? At your age? To a man you hardly know. A man you've had a couple of drinks with. The first to bat his dark lashes at you. And that's another thing, how dare he carry on behind my back, on my premises, with my sister! Last week was it, Wednesday, when I was at the catering exposition? Then he immediately asks you to marry him. The nerve! Well, see here, my girl . . . '

'It was a month ago,' Paola declared sharply, 'that he asked me. And he wanted to come and tell you right away. But I stopped him. He doesn't know I'm here. I had to come and see you alone – because I knew.'

'Knew what?'

'That you'd have an attitude.'

'An attitude? And just what did you expect when you come in here and right out of the blue . . . '

'It's hardly out of the blue, Gina. We've been going out together for nine months.' Paola's statement fell on the desk with all the effect of a live snake. But as Gina reared back, Paola continued, 'There's no point in being dramatic. Or in fighting about it. I'm sorry we didn't tell you. We wanted to, but you were always so busy, you never had time for anything, or anybody. I know, you've been doing it all for us, Filipo and me. And we appreciate it. We truly do. But somewhere along the way we sort of lost touch with you. And you lost touch with us. Don't you remember when we last sat and talked together? The night you got the job at the Starlight. Do you realize how long ago that was? I told you I wasn't a child any longer. That was 1938, when I was seventeen. It's September 1941, Gina. I was twenty years old five months ago.'

Gina, for once, couldn't cope with the figures.

Paola went on, 'And of course Johnny wasn't my first boy-friend. There were dozens at school, and a couple after who were, well . . . a bit more serious . . . you know, they . . . ' At last she smiled faintly. 'It's all part of growing up, isn't it? You understand.'

Still Gina's emotions were frayed from the abrupt abrasion of the previous moments. She chafed with uncertainty. But not merely at what to do or say; more so at the questions that had reared in her head. Was Paola's revelation really so unexpected? Had Gina truly not seen what was happening between her sister and Johnny? Had her confused motives for turning a blind eye to the situation owed much to her own feelings toward the man who had become an essential part of her life? And right now was her overriding sentiment not concern, or even anger, but rather jealousy?

Paola said, 'I got all the puppy love and teenage crushes out of my system ages ago. I now understand my emotions. I'm

248

positive of what I feel for Johnny.' She paused before adding definitely, 'I love him.'

Gina regarded her sister. She has a quiet determination, she thought. When she knows what she wants, she'll get it. Not like me, by knocking down doors; rather by persistent pushing until whatever barrier she's up against surrenders. Gina frowned as the working of her mind brought a sense of *déjà vu*. She'd been along that mental path before. With sudden recall she said aloud, 'When you had your hair cut.'

'Pardon?'

Gina blinked, pulling her memory back from that day when her sister had gone into the beauty parlour and shed not only her long youthful plait, but a part of her previous self too. Paola had been sure of the decision she made then; Gina couldn't really doubt she was any less sure of the one she was making now. The churning within her settled as she murmured, 'Just something I remembered.' She appraised Paola for a long moment; then she rose and stepped around the desk, saying, 'I hope Mister Sabato appreciates the catch he's getting.'

Paola stared, 'You mean . . . ?'

'Of course I mean.'

And they were into each others arms, laughing, and crying too; while outside the traffic hummed, along the sidewalk footsteps hurried, in the restaurant music and voices jostled. All around The Lady life busied on, unchanged. Only Gina, holding to her sister, was aware of the sadness of a childhood's end.

On the car radio Harry James was hitting notes high enough to make your hair curl. Harry Dix enthused, 'Can that man blow! The best in the world.' He grinned at Gina. 'Almost as good as I was.'

They were driving back to Manhattan after an early Sunday brunch at Paola and Johnny's new home at New Rochelle. After the wedding – the first week in October, two months ago – Gina had been shocked by the couple's decision to move out of the city, had thought they were both dyed-in-the-wool urbanites. Paola, however, had declared that after living all her twenty years above the store, she was not going to start her married life in an apartment. She'd insisted she would have, 'A real home. With a fence and a gate and a garden where children can play.' This latter announcement had silenced all

Gina's protestations. The thought of her sister, her younger sister, actually having babies, being a mother, had rendered her speechless. 'Well,' she'd said finally to Filipo, 'if they persist in living in the wilderness, we're going to have to own some means of getting there.' That had been the excuse for the purchase of the sleek, white Packard convertible which Harry had 'volunteered' to teach her to drive. Actually it was just the most massive comforter she could buy to make up one iota of the gap left in her life by her sister's leaving.

Now, as they drove along the tree-lined avenue of smart villas toward the Boston Road which would lead them back to what Gina termed 'civilization', the sun shed bright criss-cross shadows through the latticework of overhead branches. The roof of the Packard was down and the breeze was catching Gina's hair where she sat at the wheel. It had been a happy morning with Paola and Johnny, and Filipo had elected to remain with them for the afternoon. Only a small twinge of sadness had touched Gina when she and Harry drove away leaving the three grouped together, waving goodbye, at the gate.

Harry said, 'Cosy-looking, weren't they? You know, I never figured Johnny for living in the sticks, but now it isn't difficult to understand. You know, with a wife like Paola maybe I wouldn't mind laying my slippers by the hearth.'

Gina replied, 'I've never seen you as married, Harry. Besides, you're wedded to the entertainment business.'

'Sure. And we've had some times together. Back in the days when life was just one long parade of dance halls and hotel rooms, all I did was eat and sleep and play the kind of music I loved. And loved the kind of ladies who . . . ' He grinned around at Gina. 'Now you didn't think I was a you-know-what, did you? You know, there are one or two of us fellers who don't brag about their love life.' He added, 'And a few ladies, right?'

Gina bit her lip at the unexpected remark. No one had ever brought up the subject before. Since her one time with Howard Cornell she had not made love to any man. Not, of course, that she'd been short of candidates; males, young and old, single and married, rich and would-be rich were forever waving their tickets. Gina had wined and dined with several, danced with some, even touched warm lips with a few. And, frankly, there were one or two for whom she might have turned down the covers. But, somehow, she just never got around to it. There were times, when Cassie and the girls at the Lady swapped graphic details of their liaisons, that Gina's physical urges burned; on other occasions, however, the erotic gossip left her utterly empty. Still, though she sometimes wondered about the deep-rootedness of her Catholic upbringing, she never tried to analyse the reason for her feelings. She assured herself she did not need sexual relationships; her motivation and her satisfaction in life came from the building of her business, the safeguarding of her family.

Harry asked, 'Have you ever thought about it?'

'Pardon?' Gina realized she hadn't been listening as they'd reached the main highway. She wasn't sure whether the voice had come from Harry or the radio, which had switched to a newscast.

'Marriage. Like Paola. If you don't mind me saying, you'd make some guy a hell of a full-time lady.'

Gina was back in control. 'Are you offering?'

'I might at that. Except then I'd be out of a job. Being married to the boss never works out. I'd have to quit. So I guess you're going to have to settle for some young, handsome, bronzed Adonis. Tough for you, I know, but you'll just have to get me out of your mind.'

Gina laughed. 'I'll never be able to do that, Harry.' Her tensions slid away. She'd been right: with such loving friends as this why on earth should she need a man?

The radio voice was saying, ' . . . in the Philippines . . .'

Harry said, 'Me neither.' His humour quieted and he watched the oncoming road a moment before adding, 'I've never mentioned this before – you know me, as great a genius with words as I am at figures – but the day I came to The Lady . . . well . . . it was the best thing I ever did.' He held up a hand. 'No, let me finish. I just want to say that I'm grateful, Gina. You gave me . . . stability. Like I was saying about all the years I spent playing one-nighters. That's fine when you're young. A great experience. I thank God I had the chance. But comes a time you have to quit calling home the place you hang your hat, you have to put down roots. You helped me do that. And I'll always be grateful.'

The radio went on ' . . . said America will remember . . .'

'If ever you need anything,' Harry continued, 'you know you've only got to ask.'

' . . . the President said Congress would meet . . . '

Gina's foot came off the gas and her eyes fastened on the radio. In a second she was pulling to the side of the road, flicking off the motor. She sat beside Harry in stunned silence, unaware that he had reached unconsciously to grip her hand as she heard the name of the place which was as remote to her as a crater on the moon but which would remain forever branded on her life – Pearl Harbor.

Twenty-four hours later she was once more listening to a radio, in the kitchen of the Lady. Harry was again beside her, Max, Cassie and Chang too; and jammed around them the restaurant's entire staff. The whole packed room seemed to hold its breath as the announcer said,

' . . . pacifist Representative Jeanette Rankin of Montana was the only member to cast against the declaration. Thus the final vote was 388 to one in favour of House Joint Resolution 254, and as of one-thirty-two p.m. today, December 8th, 1941, the United States of America has been in a state of war with Japan.'

17

It was as if Christmas had arrived two weeks early. After their initial shock – a momentary disbelief – at the attack on Pearl Harbor, then the people went a little crazy. On streets already jangling with the festive spirit, men and women laughed louder, walked quicker, spoke with total strangers. Revenge and celebration were in the air. And when a few days later Germany and Italy declared war on the United States, the news was received with almost a sense of pleasure, as if, now that everybody knew where they stood – with either the good guys or the bad guys – they all at last could get out and get on with it and get it finished. Adolf and Musso and Tojo were going to be taught a salutary lesson, and there were few red-blooded Americans who didn't want to be personally the ones to do it. 'Over there,' they sang in the Lady every night, resurrecting the flag-waving choruses of the previous war. 'We won't be back till it's over, over there.'

Gina didn't share the euphoria.

Since the moment she'd pulled in at the side of the highway to listen to the newscast with Harry, she had been shadowed by a dark foreboding. She couldn't explain it. But nor could she dispel it. She tried; with all her will she tried. She plunged herself into the business with renewed zeal, spurring herself with the admonition that there were still hours of the day when neither the restaurant nor the club were realizing their full potential.

Monday nights always had been the worst of the week, a fact of life that had asserted itself after the Lady's novelty value had been spent by all the characters whose cocktail conversations wouldn't be complete unless they contained 'Have you been to the new place yet?' and business had settled into the nightly, weekly and monthly peaks and troughs, known to restaurants the world over, which are as inseparable from the timing of radio shows, religious festivals and local sports events as the ebbs and flows of the tides are from the phases of the moon. Gina had tried several ploys to combat the phenomenon, including special menus and cut-price wine, but still it was impossible to navigate the Monday doldrums without some loss of speed.

'Forces' night,' she now declared with counterfeit enthusiasm. 'Services personnel only. And at advantage rates. It won't interfere with our regular clientele because none of them come in Mondays anyhow. It'll be a winner, I'm sure of it.'

She was right. One small advertisement in the *Sun*, *Times* and *News* and on the first try-out Monday an hour before opening time there was a khaki, blue and black and white line a block long from the front door. The following week the assault was even greater, and by the third week it was with relief rather than annoyance that Gina learned half-a-dozen competitors were following her lead.

After a month of Forces' Mondays she announced, 'Wednesdays will be Meatless Night. There's already speculation about rationing. They have it in Europe. It's bound to arrive here. We'll forestall it. There'll be no meat whatsoever on our Wednesday menu. We'll announce that not only is this our small effort to conserve supplies but that also every dollar we don't spend on meat will be donated to the Red Cross. Customers won't shy away from the idea because they'll want to be seen to be supporting something that is aiding the war effort. And it won't cost a fortune because I can make more profit from a pound of tripe dressed up in a fancy recipe than I can from any dish using prime steak. Max, please call one of the showbusiness agencies, offer a free meatless meal to a couple of celebrities, make sure the Press is here to record them eating it.'

Max had murmured, 'Okay,' and gone to take care of it. But his face looked the way Gina felt.

His heart, she knew, like hers, wasn't in it. Max gossiped little now, had even forsaken his card-playing buddies; all his free hours he spent reading the news from Europe – more specifically from Italy. Gina understood it would be pointless to try to jolly him out of his mood, particularly as her own good humour was merely a thin mask which came off as soon as she was alone. Her despondency was further heightened when Johnny enlisted. 'He's a married man,' she protested to Paola. 'He doesn't have to go. At least make him wait to see if he's drafted.' Her sister had replied, 'Of course he has to go. And I have to let him. I don't want to watch him eating his heart out every day while he listens to the radio.' Gina was unable to put up any further argument.

Manhattan was thronged by men in uniform – with time and money to spend. The Lady was packed for as many hours as she was open despite blackouts, food rationing and gas shortages. And though the party spirit had waned, the celebrants hung on to their resolve despite the accelerating collapse of their dream.

The first months of the war had been disastrous. In the Pacific Japan had conquered the Philippines, Malaya and Burma, and destroyed the Allied fleet in the Java Sea. In North Africa the Axis armies were sweeping unchecked across Egypt, while in eastern Europe they had crossed the Caucasus to batter on the door of Stalingrad. And in the Atlantic, to the very shores of the United States, German submarines were sinking shipping at an unprecedented rate.

In later years when Gina looked back on this period, she wondered how Max had stood it for so long.

It was September of 1942 when the big man knocked hesitantly on the door of her office, entered to stand before her desk and say quietly, 'I must go, Principessa.'

Gina's throat had run dry the moment she looked up. Now she had to swallow hard before she could answer, 'I know it, old friend.' The words she saw, were what Max had been praying for. The flood of relief told her the anxieties he must have gone through to bring her this decision. She said, smiling gently, 'I'd like to hear about it.'

Max drew up a chair then, and hesitantly at first but with rising enthusiasm explained about the partisan groups acting on behalf of the Allies in Italy. With his old Albanian papers he'd approached the authorities who'd said several of his countrymen were being shipped to Europe for possible enlistment with special units who would be sent into Lombardy to join the guerillas. Max went on, detailing to Gina the reasons for his decision.

She didn't really need telling. For she knew that whatever was inside Max was in her too. When the big man ended by saying he would let Gina know when he was leaving, she answered, 'No, old friend. Don't tell me. No goodbyes between us. Just a brief parting.'

They shared a bottle of wine together that night – quietly, just the two of them at a corner table. It was the last they would share for a long time.

The autumn had gone – along with Max, and Johnny, and hundreds of thousands of young men. And with them had gone all the reckless optimism which, a year ago, had greeted the outbreak of the war. Like when the restaurant was on fire, Gina thought: the onlookers' initial aggressive expectancy had given way to dumbstruck awe as the dirt and desperation rolled in black clouds which mantled half the world.

Gina did her utmost to muster her spirits by playing her part. She allowed the services to hold promotions at the Lady; she put on fund-raising nights; provided free dinner and cabaret for the returned wounded; donated to overseas aid parcels; sold war bonds.

Still it wasn't enough. In spite of all her activity, she felt useless, rudderless, drifting with no sense of direction. Manhattan, she told herself, was no longer where her path lay, Europe was now the only place for her to be. Still for long weeks she was held back, unable to tear herself from the family. Wasn't her overriding responsibility to them? They'll survive, she silently repeated every night. I've made every safeguard for their future. Besides, I shall be away for a few months, no more. Gina strove to convince herself of this, and at last at the end of January she said to Harry, 'Remember, the day we heard the news of Pearl Harbor, you said if ever there was anything I wanted I had only to ask. Harry, I'd like to call in that favour.' Later she met Paola and Filipo and Cassie, told them that Harry would be taking care of them for a while. She did her best to explain why she had to go. And they understood. She thanked God that they understood and did not attempt to lessen her resolve; for now she was on the brink it would take all her strength to make the final step.

Alone in her room she sat wrapped in her own arms, and if anyone had come in they'd have thought from her pale face that she was ill. Later, swaddled against the hardening winter, she walked through Central Park. She looked at the birds and the leafless trees and the people, all seemingly unchanged from the days she visited here in a secondhand cloth coat. She bought a sandwich and a coffee at the outdoor lunch bar, lingered there watching young mothers strolling, some hurrying, with their children. Then she went and stood before the Bethesda Fountain. It wasn't working, and the brick terrace was silent, very silent as Gina stared out across the lake to the cold misted hills on the opposite shore.

It was late afternoon when she finally left the park and walked purposefully to the Red Cross office. Yes, they assured her, of course she'd be welcome, her particular skills would be most useful here in New York.

Gina replied that wasn't what she wanted.

A fortnight later, on a cold, blustery morning, the second week of February 1943, she stood at the rail of the ship, facing toward the prow as it ploughed into the grey troughs of the Atlantic. She didn't look back.

PART THREE

The time between

1943-1945

18

The Piccadilly Circus illuminated by March moonlight where Gina arrived was very different from the war-ravaged city of her imagination. Almost eleven p.m. yet the place was swarming. It was, after all, Saturday night she told herself; nevertheless, she hadn't expected so many people. And all laughing. Everyone seemed to be laughing as they surged along the pavement and spilled into the roadway, waving good-naturedly at motor cars, cyclists, army lorries, double-decker London Transport buses and the Red Cross van in which Gina was travelling. Though the blackout was in force, Gina could see clearly through the windscreen the moving mass of muted colours flowing against a monochromatic landscape, the contrast of which was accentuated by the white-painted kerb stones, doorsteps, lamp posts and vehicle fenders.

'This is it, girls,' announced the female driver who had brought Gina and six other S.R.A.O. volunteers from the Southampton docks. 'Welcome to the Rainbow Corner Club.' She pulled up at the bustling doorway on Shaftesbury Avenue, cut the engine, adding, 'Better known to the locals as Yanks' Paradise.'

Gina and her companions climbed out to be greeted immediately by a charge of khaki uniforms, hands grabbing their suitcases and wide, welcoming American smiles. They were exhorted, with much badinage, copious blandishments and not a little behind-patting, through a lobby which reminded Gina of Times Square on Christmas Eve. En route along teeming corridors she saw direction signs which included CANTEEN, MOVIE THEATRE, LIBRARY and BATHS.

As if reading her mind, the stocky-as-a-keg, bald-as-a-bullet character with three stripes on his sleeve who was toting her bag, yelled above the racket of laughter and music, 'They got everything in this joint. I mean everything! Guy could live and die here . . . ' he beamed ear-to-ear appreciation at a passing blonde ' . . . and not realize he'd gone to heaven. Still,' he elbowed Gina in the ribs, winked like a signal lamp, 'for those little extras you might need – you know, genu-ine French perfume, re-al silk stockings – just call my name. Tucker. Supply Sergeant Tucker R. Roscoe to you, Babe.'

Gina didn't flinch at the familiarity – an Atlantic crossing on a troop ship was enough to banish the modesty of a nun, the correctitude of a duchess, not to mention the ill-founded belief of the U.S. Army that the commissioning of all-female Red Cross personnel would render them secure from advances by male privates. She smiled at her self-appointed porter. 'Thanks. I'll remember.' The good humour however was not a reflection on the way she felt.

She revealed her true emotion twenty minutes later.

The soldiers, with promises of, 'Catch you in the bar,' had left the girls at the office on the second floor. Here the green-uniformed officer had explained the function of the Rainbow Corner Club as the recreation centre and hostel for GIs on leave in the English capital. 'We also,' he said, 'run a restaurant which makes General Motors' cafeteria look like a snack bar. Sixty thousand meals in twenty-four hours is our record.' He smiled, let the figure sink in. 'Believe me, if your particular skills are needed any place, this is it.'

Gina knew it. Though she didn't like it. After the man had explained the work schedules, and the girls had filed out to find their allotted rooms, Gina remained before the desk. She said, 'I didn't want to come here.'

The middle-aged, pleasant-faced man frowned.

Now Gina tried to explain – as she had at the Supplemental Recreation Activities Overseas office in New York, and, later, to Harry.

In 1941 the marching orders for the Red Cross simply had been to follow the Army, Navy, Air Force and Marines. It meant serving coffee to battle-weary troops on bloody Guadalcanal; it meant running a movie projector against the background din of an artillery barrage in the Algerian desert; it meant driving a station wagon loaded with doughnuts and cigarettes through a bomb-blasted pass between India and China. And these were the places Gina had expected to be. She would never be able to clarify her reasoning, not even to herself – it might have been some sort of idealism, maybe even coloured with a touch of romanticism – she merely was convinced that her role had to be played at the front lines. 'I know I've pledged to go wherever I'm sent,' she'd said to Harry. 'But I never imagined it would be London. I don't see what use I'll be there. I might as well stay in Manhattan.'

Harry had replied gently, 'I understand how you feel. If I was young enough, and had both lungs, I'd want to be where the action is too. But, Gina, you don't have to get shot to prove your worth. Your cooking – and your smile – are what our guys need. And you'll be serving more of them at the Rainbow than you would, say, in a clubmobile on a Pacific island beach. So, accept that what you're giving is enough. More than enough.'

Gina had been grateful for Harry's affection and sound advice. She knew he was right. She knew the sympathetic man in the office overlooking Shaftesbury Avenue was right when he echoed Harry's words. Still she said, 'I hope you'll be able to arrange a transfer for me as soon as is convenient.'

She carried her suitcase along the hall, angry at her own perversity, but unable to shed the feeling, particularly after she'd discovered her bedroom with its stylish furnishings, warm pink carpet and matching eiderdowns on the twin beds. So the rumours she'd heard in New York were true – this was the Red Cross's 'glamour' posting. Was it also true what some said about the girls here – that they were just snobbish, rich misses interested only in a good time with officers who were a long way from home and wifely affection? Gina feared the answer was most likely 'yes' when she opened the wardrobe to be faced by a rail bowed with the weight of her absent roommate's originals. On checking the dresser drawer she was further confronted by lingerie, stockings and cosmetics which, she was sure, would have made Supply Sergeant Roscoe Tucker's eyes fall out.

Having contrived the storage of her own few possessions she retraced the route to the riotous lobby. She considered going to eat, but her mood and her tiredness convinced her that putting on a happy face for the new surroundings would require a mighty effort. The best place for Gina Rossi was bed. She'd feel heaps better in the morning.

On that conclusion she bought postage stamps at the desk, returned upstairs to write brief news and love to all at The Lady, and was asleep while London partied on.

* * *

She was woken at eight a.m. In the still-curtained room the clock was visible in the pale light of the lamp beside the other bed. So was the female figure hanging a dress in the wardrobe. Sitting upright, Gina rubbed the sleep from her eyes, took a second to remember she was three thousand miles from home, then said, 'Hi.'

The figure turned.

Nature had been generous to Sybil Levy, née De Belvere, though not in any of the places that might have endeared her to the cameras of either *Vogue* or *Heavenly Bodies*. But while from neck to hip she was as well-upholstered as a sofa, her legs, which were revealed to Gina as she stepped out of her slip, would have run Grable a close second, and her face, softly illuminated by the lamp, was finely boned with an upturning mouth and large hazel eyes. When she reached up and unpinned her piled hair it tumbled in luxuriant, auburn tresses to below her dumpling shoulders. Turning, she saw Gina, greeted, in a voice which leapt straight from *Private Lives*, 'Hello there. Did I wake you? Sorry. Thought you were dead to the world. The way I feel. What a Saturday night!' She plumped to the edge of her wincing mattress, began to unroll her stockings; on a second thought added, 'I'm Sybil, by the way. Levy, née De Belvere.' She yawned, continued to undress.

'Gina. Gina Rossi. From Manhattan.'

Sybil pulled on a voluminous nightgown of cream silk and coffee lace. 'Lovely to meet you. Can't talk now. Absolutely too flaked.' She formed a great mound beneath the covers. 'Meet you in the lobby at three. G'night.' Within a moment her breathing deepened into sleep.

For quite a while Gina lay watching her room-mate, her previous night's suspicions of the Rainbow's girl's lifestyles deepening. She jolted out of her pessimistic preoccupation only when she realized she had better find out where she was on the duty roster.

'No need to start work today,' said the officer she'd talked with ten hours ago. 'Take a look around. Get your bearings. Meet the crew. You can pick up your schedule tomorrow. Don't worry, we aren't too rigid around here, so long as we've got all our bases covered we never argue if you girls swap around with each other. Take it easy.' He smiled. 'Enjoy yourself.'

I'm not here to enjoy myself, she inwardly fumed as she

went down the stairs. Her anger however couldn't hold its edge. Everywhere she turned there were happy faces, cheerful greetings in every American accent she could place plus several she couldn't: there was a greater slice of the U.S.A. here than ever there'd been in New York. She felt at home. Damn it, she didn't want to feel at home!

For the next few hours she checked out the building: the hugely-stocked library where *S.S. Van Dine* rubbed shoulders with Ralph Waldo Emerson; the movie theatre where Hedy Lamarr breathed huskily, 'I am Tondelayo,' in *White Cargo*; the general store where two laughing girls distributed a newly arrived batch of Hershey Kisses along with free samples of the real thing; the vast kitchens where a squad of cooks raced to keep up with nonstop orders; and the permanently full cafeteria where meatloaf, eggs, fries and pancakes were consumed at the same pace as Glenn Miller's 'Little Brown Jug' which seemed to jitterbug constantly from the indefatigable jukebox.

The Rainbow Corner Club had all the facilities, all the atmosphere, all the supplies of a resort hotel catering for a perpetual convention. While Gina couldn't help but admire its professionalism, appreciate its dedication, she was unable to shed her resentment of its vivacity; and surely, she told herself, it couldn't be reflective of the surrounding city reportedly wasted by the deprivations of more than three years of conflict.

She introduced herself around, discovered her name on the week's waitress rota, and learned that she, like all the Rainbow girls, would work shifts cooking, cleaning, serving and clerking. After eating a sparing lunch she arrived in the lobby for her date with her room-mate.

Sybil was wearing a bottle-green, sackbacked, three-quarter coat with huge shell-shaped buttons; her hair secured by a trio of gold-headed pins beneath a brown crocheted beret crossed by a pair of foot-long quills. 'Hello,' she greeted. 'Slept like a log. Quick snifter now, then a constitutional. Never miss either. What's yours? Too early? Right-ho, I'll have my swift one while you fetch your coat. See you in two minutes,'

It took exactly that time for Gina to hurry upstairs and return – pursued at every step by the mounting conviction that this entire trip was proving an unvarnished disaster.

'Fortified,' declared a waiting Sybil. 'Let's go.'

They went out to mid-Sunday afternoon in London.

263

It could have been Fat Tuesday night in Rio.

If Gina had been surprised by the activity on the streets eighteen hours ago, now she was stunned; even Manhattan, at this particular time of the week, was nothing like this. In the cold, crystalline sunshine, the crowd streamed back and forth, its mass ebbing and flowing steadily, while groups broke away to eddy around doorways or be pulled into the whirlpool of rumbustious activity around the Erosless fountain at the hub of the Circus. The carnival atmosphere was raised in the laughter and ruckus of the promenaders, heightened by the drum and brass accompaniment from a corner Salvation Army band.

So many uniforms, thought Gina: not only all three services of Britain and America, but, at a glance, she also saw Canadian airmen, Australian sailors, New Zealand soldiers, French and Dutch military police.

Sybil said, 'They call it Allied Main Street.' She pointed to distant trees along Piccadilly. 'A straight line, half a mile. From Green Park,' she swivelled around, 'to Leicester Square. If you fancy a taste of the *entente cordiale*, this is where it's always fizzing – particularly on a Sunday afternoon, when London's workers are at home, and there's hardly any traffic. Come along, dear, we'll stroll the boulevard, and, if we're lucky,' she winked at Gina, nodded toward two ambling U.S. M.P.s, 'we just might get arrested.'

They crossed the intersections around the arc of the Circus to turn into Coventry Street. Outside Lyon's Corner House, two lines – mostly couples, smiling and hugging in feet-shuffling patience – waited at the two entrances, one for the tea room, and one for the cafeteria which, Gina read on the sign, offered a variety of three courses, all with bread and butter ('or margarine,' added the rider) for 1s. 4d. Gina, after a rapid mental conversion of pence to cents concluded it was no wonder the American servicemen at the Rainbow had money to burn. But a couple of minutes later she decided so too had the British for there were hordes of civilians in a side street jostling to buy from a row of street carts: she saw one was stacked with cherries, another with rose-and-maidenfern boutonnières, another with toy monkeys on sticks. Hardly items she'd expected to see in a city supposedly starved of staple food and materials let alone luxury goods or trivia.

Her sense of depression deepened the further she walked amid the lighthearted multitude.

A further line was standing outside the Ritz cinema where the showcards depicted the burning of Atlanta, the carnage of Gettysburg and other already-legendary scenes featuring Gable and Vivien Leigh in *Gone with the Wind*.

'Been showing for four years,' remarked Sybil. 'Personally I couldn't understand what all the fuss was about. Lot of romantic tosh. Mind you, I wouldn't mind fighting a civil war with old Clark. In fact, to tell the truth, at the moment, I'd settle for fifteen minutes unarmed combat with Harpo Marx. God,' (pronouncing it, 'Gahd') she exclaimed frustratedly, 'All these prime contenders swarming the streets, desperate for a workout, yet you wouldn't believe how long it is since I went so much as a three-minute round.'

Despite her mood, Gina couldn't resist a smile at her room-mate's humorous exaggeration. Although, she wondered, if Sybil was telling the truth about her lack of male entanglement, then what had she been doing all night? Before she could come up with a reputable means of broaching the subject, they had passed the cinema, next door Forte's Milk Bar (filled to overflowing) and paused to permit Sybil to survey the display in the Dolcis shoe shop.

Surprise tugged Gina toward the window. The meagre collection of footwear was the first indication she'd seen of the war's effect on London. In America the restrictions on the use of leather for non-military goods had been noticeable but not conspicuous. When Gina had left Manhattan women were still clunking around on the latest ankle-breaking five-inch heels and platform soles in patent, suede and kid imported from Mexico, Brazil and all those other countries who at the single stroke of declaring neutrality had increased their export trade by several hundred per cent. Here, however, the array she was observing, though undeniably sturdy and ingenious, could not by any stretch of the imagination be considered either elegant or feminine, fabricated as they were from such unlikely materials as canvas, straw, gabardine, and even papier mâché.

'Imagine,' bemoaned Sybil, 'having to part with five coupons for those things. How on earth can the government expect women to keep up their morale without a decent pair of shoes?' Exhaling exasperatedly she stalked away from the window.

They continued on, past the Monseigneur News Theatre where the main feature was the latest Pathé report of the British victory in Tripoli; in front of Chris's Restaurant where, despite the cold, a high-spirited group of nurses and their boyfriends were congregated around three pavement tables; beneath the marquees of the Hippodrome where *Battle Song* was scheduled to replace *Jack and the Beanstalk*; to the corner of Charing Cross Road where the crowd U-turned to retrace its route along the opposite side of the street.

'I thought all the girls at the Rainbow would be American,' said Gina with a determined effort to put the stroll on a more personal basis and find something about her room-mate she could translate into friendship.

'I am,' Sybil replied lightly. 'By marriage.'

Gina nodded understanding. 'Levy, of course.' Added, in a jokey attempt at mateyness. 'A solid New Jersey name.'

'South Dakota, actually,' returned Sybil. 'Always reckoned he was the country's only Jewish lumberjack.' She added, 'To save you wondering, and to clear the air right away, as it were - - yes, we were an odd match. Social chalk and cheese. But at twenty-six, while I'd managed to avoid being paired off as the family prize heifer – the time-honoured strategy of consolidating the De Belvere acreage – I found the only remaining males either smelled permanently of horses or looked like them. Then I met Bernie. I'd joined the Land Army at the start of the war. He was on an exchange visit with the Forestry Commission near the farm where I was stationed. He was the biggest, darkest, sexiest, gorgeousest thing I'd ever seen on two legs. I said to myself, Sybil old girl, boats like this sail in once in a lifetime, if you miss it . . . .

'We were married in darkest secret in deepest Somerset. Ma and Pa had apoplexy, of course. I was thrice-damned. For spurning my heritage, for wedding a gentleman of the Jewish persuasion – Bernie's parents were equally stricken by his marriage to a shiksa – and, the direst crime of all, for becoming an American.' Glancing around, Sybil answered Gina's unspoken question. 'Yes, I was cut off without the proverbial bean. And, no, I have never regretted it.' She smiled. 'There you are, a swift resumé of my romantic history. You can tell me yours – if you wish – when we get back to the club.'

Gina mentally frowned, wondered whether she should, or could. 'Married long?' she asked.

'A month.'

'You were married just a month ago?'

'No. We were married for a month – November to be precise – in 1941. Before Bernie was called home, called up, and shipped to Corregidor.'

Gina, literally, missed a pace. She strode to rematch her step to Sybil. She felt dreadful, walking in a vacuum, her sense of confidence in forging companionship having been blown away in an instant.

Sybil hadn't said her husband had been killed during the infamous five-month bombardment that had reduced the Manila Bay island to rubble, but words hadn't been necessary. Gina simply knew. And it profoundly shocked her. She wasn't sure why. After all, she'd been faced by such announcements before, both at a close personal level as well as at a greater distance. Yet none had struck her so forecefully; in the dreamlike atmosphere of these vacationing streets the abrupt mention of death was an all-too-real, brutal intrusion.

'He was one of the first thousand to give his life – as they put it in all the best melodramas – for freedom and the flag,' Sybil offered breezily. 'They sent me a letter to say so. Signed by a general. Just imagine, this important chap in Washington taking the trouble personally to put his name on a missive to me, plus nine-hundred-and-ninety-nine other proud wives. Oh, look . . . .' she peered into the bookshop window. 'A new Ethel M. Dell. I must post a copy to Ma tomorrow. She thrives on the things. Yes, we do communicate again. By post and phone. Though she daren't admit it to Pa. How about a spot of tea? You know the Ritz? The last haven of sanity in a world gone mad. By the way, welcome to London. It's lovely to have you.' She linked arms with Gina. 'I'm sure we're going to get along famously.'

And they did. Though Gina took a while to come to terms with Sybil's light-hearted banter, she was dearly grateful for the English girl's warmth and wit in a situation where her own chill sense of inadequacy refused to retreat. Sybil eased Gina's path into the hurly-burly of the Red Cross club, swapped her daily duties so that they could work together, lent her cosmetics and stockings and hats ('Damn shortage of materials. Women are having to make do with headscarves, Babushka-style. A hideous indignity. Heaven help Adolf if he's ever cornered by a troop of hatless, shoeless British females'), taught her how to play bridge ('Second only to flower arranging as an essential for a middle-class English wife's social success') which Gina learned with counterfeit enthusiasm, and, on hearing about the Lady, plied her with traditional native recipes for everything from Cornish pasties and Yorkshire pudding to Bakewell tart and Bath buns which Gina accepted, and recorded, with genuine gratitude.

These were Gina's and Sybil's days together.

Their nights, however, were always spent apart.

At every seven p.m. Sybil would rush to keep some appointment, promising that as soon as she had a free evening she'd show Gina 'some super, seamy Soho spots'. For her part, Gina, though she would have welcomed a break away from the unremitting pandemonium of the Rainbow, was not overanxious to have to put on a happy face for a night on the town. Besides, she was sure – knowing Sybil's preoccupation – that any such expedition was more than likely to end up as a manhunt. And that was the last thing Gina Rossi needed right now. It was tough enough to turn a deaf ear to the never-ceasing overtures of the club's male population. For she began to understand what the GIs had been through, learned how long many of them had been at the forefront of the war, realized that their amorous advances (often bluntly physical) were intended as neither an insult nor a compliment; these were just men (civilians, she had to remind herself – butchers, barbers, bankers, bakers – in uniform) who, back from some indescribable place, needed to touch and be touched.

'That's what all the S.R.A.O. volunteers appreciate,' she wrote to Cassie. 'At first I was like everybody else back home, thought most of the Red Cross girls posted to London were good-time Annies. Not so. They're just healthy females in exotic surroundings, outnumbered by men five hundred to one (stop watering at the mouth). As normal as you and me (yes we are so, normal – well, almost). But anyone who expects them to stay indefinitely celibate in this situation is either out of touch with reality, or just a plain, old-fashioned (jealous-to-death) spoilsport. Certainly, a few of the girls are a bit more free-and-easy with their favours than average, and one of them reputedly got herself "in the club" as Sybil puts it (more of S. Levy née De Belvere on the next page), but frankly, when I recall the lurid confessions that circulated in the locker room at the Howard West, I'm astonished that such incidents here are so rare. Anyhow, what it boils down to is, we all work our buns off during our shifts, but when we're off duty . . . !!! (Do not read this sentence to Paola – or anyone else for that matter.)'

You damned hypocrite, Gina.

She castigated herself when she reviewed that part of the letter. Nevertheless, she didn't delete it.

What she did was expunge it from her mind. Tried to expunge it from her mind; as she tried to tell herself that she was immune to the constant propinquity of so many men. On her sixth day at the Rainbow she asked again about a transfer overseas. On the twelfth day when she put in the same enquiry, the officer made no bones about his vexation at her persistence.

On the fourteenth day she dreamt of Robert Fallon.

She woke, hot, sticky and confused in a tangle of sheets. In the darkness the Englishman's features were still before her as clear as if projected on a screen, and it wasn't until the outside traffic noise penetrated her consciousness that Gina realized the dream had ended.

Rising, quickly pulling on her robe, she part opened the curtains, looked down onto the early morning avenue, vehicles and people hurrying into the oncoming day, a scene that was now as familiar as that beyond her window on Forty-Seventh Street. With that thought came a pang of homesickness. Gina returned to sit on the edge of the bed. And the image of Fallon went with her – along with all she had felt for him in that time of summer laughter before winter overtook their lives; not the besotted yearning of her teenage years, but the deeper, mature affection for the Englishman, which, since a slice of her heart had been stolen, and discarded, by Howard Cornell, she'd thought she would never reconjure.

What juvenile romanticizing!

She stood abruptly, strode down the hall to the bathroom, cold showered, remaining beneath the icy needles until every centimetre of her skin was goose-pimpled and her teeth were chattering.

Back in the bedroom she dressed swiftly. Within twenty minutes of waking from her dream she was stalking along Piccadilly, the chill morning air stinging her eyes, invigorating her blood, driving out all girlish whimsies about Mister Robert Fallon. The time had come to start getting a grip. You will stop moping, her inner voice ordered. You will cease wallowing in self-pity. If you feel no sense of comradeship in this city, that's because you haven't made the effort. If you're going to sit in

269

your room every night waiting for the world to come to you, you'll wait a very long time. Get off your butt. Get out. And about. Today.

During the next six hours Gina saw more of London – the West End that is – than she'd seen over the past fortnight. From a phone box outside the Green Park Underground station she'd called the Rainbow, had no problem switching her shift with one of the other girls. Then she walked. She walked thoroughfares which were legends of her childhood: Constitution Hill, the Mall, Trafalgar Square, the Strand, Drury Lane, Oxford Street, Bond Street. Here she paused on a corner. Remembering: the corner of another Bond Street, and a second-hand clothes store, a twenty-two-year-old Italian girl exiting with her younger sister and brother toting brown paper packages tied with hairy string. Gina smiled. Looking around she spied a small café. Her appetite had risen with her spirits, and she lunched on rissoles and boiled carrots with a pot of tea. That all three were indescribably dreadful was of no account; she was beginning to feel like her old self again.

It was only early afternoon, several more hours before she was due on duty. She wished Sybil was here, wished she had a friend with whom to spend this time, that there was someone in London to share her strengthening enthusiasm.

There was; at least there used to be. How long was it since she wrote to David Lowell? Over a year. His last letter had said he'd been invalided out of the Navy. Would he still be in the city? Would he welcome the sudden arrival of a woman he'd met only once, an age ago, in Fallon's Rome apartment? (Forget Fallon.) Could Gina even remember his address?

Of course. And there was no point in standing outside this café embroiled in futile speculation for another moment. Gina found a post office, checked the telephone directory, enquired about buses that would take her to Richmond, purchased a street map.

No, the sun hadn't come out as she rode on the top level of the double-decker, it just seemed that way. The conductress giving change from the satchel around her neck, acknowledged, 'Threepence, thanks, love,' as she cranked her ticket machine, responded cheerily, 'Of course I will,' when Gina asked if she'd tell her when they reached the spot the post office clerk had marked on the map. Gina was warmed by the brief intimacy. She watched London trundle by; the Thames flowing beneath as they crossed a bridge; the congregation of the city giving way to green, open spaces, white-painted houses, colourful clusters of small boats bobbing as if in busy conversation at wooden jetties. England from a picture book.

On the opposite seat, a sandy-haired young man with an Auxiliary Fire Service arm band was looking at her ankles. She threw him a wink.

'Ferry Point,' the conductress called from below.

19

Though the trees were starkly leafless and the roadside grasses were deadened by winter, still there was almost a feel of spring in the air, an impression heightened by snowdrops, yellow and purple crocuses in the gardens of the riverside villas.

Gina's mood brightened the further she walked. By the time she reached Devonshire Close there was a bounce in her step and a swing in her arms and she was whistling ''Bye 'Bye Black-bird'. She turned into the wide street. On each side banks of laurels and rhododendrons permitted glimpses of extensive mock Tudor homes, some with large shiny motor cars on their forecourts. None of the houses however could have been mistaken for the Grange Hotel. Even without its gateside nameboard it would have been apparent as the rambling, gabled and turreted, red brick building at the end of the short cul-de-sac.

Gina approached along a gravelled drive between an over-grown shrubbery and a worm-cast measled lawn with rusting croquet hoops. The air of neglect was manifest even before she was close enough to see the flaking paintwork and last autumn's black leaves windblown into drifts against the building. Her good spirits ebbed as she pressed the bellpush, waited, reading the sign above the door which proclaimed that David Arthur Lowell was licensed to sell beer, spirits and tobacco.

Sharp footsteps across an uncarpeted floor and the door opened. Only then did Gina realize she couldn't remember what he looked like.

He was slim in grey slacks and a Fair Isle sweater. His hair

271

was blonde falling across his brow above blue eyes in a finely cut, pleasant face. 'Yes?' he said, his voice and his features admitting nonrecognition.

'Gina,' she offered. 'Gina Rossi.'

For a moment he was nonplussed, then he blurted, 'Good heavens! Well, come in. Please, come in.' And he welcomed her into the broad, oak-panelled hall, led the way past carved doors and a handsome balustered staircase, hesitated, as if unsure which direction to choose, before ushering Gina into a small room with a window overlooking the large, unruly gardens. 'Here,' he said with a mixture of embarrassment and pleasure, pulling magazines from an armchair, giving the cushion a swift swat for dust. 'Do sit down. May I take your coat? No, perhaps not. It's somewhat chilly in here.' He bent to switch on an electric fire in front of the boarded-over grate.

As Gina sat she glanced around, took in old but excellent furniture, leather and walnut, Afghan carpets, Victorian watercolours in gilt frames; but she noticed too the film of dust, discerned the smell of must in a room rarely used. Smiling brightly she said, 'I'm sorry for turning up unannounced. I didn't realize the hotel wasn't open. I thought . . .' She saw that he had only one arm. Recovering quickly, she was about to continue but was trapped by uncertainty, knowing he had caught the fleeting shock in her eyes. Before she could compose a reputable sentence he came to her rescue:

'Please, don't apologize. My fault. When I wrote and told you I'd been wounded I should have been more specific. But,' he shrugged, 'my emotions were a trifle shaky at the time. Self-pity, you know is unavoidable, even when you're aware of the thousands of people who are worse off.'

The statement was straightforward, held no affectation. Like the man, thought Gina, and she recalled with sudden clarity her one and only meeting with him in Fallon's Rome apartment when he had caused her to laugh at his hotelier's anecdotes. She knew then, as she did now, that she liked David Lowell.

'Well,' he said, sitting opposite, 'this is a delightful surprise. I don't get many personal visitors these days.' He glanced around, smiled wryly. 'Which, I suppose, is fairly obvious. No family, and all my chums are away fighting for king and country. So, how are you? How's the Lady? What on earth are you doing over here?'

Gina replied, 'I'm fine, thank you. So is the restaurant –

I hope.' She was tempted to go on, to describe her success, to say she wasn't really worried about the business because of the many good friends she had in Manhattan. Her enthusiasm however remained unvoiced; instead she said, 'I'm with the Red Cross.' As David responded with interest, she went on to explain, as best she could, her reasons for volunteering and to describe the Atlantic crossing and her first days in London. She didn't, however, mention her disillusion, and when David asked about her impressions of the city, she answered noncommittally, restricted her compliments to the architecture.

He enquired if she'd sampled any local restaurants and at her negative answer (she decided to forget the awful rissoles and carrots) said she must, that despite severe rationing many establishments were battling heroically on with dried egg, whale and horse meat, and such vegetable delicacies as curly kale and nettles. It sounded a far cry from the horn of plenty that poured into the Rainbow Club kitchen, and Gina once more was obliged to wonder if the story of deprivation was – albeit well-meaningly – exaggerated.

They chatted for another fifteen minutes before David stood abruptly, saying, 'I am forgetting my manners, aren't I? May I offer you a drink? Tea? No coffee, I'm afraid. Or how about a martini? I still have a few precious bottles of Italian vermouth. I know most of my countrymen consider it somewhat debauched to imbibe before sundown but it isn't every day I get the opportunity to demonstrate the perfection of my American cocktails to a genuine expert.'

Setting aside her usual daylight temperance, Gina said she'd love a martini and followed David across the hall and into a cosy, beamed and panelled bar. Perching on a stool, she faced him across the burnished counter as he deftly produced a silver shaker, gin and other ingredients. His one-handed skill was remarkable, and Gina hoped her eyes didn't betray the fascination she was unable to suppress.

'Nifty, eh?' He winked, swiftly recapping the liquor. Then he saw the tinge of embarrassment his remark had caused and said, 'Sorry. That was bad taste. Bit of an act I put on for the clientele. They'll buy several extra rounds a night just to see me do my stuff. I don't blame them. I'm the one at fault for showing off. But . . . . I didn't invite you in here to witness my performance.' He paused in his preparations, grinned sheepishly and added, 'Well, maybe I did . . . just a little.'

Gina relaxed, grateful to him for releasing her uncertainty. She smiled, 'Do you have many customers here to appreciate your talent?'

'Local residents mostly. But I have to keep the bar open to meet the requirements of the liquor laws, otherwise I might lose the licence. Whether, in the long term, that would matter, I don't know. But, then, there aren't any certainties left, are there? We just have to hope.' David stood two glasses on the counter and poured from the shaker. 'One moment.' Olives were produced, speared and popped into the cocktails. 'Now. Signorina. *Per favore* . . . ' His face held the hesitant anticipation of a small boy awaiting his elder's approval.

Gina lifted the glass with mock gravity, held it to the light, sniffed it, touched it to her lips and sipped. Straightfaced, she stared at him, then proclaimed, '*Eccellente!*' added, with a pronounced American accent, 'Mister, you mix one helluva damned fine Martini.'

David beamed with appreciation, chinked his glass to Gina's and toasted, 'Mud in your eye.'

She asked, 'Are there any guests in the hotel?'

He shook his head. 'Our trade used to be what I suppose you'd call genteel middle-class. Their flow was drying up even before '39. The Depression had closed so many small businesses, and the families who survived began to take extra care of their money. Holidays were no longer considered an essential of life. Then, when war was declared, our reservations dropped almost to zero. Petrol rationing was, of course, a strong factor, but the major reason was the bombing. People were simply too afraid to come to London.'

Gina considered pursuing the subject of the Blitz, but, knowing that might lead to confessing her scepticism of its intensity, she raised her glass and said, 'Well, here's to peace, and a return to full reservation books for all hotels and restaurants.'

David agreed, 'Worth drinking to,' and after they'd both downed their liquor he refilled the glasses. There followed another quarter hour's gossip about the catering trade before he asked casually, 'Do you hear from Fallon?'

Gina almost caught her breath. The question was so unexpected. Or was it? Had she known, ever since she decided on this visit, that her motive wasn't solely to renew her acquaintanceship with David Lowell, nor even to assuage her

274

depression? Had her true reason, her only reason, been to learn the whereabouts of the Reuters correspondent? Had her attempt to sublimate her deep-seated emotions been defeated? Gina indulged this self-examination several moments before answering, 'I haven't heard from him for many years.' She studied David's face, ventured, 'Is he in town?'

'He's somewhere in North Africa, following Montgomery. Been there since Alamein last October. I've received a couple of letters. Naturally, nothing strategic, usually about the enormous quantity of booze he and his fellow correspondents consume, and the number of women they . . .'

Gina saw David's jaw snap shut, watched the colour bloom on his cheeks. She enquired lightly, 'Does that mean he's still unmarried?'

David seized the opportunity to be off the hook. 'Only a hundred-and-one per cent. Fallon as a member of the slippers-by-the-hearth, potting-fuschias-in-the-greenhouse brigade? Can you imagine that? It isn't just the work that keeps him living out of a suitcase, you know. It's something more. Wanderlust I suppose you'd call it. Forever wanting to see what's over the next hill. He can't even settle down long enough to finish his book. Which is a pity because he's a damn fine writer, a caring writer. What he needs is someone to tie him to his chair for a year. Not a wife, but . . . ' He turned the stem of his glass between his fingers.

Yes, thought Gina, you have gone far enough. Yet she wanted him to say more. The desire to hear about Fallon was irresistible. The features which had woken her from sleep this morning were suddenly again in her head, even more vivid now, rivetting her attention as she watched him in Ristorante Rossi, his lips curving in a smile, his fathomless grey eyes examining the crowd while his teeth closed on the stem of his unlit pipe. She returned to David, glad he couldn't see behind her eyes.

He observed, 'He doesn't even have a girlfriend.'

She made an umming sound which she hoped conveyed vague disinterest, then remarked, 'He's been overseas a long time. Does he get a furlough?'

'He said he hoped to be home in September.'

A hard finger prodded her with the reminder that she'd asked for a transfer as soon as possible. She exclaimed, 'Is that the time? I must get back to town.'

'So soon? Yes, I realize you have to. All those hungry GIs to feed. Do me a small favour, please tell them there's a terrific bar here by the river.'

'Run by a feller who mixes the best Martini this side of the Brooklyn Bridge. I'll do that, with pleasure.' Gina slid from the stool, allowed David to lead her to the hall.

He requested, 'Wait while I get my overcoat. I don't have a car to drive you, but I'll walk you to the bus stop.' Before Gina could refuse he had hurried away. She studied the hanging sepia photographs of old Thames sailing barges until he returned in a broad-lapelled herringbone, maroon muffler and trilby. Leslie Howard, she thought fondly and when he asked, 'Do you have time for a quick tour of the old homestead?' she replied without hesitation, 'Of course.'

He went ahead, opening the doors of the ground floor rooms, explaining how the building had been extended over the years, interspersing his tale with humorous anecdotes about past guests, as well as with snippets of family history. And it wasn't long before Gina realized that despite his earlier allusions to the contrary – and perhaps in spite of himself – David Lowell felt the same affection for this place as she did for The Lady. He was as much an hotelier as she was a restaurateur.

After they'd passed through a finely corniced dining room of shrouded tables and chairs, and a vast, ancient kitchen, David went ahead up spiral stone steps.

He said, 'My great-grandfather founded the place as a coaching inn, a century ago when all the area between the local villages – Kew, Richmond, Mortlake – was still farmland. Over the years more and more bits were tacked on until we ended up with the present maze. There are four staircases, goodness knows how many corridors, and, I think, fifty rooms.'

Gina peeped through a circular window, into another hallway. 'It's fascinating,' she complimented.

'Certainly,' accepted David. 'Our guests used to love it. But few of them probably paused to imagine what a devil it was to heat, clean and upkeep. Even before the war, with rising costs, it had become quite unviable. I kept it going after my parents were killed in a sailing accident in '31 – it was the only trade I knew – but it was obvious I'd have to close eventually. I have to say, my father was typical of many of his class and generation. He made excellent profits throughout the twenties. But he spent the lot – and then some. Not a penny was ever re-invested in the business. When I inherited I carried out some modernization, though I had to borrow substantially to do so. As it turned out, all I achieved was an accumulation of debts. Nowadays, what I make from the bar, plus my pension for this chap,' he nodded at his missing arm, 'barely covers expenses and the interest on the mortgages. To be honest, if a guest turned up tonight, I doubt I'd have the wherewithal to provide heat and light for his room.'

David opened up a couple of bedrooms, darkly Victorian and smelling of damp, and a bathroom with a monstrous lion-clawed tub on bare board floors. Another landing took them along the front of the hotel with window views of the river, the purpling shades of dusk gathering amid the trees on the distant bank. The main staircase led down to the front entrance hall.

Halting beside David, Gina said, 'Thank you for the tour. It's a wonderful building. I hope when the war's over trade will pick up again. I'm sure it will.' That, she thought, sounded slightly patronizing and she searched vainly for something more to say to this gentle man whose life had been torn by uncontrollable events.

'One doesn't have to worry.' David shrugged philosophically. 'Of course I feel a certain amount of nostalgia for the old barn. But I keep it in check by reminding myself of the gloomier aspects of my childhood: lukewarm baths, compulsory breakfast porridge – because that's what the guests had – and solitary evenings in my room while downstairs my parents played the jovial hosts.'

As they walked toward the door he continued, 'Anyhow, there are more important things in life than hanging on to the past. I'd sell the place tomorrow if I could find a buyer. But who'd want it? All they'd be taking on would be a huge renovation problem. You see, it isn't just a matter of cost. It's also the shortage of materials. There are Government restrictions. Builders are allowed to carry out only essential repairs to bomb-damaged premises. Even then they have to obtain a permit from the District Surveyor. So, as guests aren't likely to stay at the hotel while it's in its present condition – and there is no way of improving that situation – I'm afraid I'm stuck here.' He gave a brief, resigned smile.

Gina ventured, 'Wouldn't the Forces, or any welfare organizations, want to move in temporarily?'

'Perhaps. But then I'd have to close the bar and give up my licence. Which, as I've explained, might be a risky step. It's a bit of a cleft stick.' He opened the door, locked it after they'd exited, walked beside Gina into the approaching evening.

They waited at the bus stop, concluding their meeting with small talk until the double-decker trundled around the far bend. As the vehicle approached David said suddenly, 'It's been splendid seeing you. I'd very much like to repeat the experience. How about lunch? Say next Wednesday, when I can get someone to look after the bar?'

Gina swiftly figured ahead to which canteen shift she'd be on seven days from now. Early breakfasts. 'That would be lovely. I'll be free at noon.' The bus drew alongside. She stepped onto its rear platform. The conductress rang the bell. And as they rolled away David called, 'I'll collect you at the Rainbow.' Gina waved, returning his delighted farewell.

Sitting on a side seat facing an old man chuckling over a copy of the best-selling Hitler's *Last Will*, she smiled as she paid her fare. She was happy; not elated, but pleasantly, relaxedly happy, moreso than she had been in months. She thanked David Lowell for that. Or was it simply that she knew she was going to see Fallon again?

Sybil shouted, 'Step on it, old thing! We're on the collection detail.' She hauled herself up to the driver's seat of the Red Cross truck as Gina dashed around the corner of Shaftesbury Avenue, roared the motor to life while Gina was calling from ahead, 'I'll change my coat.' 'No time,' returned Sybil. 'I've barely an hour before I'm off duty.'

Slamming herself into the cab Gina puffed, 'Sorry I'm late. The bus from Richmond was held up in traffic. I went to visit. An old friend. Yes, a man. No, we didn't. Is that all you ever think about?'

Sybil grinned, said no more against the din of the rattling, lurching lorry. Steered expertly through the evening's home-going bedlam.

They crossed the river, turned so many times down dark, cobbled streets, Gina lost her sense of direction. At last they halted in front of high wooden gates set in a barbed-wire-mounted wall. Sybil honked the horn and a U.S. Army soldier, helmeted, his rifle at alert, stepped through a door beside the entrance. He approached cautiously, then relaxed into a grin, hooked the gun over his shoulder and yelled, 'Hey, Angel, how ya doin'? to Sybil who briefly flashed her pass and replied, 'Fine, Joe. Open up, won't you? I've a supply list longer than your arm.' The soldier rejoined, 'You know you can come into my yard any time.' He swung around, returned through the door. Within a moment, the bang of slamming bolts was followed by the opening of the gates.

Sybil drove through into a black well surrounded by buildings. With a jerking of brakes and a crunching of gears she turned the truck, reversed it up to a dimly-lit loading bay. She climbed out with Gina close behind; together they stepped up onto the bay which fronted a huge warehouse piled from floor to rafters with wooden crates.

A man's voice called, 'Ladies. Welcome. You here to collect? Or deliver?' The chuckle accompanied the emergence of Supply Sergeant Roscoe Tucker from a tiny side office. He greeted, 'Sybil. And who else? Gina?' His eyes lit with pleasure. 'Say, this must be my lucky night. Come on in.' And he ushered them into his eight-by-six cubicle where they wedged themselves between metal filing cabinets, stacked cartons, and walls plastered with Dorothy Lamour, Rita Hayworth and Lana Turner.

After Roscoe had inspected the Rainbow's supply list and despatched three privates to undertake the truck's loading, he offered, 'A couple of the best? Sure,' and delved behind the cartons to produce shot glasses and a bottle of Martell cognac. 'From a certain colonel's personal hoard,' he grinned, 'which kinda got lost in transit.' He poured three generous measures, raised his glass to the girls and toasted, 'To Army transport. Long may its diabolical carelessness continue.' With a laugh he downed the liquor in one gulp.

Gina and Sybil swallowed their drinks less hurriedly. Gina hadn't tasted such fine brandy since she left New York; it glowed down her throat, into her bloodstream, filling her with warmth and memories.

Roscoe paced his second measure, signing and rubber-stamping the Rainbow's requisition. 'Red tape and paper,' he said as he sucked in his stomach to open a filing cabinet drawer and deposit the authorization. 'Those brains at the Pentagon figure they can wrap up a billion tons of supplies in red tape and paper. They got the imagination of turtles. I tell you, fifteen years I been in khaki, eight with the stripes up, and there isn't a damn thing I haven't seen walk. From paperclips to Sherman tanks. There's always somebody somewhere wants something, and so long as he's got the wherewithal there'll be somebody else who won't bat an eye at scissoring through red tape and flushing paper down the john.' He squinted vertically at the girls' legs. 'You okay for nylons?'

They said they were.

'Of course,' continued the sergeant, his face growing serious. 'Now we're at war, there are some places you got to draw the line. Our guys overseas need everything we can send. I know. I was in the Pacific ten months. I seen your girls – Red Cross – down there, handing out stuff. Just simple stuff – magazines, notepads, razor blades. And grown men crying as they took it. Sure, crying for a bar of soap.' He added quietly, 'That's no lie.' He looked away toward the warehouse.

Gina watched the soldiers moving back and forth with the supplies; thought of her request for a transfer; thought also of Robert Fallon.

The sergeant turned back to them, his face relighting. 'On the other hand, when it comes to this sort of military equipment.' He brandished the cognac bottle, recharged their glasses. 'Supplies that appear on a manifest as engine spares, ordered by some brass hat who wouldn't know a crank shaft if one fell on him. That's a different matter entirely.' He winked broadly, enquired, 'You okay for soft toilet tissue?'

They said they were.

Gina swallowed her brandy. In the confines of the jammed cubicle she wasn't sure whether the sweat that began to trickle down her spine was caused by the heat from without or within. She really didn't care. She was feeling good, the best she had since her arrival in London. The sense of comradeship which at last had come to her this afternoon, nuzzled her now, slipped its arm around her waist. She laughed with Sybil at Sergeant Tucker's tales of wheeling and dealing; almost choked when her room-mate recounted being snowed-in at a Devon army barracks with forty GIs who hadn't had leave for two months; heard herself telling one of Cassie's risqué jokes about a bishop and a WAC; and began to feel, if not completely oiled then certainly well lubricated.

By the time a private stuck his head around the door to report the truck was loaded, the tiny office was bathed in an amber glow as seen through the bottom of Gina's fourth glass of cognac. She hoped her wobbly smile didn't look as dumb as it felt, and that her wobbly legs would accomplish the hike across the loading bay without depositing her on her duff.

'See you later,' the sarge threw cheerily.

Gina glanced around, realized they'd made it to the vehicle. Now all she had to do was climb in.

The siren began to wail above their heads.

'Damn it!' exclaimed Sybil over the din. 'Of all the times to choose. Well, we're not hanging around here till some near-sighted spotter decides it was a false alarm. Come on.' She yanked open the driver's door. 'And even if it is the real thing, with my foot down I can have us back in the West End before the first one drops.' She hauled herself up into the cab.

Gina had sobered instantly. She had never been so close to a siren. The howling row seemed to be penetrating her very skull, driving right through to her brain. She climbed swiftly in beside Sybil, never thinking of bombs, wanting only to escape from the eardrum-splitting racket.

Woomp! Gina felt it as much as heard it. The truck didn't rattle, the ground didn't shake, it was simply as if the surrounding air had throbbed. Gina's own pulse missed a beat but before her mind could even begin to consider what to do the second detonation blew the roof off the building across the yard. Just like in the movies, she thought spontaneously when the column of flame and debris shot into the sky; then reality seized her and she threw up a protective arm, ducked as rubble rained down on the truck roof.

Chunks of brick bounced off the hood. Gina saw them clearly. Beyond, rubble was showering across the yard. The noise of the bombarding masonry and the yowling siren was deafening, crushing rational thought. She slammed her hands to her ears, squeezed her head as if to force her mind to function. The next one will land directly on top of us, was all she could think. She swung reflexively toward Sybil who turned at the same instant, and without a word they plunged into each others' arms, huddled down, clung together in mutual paralysis until the third bomb exploded.

Gina didn't see it, her eyes were tight shut; she only heard its fury, felt its hurricane force slam the vehicle's side tilting it onto two wheels. The impact flung her from the seat, out of Sybil's grasp. She seemed to be sailing through the cab in slow motion. Opening her eyes she glimpsed the steering wheel above her head, the roof beneath her feet, arms and legs tumbling before her face. Have I been blown to bits? she wondered impassively as she flew amid the maelstrom.

Then the back of her neck struck something very hard, there was an instant's blackness and when she regained her senses the first thing she saw was a shoeless foot high in the air. It was a moment before she recognized it as her own, another second before she realized she was upside down and the sharp object pressing into her cheek was the clutch pedal.

'Bloody hell!' complained a loud female voice, and Sybil's knee crossed Gina's vision.

Sounds of scrambling and a couple more curses were accompanied by a cloud of dust which showered into Gina's inverted nose causing her to sneeze violently.

'Good God!' gasped Sybil. 'You're still alive.'

'But I won't be very . . . aitchoo . . . much longer if you don't get me . . . aitchoo . . . out of here,' spluttered Gina. 'I'll choke to . . . aitchoo . . . death.'

'Hold on.' More shifting and unidentifiable detritus falling around Gina's head, then Sybil's face appeared and her hands reached downward to grip Gina's arms. After much tugging, grunting, exhortation to 'Watch out', an expletive or two, and a sharp, rasping tear, the pair toppled sideways through the truck's open doorway, fell with a thump on the littered yard. They lay, still holding on to each other, their breath knocked out, for several moments before Gina, sucking in air, pushed herself to a sitting position and stared down at her coat which was ripped from waist to hem. 'Damn it!' she exclaimed angrily. 'I told you I should have changed before I came out.'

Beside her, Sybil sat up, peered at the ruined garment and breathed, 'Oh dear. That's terrible.'

And only when they turned to face each other did they simultaneously register the incongruity of the situation and erupt into laughter. Hooting like loons they remained there until Sergeant Roscoe Tucker's voice hollered, 'Over here! They're hysterical. Get that ammonia carbonate under their noses.'

'Don't you dare,' shot Gina, swallowing her mirth. She raised her eyes to the sergeant. Covered head to toe in brick dust she looked like a terracotta figure. But Gina's laughter had died. She understood that he was right: she had suffered momentary shellshock, the reaction to the blinding instant when the blast had hurled her within the cab and she thought she was dead. Now she blotted out that image, regained her mental equilibrium. Allowing Roscoe to assist her to her feet she acknowledged, 'Thanks. We're fine. Really.' She glanced at Sybil who had been helped up by another soldier. 'Aren't we?'

'I think so,' replied the English girl, inspecting the holes in her stockings' knees.

Gina looked across the yard. A twenty-foot section of the perimeter wall had disappeared; in its place, a smoking crater from which a geyser of water was fountaining into the street. The building over there was a terrace of houses, every window shattered. One by one the doors opened and the people came out to stand on the pavement, confronting the downpour, peering bemusedly around, like sleepwalkers awakening in a strange place. The siren, Gina realized, had ceased, another had opened up further away. Overhead, search lights still crawled across the sky, but there were no black shapes amid the lacing white fingers.

'Single aircraft,' remarked Roscoe. 'That's how come it got so far without being spotted. Only three drops. It's gone on to dump the rest of its cargo further north. But they'll be waiting for it now. That's one crew of mothers' sons who won't be home tonight.' He beckoned to the half-dozen soldiers. 'Let's go. Check the building that was hit. Make sure there's no gas escaping from that crater. Keep those folks back. Stay away from what's left of that tottering wall.' He glanced at Gina and Sybil. 'You two better sit inside awhile. Let the medics look you over.' He strode rapidly away, firing more instructions at his men.

Just like that, thought Gina. A few minutes' savagery and then with calculated efficiency they were picking up the pieces. Now she began to understand something, an iota, of what had happened during the Blitz. Her imagination could at last conjure the horror that had produced the devastation. She also realized that the past minutes had been a mere glimpse of what was taking place a millionfold across half the world. It was insane. A period of madness that had overtaken humanity; for no civilized beings could have launched themselves, rationally, into such violence and hysteria and fear.

'I don't need to sit,' Sybil interrupted Gina's thoughts. 'The people over there might want our help.'

As they picked their way through the rubble into the street, the rising clangour of bells heralded the arrival of a fire engine, closely pursued by an ambulance. The vehicles rushed to a halt, their teams jumped out, running into the shambles of the warehouse yard. A warden wearing a tin hat cranked urgently around the corner on a bicycle. A dog dashed under the water shower barking crazily. Voices were calling: 'Where's Susan?', 'Have you seen the cat?', 'Is Mum all right?'

Gina stepped toward an elderly man who appeared to be in a daze. She asked which was his home, and when he pointed led him inside, sat him at a table amid a litter of broken glass and smashed ornaments. An ambulance man followed her in, said he'd take over.

She returned outside to people hurrying back and forth. Looking around into another house she saw a woman on her knees with dustpan and brush sweeping the carpet; next door a girl was sitting on the step quietly crying. Gina whispered aloud, 'Dear God.' Her only emotion was anger.

She helped wherever she could for the next hour as the firemen doused the building that had been hit, Roscoe's men pushed down the remainder of the dangerous wall, Water Board plumbers patched the fractured main, and injured residents were either transported to hospital or treated in their homes. No one had been seriously wounded, the warden explained, thanks to the heavy blackout curtains plus brown paper strips pasted to the windows.

Sybil called, 'Hurry. I'm thirty minutes late.'

Gina saw her dishevelled room-mate clambering up into their battered truck which, miraculously, was spluttering with life as Roscoe clanged shut the mangled hood. She hurried over, climbed in beside Sybil who, torturing the gears, said impatiently, 'I'll have to go directly there. You won't mind dropping me off, driving back alone, will you? I really can't spare another moment.' She already had the protesting wagon bouncing along the street.

Clutching her seat lest she again be catapulted through the door, Gina replied, 'Of course I don't mind.' What she thought was: Really, Sybil, you've been out every night for the past fortnight. Can't you stay home even after being blown up? Surely your friends wouldn't miss you just this once?

But that was before she knew her destination.

20

'Where are we?' Gina asked, peering out at the gloomy street, the vast, high brick building curtained in darkness beneath which her room-mate had halted the truck to climb quickly down with a brief, 'See you later.'

'Whitechapel,' Sybil replied from the pavement.

'Is this where you're meeting your friends?'

'In a manner of speaking.'

Gina wasn't sure why she was concerned. Perhaps because of the district they were in. Sybil had not driven back toward the West End from the supply depot, instead had taken a route through crowded old buildings which were barely more than looming shadows in the blackout. They had crossed the inky river into a similarly murky area, to arrive eventually at this destination where Gina had lost all sense of direction. 'Which way back to Piccadilly?' she called.

Sybil surveyed the distance. 'Take the second left. Then make a right into . . .' She bit a vexed lip. 'No, that street hasn't been repaired. You'll have to go all the way to the church. Keep following the kerb bollards – you know what bollards are? Sorry, of course you do – when you reach . . .' Rummaging through her purse: 'I'd better write this down . . . Drat! No pencil. Have you . . . ?'

Gina shook her head.

Sybil hesitated, glancing up and down the street as if for inspiration. Then, decisively: 'Come along, they'll have an *A-Z* inside.' She strode to an archway in the hall, waited until Gina had locked the truck, led the way into an unlighted yard where Gina scarcely could discern STAFF ONLY on the door which Sybil opened.

Bright lamps reflected from the long corridor's green-painted walls. A black rubber mat ran to the distant junction. An elderly woman was scrubbing the perimeter floorboards. There was a strong smell of carbolic. To one side a wheeled hamper was stencilled ST MAUD'S.

Gina exclaimed, 'It's a hospital!'

The elderly woman said, 'Evenin', nurse.'

Sybil replied, 'Hello, Elsie. This way, Gina.'

Four hours later, stirring a giant jug of cocoa, Gina said, 'I've been so wrong. About so many things.'

After they'd phoned the Rainbow, Sybil had changed into her auxiliary nurse's uniform (the quest for the *A-Z* forgotten behind Gina's bombardment of questions), saying resignedly, 'Very well, if we must confab, you'll have to put up with watching me unblock the basement lavatory.' Armed with brushes, lengths of wire and a lethal-looking plunger she had descended to subterranean passages and a toilet whose rim-lapping, noxious contents were a beacon at two hundred yards. There they talked; and as Sybil lunged and trawled, Gina (breathing as shallowly as possible) was hard put to reconcile the intense, puffing, tumbling-haired figure with the flippant, pedigreed girl who sported her way through her shifts at the Rainbow. Discovering about Sybil, however, was just part of her education in that dark, smelly cellar beneath the packed wards of St Maud's General Hospital, Whitechapel.

By the time they ascended to the relative fresh air of ground level, Gina had learned the truth about the Blitz, rationing, evacuee children, broken families, the huge increase in suicides since 1939, women driven literally out of their minds by unconquerable fear, the appalling waste of life in something as mundane as traffic accidents caused by the blackout – twelve hundred deaths in one month alone.

Sybil, scalding her triumphant plunger in the pot sink of a tiny scullery, had said, 'Yes, when you first saw Allied Main Street, I can understand why it seemed somewhat crazy for people to be buying luxuries like cherries or boutonnières or monkeys on sticks. But, then, when I received the letter from the Washington general about my husband, I went out and bought a sable jacket, sat on my bed wearing it for seven hours, before taking it to the boiler-room and incinerating it.' She'd pushed an escaping lock under her auxiliary's cap. 'Then I came and signed on here.'

By midnight, Gina had followed suit.

After being drafted immediately to the kitchen, she spent the next six hours peeling mountains of turnips, slicing acres of bread, and brewing oceans of cocoa, which, she discovered, was the *elixir vitae* of the British hospital system.

Throughout the night there were few lulls in St Maud's activity, and when Gina re-met Sybil at the end of their shift, her body was fervently reminding her that she had rarely ceased running it from pillar to post since a dream of Robert Fallon had woken her twenty-four hours ago.

Heading toward the exit, Sybil said, 'It's as if the world's time-clock has gone haywire. People doing things at the most outlandish hours. Even here. Doctors performing operations at two in the morning. Patients coming in for routine examinations at dawn. See . . . ' Dozens of people were waiting on the benches in the foyer, others were to-ing and fro-ing along corridors, entering and leaving the building. As a group passed by, Sybil, pausing in her stride, addressed a gaunt, fair-haired girl in a tired-looking brown coat that was far from heavy enough for the time of year. 'Hello. How are you? Peggy, isn't it? Peggy Atkins. We met last week when you came in for your check-up. Has the doctor given you the results?'

The girl had halted, snapped out of some preoccupation at Sybil's approach. Her fingers laced and unlaced around a frayed straw purse, and she glanced from side to side when she spoke. 'Yes. Thanks. Yes, he told me I'll be all right.' She looked down at her scuffed shoes. 'The baby too. It'll be okay when it arrives.'

'Well, that's fine then,' Sybil responded encouragingly. 'Remember to keep coming in for your appointments. And don't forget to use your cod liver oil coupons. Everything will work out for the best. Believe me.'

The girl offered a wan smile, but it never reached her eyes as whatever she was about to say died unspoken and she quickly walked away.

Sybil watched the distant door swing behind the slight figure before she observed, 'I wish to God there was one iota of truth in what I said.'

Gina was surprised by the abject resignation in her friend's tone. Over the past hectic fortnight, and throughout the traumas of the previous twelve hours, Sybil had shown no sign of flagging, either physically or mentally. It was doubly disconcerting therefore to see her now drop heavily onto a bench by the wall, the determination slipping abruptly from her slumped shoulders. Gina, sitting swiftly beside her, masked her concern with false cheeriness: 'Hey, you look as worn out as I feel. I guess getting blown to bits has finally caught up with us. Hold on here, I think I can raise a last dreg of strength to go rustle up some tea or coffee.'

'No.' Sybil's hand restrained Gina. 'I'm fine. Really. Just

stricken by a sudden flush of the glooms. Foolish. I've seen it all before. So many times before. Seen so many Peggy Atkins.'

'Is she ill?' asked Gina.

'Not with any curable ailment,' Sybil replied tiredly. 'Unless you consider abortion a remedy.' Staring ahead, not seeing the effect the remark had made on Gina, she went on, 'Peggy is from some town up north. Came to London before the war believing that, for pretty girls, the streets were paved with gold. It took her about six months to discover there were a million other females off the bus with the same notion, a further year to have an illegitimate daughter by a character who hasn't been seen since she gave him the joyous news. She stuck it out down here a while, but with no money, no job and the sort of acquaintances who were in much the same boat as she, there was eventually nothing for her to do but return home. Home – as big a misnomer as Parents. Peggy's mother and father agreed to take care of the child, but told Peggy she was nothing but . . . Well, what could she do? She came back to London. Two years later she's pregnant again. A GI this time, who forgot – how careless – to give her his U.S. address before being posted.'

'But if he's a soldier,' suggested Gina, 'surely the Army will trace him for Peggy?'

Sybil laughed hollowly. 'The Army,' she said, 'cares as much for Peggy Atkins as do her parents. Or the Government. Or the Church. Or any of the holier-than-thou women's organizations who preach sisterly love but wouldn't soil a delicately gloved finger by reaching out to anything as unsanitary as an unmarried mother. Peggy – and the thousands of other girls who are either too poor, too simple, or just too damn nice to fight for themselves – has as much chance of discovering the whereabouts of the GI as she does of finding a decent place to sleep once her baby's born.'

'Aren't there any hostels?'

'You really don't know a lot about the Blitz, do you?' Sybil's remark was hard but not harsh. She sighed, stood and walked toward the exit. Pausing, she half turned, waited for Gina to reach her before opening the door.

They came out into the chill, grey light of dawn. To Gina it was like stepping into a cracked, black and white photograph. She had never seen any place so lacking in colour. The high hospital, the factories opposite, the rows of terraced houses down the street, were as drab and sombre as the lowering sky, their depression reflected in the wet cobbles of the road. She pulled up her collar, shivered, inwardly.

'Somewhat different from the jolly West End,' said Sybil. 'Every capital has a side the guide books don't mention. This was it – until Herr Hitler decided to put it on the map. Or perhaps I should say, tried to wipe it off the map. Sorry – bad joke.' Jamming her fists into her pockets and adding with sudden harshness, 'God, I hate this bloody war!' she strode toward their truck.

Gina, somehow not surprised by the vehemence, followed. She shut herself in beside the English girl, hunched silent on the seat as they rumbled away from that place.

But Sybil did not head toward the heart of the city. She turned down a side street; and another; between ever-older, grimier buildings. The tenements here, scabrous with damp, veined by rusted fire escapes, huddled around refuse-strewn yards like derelicts in forlorn communion. Then they rounded a corner, onto a scene which caused Gina's fingers to talon the edge of her seat.

The street ran through a shattered landscape. On both sides a wilderness of piled rubble; giant broken faces of brickwork reaching upward, holed by glassless windows staring at nothing; slabs of linoleum-patched concrete ruptured above steps descending to nowhere; craters in the red clay as raw as open wounds. Here and there some high floors hanging in space, still supporting a sofa, a birdcage on a stand, a lavatory, an aspidistra in a pot. A man sitting amid this rubble staring at his boots. Two women stooped, picking at the ground like crows. Three children beside the pavement, eating something – as Gina went past, she saw – potato peelings.

Sybil drove wordlessly.

Gina's mind had become numb. She could remember no statistics – the acreage destroyed, the tonnage of bombs dropped, the number of lives obliterated – she could think only, Is there no end to it? For at every turn she faced more of the same. And always there was the thin smoke; no visible fires, merely the grey threads, ragged on the breeze, carrying the acrid stink of gas, sewage, putrefaction and burning timber.

She had no idea of how far they travelled, lost all sense of time and distance. In the relentless gloom the day and the devastation seemed endless.

Then, as if coming out of a tunnel, they were once more onto a busy thoroughfare. People hurried in front of stores and cinemas, traffic sped and honked, a news vendor yelled beside a billboard which announced, MINISTER DENIES NUTMEG SHORTAGE. Gina choked back a cry of bitter laughter at the absurd message.

Within minutes the familiar landmark of Tower Bridge was on their left. They trundled beside the river, turned into the wide avenues of the city and soon were pulling to a halt outside the bustling entrance of the Rainbow. Looking around, Gina had to make a conscious effort to accept the reality of all she had seen. She sat in silence watching the morning hurrying around the Circus, didn't move until she heard Sybil say raggedly:

'I'm sorry. I don't know why I did that, took you there. It was hurtful, I know. I didn't really want you to see. But, I . . .' She reached out and held Gina's hand, very tightly; whispered, 'Forgive me.'

Gina returned the grip, said softly, 'No need to apologize. I understand. And I'm grateful.'

They sat together there for quite a while.

The experience of those hours profoundly shocked Gina. Nevertheless they also gave her a new sense of perspective. She was calmer now. Rational. While her life was utterly removed from normality, at least its old rhythms had begun to return: she once more slept her customary five hours, ate at her regular intervals, renewed her consumption of newspapers and magazines, even commenced a new journal which she fattened daily with gleanings from her reading, culinary snippets from the Rainbow's cooks, household hints from Freddie Grisewood's *Kitchen Front* wireless programme, and recipe leaflets from the Ministry of Food for such unlikely items as carrot marmalade, meatless meat pie, mock lemon curd, and prune pancakes (without eggs).

Gina also thought daily of Fallon.

Her efforts – and she tried, she truly tried – to bar him from her mind were futile, had been from the day she had kept her lunch date with David Lowell. During the intervening week, as she came to mental terms with the scenes of blitzed White-chapel, the Reuters correspondent had not entered her head. It was after David had picked her up in a taxi at the Rainbow, saying, 'Special treat,' and they had driven the short distance down the Haymarket, around Nelson's Column and along the Strand where they alighted in a covered courtyard, that Gina's senses had faltered, halted, caught on the threshold of memory.

It was the legend above the entrance that had jolted her toward the past – SAVOY – and, with the letters still hovering before her eyes, as she went beside David into the reception hall she'd said, 'In 1923 the Mirror Room was renamed the Abraham Lincoln Room.'

'Yes,' accepted David, somewhat surprised, adding, in a chivalrous attempt to pick up the abrupt conversation, 'Did you know, most of the others are named after Gilbert and Sullivan operas – Mikado, Iolanthe, Pinafore and so on – on account of D'Oyly Carte, the impresario who built the place?'

Gina didn't hear. She was in a bedroom of the Howard West, a chambermaid again, reading an abandoned magazine, a feature on London's Savoy which, moments before bringing about the confrontation with the searcher, had caused her to think of Robert Fallon.

As it did now as she accompanied David in to Lunch. And the image of the correspondent refused to recede throughout the entire meal. Gina chatted and laughed with David, discussed everything from the Allied advances to the recent announcement that Conrad Hilton had bought the Plaza in New York. She enjoyed each minute of the Englishman's company. Still it was Fallon she took home to her room. He would not leave. Or did she refuse to let him? She avoided answering the question; knew only that whatever happened, she would see him again.

Toward the end of March a letter arrived from Harry. Ten pages chronicling every minute since Gina had left New York: the price of prawns had become outrageous; the basement boiler had sprung a leak; one of the hat-check girls was pregnant; a beer barrel had exploded; somebody had stolen an entire roller-towel cabinet; the kitchen cat had eaten a pound of caviar; the sidewalk in front of the entrance was being dug up, again; a waiter had dropped $100-worth of crystal champagne flutes; a twenty-fifth wedding anniversary party had ended in a fist fight; the electricity bill was unbelievable; the window cleaner had been drafted; one the trombonists was going to marry the hat-check girl; a tarantula spider – everyone swore it was a tarantula – had jumped out of a crate of oranges. In other words everything was fine. Gina was pleased that so far Harry hadn't had to cope with anything out of the ordinary. On the last page Harry had written 'PTO'. Gina did so. At the centre of the sheet he had drawn a small heart with Gina's name upon it; surrounding this, covering the paper, were the signatures of every person who worked in the building. Gina pasted the page on a piece of card and hung it on the wall beside her bed.

The year turned through the arc of summer.

Gina scarcely noticed the months pass. Her days and nights were filled with the Rainbow and St Maud's. Even during her first year in Manhattan, toiling at the Howard West, caring for Paola and Filipo, she had never been as busy as this. Yet she revelled in it, gave herself to it with all her heart and all her strength. In the midst of the world's self-destruction she at last felt she was doing something worthwhile; the sense of necessity which Max had tried to explain that time at the Lady before he'd come to Europe, Gina now understood, fully.

She thought frequently of Max, Johnny too, and wasn't sure which troubled her most.

On the one hand she had heard nothing of the Tuscan giant since he left New York, had no idea where he was, whether he had been killed months ago, was unable to envisage what he might be going through with the Italian partisans whose operations were little more than rumour and speculation. When she mentioned this to Roscoe Tucker, the sergeant said, 'Don't worry. Information in this man's army is as easy to come by as any other commodity – so long as you can tap in to the right telegraph. Leave it with me.' Gina had offered her thanks – but with scant confidence. On the other hand she knew her brother-in-law was with General Eisenhower in western Tunisia, and that he was still alive. Gina could conceive only too easily Johnny's situation; the descriptions of the war brought to the club by furloughing GIs left little to the imagination.

The information about Johnny came in a letter from Paola, who now wrote every week. Harry continued to send frequent news too, and there were regular letters from Cassie, Chang, and Mrs Ponti. Between them they kept Gina in touch not only with the daily goings of everyone at the Lady but also with the intimate details of who was committing what, and with whom, where, when and why throughout the island of Manhattan. They all brought Gina immense pleasure.

But none more so than the single page in June from Filipo which opened, 'Dear Sis,' ended, 'Your loving, handsome, intelligent, strong, virile!!! brother,' and was postscripted, 'Don't let the Army (or the Navy or the Air Force) get you down.'

How old was he?

London by mid-1943, it seemed to Gina, though still chronically short of food and fuel, was beginning to build a fresh sense of hope. Maybe it was the infrequency of air raids on the capital – the *Luftwaffe* having shifted its attentions to other cities; maybe it was the weather – a record period of sunshine in May; maybe it was the strengthening understanding that Britain truly was no longer alone – the country appeared to be packed with American forces. And then on July 9th the growing mood of confidence was boosted a hundredfold with the news that the Allies had landed on Sicily. Ten days later the optimism flared to exaltation when Rome was bombed for the first time. Though Gina couldn't share the unholy joy, neither did she feel any special grief; the name Rome was simply one more to add to a list – Coventry, Hamburg, Southampton, Cologne, Bristol, Dusseldorf – the tragedy of which was nullified by its enormity.

She renewed her efforts at the club and the hospital as if the intensity of her labour might somehow help to end the war. For now that she comprehended it, she desperately wanted it to finish. Each day she felt further distanced from New York, further misplaced from reality. One evening in mid-August after pasting a recipe from *Housewife* magazine in her journal she wrote beneath the clipping, 'I wish I was home.' The admission had been spontaneous. She did not delete it.

Her despond however was shortlived, for when September arrived, summer refused to retreat.

As the sun shone like a good omen, the open-neck shirts and cotton dresses of the previous month carried a holiday air into the unseasonal heatwave. Gina, along with most of the Red Cross girls, spent a precious hour every day on the narrow but flat roof parapet, where, in bra and pants (with the stairwell door securely locked), they acquired tans which would have caused envy on the beach at Acapulco.

On the 8th, Peggy Atkins – the girl Gina had met during her first visit to St Maud's – gave birth to a healthy, seven-pound boy. Gina and Sybil assured Peggy everything would work out fine. They toasted the infant in Indian Pale Ale.

On the 9th, Roscoe Tucker brought the news – via what devious route Gina prudently did not ask – that among the partisans aiding the Allied advance in southern Italy was one Max Barzini. Gina and the sergeant celebrated with liberated Dutch schnapps.

On the 10th, David Lowell telephoned – on what pretext Gina never would remember – and conversationally mentioned that Fallon was home. Gina was able neither to drink nor eat for the remainder of the day.

She spent that night in a ferment of indecision. Why shouldn't she visit Fallon? He'd be delighted to see her. After all these years there'd be so much to talk about, all the old times to discuss, the happy evenings they'd spent at Ristorante Rossi, even the bleak months that followed; Fallon had been a part of them, they each had been a part of the other's life during a period which they surely never could forget.

So why hadn't he written?

Because he'd wanted to leave the past dead and buried. Because he'd had no desire to dig up an ancient episode which was no more significant to him than the thousand adventures he'd had across the globe. Because one Italian girl was no more memorable to him than any of the squads of women (regiments more likely, from what David Lowell's slip of the tongue had suggested) he'd bedded wherever he datelined his reports.

Gina's brain was wrecked on the rocks of reason.

At least, that was the excuse she gave herself for her subsequent actions.

The streets here were narrow, some cobbled, the pavements barely wide enough for two people to walk side by side. The buildings of ancient brick were huddled, locked together by gateways, arches and roofs as if not only to confuse and impede strangers but also to prevent the encroachment of time itself. Yet Gina walked unerringly, guided by an inherent sense of direction born in a city maze so similar to this that she paused on a corner to right herself in time, to remind herself that the massive dome dominating the reddening evening sky was in fact London's St Paul's and not Rome's St Peter's.

She went on.

The courtyard bearing the name of Wren's church was unevenly flagged beyond old wrought iron gates in a lichen-mortared wall. Its encompassing houses were three-storeyed with stone mullioned windows and a short flight of steps to each front door. A single gas lamp leaned at the centre of this small enclave of silence.

Silent it was. As Gina had stepped through the entrance it was as if a switch had been thrown on the hum of the city. The wind too had been left outside the wall. Here there was only stillness, an aura of calm which Gina felt had been undisturbed since the weathered paving had been laid on river meadow soil. But she did not feel like an intruder. The court was not unwelcoming, and her uncertainties subsided as she headed toward the nearest house.

They rose again – tenfold – when she stood before Fallon's door. She had found his apartment at a corner of the square. The small brass nameplates beneath the three mailboxes advised that he occupied the top floor. Gina had climbed the carpeted staircases to halt on a landing in front of 17c. She remained there for a long time. Looking to her left she met the smile of a round-faced, bewigged gentleman in a worn gilt frame. Glancing to her right she viewed tiled alleys and slopes beneath the soaring pinnacle of the cathedral through a dusty window. Facing ahead again she saw a fist raised against a panel of varnished oak.

It was her own fist. What on earth was it doing there? What on earth was she doing here? How could she have come to be standing on this spot? How could she have ignored all the warnings of her common sense? This was ridiculous, childish, the pursuit of fantasy, the result of . . .

She struck the panel.

The sound reverberated through the building like the detonation of a bomb. Gina shrank from the din, recoiled from the assaulted oak. Jamming her treacherous fist into her jacket pocket, she prepared to flee. There was still time. If she turned now, ran down the stairs, she'd be past the lower landing, out of sight, before he saw her; he'd never know she'd been here, she'd never have to face the mortifying embarrassment of his rebuff.

Why didn't he answer the door?

She raised impatient knuckles.

He stood framed against the sunset-lit room.

Gina thought her entire body had turned to rubber. She didn't seem to have any control over her dissolving muscles.

Her legs refused to move either forward or back, her still-hovering fist would not withdraw its apparent threat to Fallon's jaw, and her mouth was adamant in its recalcitrance against the brain's commands to form any sort of lucid sound. Plus, she felt like the biggest dope in all the world.

He said, 'What a fantastic tan.'

She said, 'I've been sunbathing on the roof.'

'I thought the Red Cross ran you off your feet.'

'I use my lunch breaks.'

Nodding understanding he ushered her into the room, closed the door. 'Tea? I just brewed.'

'That would be lovely.' She stood by a scuffed leather sofa while he disappeared through an archway where he began making crockery-rinsing noises. The room was large. The patterned carpet was faded but not worn. With the sofa were two armchairs grouped about a brown tiled fireplace (no fire) with a brass fender and a polished wood mantle which was full-laden with books, postcards, stacked letters and notebooks. A similar litter covered the oval gateleg table flanking the archway, as well as the double-pedestal desk in the tall bay window, where, beside a battered Remington typewriter, a steaming mug testified to the truth of his recent brewing. A few interesting lamps and photographs perched on stands, but what dominated the room were the walls – or lack of them: from corner to corner, floor to ceiling, every available inch was covered in books.

Gina stepped to the nearest shelf. At a glance she saw Hugo, O'Neill, Kipling, Yeats, Steinbeck, Galsworthy. She reached up and took down a volume whose cover had been much fingered, whose pages had been often turned. On the flyleaf, written in blue ink was, 'And if you work at it, real hard, one day you might also be able to drink as good as me.' The signature was a scrawled S. On the title page was: *Elmer Gantry* by Sinclair Lewis.

Fallon said, 'Sorry, no sugar.' He stood holding a white cup and saucer. When he saw she was not going to put the book down until he answered the question in her eyes he shrugged. 'Back in the late twenties. I interviewed him. So did a lot of other young hacks.' He came and set the tea on a small table by the sofa, went and fetched his own mug.

Gina countered, 'Don't sell yourself so short.' But before she was able to pursue him further, she was hit by the sudden realization, he did it to me again. He'd caught her with that same line he'd used – how many years ago? – when he'd appeared in the doorway of that terrible hut in Baremo. And today she'd fallen for it in exactly the same way. With those four words he'd quelled her doubts, dispelled her fears, led her into his room and back into his life with ease and caring. She thanked him for that. She loved him for that.

She shot, 'You knew I was at the Rainbow!'

'I heard.' He examined her over the vapouring rim of his tea mug; an impenetrable searching gaze that at once quickened Gina's pulse while throwing her off balance.

She said, 'Don't say I haven't changed.'

'You've changed a lot. In all the right ways.'

'You always could charm the whiskers off a cat, Mister Fallon.' What a cliché! She was beginning to feel awkward again, a gawky girl standing here in front of a romantic vision become real. Only now did she study his face. Time and weather had sculpted his features since last she saw him. His hair still tumbled in every direction, but now it was charged with grey. Green cord jacket, maroon shirt and loosened blue tie observed his consistency in dress. Reporter's pad, pencils and, yes, the pipe sprouting from his pockets witnessed his continued energy. He was all he had been – and more. He was all Gina Rossi had seen when she was seventeen years old. He was all she ever had wanted in a man. He was what she wanted right now.

The admission stunned her. So did her abrupt, reflexive sexual response. Her teenage desires, later life urges, none had been so intense, so unexpected as this. The flood of heat through her stomach and between her legs caused her to bite her lip for clarity, to reach for the sofa's arm for support. Summoning what was intended to be a nonchalant smile but which she was sure appeared as a goofy grin she swiftly sat, searched for something alluring and meaningful to say, came up with, 'How've you been?'

'Fine.' He sat opposite.

'Good. That's good.' Gina cringed mentally. Her powers of conversation seemed to have evaporated. She peered into the depths of the tea, probing for the gem that would light the sparkle between them. Brightly, 'This is a nice apartment.'

'Flat. In England we call it a flat.'

'Really? That's interesting.' No it isn't, it's a dull response to a boring remark. And I've known the word was 'flat' for as long as I can remember. She was beginning to shrivel inside. 'Yes . . . ' looking around, 'well, you've made it very . . . attractive.'

'Thank you.'

'And collected a lot of books.'

'I don't collect really. Just never give any away.'

'Not ever?'

'Once or twice. Perhaps.'

'Yes, of course.'

The silence grew opaque. Concentrate as she might Gina was unable to break it. Oh, God, this was mortifying! An unmitigated disaster. The biggest mistake of her life. She should never have come. He was disconcerted by her arrival; was being gracious, but no doubt awaiting the opportune moment when he politely could bid her goodbye. He'd never wanted her here in the first place. Of course he hadn't, otherwise he'd have been in touch. After all, he'd known she was in London. Yes, he'd known – obviously, David Lowell had told him – but he hadn't phoned even to say hello. Gina burned. Why on earth hadn't she listened to her own cautions? Why had she forged ahead unheeding into this appalling situation, trapped not only herself but Fallon too in this uncomfortable corner?

Facing him she felt asinine, ashamed, and miserable as hell. Her sexual surge had ebbed as suddenly as it had risen. She no longer wanted to rush him into the bedroom (yes, that had been the startling thought that had seized her), now her sole desire was to dash out of here, as fast and as soon as possible, to save them both from further embarrassment. She plonked down the cup. Stood. 'Fallon, I . . . '

He too was on his feet. All uncertainty evaporated from his features. His hands gripped her waist, he pulled her into him, and kissed her. It was a kiss that flamed down to the depths of Gina's insides. She wasn't startled by the suddenness of it, but was shocked by its urgency; it was open-mouthed, searching, fierce, with as much wanting in it as there was in her.

She returned its passion, consuming his mouth with her lips, her teeth, her tongue. All her doubts and fears had flown. A million questions were in her, but no uncertainties as she pursued the kiss until she felt her lungs might burst. Then

Fallon briefly held away and gasped for breath. Gina stared into his face, and there in the gathering evening dark she could see his heart in his eyes. Her own emotions surged, an abruptly mounting need that threw her against him with physical force.

Destiny, she thought. There is such a thing, of course there is. It led me here, across three thousand miles and five years, to where I was meant to be.

They undressed each other in silence. At last they were naked, on the floor.

Fallon's mouth moved swiftly but gently across Gina's throat and shoulders, licking into every hollow and curve of her. His lips travelled downward to the swell of her breasts with light, caressing touches, almost tentatively as he whispered his pleasure while expressing a sense of disbelief at what was happening. And as his hands explored, there appeared a sort of wonder in his face, as if he was examining something infinitely precious.

Gina reached down to where his head moved, ran her fingers over his back. A broad back, as tanned as her own, with dark hairs and a blue scar running six inches horizontally from the middle of his spine. She didn't question it, for his hand was between her legs now, opening her, intimately, but gently and patiently. So sensitive was she there now that she bit her lip to prevent a cry escaping.

He moved upward. Entered her. And Gina's mind was caught by a brief remembrance – the bright morning when Howard Cornell had made love to her in the Plaza Hotel.

But this wasn't how it had been with Howard. That, Gina could see, had been something different. Not infatuation; certainly a sort of love, but not truly for the man, rather for what he had brought to her life at a moment when – even though she might not have been aware of it – she was desperately in need of physical contact. Howard also had given her the joy in the experience of sex, while driving out the dread that had stalked her for so long. And, despite his subservience to his mother, she was grateful to him for that; a small part of her would love him forever for that. But not in the way she loved Fallon, the all-consuming way she always had loved Fallon. Now there was no doubt in her mind, Fallon had been her love from the first moment she set eyes on him; she should have believed her instincts, never should have wasted all the years between. But, then she thought, maybe that's the way it has to be; you must lose something and find it again before you fully appreciate its worth.

Fallon moved over her, under her, with her. He was a very part of her. They were one: a merging of hills and valleys, hardness and softness, light and shade. Gina's senses were at once numbed and heightened; she was in a dream while experiencing the utmost reality. She wanted to weep, needed to shout for joy as Fallon carried her upward toward fulfilment, pacing his own pleasure, matching his rhythm to her mounting need, so that when he finally climaxed it was only moments before her.

Yes, Gina climaxed too.

Erupting volcanoes. Soaring angels. Exploding surf. All the poetry, movie, erotica clichés rolled into one. Gina choked with it, arched with it, yelled with it. Sailed with it for what seemed an interminable moment before she fell back, heaving and gasping, burning and aching; satiated yet still wanting; amazed, yes, amazed, by what had happened inside her. So that was it, that was truly how it should be! And was that how it was for all women? Never. It couldn't be. Because no one else had Fallon; no one else – she refused to believe otherwise – possibly could be as close as they. But, the thought sidled in on her, will it ever be as sensational again? Could she tower to such incredible heights of sensuality a second, a third, a lifetime's number of times? Of course. Why should there be any doubt? This was the way their lovemaking always would be. For ever.

The thought caused her heat to rise again. She squeezed her thighs together. God, she felt so . . . Randy. Sybil's word. Gina bit her lip as she almost laughed out loud. If Sybil could see her now. If Sybil had seen her two minutes ago. If anybody had seen her two minutes ago. Cassie or Paola or any of the girls at The Lady, or Harry even. She burned at the image, wondered if too much of a good thing had unhinged her senses. So what if it had? She didn't care. She suddenly wanted to shout, Hey, take a look, everybody, take a look at what Gina Rossi has discovered!

Maybe Fallon wouldn't appreciate that too much.

Smiling in the darkness, she turned on her side, wound her leg across his knees, raised it to press the inside of her thigh against the damp softness of him; laid her palm on his taut stomach, slid it upward to cup his chest, to turn his nipple between her thumb and forefinger; lowered her head to kiss his throat, moving downward.

He sat up abruptly. 'I didn't use anything.'

'What?'

'I forgot. Gina, I'm sorry. Did you?'

For seconds she had no idea what he was talking about. Then understanding dawned. She was glad he couldn't see her blush. Yes, at her age, the subject of contraception still made her flush with the same co-mingling of embarrassment and uncertainty she had experienced that day when, cleaning one of the Howard West bedrooms, she had found, and stared uncomprehendingly at, a packet of male rubber sheaths. Cassie, casually regarding the find, had advised, 'Don't take those to use, Hon. There are jokers purposely leave them lying around, having first made sure they've all got an invisible but effective pinhole. If you want to be on the safe side, just in case you get lucky one night,' she'd winked broadly, 'but the feller has forgotten his merry widows, call in the druggist around the corner opposite the planetarium, they'll fix you up with some of that new jell. It's good stuff.' Grinning, she'd assured, 'Believe me.'

Gina had been too shocked to pick up the levity. That subject was taboo. Though an Italian girl might indulge, even share with her pals the most erotic fantasies (surrounded by citiesful of graphic nude art, they were perhaps more knowledgeable on the details of the male body than their contemporaries anywhere else in the world), the practicalities of birth control, even in a household as enlightened as the Rossis', were never mentioned. And, for all the sophistication of New York and the easy attitude of the girls with whom she'd worked over the years, the matter remained one which Gina found impossible to discuss. She had wondered, sometimes, how Paola had coped with her teenage years; had assured herself that her sister, Americanized though she may be, would never flout two thousand years of teaching.

Contraception was a sin: a greater sin than the act of sexual intercourse itself. That was the lore. Gina could no more unlearn it than she could the Commandment not to kill.

Beside her, Fallon prompted, 'Did you use anything, Gina? Will you be all right? I'm sorry for being so damned thoughtless.' He touched her cheek with anxious fingers.

Gina held his hand, tightly. Confusion chafed her. She loved him for his caring, but at the same time was wounded by his presumption that she might not want their child. She answered quietly, 'Don't worry.' Because there was no need for concern. It didn't matter if she became pregnant. In fact, she'd love to be pregnant. Yes, she would. She repeated the word in her head. Pregnant. Previously she had shied from it – grim associations with Baremo, perhaps – had refused to acknowledge its possibility even after her lovemaking with Howard. Now, however, she allowed the thought to build. She wanted it; yes, wanted, fiercely, to conceive a child. What a monumental idea that was! Her head swam with it.

She straddled Fallon, gripped his hips with her knees, said throatily, 'I hope you aren't one of those Englishmen who believe in moderation in all things.'

21

That was Monday. On Wednesday he said over the phone, 'Come to the country with me.'

Gina answered instantly, 'Yes.'

She was astonished by her own audacity, not to mention her desire. She wanted Robert Fallon with a passion beyond good sense. Her every waking moment (and there were a lot of them because she barely had slept a wink since that first time with him) was filled with libidinous mental rehearsals of their next meeting.

After three fervid hours at his apartment, Gina had hared to her shift at St Maud's, the pain of tearing herself from him made the more acute by his admission that he must spend the following three days at a war correspondents' conference somewhere in Cornwall. Back at the Rainbow, over a cauldron of corned beef hash, Sybil had pierced her with a look that could have penetrated lead and said, 'You're liable to get arrested for what you're thinking.' Gina had begun to protest, but, knowing her face was more steaming than the hash, she decided denial would be futile. Moreover, to be honest, she'd spent the night hours feeling like a boiling bean can, knew that if she didn't spill all – well, almost all – very soon, she surely would explode.

At the end of the confession Sybil proclaimed, 'Scandalous. Brazen. Depraved.' Urgently: 'Tell it again.'

Gina did; and would have a third time had they not been drafted to separate duties. For all she wanted to do was talk, talk, talk about Robert Fallon. And to Robert Fallon. She was on tenterhooks every moment awaiting his phone contact. When none came it took her whole will to convince herself that his Cornish assignment was all-involving. On Wednesday evening she flew to the reception desk when Sybil, passing her in the hall, mentioned offhandedly, 'Oh, by the way, I almost forgot, I think there's a call for you.'

Fifteen minutes later the English girl insisted, 'Certainly you must go. You haven't taken leave since you arrived here. And don't worry about St Maud's. We'll miss you there, greatly. But we'll manage. Come on, I'll help you pack. Of course, if you'd prefer to remain in London, I'd be more than happy to play substitute.'

The further they travelled from the city – in a green, 1939 Ford 8 borrowed from one of Fallon's pals – the more Gina felt distanced from the war. The English countryside – Suffolk he'd shown her on the map – was idyllically peaceful. It was all she had ever imagined, and more.

Really, she thought, looking out at emerald fields, goldening woods and pink-washed cottages, I've travelled hardly at all since leaving Italy. In Manhattan she'd considered a trip to Paola's home at New Rochelle, barely seventeen miles from Forty-Seventh Street, a major exploration; knew, she had to admit, little of the geography of New York State, let alone the rest of the country. I've become insular, she mused. It's about time I started getting out and about more. Of course, now that she had Fallon, her personal life would be different. Once the war was over – won, she had to believe that – there would be so many places to visit, things to do, an entirely new existence to lead, out of the rut and onto a fresh and exciting route, her lover at her side.

She studied his profile; was tempted to bite his neck. Yes, Sybil, I think I am becoming depraved.

Evening shadows were fissures across the landscape when he said, 'I'll pull in for supplies. Meat, bread, vegetables. So long as we're here I'll cook. No arguments. Why the look of anxiety? You won't be poisoned. Not all men are limited to opening a tin of Spam, you know.'

'It wasn't that,' responded Gina. 'But – you're going to kill me for this – I forgot to bring my Red Cross ration warrant.'

Fallon's face closed into exaggerated severity. Then with a shrug he said, 'Well, I assure you I'm too long in the tooth to live on love for more than one meal. So, you'd better rustle up your heart-rendingest smile and hope that Mrs Bridger takes pity on you.' He tugged on the hand brake outside a stooping, thatched cottage, and led Gina beneath POST OFFICE and HOVIS signs to a tiny interior whose floor, walls and ceiling sagged with their burdens of barrels, cartons and crates.

'Aladdin's cave,' remarked Fallon, 'was a non-starter compared to Bridger's Stores. You name it, they'll have it. When Monty was passing, called in for a sprocket for his scout car – no problem. Mind you, he hadn't forgotten his ration book. Ah, Mrs Bridger. How are you?'

'Mister Robert. I'm fine, of course I am. And you, you're looking so well. I read all your stories in the papers. But those places you've been. They sound so terrible. You should tell the newspaper's editor to send someone else for a change. You didn't ought to always be the one to go. Besides,' the plump, grey-bunned woman's bright blue eyes moved to Gina, 'you're too old to be off on those sort of trips. At your age you should be settled. At home.' She smiled, warmly and genuinely, at Gina. 'Always the same he was. Running about I don't know where. But, then, never any different, are they? Men. Just boys in big skins. What a way they'd be in if women weren't around to make sure they washed behind their ears and went out with a clean handkerchief.'

Reflexively, Gina replied, 'And with a haircut.'

Mrs Bridger, with an askance eye toward Fallon's unruly head, agreed, 'Isn't that the truth. Now, my dear, weekend groceries is it? For the two of you?'

The question was natural, no edge of nosiness, and Gina was about to reply when Fallon laid a pious ration book on the counter and said, with a retaliatory gloat, 'My friend left her coupons in London.'

Mrs Bridger shot him a look that could have curled toast, before bobbing below the counter, coming up with an empty carton. Moments later she had packed bacon, sausage, eggs, a crusty loaf, fresh vegetables, jars of pickle, cheese and even a generous pat of butter. Making change for Fallon's ten-shilling note she clucked at him like an admonishing mother hen. Then she carefully tore from his ration book enough coupons to cover all the provisions, beamed at Gina and advised, 'There'll be scissors at the lodge to cut his hair.'

Back in the car he observed darkly, 'If you grin like that for much longer your jaw will lock.'

It was dusk by the time they reached Monk's Lodge. In the car's headlights Gina discerned a tiny house sheltered amid shoulder-high wild roses and titanic gone-to-seed cow parsley. Fallon said, 'This was my parents' summer spot, since I was a teenager. They retired to Scotland in 1937. Dad has refused to bring my mother south since war broke out. I use the place sometimes. Not for anything special. Just for being alone. Staring out the window for a couple of days. Reminding myself not everybody in the world is killing each other.' He had opened the trunk, carried their two small suitcases to the honeysuckle-smothered porch. Unlocking the door he ushered Gina inside, flicked on a switch.

'It's wonderful,' she declared, genuinely gasping at the heavily beamed ceiling, timber studded walls and ancient inglenook fireplace. She stepped amid the clustered chintz armchairs, oak cabinets, pewter and copper and brass. Though there was a strong smell of must, the room glowed warm and welcoming. She turned to Fallon. He gathered her into his arms, and they kissed deeply and lingeringly.

She could not remember when she last had felt so relaxed, so much . . . at home.

True to his word, Fallon cooked dinner while Gina lit a wood fire, aired the blankets, dusted and plumped cushions. As they ate they talked. And later, sitting on the floor in front of the smouldering logs, they talked more. There was so much about each other to tell, all their separated years to recount, their lives to exchange.

Fallon, Gina learned, had been born a Welshman (she thought of dark and passionate Celtic blood); had spent his first nine years in a pit village where his doctor father watched half his male patients cough themselves to death before they were fifty. 'No, there was no savage beauty,' he said, 'No iron-forged indomitability. That's fiction. My most vivid memories are of grass that was permanently black, a roadside to the mine forever stained by men's spit, our cottage saturated with the stink of disinfectant, and the resentment in the eyes of all the other kids who knew I was the only one who wouldn't end up like their fathers.'

After the pit had shut, a succession of surgeries had led from Wales to north London from whence Fallon had entered Edinburgh University, emerged with a degree in European history, and promptly joined the army, 'to spend two and a half years propping up bits of the crumbling Empire in Palestine, India and West Africa. The landscapes were different, but the people were always the same. The faces held the identical resentment I'd seen in my childhood.' Signed out of the service, he'd returned to London and a job with Reuters, 'because I was too dumb to do anything but write'. Six months later he was covering the Japanese occupation of Manchuria; then the Paraguayan-Bolivian conflict; then the Italian invasion of Ethiopia; then the anarchist uprising in Spain. 'I've been asked,' he said, 'the colour of my politics. If there's one thing I've learned, it's that when you come right down to it, there are no colours. There are just people, with resentment in their eyes.'

Hearing all of Fallon's adventures, Gina felt the tale of her life in America seemed somewhat inadequate, nevertheless she recounted it, told Fallon about Cassie and Harry and Johnny (omitted Howard Cornell) while he listened with interest and enthusiasm, prompting her here and there for additional details of the exploits of Paola and Filipo and his old drinking and debating buddy Max.

They talked beyond midnight. Only their subsequent love-making, in the big, old bed beneath the bird-rustling eaves, interrupted their gossip; and when Gina finally drifted to sleep gathered in Fallon's arms, her dreams continued to be filled with the smoky timbre of his voice.

She awoke with the sun like diamonds through the window. The curtains were open, through the glass Gina could see blue sky, copper tree tops, this side of the casement a pot of red geraniums, shades as vivid as fresh paint. She stretched, basking in the warmth, luxuriating in her happiness. Another four whole days, she thought. I've got him to myself for – she mentally calculated – almost two hundred more hours. More than a body can stand. Don't you believe it?

Throwing back the covers she realized she was naked. So

what? This was the way lovers were supposed to wake in the morning. This was the fantastic feeling she'd been missing all these years.

She padded to the window. Below, a moss-grown terrace supported time-bleached timber chairs, was flanked by stone urns overflowing with scarlet sedums above which clouds of butterflies fluttered like welcoming coloured handkerchiefs. Steps led down to a lawn turned to hay running to a wooden jetty at a lakeside. The water lay perfect as glass, and on the far shore orange-tiled white and ochre houses nestled in the folds of the tree-clothed hills. Gina had never seen anything so picturesque. Her memory briefly approximated the landscape to that around Lake Maggiore where she had holidayed with her parents, but this was lusher and gentler, and wafting over the sill were not the heady perfumes of azaleas and camellias but the subtler scents of sage and lavender – and bacon!

She was ravenous. She swung around, strode across the rug, and was opening the door before she remembered she was nude. Halfway into her bra she changed her mind, made a rapid sortie of the wardrobe, extracted and donned one of Fallon's white cotton shirts, cinched the waist with her skirt belt, stepped into her high heels. Did you ever see legs that went this far, Mister World Authority on Women?

Shameless!

Damn right.

He turned from the kitchen stove where he was ladling fried eggs onto a plate and Gina flamed with satisfaction at the expression on his face. Cranking his jaw up he greeted, 'Just in time,' and added bacon and fried bread to the sunny-side-ups, set the spread on a scrubbed pine table and commanded, 'Eat.'

'But that was yours,' protested Gina. 'And, anyhow, I couldn't possibly. I never touch breakfast.'

'Don't argue. Besides, you know you're starving. It does it every time. To me too.' He grinned over his shoulder as he piled more supplies into his frying pan. 'No, not that. The country air.'

Gina smiled, knew that she was blushing. Good heavens, what was the matter with her this morning? She felt weird, lightheaded, almost delirious. A thousand moths were whirling in her stomach. An empty stomach. She focused on the food, a sight which under normal circumstances would have curdled her blood. But these circumstances were far from normal. She

307

sat at the table. Ate like a starving lumberjack. Gradually, some sense of reality returned. When she glanced up Fallon was watching her. It was as if he were studying the very pores of her skin. Oh, God, she thought, I forgot my hair, and my make-up. I must look hideous. Medusa on a bad day.

He said, 'You're very beautiful.'

Her knife and fork hovered. The euphoria and delirium faded, replaced by an unheralded sadness, an overwhelming surge of self-pity for all the years she had let slip by, all the mornings she had spent alone with coffee and account books. She pushed that emotion aside, continued to eat as Fallon returned to his cookery.

When they had finished, they sat on the terrace, and keeping to their pact to eschew both radio and newspapers for the duration of their stay, they again talked, far into the morning.

At last Gina asked, 'Where's your novel at?'

'Such mangled American grammar.'

'Don't be so pedantic. And don't avoid the issue.'

After a pause: 'It's nowhere.' Fallon stared off toward the lake, his eyes fixed on the reflecting glare of sunlight. Eventually he returned to Gina's determined silence and said, 'I put it aside. A couple of years ago. Because everything I'd written paled to insignificance in the face of what was happening. I knew that if I was going to produce anything it had to be about this war. But I didn't know if I was capable; wasn't certain I'd find the words to tell it as it is. – Please, no well-intentioned contradictions. – When the last shot has been fired, a thousand authors, good, bad and indifferent, will try to put the unprintable on paper. They'll record the adventure, the romance, the tragedy, even the comedy. Some will succeed marvellously. Others will produce dross. If – repeat, if – I'm one of them, I honestly am not sure which category I'll fall into But I am certain of one thing: I'll write simply about the ordinary people – the clerks from Manchester, the welders from Toronto, the,' he smiled, 'restaurateurs from New York – made extraordinary by events, and maybe, if I'm able, how this massive wound on history scars the brief span of their lives.'

Fallon halted there. 'End of subject,' he declared. 'Now,' he stood, held out his hand, 'we'll swim.'

Gina hesitated, still caught among his words.

'You can swim, can't you?'

She accepted his decision – for now – to close that discussion. 'Of course,' she replied, and wondered if after so many years she'd sink like a rock. Then she exclaimed, 'I don't have a costume.' But the expression in his eyes told her how futile that excuse was going to be. What about the opposite shore? her inner voice ventured. The folks over there might have binoculars. She stared across there. This is madness, she thought. 'So let them look,' she said aloud, kicking off her shoes.

'Whatever happened to that demure young thing I once knew?' growled Fallon. And he grabbed for her and she yelped and fled and he chased her off the terrace, down the lawn, whooping and promising exquisitely terrible assaults upon her body. At the jetty she hesitated only a moment, turned to face him, then yanked the shirt over her head, threw it aside, let him take one long, boggle-eyed look before she leapt into the lake.

She swam swiftly out, rolled onto her back, the cold and exhilaration sucking her breath as she dived and resurfaced in a glittering cascade, revelling in the long-forgotten joy of being a water-baby. Sluicing her hand across her face she saw Fallon dive, disappear, burst into view only feet from her, cleaving the swell with powerful strokes, his streaming features alight with passion.

Gina spun and surged away, felt his hand seize her ankle, thought she'd swallowed ten gallons as he pulled her beneath the surface. When he released her she shot upward, erupted into the sunlight like a cork from a bottle, wallowed, spluttering and gasping. Once more she was in his arms, and the sliding of his slippery body against hers was the most erotic sensation she had ever conceived. She melded herself to him, caressed him with every inch of her skin, slid her hands over his back, his buttocks, his thighs, plunged and played and splashed with him. Suddenly realized she was one with him. Her mind reeled as his lips found her mouth. She was in some crazy dream from which she was sure she would wake. This couldn't be happening. No one could be as ecstatically, as sensually happy as this.

She didn't know how long they cavorted in the water, or how many times they made love during the remainder of the day. When she finally sank back beside him on the bed that night, she had only a kaleidoscopic remembrance of swimming, lying naked on the lawn, drinking, dry, aromatic white wine, arranging marigolds in a heart shape on his chest, eating charcoal-grilled sausages on the moonlit terrace. No wonder teenagers started acting strangely when they discovered simultaneously sex and romance. Who at seventeen could be expected to cope rationally with this outlandish sensation? Who at twenty-six could be expected to cope?

The second morning Gina lay on a lounger on the jetty while Fallon rowed an ancient skiff out onto the lake and waited beside a fishing pole. Occasionally he waved, and she watched him, studied the hard, tanned muscles of his shoulders and arms and ached for their strength around her. It must be something to do with my age, she thought, for she wanted him every moment, was besieged by visions of their bodies entwined in every conceivable embrace.

They lunched on the trout he proudly brought ashore, then strolled through the woods, hand-in-hand, to a stile in a hedge and, beyond, meadows where slow-browsing, cream-coloured cows were the only other signs of life. Gina realized she had never known such solitude, never experienced such an overwhelming sense of peace. It settled on her like thistledown, and she held it, carried it with her as they retraced their path to the house.

And so the precious hours passed.

As their time together wore away, Gina wound down and down, her recalls of the tumult of the Rainbow and St Maud's becoming ever more infrequent. This was a different world, without a single reminder of German retreats, British advances, American losses in the Pacific. This was a magic time, when war clouds had been bewitched from the horizon. The days settled into languid patterns of lazing and loving; the wheeling of swallows was the tempo of the mornings, the throb of crickets was the rhythm of the afternoons.

On Sunday, on the terrace, they sat watching the swallows. Fallon said, 'You know, they rarely come to earth. Don't ask me why. Maybe it's because they know they're too vulnerable once they land.' The years at the corners of his eyes deepened as he squinted at the high turning birds. 'Or perhaps it's just something inside them, something they can't overcome, that keeps them forever in the sky.'

That night he said, 'We have to go back.'

Gina answered, 'I know it.'

They laid their suitcases in the trunk of the little Ford, locked the door of the old house.

Gina looked around at the rioting wild roses, the forest of cow parsley. I will see you again, she promised. There'll be other days. With Fallon. All the days of my life.

Gina quit her room at the Rainbow Corner, moved into Fallon's apartment. Sybil said it was a shocking thing to do – in these days of chronic shortages, hogging a whole man instead of sharing him among the needy.

They passed this autumn time like any married couple (except, they weren't married).

Both arranged their hectic work schedules so that they could spend at least their evenings together. Gina would cook, then they'd eat, sharing a bottle of Chianti – courtesy of Sergeant R. Tucker – and Fallon would marvel at the dinner she'd produced from a few dried vegetables, herbs and offal. Later they'd sit on the sofa, Gina's head on his shoulder, the lights out, illuminated only by the flickering glow from the tiny, rationed coal fire, and listen to the big, old wireless – Tommy Handley in *ITMA* broadcasting from the mythical Westminster Office of Twerps (Gina never could understand why this word caused Fallon such amusement), Henry Hall's dance band, and the B.B.C. Home Service nine o'clock news which Fallon said was the only remaining more-or-less-unvarnished truth in the world.

Some nights they'd walk around the corner to the pub where Fallon would become deeply involved in protracted, intellectual discussions on the relative qualifications – more accurately, lack of them – of the Saracens, Harlequins, Wasps, London Scottish and others to appear at some place called Twickenham. Unable to push a quiet word in edgewise during these loud debates, Gina for several evenings sat silently by until a trio of housewive regulars, similarly abandoned by their rugby and soccer expert spouses, invited her over to join in Guinness, chat and bawdy jokes which, before bed, Gina scribbled into her notebook for recount the following day to Sybil and later transmission to Cassie.

A few times they went to the cinema where during the intermission a man seated at an organ rose out of a pit before the screen to play trilling tunes while the audience gossiped about the patriotism-rousing epic they'd just seen in which Leslie

Banks had destroyed the entire German navy or Errol Flynn had single-handedly defeated the Japanese. Afterwards Gina and Fallon would stroll home, detouring to the fish and chip shop for roe and a penn'orth, later pausing in the dark of the stairs below the apartment to kiss with fishy, salty, vinegary lips.

On Sundays they would simply walk – the park, the riverside, the winding alleys around St Pauls, anywhere but Allied Main Street – or they would take the bus to Richmond and visit David Lowell.

It was on one of these occasions, when the conversation touched, inevitably, on rationing, that Gina, remembering, mentioned the children she'd seen eating potato peelings.

Fallon remarked, 'That's not so unusual. And it isn't wholly the fault of the war. Even before 1939 thousands of London's youngsters, contrary to their media image as rosy-cheeked rapscallions, were as half-starved as many of their counterparts in the slums of Paris, Detroit, Madrid.' To the disbelief on Gina's face he continued, 'At the agency we've been following the reports from country families who are housing evacuees. A disturbing number say how utterly astonished, and concerned, they were at the children's attitudes toward food: many had never eaten a fresh vegetable in their lives, some had no idea what a milk pudding was, several said their mothers hadn't ever produced a hot meal. The roe and a penn'orth we pick up as a snack is the staple diet of a lot of city kids. Others subsist entirely on sandwiches. And they're the relatively well-fed ones.'

'But what's being done about it?' Gina demanded sharply. Then, seeing the patronizing flicker pass between the two men, she added angrily, 'And that's as much as any male cares.'

It was the spark that lit her first row with Fallon. Not so much a row, more an exchange of her indignation for his quiet understanding. It lasted all the way home to the apartment, until, as he wound the alarm clock he said gently, 'We can't save everybody, Gina. Sometimes it's all we can do to save ourselves.'

She lay in bed with that, for five hours. She didn't need the alarm because she didn't sleep. When Fallon awoke, Gina was putting on her coat. She came to him, kissed him briefly, said, 'Coffee's in the kitchen. See you tonight, sometime.' Before he could restrain her, physically or verbally, she was heading for the door.

On the street, she strode past the bus stop. It was a long walk to Shaftesbury Avenue, but she needed it; needed this chill November morning to clear her mind of a growing confusion – an admixture of pain at the abrupt rupturing of her idyll, resentment of Fallon's ability to find words which sounded so frustratingly right, and an unshakeable belief that she could prove him wrong.

'I know there's no point in agonizing for the world,' she conceded to Sybil. 'But, surely, if just one child could be given a single ray of hope in all this darkness, it would be worthwhile.'

'Don't you think you're already doing enough?' the English girl returned. 'All right, you've heard that before. Although . . . ' She paused in her scouring of a saucepan, sighed and accepted, 'Yes, I agree, of course I do. None of us can ever do enough. But we won't accomplish anything by beating our breasts. We have to produce practical solutions. I'll help you save that one child, you know I will. Just tell me how. Also,' she held Gina with genuinely caring eyes, 'tell me which one.'

Gina knew her friend meant well, knew at the same time that, like Fallon, she was trying, in her own gentle way, to lay the ghost which suddenly had risen in Gina's life. Gina herself wasn't sure what had caused her to be haunted by a spectre of lost children. It wasn't wholly due to the conversation about evacuee youngsters, something else had been on her mind that afternoon at David Lowell's. Something? Don't pretend you can't remember, she rebuked herself. You know what was in your head. A question. A question you daren't ask because you're afraid of the answer.

Why hadn't Fallon mentioned marriage?

Eight weeks had passed since their days in Suffolk, in all that time they had discussed every subject under the sun – bar one. And, because Fallon never broached it, Gina avoided probing their relationship too deeply. They were compatible in so many ways, could fulfil each other's needs without demand or commitment. That was enough. She told herself so every night.

Drying the pan Sybil had washed and handed over, Gina exclaimed aloud, 'The Grange Hotel! A children's home.

Wouldn't it make a marvellous children's home?' Her abrupt enthusiasm was firecracker-bright.

By noon it had sputtered out like a damp squib.

At a corner table in the Grange's bar, David said, 'It's a lovely idea, Gina. And I'd have no objections, of course I wouldn't. This old place has been dead too long. It needs an injection of life. So do I. I'm beginning to feel useless, fossilizing here. That's why I'd love to offer you a practical alternative to sympathy. But it will take more than our combined enthusiasm – Sybil's too, I know she's with you on this – to get this barn habitable. When you first visited maybe you didn't fully appreciate the state it's in. The plumbing's falling apart. Some of the electrics could be lethal. There's enough damp in the north wall to breed fish. And half the bedroom floorboards are supporting the furniture by nothing but will power. I'm sorry. I truly am. But, even if we could afford to make the place safe, the materials just aren't available.'

Gina faced the genuine sadness in the fair-haired man, who, over the past eight months had become a true and trusted friend. And she scolded herself with self-reproach for rushing in here with her unlikely scheme and causing him such concern. She had never done that before, gone off at half-cock before thinking her idea through. She told herself her recently decimated emotions were to blame; but added that that was no excuse.

She said, with a pale smile, 'Thanks for hearing me out, David. Please don't think me too hare-brained.'

'That I'd never do.' He reached across the table, squeezed her hand, encouraged, 'Don't worry so. Everything will work out. For the young, and the old. For all of us. I don't believe in brave new worlds, but something good, something constructive, has to come out of all this waste. And that day's getting closer. There's light at the end of the tunnel. Certainly there is.' He grinned. 'For the first time in two years, Woolworth's have got knicker elastic on the counter. Means Winston will be able to devote his entire efforts to winning the war, won't have to spend so much time reminding us to pull our socks up.'

Gina responded quickly, 'Though it might slow down the advances of some of our less determined troops.'

David laughed out loud.

And, for now, Gina's demons were gone; though the ghost of

the idea with which she had rushed here was still within her. It remained undisturbed there for one more month.

In the week before Christmas the weather turned bitterly cold. Fallon reported he'd be staying in London at least until next spring. St Maud's had to cope with an outbreak of influenza. Sybil went to lunch with David Lowell, alone, twice. The Rainbow became festooned with holly, balloons, streamers and pictures of the Andrews Sisters who were scheduled to visit in March. Harry wrote to say business at The Lady was booming.

None of these, however, was the factor which precipitated Gina Rossi's renovation of the Grange Hotel.

22

Pregnancy was the last thing she had thought about.

Not true. Pregnancy was what she had striven to keep as far from her mind as possible. Since that night Fallon had mentioned contraception Gina had shelved not only her conscience, but also any speculation on the potential of their sexual relationship. What the eye can't see, the heart can't grieve over – or look forward to. Today, reliance on any such maxims was at an end.

Sitting on the straight-backed but comfortable chair in the small but neat waiting-room, Gina presented a picture of elegant calm to the half-dozen pine-framed, watercoloured British birds who chirrupped at her from a facing wall. Inside her head, it was a different story. Her brain was as relaxed as a well-stirred hornets' nest. The stick that had caused the ferment was, of course, a missed period.

'A missed period!' Cassie had exclaimed that time one of The Lady's young hat-check girls had sought big sister reassurance after a loving but careless weekend with the band's curly-haired alto sax player. 'Just one! Kiddo, I've missed more periods than you've had hot dinners. How long you miss it by? Two weeks. Uh huh. Sprint round the block three times. Swallow a coupla dry Martinis – real dry. A hot bath. Quit worrying.'

Gina smiled at the suspended blue tit – thought her heart wasn't really in it. For the past three days she'd been considering, seriously, running thrice around Soho Square and following with the other ingredients of Cassie's remedy. She'd also spent that time imagining what might happen if she let nature take its course. There were so many questions in her, so many doubts and fears.

Just a few weeks ago – up until her first time with Fallon – she would never have believed she could be hesitant about the correct course to follow in this circumstance. Beside abortion, the sin of contraception paled to insignificance. Yet the day she'd realized the clockwork regularity of her menstrual cycle had missed a beat, she'd been assailed by uncertainty. She couldn't even rationalize her motives. And her emotions were out of control; one minute she was on the crest of elation, the next she was in the slough of despond. Thank goodness her Rainbow and St Maud's schedules were too busy for her mood to become apparent to Sybil, and that Fallon's equally taxing workload caused him to be too preoccupied to notice anything amiss. Or was he merely avoiding confrontation when, last night, as his reaching arms had been rebuffed by her muttered, 'Tired,' he'd responded, 'Getting like an old Darby and Joan,' and gone to sleep holding her hand?

This morning, with that memory still painful in her mind, Gina had at last been struck by logic. Serving coffee around the canteen, she suddenly declared aloud, to the startlement of the four marines at the table, 'This can't go on.'

At the end of her shift she'd discreetly checked the directory in the club's library, then made one telephone call. An hour later she was at the Harley Street consultancy.

'Miss Rossi.'

Gina, startled, turned from the watercolour birds to the morning-suited man in the doorway. Rising, smiling with counterfeit nonchalance, she followed him into his consultancy room. The walls were oak-panelled to complement the cabinets and desk. The upholstery was burgundy leather, the drapes were matching velvet. The air of respectability was as heavy as Gina had expected on this famed thoroughfare. As she sat she felt a brief wash of shame that she, earlier, had sullied it.

On her arrival and explanation of the reason for her visit, the doctor had agreed to carry out an immediate examination, but had then explained that the results would not be available for another forty-eight hours. When Gina's protestations and importunings had met only with the man's adamancy, she had offered him money. 'Three times your usual fee,' she had blurted, pulling cheque book and pen from her purse. 'Please. I can't wait any longer.' That had been the truth. The gross bribe (what else could you call it?) had sprung from neither crassness nor conceit, but from sudden genuine desperation. And perhaps the doctor had recognized that in Gina's eyes, for, with not the slightest glance toward her cheque book he had said flatly, 'After your examination I shall require a further hour.'

It was more like two. But, then, the physical exploration also had taken much longer than she'd expected.

At his desk, Mr Mayne scrutinized a sheet of paper, looked across at Gina.

'Am I?' She could contain herself no longer. 'Please, Doctor, am I pregnant?'

The doctor replied, 'No, Miss Rossi. You are not.'

Gina didn't know whether she was relieved or disappointed. Both, she guessed. She couldn't help beginning to analyse her response, to try to make some sense out of the emotional upheaval that was climaxing within her. All she wanted now was to be out of here, to find some quiet place and regain a modicum of composure before returning to the apartment and Fallon.

'Miss Rossi.' The doctor steepled his fingers above the desktop. For a second he seemed unsure of what he was about to say, but when he at last spoke his voice was level and sure, its tone instantly capturing Gina's attention. 'Ordinarily I would not broach what I am about to discuss without first contacting your regular physician in New York. However, these are not ordinary times, and transatlantic communications are hardly satisfactory at the moment. Besides, the very fact that you came to me for a confirmation of your condition, is evidence that you have, in the past, sought your doctor's advice but rarely, and certainly have never undergone his thorough physical examination. Please, correct me if I am wrong.'

Gina replied, somewhat bemusedly, 'You're absolutely right. I'm registered with a doctor in Manhattan, but the only occasions I've seen him have been when he's visited my younger sister and brother to prescribe for their minor childhood ailments. I've never had a day's illness in my life.'

The doctor nodded. Again he pondered before asking, 'Do you have friends or relations in London? Someone with whom you're staying?'

Perplexed by this odd turn in the conversation, Gina answered simply, 'Yes.' She hoped she was not about to receive either a lecture on sexual morality or advice on contraceptive practices. At her age. How mortifying! She decided she should have waited at least a couple more days before rushing in here like a frightened hat-check girl.

'You suffered an accident several years ago, Miss Rossi. Please believe me when I say I am not being presumptuous or making an unconsidered diagnosis, but, in my opinion, the medical treatment you received at the time of the accident was somewhat inadequate. I stress that this is merely an opinion. Ethically, and legally, I cannot make judgment on a fellow doctor's work, particularly when I am not cognisant of the circumstances, however . . . '

The doctor went on. Gina didn't hear. What had he said? An accident? She'd had no accident. Several years ago? When she was an infant perhaps. Something she couldn't remember. Something her parents had never mentioned? But what could it be? She was fine. I've never had a day's illness in my life.

' . . . the damage was considerable. The results compounded by what I surmise was unchecked haemorrhaging. There is evidence to suggest . . . '

'Accident?' interrupted Gina. 'I didn't have any accidents as a child. I don't understand.'

'Not when you were a child,' frowned the doctor. 'Later. Much later. You certainly had reached maturity. Surely you recall, Miss Rossi? You must know what I am talking about. Such massive internal rupturing could not have occurred without your knowledge.'

Internal! The image in Gina's head flared like a suddenly re-opened wound. Blood poured across her mind. The blood of Galeazzo Sturzo blooming like an opening flower around his smashed skull. And her own blood; not seen, but felt, foaming inside her, coursing down her thighs as she fled across a luminscent landscape. She snatched her knuckles to her mouth, pressed them against her lips until the acute pain cancelled the agony in her belly.

'Miss Rossi.' The doctor was halfway out of his chair. 'Are you all right? Shall I call my nurse?'

Gina ground her jaws, breathed deeply through her nostrils. When she spoke her voice was as rigidly under control as her inner feelings. 'I'm fine, thank you. A brief spasm of toothache. I must visit a dentist. Now, doctor, my accident. Yes, of course I remember. A fall in my late teens, one day when I was out riding. I was a long way from home. It was several hours before I was found and taken to a village doctor. He did his best, though,' she smiled drily, 'perhaps not his neatest. However, there is no need for your concern. I assure you it never troubles me. Indeed, as you have just witnessed, there are times when I completely forget about it.' Gina arranged the businesslike set of her shoulders. 'So, I hope you will accept my apology for my earlier conduct. My offer to multiply your fee was not intended as an insult to your personal, or professional, integrity. I allowed my impatience to overcome my manners. Thank you for your time, and for indulging my discourtesy. Also, of course, for your reassurance. Shall I settle your account with your nurse, or will she mail it to me?'

The doctor shook his head, raising a stilling hand. 'One moment, please. There is something more. You came here seeking confirmation of pregnancy. Forgive me, there is no easy way to say this.' He paused before continuing, enunciating each word as if addressing a foreigner. 'Such a likelihood is so remote as to be virtually impossible.' He leaned slightly forward across the desk. 'Do you understand, Miss Rossi? After examining you, I believe the extent of your internal injuries precluded you from conceiving a child.'

Gina said lightly, 'Really? I didn't know that.'

'I'm sorry to give you such news,' said the doctor. 'However, I repeat, this is solely my opinion and . . .'

'Quite. Yes. I understand,' clipped Gina. Her muscles were becoming steel cords and she could feel the ligaments of her jaw tightening to where she would be unable to speak. Her arched fingers were clamped over the chair arms, suspending her above the pit of anguish. She could see the doctor had begun talking again but his voice was unintelligible. The only clear words in her head were those he had already uttered: 'Precluded you from conceiving a child.'

Yet had the fact come as such a shock? Or was it its vocalization which was so appalling? For had Gina known – yes, known, not suspected – had her deepest female instincts unequivocally known the truth about her own defectiveness?

Defectiveness. Was that the word from which she had shied for over five years?

'. . . not without hope,' intoned the doctor. 'Medical advances are being made constantly. And, once you are married, you could consider adoption. In your own country, as well as Britain, there are thousands of youngsters awaiting loving parents. Please, remember these things. Believe me, there is no reason for you to be depressed. Come and see me again, for a check-up, next week. In the meantime I'll ask my nurse to make up this sedative . . . ' He began to scribble on a prescription pad.

'Thank you,' Gina said sharply, rising as suddenly. 'You've been most kind. No, that won't be necessary,' she dismissed the prescription. 'You're quite right, barrenness is something any woman can cope with. Thank you again. For your understanding.' She strode across the room, unfaltering as the doctor hurried from behind his desk to open the door. She paused, shook his hand, said, 'Good day,' went past the forever bright eyes of the watercolour birds, the equally permanent smile of the nurse at the reception desk.

On the street the air had become iron. Passers-by leaned into the winter, faces tight closed against the cold.

Gina didn't notice. Anaesthetized by desolation, she walked. She walked into the darkling afternoon, into the frost-cast evening, clutching her purse to her chest, cradling it there like a last grasp on reality. Her mind was no longer in the present. It was in the future: a future which until today had been full to overflowing, but which now was a hollow shell, as empty and vulnerable as Gina felt. For it was without Fallon. How could it include Fallon? How could she ask him to share a life that was incomplete? With a woman who was incomplete?

The despair stalked her into the blackout; through the city; across midnight.

'Are you okay, ducks?' asked a female voice. 'You look a bit peaky. This wevver I shouldn't wonder. Enough to freeze 'em off a brass monkey. Wiv a bit of luck though, it'll be twice as perishin' in Germany, give old Adolf chilblains where he'll feel 'em most. Eh? Eh?' Racking laughter was accompaniment to an elbow jagging Gina in the ribs.

She looked around at a face the colour and texture of dried figs, wrapped about with scarves and cloths, shrunken into the neck of a voluminous khaki overcoat, the belt of which was festooned with bags, tatty parcels and an unlit railway lantern. Beyond this figure the earth was silver, dappled, reflecting derricks and black buildings. Gina shook her mind, dragged herself back to reality. She was beside the river, on a rank-smelling wharf. The woman was tugging her arm, inviting, 'Come on, ducks. Aht of this wevver. Shrivel yer vitals it will. Come over 'ere. Join the gels.' She pulled Gina along the side of a wall, into deeper dark, into viler stink; until suddenly they came into a cave walled by rusted drums and rotting crates, roofed by sagging timber and tarpaulins, lit by the rufous glow of smouldering garbage.

Gina recoiled, wrenched herself from the crone's grasp. Her pain had fled as comprehension returned like a lancing knife. She stared into the semi-circle of faces, half-a-dozen women, as leprous as the one at her side, squatting around the fire returning her gaze with a co-mingling of fear and pity and expectancy and . . . welcome.

She yelled, 'No!' And the cry cracked amid the encircling buildings like fracturing masonry. The women stumbled, slithered into the recesses of their pit. Gina turned. Ran. Out of that place, down alleys and yards and streets. She ran until her breath was ragged in her throat, until the sweat was pouring down her body, until she was as far away from those women as her legs would carry her.

It was after one in the morning when she reached the Rainbow and was allotted the still-vacant bed in her old room. She asked the girl at reception to call Fallon, tell him she'd been sent out on long-distance collection detail, would phone him tomorrow. Unable to piece together her shattered reasoning, she knew merely that tonight she must sleep alone.

Removing only her hat, coat and shoes, Gina climbed into bed, pulled the blankets to her chin, and slept. She slept as though drugged, a deep dreamless sleep during which neither her body nor her mind moved.

She remained that way for ten hours.

When she swam back to consciousness the room was cleft by a sliver of sunlight slicing between the still-closed curtains. Sybil was hunched on the edge of the facing bed rolling off her stockings; her face was drawn, and even in the half-light Gina could see the fatigue shadowing her eyes. Pushing herself to her elbows, Gina asked, 'Tough night?'

Sybil started. 'I woke you. I'm sorry.'

Gina, glancing at the clock, exclaimed, 'After eleven! Good heavens, I must have been dead to the world.' She swiftly swung her feet to the floor, began to rise. Then she remembered. She remained sitting erect, clenching her fists against a return of last night's anguish. It didn't come. There was nothing inside her. Better if there had been, because she desperately wanted to break down. Why couldn't she be permitted her moments of grief?

Sybil said flatly, 'Peggy Atkins died.'

Gina could only stare.

'She came back to the hospital last night. Sister Carey said she looked dreadful. She'd probably been sleeping rough in the bombed-out buildings with the derelicts. When she came in she didn't speak, wouldn't speak to anybody. Wouldn't eat or drink either, even though, of course, it was offered. But she did let them feed the baby. Contrary to Peggy's condition, the kid was well-nourished and, wherever she'd been living, she'd made certain he was kept warm and clean. She'd even washed his clothes, the ones she'd been given at St Maud's, and he was wrapped in a new blanket – maybe she bought it, stole it, who knows?' Sybil bit her lip, held her breath a moment.

Gina thought her friend was about to cry, though she herself was still too confused to offer sympathy. What had Sybil said about Peggy? She died?

'She left the baby.' Sybil's voice was taut with suppressed sadness, anger too. 'She watched him being fed, then said to take care of him while she went to the cloakroom. That was the only time she spoke. It was also the last time she was seen. When she hadn't returned twenty minutes later a search was made but Peggy was nowhere to be found. She wasn't in the hospital. No one had seen her. That was shortly before I went on duty. We told ourselves she might have just slipped off for an hour or so to be alone. But, I suppose, that was wishful thinking. A forlorn hope. Frankly, none of us was surprised when, by this morning, she still hadn't come back. She never had any intention of doing so. She'd visited only to bring the baby. To leave him there, where she knew he'd be . . . looked after . . . where . . . ' Sybil's words caught in her throat and she bit her lower lip. After a hard moment she exclaimed harshly, 'Oh, God, we should have seen it coming.'

Gina rose quickly, moved to her friend's side. Never had she thought of Sybil as vulnerable, even now was loath to place a comforting arm around her shoulders. 'Hey, take it easy,' she consoled. 'Don't make it so personal. There's no reason for you to blame yourself. You've given more than your share in this awful war. Truly, I wish I could have done half as much.'

Sybil turned to her, drew a deep steadying breath and re-gathered some of her usual spirit. 'Sorry, old girl, I shouldn't have let it get to me. There've been thousands of Peggy Atkins over the past four years, and there'll be a lot more before this mess is sorted out. Like I told you, the first time we were at St Maud's, we can't weep for them all.'

'You said Peggy died,' probed Gina.

'Maybe not yet,' returned Sybil. 'Perhaps she isn't yet physically dead. That might not come for several days, even weeks. But, whatever it eventually says on some coroner's report, the fact will remain that Peggy Atkins died last night – when she walked away from her baby.' Pain once more tightened her voice, but she took another composing breath, pulled out a lace handkerchief and blew vigorously. When she again faced Gina her features were calm.

They began to break apart as, eyes widening, she exclaimed, 'You were in bed with your clothes on!' Suspiciously: 'Why aren't you at home? With Fallon? Have you two fallen out? Is Fallon alone? In need of a bosom to cling to? The poor lamb.' She was off the bed, reaching for her hat.

'Sit down,' said Gina, unable to resist a smile. 'It's nothing like that. I . . . .' Memory stilled her. For the past minute or two she'd been so wrapped up in Sybil's story she'd forgotten the real reason for being here. Could it be wiped out, just like that? What was the matter with her? It was as if there was something missing inside, a part of her that had been cut away while she slept. Before she could reach back for it, into yesterday, she was rejoined to the present by Sybil plumping down onto the bed with a huffed:

'Harumph! Why is it that in a world of splintered love affairs, I'm never around at the right moment to pick up the male pieces? Are you sure you haven't broken Fallon's heart? Not just a little bit? No. Then you can jolly well clear off back to him. Let me get some shut eye.' She returned to the removal of her stockings.

Gina smiled fondly. She stood, gathered her coat; bent and kissed Sybil on the cheek, said quietly, 'Thanks,' adding, to

Sybil's quizzically raised face, 'I'll explain. One day.' She went out and down the stairs.

'Hey, Babe. How ya doin'?' Sergeant R. Tucker barrelled through the lunch-room-headed crush stuffing his scarf into the throat of his greatcoat. 'You okay for suspender clips?'

'Roscoe,' greeted Gina, genuinely pleased to see the cheerful face. 'Yes, I am, thanks. Off to the stores? Or have your nefarious deals at last brought about your banishment to a depot in Iceland?'

'No such luck,' the sergeant responded jovially. 'Now, if I was way up there, where it's too cold for thin-blooded lieutenants to stick their noses out the officers' mess, let alone into my business . . . ' He gazed upward into some blackmarket heaven, his face becoming positively beatific. Then, shrugging out of this reverie, he observed, 'Still, plenty of opportunities right here, so long as you reach out and grab 'em before the next guy. We all got to do that, don't we, Angel, because come tomorrow . . . ' His spread hands said the rest.

Gina nodded. There were voices in her head.

Roscoe was saying, 'See you later,' starting away.

Gina muttered, 'Yes. 'Bye.'

She went through to the canteen, apologized to the duty officer for her lateness, reported for kitchen detail. But as she worked, her mind was elsewhere, embroiled in mental argument of right and wrong, moral commitments, uncertain futures; it was a discord of jangling bells through which she strove to discern the words she had heard during the past twenty-four hours – the platitudes of a Harley Street consultant, the camaraderie of a female derelict, the sensitivity of Sybil, the veracity of Roscoe Tucker. Gina groped amid the conflict; sought an answer to her question.

When she stepped out into the dark of a late afternoon she had discovered no truths. But she had reached a decision. No one would dissuade her now.

Fallon pronounced, 'Never. I won't permit it. Gina, that's crazy. I know you mean well. I admire you for it. Love you for it. But it isn't realistic. All right, it is. In the present lunatic world anything is possible. I still can't let you go through with it. You know where you'll wind up? And not just you. What about the others you're involving in this . . . . this . . . crime?'

Gina smiled and kissed him.

The following morning she put the proposition to Sybil. The English girl sat and listened, her intent expression punctuated by disbelief, wonder, amusement. Later, together they visited David Lowell. The hotelier sat and listened, his expression punctuated by incredulity, admiration, anticipation. In the afternoon they invited Sergeant Roscoe Tucker to the Grange, showed him around, laid it on the line for him in the bar. He sat and listened, his expression as deadpan as a blank requisition sheet. Afterwards, they shook hands, wished each other, 'Merry Christmas.' A fortnight into the new year, on a Friday evening, they regathered, jammed into Roscoe's cubby hole at the supply depot. Gina asked, 'Are you all sure? Once the wheels are in motion, there'll be no stopping them, no going back.'

David said, 'Well, as far as I'm concerned, no matter where we end up, at least I'll have moved somewhere, had some sense of direction. And that has to be a whole lot better than mouldering in that mausoleum, until it crumbles on top of me, or the men in white coats carry me off to a home for slightly dotty, destitute hoteliers.'

Sybil said, 'Really, old girl, you couldn't pull me back now with wild horses. I'm looking forward to the relaxation. Supervising our venture, once it's under way, will be a doddle compared to dishing up dinners for permanently starving GIs. I'll miss their lecherous little bodies, of course, although I'm sure quality will more than compensate for quantity.' Her smile broiled David's face bright crimson.

Roscoe said, 'Certainly makes no odds to me. In fact it'll be kind of an interesting challenge getting this lot together.' He tapped the list they'd made at the Grange. 'Piping and plaster and paint will be a pleasant change from radios, razor blades and wristwatches.'

Gina said, 'That's settled then.'

Beaming around at her companions she felt flushed with enthusiasm, and, even though this was merely the beginning, accomplishment. This was the exhilaration she'd been missing all these months. Her work at the Rainbow and St Maud's were satisfying and, she knew, beneficial; still it hadn't been enough, hadn't been sufficiently constructive to fire her old zeal. Now she was experiencing that pumping of the blood that had come when she was first planning the Lady. Well, the

Grange Hotel wasn't going to be in quite the same category, but it was a scheme which, from the moment it had shaped itself in her mind, had captured her imagination along with her determination. All the old financial skills and strategic ingenuity had been rekindled as she toiled in the Rainbow's library with scratch pads, adding machine and a stack of construction manuals. She had devoted her every spare moment to the project during those first two weeks of 1944, holding meetings not only with Sybil and David but also seeking advice from a parade of experts – plumbers, electricians, carpenters, even an architect, all of whom were currently masquerading as soldiers, sailors and airmen on furlough at the Rainbow – while forbearing at this stage to mention to any of these that in the near future she would be requesting (enlisting) their more practical co-operation.

Only once during this frenetic activity had she faltered. Sybil had asked casually, 'But what sparked off the idea?' Gina's pen had hovered above a column of figures as a far voice had echoed, 'Precluded you from conceiving a . . . .' She had shut out the words, just as she had obliterated the whole of that morning in the Harley Street consultancy. Shrugging aside Sybil's question she had returned to her abnegation of all but work.

Even her lovemaking with Fallon had been cancelled. She had pleaded commitment to evening and night shifts, assured him it wouldn't last long, and salved his sore looks – and her own conscience – with lunchtime rendezvous in the pub around the corner from his office.

Tonight, she promised herself, the self-imposed celibacy would cease. Her intense, almost religious fervour of the past weeks, if not entirely exorcising her ghosts had at least subjugated them.

The blueprints, specification and bills of quantity for the renovation of the Grange Hotel were complete. Gina and Sybil had each contributed a thousand pounds towards what, at current blackmarket prices, the scheme was likely to cost. David, unable to offer any financial assistance, had insisted on assigning each of them a quarter share in the building. Sybil had protested, 'But that's worth far more than our investment.' David had insisted, 'Only so long as the place is standing. Which it won't be for much longer without your money. Sort of chicken and egg, isn't it?' Sybil had continued to argue until the deals were signed. Gina had not - though she didn't probe her motives.

In the depot office Roscoe cracked the seal on a bottle of cognac. 'Here we go then. Tomorrow I'll put the word on the grapevine. Don't hold your breath though. This will be a hefty order to fill. And we can't pull it all out of one place. That'd leave a hole in an inventory that even the dumbest O.C. Construction would spot. We have to chisel out a little here, a little there, leaving gaps that quartermasters can easily paper over. It'll all take time.' He filled generous glasses.

Gina asked, 'How long?'

'Reckon on the first delivery arriving next week. Sure, that soon. I just happen to have a good buddy down at the new rest camp they're building in Sussex. I know he'll be more'n happy to trade a truckload of floorboards for a hundred gross of nylons. That's the first easy step. From there on the going gets tougher, and we gotta tread more careful. But don't sweat it. Come May, I promise, you'll be tucking your last . . . er . . . guest . . . I guess that's what you'll call 'em? Sure . . . tucking the last one into brand new sheets.'.

Gina said happily, 'Roscoe, you're a doll.'

The others echoed the sentiment. They all raised their glasses. For a moment they looked from one to another, their poses stiffened by brief last-minute hesitancy. Recovering, it was Sybil who offered the toast:

'The Grange Home for Unmarried Mums.'

They drank.

Gina held to the exquisite moment, wondered how long it could last.

The months sped, and Gina's joy was undiminished. Nothing could jar her enthusiasm. Germany had launched a desperate series of fresh air raids on London, yet even these - and the accompanying strain they wrought on the understaffed, overworked St Maud's - she took in her stride as she hustled winter into spring.

The letters she continued to receive from New York further boosted her spirits. Everyone there seemed to be thriving as they rallied to the call of the War Manpower Commission. Paola had taken a full-time job at a blanket-weaving plant as well as spending four evenings a week making up overseas aid parcels at the Church of the Holy Cross. Somehow she'd also found time to cultivate the garden and was supplying vegetables to one of the local relief agencies. Cassie similarly was sharing her shifts at the Lady with packing ammunition at a factory in the Bronx. Also she'd learned to drive and spent Saturdays running a Hudson Transit bus to and from Atlantic City. Harry was still holding constant Services fund raisers at the restaurant and the club, the latest of which was in response to the Government's exhortations to collect various materials for recycling. Now every customer who brought in an item of rubber received a free champagne cocktail. The rear yard, Harry reported, was currently seven-feet deep in everything from tyres and galoshes to hose pipes and at least one pair of 1920s corsets. Filipo's collecting effort had been concentrated on metals, and in April his class had been awarded the Stack of the Month Award. Harry wrote he was sure (with fingers crossed) that this was in no way connected with the recent disappearance of garbage bins from several neighbouring premises.

Gina replied affectionately and encouragingly, recounted her London life, but, although she itched to tell all, mentioned nothing of the project which now filled her every sleeping as well as waking moment. No letter going astray must be permitted to jeopardize the Grange's refurbishment, which was advancing by leaps and bounds.

Roscoe had come through all the way – in aces. Parlaying, wheeling and dealing, dipping into the two-thousand-pound kitty if necessary but bartering quid pro quo whenever possible, he made Gina's head spin with awe as he explained how a crate of cameras from Ontario became six bales of BVDs in Boston turned into a wagonful of condensed milk in Liverpool and showed up as ten bathroom suites (complete with taps) in Richmond. 'You want I should get the john seats changed for that new-fangled plastic?' he suggested. Gina replied, 'I'm sure the wood will be fine, thanks all the same,' and exited swiftly, tracked by a vision of ten recently-housed colonels ranting, bathless, somewhere in England. She pulled the shades on that, before it led to a picture of a Manhattan ex-restaurateur, growing very old in the U.S. Army equivalent of the Chateau d'If.

Her recruited experts (remunerated alcoholically from Roscoe's apparent direct pipeline to a distillery), handled the professional necessities of wiring, plumbing and joinery, while

Sybil and David tackled those tasks requiring only a modicum of accuracy in the wielding of hammer, saw or paintbrush.

Sybil, having resigned from the Red Cross but continuing as a St Maud's auxiliary, also drew up the rules, working schedules and economics of the Grange's future persona. She devoted all her energies to the project; and Gina was hard put to subdue a twinge of envy at the English girl's deepening sense of commitment. For, while Gina's initial enthusiasm had never waned, and her concern for the plight of the husbandless girls who checked into the hospital's maternity wing grew daily stronger, she could no longer deny that her motivations sprang from a more complicated, but less altruistic, well than Sybil's.

Still her sun refused to be eclipsed. Life, as Johnny used to say, was running on wheels.

On May 1st (they had to explain to Roscoe the tongue-in-cheek significance of the garlanded pole they erected in the Grange's one-time croquet lawn) Gina climbed down from a 'borrowed' Red Cross truck at the hotel's front porch to be greeted by a widely beaming Sybil and a shyly smiling David, walked around the vehicle, unhooked and dropped the tailgate and declared, 'Here we are, ladies. Welcome to your new home.' She stood aside; waited.

A fair-haired young woman in a blue and white spotted frock, cradling a silent infant, hesitantly stepped down to the forecourt gravel. Slowly, eleven more followed. For an aching moment, as they stared up at the sombre red brick gables and turrets, Gina thought this all had been a crazy mistake, that the girls would turn away, refuse to enter. Then Sybil was striding forward, greeting cheerily, 'Mary, how are you? Alice, so glad you decided to come. Betty, my, isn't the little chap looking grand!' She moved swiftly amid the group, addressing each girl by name, affectionately touching each child, eliciting both smiles and wails, but lighting the small band one by one as surely as if she were flicking on switches. Then, 'Come along,' she called, 'Let's get you all settled. Mind the builders' trestles in the hall. Still a lot to do here. More rooms will be ready by next week. David, please hold the doors open, won't you?' And she marched ahead as a dozen suddenly gossiping girls lifted their suitcases and paper parcels, carried these, and their daughters and sons, in beneath the string of red, white and blue bunting.

Gina watched the last disappear inside. David waited for

her. She said, 'I'll be in in a minute. You go ahead. Sybil will need you.' After David had gone, she stood alone in the sunshine beside the empty truck. Voices, laughter too, came from within the hotel. A breeze stirred the little flags above the entrance. No sad thoughts, she told herself, not this lilac-scented morning. She went on inside.

By late afternoon Sybil had implemented a duty roster, was taking each event of these extraordinary hours in her stride as if this was the routine thousandth, rather than the monumental first, day in the new life of the Grange. At a desk in what used to be David's sitting-room, she protested, 'But you must stay for the party. The girls will be so disappointed if you don't. If it wasn't for you none of them would be here, half of them would be sleeping in dosshouses tonight.'

'Thanks,' returned Gina. 'But it's you, and David, the girls need now. I'll continue to help, of course I will, just as much as my shifts at the Rainbow and St Maud's will allow. Right now, though, I really would prefer to get back to town. I think it's about time I did a little confessing, and explaining, to a certain Mister Fallon.' She leaned to kiss Sybil's cheek. 'No, don't walk me to the door.' Her chest was tightening. 'Have a lovely party. I'll see you tomorrow.'

All the way to the city, driving beside the river, she silently repeated, Don't look back. Only forward. Only ever look forward.

'We did it,' she proclaimed as she entered the apartment, her melancholy eclipsed by the delight that Fallon was here to receive her news, share her success.

'Did it?' He looked quizzically from his typewriter.

'Got the stuff for the hotel.'

'Your English is improving.'

'Don't be so pedantic.' Gina made a face, strode to him, kissed him on the mouth . 'Mmm, I think I'll ravage you. But later. First we have to toast the almost completely rewired, re-plumbed, redecorated Grange Hotel. Isn't it *fantastico?* Where's that bottle? I mean the real Scotch you hoard for when your fifteen overgrown English hooligans squash fifteen equally retarded Welshmen into the Twickenham mud. Yes,' she yanked open the cupboard, extracted the precious whisky, 'I am blasphemous tonight, aren't I?' She sloshed out two hefty measures, handed one to Fallon, raised her glass. 'To the good ship Grange, and all the unmarried mums who sail in her.' She tipped back the liquor, grinned at Fallon's incredulous face.

His drink remained suspended. 'You didn't.'

'Of course we did. And no, David won't lose the licence, because the bar has been totally walled off from the rest of the building. And yes, it is a viable proposition, because all the girls have jobs. And certainly, we expect the local council, Member of Parliament, League of Decency, armies of outraged citizens to come beating upon the door. But, fear not, it will take more than mass moral indignation to shift a bulwark named Sybil Levy née De Belvere.'

Fallon sighed. Gina thought he was about to speak, but the retaliatory speech she had been polishing all the way here remained undelivered against his continuing silent stare.

She urged, 'Hey, come on, lighten up! All right, so now you know why you haven't been invited to the Grange since Christmas. I'm sorry we had to be secretive . . . '

'Underhand.'

'If you like. But what would you have done if I'd let you in on it? Lectured me. Every night. It would have led to a fight, for sure. I didn't want that, Fallon. I never want to fight with you. Though it wouldn't have stopped me. Because I believed in it. I admit maybe the whole thing was slightly mad, but you yourself said that sometimes the only way important things are achieved is by people acting a little crazily.'

'Are your unwed mothers so significant?'

'Definitely. Do you realize there are still English cities where they can be imprisoned under Victorian vagrancy laws? Up until the war there was an organized political lobby to deny them the vote. They had never . . . ' Gina halted, realizing she'd fallen into her prepared speech. This was not the time. Besides, it would sound fine coming from Sybil, but somehow in her own mouth the words had a faintly hollow ring. Shelving that disquieting thought, and her serious face, she swiftly changed course. Brightly, 'Anyhow, I haven't committed the crime of the century. I won't land in jail. And if I do you can smuggle me a file in a cake, buy me a passage on a clipper to the China seas, then sell the story to the *Sunday Dispatch*.' She gave him her best, cheeky grin.

Fallon's eyes remained shadowed.

Gina probed his expression. 'Are you okay?'

He stared at her for quite a while, his chin braced back; then his big hand was holding hers and his mouth was curving into a smile as he avowed, 'Of course I am. And I support you whole-heartedly. I'm very proud of you. I want to hear all about it.' He pulled her onto his lap. 'But first . . . ' raising an anticipatory eyebrow ' . . . didn't I hear something about ravagement?'

Gina joined his laughter. And yet? There was still something behind his eyes, a look she'd learned to recognize in this complex, caring man, the far-off light that said in spite of all contrary appearances, Robert Fallon wasn't really here. Her question formed in her head. She left it there; knew he wouldn't accept her, 'Penny for them.' Or was it that tonight, this warm, apple-blossom night, there was a deeper, unfathomable reason for her not wanting to know what was on his secret mind?

She unfastened several buttons of his shirt, ran her fingers down his strong throat, through the greying hairs of his chest. Taking his glass she placed it beside the old Remington, saw typed on a sheet of paper there the dates of three days early next month, June, followed by a string of question marks.

Noticing the direction of her gaze, Fallon shrugged, 'Just some notes on a rumour I picked up.'

Gina turned to him; wondered, why am I afraid?

Soon they made love.

It was five more weeks before the world fell apart.

23

This Saturday evening, though the sun continued to shine, ragged trails of cirrocumulus streaked the high atmosphere. Gina and Fallon had visited the Grange. As predicted, over the past month all manner of retribution – from the wrath of God to the discipline of the District Council – had been threatened against the hotel. So far none had come to pass. As Sybil said, 'Eighty young mums and their children, driven onto the streets. That would look splendid in the headlines. Just the sort of furore the Home Office needs right now. Don't worry, the tub-thumpers will have their say, but they won't bring our walls down.' When Gina had left she'd been glowing confidently. Beside her, Fallon had been scrutinizing the mackerel sky. But, Gina frowned as they strolled past the National Gallery, he'd seemed unusually concerned about the weather all day.

They went on past the Odeon where Frank Sinatra's film *Higher and Higher* was billboarded for next week. (The record of the title song had sold out nationwide within three days of issue despite the fact that people buying a new record were asked to take back an old one which would be used to make more new ones.) For the first time in several months Gina experienced a pang of nostalgia for New York, her memories kindled by recall of Cassie's umpteen visits to a Tommy Dorsey movie because it featured one song by the then little-known band singer who, over the intervening three years had eclipsed all his contemporaries.

Fallon observed, 'It might rain.'

Later he said, 'I have to leave tomorrow.'

The report on the front page of the *Daily Mail* read: 'Invasion operations were postponed 24 hours because meteorological experts predicted that the weather would get worse. They were right, but after a few hours they said an improvement was on the way. The Allied commanders decided to act on this forecast and to proceed with the operations.'

On Tuesday, June 6th, 1944, while letters of fire burned the beachhead codenames Utah, Omaha, Gold, Juno and Sword across the pages of history, Sergeant Roscoe Tucker sat between two M.P.s in the rear of a U.S. Army truck en route to military detention. At the same time, Gina Rossi was seated before a desk in the Rainbow Corner Club listening to a Red Cross officer:

'I'm sorry, I truly am. I understand your motives. And I sympathize, greatly, with your ideals if not with your methods. However, my first loyalty – as yours should have been – is to our organization. You know full well that the countless selfless acts of tens of thousands of our girls can be obliterated totally by one scurrilous rumour about a single individual. You may be right in your opinion that the Army's refusal to prosecute is due to a reluctance to wash dirty linen in public – they admit increasing concern over the problem of G.I.s and their English girlfriends – nevertheless, I am hugely grateful that the reputation of the Red Cross is not going to be undeservedly tarred.' The man took a breath as if about to say more, instead looked down at the papers on his desk.

Gina watched him in silence. She considered prolonging her self-defence. The strength though had gone from her, battered away by the blows of the past three days. She ached as she thought of Roscoe. Some minor knot in the threads that knitted his network of deals had become a noose around his neck. Still, he'd kept quiet about the Grange. Unfortunately, one of his corporals had proved less stoic. In the ensuing maelstrom the only straw which had saved the hotel from drowning was the Army's appreciation of the prudence of discretion. Gina understood it too. So far the Grange had withstood the assaults of its opponents. But what chance survival if it was smeared with the mud of blackmarketeering?

Before the desk in the Rainbow, Gina said nothing.

The officer looked up, stated crisply, 'Your overseas transfer has been ratified. You are to report to our Dover headquarters by twenty hundred hours tonight.'

She didn't know where she was.

But, then, who did? 'Somewhere in Europe,' the troops wrote on their letters home. The world had shrunk while becoming interminable, reduced to a parade of names – Amiens, Lille, Charleroi, Namur, Eindhoven – while marching into an infinity of ravaged fields, cratered roads, shattered buildings. Time too had telescoped. Each week was a minute, every hour lasted for days. The only sounds on this contrary earth were the tramp of boots, the thump of artillery, the strident rattle of tank tracks. The only living creatures were humans and birds; no cattle, sheep, pigs or horses, 'and, in some cities,' Gina was told, 'no dogs, cats or rats'. The only smells were smoke, sewage and coffee.

Coffee was Gina's very existence. It was a part of her from the instant she woke to the moment she crawled into her bedroll. Coffee was in her hair, beneath her broken nails, ingrained into the cracks which had opened in her fingers. Eighteen hours a day, as the Red Cross trucks rolled behind the battle wagons' toiling but inexorable advance, Gina brewed endless gallons of the bitter, scalding liquid, ceaselessly served it to men who clasped the mugs in blackened hands and thanked her with eyes she would remember for the rest of her life.

334

This was how it was with her, Gina's war.

One brief ray of light in the darkness came via a several-times-rerouted letter from Sybil. Before leaving England Gina's overriding concern had been for Roscoe Tucker. She'd written a dozen pages to the U.S. Army taking full responsibility for the acquisition of the materials for the Grange, pleading on the sergeant's behalf, emphasizing that all his actions had been for the benefit of the unmarried mothers, that he hadn't made a cent of profit from the deals. Further, Gina had asked Sybil whether there might be someone amongst her British officer contacts to petition for Roscoe. The letter from Sybil reported success for their efforts. Justice had been tempered by mercy – and Army discretion – and Sergeant R. Tucker had suffered only the loss of his stripes plus banishment to a supply depot on the northern coast of Scotland. Almost, Gina thought with relief and a ray of humour, as good as Iceland.

The battle lines advanced into a new year.

Gina ate, slept, boiled coffee, shared of herself what she could, while in an adjacent tent someone screamed, while over France Glenn Miller's plane was lost, while on the road before her eyes a soldier was blown to pieces, while in Sweden the Nobel Peace Prize was awarded to the International Red Cross, while beside her a fellow volunteer perpetually recited the Bible, while in London the advertisements for Eve toilet soap asked, 'Will you be as young and lovely when he comes home again?'

On April 28th, 1945, half a mile from the Austrian border, Italian partisans halted a truck carrying deserting German soldiers. Amongst these captured troops, disguised as a *Luftwaffe* pilot, was Benito Mussolini. He was marched to the side of the road and summarily executed. His body was then driven to Milan where, in the Piazzale Loreto, it was strung by the heels from the canopy of a gas station and stoned by the mob.

The train rattled southward.

The compartment was packed – children, women, men with faces grown old from tiredness and defeat, all in dull, shabby clothes; nothing new here, only the detritus of the past wrapped up in rope-tied bundles and battered suitcases. There were soldiers too, Americans and British; they smoked and laughed a lot, played cards on their upended kitbags, smiled at the Italian people they had conquered. In spite of the open windows, the air was acrid with the stink of tobacco, babies' urine, sweat and engine smoke.

Gina was grateful that, on the slatted wooden seat, she was crushed up against the glass; at least she got the best of the ventilation, while, with her back to the locomotive, missing the cinders that frequently blew in onto the young couple (pale and drawn, holding close together) sitting opposite.

She was on the inland side of the train, looking out over the ochre and olive Tuscan landscape. Across the aisle the passengers stared beyond a rocky shore to the sun-dazzling Ligurian Sea (the Allied soldiers referred to it as the Mediterranean). The train was making little speed, nevertheless it swayed constantly, causing the passengers, wedged three to a seat, to squash against each other as it clack-clacked around curves, over bridges and through coastal villages – Cecina, San Vicenzo, Follonica, Orbetello.

The names stirred in Gina's mind like half-forgotten words in a long-ago-read book. The small stations – many were no more than a patch of weed-sprouting flagstones beside the track – were also familiar. Yet they were different somehow; something was missing. Gina had been travelling for over an hour before she realized what it was. Nowhere was there a picture of The Leader. The portrait, and the accompanying slogans, which once had plastered every building, wall, rock and tree, had been expunged, utterly.

But it gave Gina no joy. She felt only a mounting despondency. It came, she knew from her sense of isolation. She had never been so alone as she was in this crowded compartment.

Yesterday, when she'd been granted leave from her Red Cross unit in Munich, she'd told herself she must return to England. Just as the war was over, so also was the part Italy once had played in her life. She should not go back. Nothing was there for her now. Max and Johnny were waiting for her in London. Fallon too. She ached to see Fallon. Their fifteen months' separation had been an agony.

Still she requested a travel permit to Rome.

'Hey, a cookie?'

Gina turned to the male voice.

The young U.S. Army private, standing, hanging on to the overhead rail, was grinning amiably, proffering a brown paper carton. 'Direct from Mom in Topeka, Kansas,' he said enthusiastically. 'Can't beat 'em. Can't beat home cookin', eh?'

Gina stared, on the brink of answering, of reaching out. But she held back. He'd spoken to her in English; he assumed she was American, or at least British, certainly not Italian. Why? Her clothes, plain but too fashionable in this drab company? Her make-up, slight but over-professional, damning evidence of being the victor not the vanquished? She replied curtly, 'No, grazie. *No parlo inglese*,' and turned back to the window. From the corner of her eye she saw the young couple take cookies from the bag. She glanced toward them. They did not return her smile.

It was three p.m. when Gina walked from the terminus station into Rome's brilliant September sunlight. Over eight years since she stood amidst the grandeur that had been her beloved Eternal City. Could it truly have been so long? She'd expected change, a war-torn capital, reminders of London's shattered East End. There were no visible changes. It was as if she had been here yesterday. With just one difference: eight years ago, at this time in the afternoon, all windows would have been shuttered, cafés closed, no one on the streets during the heat of the day. Now, the piazza in front of the station was swarming.

Gina felt almost a touch of fear at the density and vigour of the throng. There was no strolling, no pausing for easy conversation. Everyone seemed to be in a hurry, rushing excitedly, almost desperately toward their destination. Allied soldiers were everywhere, carrying the same laughter as they had on the train. Genuine friendliness toward the local civilians? Or the unquenchable joy of being winners? Gina took a firmer grip on her suitcase.

She had told herself she'd go directly to Cousin Letti's. Instead, she turned toward Piazza dell' Esedra, drawn irresistibly westward in the direction of Via Condotti.

Memories crowded in as she walked around the square's fountain and headed into the back streets, not consciously to avoid the multitude, simply because this was the short cut any Roman would take, the route Gina and her family had used whenever they went between home and the station.

Crossing the square, she paused to look up at the stone cataract of the Spanish Steps, saw a teenage girl there, laughing as she joked with the flower-sellers before the twin towers of the Trinità dei Monti – Gina Rossi homeward-bound to aid her father during the lunchtime rush. She pulled her gaze away; walked across the wide street. Into Via Condotti.

She was moving blindly now, was fixed only on her destination, drawn as a moth toward a flame.

In front of the building she halted. No sign had been necessary to lead her to this spot. Her subconscious had counted the number of paces, set her before Ristorante Rossi – even though no vestige of her former home remained.

Gina's senses returned in a flood. She stared. Where ancient timber had once framed the yellowed, centuries-old window, gleaming chrome now edged polished glass. The door similarly had been stripped of its history. And the ages-mellowed stone facade, the lower half of which had witnessed the passing of Caesar's train, had disappeared beneath glaring cobalt tiles. 'Fascism,' Mussolini had declared, 'must leave its mark, on every aspect of Italian life. For ever.' Roman architects had rushed to make his word concrete – literally. The result had been manifest throughout the city. Gina, in her youth, had scarcely noticed.

Today she was assaulted by the sight before her.

Ghosts gathered at her shoulder. There is nothing for you here, they insisted. Leave this place. Go home, to where you now belong. Let your dead rest in peace.

She pushed the door. Entered.

And recoiled. The stark modernity struck her like a physical blow, a fist in her stomach which caused her almost to cry out with pain so that she automatically threw up a hand to ward off further assault from the glaring ceramics and steel. Nothing of the old Ristorante Rossi remained: frescos, patinaed timber, gilt lamps, none had been spared. All trace of the home where Gina and Paola and Filipo had spent their childhood had been obliterated, totally. Her heart spasmed, sought to tear itself from the cruel spike of betrayal. Customers' faces, white in the soulless electric light, stared around at her; ranks of alien eyes repelling her with the coldest exclusion. Gina was the stranger here; the uninvited one; the intruder.

Gall seared her throat, the sickness of despair burning pitilessly through her. Not since Max, in the cabin of that rusting freighter ploughing from Taranto, had told her of Alfredo's execution had she felt such an inconsolable sense of loss. This was worse than a family death. This was annihilation; the wiping out of generations.

Gina swung around, groping, blinded by grief. A voice called, 'Signora? Are you all right?' A hand sought to steady her. She thrust the offer aside, snatched at the door, at the old brass knob which was no longer there. Her nail tore. Wracked by anguish and frustration she raked her knuckles across her tears, saw the blurring chrome handle, grabbed it and pulled, dashed staggering into the street.

She fled along pavements that were as alien as the surface of the moon. She didn't know where she ran or for how long. Only when her chest was heaving with exertion, her breath sucking in harsh rasps, did she halt to look despairingly around. Finding herself beneath trees, amid statues, with half-a-dozen more strides she reached a stone bench, dropped down there as the dam within her began to crack. Her arm along the seat's back, she buried her face in her sleeve. And, at last, the barrier that had long buttressed her emotions collapsed. She wept bitterly. Gina wept for a long time.

It was the cool of lengthening shadows cloaking her shoulders which eventually brought her around. Raising her head she stared at the wet mascara patches on her jacket. She swallowed and ran the back of her hand under her nose and eyes. Slowly she turned, placed her wrists between her knees, hunched forward until the aching gasps were under control.

Later she sat back, shivered slightly.

Far out, beyond where the day was retreating, a ship's horn lowed, brooding and ghostly. Or maybe Gina only imagined it, saw in her mind's eye the old merchantman, the Conti de Savoia laden with almonds from Sicily, wine from Capri, olives from Sardinia, steaming into Civitavecchia harbour to discharge its cargo to the warehouses where she would visit with her father, revelling in the commercial skirmishing amid the mêlée of buyers at the vast trade tables.

Two policemen paused on the flagged path, lighting cigarettes, their faces harshly yellow in the sudden match flare. They stared in her direction, examined her, exchanged remarks, a laugh, continued into the darkness.

Gina stood and walked.

It was an hour later when she bought the knife.

She would never remember buying it, would barely recall checking into the dingy hotel overlooking the grimmest bank of the Tiber where a few telephone calls told her all she needed to know and that she must wait a day to carry out what she intended.

She spent the twenty-four hours sitting on the wooden chair beside the fly-grimed window watching the river flow. She didn't agonize, didn't scheme, didn't hope, didn't think. Once, someone came and knocked on the room's locked door, rattled the handle, and a man's voice enquired gruffly if she was okay. When he received no reply he went away. Gina remained immobile, erect, her hands folded on her purse which contained the knife. It was a long knife – ten inches – straight and double-edged, very sharp. The man in the Piazza del Biscione junk shop from whom she'd bought it had warned her, laughing, to be careful, not to cut herself.

She left the hotel, walked into the night.

The villa stood amid high cedars, beyond double gateway pillars topped by orange-glowing lamps. Gina skirted the building. Through lighted windows she saw wealth. Tapestries and paintings covered the walls; fabulous antique furniture crowded the floors; crystal and silver and jade covered every surface. The home of a baron; overflowing with the spoils of war.

Headlights arced through the gateway, raked the ornate portico columns behind which Gina stood.

The black, brand new Cadillac limousine swept up the drive, halted before the mansion. A black-uniformed chauffeur stepped out, moved briskly to open the rear door. Gleaming shoes swung out over the sill, followed by white trouser legs, tight around huge knees and gross thighs. Sausage fingers reached up to clutch the top of the door, to haul the obese bulk of the man from the interior of the car.

Gina did not recoil, experienced no sense of shock. She was calm. She felt nothing as she stared into the sweating features of Ugo Balbo.

This was how she had been for the past twenty-four hours, since the moment she entered Ristorante Rossi to be savaged by the appearance of the place that once had been her home. From that instant her mind had become lifeless, stunned by grief. All that continued to pulse within her was the seed that had been planted the day she faced the gross hotelier's triumph

340

across a crowded courthouse corridor. The seed of vengeance. It had lain inside her all these years, deep buried, swelling only during those moments of nightmare, but, in the far away astmosphere of New York, never drawing enough strength to burgeon. Here, however, in the storm of Gina's anguish it had burst forth, towered uncontrollably to strangle her self-will. Now her mind was drowned by the roar for revenge.

Balbo spoke with his chauffeur, who climbed into the limousine and drove around the rear of the villa. The fat man turned toward the doorway. Toward Gina. Mumbling, he swayed drunkenly, staggered, then started for the house.

Gina stepped from the shelter of the column. As the lumbering figure approached she calmly opened her purse and took out the knife. She didn't look at the weapon, held it obliquely across her chest pointed downward, her eyes fixed on the creature of her nightmares. She watched him in an almost detached way, like an observer at an event the result of which she already knew. She seemed to be standing outside her own body, several yards from the swaying hulk who was in fact less than ten feet away. Her mind drifted. She was in The Lady, elegant in a white silk evening gown. Cassie and Harry were with her, laughing as she examined the new consignment of cutlery. It was first-class cutlery, she told them, except the knives. The knives were far too long. She lifted one, held it to the light, examined the blade, the ten-inch, double-edged blade. Beyond the glittering steel the faces of Cassie and Harry fractured into horror.

Balbo screamed. His mouth nailed open, he screamed the high-pitched feminine shriek of a terror-struck animal. The cry howled across the night, echoed against the high façade of the villa, panic-laden, pleading for mercy, and quivered on the air long after it had ended.

Then, his breath spent, the gross man's face began to purple as he strained to drag air into his fear-paralysed lungs. His fingernails raked at his cheeks, his massive shoulders started to shake, and all the while his eyes bulged toward the knife which hung suspended before him. He hadn't even looked at his attacker, his gaze had leapt onto the weapon as it had flashed upward, had remained riveted there when dread and his evening's alcohol consumption had petrified his legs. His brain also was frozen; it was capable only of telling him that he was about to die. He knew implicitly that he was a dead man.

Gina knew it too. She understood that the knife would plunge downward, splintering bone, lacerating muscle; again and again it would smash through Balbo's chest to explode his heart, to slash apart his life as he had torn asunder the Rossi family. And then she would be free. Her father would be avenged.

The knife would not fall.

Gina stared up at it. She didn't recognize it. Somewhere a motor horn bleated. An overhead light flicked on in the villa's porch, and a voice called. Gina jolted out of her trance as abruptly as Balbo's paralysis snapped.

The huge man bellowed and bolted. Like a fright-crazed bull he lumbered wildly, blindly away into the shrubbery while Gina stared after him, briefly pinioned by her own mounting horror. Reality slashed her face. She swung around, toward the villa. Through the window beside the door she saw a figure approaching along a wide wall. She turned again in the direction of the gateway, broke into a stride, felt the knife still gripped in her fist. Halting, wrenching her arm back, she hurled the weapon with all the strength of her erupting emotions. It flew high and far, turning and glinting. She heard its clattering fall on stone, the sharp noise striking her like a physical blow, sending her dashing for the distant street.

Behind her, shouts, a dog barking.

No one following.

Gina ran from that place pursued solely by the sure knowledge that she never again could kill.

As the train rattled northward, she stared out at the rushing blackness, gathered her tattered nerves, rewove her self-possession. The further she travelled the less real the past two days became, until there were whole minutes when she was sure the entire episode had been no more than a nightmare. But deep down she knew the truth of it. She knew too that she would not forget, would never forget Ugo Balbo. The seed of vengeance that had burst briefly, though buried again, was not dead. One day it would flower again. Then the debt to the Rossi family would be settled. Ugo Balbo would pay. Gina would make him pay – in full.

24

Sybil asked, 'Seconds, anyone?' not waiting for David's response before ladling more treacle dumpling onto his plate.

Gina and Fallon hastily extended defensive hands against similar attack. As the English girl shruggingly set aside the formidable pudding, they both sank back, hands on stomachs, to watch David stoically, though not unwillingly, plough toward the end of Sybil's Traditional English Sunday Lunch. ('Hitler should have known,' Fallon had once said, 'any people capable of withstanding such a gastronomic onslaught every week from the day they are old enough to chew, have got the stomach for anything.')

Gina smiled at David, a round-faced, happy fellow, twenty pounds heavier than the slim, rather sad man she'd first met that winter day soon after her arrival in England. The intervening years had been good to him. So had Sybil. The unlikely partnership had bloomed. While Sybil took care of the day-to-day organization of her young mums and their infants, David coped with the longer-term details of financing, provisioning and maintenance. In mutual support they had fought off bureaucracy and prejudice to make the Grange a resounding success. A common cause, thought Gina, that's what binds them, makes them doubly strong. She looked out at the slate-grey November afternoon, the year become old and chill, wondered, So what ties Fallon and me?

It was two months since she'd transferred from her Red Cross unit in Munich back to the British headquarters; and last night was the first she'd spent without the nightmare, the first time since her confrontation with Balbo that she'd slept free of his image.

After she'd fled from Italy she'd met Max and Johnny in London. That day her memory of the dark events in Rome had been curtained behind the bright joy of her reunion. Both the men seemed bigger, happier, handsomer than ever. Max, resplendent in brown striped suit and red waistcoat, silver hair and whiskers curling magnificently, had seized her waist in his huge hands and lofted her three feet clear of the railway station platform, boomed delightedly, 'Principessa!' so that a hundred or more passengers and porters stared around at Gina's suspension and the tears pouring down the giant's cheeks. It was when she was replanted on the ground that she noticed Johnny's walking stick.

'Don't even think about it,' Johnny said swiftly. 'Look, it ain't nothing but a sympathy rouser,' and he executed an accomplished soft-shoe shuffle ending with a twirl of his cane and a finger-flip at the brim of his fedora which brought a burst of applause from the onlookers who only went on their way when no further entertainment was forthcoming from this strange trio.

Later Gina would learn that a piece of shrapnel had removed Johnny's kneecap in a German field a month before the war in Europe had ended. He'd been home since March. The family had decided to keep the news from Gina, knowing she'd only worry. Now Johnny was back on this side of the Atlantic, 'To do a little business,' he winked. 'Best step I ever took, signing up with Uncle Sam. While the rest of the guys in my unit were sweet-talking the mademoiselles, I was parley-vousing their poppas. Made some very useful contacts. You know, some of those French farmers had never heard the word "export" till they met me.'

That was all Johnny ever said about his war. Max, likewise, revealed little, though he did show Gina a photograph of himself, posed, grinning self-consciously, on a scrubby hillside, bandoliers of bullets criss-crossing his chest, machine guns on both shoulders. Gina never could reconcile this violent picture with the gentle man who shared her life.

Gina's celebrations with these two had lasted ten hours.

The following morning Johnny left for France, Max for America. The Tuscan's partisan unit had been demobilized several weeks earlier. He'd spent the intervening time visiting relatives and friends in Italy. Gina asked, tentatively, if he hadn't considered remaining in his native land. Max had replied, 'I had to be there when I was needed, Principessa. But my life is with Paola and Filipo . . . and you.' He held her that moment before they parted, and said, 'You will come to us soon? *Si*?' Gina had promised to fly to New York the moment the Red Cross would grant her discharge. That this was available whenever she chose to ask for it, she did not mention.

Fallon returned to London that evening after a week in the Midlands visiting ex-P.O.W. camps.

Fifteen months after last seeing him, Gina awaited him at the apartment. 'Hey,' she greeted from the kitchen stove when he entered. 'You're late for dinner.' He walked up behind her, peered over her shoulder, growled, 'Not spaghetti bolognese again.'

Her celebration with him had lasted three days.

That was all they had had together before she'd returned to Munich. She made every second count, never leaving the apartment, rarely quitting his bed; so that when the time for her departure inevitably arrived, Fallon observed, 'A good thing you're going. I'm getting too old for all that strenuous stuff.' Gina riposted, 'Nonsense. You're as young as you feel.' She tweaked his backside. 'And you still feel pretty young to me.' As he drove her to the airport, she added, 'Which is just as well, because I've put in for the earliest possible transfer home – here. So take a deep breath, Bub. You're gonna need it.'

During those three days she hadn't mentioned the nightmares, which woke her, sweating, beside Fallon. She knew they would pass; knew too that Ugo Balbo was a kernel of her emotions which she would reveal to no one.

Her transfer to London was through within a week. Life settled into a routine. Gina went daily to the Red Cross office, Fallon attended the numerous political conferences taking place in the capital. Letters arrived from New York. Gina replied, Yes, she'd be coming over at the earliest opportunity. The autumn turned from gold to grey. Why was she waiting? For what was she waiting? The initial exaltation of those reunion days with Fallon slowly faded. To contentment? Or anticlimax? One moment Gina's growing uncertainty would chafe her with irritability, the next she'd be unconcerned to the point of apathy. While Fallon was as committed as ever to his work, deeply caring for the social pains being suffered in the wake of war, Gina, try as she might, could not share his dedication. The fire that had flared within her, driven her to reforge the destiny of the Grange, had burned to embers. She still loved her visits with Sybil and David, rejoiced there in the smell of new paint and new babies, but they were not enough to fill the void which was opening across her life. She was in limbo.

Stacking the luncheon crockery, Sybil remarked casually, 'Fallon, you've been in England three whole months. When are you off to find another war?' (Hours later she'd admit to

345

David, 'I don't know why I said it. My mind was wandering, I suppose. Oh, hell, I could bite my tongue off! Did you see Gina's face?')

They had returned from Richmond in silence. Entering the apartment, Fallon said, 'Won't need another meal till next week.' He went directly to his typewriter, began hacking steadily.

Gina watched him awhile. Then she took her coat to the bedroom, hung it in the wardrobe, moved her cosmetics around the dressing-table, peered at herself in the mirror, wondered if she should cut her hair, sat on the edge of the bed, flipped through a magazine, didn't see any of the pages. She returned to stare at Fallon's back. Her throat had gone suddenly very dry, and when she spoke her voice was hoarse, 'When are you leaving?'

Clack-clack-clack. 'What?'

'You didn't give Sybil an answer.'

Clack-clack-clack.

'Fallon, we have to talk.'

Clack-clack —

'Fallon, for God's sake leave the bloody machine alone.' Gina recoiled from the vehemence of her own voice. Silence had struck the room like a bomb. An apology rushed into her head, an explanation for the irrational outburst. The walls began to reel.

Fallon was on his feet very swiftly. He was at her side, arm around her waist, leading her to the sofa, sitting her down there like a child, like an invalid. He said, 'Take it easy,' brushing a stray lock from her forehead. 'A couple of deep breaths. Come on, no argument. Okay. Now, steady. Don't say anything. Just sit quiet.' He was holding both her hands cupped in his, squeezing them with gentle pressure; looking into her eyes as if afraid of what he might find there.

Gina felt . . . She didn't know what she felt. Confused. More than that. Shrinking; as if her mind was draining gradually away. What on earth was the matter? And what had happened? A moment ago she'd yelled at Fallon, had been about to attack him verbally with all her strength. Now she seemed as timid as a kitten, incapable of saying boo to a goose. She thought she also wanted to cry. Ridiculous. She never cried, couldn't remember when she had last cried. Couldn't remember anything. Not even what day it was. Her brain was turning to mush. 'Fallon, am I having a nervous break-down?'

'You're entitled.'

'That's for crazy people.'

'No, just for folks who are a bit too sane.'

'I'm very tired.'

'I know it.'

He was lifting her then, carrying her to the bedroom, laying her down amid cool sheets. This was pleasant. Really lovely. She still couldn't remember anything, but it didn't matter anymore. She didn't care. So long as she could sleep, lying here holding Fallon's hand, it wasn't important if she never, ever again, recalled a single thing. She said, 'I love you, Robert.'

He answered, 'I love you too, Gina.'

The doctor explained it four weeks later, assured her it was nothing to worry about, was not a recurring ailment, merely the delayed reaction to the traumas of the past two years.

Gina had spent half the month in bed, the other half pottering around the apartment in slippers and dressing-gown. Fallon and Sybil and David shared their hours with her, fed her on delicacies, talked to her about nothing more disturbing than gardening, the Royal Family, and raising chickens (David had a bee in his bonnet about the price of eggs). Gina gratefully accepted their gentleness, didn't bother to read or even listen to the radio, was content to let her scars slowly heal as the early winter snow melted on the window turning the view to St Paul's into a roofscape by Monet.

By the time of her chat with the doctor she felt a hundred per cent better. Her perspective was clear, her equilibrium was level, and her memory had returned. She felt strong enough to cope with the present, the future, and, most importantly, the past. At first, as she looked back down that dark road, she hesitated with childlike fear. But, obeying the doctor's advice, she did not force herself to face realities until she knew she was able. When she finally, mentally returned herself to a Harley Street consultancy to hear words which once had sent her fleeing into the night, she listened with quiet acceptance, came away saddened but not stricken.

On the afternoon of December 22nd, alone in the

apartment, she had the sudden, overwhelming urge to see a newspaper.

Thirty minutes later she was buying vegetables from a grocery shop beneath the cathedral.

At five-thirty, dressed in her elegant blue flannel suit, white lace hanky in her breast pocket, pearls at her throat, she was laying the table with china and crystal flanking a centrepiece of holly, silver-painted fir cones and two flickering, red candles. From the kitchen drifted the aromas of herbs and roasting meat. From the radio came the voices of celebrating choristers. When Fallon entered, she kissed him, placed a glass of whisky in his fist and said, 'Happy Christmas.'

It was.

She had never felt so close to Fallon, at the same time was able to accept that she would be parted from him. They had talked their way into the new year. Gina had told him all her experiences (except the encounter with Balbo). And she felt no qualms at the telling, not even at the revelation of being unable to bear a child. Fallon had said, 'You've already got a bigger family than most. And my knee is rarely in one place long enough to dangle an infant.' They never mentioned marriage; Gina simply knew that once he joined her in New York, she would easily get him to settle down to his novel, allow him to adjust in his own good time to the idea of domesticity. For now he was operating out of his London office, was due to spend some months on assignment in Europe later in the year, after which, he agreed, he'd join Gina in Manhattan. She was going back. She'd decided. Was happy with the decision. Fallon asked, 'When?' She answered, 'I'll know when the moment arrives.'

The cable came the last day of January.

Simply: FRONT OF HOUSE HAS BLUE RIBBONS

It was signed: LOVE STOP J & P & F SABATO

Gina was too elated to mind when the Red Cross asked her to remain another month while they found a replacement.

PART FOUR

Arrival and Departure

1946-1949

25

He was the brightest, bouncingest, boyiest baby in the world.
Gina could have eaten him, he was so gorgeous. From the
moment she'd arrived at Paola's home, she'd nursed him,
cuddled him, kissed his chubby cheeks, stroked his fuzz of
black hair, tickled him all over, hadn't released him for one
second during the hour she and her sister caught up on the past
three years. Now, as his tiny fists squeezed Gina's fingers,
Paola asked,

'Would you like to give him his feed?'

Gina momentarily did not understand, then, seeing the
bottle her sister had brought through from the kitchen, she was
taken aback. 'You give him that! You don't breast-feed him?
Paola, what are you thinking of? His hair will fade. He'll be
anaemic. His teeth will grow crooked.'

Paola laughed. 'Really, Gina! You're the one who's
supposed to be so modern, who always dinned it into Filipo
and me to forget the old ways, old superstitions. Anyhow, the
doctor explained there might be difficulties with my natural
milk production – nothing to worry about – and the powdered
feed would be much better for Frankie.'

And that, reflected Gina, was another thing. Frank John
Alfred. Utterly anglicized names. The third was a nod in the
direction of his grandfather. But where was a sign of his Italian
heritage? Paola had countered Gina's initial disapprobation
with, 'He's American. He was born an American. Yes, I want
him to be aware, proud even, of his ancestry. But I won't make
him grow up waving flags for a country he's never seen. Nor
will I saddle him with Mario or Dino or Pauli. Frank's a fine,
sensible name. Besides, if it's good enough for Sinatra . . . ' At
least, as Paola's declaration had slipped away, she'd had the
good grace to blush.

So, thought Gina, taking the banana-shaped bottle from her
sister, while she'd been away, not only had her nephew been

named after a skinny crooner with a kiss curl and a predilection for oversize bow ties (never mind the fact that his 'I Couldn't Sleep a Wink Last Night' sent goosebumps – though she'd never admit it to a soul – along her spine), but also he'd been weaned on imitation milk. A good thing she'd come home when she did, before matters got entirely out of control.

Little Frankie clutched her hand, sucked voraciously on the yellow rubber teat. And, at last, Gina turned to her sister to discuss something other than the infant in her arms.

Paola, having been unable to alter Frankie's regular clinic appointment this morning, had not attended the spectacular homecoming party which had greeted Gina at the Lady. Now though, with no one to interrupt, the pair of them traded their experiences of the past four years. There was so much to tell. Gina left out only her confrontation with Ugo Balbo and her visit to the Harley Street obstetrics consultant. Paola was thrilled by the tale of the Grange, fascinated by the goings-on at the Rainbow, and agog at the revelations about Robert Fallon. In turn she recounted her experiences at the now-closed blanket factory, the birth of her son, and her commitment to numerous fund-raising activities for the church and local organizations.

Listening, Gina felt a burgeoning pride. Her younger sister had matured into a fine woman, had found her own way, her place in life as a wife and mother and dedicated member of her community.

They sat and talked through the afternoon while Frankie slept in his cot, and were still happily exchanging news, anecdotes and gossip when Johnny arrived home.

Gina was as elated to see her brother-in-law as she had been that day of their London reunion last September, with the added pleasure of noting he no longer needed a walking stick. They embraced and kissed, laughed and kidded each other about how great they looked, broke off their banter only for Johnny to spend time with his son. When he returned to the sitting-room, he sat with Gina and Paola sharing wine and more reminiscences before the log-crackling hearth.

Johnny had been back in New York three months. Business, he reported, was booming: he had two warehouses full of post-war Army surplus supplies which were increasing in value every day; a new iron in his fire was wine-importing following a deal with a vineyard owner Johnny had met while liberating

Burgundy; and he was expanding his vending-machine operations 'just as fast as I can make locations. That's where the money is. Profit without labour. Once the machines are installed all I do is sit back and wait for the monthly percentage cheques to roll in.'

Gina suggested, 'Isn't it a risky proposition? You have to rely on the honesty of the operator?'

'Naturally,' agreed Johnny, 'once in a while there's a character who tries to skim off the top. But I research my locations carefully, know what a machine in a particular bar or lunchroom ought to take. So, allowing for fluctations in income, I can spot a fiddle within a few weeks. Then I just pull out the operator's machine, no arguments.' He added, with a touch of self-conscious pride. 'Of course, I make sure that our Vendomats – that's what we call them – are maintained in tip-top condition, and that their stock is always fresh. So the customer who pushes in a nickel doesn't lose the coin, gets a fair shake, and, most important, learns to trust machines with the Sabato logo. That's the name of the winning game – reliability. The outfits that stack the deck against the public can only get away with it for so long. Folks aren't dumb . . . '

Johnny continued talking. But Gina's attention had wandered. Her brain was ticking, ticking. She stared into the flames of the fire, unseeing. All that Johnny had said was tugging at her thoughts; a conception was forming, an idea that wanted to be seen yet remained indistinct, a shape part-hidden by mist. Paola had interrupted her husband to say something about supper. Gina didn't really hear; she was trying to catch the words which whispered on the boundary of her consciousness.

'Gina. I said, how about *pizza rustica*?'

She looked up, stared at her sister before mentally shaking herself and replying, 'No. No thanks. I must be getting back to the Lady.'

'But you've been here for such a short time. Surely you're not working tonight? This is your first day back.'

Is it? The question voiced itself in Gina's head. She glanced at her watch. Seven p.m. Had she been home only twelve hours? It seemed days ago that she was once more standing on American soil at North Beach Airport. The mind works in mysterious ways, she thought, makes life like a movie, a series of bright, memorable scenes with all the duller material edited out, and the action of the moment always seems more vivid than that which has gone before. On the fourteen-hour flight from London, Gina had read her magazines, and whenever her thoughts drifted, it had been toward what lay ahead, not what had been left behind. David Lowell, Rainbow Corner, Sybil, even Fallon's cottage, though still bright in her mind's eye, had already lost the clarity of their detail. The only image which remained acutely sharp, the memory she carried as hard and as real as a stone in her pocket, was that of Ristorante Rossi, the harsh ceramics and steel that had obliterated every vestige of her childhood home.

Johnny said, 'Are you sure you should drive back alone in that tank? Maybe I ought to come with you, in case you have a flat, need to change a tyre.'

Gina pulled out of her abstraction. 'Mister Sabato, I'll have you know, when I was up to my neck in muck and bullets . . .' She shared their laughter, went out with them to the hall but couldn't resist detouring to the rear bedroom where Frankie was sleeping.

His cot was a neat, white oasis amid multi-coloured mountains of dolls, locomotives, erector sets, teddy bears, racing cars, cowboy suits, picture books, all the essentials deemed necessary for the development of a small boy, a large proportion of which had accompanied Gina here in the trunk of the Packard (the rear seat being buried beneath enough bootees, smocks, bonnets and rompers to kit a baby battalion).

Her desire to touch him was so great she had to stick her hands in her coat pockets when she recognized the please-don't-let-her-wake-him look in her sister's eyes. 'They've got much prettier blankets in town,' she whispered. 'I'll pick up a dozen tomorrow. Pillowcases too. And matching coverlets. And this cot's rather plain. I saw one with a lace canopy . . .'

'Gina,' Paola interrupted. 'I wanted a plain cot. It's fine. Besides he'll have grown out of it soon.'

'That's not the point,' countered Gina, not really hearing anyway, never shifting her gaze from the infant sleeper, willing him, willing him with all her might to open his eyes so she could lift him, hold him once more.

Paola said, 'It was lovely to see you. We'll have a proper get-together. Soon. You'll come over to dinner. Max and Cassie and Harry too. We'll . . .'

'No, not here.' Gina tore herself from her nephew. 'At The

Lady. You missed the party this morning. We must have another. To celebrate that we're all together again, and with a brand new member of the family. I'll make the arrangements, draw up a special menu. How about Abbott and Costello for the cabaret? They'll be perfect. Frankie will love them.'

Paola laughed, 'He's only five weeks old.'

Gina shrugged. 'So?' Surely that didn't mean he lacked a sense of humour? Did it? She mentally frowned. To be honest, despite all her involvement with the Grange, she had to admit she didn't know a whole lot about babies. Still – she brightened – now she had Frankie there'd be so much they could teach each other, and do for each other. She regarded the cot, couldn't for the life of her see why Paola had chosen it. And the curtains – blue cotton with pictures of Mickey Mouse and his buddies – were okay, but the ones on display in the new Little Angels shop (where Gina had spent two hours purchasing the Packard-load she'd brought today), cream silk with appliquéd and embroidered woodland animals, weren't they what Frankie ought to have? Definitely. And he would. And after Gina collected, delivered and personally installed them tomorrow, Paola would love them. Of course she would.

They exchanged goodbyes beneath the streetlamp. Gina waved from the Packard, drove away along the avenue.

When she reached the Lady, the lobby was thronged, evening-dressed customers were shoulder-to-shoulder in the bar, waiters were attendant on every table in the restaurant, and upstairs the dancers certainly hadn't the space for any fancy chassés on the packed floor. As Gina had entered the building beneath the pink neon-scripted marquee, she'd experienced a charge of excitement as tangible as an electric shock. Arriving this morning from the airport, she'd been thrilled to be home, had spent a marvellous three hours' laughter-and-tears reunion with all the gang, but still that pleasure was no match for the way she felt now. All her ambitions, hopes, schemes came surging back in the rush of adrenalin. This was what her life was all about, this was the wellspring of her being, this was what she had missed even though she hadn't realized it. There could be no substitute for the exhilaration that came from the sight, the sound, the smell, the very touch of the air in this place that was the realization of her dreams.

Pausing in the hall that led to the offices, turning to survey the scene in the club, Gina concluded that at this moment her life was perfect: she had The Lady, her family, a delicious new nephew, and soon Fallon would be here too. What more could she want?

As she entered her office, Filipo looked up from her desk, greeted, smiling, 'Hey, Sis!'

Her rejoinder went unvoiced. It was the shock of seeing him; no less than it had been this morning. When he'd stepped from the crowd in front of the WELCOME HOME bannered bar, grinning widely, proffering a glass of champagne, it had been moments before she'd recognized him. Three years had stretched his frame, sculpted his features, erased his boyishness, begun to chisel the shape of his adulthood. Not until his mouth opened to speak had Gina cleared her confusion and whispered hoarsely, 'Don't you dare call me Sis,' as she'd seized him and kissed him and realized that he was taller than she.

In her office she nodded toward the ledger he'd been studying and said, 'You were never interested in figures.'

'You mean in the school stuff,' he rejoined. 'Algebra, geometry, equations yet.' He raised his eyes to the ceiling with exaggerated aversion, then, tapping the columns, 'This is different. This is business. Dollars and cents. Profit.'

'Are we making any?'

'Like bees make honey. We're running capacity six nights out of seven. Lunches, we couldn't serve any more if we shot it in on chutes. Morning coffee, a list of ladies' clubs' reservations from here past Thanksgiving. Tea dances, we make Roseland look like an abandoned building. Remember the late-night dinners we served to cinema customers? We introduced a similar after-theatre menu, tied up a promotion deal with the managers at a dozen top Broadway houses. Something else new is our Wedding Anniversary Table for Two. A table d'hôte five courses with the works – caviar, foie gras, pheasant, champagne. Any couple choosing it gets courtesy limousine service from home and back within twelve miles of the restaurant. That expense is cancelled by the free transportation the limousine company provides for our staff – your ride in from the airport didn't cost a dime.' He smiled, 'Of course, they'd probably have carried you gratis anyhow, just for the privilege.'

356

'So,' returned Gina, 'I do still warrant some recognition around here? I was beginning to wonder if anyone would remember me since the new management,' her arm swept his position at the desk, 'took over. Do you think – seeing as how you've got the entire administration running on jet-powered wheels – that there might still be some simple task suited to my limited talents?'

'Well . . .' Filipo pursed his lips. 'Okay, I guess we can always use another cigarette girl.' He half-rose, leaned forward to peer down over the front of the desk. 'So long as your legs will stand up in fishnet tights.'

Gina advanced a swift pace, her finger extending to prod his chest. 'Down, buster. When you're old enough to audition knees I'll give you a certificate.'

Dropping back onto his chair, straightening his tie (which Gina reckoned he must have bought at a florist), in an excellent James Cagney he warned, 'Take it easy on the tailoring, doll-face. You don't wanna wind up eating half a grapefruit the hard way.'

Gina removed her coat, responding casually, 'That's not a bad impersonation. One of the best W.C. Fields I've heard. Now, may I sit at my desk? Please.'

Smiling, Filipo vacated the spot, bowed his sister into it. He crossed toward the door, looked back, 'Some stuff I have to do in my room. Homework, would you believe? But we haven't really talked yet. I'd like to hear all the serious stuff about London. You know, a detailed description of the show at the Windmill Theatre, the place that never closed; an account of the educational facilities in Soho; what the WACs wear under their . . .' He cut off, held up his hands against the look in Gina's eyes. 'Okay, maybe we'll find something else to discuss.' He stepped to the door, added more seriously, 'But it is a date, right? Tomorrow night? Dinner? I hear there's a pretty fair restaurant downstairs. I might just about be able to afford it on my pitiful allowance.'

Gina faced him. How old was he? Going on eighteen? Did boys of his age always act this way? She guessed he wasn't a boy, suddenly realized that if the war hadn't ended, within a few more months he'd have been drafted. Perhaps he still would be. On that harsh thought the door opened and Harry entered, greeting:

'Filipo, how's it going?'

'Can't complain, maestro. At least two dozen cheerleaders standing on line to demonstrate their baton routines.' He looked back toward his sister. 'Our date tomorrow night?' When Gina, temporarily lost for words, nodded affirmation, he grinned, 'Great,' strode out to the hall, glanced around. 'By the way, forget the cigarette girl job. With legs like yours, you're a cinch for the centre spot chorus.' Winking broadly, he was gone.

After Harry had closed the door and come to sit before the desk, Gina asked, 'Doesn't he ever deliver a sentence without relating it to sex?'

'Rarely. But, then, that's probably all he ever thinks about.' Harry smiled. 'Don't worry. It's natural. He's doing all right. And he's taken to the club like a duck to water. He's got a feel for show business. It's been a real help having him around.'

Gina's expression clouded. 'Yes, well, now that I'm back, you won't need him any more. He'll be able to concentrate on his schoolwork. If he's going to enter law school he'll need to give all his time and effort to his studies.'

'He's never mentioned law or . . .'

'He's very young, Harry. Just because he's maturing physically doesn't mean he's yet old enough to know his own mind. He has to be kept on the rails as far as his future is concerned. I'm grateful for all you've done to raise him while I've been away, but from here I'll take the responsibility. I'll ensure that Filipo succeeds in college, goes on to a solid career in a profession we can be proud of.' She placed her hands flat on the desktop, surveyed the office, breathed deeply. It was good to be back. She said, 'By the way, we're having a party. I promised Paola we'd book Abbott and Costello for little Frankie.'

Harry switched his thoughts from Filipo's future, struggled to retrack himself as abruptly as Gina. 'Sorry,' he said. 'No can do. Bud and Lou are playing Las Vegas.'

'Where?'

Harry said, 'Of course, you haven't heard. It all happened while you were overseas. Remember your old admirer, Benny Siegel? He opened a casino in the middle of the Nevada desert. Gambling's legal out there – everything from blackjack to roulette, craps to poker.'

Gina slowly nodded, frowning. 'Yes, I knew that. But I thought Reno was the centre of activity. Where's Las Vegas?

What's so special about Mister B. Siegel's place? And why on earth is the number one double act in the world playing out there? Have they slipped down the ladder since I've been away?'

Harry shook his head. 'They're still at the top. That's why, for them and the Xaviar Cugat Orchestra as opening head-liners, Benny shelled out a record fee of twenty-five thousand dollars.' Harry paused to watch Gina's jaw gradually sink.

When she had recovered from the stunning revelation she listened without interrupting as Harry went on to recount how less than ten years ago folks en route through Vegas would have passed only a few small casinos and hotels. They'd perhaps have seen a Paiute Indian woman with her baby on her back, campers and hunters on their way to the Charleston and Shoshone Mountains, a cowboy or two, and the occasional prospector looking for a new grubstake. The city, so called, had been growing, though not so's anyone would notice. But its highway, running straight to Los Angeles, did carry a steady trickle of gamblers from the movie colony. By 1944 the flow had increased to a stream, supplemented by cross-countrying GIs. The little casinos had expanded, polished their image. Then along came Mister Siegel. With the genius of simplicity he had figured two things. First: the bigger the casino, the greater the flood of gamblers. Second: if casino is just a few yards closer to L.A. than other dens of chance, flood will be guaranteed to pour through its doors. Harry said, 'Because – and Max will confirm this fact of life – inveterate addicts of the green baize will not travel one step further than necessary to get their chips on the table.'

'So Siegel's place isn't actually in Las Vegas?'

'Five miles south-west, surrounded by nothing but rock, sand, lizards and coyotes. By all accounts, one of the weirdest sights out west. Like an ocean liner stranded on a dried-out ocean bed.'

'And is it big?'

'Word is, the biggest. And the plushest. And the neonist. The whole of the exterior is clad in pink bulks. So is the name sign, which is reputedly six storeys high. The name, by the way, is the Fabulous Flamingo. Benny's spared no expense – or, shall we say, his partners have spared no expense. The grounds are landscaped with palms, sycamores, a lagoon, and a waterfall, and the interior was designed by a top Hollywood decorator. It's so ritzy even the janitors wear tuxedos – no kidding.'

Gina asked, 'Is it making a profit?'

'Ah,' smiled Harry, 'there's the rub. Rumour has it that Benny's partners are none too happy about the continuing lack of return on their investment.'

Gina observed, 'But that might well have more to do with Mister Siegel's creative book-keeping than with the establishment's true viability. Max always has maintained that in any betting operation the odds are permanently in favour of the house. In the long run, the gambler must lose and the casino must win.' She doodled on her pad. 'It will be interesting to watch what happens to the Fabulous Flamingo.' Added thoughtfully, 'I might even go take a look-see for myself.'

'You'll need the best part of two days to get there, even by plane,' said Harry. 'And that, despite B. Siegel's optimism, is what will ensure the Flamingo, sooner or later, turns into a giant white elephant. It can't rely solely on gamblers from Los Angeles. But who else is it going to pull? There aren't enough potential customers prepared to travel hundreds of miles just to play roulette – not even with the added attraction of Abbott and Costello, or any other artiste for that matter. No, Gina, you can forget Las Vegas. New York has always been the heart of the entertainment industry, and it always will be.' He nodded emphatically.

Gina didn't reply. There were a lot of 'maybes' in her head. She suddenly felt it had been a very long day; and she remembered she hadn't eaten since noon. Arrangements for the party could wait until morning; so could her review of the ledgers. She came around the desk, and as Harry rose she kissed him on the cheek, held her face to his for more than a moment. She said, 'It's great to be back, Harry.'

Colouring he returned, 'And it's great to have you back. I missed you. We all missed you. I didn't get chance this morning to say you're looking . . . radiant.' He smiled self-consciously. 'That's what they say about women who are having babies, isn't it? Still, you know what I mean. I guess Europe was good for you. But not too good, I hope. I . . . we wouldn't want you to go flying back there for a while. You're loved, and needed, here. We want you to stay.'

Gina reached out, squeezed Harry's hand. She appreciated the depth of his sincerity. She also knew what it had taken the usually shy man to make the short speech. She responded, 'And I intend to stay. You're right, I needed London, the chance to get my bearings again – something like that. But now . . . ' she added a dash of briskness to her voice lest he think she was becoming maudlin, 'it's time to get back on the rails. We're going places, Harry. I don't know quite where, but, like the man said, you ain't seen nothin' yet.'

Harry grinned. 'Now that sounds like old times. Coming down for dinner? Chang'll be mighty disappointed if you don't let him cook you something special your first night home.'

Gina had been about to say she'd forgo food and turn in; she really was beginning to feel faded. She replied breezily, 'Tell him what I truly fancy is roe and a penn'orth – double – lashings of salt and vinegar.' To Harry's bemusement she added, 'But I'll settle for *panzerotti*, a helping of *anguille carpionate*, and zabaglione to follow. The heck with my waistline! See you in twenty minutes.'

After Harry had departed happily, Gina showered, vigorously brushed her hair, donned a clingy blue silk number (you know, she hadn't bought a new dress in over three years – tomorrow she'd raid Fifth), applied a whisper of eye shadow, a lick of lipstick, paused at the door, took a deep breath, strode out to play the game.

Spring sped by in a flicker of green and yellow. New York hurried toward summer as hopefully as the world ran away from its past. The streets were busier and brighter than even Gina remembered, an impression accentuated by the final image she carried of London, imprinted on her mind that last day she said goodbye to Fallon – a tired, dusty, colourless place where the euphoria of victory had dissolved into bewilderment and uncertainty. Though the admission pricked her with guilt, she was glad to be out of Europe, she was elated to be home. Yes, home, unquestionably, that was how she now thought of this city which once had filled her with such isolation.

The day after her return she'd kept her promise to herself and in an orgy of self-indulgence bought new underwear, dresses, suits and hats and – the greatest pleasure of all – shoes; Sybil had been right, the way to a man's heart might be through his stomach, but the route to a woman's was without doubt via her feet.

Gina also had pursued her resolve to kit out little Frankie

with fresh furnishings. After Paola had given her blessing the infant was transferred to an Angel Rockabye, a white and gilt and laced affair which, the sales literature assured, was an exact replica of the crib which had brought sweet dreams to seven generations of Ruritanian princes. And, to complete the lad's environment, André de Sath, who had designed the award-winning sets for the recent Broadway smash-hit *Golden Melodies*, was inveigled (one champagne supper evening at the Lady) into transforming the Sabato nursery into a cross between Munchkinland and Bronx Park Zoo.

Over the following weeks, when Gina wasn't adding to Frank John Alfred's wardrobe (or supplementing his diet, or advising on his education, or driving him, in a specially constructed rear-seat cot in the Packard, around Central Park), she spent hours with her notebooks and ledgers rehoning the business's profitability; discussing and perfecting new recipes with Chang; visiting all the rival clubs with Cassie to make sure none had introduced innovations which could put them so much as half a step ahead of the Lady; auditioning fresh acts with Harry; keeping Max as involved and busy as possible (for there were times she felt that the big man was not where he should be – though, for the time being, she was unable to come up with an alternative); ensuring that Filipo spent more time upstairs with his homework books than he did backstage with the chorus girls ('Sis, it's crucial I see a minimum of two stocking tops a day or I get these terrible headaches.' 'I'll tell the drugstore to deliver a truckload of Alka-Seltzer.'); and, at least once a week, writing to Fallon.

Letter composition never had been her favourite occupation; now she went at it like Pepys at his diary, covering reams of paper with her daily doings, from the ransom price she'd had to pay for a case of Maine lobsters before this morning's breakfast, to which celebrity had clocked his girlfriend around the ear with one of the crustaceans' claws during this evening's supper show.

Gina punctuated her reportage with paragraphs of passion, outpourings whose literary influence ranged – according to her lust level at the time of composition – from the elegant poignance of Jane Austen to the explicit intimacy of D.H. Lawrence. These were the first love letters she had ever written, and she wondered, once or twice, if their content was what a woman of her age ought to be feeling. But, then, she

362

told herself, just because she'd turned thirty (all right, thirty-one) didn't mean she should be any more immune to sexual imagery than someone ten years younger. Her conviction thus fortified she penned her impetuous prose with renewed vigour, airmailed it to Robert Fallon, Esq, 17c St Pauls Court, London EC4.

His replies, though not as frequent as Gina might have wished for (one every month or so), she placed in the same class as *The Grapes of Wrath*. She knew indubitably that once Fallon stopped chasing wars around the globe, settled down at home (their home) to complete his novel, the top of the world's bestseller lists would inevitably be the position from which he collected his Nobel Prize for Literature.

And then, as Sybil used to say, everything in the garden would be absolutely lovely. Fallon would be famous. Gina would be rich. No question, Gina would be rich.

She couldn't remember when she'd decided this, it was merely that one day she knew that it was what she wanted. 'I want to be rich,' she told Max. 'No, not rich the way we are now. I mean Rockefeller-rich, Hughes-rich, Woolworth-rich. Of course it's possible, old friend. Anything is possible, anything is achievable so long as you want it badly enough.'

Max had frowned, said no more. Gina hadn't noticed his concerned expression. She was beyond noticing anything but good things, was incapable of feeling anything but enthusiasm. Ambition was quicksilver in her veins as she mentally laid the foundation of her future – the entire family's future. She now had the grains of a concrete idea, a base to build upon, that brief conversation she'd had with Johnny about his vending-machine operations. Gina made notes, multiplied figures, crossed them out, began again, all the while her determination hardening as she strove for the plan which would lead her to the pot of gold.

Only once did she falter.

One of Sybil's regular letters reporting the continuing success of the Grange mentioned in passing Fallon's posting to Cape Town. Gina swayed between dismay and anger. But when he telephoned a week later – actually telephoned from halfway around the world – her chagrin turned as weak as her knees and she assured him, 'Certainly I understand. Yes, the political situation in South Africa is very important.' She told him how much she loved him and missed him, went on to recount her host of improvements at the restaurant and the club, the outline of her strategy for becoming rich. 'Rich,' she repeated to him. 'Everybody wants to become rich. Of course they do. Don't knock it till you've tried it.' Gina laughed, quickly.

She re-applied herself to the future, strengthened by Fallon's promise to be in New York by next April. Seven more months. She could wait that long for him to get this final assignment out of his system. Then, after he'd completed his book and become famous, and she'd implemented her plan to become rich, everything in the garden, for sure, would be absolutely lovely.

It had to be. Gina had plotted it that way.

26

Life, of course, is no respecter of timetables. It makes its own decisions on when to schedule fame – also on whom to bestow that dubious gift.

Operation War Brides was launched by the President of the United States and the Prime Minister of Great Britain when they recognized the plight of the English GI wives separated from their husbands after the war was ended and the troops were shipped home.

'Hogwash!' wrote Sybil. 'At best the American and UK Governments hoped it was a problem which would go away. At worst they didn't give a hoot about British females who'd fallen for the slow talk and fast money of soldiers who were either too dumb or too decent to heed their commanding officers and avoid putting rings either on their girlfriends' fingers or through their own noses. But now, with a volcano threatening to erupt in Washington as well as Westminster, we get a speedy political placebo; a sugar-coated pill which will be swallowed by voters on both sides of the Atlantic, thus curing the nasty headache currently plaguing Mr Harry S. Truman and Mr Clement Attlee.'

Gina read this letter twice, thought perhaps it was Sybil who should write a book. The English girl seemed more committed with every passing month. She had put the Grange in the vanguard of Britain's postwar wave of social reform, had been on the Southampton quayside, lobbying the Press, when the liner *Argentina* – one of the seventeen specially fitted ships – set sail with its share of the fifty thousand GI brides who had accepted the United States' offer of free passage to their husbands' homelands.

Not for the first time Gina was touched by a mite of envy at Sybil's idealism. Still, she set aside that invidious emotion; went busily about her own life; temporarily shelved memories of Peggy Atkins, blackmarket bathroom suites, and a dozen hesitant girls stepping down with their babies from the rear of a 'borrowed' Red Cross truck.

'Tell me, Mrs Quinn,' prompted the *New York Mirror* reporter. 'Are you pleased to be here? Happy to be reunited with your husband? Satisfied with the organization of Operation War Brides?'

'Oh, certainly,' the pretty blonde girl replied in a Cockney accent. 'Me and Bernie,' she squeezed the arm of the big, grinning red-haired man who was holding an equally red-haired toddler, 'we're both grateful for all the help we've had. We don't know what we'd've done if it hadn't been for President Truman and the U.S. Army, and Sybil – Mrs Levy – and, of course, Miss Rossi.'

'Who?'

But that was the last time anybody had to ask.

It was Max who started the scrapbook, took out a subscription to a press-clipping agency, spent an hour every day, religiously pasting in the paragraphs and pages and pictures, neatly captioning them with the dates and publications' titles.

Gina said he shouldn't indulge in such nonsense; couldn't resist the temptation to wait until he was out, enter his office and peek at the hundreds of column inches about herself in newspapers from the *Providence Journal* to the *Denver Post*, from the *Chicago Tribune* to the *Kansas City Star*, in specialist periodicals as diverse as *Variety* and the *Wall Street Journal*. For not only had Gina Rossi's story an angle for everyone, the lady herself was an editor's dream: she was forthright, lucid, talked dollars and cents like a banker, management and labour like a union organizer, while all the while lighting up camera lenses like the Fourth of July.

Within two months of that *New York Mirror* reporter asking, 'Who?' Gina had become a pin-up in baseball club locker rooms, stockbrokers' offices, sorority house dormitories, the gamut of restaurant kitchens from Michel's Splendide, Boston, Mass., through Al's Kwik Eats, Aking, New Mex. There could have been hardly a living soul within the fifty states who didn't know her favourite movie star (Clark Gable), midnight snack (Scotch smoked salmon), lingerie colour (mauve) singing group (The Ink Spots), or variety of rose – this last question from *Mid-west Gardener* who decided if a cover photo of Miss Rossi could boost circulation for everybody else, why not for them also? Gina scored them ten out of ten for initiative, replied, 'The American Beauty.' (By now having a shrewd idea what columnists' questions were likely to be, she mugged up her answers in advance.)

'I feel such a phoney,' she told Cassie. 'Yes, I don't mind offering an opinion on how best to preserve turbot or what sauce to serve with stuffed cabbage rolls, but what qualifications do I have to expound on the financial ramifications of a rise in gasoline prices, or the even more serious subject of whether the New York Yankees are going to snatch the crown from the St Louis Cardinals in next year's World Series?'

Being regarded as a universal authority, however, was not the only reason why Gina felt she was a fraud. Following the revelation of her link with the Grange, a hero-hungry media had blown out of all proportion her contribution to the rescue of Britain's abandoned mothers and their infants. At every interview Gina stressed that it was Sybil and David who had devoted their lives to the project for the past two years, while she had merely helped at the outset. Somehow, though, this was never how it came out in print.

Harry consoled, 'Why look a gift horse in the mouth? It may seem a mercenary viewpoint, but have you seen our profits since you became a celebrity?'

Gina couldn't deny that truth. Once upon a time she'd striven to dream up schemes to turn a dollar on the Lady's every available hour. Now she had to devote an even greater effort figuring how to squeeze a spare minute out of the restaurant's frenetic schedule. Rarely was the last customer out of the door before four a.m., the first, for morning coffee, was waiting on the sidewalk less than five hours later. It was apparent that the country's entire population was determined to say it had eaten, drunk or danced at the establishment owned by the famous Gina Rossi.

Wasn't Fallon the one who was supposed to become famous? Gina seemed to remember thinking something like that, an age ago. No matter, she told herself, he wouldn't mind. Besides, the windfall of national fame would be the booster that soon would shoot her toward her ultimate objective – in which they both would share – the state of being, as she had printed in capitals on a page of her notebook, RICH.

On a frost-bright morning of January 1947, she set her pen aside, switched off her new electric adding machine. The route to her goal was now crystal-clear.

Two hours later, facing Max, Harry and Cassie across her desk, she shook her head. 'No, not another Lady. One in town is enough. Nor identical restaurants in other cities. That would pay off for a while, but if the national economy takes a dive – as some pundits think it might – then luxury spots will become unviable.'

Cassie ventured, 'But you insist we must expand.'

'Definitely. We have to make it to the major league. Okay, so we're the tops in Manhattan, but compared to the national outfits we're a fly on the wall.' She saw the remark fall hard amid the trio of faces, went on determinedly, 'But I intend to change that. I intend to be number one. Not just in New York, not even just on the east coast, but across America.'

Harry raised circumspect eyebrows.

'It can be done,' Gina stated emphatically. 'It isn't an impossible goal. Schrafft, Childs, Huyler, all started out with one café. If they can do it, so can we. But to succeed – before we're all in our dotage – we have to forget the de luxe policy we've pursued here. We have to aim for a wider, but lower, market.' She searched amid the faces for responses.

It came, tentatively, from Max. 'Bistros?'

'Exactly. But not the type we already have in America – mock Italian trattorias with chequered tablecloths and dreadful colour prints of Venice on the walls. What I envisage is a restaurant with top-class decor, upholstered furniture, cruets that don't look like they came from the Red Cross canteen.'

'Gina,' put in Cassie, 'I'm getting confused. You said we had to forget the de luxe approach.'

'We do. But I meant our prices, not our presentation. Why should inexpensive meals be eaten in second-rate surroundings? Why should candle-lit elegance only be available to customers who can afford imported champagne? A fellow who works on the line is entitled to a bit of glamour too. And not just on his wedding anniversary, but whenever he wants to take his wife, his girlfriend, his family somewhere special – without having to blow a month's pay.' Gina saw the flicker of acknowledgment run around her directors. Pressing her point home she continued, 'The best example of what I'm talking about can be seen in the cosmetics industry. Take a look at the magazine ads, the billboards, the packaging of Revlon and Rubinstein. Do you see any difference? I doubt it. Basically they are both terrific. They both reflect quality. Their products are of similar excellence. Their presentation is equally expensive. But, the point is, whereas Rubinstein pushes chic to the chosen few, Revlon sells class to the masses. Revlon tell a woman she can look as beautiful and sophisticated as the model on their showcards for the mere price – reasonable price – of a lipstick and bottle of nail enamel. Do you see?'

As Gina transmitted her enthusiasm across the desk she glowed with satisfaction as she saw the light dawn, first in Cassie, then Harry, at last Max.

She pressed on, 'That's what we must aim for. A restaurant that makes any man and woman feel like . . .' she searched for an example, came up with, 'Cole and Linda Porter,' added, 'for the cost – affordable cost – of cocktails and dinner.' That, she thought with a surge of exhilaration, is it in a nutshell. It was the first time she had vocalized the scribbles that had swarmed through her notebooks, and now that she had heard the idea expressed out loud, she knew it was right. Excitingly right. It was what would give them success, carry them all the way to the top of the hill. She still wasn't sure why she wanted to get there, but did that matter? It was the doing that counted. The accomplishment. Don't compromise, she'd always instilled in Paola and Filipo, set your sights on your destinaton, and go for it; if you sit around pondering the wherefores and whyfores, your ship will sail and you'll still be on the beach.

Max interrupted her thoughts: '*Si*, Principessa, I understand. But is it possible? To have such a restaurant with such prices? Where would be the profit?'

'The same place as always, old friend,' rejoined Gina. 'In the food and the wine. The economics will be no different to those of our After Theatre dinner. By restricting the menu we are able to keep tight control on our stock, cut down on wastage, and increase our bulk purchasing power. At the new Rossi restaurants we will offer a good but limited choice of dishes; say, three or four starters, half-a-dozen main courses, two or three simple sweets included in the price. The wine list will be similar. You know, half the pretenders who come in here haven't the foggiest idea what they're drinking. They choose on price, usually the most expensive, to impress their girlfriends or buddies, also because they think high cost equals best quality, not realizing it sometimes means merely scarcity or heavy transportation overhead.'

'Or,' interjected Harry, 'in some unscrupulous establishments, sheer profiteering. In the good old bad old days the speakeasies stuck impressive tartan labels with Scottish-sounding names on quarts of red-eye, sold it as the real McCoy. There are still plenty of similar gypsters who know a gullible Joe Public will pay over the odds for anything with foreign writing on the bottle.'

'Unfortunately so,' agreed Gina. 'But that won't be the case in our restaurants. Our customers will get real value for money with genuine French and Italian wine. The first because it is the best and comes from the only reliable vineyards in the world. The second because some folk,' she smiled at Max, 'won't drink anything else, in spite of the fact that Italy's wine trade has always been as disorganized as a barrel-load of monkeys.' To the big Tuscan's unhappy reaction at this, she added placatingly, 'Though that doesn't mean some of their product isn't excellent. You just have to know where to look for it.'

Cassie grinned at Max, then said, 'I'm beginning to see it. Sure, I guess it will work. But, Gina, have I got this straight – every one of the Rossi restaurants will have the same menu and wine list?' To the affirmation in Gina's eyes she added, 'And will they all look identical?'

'Peas in a pod,' responded Gina. 'To ensure the customers will instantly recognize them, also so that whether they're in an Oregon forest, up a Colorado mountain, or on a Florida beach, as soon as they walk through our door they'll feel at home. That's what the Rossi sign will stand for – familiarity, reliability, and relaxation. That last is the most important, because we'll be catering to a great mass of people who aren't accustomed to dining out, folks who treat fancy restaurants with awe. We have to impress them, give them style, offer the top-class service our Lady clientele takes for granted, but – we stand or fall on this – we have to do all that without frightening them to death.'

Harry murmured, 'Tall order.'

'But not impossible,' persisted Gina. 'It's all a matter of reception and presentation – the staff and the decor. The first is easy. We've never tolerated bartenders who give short change, waiters who hustle for tips, doormen who favour customers in big limos. That policy will continue. When there are a thousand Rossi restaurants, the lowliest employee in the farthest-flung outpost will be in that job because he, or she, truly wants to be there, to build a career in catering, not merely because they figure it's easier than slinging rivets or hammering a typewriter. The second necessity, presentation, is not so simple to . . . '

'*Mille ristoranti!*' exclaimed Max. 'Principessa, *scusi*, you said a thousand. But that was only . . . *retorico* . . . how do you say, a figure of speech. Yes?'

Gina interrupted in full flow, pulled her attention to Max, answered crisply, 'No.' She scanned the trio. 'Is that what you all thought? Didn't I make myself clear from the outset? I said we'd be number one. Nationwide. That meant ahead of the rest. That means a Rossi Tavern – do you like that name – in every major city throughout the U.S.A., and at every watering hole in between.' Her voice was shaded with impatience. 'Are we all on the same wavelength? Max?'

The Tuscan, in a defensive reflex, tugged his moustachios, answered haltingly, '*Si*. Yes. I'm sorry, Principessa. I . . . '

Harry said quietly, 'I think Max was just speaking out for all three of us, Gina. Voicing our surprise. You know your proposal takes some swallowing in one gulp. I think we need to chew on it a while.'

A while, Gina's mind protested. Why? Can't you see . . . She drew a deep breath. All right, take it calmly. Don't keep expecting so much. They're loyal and loving and with you all the way. Just let them absorb it at their own pace. She smiled, said, 'Yes, I suppose I did sort of drop on you out of the sky. However,' she restrained restless fingers from drumming the desktop, 'we can't let the grass grow, we have to expand, otherwise we'll just stagnate.'

Cassie glanced sideways at Harry and Max. Returning to

Gina, on behalf of them all she acquiesced, 'Sure, we see it, Hon. Of course we do. Go on ahead now.'

Gina reassembled her thoughts. 'As I was saying, presentation. That means decor. No point in spending our time throwing around personal preferences. We need expert advice. André de Sath – the Broadway set designer who did little Frankie's nursery – I've arranged a meeting with him tomorrow. Now,' she opened a folder, distributed typed sheets, 'these are my projected costings, based on average throughput, profit per capita, allowing for national inflation next year of, say two per cent.' She surveyed her own handiwork.

The others applied themselves.

For the next three hours they planned the menu, the wine lists, the manning levels, the stock control system for a chain of restaurants across the United States.

When Gina eventually sat back, regarded the intense expressions of her three directors, who were now avidly discussing minor details amongst themselves, she felt like a mountaineer who had scaled a mighty peak. Well, almost. She still had a couple more steps to take to plant her flag, but she knew they were no problem. The future was as bright as the clear winter sky beyond the window.

'About time we ate,' she declared. 'How about lunch up here? And a celebratory bottle with a gold top? I'll go rustle up something.' She rose quickly, declining Cassie's offer to help, went out to the hallway. She didn't really want the drink, but did need this moment alone to enjoy her own exhilaration. Self-indulgence? So, she was entitled, wasn't she.

She walked past the adjoining offices, exited through the door opening onto the upper lobby. Crossing the expanse of ivory carpet, she stood at the balcony rail, looked down at the elegant turmoil that was midday in the Lady. Conversation, laughter, music, the clatter of crockery, pop of corks, the hubbub was like a turbulent cloud beneath where Gina stood. Yet she was able to distinguish every component of it, pick out each waiter's voice, could tell precisely which customers had just been seated, which were on the verge of leaving. Above all she knew how rapidly the cashier was taking money; from a screened booth in a far corner, the opening slide and closing thunk of the register's drawer was as distinct to Gina as if she was right beside it. She listened for several minutes. Imagined it multiplied by a thousand.

In her secretary's office, a list of the morning's telephone calls was beside a stack of mail. Gina swiftly noted all the red-flagged communications she would have to handle herself. She lifted the envelopes marked, 'Personal'. Four, three with unfamiliar handwriting – par for the day. Celebrity had its price, coined in hate, love and importunings. Later Gina would read the letters from three strangers, discover a gas-station clerk in Minneapolis believed her to be the daughter of Satan, a lady dachshund breeder in Chattanooga thought she had the world's most beautiful breasts, and a short-order chef in Cheyenne knew she'd be delighted to receive his secret recipe for aphrodisiac cola, for a mere five thousand dollars.

For now, Gina opened the fourth envelope, the one bearing Sybil's recognizable scribble. From within she extracted a blurry black and white photograph of Sybil and David, holding hands beside a signpost which was barely distinguishable as GRETNA GREEN. On the reverse of the card, again Sybil's scribble:

'En route to skiing hol. Seemed like a good idea at the time. Further missive when strength permits. Love, Mrs David Lowell, née De Belvere.'

Gina's mouth had gone very dry. Of course she was pleased. She was delighted. Happy for both of them. Certainly she was. Why shouldn't she be?

Cassie avowed, 'He's terrific! Really, he is, Hon. I've heard him a hundred times. He's better than Sinatra even.' She coloured. 'Well, he will be, one day. He needs professional backing is all. A chance. He deserves a chance. Please, Gina, say you'll listen to him. You won't regret it. I promise.'

Gina regarded the redhead. Cassie's hobby was having crushes, 'The hots,' she'd enthuse. 'Holy Moses, I've got the hots for that guy!' Usually, however, the object of her passion remained on the scene for about the same length of time as Cassie's latest hat. Paraded perpetually around the city for a month – at most – it would then be cast aside in favour of whichever new model had captured her eye.

So, Gina asked herself, was the object of her friend's present canvassing just the flavour of the month? No, it wasn't. Gina couldn't define it, but there was a discernible difference in Casssie's attitude, an intensity which she'd never shown before. It had been apparent from the moment, fifteen minutes ago, after a brief lunch and rounding off of the new restaurant proposals, when Cassie had approached Gina with, 'Have you got a minute, Hon? Just a minute. It is kinda important.'

Gina, her head still echoing with the bombshell news from Sybil, had agreed abstractedly and half-listened while Cassie extolled the virtues of some young singer she'd met in a jazz joint downtown. He was a bellhop at the Pierrepont, did a solo spot with the resident six-piece on Saturday nights, had played a summer season last year at one of the vacation lodges in the Catskills. Gina's nerves – for reasons she chose not to probe – had been, to say the least, on edge. The enthusiasm she'd felt early this morning had been replaced by a fragile patience that was threatening to crack.

But it was then she'd caught the tone in Cassie's voice. Pocketing her preoccupations, Gina had turned her full attention to her friend's urgent monologue.

For that is what it had become, a breathless dissertation on musical technique, vocal qualities, and popular singing trends, and a certain Mister Tony Snow's mastery of all three. 'We've all had our breaks, Hon. You, me, Harry. Tony deserves his. He does. You know I wouldn't waste your time. And I never asked a favour like this before. Please, Gina. Please let him come audition.'

Cassie's shoulders were tilted forward, the upper part of her body as tense as a spring. Her face was tight with supplication. The desperate posture was so unlike her usual happy-go-lucky attitude that Gina experienced a stab of fear. It was this, she decided later, which caused her to answer, 'Yes, Cass, why not? Remember though, Harry has the final say in who appears in the club. I'll suggest we give . . . Tony, did you say? a try out, but that's as far as I'll go. Can you get him here later this afternoon?'

'No problem. Oh, Gina, you're a pal. Thanks. Thanks a mill,' bubbled Cassie. 'And don't worry, Harry will love him. So will you. Same as I do. Sure, dumb isn't it? I love him. I never thought I'd hear me say it either. But, we all gotta fall someday, right? Wait'll you see him, and hear him, you'll understand. You'll know why I get goosebumps just standing near him. You'll realize what makes Tony so special.'

He wasn't tall, maybe only an inch taller than she, but he was broad-shouldered and deep-chested, and as slim-hipped as a boy. It wasn't however his body which caused Gina's pulse to jump. It was the face. His mouth was wide, and when he smiled, as he was doing now to Harry Dix, his teeth were white and even. Beneath intensely blue eyes his cheekbones were high giving him a faintly oriental appearance, this contested by the corn-blond hair falling casually across his brow. Beautiful, thought Gina as he walked toward her flanked by Harry and Cassie. So why did she dislike him even before she'd been introduced?

Halting in front of her he extended his hand. 'Hi. I'm Tony.' His voice was deep and easy, his smile friendly and polite as he made unwavering eye contact.

Gina took his hand briefly, released it as an unbidden heat spread through her stomach. Chagrined at herself for the reflex response she replied brusquely, 'I'm pleased to meet you. Cassie's told me a lot about you.' You wouldn't believe how much, she added to herself, and that raised a mental vision of Cassie's graphic account of an evening she'd spent at his apartment. My God, Gina thought, he can inspire sexual imagery just by his presence, and she understood why her usually easy-come, easy-go friend had seemed so obsessed when she first described this man. Even here in the gloomy, unlit nightclub there was an excitement charging the air around him, filling Gina with a co-mingling of arousal and unease. She said, 'You're a singer.' The remark was curt, but purposefully so. She had no wish to seem rude; equally she must maintain a sense of rationality in this situation, not be railroaded into hiring someone with no talent simply because he was Cassie's infatuation and flaunted a devastating smile.

Modesty veiled his eyes. 'I try, Miss Rossi.'

'Then I'd like you to try for us,' answered Gina. 'We don't have the band here, so I hope you won't mind singing with a phonograph record.'

'That's just fine. I don't sing with anything in the bath.' He reached out and squeezed Cassie's hand, causing the redhead to flush to the roots of her hair, and Harry to chuckle appreciatively.

'Very well,' Gina's response was clipped. 'What are we waiting for?' She pulled a chair from a table and sat, stared in the direction of the small stage with a poised display of authoritative attention.

Harry hurried behind the wing curtain where he would wind

the gramophone which was used when the band took five. Cassie walked with Tony to the small stage, touching his arm, whispering to him, looking into his eyes with love and wonder. He laughed, kissed her cheek, stroked a curl from her brow.

Gina snapped, 'Are you ready, Harry?' She bit her lip, blew out her breath, drummed her fingers on her knee. Childish reaction to someone else's pleasure, she chastised herself. What was the matter with her this afternoon? Why should a good-looking man unnerve her this way? She saw plenty, just as handsome, every day, actors, singers, sportsmen whose female fans camped at the door while they ate in The Lady, yet none had ever caused her to feel either embarrassed or intimidated. But, then, those weren't the emotions she was experiencing here. It was something else. A sense of apprehension that was disquieting her.

'If you go too long without a feller, you get a bit screwy, you know.' Recall of Cassie's prognosis, pinched Gina out of her introspection. She allowed herself a small inner laugh. Maybe her friend was right, maybe she'd just about last out till Fallon got here.

'All set,' called Harry.

Cassie released Tony and he stepped up onto the stage, walked behind the dead microphone, smiled at Gina and said, 'Just so it looks right,' then glanced toward Harry and declared, 'Ready when you are, Maestro.'

Silence ensued for several moments before the loud record hiss issued from the speakers behind the bandstand, followed abruptly by a saxophone intro to 'The Way You Look Tonight'.

Gina watched Tony. He was staring over her head at some unseen spot, his head nodding slightly to the tune's beat. He let the first four bars ride, picked up on the fifth. And Gina didn't need to hear any further than the eighth to know he was good. Better than good. His voice wasn't Crosby, it possessed a harder edge, but it had that easy slide between notes, the melodic quality that was God's gift to a chosen few, blended with a unique phrasing which came from years of practice and listening to – studying but not copying – one's peers. The effect was electric.

An emotional description, thought Gina, but not an exaggeration. Reaction to the man and his voice was clearly visible on every face in the room. Cassie was standing transfixed. Harry had appeared from behind the curtain to stare in appreciation. Chang and his six kitchen hands had been drawn to the room. Their expressions said it all as Tony took the song its course, becoming more relaxed, self-assured in his rendition as he reprised the chorus, atuned now to the band's timing. He wasn't thrown even when the record ended before he did, skilfully holding the last note as if the finish had been rehearsed to this perfection. He cut off with a brief hand motion to an imaginary orchestra, dropped his head in a sharp bow, then stepped back and threw a smile across the deserted tables as if he'd just played Saturday night at the Coconut Grove.

For a moment silence hung stunned, then spontaneous applause erupted. Harry was striding across the stage, shaking Tony's hand. Cassie was yelling 'More!' Chang and his staff were chattering excitedly. Tony was smiling, nodding thanks, looking suitably grateful; most of all he was watching Gina.

As the hubbub died down, she stood and walked toward the stage. She said in a businesslike manner, 'Thank you, Tony. I enjoyed that. I'm sure we all did. Now, if you'll excuse me, I have several matters to attend to. Harry, when you've finished here, perhaps you could spare me a few minutes in my office?' She turned and strode from the room.

At her desk she signed the day's mail, penned a swift congratulations to Sybil. Her secretary brought in a list of telephone callers. Gina scanned the two dozen, knew more or less what each wanted. Except one. The woman's name was familiar. She remembered: an editor at one of the publishing houses who occasionally came in for lunch with authors and agents; Gina had chatted with her a couple of times, mentally filed her name as a possible contact for when Fallon's novel was ready. She briefly wondered about the call, but shelved the speculation as Harry entered.

He came and sat opposite, without preamble, said, 'The singer. Something bothering you?'

Gina pursed her lips. 'Perhaps.'

'You don't trust him?'

Gina was surprised. 'You sensed it too?' To Harry's indecisive shrug she said with a wry smile, 'Maybe I just don't go for guys who are prettier than I am. I'll bet the bell-captain at the Pierrepont has him doing more than tote baggage.' The remark, she knew, was unfounded. Not all good-looking young men who worked hotels hired their talents to the female guests, and even those who did weren't necessarily villains; after all, Cassie had been accepting 'presents' from admirers for almost half her life, and though Gina didn't wholly approve she still considered the happy-go-lucky redhead her dearest friend. Annoyed with herself for her tangled emotions, she said briskly, 'The point is he can sing.'

'Like a lark,' agreed Harry. 'A natural. He has a few rough edges, but I can smooth those.'

'You suggest we hire him?'

'He's better than half-a-dozen recent *Billboard* top-tenners who cost us an arm and a leg. Sign him now, on contract, before the wife of some radio producer hears him singing in his bath.' In response to Gina's raised eyebrow, Harry conceded, 'Yes, I guess you're right, his boyish innocence is as phoney as our Italian chef. But that's what this game is all about. Illusions. The restaurant business, night club trade, entertainment industry, it all boils down to the same thing – sprinkling stardust in the customers' eyes, never letting them see the garbage cans out back. So, as long as the kid can warble every night the way he did this afternoon, why worry about his morals? Let me work with him for a couple of weeks to polish his timing and I guarantee he'll pack 'em in. Specially the women. You must've seen that.'

Gina smiled. 'Just slightly. All right, we've got ourselves a new headliner. Have him photographed, and a showcard designed for the lobby. What was his name? Tony Snow. That's terrible. We need something sharper, more memorable.' She drummed on a contemplative desktop. 'The Italian for snow is *neve*. Tony Neve? That's awful too.'

The voice from the doorway suggested, 'How about Nevada?' Filipo strolled forward carrying his schoolbooks. 'Like the state. It's Spanish for snow-capped. Near enough, isn't it?'

Gina enunciated speculatively, 'Tony Nevada.'

Harry silently mouthed it, bit it on his lip as if tasting it, and finally declared, 'I like it. And nobody is using it. Better yet, the name of that state has gained a sort of glamorous reputation since B. Siegel's casino opened. Tony Nevada. Sure, it gets better all the time. Phil, you're a genius.'

Filipo grinned, chewed an imaginary corn stalk. 'Shucks, 'twarnt nuthin', Pappy. Jest a nachel-born talent I got fer showbiz.'

Gina clipped, 'And we're very grateful for your assistance. How did you do in the history exam?'

'Pardon? Gosh, look at the time. I'll be late. So long, Harry. See you later, Sis.' And Filipo had beat a hasty retreat before Gina could open her mouth to ask, Late for what?

She fired a beam of frustrated retribution at the door through which her brother had exited, before turning to Harry's grin and saying, 'It isn't funny. His school reports are atrocious. All he ever thinks about is movies. And television. Cajoles me fifty times a week to install a television. Have you seen the programmes? Moronic. I wouldn't have one as a gift.'

'Of course you wouldn't,' agreed Harry.

Gina looked into his deadly stern face, then, seeing the sparkle at the corner of his eyes, she slowly smiled. 'All right, perhaps the box has some virtue. I guess inexpensive entertainment for folk can't be such a bad thing. I don't know . . . ' she sighed, 'maybe all this new-fangledness is getting too much for me. Doesn't the world seem to be spinning twice as fast as it used to, Harry? Don't we seem to have to run six paces to make four? Or is it just me? Am I growing too old for the game? Don't answer that. Did I tell you, Sybil got hitched? Remember we once talked – I seem to recall we were in an automobile someplace – about marriage? You said you weren't the settling kind. You know, I sometimes wonder if I'm not the same. Sybil's done the deed. And Cassie – Cassie of all people, is strangely smitten. Yet I . . . I want Fallon here, I want it so much, but at the same time, I think of all the things I have to do, and I feel, sometimes, I'd rather do them alone. Does that make any kind of sense? What was I just saying about Filipo? I'm really going to have to do something about him.' She paused, suddenly aware that she was watching her pen doodling across her notebook. She looked up, into the quiet understanding of Harry's eyes. She said wryly, 'I was rambling, wasn't I? Another sign of senility.' To his gentle smile she added, 'Thanks for listening.'

Harry said, 'I enjoy the sound of your voice.'

Gina remained silent a moment longer, then she reset her shoulders, snapped shut the notebook and, rising, declared, 'Well, can't sit here gabbing all night. A hundred and one things to do. Not least of which is getting Rossi Taverns under way. By the way,' she paused, as Harry stood, 'I'm sorry if I got a bit snappy at the meeting this morning.'

'Likewise,' he returned.

'Anyhow,' Gina forged on, 'I haven't had a chance to ask you what you really thought of the idea.'

'Frankly,' he replied, 'I thought it was the most outrageous, extravagant, preposterous scheme I'd heard since a bold-as-brass, blonde eager-beaver buttonholed me at the Starlight, insisted she could double my profits. I knew then I never should have listened. Instead, look where I finished up. And now, I have this terrible feeling I'm going to become,' his long face adopted its old doleful expression, 'a millionaire.' He forlornly shook his head.

Gina, donning an equally crestfallen expression, murmured with exaggerated repentence, 'I hope you'll forgive me.'

They linked arms, went out of the office.

It was later, as they sat together over supper in the club, that Harry ventured, 'There was just one thing. A minor detail. These thousand restaurants. How are we going to pay for them?'

Gina, knifing Stilton cheese onto a graham cracker, answered casually, 'Oh, that. Didn't I mention it? Well, we, actually, won't be paying anything. That is, people – lots of people – will be paying us.' She popped the morsel into her mouth, chewed as she watched the dancers slow waltzing around the floor. After she had swallowed, she faced Harry's expectancy, said, shrugging, 'It's obvious. Franchises.'

27

'It's like a licence,' she explained carefully to Max. 'We grant someone the right to use our name on their business. And they pay us a lump sum for that right. No, there was never anything like it in Italy. The idea's hardly been heard of in Europe. But it's where the future of the major service industries lies. Without massive amounts of capital it would be virtually impossible to open a chain of restaurants or hotels in one fell swoop. Normally it would take years. A lifetime. As I said yesterday morning, we need to reach the top of the hill while we're all young enough to enjoy the view. We also want to get there without breaking our backs en route. Franchising is the vehicle we'll use. It'll ride us up to the summit as smoothly, and as rapidly, as an express elevator. Believe me, old friend, when we announce Rossi Taverns Incorporated, folks will recognize it as the gravy train of the century. They'll be climbing over each other to jump on board.'

Gina smiled warmly at the big man, hoping her simple explanation of the scheme had cured the bemusement he'd shown when she broached the subject. She wanted him to understand, because she wanted him to share her enthusiasm. Why was it she always worried so about Max? Of all the family he was still the one who seemed misplaced. He was excellent at what he did, diligent, painstaking, caring in his managership of the Lady, indispensable to Gina, freeing her from the every-day, nonetheless important, routine which kept the ship on an even keel. Nor did Max ever complain. He was, seemingly, happy, proud too of his involvement, ofttimes to be seen hands clasped behind his back, semi-concealed by a pillar or floral display, observing the hectic yet impeccable commerce of the restaurant, his moustachios positively curling with satisfaction. Always, though, Gina felt the Tuscan giant should be doing something else.

But what? What was she missing?

She said fondly, 'I hope you're not going to lose your first million to your pinocle-playing buddies.'

Max, relaxing the frown which had continued to knit the enigmas of franchising across his brow, grinned, 'Principessa, lose? *Non capisco*. What is this word?'

Gina, happy that another minor bump on their future path had been ironed out, went on to discuss their more immediate plans to introduce a new staff bonus scheme. By the time they had that subject put to bed, her secretary had called through to say Mrs Dorothy Hamm was waiting downstairs.

As she crossed the bar where Mrs Hamm was finishing a mid-morning coffee, Gina recognized the fiftyish woman, elegant but faintly awry in a grey tailored suit and matching toque, whom she'd yesterday placed as an editor at one of the New York publishing houses. Gina had returned her telephone call, agreed to this prompt appointment as the matter had sounded most urgent. Extending her hand, she greeted, 'Hello there. Lovely to see you again.' She sat opposite.

More coffee was refused and they exchanged pleasantries for several minutes, inevitably swinging the chat around to the literary scene. By now Gina had decided Mrs Hamm was here to arrange a luncheon or dinner for her authors, and was mentally figuring what discount she'd offer as a sweetener to a deal, on Fallon's behalf, for what, she would assure the editor, was going to be The Greatest War Novel Ever Written. Maybe I should go into agenting, she mused along a sidetrack as the woman talked on. Not representing writers, of course, but entertainers. Harry could handle that. He knows more about showbiz than all the promoters of Times Square put together. Where was I? Fallon.

She said, 'There are some fine English authors.'

The woman responded, 'Have you ever considered writing a book yourself?'

Gina thought her hearing had become impaired.

'You wouldn't have actually to write it, of course,' hurried on Mrs Hamm. 'We'd help you with that. I personally, if you wished. I hope you'll permit me. After all, this was my idea, you see. Mine and our publishing director's. He's so eager to meet you. Although you've already spoken. When he's dined here. You do remember him?' She teetered toward a frown, then beamed enthusiastically at Gina's pale acknowledgment. 'We'd guarantee a record promotion budget, naturally,' she continued. 'I just know it would be a dream of a success. A runaway bestseller. We're all so excited by the prospects.'

As the editor continued to paint exuberant word-pictures framed by world rights, broadcasting rights, serialization and other gilded jargon, Gina was struggling to re-orient herself into a new dimension. Write a novel? But how? About what? She vaguely listened to the voice saying, 'The battle's all but won, you see. The entire country already knows your name, recognizes your face. Every woman in America hangs on your briefest word.'

Gina attempted to lay hold of the proposition. The light of reason began to penetrate the fog of confusion which Mrs Hamm's astounding suggestion had wrought. Was the idea so unlikely? Well, she wasn't illiterate, was she? And imagine – the thought seized her with a hot hand – imagine the publicity value. All right, she was already famous, riding the crest of the wave generated by her link to the GI war brides brouhaha, but that surge wouldn't last for ever. A further thrust would be extremely useful, particularly as an extra impetus behind Rossi Taverns.

She fixed her undivided attention on Mrs Hamm.

Who was saying, 'Of course, it's early days yet, a great many details to discuss, and certainly we'd respect, value, your opinion, but I, we, thought it would be just so wonderfully apt, succinct, with your photograph. The title . . . ' Her hands made a small fanfare in the air in front of her face. '*The Lady's Cookbook.*'

During the ensuing weeks Gina conducted every conversation as if she were walking on glass. She was reminded of the posters of wartime London: CARELESS TALK COSTS LIVES. Here and now it might cost thousands of dollars.

Plans for what were intended to be the two most newsworthy events of the year, bar none – publication of Gina Rossi's tome of genuine Italian recipes, plus her launch of a nationwide restaurant franchise specializing in said cuisine – were progressing at full tilt. Trouble was, both were more hush-hush than a Pentagon secret weapon.

While she attended interminable editorial meetings with Mrs Hamm to flay back and forth across fields of typography, photography, illustration, the thousand and more details of publishing essentials which were, apparently, far more important than the actual content of her book, she had to keep a tight cork on her fizzing desire to mention Rossi Taverns Inc. Equally, when she discussed the latter with her small band of directors and expert advisers, she was obliged to swallow all urges to reveal her upcoming move into the ranks of authorship. 'If one word leaks,' Mrs Hamm had cautioned, 'every publisher in the country will be rushing into print with whatever culinary concoctions they can pin to the name of any celebrity – no matter how unlikely – willing to be nailed to the dotted line.'

Thus, Gina's waking hours were spent in a state of perpetual mental suppression, so that each night, the instant her head touched the pillow, her imaginings leapt their fences, careered off in a hundred different directions across Technicolour landscapes so exciting as to make more than ten minutes' sleep impossible.

Could she conceivably reach April 30th without brain damage? April 30th, the date Fallon was due to arrive in New

York, the day Gina, within thirty seconds of dragging him into her bedroom, would yank the stopper on not only the bottled-up secret of her book, but also, simultaneously, on her other inner volcano (no, not Rossi Taverns) which by now was threatening a blood-boiling climactic eruption.

Less of those thoughts, she warned herself ten times a day as she swept, a rigger in full sail, across the often uncharted, sometimes familiar seas of publishing, financing, franchising, interior decorating, advertising, cooking which were the routes to her new horizon.

The days counted down.

March 29th, the first layout for *The Lady's Cookbook* was complete. March 31st, Gina had presented all her recipes to Mrs Hamm. April 4th, André de Sath had finalized plans and colour drawings for a Rossi Tavern the lobby of which was a moonlit Venetian quay before a slow-flowing canal where diners would cross, via an arching stone footbridge, to a restaurant which was a glowing, beamed and tapestried taverna opening onto a terrace where cages of live doves hung in the branches of real trees. (Gina didn't need Cassie's, Harry's, and Max's boggling eyes to know that customers would scale mountains, trek deserts just to get a look at such a place.) April 10th, Tony Nevada opened at the club. April 11th, Nightjay of *The Star* said, 'Catch him this week; next week reservations will be worth gold.' April 20th, Mrs Hamm reported publication would be November – 'S. Claus will need to hire extra sleighs for delivery either to or on behalf of every woman in the country.' April 22nd, the accountants and lawyers were putting the finishing touches to the outline franchise proposals. April 24th, Paola mentioned that Johnny was flying to Phoenix to investigate vending-machine prospects in Arizona. (Harry told Gina he thought her brother-in-law must have lost a marble – there was less potential for his business in that entire state than there was on any single mile of Fourteenth Street. Gina didn't have time to ponder this.) April 26th, she bought a new suit and hat. April 28th, she had a special showcard made for the lobby, personally polished and dusted and straightened the guest bedroom, (Cassie peered around the door, grinned knowingly. Gina riposted, 'Yes, he will too be sleeping in here,') and ordered a limousine for collection at the airport.

April 29th, she never remembered what happened.

April 30th arrived.

Gina was out of bed less than two hours after getting into it; had swallowed a mug of coffee, checked the day's menus and reservations, scribbled her stack of memos, repolished and redusted and restraightened the pristine guest bedroom, and was purchasing vegetable and fruit supplies at Gansevoort Market while the growers were still unloading their trucks.

She was back at the Lady by five-thirty a.m.; changed into the new navy worsted suit – calf-length skirt built out at the hips, extravagantly-peplummed jacket cinched into a twenty-inch waist by a broad patent leather belt – an enormous silk bow at her throat, and the dipping and curving portrait hat, which could have doubled as the roof of a Chinese pagoda, on her head.

Thus garbed, she spent the next three hours prowling the building in an agony of impatience, fidgeting and ferreting into anything and everything, getting in folks' way and in their hair as they set their own daily rounds in motion, relocating the special lobby showcard in a dozen spots, even hurrying (twice) down to the corner of Forty-Seventh to peer amidst the teeming morning traffic lest the airport (she had called them three times) had been mistaken about the plane's E.T.A. and the limousine bearing Fallon was already heading up Fifth Avenue.

Of course she was aware, just as well as everybody was, that aircraft, true to the tradition of all forms of public transport, had never been known to arrive early in the entire history of aviation; nevertheless, thirty minutes before the limousine she'd despatched was due to appear, Gina was on the sidewalk, stalking back and forth beneath the marquee, scanning the distance where she imagined Fallon to be bubbling in a similar stew of excitement and trepidation.

Miracle of miracles, the limousine was five minutes ahead of schedule. It came nosing out of the wave of vehicles, taking Gina by surprise. Before she'd had time to flick another imaginary speck of dust from the chest of her jacket, the car's door had sprung open and Robert Fallon was standing at the kerb, gazing around like Stanley emergent from the jungle but not recognizing Livingstone even after a full five seconds' stare.

Gina's legs were working about as well as his eyes. They

seemed exceedingly reluctant to do anything but shake, so, discretion overcoming passion, she stayed put, raised a casual hand and called, Hi!'

The penny dropped as abruptly as Fallon's brows rose. Then he crossed the sidewalk to stand before her, pipe clenched between his teeth as if to hold back the astonishment that was straining behind his face.

She warned, 'If you mention my tan I'll brain you.' Her overwhelming impulse was to seize him and kiss him, to plaster him with kisses. But she knew that public displays of affection were not Fallon's style, so she settled for a peck on his cheek; which left them standing dumbly looking at each other with the uncertainty and vague embarrassment of strangers introduced and abandoned at a cocktail party.

At last he observed gruffly, 'I didn't know Lockheed had gone into hats.'

And that broke the moment and she jabbed him in the ribs, regarding his usual rarely assorted clothing, and mentally shooting back, And I wasn't aware that Heinz had gone into menswear. But she swallowed the rejoinder before it surfaced, realizing suddenly that it might sound like Miss Smarty Pants. In fact, maybe the hat was a trifle exaggerated. Perhaps she should have rethought the entire ensemble. Damn it, why hadn't she given it more consideration? And, damn it again, why did he always make her feel this way, sending her self-assuredness sailing out the window while filling her with romantic longings (lust)?

That word popped into her head with all the effect of an unexpected hand on her breast, causing her to blurt, 'Well, what the heck are we standing here for?' Swiftly seizing his arm she propelled him toward the entrance.

As they entered the lobby she winced, confronted by what she now knew was her second almighty error. The large, gold-on-black showcard fanfared: THE LADY WELCOMES ROBERT FALLON, BESTSELLING NOVELIST (TO BE)

Gina hurriedly dismissed it: 'We do it for all our visiting VIPs. You get to take it home so you can frame it, throw darts at it, whatever.' Not daring to look at his face and the disaster she was certain was written there, she towed him beneath the archway to the restaurant, gasping with relief to see Max striding toward them.

The two men grabbed each other's hands, embraced,

laughed, appraised each other, exchanged greetings. Fallon was saying, 'Hey, old buddy,' surveying the room's pink and ivory splendour, 'some hell of a place you've got here.' And Max was replying, 'Just a modest little trattoria. But it pays for my bookie's vacations.' Then they were joshing, slapping shoulders, heading for the bar.

Gina felt as cheerful as a cast-off sock.

By the time she'd followed them (tossing the damned hat onto an empty table), Cassie and Harry had appeared. The club's vice-president's long face was beaming as he welcomed Fallon, while the redhead's eyes were firing a twenty-one gun salute. Amid the gabble they reached the counter where Max played barkeep, and within a minute everyone but Gina had a drink in their hand, and were toasting and swigging their liquor as if celebrating the homecoming of a long-lost brother. When Max eventually noticed Gina, he poured and handed her a club soda, barely pausing in his banter with the jolly gang.

Gina gripped the glass in sorcerous fingers and willed them all to disappear.

They were about to embark on their third round when she jammed a shoulder into a gap in the confab and said loudly, 'Fallon, I'll show you your room.'

As these were the first words she'd uttered for ten minutes they were received like gunshots at a wedding reception. However, she had no intention of allowing this revelry to continue for one second longer. Despite her burgeoning irritation, her overriding emotion was still desire. 'Cassie,' she prompted, 'remember it's the Women's Civic League coffee morning. Max, the beer truck will be here in thirty minutes. Harry . . .' offhand she couldn't think of anything for Harry, settled for, 'Fallon and I will be up tonight for the supper show.' Then, before anyone could get off a returning salvo, she was striding the Englishman toward the exit (only slightly burning from Cassie's knowing grin), up two flights, along the hallway and into the room next to her own.

As he turned to her she kissed him.

Not a peck this time, not a brushing of lips, a deep open-mouthed kiss that was the realization of a thousand fantasies of this last, long year.

Her entire being was centred on that kiss. She wanted it to last for ever. She clung to him, her arms around his neck, pulling his head down, digging her fingers into his hair, melding her body against his. She hadn't realized the intensity of her need, wouldn't have believed there could be so much voraciousness in her. Her mouth moved from his for an instant as she gasped for breath and rasped, 'Fallon.' Then she was kissing him again, passionately, fiercely; her hands were squeezing his shoulders, sliding inside his jacket, kneading his chest.

He pulled away from her and breathed, 'Hey! Take it easy. Give a fellow a minute.'

It was the first time in all the years she'd known him she had ever seen hesitation in his eyes. The look pricked her with uncertainty. Inhaling raggedly, she said, 'I guess I was a little sudden. But it has been kind of a long time.' The question, Has it been as long for you? sidled into her head, nudging her desire to one side.

Fallon held her at arm's length. 'I'm sorry,' he smiled. 'Of course I feel the same way. It's just that I had a heavy night. A long interview. Didn't get to bed till three a.m.' To the rising confusion in Gina's face, he confessed, 'Yes, I arrived in New York yesterday. I appreciate I should have phoned, but I knew you'd be busy, and I had this feller to track down. It was important, Gina. A feature I'm working on. An opportunity I couldn't miss.'

She wanted to yell, An opportunity that was a bloody sight more important than seeing me! Her romantic notions had been incinerated as abruptly as rosebuds under a blowtorch. She was a child who'd just heard Santa Claus had cancelled Christmas. She wanted to rage as well as weep. She wanted to tell Robert Fallon he was a selfish, inconsiderate, self-obsessed skunk who didn't give a damn about other people's feelings, and that he could get the hell out and not come back and good riddance.

He reached out one hand, cupped her face, leaned forward and gently kissed her. Moving back, he shrugged, unsuccessfully pushed his hair from his brow. 'Forgive me?'

What unmitigated gall! She asked softly, 'You will be staying here tonight?' She heard her own words with disbelief. How pathetic! Why didn't she just prostrate herself at his feet and implore him to stay?

Fallon said, 'I'll send for my bags.' Surveying the gleaming immaculateness, he added, 'I'll have them scoured and waxed before bringing them in.'

Sarcastic? No, that envy-seeded churlishness wasn't within Fallon. Still there was a tension in him. There was an invisible barrier which Gina felt she could not cross. She, literally, didn't know what to do, though she was certain that to make any further romantic overtures would be her biggest, maybe last, mistake of the morning. She suddenly realized that with a supportive hand on the dresser she was standing on one foot the other hooked behind her upright calf, a stance she hadn't adopted since her pre-teen schooldays. Swiftly rearranging her pose she clipped, 'Come on, I'll show you New York, my home town.'

Fallon said, 'Sounds like you've put down roots.'

'For sure.'

'This is where they'll stay?'

'I couldn't possibly afford the freight charges for moving my shoes and hats.'

He laughed. A crack in the wall between them. Gina took his arm, led him out to this spring morning in Manhattan.

Despite a continuing vague unease, she couldn't remember when she last had felt such happiness. Not the joy of the day of her return from Europe, nor the euphoria of the day she was first fêted as a heroine of unmarried mothers, but the gentle happiness of sharing her time, and herself, with a much-cared-for friend. For that was what Fallon was: not merely her lover, but a confidant with whom she could trust her most intimate secrets (soon, she promised, she'd tell him about her cookbook). Also, she was sure, he was the only man in the world who would ever satisfy her as completely out of bed as in it, able to fulfil her mentally as well as understand her physical needs. What more could she ask? His arrival had made her life complete.

She gripped his hand; ran with him across the intersection just before the traffic lights changed; clung to him, panting, on the sidewalk; kissed him, yes right there amid the crowds, bringing a blush to his cheeks, sending her own blood thumping; hooked her arm around his waist, conscious of her breast pressing against his side; strolled with him into the sunshine.

She guessed this was how Paola and Filipo had seen the city that first day when they'd walked all the way from Broome Street, kitted in their new secondhand winter clothes, to explore Times Square, to become, in the space of one day,

Americans. The carefree excitement she'd observed in their faces then, Gina now felt in herself. In all her years in Manhattan she'd never seen it this way. The buildings were taller, the windows brighter, the mounted cops cheerier, the aroma of petrol and people and the sea sweeter than the English countryside. Gina Rossi was intoxicated.

She would not permit herself to think otherwise.

She couldn't really show Fallon New York, for during the time he'd lived here as a correspondent during the thirties he'd become more familiar with the city's labyrinthine byways than many of its lifelong residents. This didn't bother Gina however, just being beside him was enough. Nevertheless she was pleased that he was a stranger to the recently completed Rockefeller Center; and she couldn't resist a flush of chauvinism when he marvelled at the towering architecture, the esplanade with its pools and yew hedges, the vast murals, the massive bronze figure of Prometheus rising above spouting streams in the lower plaza. 'He's nicknamed Leaping Louie,' Gina gibed, pricking the metal giant's grandeur lest Fallon think she was becoming too puffed up with civic pride.

After exploring the roof gardens of the RCA Building (where Gina made sure she pointed out that of the six different countries' landscapes the English, with its sundial from Donnington Castle, was by far the most popular), they returned to street level to stroll west into the theatre district and lunch on corned beef and cabbage at Dinty Moore's.

While they ate, the coming and going Broadway regulars greeted Gina, exchanged snippets of entertainment gossip, said they'd caught Tony Nevada's spot at the Lady, thought he had a great future; several table-touring autograph collectors stopped by for Gina's signature; two press photographers snapped them; and a columnist came over hoping there was a story in the town's most eligible restaurateur lunching with a tall, dark and handsome (if eccentrically dressed) stranger.

Putting together a conversation was impossible. As Fallon pushed aside his unfinished meal, Gina apologized for the constant interruptions. She shrugged, 'The price of fame.'

'And fortune,' he added.

'Well I'm not yet the second-richest person in New York,' Gina smiled. 'That position's held by the doorman at Twenty-One. Though I guess I can't complain.'

'You're wealthy.'

'It isn't a crime,' she countered. 'I've earned . . .' She'd been about to launch into a defensive speech. Why? And why such sharpness in her response? Still that indefinable something in Fallon's attitude? What was lurking between them? Nothing. She was totally happy. Of course she was. She asserted that it was simply because her sexual nerves were on edge. Having enjoyed every moment of this relaxing morning, she was once more itching to get Robert Fallon into bed. Could she really be feeling this way? Yes – and then some. Gina surprised herself with the admission; hoping her face hadn't gone as red as it felt. Dragging her mind away from visions of his naked arms and chest she said nonchalantly, 'So, tell me about the story you're researching over here?'

'Not a lot to tell,' he answered. 'I'm interviewing service-men who were invalided out and now can't get a job.' His eyes went on, Nothing that would interest a rich lady like you.

Damn it, why was she imagining these things? She blurted, 'Hey, bet you've never been to Coney Island.'

The spur-of-the-moment trip wasn't such a mistake as she thought it might have been.

Rather than take a cab, they rode the subway to the Stillwell Avenue terminal, emerged with the laughing, pushing, hurrying crowd to head for the boardwalk. As Gina removed her jacket, slung it around her shoulders, it was as if she'd shed another self. Fallon too, tie shoved in his pocket, shirt unbuttoned, seemed to lose the tension that had been binding him since his arrival this morning.

They did all the childish things that all the other crazy adults were doing while the city's youngsters were still in school. Amid the wild tangle of dance halls, freak shows, shooting galleries, souvenir shops, waxworks and penny arcades, they played skeeball and hoop-la and beano and ping pong; they rode the Thunderbolt and the Loop-o-Plane and the Dodgem Speedway and the Whip; they ate cotton candy and ice cream and corn-on-the-cob and hot knishes; they watched bathers splash the water, tots dig the sand, adolescents throw balls, couples share each other.

It was a magic time. When dusk fell, Gina did not wish the spell to end. She said, 'Do you really want to have to get yourself up like Mister Esquire to eat at that fancy Lady's joint downtown? Come on, I'll take you to the oldest, largest and best restaurant in Coney.'

She was delighted that he'd never been to Feltman's, where, she informed him, in 1871 the frankfurter was introduced to America. 'See, an evening out with me is a feast of intellectual titbits.' There were no news-story gatherers, no celebrity-seekers here. Apart from Gina being greeted with happy fellowship by the owner, she and Fallon were simply two more tourists in the multitude of noisy diners. Despite all the junk they'd eaten earlier, they now consumed oysters, soft-shell crabs and huge bowlfuls of clam chowder. By the time they were on to their fourth steins of foaming beer, Gina was loudly la-la-la-ing along with everyone else to the songs and accordions of the Bavarian troupe, while Fallon (she hardly could believe her eyes) was gambolling with a dozen other male customers in a thigh-slapping, leg-kicking, utterly ridiculous imitation of the entertainers' *Shuplatt'l*.

It was turned midnight when, in an embrace of mutual support rather than desire, they wandered their weaving way to the station, leaving behind the litter of banana and orange skins, discarded magazines, forgotten towels, lost sandals, sleeping drunks, murmuring lovers, and the sighing goodbye of the abandoned surf.

They spoke not a word as they rode in the swaying, rattling, end-of-the-day smelling train.

Gina shook her head as Fallon turned beneath the Lady's marquee. With a nodding smile to the doorman and a brief wave to an entering quartet of evening-suited revellers, she led Fallon along the front of the building and into the dark side alley where, scooting a refuse-bin-exploring moggie protesting into the blackness, with a finger to her lips like a cautionary cracksman, she unlocked the service door and tugged him into the delivery lobby.

Sliding swiftly past the portholed kitchen door behind which Chang was yelling something about burned veal, she pulled Fallon down the corridor, up an inky stairwell, at last into the brightness of her apartment's hallway, thence into her bedroom.

She never did remember undressing him, or herself. Later, she would recall only their nakedness and their lovemaking. She was glad they hadn't spent themselves this morning in rapid, urgent lust, for this was so much better: a strong but easy sexual sharing tempered by tiredness, erotic but gentle, powerful but considerate, a mutual giving and taking between two people who, despite the months apart, remembered and appreciated each other's passions.

When she eventually was lying back, her head on Fallon's shoulder, listening to the faint but distinct sound waves – music, electrics, voices, plumbing – which were the pulse of the Lady, Gina mused on what they had discussed all day.

Very little. Contrary to what she'd told herself about him being her confidant, during the past eighteen hours their talk had consisted mostly of trivia. Fallon, on his part, had mentioned nothing of his South African assignment, little of his New York schedule. They hadn't exchanged any fresh opinions on literature, politics, movies which had formed their long-into-the-night conversations in London.

But everything's fine between us now, she told herself. Of course I can tell him about my book.

She said, 'I'm going into franchising.'

For the next hour she talked about nothing else.

With Fallon, arms folded, propped silently against the pillows, she perched, cross-legged before him, having chased back and forth to bury the bed beneath financial programmes, floor plans, furniture catalogues, wine lists, sample menus, scores of designs for Rossi Taverns' logo, André de Sath's huge colour drawings, and a hundred-page market research report evaluating the family eating habits, dining-out annual expenditure, and culinary preferences of the inhabitants of fourteen sections of the United States which, the experts assured, were as definable as the different countries of Europe in their lifestyles, tastes, and attitudes. 'Isn't it exciting?' she enthused, surveying the drifts of bumf. 'It'll be the biggest thing since Mister Biedenham bottled Coca Cola. Don't you think so? Don't you think I'm going to be the most successful lady in America?'

Fallon had listened in silence as Gina had ardently laid out the future. Now, scanning the manifesto which was heaped between them, he said impassively, 'Yes. I do, Gina. I think you're determined that is what you'll be.'

Gina returned breezily, 'Then don't look so glum about it.' Added in her attempt at a Cockney accent, 'Come on, give us a smile, ducks.' And when, at last, his lips curved in response, she scrambled back into bed with him, sending half the paper mountain avalanching to the floor, burrowed down beside him, seizing his thighs, squeezing an appreciative grunt from him.

You didn't tell him about the book.

I'm aware of that. Why rush it? A surprise. I'm going to keep it as a surprise. Isn't that the sensible thing to do? No question. Imagine his face when I present him with a copy. He'll be over the moon. Of course he will.

28

Gina Rossi's leap from restaurateur to franchise magnate became public knowledge a week after Fallon's arrival in New York. It wasn't, as she had predicted, the biggest thing since Biedenham bottled Coca Cola. It was bigger.

Advertisements had been scheduled for two hundred major daily newspapers. They were a total waste of money. Gina had said, 'We'll set the country alight in one fell swoop. Complete secrecy to be observed by all the press carrying our ads prior to publication.' Twenty-four hours before the announcement was due to appear, the secrecy, via a casual word by someone from a print room to someone in a bar within earshot of someone from a radio station, was blown. 'Miss Rossi?' the voice on the phone had probed. 'Is it true? What we've just heard on KLFW?' Gina had denied it. The moment she'd replaced the receiver, it was ringing again. Two minutes later as the fourth newshound was firing the same question along the line, three reporters were advancing across the restaurant simultaneously peppering Max with quizzing insistence. Within thirty minutes the building had been besieged.

Within twelve hours it had been stormed.

Would-be concessionnaires. They arrived by cab and car, by bike and foot, one – to prove he was the sort of go-getting, showmanship-conscious type perfectly suited to operate a Rossi Tavern – arrived, inevitably, by horse (it took an hour to propel him from the office, twice as long to extricate the nag from the bar). They came in all ages, colours, shapes and sizes. The jelly doughnut salesman ready for bigger things. The out-of-work opera singer eager to serenade his customers. The Pullman car steward wanting to settle down. The Depression-bankrupted hotelier desperate for a second chance. The public relations man full of his own big ideas. The fourteen-year-old schoolboy with his life savings to invest. The septuagenarian couple looking for a fresh start. They brandished cash, cheques, political pamphlets and religious tracts. They jammed the lobby, the restaurant, the staircase and the club. They yelled at the staff, the customers (the few who hadn't fled), each other and the cops who sirened in when they jammed the street. They gave the press a field day which subsequently would fill forty pages of Max's scrapbook.

Max said it was *stupendo*. Cassie said it was terrifying. Harry said he hadn't seen anything like it since the day prohibition ended and the Brooklyn Ferry Inn advertised free beer.

Gina said nothing.

She was too busy replanning her strategy to speak to anyone. If this was the result of a couple of premature radio reports, what was going to happen when two hundred advertisements hit the country? While the turmoil fumed beyond her barricaded door, having grabbed the phone in a split-second when it wasn't shrilling, she relayed instructions via Johnny for swift moves to deal with what threatened to be a tidal wave of franchise applications. By the following morning a temporary ROSSI TAVERNS INC. sign had been affixed to the door of a suite of offices four blocks down the street, where two dozen phones had been rapidly installed along with treble that number of staff whose sole task would be to issue the questionnaires (designed for the initial winnowing of seed-corn applicants from the chaff) the original fifteen thousand of which had been multiplied – with triple-rate paid to the printer – tenfold, overnight.

Not a moment too soon.

Harry observed, 'The Post Office ought to put us on commission.' He was with Gina at her office window, watching another mail truck being unloaded. Inside four days the printer had been recalled to extra shift five times. The staff coping with the flood had been doubled and were working round the clock; so too were the ten Pinkerton men hastily assigned to the Lady and the temporary offices when it had been realized that some would-be Rossi Tavern-keepers were far from willing to be fobbed off with kind words and questionnaires.

Gina answered, 'What a good thing we didn't launch a simultaneous campaign in Canada.'

'Canada?'

'People eat there too.'

'But it's . . .'

'It's a ten-cent bus ride from Buffalo, across an imaginary line drawn on a piece of paper over two hundred and fifty years ago. Administering a franchise chain there won't be a problem of communications, merely a question of logistics.'

Harry had stopped breathing; when he started again it was with extreme caution. 'You said, Won't be. Future tense. Definite.' He peered into Gina's face, then took a rapid pace backward. 'Now hold on. I know those eyes. If you're looking for a vice-president i/c Ottawa, don't stare at me. I haven't been off this island in fifteen years. I get travel-sick north of Fifty-Ninth Street. I can't speak Canadian. I . . .'

Gina laughed. 'Don't worry, Harry. When we set up over the border – I reckon six months from now – it will be with someone born and bred there in charge. The same when we open Rossi Britain, and Rossi France, and Rossi . . .' She nodded positively at Harry's incredulity. 'Yes, I am serious. The world's shrinking. The corporations who take advantage of the fact will become the strongest. I know we aren't in that league yet, but we will be. And then we'll tackle Europe. Say, within six years. By which time they'll be back on their feet, and we'll be on top of the whole North American continent.' Her shoulders set with determination as she turned to watch the emptied mail truck pull away. Re-facing Harry, she added on a lighter note, 'Anyhow, as I was saying, you won't be the one who has to figure the exchange rate on the Canadian dollar.' She laid a gentle hand on his arm. 'Because I couldn't possibly do without you here.'

Harry had sagged with relief.

Gina held his smile a while, then gathered up some papers, walked to the door, paused to regard him affectionately before exiting. Seconds later her voice came from down the hall, 'Especially when we open the talent agency.'

Harry galloped after her.

'It was an idea I got,' Gina said to Fallon over breakfast, 'the first time I talked with Mrs Hamm.'

'Who?'

Slip of the tongue, Gina. 'Oh, er . . . A woman I know. In publishing, actually. An editor . . . She edits. Books . . . You ought to meet her. You'd get along famously.'

395

Fallon regarded her from beneath dark brows, returned to the newspaper. 'How come you aren't beneath the masthead today? No one here but also-rans – Truman, Princess Elizabeth, the Pope.' He rummaged through the pages. 'Ah, relegated to the gossip column. An out-of-focus picture with . . . ' The veins in his temples knotted like blue cords.

Gina rose rapidly from the table, stepped behind him, stared down at what he was seeing.

The photograph was the one of the pair of them, taken during lunch at Dinty Moore's the day of Fallon's arrival in New York. The caption read: 'Hands across the ocean. And under the table? Just a tête-à-tête. Or a putting of heads together? Sources report craggy member of G.B. Fourth Estate and svelte tavernerette of N.Y. 47th Street are long-time allies. Closer co-operation leading to signed treaty? Watch this space – and other intimate corners.'

Fallon growled, 'Bloody nonsense.'

Gina said, 'Don't be such an old grouch. Most folks would give their eyeteeth to see themselves in the paper. Besides, it will be . . . ' She'd been about to go on about how useful the publicity would be for him when she introduced him to Mrs Hamm for early discussions on his novel; she pulled up sharply, however, when she saw the red light in Fallon's eyes.

He said, 'And that's one of the reasons I don't finish the book you're always on about. I have better things to do than become a circus act, jumping through hoops for some publisher's smart-arse press agent.' Dumping the newspaper, he pushed out from the table, hoisted his battered, old briefcase under his arm. 'I'll see you tonight. Around eight. Unless you have other plans, like taking over the world.'

That was biting. Annoyance pricked Gina. Though she wasn't surprised. She'd seen this coming, felt the tension building over the past week. And it wasn't only because of the Rossi Taverns hullabaloo, it had begun before that. What Gina had once seen as trenchant wit in Fallon, she now felt was a causticness verging on intolerance. Any section of society whom he regarded as pretentious or useless was axed with one incisive verbal blow. Gina hadn't retaliated until the evening he'd been particularly critical about a ructious but not untoward celebratory group at one of the Lady's tables. She'd countered, 'Just because they're wealthy doesn't automatically mean they're wastrels. And I've seen much worse behaviour from your beloved Common Man both sides of the Atlantic.'

She hadn't meant to retort so hostilely, but at that moment her dander was truly up. The beginnings of a rift? No, we're as close as ever we were two years ago. It's just the pressure of our lives, our overfull schedules making us snappy. Everything will be fine when we settle into each other's routines, the way we did in London. We just need to spend a few regular hours together.

Next morning Rossi Taverns had hit the airwaves.

Now, as Fallon strode with his briefcase to the door, she offered conciliatorily, 'How about an old-fashioned stroll this afternoon? Just you and me. I'll make time. Come what may. Please, Fallon, say yes. We have to get away awhile. Will you be here? Three o'clock.'

He looked back, pursed his lips. Then: 'I'll try to cancel my appointments.' He returned, kissed her forehead, and, smiling, patted her butt. 'Go on. Back to empire-building. I shall expect you to be at least twice as famous by lunchtime, and even more able to keep me in the manner to which I am becoming accustomed.'

Gina was still glowing warmly twenty minutes later when the phone rang.

'Paola. Come over? Heck, why not! There are enough troops here to hold the fort. Besides, I haven't had time to thank Johnny for lining up the temporary offices, the phones, staff and everything when the dam burst last week. How's little Frankie? I have missed him so. There are some gorgeous Swiss embroidered romper suits in Little Angels. Of course he doesn't have enough. I'll bring half-a-dozen. By the way, I was talking with the principal of Columbia's College of Physicians and Surgeons. He says a whole new world is opening up in medical science. Tremendous opportunities. In research and consultancy. Pardon? Little Frankie, who else? Certainly he'd be a wonderful doctor. Well, you can't just leave his education to take care of itself, Paola. Yes. All right, we'll talk about it later. Noon. See you then.'

Gina sped through the morning.

Before leaving she asked the kitchen to make up a small picnic basket with English-style teatime sandwiches, pâté and crackers and a bottle of Chablis; late afternoon with Fallon someplace away from their hurdy-gurdy existence would complete a happy day. She went out via the rear entrance;

waved to the crowds milling in and out of the front entrance as she drove by in the Packard.

She was whistling with the birds when she carried her armfuls of packages up Paola and Johnny's tulip-lined path.

Before she could ring the bell, the door opened and she was greeted by a flurry of small animals, yapping and leaping up her legs like demented mop heads. Only when Paola shouted, 'Boys! Boys!' did the commotion separate itself into what Gina perceived to be a couple of white dogs skittering back past her sister into the hall where they were scooped up by Johnny who, as Gina entered, grinned, 'Okay, I owe you for a pair of nylons.'

'If these crazy beasts are going to become permanent residents,' returned Gina, 'You'd better provide me with dungarees.' She rubbed the pups' heads to a response of frenzied licking.

'They're Scotties,' Paola said, closing the door. 'Johnny thought . . . ' she glanced at her husband ' . . . that they'd be company for me while he's away on business. For Frank too.'

'Where is he?' asked Gina. 'Out back? I'll go see him. Just for a minute.' She started for the rear of the hall, thrusting the stack of parcels into Paola's arms.

'Leave it for a moment,' her sister said sharply, and the clipped tone turned Gina around. Paola smiled palely. 'Sorry. Didn't mean to snap. But you can see Frank later. Come in now. Let's visit awhile.' She waited, loaded with packages, beside her husband, loaded with dogs.

Gina thought, Don't they look so . . . together. 'Of course,' she conceded. 'It's been over a fortnight since I saw you.' She returned to them, went ahead into the sitting-room and swiftly to the window to look out to the lawn where Frank John Alfred was clutching the top rail of his playpen, bending and swaying on chubby legs like a boxer limbering up between rounds. The contest was obviously going well, a number of opponents – two teddies, a panda and Donald Duck – were already out for the count several feet beyond the ring.

Paola said, 'You really shouldn't bring so much. Frank has closets full of clothes. Most of them from you.'

'Which is how it should be,' rejoined Gina. 'I'm his only aunt. And his *madrina* – godmother.' Tugging herself from the window, she sat on the sofa, opposite Paola who was perched, straight-backed at the front of an armchair. Johnny,

398

who had deposited the Scotties elsewhere, came and stood at his wife's arm, his hand on her shoulder, so that Gina felt as if, rather than being entertained as their relative, she was being interviewed as a prospective housekeeper. Oh dear, they're going to lecture me, she decided. About overspending for little Frankie. Or sending the decorators round last month to re-do his room. No question, Johnny was looking decidedly ill at ease, no doubt under instructions from Paola to play the heavy brother-in-law. I expect she means it for the best. And she is, after all, an excellent mother. Nevertheless . . .

Paola announced, 'There's something we have to tell you.' She paused into a meaningful silence.

Johnny remained waxlike.

Gina adopted a receptive pose. 'Yes?'

Paola: 'We're moving west.'

Gina's one track thoughts almost became derailed as they swung to follow the abrupt sideline. 'West?' But who wants to live in New Jersey? It's miles – at least thirty – from civilization?' She repeated, 'West? Where west?'

Johnny said, 'Arizona.'

Gina knew she'd heard right.

Paola said, 'We have to. For Frank's sake.'

Little Frankie? Gina became suddenly very cold.

'Don't worry,' Paola added quickly. 'He isn't seriously ill. Not incurably. It's simply his chest. He has an asthmatic condition. Do you understand?' Her hesitancy was gone now, she was facing her elder sister with control and determination, transmitting confidence as Gina felt her own draining away. 'Let me say it all, briefly. Please. The doctors have examined Frank. Specialists. The best. We didn't call you before because you had so many things to take care of. And it wouldn't have helped. Your love would, but not your anxiety. I promise you, we've had the finest advice available for Frank. All the experts confirm, there is no need for concern. His condition is not chronic asthma. It's containable, even curable, so long as he gets to a dry climate, as soon as possible. That's why Johnny visited Phoenix. He's rented an apartment on the outskirts. We'll live there until we find a house. It's a beautiful city, truly, Gina – Johnny brought lots of photographs – clean and fresh, surrounded by desert and mountains. And with the sort of bright sunlight I haven't seen since we left Italy. Do you remember that? Really, even if we didn't have to go because of

Frank, I know I'd want to live there. You'll see, when you come to visit, you'll love it.'

Gina stared at Paola. Her thoughts had been racing so desperately during the past moments, she scarcely had heard all the words. She queried vaguely, 'Visit?'

Johnny cut in, 'Sure. Contrary to the belief of most Manhattanites, trains, buses, airplanes do not disappear into a black void once they cross the Pennsylvania border. A great many of them, complete with passengers, go all the way to the Pacific Ocean. Phoenix is on route, with a real highway, gas stations and all, and there hasn't been an Indian attack on the Pony Express for weeks.' He stepped across to Gina, sat beside her. 'Hey, come on, don't go blue on us. Like Paola said, the boy's going to be okay. And that's all that matters, isn't it?'

Gina still felt frozen. With great effort she nodded.

'Right,' said Johnny, his eyes concerned but smiling. 'And I wasn't kidding about Arizona. It isn't the end of the earth. In fact, I reckon the west is where the future lies. The potential out there's been hardly tapped. I'll be concentrating on opening up the territory myself, putting a manager into my New York office.' He added with a gentle nudge, 'And I promise, when I'm on the road, wherever I stop off, I'll always eat at a Rossi Tavern.'

Gina stared mutely. A Rossi Tavern? Her mind was locked on New York – without little Frankie. Her life would be bereft. No, don't overdramatize. Johnny's right, look on the positive side, the news could have been much worse. Facing her brother-in-law, she breathed deeply, the quivering intake of air dispelling her initial shock. 'In which case,' she said with artificial levity, 'you'll qualify for discount. Ten per cent for diners who visit more than eight times a month.'

'I'm sold,' grinned Johnny. 'By the way, these tavern concessionnaires, I assume they'll be allowed to install only Rossi-approved equipment – ovens, fridges, waste disposers . . . ' He raised hopeful brows ' . . . vending-machines?'

Certainly, Gina mentally returned, but I shall nail you to a very tight contract. As her shadows retreated, her gratitude went to Johnny for knowing how to bring her into the light. She reached out, squeezed his hand.

'I reckon that means I just made a sale,' Johnny said happily. 'Paola, you won't have to get a job cattle-punching after all.' He stood. 'Now I'll go fetch my son, heir and junior partner.' To Gina, 'I'll have him close the deal. Sharpen your pencil, lady, the kid drives a helluva bargain.'

After he had gone out, Gina turned to Paola. 'Did you tell me everything? Frankie's illness isn't serious?'

'Honestly. I'll show you the specialists' reports later. He doesn't have what they call true asthma – which is a sort of allergy – rather a bronchial reaction to damp air. That's why it took us a while to realize anything was wrong. He's always been in a warm, dry house. When he was a bit chesty after being outside last winter – you remember – we thought it was just a common cold. But, I promise, so long as we move to a suitable climate, the problem won't get any worse.'

'When will you go?'

'Within a fortnight.'

So soon? 'Of course. You must. Do you have the photographs Johnny brought? I'd like to see.' Gina radiated an enthusiasm she was still unable to feel. As Johnny re-entered the room toting his gabbling, fist-waving son, she stood quickly, strode to him, took Frankie into her arms, held him very close, for all the time she could.

She carried him, in her heart, back to Manhattan. A fortnight. Such a short time to be with him. Also – the thought occurred as she drove past the first department stores on Fifth Avenue – so few days in which to purchase all the things he'd need for his trip. A complete new wardrobe, naturally, lightweight for those desert temperatures. Bedlinen too. Plus a sun canopy for his buggy, a bigger one for his playpen. The heartache which had gradually receded during the last three hours, withdrew further now as Gina scribbled her mental shopping list. So many items to buy. And not a moment to lose.

She parked the car around the side of the Lady, walked back to the Avenue shops.

By the time the afternoon was giving way to evening, she had brought delight to the commission books of salesladies in every baby department within a six-block radius. She felt so much better, a heady combination of satisfaction and renewal. No question, shopping was one of the finest restoratives for the spirit as well as the flesh. She accepted now that little Frankie must go, refused to dwell on the chasm his departure would leave in her life, considered only the pleasurable prospects of the situation – the long telephone conversations she would have with him, the letters and cards she would write, the vacations she would spend in Phoenix. The more she thought about it, the less bleak the future looked. She'd been whistling happily when she'd walked to Paola's door this morning, was doing so again now as she made a last-minute sortie into Vincent Cartiér's new beauty store.

Self-indulgence, purchasing a ludicrously expensive lipstick she likely never would use? So, wasn't she entitled?

She turned abruptly from the perfume counter to the male voice which said, 'You should never wear any scent but your own.' Tony Nevada, in a white, short-sleeve shirt which accentuated the deep gold tan of his arms and throat, smiled his ingenuous smile while his eyes held Gina's with all their usual bravado. Later Gina would tell herself she didn't understand why she responded the way she did. Extending her wrist with the sample she'd dabbed there she asked, 'What do you think?'

He took her hand, raised her upturned palm. Never for an instant shifting his gaze from Gina, he inhaled, then exhaled slowly through his part-open lips.

The damp heat of his breath sent a charge straight up Gina's arm. So sudden was her involuntary reaction that she tugged her hand free and pulled on her glove as if to smother the burning spot where his mouth almost had touched. The noise in the store seemed to have grown louder, the lights brighter. 'Well, should I buy it?'

'You're the boss.'

'That's a great help.' She was leading him. Leading herself. Into someplace she wanted to go? She said, 'Perhaps today isn't so good for such momentous decisions. Besides, I have to be getting back to the Lady.'

'Me too. Rehearsal for the new Berlin number.' He fell into step alongside her. 'You know, he was born only a block away from me on the East Side. Irving Berlin. Israel Baline, actually. He started out the same way too, a singing waiter at the Chatham Club. In fact, I guess the only difference between us is that he's richer, while I'm younger.' Tony flicked Gina a wink as they headed toward the exit. 'Of course, that gives me the advantage. Berlin can never match me in years, whereas I'll more than equal his wealth before I'm thirty. Three years from now.'

On the avenue Gina said, 'Just like that? Mister Berlin is a very talented man.'

'So am I. Also I'm determined. That's what success is all about, isn't it? Exploiting your skills, never believing you'll be anything but number one, letting nothing – and nobody – stand in your way.' He stared at Gina as they waited at the intersection lights, and she saw again that inner coldness she'd glimpsed the first afternoon Cassie had brought him to the club. It repelled her, at the same time fascinated her. Like the gaze of a snake, she thought involuntarily. In India, she'd read, there was a type of dove which not only could be trans-fixed by a cobra, but would actually throw itself at the serpent's lips. To be kissed to death.

Gina snapped off that overcoloured image.

Tony Nevada held her arm as they crossed the street. At the opposite sidewalk he maintained his grip for several paces before releasing her and saying, 'Isn't that your philosophy?'

Gina was recovering from the touch of his hand; not where it had circled her upper arm, but where its knuckles had brushed the side of her breast. 'I believe in making the most of one's opportunities, yes. A certain amount of luck comes into it too.'

'There's no such thing as luck. Fate. Fortune. God's will. That's all garbage. Mumbo jumbo put out by bookies and priests to separate the saps from their wages. Kids should be taught in school, they're never going to be handed the world on a plate.' The singer's voice had hardened. 'To get any place in this life you've got to fight for your spot, take it the best way you know how, and hang on to it.' As he spoke he did not look at Gina; his eyes were fixed dead ahead.

Yet Gina felt she was still held by that intense coldness. By his words also? No, I do not agree with that credo. It's immature and simplistic. Furthermore, what am I doing listening to it? I hardly know this man. We've held no more than half-a-dozen two-minute business conversations since he started at the club. Gina, from the corner of her eye, studied his profile, the slightly oriental cheekbones, the full lower lip, the sharp line of his jaw; and she experienced again that instinctive sexual response. She said quickly, 'We're in the process of setting up a talent agency. Harry Dix will be in charge. He'll be asking you to join us.'

Tony Nevada turned, the hardness which moments ago had sculpted his features relaxed as his mouth curved. 'That would be a switch. Right now we're employee and boss. Your suggestion would make us client and agent. You'd be working for me.' His gaze deepened. 'Do you figure that will work out? Or do you think we should be more equal? After all, aren't we the same, you and I? Don't we both come from the same place? Aren't we both headed for the same summit? Maybe we should forget all the client-employee-boss stuff, get ourselves on a more even footing. Form a partnership.' His gleam of a smile was humorous, casual, jaunty . . . taunting? He halted.

Gina realized they had reached The Lady.

The singer said, 'Now wouldn't that be interesting?' He again reached for her arm to lead her beneath the marquee. As Gina stepped aside, avoiding his hand, he ran his tongue along his white, even teeth, gave a brisk, deferential bow, said, 'After you . . . Miss Rossi.'

Gina went swiftly ahead, briefly acknowledging the door-man's greeting, into the busy lobby. Relief claimed her as she paused amid the familiar activity, among the safety of numbers. A local Congressman and his wife waved from over by the hat-check booth; a well-known tennis star, glancing back from the other side of the pink silk rope across the entrance to the restaurant, lobbed a smile, raised an imaginary glass, mouthed, Later; Mrs Hamm, turning from chatting with Filipo, brandished a fat manila folder. Gina gathered her composure, strode back into reality, didn't look around at Tony Nevada.

Filipo, in blue, baggy yacht pants, white V-neck sweater, sleeves pushed to his elbows, no shirt, called, 'Hi, Sis! Lady here to see you. Been telling me all about publishing.' He flicked expressive eyebrows up and down.

He doesn't know anything about my book, Gina assured herself as she approached. He's just fishing, as usual. And if I've told him once, I've told him a thousand times not to come down here looking like a Greenwich Village bohemian. She lit her face. 'Dorothy. How lovely to see you. Filipo, don't you have some studying?' She attempted to fry him from behind gleaming charm.

Not even mildly singed, he grinned. 'Sure. There are some important figures I have to check out tonight.' Behind Mrs Hamm's back he made a swift hourglass in the air. 'See you around midnight.' With a lurid wink he was gone.

Midnight! You're supposed to be in by eleven.

'Such a charming young man,' said Dorothy Hamm. 'And very handsome. If I was thirty years younger . . .'

Gina glimpsed Tony Nevada heading down the hall. But you're not, Dorothy. You're like me – too old and sensible to let pretty boys turn our heads. We have mature lives to lead, important businesses to run. You have a staunch, fifty-four-year-old husband. I have a . . . Her mind caught its breath, gasped, My God, I was supposed to meet Fallon here at three o'clock! She spun around, searching the lobby, half expecting to see him standing, fuming in the corner. 'Please excuse me,' she shot. 'I must go. Someone waiting.'

'But, the final galleys,' protested Mrs Hamm, offering the manila folder. 'I'd like to discuss . . .'

'Leave them at the reservation desk.' Gina was already striding away. 'I'll read them later, and call you.' She didn't look around. If she had she wouldn't have seen the baffled editor; the only image looming in her mind's eye was that of Robert Fallon, with steam spurting out of the top of his head.

When she spotted him at a corner table in the bar, there was no visible steam but his face certainly looked as iron-cast as a boiler door. Girding her loins Gina strode across, greeted lightly, 'Hi.' She almost flinched as Fallon's head jerked up but the only response he threw was a twitch of his left cheek. Noting there was nothing before him save his fists clenched around the unlit pipe, she coaxed, 'What, no bourbon? Don't tell me you climbed on the wagon. How about a shot?' She probed his armoured stare. In imitation of his best growl: 'Sure. Have a seat, Gina. Join me, why don't you?' In her own voice: 'Thanks, Fallon. I'd be delighted.' She sat, smiled at him like an Easter Parade.

He muttered, 'Sorry.'

'Of course I am. I . . .'

'I know I should have phoned,' Fallon went on, 'but I couldn't interrupt the interview. You understand how it is when a subject opens up. And this was important. I had to nail it.'

Gina said nothing as she dawningly realized Fallon was explaining why he had been late for their appointment. She listened without comment as he continued, his apology gradually metamorphosing into an exposition of the current welfare inadequacies toward veterans; but now her initial dislocating surprise retreated. She was enmeshed in a web of anger, sorrow, self-recrimination. How could Fallon consider his interviews more important than her feelings? How could she so utterly have forgotten him this afternoon? That question scalded her. She answered that it was on account of her concern for little Frankie. Fallon, she contended, could offer no such mitigation. This, however, she kept to herself; together with a confession of her own lateness for their date. The gap between their lives was widening, to raise further reproaches would not help matters. Gina mustered a smile, told Fallon it was okay about his interviews, that they could spend time together next week, this afternoon was no great loss.

This was what she continued to tell herself for the remainder of the evening. They ate dinner. Fallon retired to the apartment to work on his notes. Gina spent three hours in her office with Harry discussing the talent agency. It was after midnight when she went upstairs, took a shower, climbed into bed beside a sleeping Fallon.

She lay on her back listening to his breathing.

The room was lonely and full of shadows.

29

The sun bounced white and hot off the airport concrete. This first day of June New Yorkers were sweating in temperatures which they usually wouldn't have to suffer for at least another month. At the outside departure gate, Paola, in white cotton frock, hoisted Frank John Alfred from his buggy, held him on her arm, turning him away from the glaring noon sky. He struggled, protesting, 'Wanna walk. Auntie Gina, wanna walk.' As his hands flailed and his feet kicked, his mother said firmly. 'You can walk later. Be still now.'

Johnny, folding the buggy, wedging it into his fist along with a bulging linen carrier – his other hand loaded with briefcase, a Bloomingdale's bag plus a bundle of magazines and newspapers – said, 'Take it easy, Buck.' (This nickname, donated by Filipo, immediately upon learning of his nephew's western emigration, had been, to Gina's dismay, adopted universally.) 'Just a few more hours and you'll see that horse I promised you.'

'Horsey!' yelled Frank.

'Horse,' corrected his mother.

Gina croaked, 'Take care now, you hear.' Her throat had

been constricting ever since yesterday afternoon's farewell party. While everyone else had chatted and laughed and chinked glasses in the Sabato sitting-room as if it was already the Fourth of July, she had sat with a happily gossiping Frank on her knee feeling as miserable as a wet week in November.

As the huge double propellers of the distant aircraft roared into life, Johnny urged, 'Come on, Paola, that's us. *Arriverderci*, sister-in-law.' He bent and quickly kissed Gina. 'See you when you visit in three weeks.'

Gina mumbled, 'It seems so far away.' Johnny returned, 'Less than a month.' She said, 'I meant Arizona.' Then she was hugging him, hugging her sister, hugging Frankie. They were all talking at once, exchanging farewells, kissing and hugging again; passengers were striding past them, someone was calling and a whistle was blowing; and before Gina realized it she was alone watching them hurrying away across the concrete. She fumbled in her purse, found her hanky to dab her streaming eyes, fluttered the sodden lace as Paola and Johnny turned at the aircraft steps. Paola swivelled Frankie's head, pointed back toward Gina, but he was too interested in a man waving orange semaphore bats. They went on up the steps. Within a moment had ducked into the cabin.

Gina was still staring at the closed door as the plane began to roll away. She was still watching the sky long after the sun-reflecting silver dot had disappeared.

She plunged herself into the franchise programme: the costings for Rossi Taverns, the locations of the restaurants, the final criteria for selecting suitable concessionnaires. The original mountain of applications had been chiselled down by the team of independent consultants Gina had engaged to handle the monumental task. The next step would be to hold personal interviews. The grand opening of the first tavern – provisionally proposed for somewhere near Columbus Circle – was scheduled for September. 'Impossible!' Max had exclaimed. To which Gina had replied, 'That's what they told Monsieur Eiffel when he said he'd build his tower in less than six months.' (When Max had relayed this to Fallon, the Englishman had replied, 'A pity she and the Frenchman weren't around when God was struggling to create the earth.')

As the days passed Gina grew ever more aware of the widening gulf between herself and Fallon. Whatever good intentions she'd had toward culling her workload had flown out of the window. But, then, she countered when a warning voice admonished, he was no better, out day and sometimes most of the night on his assignments. But, Gina, you promised to make the effort to spend more time together. Do you want to, or don't you? Certainly I do. I asked him to come with me to visit Paola and Johnny, didn't I? He told me he had to spend three weeks in Washington interviewing some Foreign Office spokesman about Korea.

Does he bore you? Of course not? He's still the most aware, involved, concerned man I've ever met. It's just that, wasn't he the one who once said we can't save everybody, yet he now seems to think he can carry the entire burden of mankind on his shoulders? And, much as I'd like to, I can't share that load. My own life is more important. Is that so wrong? Furthermore, why can't he try to understand it?

But it was impossible to convey to Fallon how she felt about business. In fact, it was becoming more difficult to hold any kind of meaningful discussion with him. She tried, she truly made an effort to follow him when he went off toward the social upheavals taking place in Asia and Africa in countries she'd never heard of. The problem was, her mind always drifted, to the next financial move she was going to make in what she was beginning to regard as her private, massive chess game. The ploys and gambits of this match – Gina versus the World – filled her dreams, so that each morning when she awoke she scribbled the manoeuvres – no matter how outlandish – into her notebook; then, during the day, in her brief moments of solitude, she would mentally review the notes, search them for grains of reality which might yield some future profit. And this was what she tended to do whenever Fallon's conversation delved too deeply into world politics and economics.

It's a problem that will pass, she told herself yet again, as she once more totted up the potential annual earnings from the initial hundred franchises.

'Principessa,' Max said, wonderingly shaking his head as he stared at the astronomical figures, 'I still don't see what we're going to do with all this money.'

Gina placed her air ticket for Phoenix in her purse, smiled across her desk at the perplexed giant. 'Neither do I, old friend,' she responded. 'But it will come to me. I'm sure it will.'

* * *

The Western Press Agency news report was issued from the company's Los Angeles office at ten p.m. June 20th.

'Amid conflicting reports from alleged eye-witnesses, L.A. Police Department neither admit nor deny an arrest has been made. However, in a brief statement Chief Jack Briskin confirmed that earlier this evening at a Beverly Hills mansion an unnamed assailant fired several bullets into businessman-celebrity Benjamin Siegel. Mister Siegel died before reaching hospital.'

Before Gina Rossi flew out to visit Paola, Johnny and Frank Sabato, she'd been unaware that she'd be spending that long weekend less than three hundred miles from the city of Las Vegas. She wasn't alone in her ignorance, however; up until that month a scant percentage of the U.S. population could have pinpointed accurately the state of Nevada, let alone its desert-surrounded casino city. But by the time Gina returned to Manhattan, she, and just about everybody else in the country, knew the precise location of the gamblers' mecca 'discovered' three years previously by the late B. Siegel. As Harry put it the following week: 'Not only has Benny's enforced demise put his business – his partners' business – into instant profit, the coast-to-coast headlines of the event have placed Vegas squarely on the map – in aces.'

Gina said, 'The Flamingo's no longer a loss-maker?'

'Word is, as you suggested, the expense columns in Benny's account books showed a great flair for fiction; though, as it turned out, his talent was the death of him.'

'So, Max was right, all gambling operations must, in the long run, come out ahead of the client?' Before Harry could reply Gina was reaching for her desk phone, instructing her secretary to track down maps, hotel listings, airline schedules. Recradling the receiver she flipped open her notebook, poised her pen, halted. 'Darn,' she muttered to herself. 'I don't know where to start!'

Harry, smiling, watched her furrowing brows. Starting for the door, he said, 'But you will. As always.'

That evening Gina said to Max, 'It's time you took a vacation. Of course it is. You haven't had a day off since the end of the war. You should have a furlough, old friend. We'll fly out next week. Yes, we. No, I don't need the break. I need the education.'

* * *

It was night when they arrived in Las Vegas and made the short drive along the Desert highway to the casino-hotel whose name – The Fabulous Flamingo – had become legend. Gina was dumbstruck. As she climbed from the limousine she couldn't take her eyes from the pouring column of orange and pink neon. Even though it had been visible from ten miles away, taking shape with her approach until she was able to distinguish the towering flamingo figures, its power had in no way been diminished by familiarity. Now, standing virtually beneath it, staring upward, Gina could no longer identify its details; all she could see was a coruscating pillar of lurid colour which suddenly gave her the impression that it might topple and drown her. She stepped back, blinking.

Max concernedly gripped her arm. 'Principessa . . . ?'

She smiled. 'I'm all right, old friend. Just a bit dizzy with shock. It may not be the most tasteful sign in the world, but it's certainly the most impressive. I guess it's a good thing they've got the Hoover Dam down the road, just to supply the million volts for this monster.' She turned toward the marquee. 'Though they certainly aren't overcharging their customers to pay for the electricity.'

The illuminated fascia announced Jimmy Durante (recently polled as one of the world's top three entertainers) as the headliner. The eight p.m. show complete with 'gourmet dinner' was advertised at $3.50.

Gina shook her head in disbelief at the cost. 'Max, with good storage and transportation costs out here in the desert at least double what they'd be in New York, that price can barely be breaking even. And that's before they start paying Durante. If the rumours of their profits are true, then not a cent of it is coming from the catering. It's all being generated by the gambling.' As the liveried footman carried their bags toward the entrance, she said, 'Old friend, I have a feeling we just arrived at the richest goldmine in the west. But, frankly, I don't know the difference between a stacked deck and a busted flush. You're the one who understands all that according-to-Hoyle stuff. So, from here on, it's up to you to discover just how many carats these ex-partners of Mister Siegel are digging up each week.' She beamed at Max. 'Ready?' And without awaiting his reaction strode after the footman.

The lobby – the biggest Gina had ever seen – lushly pink and orange, was lined with fruit machines, forty or fifty, every one whirring and thunking as the players fed in their dimes, yanked eager handles. Scores of guests, male and female, stood around watching the action, swiftly stepping in whenever a player gave up on an uncharitable machine. A beautiful, young blonde in a pink silk evening gown which, Gina figured, couldn't have cost less than four hundred dollars, weaved amid the crowd carrying a tray loaded with mint-packed rolls of coins, permanently smiling and rapidly making change for whoever needed it. Another girl, identically dressed, equally stunning, sashayed in to dispense a dozen cocktails.

Though there was no hustle and bustle, few voices – the gamblers only moved their hands and arms, rarely spoke – amid the music and mechanical rattle excitement charged the air like static electricity. Gina had felt it the moment she stepped through the door; or perhaps, she speculated, it had been building within her ever since she left New York, had burgeoned as she was confronted by the stunning exterior of this building, and had rushed through her blood when, on entering here, her anticipation had been fulfilled.

This was it, she thought. There had been no anticlimax. Everything she'd heard about the Flamingo had proved true. Like a child whose Christmas Eve dream is of a huge, gaudy package, she had wakened to discover reality was even more fabulous than the fantasy.

A cry went up from across the lobby; bells began ringing; the unmistakeable chattering clatter of coins announced the woman in a crimson sequined sheath, hopping on one leg, yelling, 'My God, my God!' had hit the jackpot. As nearby fellow players called congratulations, some bending quickly to help collect the silver shower which was spilling to the floor, a white-tuxedoed photographer pushed through the throng to record the happy event.

'Miss Rossi?'

Gina turned to the silver-haired, elegant man in black evening suit, answered, 'Yes. I am she.'

'Charles Lehman. Your host.' He briefly but firmly shook Gina's hand. Acknowledging her surprise he smiled, 'Yes. I do recognize you. Your face has become quite familiar to newspaper readers on the west coast. Besides, when we received your reservation we checked to make sure you were the G. Rossi we thought you might be. We like to know when we're due a visit from a VIP. I'm sure you do the same at The Lady.'

His statement was straightforward, unpatronizing. He looked and spoke, thought Gina, more like a banker than a casino executive. But, then, what did she expect? A brilliantined Sicilian with a Brooklyn accent? Times were changing – rapidly. Gambling – never mind who was still backing it – was, here in Nevada, putting on a respectable face. She said, 'I'm pleased to meet you, Mister Lehman. This is my partner, Mister Max Barzini.'

The two men exchanged pleasantries, then Charles Lehman led the way to an annex off the lobby where, at a long, imposing reception desk, Gina and Max signed the register.

Lehman said, 'You're our guests, of course.' Stilling her protest before it arose he added, 'No, I wouldn't dream of presenting you with a bill.' As he accompanied them along the richly carpeted corridor, he explained, 'In any case, we charge only a nominal sum for accommodation. As I'm sure you'll understand, we are not here to make huge profits from the hotel. The bedrooms are for the convenience of our guests; as are all our facilities. Our gourmet restaurant – and I'd be honoured if you join me there for dinner tonight – has one of the finest menus you'll see outside of New York. And our cabaret equals the best in the country, perhaps the world.' He paused at a door gold-lettered SUITES. 'Our prime concern is to keep our guests happy.' He then smiled and added with a shrug, 'Just as long as they keep on gambling.'

Thirty minutes later, Gina said to Max, 'And it's a neat trick if you can get it right.'

Charles Lehman had left them to settle in. Their suites were opulent, and then some; and for the first time since Fallon had left for Washington, Gina had experienced a co-mingling of melancholy and sexual need as she'd surveyed the vast, pink-covered, silken-pillowed bed. She had cold-showered both feelings down the drain, pinned up her hair, and donned her Schiaparelli black evening suit of pencil-slim, floor-length skirt with matador jacket over a high-collared white blouse. She didn't need to glance in the mirror to know she looked dramatic; and it wasn't without a flush of satisfaction that she noted the more-than-fatherly appreciation in Max's eyes when he came to collect her from her room.

Placing her lace gloved hand on his arm she said, 'Let's go knock 'em dead, old friend.'

And they did.

Heads turned, handle-pulling fists faltered, and a ripple of intrigue ran around the lobby as the exquisitely svelte blonde and the magnificently moustachioed giant crossed and entered the main casino.

Gina halted, stared. Several hundred people thronged the vast room, laughing, talking, shouting as their numbers came up. The cacophony of voices competed with the machine-gun rattle of roulette balls in their wheels, the rapid patter of craps dice on their beds, and the thumping bass rhythm of a boogie-woogie 'Bye Bye Blackbird' from an ivory Steinway grand on a dais in a packed lounge area off to the left. White-jacketed waiters glided as smoothly as skaters amongst the swaying mass, silver trays aloft, crystal glasses flashing lights like fire-crackers. Cigarette smoke hung in blue layers beneath the chan-deliered ceiling, while the lower atmosphere was rich with the scent of Cuban tobacco, French perfume and Scotch whisky.

Gina's pulse was hammering. The sudden plunge into such saturating luxury was a physical as well as mental shock. There was no subtlety here. Voluptuousness seemed to ooze from the very walls. And now, as Gina steadied her breathing, she began to understand more of what Charles Lehman had said about his clientele. These people weren't merely happy – they were intoxicated, not by alcohol but by the overwhelming sense of existing in a sensual, almost erotic, dream.

She and Max advanced around the room's perimeter.

There was action at every table. It was loudest amongst the craps players where folks were hollering, clapping, cheering as chips were tossed down or raked in and the dice were flung along the green felt.

Gina hadn't the foggiest notion what was going on.

Max observed, 'A very professional operation. See, the dealer and the stickman, the speed at which they move. Experts. And look at their faces, alight all the time, infecting the players with enthusiasm. Also,' he smiled with appreci-ation, 'listen to them yelling, as if they're rooting for the gamblers. Of course, they're not. They're keeping them on the boil, urging them to make high-risk plays – field bets, single elevens, one-roll craps – which give the house a huge advan-tage, as much as eighteen per cent.' A diamond-dripping matron with lilac hair threw the dice, shouting something Gina didn't understand. Max bellowed, 'Make them dance! The hard way.' And as the flying cubes came to rest, the crowd roared, and the woman beamed Max good humour and appreciation.

And from thereon Gina knew that the idea, which had been quietly germinating since that day she returned to New York from Europe when Harry had first told her about Benny Siegel's casino in the desert, could flourish from a strong root. Her confidence was drawn from the gleam in Max's eyes, from the authority with which he had spoken. She had been right: at the Lady Max was always competent, yet his heart was never truly in it; here however, his self-assurance had been apparent from the moment he stepped into this room, and whereas Gina was a stranger in an alien land, the Tuscan was the expert in a world he had made his own.

The dice fell on the floor, were retrieved by a player, but before being returned to play were examined by a sharp-faced character sitting at the centre of the table.

Max explained, 'The boxman. He watches the tables like a hawk. Makes sure nobody switches dice – the casino dice will be marked in some special way that he alone can detect and identify. He checks the plays, monitors the supply of chips, and settles all arguments. He also keep an eye on the dealer. Notice the dealer never directly takes a chip from a player's hand. It is forbidden, so he can't work with a buddy, switching low denomination chips for high ones. He wears no jacket because the only pocket he is entitled is on his shirt's chest – where players can slip their tips. Look at his tie. Very narrow. Nothing could be hidden behind it.'

The man Max was talking about, now stepped back, held his hands in the air, quickly turning and wringing them in a washing motion before walking away as a replacement dealer took his spot at the table.

Max said, 'He must do that whenever he leaves.'

'So that the boxman can be certain he hasn't secretly palmed anything,' said Gina.

Max smiled. 'You're learning, Principessa.' As they moved on he said, 'Security is the biggest headache of any gambling operation. There has to be a man watching the man who watches the man. There, you see?' He indicated an innocuous-looking, middle-aged gent sauntering behind the dealer at a blackjack table. 'A floorman. You'll spot several around the room. There are a number for each pit. A pit is a collection of tables all with the same game. We were just at the dice pit; there is also a pit for blackjack – in Europe we call it *vingt-et-un*, in England it's pontoon – and one for baccarat. The baccarat pit, in addition to its floormen, has laddermen who can look down onto the dealers' hands.'

Gina had wondered about the men on high stools.

Max went on, 'Each pit has a pit boss. Overseeing all of them will be the shift boss. And he is directly responsible to the casino manager. The system is the same throughout the world. Perhaps it has been since the ancient Egyptians opened the first casino.' He nodded seriously. 'They were playing dice games in three thousand BC. Also they invented roulette. Yes, fifteen hundred years before the French had even heard of it. And those Pharoahs were a lot smarter than the Bourbons too: their wheels had three zeros – all of which paid out to the house – the modern versions have only one.' Max suddenly stopped speaking. He smiled self-consciously, and Gina understood he was embarrassed by his little lecture.

She said, 'Please, don't apologize, old friend. It was fascinating. I never realized gambling had such a background. Or that you knew so much about it.'

The big man shrugged. 'When I started playing pinocle for money – I guess I was about ten – I met an old addict who gave me a book on the history of card games. It was the first time I ever read anything cover to cover. And from there on I was hooked.' He grinned sheepishly. 'Maybe I couldn't tell you a lot about American history, but I do know that back last century, when Nevada was still a territory under federal law, any district attorney was awarded a hundred-dollar bounty for every citizen he convicted of gambling.'

Gina, pausing to observe the action at a roulette table where enough chips had been laid to cover fifty such bounties, remarked, 'My, how times have changed!'

'People have always gambled,' said Max. 'And authorities have always tried to prevent it. But they've never succeeded. Making it illegal has merely driven it underground. Like liquor during prohibiti. If folks want to do something badly enough, they'.. f ... a way – law or no law. And there'll always be somebody around to fulfil their needs – usually at a hugely inflated price.'

'So the sensible thing to do with gambling, alcohol or whatever is to legalize it, and regulate it.'

'And,' said Max, 'make a profit out of it. You know the Nevada state legislature has just upped the gambling tax from one to two per cent. Why? Because it knows a good thing when it sees one. The tax is on gross income. Last year the casinos in Nevada took in ten million dollars. So the tax they paid was a hundred thousand. Also, they now have to pay a licence fee for every table they operate.' His arm swept the room. 'Who said state officialdom was dumb?'

Gina said, 'But they mustn't get too greedy, or they risk taxing the casinos out of business.'

'Don't worry on that score,' returned Max. 'I've asked around, and word is the gross take throughout the state this year will be over thirty million.'

Gina quietly whistled, let the figure percolate through her brain. Then her brow puckered and she queried, 'You asked around? You mean you've been making specific enquiries to learn all this stuff about tax percentages, licence fees and so on?' She nailed him with a slitted eye. 'How come, Max?'

Colour suffused the big man's face. 'Well . . .' he muttered. 'I was . . . I suppose . . .' He stared down at his shoes; but there was no encouragement reflected in the patent leather, and when he returned his gaze to Gina it was with the look of a schoolboy who knows that the cat is three parts of the way out of the bag. He grumbled, 'Oh, shucks.'

And Gina had to gulp back a laugh at both the down-home Americanism coming from the giant Tuscan and the cartoon of extreme discomfiture sketched on his face. Laying her palm on his lapel she smiled, 'I'm sorry, old friend. That was abrupt of me. And presumptuous. I had no right to pry. Put it down to me getting nosy in my old age.' She added wryly. 'Though maybe you'll say I always was a busy-breeches.'

Humour returning to his eyes, Max growled, 'More restless than a pocketful of kittens.' He enclosed her hand in his vast fists. 'But if you hadn't been, if you hadn't always wanted to be up and doing, where would we all – Paola and Filipo and me – be now? I don't doubt I'd be still dockwalloping, and shooting craps in backrooms for a fistful of tatty dollars, instead of standing here, gussied up like the King of England, with more money in my bank account than I know what to do with.' He added nonchalantly, 'And on the verge of making a lot more.

Just as soon as we open our casino.'

Gina stepped back a startled pace. Before her exclamation of surprise could escape, Max confirmed:

'Yes, Principessa. We knew what was on your mind. You've caught us on the hop before. But not this time. Harry remembered talking to you about Las Vegas eighteen months ago. When you brought up the subject again last week, we added two plus two and . . . ' He gave an eloquent shrug of his wide shoulders.

Gina nodded quiet understanding. 'Which is why you've been digging up all the facts on local taxes and such. Max, I never knew you were such an old slyboots.' She grinned at him then glanced around as if suddenly remembering where they were. 'Come on,' she said, 'now that you've put the kibosh on my Great Announcement, the least you can do is buy me a beer. I'm parched. I guess it's the desert air. Folks must drink gallons out here.' Her eyes narrowing as that observation set her mental wheels in motion, she walked thoughtfully away, murmuring, 'And that all adds to the profits. I'll negotiate a new deal with the liquor supplier. I wonder if these gambling types drink wine. We'll need a massive ice-making facility.' Rummaging in her purse: 'Where's that notebook?'

Smiling with great fondness, Max followed her blonde head through the crowd.

When they flew home to New York five days later, Gina was feeling even more intoxicated than she had that first evening at the Flamingo. This, however, was the elation of success; more precisely, of knowing she was a success, that everything she did was a success. It was as if she had been blessed with Midas's gift: everything she touched turned to gold? But why shouldn't it? She worked at it, didn't she? She worked damned hard. None of her success was a fluke. She hadn't flown up the stairway of fortune, like an Horatio Alger character, on an unlikely series of lucky breaks. I've recognized life's opportunities and turned them into accomplishments. I've seized the moment when more timorous individuals would have hesitated. No, I don't consider that either an insulting or conceited remark. Why shouldn't I acknowledge my ability? And why shouldn't I enjoy some of its fruits? I'm richer – will be even richer once the franchises pay off – than any of those Hollywood poseurs who were flaunting their jewels at the

Flamingo. Also, I'm more famous – almost. It's about time I started showing it. For a start, a new apartment. I've been living above the store quite long enough. A move to privacy: somewhere that reflects my social position. Park Avenue, of course. A six-room layout currently costs around nine thousand a year. I'll be more than able to afford that by the end of the year. Secondly, the old Packard can go – a long overdue move. I'll replace it with one of the new Cadillac limousines, finished to my own specification – mauve bodywork, purple interior, ivory leather upholstery. And how about a chauffeur in matching livery? Wouldn't that make 'em sit up and take notice when I cruised the park with little Frankie?

Little Frankie is in Phoenix.

Gina came down to earth as the plane touched the runway at New York's La Guardia Airport.

But the changes which had overtaken her on that flight from Las Vegas, did not retreat; they merely remained unseen as she walked with Max from the terminal, deeply breathed the fresh sea-scented air. No one would notice the changes for several weeks; then, however, they would become progressively apparent to everybody, until they eventually would cause Harry to say, 'You're rushing, Gina. Too far, too soon. And when you go forward so fast you often leave some good things behind.'

For now, though, she hadn't much of the rush in her. The past short week out west had been hectic. While Max had played the Flamingo tables every day, Gina had visited all the other gambling halls, saloons, hotels and restaurants in town, instinctively assessing from customer flow, staff attitudes and the pace of business, the percentage of profit being rung up, and whether the wilderness oasis genuinely had a future or if history, along with the visitors, was just passing through en route to someplace else.

In fact she'd only needed half the time to come up with the answers. There wasn't the remotest doubt in her mind – Las Vegas was planted as soldily in the arid earth as the NEW CASINO OPENING SHORTLY signs which sprouted incongruously mesquite-dotted lots along a five-mile stretch of sun-scorched highway. And when Max had at last dropped beside her into the pink velvet booth of the Flamingo's showroom and whispered above Durante's clattering piano, 'Principessa, you aren't going to believe me,' she'd required no further proof for the case she would present to her directors.

Tomorrow will be soon enough, though, she thought in the rear of the limousine carrying her and a snoring Max from La Guardia. I'll tell them my plans in the morning. What I need right now is six hours' sleep. This flying back and forth between night and day takes some getting used to. I'll ask Fallon how he copes.

Fallon is in Washington.

She was still dwelling on that as she sat at her dressing table, brushed out her hair. She unbuttoned her blouse, began to slip it from her shoulders.

Tony Nevada's voice said, 'Cute dimples.'

30

Gina swung around, swiftly pulling on her blouse. 'What are you doing here?' Angry heat suffused her as she fumbled with the buttons, poised stiff-backed on the chair's edge while the young singer leaned against the doorjamb piercing her with eyes that sent a shudder through her lower stomach.

'How was Vegas?' he asked, and Gina could hear the liquor in his voice. 'I missed you last week. You should've been here. For my celebration. A contract. You know I got a contract with Columbia. I'm cutting a record tomorrow.' Smiling lopsidedly he advanced into the room.

'Harry told me,' Gina returned quickly. 'I'm pleased for you, Tony. You deserve it.' She watched him drop into an armchair. He lounged back, one leg thrown casually over the other, an arm hanging loosely over the chair's side. He was wearing a pale blue, silk sports shirt which clearly outlined the muscles of his arms and chest, was tight across his flat, ridged stomach. Gina's scalp was prickling. She stood abruptly, on the verge of saying something about this being her private apartment; but deciding that sounded childish she clamped shut her jaw, quivered with suppressed . . . Annoyance? Self-recrimination? Desire? That latter possibility scalded her as she was held motionless by the look on the singer's face.

His high-cheekboned features glowed with a confident humour; but there was something more deep in his gaze. At first it was half-hidden, like a fire smouldering in the shadows, then it suddenly blazed.

Gina felt its heat.

Tony Nevada's eyes remained on her face for a suspended moment, then they travelled down her throat, lingered on her breasts, moved slowly downward to her thighs. They paused on her long legs before returning upward to lock on her own gaze.

She stared at the brilliantly blue irises, into the black pupils. And she saw the flames there, a scorching sexual furnace – reflecting her own. That realization stifled her. She gasped for breath as if choked by her own feelings. She said, 'Well, Tony, much as I'd love for us to chat awhile, I really have had a long day, and I'm going to turn in early.'

The corner of his full mouth quirked.

Gina remained standing. Tell him to get out. Now. She said, smiling woodenly, 'It was wonderful about your contract. We must talk about it. Tomorrow.'

'And my wages.'

'What you earn here?'

'Sure. It isn't exactly gold dust, is it?'

'Your salary is generous, Tony, considering you were an unknown when you started here.' Gina's palms were damp. This conversation was meaningless. She knew exactly why Tony Nevada was sitting in that chair, and exactly what was on his mind. Did he know what was on hers? Were her thoughts as naked as her body felt? She had to end this right now before it was too late. Somehow she was unable to move; she was riveted to the spot by his penetrating gaze. When she spoke her voice had a far-away tone, as if she was outside herself listening to the words. 'Perhaps, in view of your becoming a recording star . . . ' she jokily emphasized the title ' . . . we might renegotiate your contract. Harry will talk to you about it.'

'I'd rather you talked to me.'

'Harry handles the entertainment . . . '

'Harry is hired help.'

That stung Gina. Still she didn't move.

Tony Nevada uncrossed his legs, planted his feet apart. When he stood it was with a languour and arrogance that sent icy darts down Gina's spine. He walked slowly toward her, his hands in his pants pockets.

Gina retreated a pace, felt her legs back up against the dressing-table stool.

The singer advanced. He spaced his words on sensuously curving lips. 'Hey! Lady. Don't try to fool me. Even if you think you can fool yourself. You want me. You know you do.' He was directly in front of Gina now. Their bodies were less than twelve inches apart. Gina imagined she could feel the heat of him. She knew that was illusion, understood it was her own desire causing sweat to pour inside her blouse, threads of liquid like erotic fingers on her flesh. A voice warned, This is madness. You don't want this. She resented the voice, resented the truth of it, just as she resented her own unquenchable response to the man before her.

Tony Nevada reached out, strong hands on her waist, drew her forward. The smile on his face was one of absolute confidence. He knew Gina was powerless. His hands moved slowly up the sides of her ribcage until his thumbs were below her breasts.

She held her breath, knowing that when she exhaled their bodies would touch. There was nothing she could do to prevent it.

He said, 'You're going to love it, baby. You're going to thank me for the privilege.'

His arrogance shattered Gina's paralysis. Her hands jerked up, rammed forward in one rapid motion, thumping into Tony Nevada's chest taking him off guard, sending him jolting backward. He almost stumbled over his own feet, bounced against a chair, grabbed at the air for support before regaining his balance, standing red-faced and tight-lipped, his fists bunched at his sides. Gina's blazing eyes seared him with all the contempt she could muster, and she burned with satisfaction when she saw it drain his blood until the lines of his face were as white as scraped bones.

She strode past him, through the sitting-room, opened the front door, didn't look back, only waited until he came from behind her and went out into the hall. Not until the door was swinging from her sharp push did the singer glance around.

It wasn't anger she saw in him, nor hate. At that instant as the door cracked shut she wasn't sure what emotion had flashed in Tony Nevada's eyes. Only after she had turned away and walked slowly back to her bedroom did she realize what she'd seen. Spite. Icy vindictiveness had been all the young singer had carried away from their encounter. The most immature of all sentiments. 'What did you expect,' she asked herself, 'from a boy?'

Well, she went on as she undressed and stepped into the shower, no more boys for me. No more high cheekbones and white teeth and tanned throats. No more aberrations, no matter how minor or brief. She leaned back beneath the hot water, her face raised to the spray, remained there until the warmth permeated her blood, washed away all her tensions.

By the time she had vigorously towelled herself, then, wrapped in a white terrycloth robe, warmed a mug of milk and curled into the armchair beside her bed, her nerves had unravelled and she had all but dismissed the incident with Tony Nevada. Her reaction to him she put down to the tiring and tiresome journey from Las Vegas. Was it only last night she and Max were at the Flamingo? It seemed an age.

It wasn't until halfway through the following morning that she enquired, 'Where's Cassie?' when she realized she hadn't seen her friend although she herself had come down to the Lady at five a.m. refreshed and revitalized after a long, deep sleep in which she'd dreamed of a silver palace in the middle of the Nevada desert. After Harry said Cassie hadn't been around since last night, Gina phoned the redhead, gave up after four attempts which met with the busy signal and took a cab to her apartment.

She'd leaned on the bellpush long and hard before the door opened and Cassie, uncombed and bleary-eyed in short wrap-around green robe, gasped, 'Oh, Gina . . . Hon . . . I over-slept. Sorry. Didn't get to bed till this morning.' She stood on the threshold, pushing a hand through her mass of flaming hair until she came suddenly awake and said, 'Hey, gosh, what'm I thinking of? Come on in. Come in,' and she ushered Gina through the hall and into a sitting-room – which looked as if a bomb had hit it.

Gina halted, stared at the overturned coffee table, two fallen floor lamps, a Boston fern lying amid the shattered remains of a pot, and a wall mirror riven from corner to corner.

Cassie laughed, a short, cracked sound. 'Darn cleaners didn't show up again.' Her smile struggled for survival. 'Don't buy that, eh?' Surveying the wreckage: 'Is kind of a mess, isn't it? I guess we got kinda carried away last night. Tony and me.' Again the crooked smile. 'Mad, passionate love, you know.' She bent and lifted the fern, stood it lopsidedly in a crystal bowl on the sideboard. 'I'll make some coffee.'

'No.' Gina's voice jumped out of her mouth. Her pulse rate had risen and she was trying desperately to disbelieve what had happened here. 'No coffee for me, thanks. I have to be getting back. Just came to make sure you were all right, weren't sick.' She hesitated, wanted to say more but didn't know where to begin. 'Well . . . I'll see you later.' It was then, as Cassie again pushed her hair from her forehead, she noticed the dark bruise on her temple. Gina's heartbeat leapt as abruptly as her hand instinctively reached out toward the lurid mark.

Cassie recoiled. 'It's nothing.' She tugged at her hair in an attempt to conceal the discolouration. 'Look, I have to shower. Let me get on, okay?'

'Cass, what happened?'

'I hit my head, is all. That's it. You know, we, Tony and me, we were horsing around. One of the lamps got knocked over. My head didn't see it coming. So what? You know my head, solid wood. No . . . .'

'Cass, stop talking nonsense.' The instant Gina had said it she wished she hadn't. She shouldn't pursue this. It was none of her business. Too late though as Cassie retaliated:

'I think you'd better leave, Gina. I didn't ask you around in the first place. Okay, so I was late for work. It won't happen again, all right? In the meantime, remember, you may be the boss but that doesn't mean you can come butting into my private life.' She tightened her robe. 'Speaking of which, you might as well know, I'll be quitting this apartment, moving in with Tony.'

'What!' blurted Gina unable to contain herself. 'You can't be serious, after he did that to you.'

'I told you it was an accident,' snapped Cassie. 'It was.' She avoided Gina's eyes. 'Sort of. Tony didn't mean it. Didn't mean to hit so hard. He'd had too much liquor, is all. Besides, it was my fault. I shouldn't've gone on at him for not keeping our date. I should've seen he was upset over something. He gets upset easy, you know. Because he's so talented. Talented people are highly strung, aren't they?' She began to collect the broken pottery.

Gina watched, trapped in an agony of indecision – whether or not to tell Cassie, somehow or other, about her confrontation with Tony Nevada last night. Couldn't her friend see what he was? Or didn't she want to see? Was she too blinded by infatuation? Gina knew that was the truth of it. Cassie of all people! Perhaps it would pass. Surely she'd come to her senses. In the meantime the redhead's nerves obviously were too frayed to stand further abrasion. Gina stepped toward where her friend was re-standing one of the floor lamps. 'I'll help you tidy up.'

'No, it doesn't matter.' Cassie didn't bother to adjust the lamp's tilted shade. 'Like I said, I'm moving in with Tony. Tonight. He needs me. Needs someone to look after him.' She walked briskly past Gina. 'Now I'm going to grab that shower.' She was into the hall. Her voice called, 'Let yourself out, won't you?' and a door closed.

Gina remained motionless until she heard water begin to run. She took a final glance around the apartment before sighing deeply and leaving.

A much happier encounter was awaiting her at The Lady.

'Mrs Ponti,' she exclaimed joyfully, '*Come sta*?' as she reached the upper lobby to find her ex-landlady perched neatly on the pink velvet sofa.

Rising rapidly, Mrs Ponti, in smart navy and white dress with matching bag, shoes and half-veiled hat, met Gina, embraced her, kissed her on both cheeks and answered in her ebullient, Cockney accent, 'I'm just splendid, love, thanks. And yerself?' She approvingly appraised Gina. 'Yer lookin' elegint. Elegint as ever. And brahn. Look at it. Brahn as a berry. All that wild west sun, I shouldn't wonder. Max has bin tellin' me about yer trip, as how you've bin givin' that gamblin' palace the once over. A fortune to be made out there, he says. And I can believe it. Though I must say I never bets meself. Never so much as bought a number in me entire life. Nor did Mister Ponti, God rest his soul, neither.'

'It is lovely to see you,' shot in Gina before her garrulous old friend could get another word out. She was genuinely delighted to see Mrs Ponti who, though a frequent visitor to the restaurant, rarely caught Gina at a convenient moment. This morning, however, following her sharp exchange with Cassie, Gina was in need of a friendly face and a lighthearted chat, even though, she thought wryly, she probably wouldn't get a comment in edgewise once Mrs Ponti opened up. 'Well,' she offered brightly, 'don't let's stand here all day. Come into the sitting-room. I'll call for some coffee.'

'No, not for me, love,' interposed Mrs Ponti. 'I wasn't really here on a social call. Not exactly like. What I wanted to talk about was a spot of business.'

'Oh?' That was all Gina, taken by surprise, could come up with. 'Right you are,' she said, gathering herself in response to what she now saw was a distinctly professional air about the stylishly clad woman, 'let's go into the office.' And without further delay she led the way.

When she was seated one side of the desk and Mrs Ponti the other, Gina exchanged brief pleasantries before smiling encouragingly and prompting, 'Well, then . . . ?'

'It's about the Rossi Taverns,' began Mrs Ponti. 'Gina, I'm sorry to have to do this. I suppose I oughtn't really. But needs must when the devil drives. And I was gettin' absolutely nowhere with those blokes down your office. I can see from the look on your face they told you nothin'. I knew it. Reckon they thought I was tryin' it on when I said you and me was old mates. Still, I appreciate they got their job to do, keepin' a weather eye out for nutcases, you can't be too careful . . . '

'You've been to the Rossi Taverns' office?' interrupted Gina, trying to latch a hold on the verbal gallop.

'Exactly,' returned Mrs Ponti. 'Six times. Six lots of forms I filled in. Five interviews I've had. Lor love us, Gina, those interrogators of yours know more about me than the bloomin' Government! And still they says they'll let me know. So I told myself, I'll do what I should've in the first place. I'll go direct to Gina. I hope you won't think badly of me for it, love, but the more I think about it, the more I want it. And I know I'd be right for it. I'd be right for you too. Because you've got to have somebody you can trust. Somebody who won't let you down. And . . . well . . . ' she smiled hopefully through the half-veil, 'here I am.'

Gina was rapidly piecing together the broken bits of Mrs Ponti's effusion, and now, as at last some of them clicked into place, she exclaimed, 'A franchisee! Ethel, you want to be a tavern-keeper.' She suffused with mingled surprise and delight, didn't realize she'd called the elder woman by her Christian name for the first time in all their years of acquaintance.

Mrs Ponti beamed appreciation, and – also for the first time since Gina had known her – she was temporarily lost for words.

Gina said enthusiastically, 'But of course you should have come to me from the outset. Good heavens, Ethel, what are old friendships for?' To Mrs Ponti's slightly embarrassed shrug, she added, 'There's no question, I'd be honoured to have you running a Rossi Tavern.'

Mrs Ponti gave a small sigh of relief. 'I was worried, thought you might not be accepting folk who haven't had any experience of restauranting.'

'Business acumen is what's needed. All franchisees, whether or not they've been in the catering trade will receive training at a centre we're setting up in the office building. It is my intention to have full-time teaching professionals – chefs, *maître'd*'s, managers, even bartenders. As back-up, we're producing a comprehensive instruction manual which will cover all aspects of operating a Rossi Tavern.'

Mrs Ponti's usual ebullience had given way to rapt attention. 'I knew when I met those interrogators that you were aiming for something special, Gina, but I didn't realize it was going to be nothing like that. Though Max did say as how you were plannin' on a thousand restaurants.' She paused as if to contemplate the enormity of the figure. 'Yes,' she mused, 'I suppose it is possible, in time. In what? Ten years maybe?'

'Two,' said Gina. 'And that will be just the start. From the studies I've received of the dining-out habits of all the major cities in the country, given a stable national economy, I see no reason why, within a decade, there shouldn't be at least six thousand Rossi Taverns in operation. By then we'll also have expanded into Europe, and the training centre will be a fully-equipped school, perhaps even a residential campus, incorporating everything from financial planning to sales promotion.'

'It sounds big,' said a subdued Mrs Ponti.

'The biggest thing the U.S. catering industry has ever seen. But,' stressed Gina, 'we won't lose our personal touch. The Rossi Corporation will be a family. That's a promise, Ethel. We'll be one big, happy family.'

Mrs Ponti managed a small nod. But she didn't return Gina's enthusiasm, and the breeziness had gone out of her. Slowly, she said, 'I reckon as how I've made a bit of a mistake, love. A bit of a chump of myself too. Here I was thinkin' you could use some help. That you'd be wantin' a familiar face to give you a bit of confidence like. Someone you could trust in your first tavern. But . . . well . . . I see now you won't be needin' me. I'm sorry I took your time this morning. I realize how busy you must be. I'll be on my way now.' She began to rise.

'You'll be no such thing,' rebutted Gina. 'Since when have we had time between us? My time is no more precious than yours.' She smiled, but felt a stab of annoyance at herself for the note of sharpness in her voice. It had come, she knew, because she'd seen a hint of truth in her ex-landlady's words.

Mrs Ponti had resat, hesitantly.

Gina said, with considerable amicability, 'Where exactly had you in mind for a Rossi Tavern?'

Mrs Ponti smoothed her skirt, regained some confidence. 'Max mentioned Columbus Circle.'

'Yes, but perhaps you didn't quite understand. That is where we intend to site the first tavern. You've seen our prospectus. Did you read that all franchisees will be obliged to own, or hold a long-term lease on their premises? A property in Columbus Circle will be extremely costly. However, there's no reason why your tavern shouldn't be equally successful in a somewhat less expensive location.'

'Money's no problem,' rejoined Mrs Ponti. 'My husband, Mister Ponti, God rest his soul, left me well provided for with his insurances. I've always been careful, saved from the first day we set up shop. And I've been offered a good price for the grocery story. With a loan – I've already spoken to the bank – I'll have more than enough for a spot on the Circle. In fact, I've seen one. Next to the old Park Theatre. It's an omen. You know before the war the building was Pabst's Grand Circle, a fine restaurant, famous it was for its free lunch, an orchestra and the best oyster bar in Manhattan. Opening up there with a Rossi Tavern would be continuing a New York tradition like. It'd be the sort of story the newspapers would love. Good for publicity. That's what we need, isn't it, love? Publicity. Oils the wheels of commerce, as Mr Ponti, God rest his soul, used to say.' The elderly woman's face had relit, and she was braced expectantly forward against the desk.

Gina, frankly, was somewhat nonplussed. She'd known Mrs Ponti was a provident and nimble-witted character, but she'd never credited her with being quite so shrewd as to understand

427

the value of press promotion. Also, this was the first time Gina had been involved directly with a potential franchisee – so far she'd only studied reports and profiles prepared by her consultants – and she found the experience novel, at the same time stimulating; for despite the mountains of work that had gone into the project over the past packed weeks, it had never seemed as personal as her involvement with the Lady. During the last few minutes, however, it had stepped several paces closer. In the persona of Mrs Ethel Ponti it had assumed flesh and blood.

Gina was thrilled by it.

She asked, 'Do you know the franchise fee?'

'A thousand dollars,' replied Mrs Ponti. 'Plus an annual royalty of seven-and-a-half percent of total sales.'

'A third of which will be spent wholly on national advertising of Rossi Taverns,' said Gina. 'We're planning a powerful programme of press and radio commercials which not only will put us squarely on the map but also will guarantee higher than average profit for all the individual taverns. Have you been given any idea about costs and return?' To Mrs Ponti's headshake, Gina pressed on, 'Based on national statistics as well as our personal experience here in New York, we estimate that after food costs, local taxes, wages, overheads and utilities, plus the royalty fee, a tavern-keeper who is running his business efficiently – and under our guidance that will be assured – will make a gross profit of at least seventeen per cent.' She glowed with enthusiasm at the sound of her own words.

Mrs Ponti gave a profoundly impressed nod.

Gina, smiling, studied the woman.

My first franchisee, she thought. Mrs Ponti. The first person I had a cup of coffee with in this alien land. A lot of years and a lot of beers between, as Johnny would say. Who'd have thought we'd end up here? Not end up. Begin. We're beginning here. Just beginning the story. Everything that went before was just a prologue. There's so much ahead. So many horizons.

Gina felt a quickening of her blood. The future tumbled through her head. Rossi Taverns. Las Vegas. Could you franchise casinos? Europe. The Rossi catering college. And how about hotels? Hotels were the next logical step. And, you know, come to think of it, the lodging business is an almost untapped industry. There are luxury hotels and cheap hotels.

What, nationally, is there in between? Who is providing first-rate, family accommodation, with standardized quality and service, at a price that isn't out of this world? What do you know about hotels? I know a great deal about scrubbing their floors. Cesar Ritz wasn't born a hotelier. Claridge of London was a butler before he opened a lodging-house for England's gentry. Pierre, here in New York, started out as a page boy in Monte Carlo. Jammet of the Bristol in Paris was a chef. And, you know, Poppa's old friend Signor Rusconi who nowadays is the managing director of the Ambasciatori in Florence began his working life as an eleven-year-old kitchen hand at the Raffles in Singapore. Of course, the Las Vegas casino will in fact be an hotel. That will be a start, somewhere, as it were, to learn the trade. But then . . . Imagine, a Rossi hotel in every major city. Today really is only a beginning. The first step toward . . .

Toward what?

'Well, then, Gina, I'll have my attorneys get cracking on the Columbus Circle property.'

Gina blinked; returned to earth and Mrs Ponti. 'You definitely have made up your mind? It's what you want? Unsociable hours. Non-existent holidays. Truculent diners. Temperamental dishwashers. Eccentric electricity supplies. An itinerant caterpillar in the cabbage the day the health inspector turns up. An exploding oven two minutes before opening time. All this is your idea of heaven? You wouldn't trade it for star billing in an MGM musical?'

'Not even alongside Dick Powell,' said Mrs Ponti.

Gina stood, offered her hand across the desk. 'In which case, Ethel, I reckon we're both in business.'

She loved it. Gina loved the thrill of it, this headlong rush in her life; like a roller-coaster ride of breathtaking climbs, pell-mell plunges and unexpected curves. Even when sitting at her desk, or attending some meeting, she felt the sun was on her face and the wind was in her hair.

During the fortnight following her meeting with Mrs Ponti, attorneys and accountants had been spurred into moving six times faster than their usual somnolent turtle's pace, the Columbus Circle property had been signed, sealed and delivered, and an army of construction workers mobilized to transform the building into a Rossi Tavern. As predicted, the press ate up the story. They also ate up Ethel Ponti. From the moment she opened her mouth at the public signing of the initial franchise contract she was a hit. Her Cockney accent and natural drollery turned her into a minor celebrity overnight. The success of her tavern was assured three months before The World's First Rossi Diner was due to be welcomed over her threshold.

While Ethel was supervising the decorating of her restaurant, Gina was overseeing the furnishing of her new apartment.

On the crest of her exhilaration she'd renewed her determination to move from 'above the store'. Oblivious to the eyebrows her decision raised, she took a lease on an eight-room duplex in Van Clare Mansions overlooking the manicured grass, immaculately groomed flower beds and scrubbed sidewalks of Park Avenue, whence she could gaze diagonally across to the huge figure of the Spirit of Achievement above the entrance of the Waldorf Astoria.

She told Junius Flick, the current décor darling of Manhattan's beau monde, 'If I'm going to do it, I'll do it right.' Thus the apartment acquired an elegance as lustrous as the pastel Chinese silks which were chosen to cover the walls. Complementary swagged and draped velvet was hung at the floor-to-ceiling windows. In the stylish but tasteful sitting-room the furniture was bird's eye maple to match the panelled ceiling and block floor, the upholstery was mauve kid, the tops of the occasional tables on white jade; on a raised area the dining-table and chairs easily could accommodate sixteen guests. The classical lines of the kitchen and bathrooms were reflected in the latest gadgetry, while the stately library was unobtrusively equipped with electric typewriter, dictaphone and ticker-tape machine. Last, but far from least, the master bedroom: a coffee and cream, satin and lace confection with a custom-built brass and onyx half-tester which was, growled Fallon, 'Like an ice-cream sundae. Great for a kids' picnic, but too much for any adult to swallow. Particularly,' he added after his first dinner at the apartment, 'on a full stomach.' Gina called him an old grouch, made love to him amid the static-crackling, shiny sheets, almost slid out of bed three times, instructed May Ling to exchange the satin for cotton the following morning.

May Ling was as quintessential to the apartment's social status as the gold-and-purple uniformed doorman was to Van

Clare Mansions. 'Not to have a maid,' Gina informed Fallon (who muttered about *anciens régimes*), 'is simply unthinkable.' Anyhow, May Ling was Chang's daughter, and according to her father, like all teenagers she was in need of 'discipline'. Gina could sympathize with that. Since Filipo had started college his grades had been as bad as they had in high school. At nineteen years of age it was time he buckled down. Gina had made a mental note to have a long, serious talk with him.

Also, she'd reaffirmed her intention to spend more time with Fallon – as soon as she could.

Meanwhile, she held a Get-To-Know-Each-Other party in her old apartment above The Lady (kept on for just such occasions, when the richly elegant atmosphere of the Van Clare Mansions apartment might have been too rarefied) for the first hundred accepted and contracted franchisees who were scheduled to be in business before Christmas. The following day she phoned Paola and Johnny, told them what a terrific success it had been and that they'd be guests of honour, along with the Governor of Arizona, several movie stars and a herd of local worthies at the grand opening of the Phoenix Rossi Tavern.

The same day she air-mailed a long, enthusiastic letter to Sybil and David, along with an invitation to the launch of Ethel Ponti's Columbus Circle tavern in October.

Sybil's reply came a month later. She thought, regretfully, that she and David would be too busy to get away, but wished Gina the very best of luck, sent love to all. She enclosed a score of photographs of happy mums and their infants, plus a number of forms for Gina to sign so that the Grange could become a Limited Company. Gina complied with the request, stuck all the photos in her latest journal, on the page following the large picture of a sun-baked, sagebrush-patched stretch of land she'd received from the real estate agent in Las Vegas.

'Principessa,' Max had said soon after their return from Nevada. 'Do I want to be the boss of our own casino? Does a footballer want to be signed by the Giants? But,' he tugged his whiskers, 'you still haven't explained. *Perchè*? Why are we doing it?'

Gina had replied patiently, 'Because we have to. There's so much talk about Las Vegas. Everyone knows the Flamingo has been making money hand over fist since Ben Siegel's death.

Major corporations are now looking in that direction. I heard a rumour last week that convinced me we have to move on it before acreage prices out there hit the sky. Land, Max, always has been the finest investment anyone can make. You know the old story? When Jacob Astor was on his deathbed they asked him if he had any regrets. He replied, only one – that he hadn't bought up every square foot of soil in Manhattan. Well, we also were too late to stake out a plot in this city. But Las Vegas is our chance. Our opportunity actually to own a piece of America. Just like the old western pioneers. Imagine what an original Californian homestead is worth these days.'

Max frowned. 'We're to become landowners?'

'It will give us permanence. It will be the foundation on which we'll build our future. More importantly, the future of the Rossi family. The future of Filipo and little Frankie and their sons and daughters, all those who will come after us.'

Max smiled. 'So when you're a very old lady you can sit with the generations around your feet and tell them how it was for a young Roman girl and an old Tuscan gambler the day they tramped through the fog of Ellis Island.'

Gina stared. A lump sprang to her throat as she recalled the chilling reception hall of the immigration centre. Lest the memory get the better of her, she quipped, 'Max, I never knew you were such an old sentimentalist.'

He reached out, touched a big hand to her halo of blonde hair. After a moment that way he asked gruffly, 'So, tell me, can we afford this piece of Nevada?'

Gina swallowed her emotion, regathered her briskness. Tapping the stack of contracts on her desk she replied, 'Old friend, I think we can safely say that during the coming months our assets will achieve what the financial wordsmiths might call, a modestly encouraging yield.'

'It amounts, in our first year,' she informed the president of the Eastern Commercial Bank & Trust Company, 'to one million dollars in franchise fees alone. That sum, as you see,' her gold pen tapped the page of her financial report, a copy of which was before the dark-suited balding man, 'is derived simply from the initial thousand franchises. The only reason it isn't double that number is because of the time which will be required for administration. Not only do we insist on all the potential franchisees being vetted meticulously, we also ensure the same precise investigation of their intended Rossi Tavern building and its location. This all requires, Mister Hoyt, diligence, patience and time. You understand?' Gina spoke not sharply, but with sufficient brittleness to cause the bank president's eyes to jump up from the document and register prompt affirmation through his gold-rimmed spectacles. Yes, thought Gina, you'd do well to pay attention when I speak, otherwise I might take a short walk up or down Wall Street to any one of the other patronizing moneylenders who'd dearly love to get their slippery hands on the Rossi Taverns account.

Gina did not like bankers.

'I'd sooner sit down to eat in a snake pit,' she'd averred to Max with no small tinge of bitterness when he'd relayed a luncheon invitation from the bank's board of directors a year ago. She'd turned down the invitation, and every one since; because Gina hadn't forgotten, never would forget, that merciless day she'd sat before a man (the one facing her now was so similar she involuntarily shivered whenever she met him) and had all her carefully typed plans and costings for The Lady spurned as disparagingly as a child's scribble, had all her hopes and dreams flicked aside as disdainfully as a speck of dust from the moneylender's immaculate desktop.

Nowadays she derived no pleasure from being bowed into the bank president's office, gained no satisfaction from the man's deference. She still saw him as an enemy; for in him she always sensed not merely condescension but also suppressed resentment that a woman should be admitted to these hallowed halls. 'America,' Gina had remarked to Fallon, 'may be thirty years ahead of Europe as far as female emancipation is concerned, but there are still plenty of institutions who believe a female's place is, at worst, chained to a stove, or, at best, stuck behind a typewriter. I know, I meet it every day of the week. There are hundreds of clubs and organizations from which I'm barred. There are scores of companies – local and national – who won't deal with me because they consider I'm a bad risk. And there are thousands of individuals – including members of my own sex – who think, because I run my own company, drive my own car, and don't jump into bed with every drummer who comes pushing his wares, that I'm either frigid, a lesbian, or in need of psychiatric treatment.'

In Wheldon J. Hoyt's rosewood-panelled penthouse office of the Eastern Commercial Bank & Trust Company, she now said firmly, 'Within a month, I shall have signed contracts from five hundred of those first thousand franchisees. Contracts worth half a million dollars. Collateral to stand against a loan of that amount. I fail to see a reason for your hesitancy, Mister Hoyt.'

The bank president's expression remained as bland as a sugared almond. 'Not hesitancy, Miss Rossi. Caution. Please appreciate my concern to advise caution. It is not the worth or the validity of the contracts which is causing me, and my fellow directors, a not inconsiderable degree of anxiety, but the venture into which you propose to invest not only the total income from the franchises, but also, as I understand it . . . ' he briefly perused the financial report as if it had been on his desk for only ten minutes rather than a fortnight, 'an additional sum of twice that amount. A total of one and a half million dollars, Miss Rossi.'

'Precisely,' Gina rejoined with impulsive sharpness, unable to keep the exasperation out of her voice. 'That is what it will cost for the land and the construction of the casino.'

Wheldon Hoyt's face visibly twitched at this latter word. 'All of which,' he said, 'will be paid out – should I, and my directors, agree to this venture – considerably before the sum has been recouped from the franchises.'

Provoked, Gina wanted to retaliate, 'Isn't that what usually happens?' But she knew it would be pointless. In the world of banking, investment in a casino was less usual than the financial backing of a brothel (Gina had heard of at least two major financial institutions who had considerable funds – their virtuous clients' funds – earning profits from red light districts both at home and overseas). 'Gambling,' Wheldon Hoyt had said when Gina first made her presentation, 'is a very risky business.' And there hadn't been the slightest flicker of humour in his face.

Keeping her vexation under control, she now said, 'On pages eight to twelve of my report you will see – have seen – ample evidence that a casino has a far lower risk factor than, say, a grocery store or a gas station. In gambling, the long-term odds in favour of the house are irrefutable. They are fixed. Who else can offer you that sort of guarantee?'

The bank president pursed his lips, adjusted his spectacles. 'Why must you open this establishment so soon? Scarcely more than a year for completion of such a vast project seems precious little time, particularly as, at the moment, you have nothing more than an artist's impression of the building. Perhaps, if you did not seem to be rushing into this venture, if you were to start with a more modest building, and set your proposed opening date two years from now, then, Miss Rossi, I, and my directors, might be prepared to favourably . . .'

'Even one year from now isn't soon enough,' cut in Gina. 'Mister Hoyt, you haven't been to Las Vegas. I suggest you do. I suggest you check out all the real estate offices. Ask them what land was fetching per square foot last week, and what they'll be asking seven days from now. And if you require further confirmation of Las Vegas's future, I suggest you telephone Mister Del Webb.'

Hoyt's eyebrows stood to attention. 'Webb? The builder?'

'He constructed the Flamingo for Siegel. I understand he's now considering erecting a casino of his own.'

That gave Wheldon Hoyt pause for thought. As it had Gina a month ago. It was the rumour she'd mentioned to Max when telling him of her intention to buy Nevada land. It had been the major factor influencing her decision to head west. When she'd heard Del Webb's name she'd recalled meeting him at one of The Lady's charity nights. She'd only chatted with him for a short time but it had been sufficient to make her understand why he was the man who, after starting his working life as a carpenter in Phoenix, had built up a company which during the war had handled government contracts for airfields, training camps, munitions factories and hospitals – all before he turned forty-five. Such a character had more marbles in his box than most, and if he was seriously considering a casino-hotel in Las Vegas as a viable proposition, that was good enough for Gina Rossi.

Perhaps for Wheldon J. Hoyt also.

He cleared his throat, re-examined the financial report, took off his spectacles and began to polish them with a small silk square. 'Very well, Miss Rossi. I'm prepared to give your request my further consideration.'

Gina'a gratitude rose.

'However,' added the bank president, 'as you have seen fit to mention Mister Del Webb, I must reply that you are hardly able to offer the same reliability of collateral as the Webb Corporation. If you insist on completion of your Las Vegas project within a year, then I have no alternative than to insist upon taking not only your franchise contracts as security, but also your personal majority holding in your restaurant, The Lady.' He replaced his spectacles, stared through them at Gina with eyes as cold and as hard as washed pebbles.

When she came out into the sharp sunlight fifteen minutes later, Gina was striving to remain calm and confident. She told herself everything was fine. Yes, she had incurred another huge debt, stretched her finances to their limit while deepening her financial risk by acceding to Wheldon Hoyt's demand for security. But nothing could go wrong, she mentally insisted. Twelve months from now the casino would be complete, there would be Rossi Taverns coast to coast, the foundation of the Rossi empire would be as solid as a rock. The future of Gina, and her family, would be secure. And Wheldon J. Hoyt and all other merciless moneylenders could go hang.

She boosted her positiveness with a smile, determinedly raised her hand, and her new ivory limousine came swiftly to carry her away from that chill street.

31

Sitting on a bench amid the hubbub of the main concourse of Grand Central Terminal, Gina studied her brother's profile.

Filipo's looks had matured dramatically. His deep hazel eyes seemed intensified by their thick lashes. His nose was Roman straight with flared nostrils above a wide, permanently tilted mouth. The jaw was square, dark with shadow which he could barely keep at bay with twice-daily razoring. Topping all this was a shiny mass of wavy black hair which barbers rarely got a shot at.

You're far too handsome, my lad, Gina thought affectionately. And so much like Poppa. Yet inches taller. The long legs you get, like me, from Momma. No wonder all the girls of the chorus are doe-eyed over you. They'd make you top of the box-office if you were a movie star.

What? Where did that thought spring from? A movie star is the last thing I'll have him be. That's what the previous thirty minutes' discussion has been all about.

Filipo had spent the past three weeks of August in Phoenix with Paola and Johnny. He'd returned by railroad in response to Fallon's assurances that it was the best way to see the country. Gina had come to meet him, this sunny first afternoon in September, had sat him beside her on the bench saying it was one of the few places they could chat without interruption. She'd been preparing her succinct speech for days, had delivered it non-stop while Filipo sat and stoically heard her out. Now she said, 'We aren't going to fight about this, are we? You agree, you have to pay more attention to your college work?'

Filipo sighed. 'I told you, Sis, I'm not cut out to be a lawyer. Do I look like a lawyer?'

'Please, don't be flippant. Nobody's cut out to be anything. We all have to decide what we're going to be, then set about becoming it. Don't you see? Of course you do. Well, then . . .' she pushed a stubborn lock of hair from his brow, 'I've enjoyed our chat. It's been too long since we talked together this way. You're always on the hop. I can never pin you down.'

'The last time I stopped by your office, your secretary said I didn't have an appointment.'

'That isn't so. Well, it might be. Maybe I was overbusy that day. Things will start to ease up now we have the staff at our new offices. How about that place? Exciting, isn't it? Our family name right there on the reception wall. All those people beavering away on the franchise applications. And one day, soon, there'll be even more. I've leased two more floors of that building. One day we'll buy it. We'll have whole suites of executive offices. Mine, yours, Harry's, Max's . . . No, perhaps not Max, he'll be in Las Vegas. He'll be so happy there. Did I tell you, I bought the land for the casino? The architects are drawing up the plans. And the name . . . Wait till you hear this.' She paused for dramatic effect. Announced, 'The Silver Lady. Hey? How about that? Corny, isn't it? But you will understand when you see the artist's impressions. A silver pyramid. Glass and chrome, to reflect the sunlight – the sun never stops shining in southern Nevada – so the place will be visible from miles around. Nobody else has thought of that. They've only concentrated on lighting up their buildings at night. What do you think? Isn't it a great idea?'

Filipo studied his sister's overflowing enthusiasm. Nodding, with a half-smile, he said, 'Terrific.'

'I did so want your approval,' Gina said happily. She stood. 'Come on, can't sit here confabbing all day.' As Filipo rose, lifting his suitcase, Gina linked her arm with his, started toward the exit. 'By the way, I've arranged for you to board at college, Mondays through Fridays, this coming semester. Don't pull a face. It will give you more time to study, instead of travelling home nights. You'll still be here weekends. I'm sure it's for the best. Don't I always know what's for the best?'

The reporter with *L.A. Herald* tabbed in his hatband hurried alongside Gina and Max as they strode into the glaring morning outside Los Angeles' airport. He'd been firing questions like a machine gun since he'd spotted them at baggage arrival. The price of fame, Gina told herself whenever such attention insisted to the point of aggravation. Also, she added the consolation, imagine all those characters – business types as well as celebrities – who'd happily cut off an ear for less than half the column inches Gina Rossi received whenever she publicly opened her mouth.

As the *Herald* legman pursued her to the waiting hotel limousine, she continued to answer briefly and politely. Max stowed the suitcases in the trunk as the chauffeur stood neatly beside the rear door waiting while Gina bent to enter.

'How about the Mafia?' shot the reporter.

Gina straightened. 'Who?'

'Word is they've got their eyes on Vegas now. They might be your neighbours. Does that worry you?'

Gina looked down at the poised pencil, into the man's perfectly serious face. Smiling, she replied, 'I've lived in three of the biggest cities in the world, I've never had any problems with my neighbours. Besides, it's always been my experience that the Mafia aren't much different from other folks – so long as you don't bother them, they won't bother you. Bye now.' She ducked into the limousine.

When they were gliding away she said to Max, 'The trouble with the press, they believe in their own lurid stories.'

Within an hour of checking into the hotel they were out again and chauffeured to the showrooms of the furnishing wholesaler with whom Gina had made an appointment. In New York Max had suggested that wasn't it somewhat premature to order equipment for the Silver Lady (the name had been announced by press release that day three weeks ago when Filipo had returned from Phoenix) when the architects hadn't yet completed their drawings? Needless to say Gina had rejoined with, Not letting the grass grow, Never putting off today what you can do tomorrow, etc., and had informed him that while she would take care of the furniture he would be in charge of the purchasing of all the gambling equipment, from the dice and decks of cards to the craps tables and Big Six wheels. That had got him going in no time flat, and his enthusiasm had burned more brightly than Gina's as he'd phoned manufacturers around the country, eventually settled on one in Los Angeles who was offering top quality as well as a great deal due to low transportation costs over the less than three-hundred-mile route to Las Vegas.

He wasn't able to apply his expertise, however, until he'd observed Gina's.

As she walked (stalked) with him around the Los Angeles furnishing showroom he recalled the day they'd bought the equipment and fittings for the Lady, when Gina, after explaining the practical design requirements of crockery, cutlery and glassware, had gone on to the purchase of furniture, her choice dictated by something she called anthropometric data.

Max never had grasped a satisfactory Italian translation of this term, but it meant, for instance, that the height of a chair's seat from the floor, for an average man aged between eighteen and fifty-nine, must be 435 millimetres, and for a woman in the same age range 418 millimetres. With what Max thought was a somewhat macabre exactitude, Gina had added that the measurement reduced to 404 millimetres for both sexes when they began to shrink physically once they reached sixty years. He had also learned that the seat's depth must be 350 millimetres, the maximum height of the backrest 330, and the radius of the backrest's curve 430. There was too a lot of stuff about angles and clearances and body weights, most of which he'd given up on. He had understood, however, Gina's reference to seat width, and had rubbed his palm over his whiskers in order to conceal his grin when she'd admitted that the average female posterior (due, she'd said, to the child-bearing hip spread) needed fifteen millimetres more than the average male.

That day, Max reckoned, he'd learned enough about furniture design to write a book.

Now, beside Gina in the Los Angeles showroom, he realized there were still a few chapters to complete.

'Wardrobes,' Gina declared opening the door of a rosewood cabinet, 'must have ample internal space.' She speedily aligned her tape measure side-to-side, up-and-down (rather, thought Max, like an efficient undertaker) before approving. 'Excellent. See, the hanging rail has over 100 millimetres clearance from the top, and the drop below it is almost two-and-three-quarter metres – sufficient to hang the longest fur coat. The depth from back to front is 550 millimetres, adequate to prevent shoulder-rub.'

Closing the door she said, 'The average rail space for each garment should be eighty millimetres. Short-stay guests – those booked in for no more than a night or two – generally carry six hanging garments. So for them this wardrobe,' she tapped the model she'd measured, 'would be fine. Long-stay guests, of course, need extra width – one-and-a-quarter metres in a single room, not much less than two metres in a double. Naturally, in the double the hanging space must be divided by a partition to separate the woman's and man's clothes.' To the mystification in Max's eyes she explained, 'To prevent the transference of perfume and heavy tobacco odours.'

Max nodded sagely. He considered suggesting that in a few rooms such niceties could be omitted for those wardrobe-sharing couples both of whom smoked and/or wore scent, but decided that when Gina had her hat set at this magisterial angle, such frivolities were best left unvoiced.

They moved on to dressing-tables.

Gina tugged a drawer, peered in, muttered something about, 'No proper dovetails. Fall apart in a week,' and dismissed the piece without further inspection.

At the next example however, she murmured satisfaction. 'Almost two-and-a-half square metres of drawer bottoms. More than enough for a long-stay double room. Deep drawers, and one extra-deep for woollies. And this shallow one for cosmetics.' Sliding it open she exclaimed, 'Excellent! They've lined it with that new-fangled thin plastic, much more effective, and neater, for protecting against spilled nail lacquer than the rubber mats or pieces of Rexine we used to use in the good old bad old days at the Howard West.'

Scribbling frequently in her notebook she progressed amongst the ranks of merchandise samples like a general inspecting troops, Max half a pace to the rear, hands behind his back, pausing to observe each time Gina made an examination, wincing and smiling palely in the direction of the patient showroom manager as she prodded and probed, pulled and pushed, lifted and dropped to test what she termed the Guest Assault Resilience of every potential purchase.

The big man was greatly relieved when they eventually exited beneath the CABINET FURNITURE sign and headed toward CARPETS & DRAPES.

That was before they detoured into BEDS.

'Oh, please, Max. Good heavens, anyone would think I was asking you to put on your nightshirt! All you have to do is lie on the thing. Nobody's watching. Those half-dozen customers aren't going to stop and stare. Well, I'll stand so that you're part-hidden. Please? I'll be truly grateful. Will you slip your shoes off? There isn't a hole in your sock, is there? I'll hold your jacket. Now, full length. A bit nearer the middle of the mattress. Could you be a touch less rigid? You're supposed to be asleep, not dead. Lovely. How's it feel? Level and firm? And warm to your back? Reflected body heat from the layer of fleece wool between the springs and the cotton ticking. It's an expensive addition but if guests are snug in bed they don't notice when the central heating is turned lower in the middle of the night. Bounce, *per favore*.'

'Bounce, as in up and down.

'I'm sure you can do better than that. Put a bit of passion into it. Yes, passion. That is what hotel beds, nine nights out of ten, are used for. We have to be sure the frame won't disintegrate under the rigours of vacation lust, and that the springs won't howl and keep the folks in the next room awake – or make them envious. There's no point in turning red around the gills. Once you're a hotelier you'll learn a lot more about human appetites than you ever did as a restaurateur.

'Yes, this model seems fine. Comfortable and tough enough for whatever goes on on top of it, with a clearance from the floor of 250 millimetres so a chambermaid can clean easily underneath it. Thank you, old friend. You really were a terrific help. I don't know what I'd do without you.'

The other customers waved goodbye.

Thereafter, through the purchasing of drapes, rugs, sheets, pillowcases and towels, the anthropometric or whatever other data guided Gina's decisions, largely passed Max by. She continued to seek his opinion, however, plus, whenever necessary, his further practical assistance. Thus, that evening after dinner and inventory review when she mentioned that tomorrow they'd visit the bathroom equipment showrooms, he suffered a sudden burst of coughing then said that he had an unbreakable appointment with the man who made roulette wheels.

It took four days to finalize all their orders. Long enough, they agreed, to spend in this town where there was nothing to do during the day except sit in the sun, and nothing to do in the evening except watch movie stars eat. On their last day they took time to visit a contracted franchisee whose Rossi Tavern was to be sited on Sunset Boulevard. They spent a pleasant afternoon at his home overlooking the Pacific. In the limousine on the way back to the hotel Gina remarked to Max, 'I reckon his restaurant will become Los Angeles' biggest tourist attraction. At the moment this town might be a great stomping ground for the well-heeled, but it has precious little to offer ordinary folk except the beach, bus-rides round Beverly Hills, and very bizarre architecture.'

They drove on amid the mishmash of stuccoed, Spanish-style houses, cathedral-like movie theatres, concrete apartment blocks and varicoloured office towers.

As they motored along a shabby downtown street, Gina cried suddenly, 'Hold it,' and as the startled driver jerked to a halt she swung open the door, swiftly exited and strode across the sidewalk and into the pawn shop. Minutes later she reappeared toting a three-foot, lumpy, brown paper-wrapped package. Climbing back into the cab she sat her purchase beside her, said to the driver, 'Thank you. Go ahead now, please.'

At the hotel she untied string, peeled away the wrapping and the underlayer of newspaper to reveal her impulse buy.

Max exclaimed, '*Che cosa* . . . What is it?'

'That's Twickenham,' Gina replied happily.

'It looks like a sheep.'

'Actually, it's a sheepdog. An old English sheepdog,' she said patting the head of the full-size, upright sitting, porcelain hound. 'Isn't he gorgeous? Not a chip on him. Genuine Victorian Derbyshire pottery. The twin of one they had at the Rainbow in London. Over sixty-five years old. Just think, Max, of all the firesides he's sat beside. The families who have

442

loved him. The children who have played around his paws. The six thousand miles he's travelled from the place of his birth. And yet he ended up in a junk shop window. How could anyone condemn him to that? How could I leave him there?'

Max regarded the dusty, shaggy, ceramic beast as Gina hugged it, tousled its petrified mane and plonked a lipsticky kiss on its unkempt brow. Frankly, he never had been keen on dogs of the kiln-fired species. In fact, to be honest, he wasn't overfond of the flesh-and-blood variety, always had considered the British obsession with them somewhat eccentric if not downright insanitary. Thus, this glazed canine (which Gina now was towelling vigorously as if it just had emerged from the hotel pool) stood scant chance of being invited to share his hearth. He muttered, 'A bit of a scruffy animal.'

'Don't be so hurtful. Dogs know when they're disliked. Look, he's polished up a treat.'

'Yes, well . . . So long as he's what you want, Principessa.' Maybe he should be grateful that it was at least a docile breed and not one of those small but ferocious creatures which some women toted around like hirsute, beribboned handbags and which were the *bête noire* of all waiters, many of whom bore the scars of their encounters with those Lilliputian monsters. 'I'm sure,' he offered, 'it will look fine in your sitting-room.'

'No, he won't be living with me,' replied Gina. 'He'll reside in a place of honour in the Silver Lady's lobby. That's when he isn't working, of course.'

'Working?'

'Twickenham is to be our fourteenth diner.'

'*Che?*'

'As a gambler, Max, you're more aware than most of folks' superstition over the figure thirteen. You know it's only once in a blue moon we get that number sitting together at the Lady. They'd snub their best friends or invite their worst enemy just to ensure they had one less or one more person at the table. I've never bothered to do anything about it in Manhattan because it's never been our policy to indulge in gimmicks. Vegas will be a different kettle of fish, however. It's a place that's going to be wrapped up in stunts and show-stoppers. So, whenever any guests at the Silver Lady are faced with the dinner party dilemma of thirteen guests, Twickenham, complete with place-setting and napkin, will attend as the fourteenth diner. You'll see, when word gets out, customers will be standing in line in bakers' dozens just to have him at the head of their table.'

Gina hugged her new recruit. What she didn't confess to Max was that she'd filched the entire idea from London's Savoy. David Lowell had told her about the famous English hotel's tradition that day he'd taken her to lunch there. The Savoy's black cat Kaspar, he'd explained, spent most of his time in the Pinafore Room. On those occasions, however, when a dinner party of thirteen was unavoidable, he was brought forth to perform the luck-ensuring duty which at the Silver Lady would be emulated by Twickenham. The only difference between the two animals was that whereas Twickenham was cast from porcelain, Kaspar was carved from wood.

Max, though still unable to warm to the pet pooch, conceded, 'It's a good idea, Principessa. All our customers will be gamblers, characters who'd hike a hundred miles out of their way to avoid walking under a ladder. They'll appreciate our concern. But . . . ' Surveying the outsize talisman, he frowned. 'What is a Twickenham?'

Gina grinned. 'Old friend, you obviously are not a devotee of English rugby football.'

32

Her regret was that she was unable to bring Twickenham to New York; but, rather than risk him arriving in several pieces from a trip which wasn't strictly necessary, she had him securely cartoned and stored in a Los Angeles depository to await commencement of his duties at the Silver Lady.

A pity, Gina mused, because Fallon would love him, would be delighted with his name which had popped into Gina's head the instant she saw him in the pawn shop window. It would have been a talking point to re-draw them together, to halt their slow drift apart. Because something had to be done, for sure. It was now or never. That was the truth, the dark blemish on Gina's otherwise glowing existence.

These were the clouded thoughts she brought back from the

sunshine of the west coast; along with a growing sense of resentment. She couldn't deny it. She was becoming increasingly irritated by her own inability to stabilize her relationship with Fallon, as well as with his lack of attempt to communicate. The more she pondered it, the more piqued she became. I will not let it get to me, she vowed as she rode in the elevator to her Van Clare Mansions apartment, determined that the air of foreboding which had beset her the minute she'd left Los Angeles would not darken her homecoming.

She'd cabled ahead, asked Fallon to meet her here for dinner. Just the two of us, she'd told herself, the phone off the hook, the porter instructed to admit no one. Tonight I will remind him of how it used to be with us, I'll see that we both turn over a new leaf, make a mutual resolution to take time out, at least twice a week, and sit quietly and talk. That isn't too much to ask, is it?

The apartment looked lovely. May Ling, following Gina's phone call last night, had given the place an extra-special polish and filled all the vases and bowls with fresh flowers before taking the evening off. She'd also, Gina was glad to see as she entered the kitchen, purchased, as instructed, the ingredients for dinner, left them on the table – beside a brown paper parcel.

Gina, frowning at this, reached out.

As soon as she lifted it she recognized it. A tremor of excitement shook her as she impatiently tugged at the knotted string, pulled away the wrapping.

There it was.

She held it before her at arm's length. Stared at the photograph of herself beneath the pink-scripted, 'The Lady's' – the same style as the now-famous logo on her restaurant's marquee – followed by, in slim tan capitals, 'COOKBOOK'.

Beautiful. That was the word which sprang into her head. Gina couldn't resist the description, couldn't subdue the flush of pride which made her face quite hot. Though she'd already seen proofs of the book's jacket and contents, the pins-and-needles thrill of this moment was undiminished. The sight, the feel, even the smell – she held it to her face, breathed the scents of fresh paper and ink – of the actual volume, filled her with . . . elation. Certainly. No point in mincing words, pretending she wasn't internally jumping with joy. Look at it! Just look at it! My own book! She hadn't felt so undeniably pleased with

445

herself since she'd read her name on the deeds of sale of the Forty-Seventh Street premises. She stood the book upright on the table. Said, 'Hello,' to it. Winked at it. Walked around it. Lifted it and took it through to the sitting-room, sat on the sofa with it and minutely read every word for the next hour. Not until she realized that the room had grown dim did she jump up and exclaim:

'Good heavens! Dinner!'

She dashed for the kitchen, the cookbook still in her hands. What to do with it? How to surprise Fallon with it? For that is what she would do? Won't he be amazed? This will be what brings us back together; better even than Twickenham. But I can't just stick it under his nose the second he walks in. I have to be sure the moment is right. Gina studied on that awhile before taking the book to the office/library, leaving it on her desk. First things first. Cook, or he'll arrive to no food and all he'll do with your tome is bop you over the head with it.

For the next hour she moved swiftly and efficiently. Ham was put in to roast; *fiorentina* sauce was prepared with tomatoes, olive oil, herbs and a not ungenerous quantity of Soave; the dining-table was set; a bottle of Chianti uncorked. When all safely was under way, Gina proceeded to preparing herself. Simple apricot blouse, toning hostess pants, pearl earrings, a matching choker. Hair brushed up and secured with two tortoiseshell combs. Elegant, if not fashionable. Simple, like her outfit, like the meal. That's the way it must be tonight.

He will show up, won't he?

Seven-thirty a key rattling in the lock. He entered, toting his battered old briefcase, halted two paces into the room, surveying the plush expanse as if for the first time.

'Hey,' greeted Gina, rising from an armchair where she had placed herself three seconds ago, affecting an air of casualness which matched the subdued lighting and misty music from the radio. 'Had a good day?' She kissed him, reached for the briefcase. 'I'll take that.'

'No. A couple of notes I have to complete. I'll use the office. About thirty minutes.' He started across the room.

Work as usual! Gina's dander rose.

Fallon paused, sniffed the air. 'Dinner smells good. I'll try not to be too long.' He smiled and went out.

That damn smile! He could do it to her every time, make her

feel like there were butterflies in her stomach and bees in her head. Her momentary annoyance had melted. Everything was going to be fine. She walked slowly across the room to where the warm, fresh evening air wafted into the apartment. She stood awhile at the open window as the breeze stirred the drapes, listened to the music of the city. The aroma of the tomato sauce drifted from the kitchen, mingled with the scent of automobile fumes and the Chanel Number 5 she had touched to her neck. Gina absorbed these familiar pleasures.

Returning to the sofa and its side table of magazines, she reached for a copy of *Billboard*.

Tony Nevada's record which had leapt to number eight in the magazine's chart, was reviewed by a critic whose omnipotent word could mean life or death in the fickle entertainment industry. The writer said the record was the best thing he'd heard in a month of Sundays and added that having seen the singer in the flesh he could guarantee that pretty soon there would be a bevy of movie moguls beating on Nevada's door.

Gina didn't doubt it. She'd set her own brief encounter with the singer aside, and figured he had too. After that evening in her bedroom he had rarely spoken to her again, but when on those occasions they inevitably did meet at the Lady, while his attitude was cool, it was not belligerent.

What continued to trouble Gina, however, was Cassie's relationship with Tony Nevada. The redhead was becoming more involved with each passing week. She had long since moved into his apartment, spent every available moment with him, ran around after him like a . . . a slave. That was the word Gina came up with. And it wasn't an exaggeration. Cassie fawned on her young lover to the point of patheticness, mixing his drinks, toting his coat to the cloakroom, carrying his music sheets. Once, Gina had plucked up the courage to josh lightly, 'Cass, don't you think he's strong enough to hang up his own hat?' She'd regretted it ever since. Her friend had turned on her with blazing eyes and in a whiplash voice had retaliated, 'Take care of your own business. And your own man.' Gina had never heard such venom in Cassie in all their years together. The following day she'd sought reconciliation by recounting to the redhead a joke she'd heard in the kitchen. When Cassie had summoned a faint smile, Gina put the previous day's outburst down to simple female possessiveness.

Still, as she now laid aside the copy of *Billboard*, the sense of unease over Cassie's involvement with Tony Nevada strengthened its presence.

She walked to the table, lit the candles.

Fallon came in twenty minutes later, paused in the amber glow and murmured, 'Special occasion?'

'It always is when you're around.' Gina went to him and kissed him. Stepping back she said, 'Bet you can't remember when we last ate roast ham with *fiorentina* sauce.'

He frowned, shook his head.

She prodded him in the ribs and chided, 'You'll never be a romantic novelist.' That was a foolish slip and she hurried on, 'It was about a hundred years ago. In an apartment – flat – beneath St Paul's Cathedral. There was snow on the window and choristers on the radio. You'd just finished a piece you were writing about post-war London, and I'd just finished having a bit of a turn – as they say down the Old Kent Road.' As remembrance unfurrowed his brow, Gina bantered, 'So the old bear does still have a soul.' Bad English grammar. Remind me of it, Fallon. Then I can tell you not to be so pedantic. The way we used to. Have you forgotten that too? She widened her eyes, said throatily, 'And you know what we did after that dinner, don't you?' She seized his hand, tugged him to the table. 'So let's get a move on.'

For the next few minutes she busied in and out, hurriedly bringing in salad and rolls while Fallon poured the wine, sat with his fists around his glass staring down the room to the glittering towers across and beyond Park Avenue. She tossed him several quips during her to-ing and fro-ing, to which he replied, 'Uh huh,' a few times before lapsing back into preoccupied silence.

Gina paused in the kitchen with the steaming ham on a silver platter. I could serve my book alongside the meat. Proclaim, 'Main course, plus instruction manual.' That might snap him away from wherever he is. Also, while he examines the book, the ham will go cold. Scrap that idea. Get the dinner under way and out of the way.

When eventually they were facing each other across their plates, Gina asked, smiling, 'So, how goes it, Doc?'

Fallon pursed his lips, seemed to be considering his answer, then, as if deciding to shelve his initial response, he replied, 'I'm still working on the Korean piece.' To Gina's relief he opened up a mite then, told her about the increasing rift in that East Asian country, that despite United States Foreign Office efforts there was an increasing possibility of the north and the south establishing separate regimes, which, Fallon said, would be economic suicide as all the regions within Korea were industrially and agriculturally interdependent. Gina didn't understand a lot of this – in fact, to be honest, she wasn't quite sure where she'd find the far-off land on the globe – nevertheless, she uttered what she hoped were intelligent noises, nodded a great deal and made a real effort not merely to appear interested but to raise a genuine concern for Fallon's discourse. I will not, she mentally affirmed, think of anything whatsoever to do with business.

She held that resolve through the meal.

When Fallon finally pushed aside his cleared plate with a satisfied grunt, Gina acknowledged, 'Thank you. It's good to be appreciated. We must do this more often.'

A flicker crossed Fallon's eyes.

Gina told herself she hadn't seen it.

She went to the kitchen, made fresh coffee. Returning to the sitting-room she found Fallon had moved to the sofa, was sitting, elbows on his knees, staring into the flower-filled fireplace. She poured coffee into large cups, placed them on the low jade-topped table, then sat beside him. Reaching to her side she switched off the floor lamps leaving the room in the flickering glow of the candles and the dark blue of the New York night.

Fallon said, 'Now I can't see how beautiful you are.'

It took Gina by surprise. Searching hurriedly for a reply she arrived at, 'Now you can't see how old I am.'

'Thirty-two. An ancient lady.'

'Sometimes I feel it. Sometimes I feel I've lived two lifetimes since the day Poppa was arrested.'

'You have. But, then, so have a lot of others, the ones who survived the past dozen years.' Fallon ran his hand through his tumbling hair, a gesture Gina hadn't seen in a long time. 'Yet, you know,' he went on, staring ahead, 'already there are some youngsters who don't understand what happened. Sure, so soon. The other day, a kid came to work at our New York office. Fresh out of college. He'd spent a few months with some so-called intellectuals in a loft in the Village; had had a couple of walk-on roles at a so-called experimental theatre; probably had smoked a reefer, once; and probably had been to bed with at least one girl. This kid was introduced to Ben Ryan, an old hound-dog newspaperman from London. He told Ben he'd done more in the four years since he'd left high school than Ben had done in his whole life. Ben looked at him awhile, then walked away. What Ben didn't tell the kid about was the bullet wound through his shoulder put there by one of Franco's soldiers, or the dent in his skull inflicted by a Mosley Fascist, or the scars nobody can see gathered during two years in a Japanese prisoner-of-war camp. But Ben should have told him. Because two decades from now that kid could be running for the Senate, and he'll still think the Battle of Britain took place in a movie.' Fallon looked levelly at Gina. 'Do you see?'

Yes, she thought, I see. Of course I do. I know it's important. But so is our life together.

Fallon said, 'Somebody has to tell it, Gina.'

'You don't have to do it single-handed.'

'Have you listened to one word I just said?'

'Don't be so sharp. Please, Fallon, don't let's argue. We must not argue tonight.' Gina reached for his hand, held it, said quietly, 'Can we just sit awhile? No more talk for now.'

'I have some calls to make.'

'Can't they wait?'

'They're important.'

'As always.'

Fallon pulled his hand away. Standing, he strode to the sideboard where he'd left his briefcase. Pulling out papers, he said, 'I don't want to argue, Gina.'

She gave a short, sharp laugh – couldn't help it. Gina couldn't help the frustration which was claiming her. Why was this happening? She loved Robert Fallon, this man before her. Damn it, yes, loved him! Had loved him from the instant she set eyes on him in Ristorante Rossi. And he loved her. He'd said so in England. And his feelings hadn't lessened; Gina was sure of it. Then what in God's name had gone wrong? Had they both changed so much that the gulf between them, despite their love, was now unbridgeable? Or, if she dared to delve the truth of it, would she have to admit that Fallon was as he always had been, and that it was only she who had altered?

The question stung her.

She offered with brittle brightness, 'Hey, I'm sorry. I understand about Ben Ryan. Go ahead make your calls. I'll go get some crackers and cheese and another bottle of Chianti. We'll take them through to the bedroom. How about that?'

He glanced around. Briefly, there was a trapped look on his face; then shaking his head, he answered, 'No, not tonight. After I make my calls, I have to go out. People to interview.' He scanned his papers, began to pen notes.

Gina clenched her fists. She teetered between anger and self-pity. Certainly, self-pity. Please, she wanted to beg. Please stay. If you don't stay tonight this will be our last time together. She knew that as surely as she knew the sun would rise tomorrow. Damn it, Fallon! she railed mentally, put down the bloody papers, turn and look at me, before it's too late, before you tear us apart. She said flatly, 'Will you be late back?'

He snapped shut the case. 'I guess so. Yes. You know I can't rush these things. If my interviewees get to opening up . . .' He shrugged, stood staring at Gina. She thought the very air ached between them. Then he questioned, 'Okay if I use the phone?'

'Since when did you have to ask?' Gina rose, walked out to the kitchen. She lifted the half-full bottle of Soave she'd used for the sauce, tipped a hefty measure into a tumbler and drank. She stood at the window and looked down to the evening crowds and traffic. So many people hurrying their lives along. She drank some more. Alone. The way she had all the years before Fallon. And what was so bad about that? 'Answer me that,' she said aloud and carried the wine along the hall to the office/library.

At her desk she listened to Fallon making calls in the sitting-room. He spoke to several people, setting up appointments for tomorrow. No, she heard him say, there was no problem about evening interviews, he could meet any time. When he was through he came into the office wearing his trenchcoat. He said he'd be back by one a.m., but not to wait up for him.

Gina nodded woodenly.

It was then he saw the cookbook.

At first he just glanced at it, then away, beginning to turn toward the door, and it was a second before what he might have seen registered across his face. He jerked back, reached down to twist the book around so that he was staring directly at it.

Gina was frozen. She'd completely forgotten the copy was

451

there. If a moment ago she hadn't been blinded by dejection she'd have buried it deep from sight; for what earlier had been the thing of promise which she'd thought would bring her and Fallon together, she now knew to be the deadly object that at this instant was blasting them apart. That there was no explosion, no sound and fury, was irrelevant. In the towering silence the waves of destruction pounded over her as tangibly as physical blows. She groped for something to say, some shred of mitigation. There was nothing, no defence.

Fallon said 'Congratulations.' Though his face remained expressionless, his voice had a cracked, strained note.

Gina murmured, 'Thanks. I was going to . . . ' Her explanation trailed away as he opened the cover, scanned the title page, the copyright page, riffled through the remainder.

Closing it, he said, 'It's very . . . attractive.'

Gina flinched. She shrugged. 'It was Dorothy Hamm. Her idea. For me to write a book.' That was the worst thing she could have said. She knew it. As Fallon turned on her, though he didn't speak she saw the words in his eyes: That isn't a book. *The Great Gatsby* is a book. *Huckleberry Finn* is a book. *Sons and Lovers* is a book. What an author sweats and suffers and agonizes over is a book. What I've been trying to tear out of myself for the past ten years is a book.

He said without rancour, 'I hope it's a bestseller. I'm sure it will be.' The trapped pain on his face was all that remained between them. He glanced at his watch. 'You can tell me about it tomorrow.' His brief smile sent darts of agony into Gina's chest. She whispered, 'Sure,' looked down at her ledgers. She didn't watch him leave, just heard the door close. When she looked up the room was hazed by moisture.

Rising slowly, she took a shuddering breath, walked to the door, opened it and looked along the empty hall. 'Now I can't see how beautiful you are.' The words echoed back at Gina. She gripped the jamb, closing her fingers until her knuckles were white. The impulse to scream towered within her as her emotions were stretched on the rack of despair – and anger. A mounting anger, made the more unbearable because it had no direction. Gina's soul cried out for someone at whom to hurl her bitter fury.

She slammed the door with all her might, causing pictures and plaques to jump and one of the wall lights to blink out. 'Damn! Damn! Damn it all to hell!' she snarled and stormed to her desk, to the cookbook, and the telephone, and her adding machine, and her ledgers and notebooks, plans, specifications, tax forms, inventories, bank statements, franchise applications, all the building blocks of her life, and with one long, torment-driven sweep of her arm she sent it crashing to the floor. It lay, a shambles at her feet, and in a final spasm of virulence she stamped on the cookbook, ground and kicked her heel into its jacket, obliterating the image of herself there, tearing it to shreds before running to her bedroom, throwing herself onto the bed, beating her fists into the pillow until her arms collapsed. Then, her strength and her outrage drained, she sagged under a flood of self-pity and sobbed into the sheets.

She was oblivious to an hour's passing.

It was May Ling's knock on the doorjamb which finally pulled her to a sitting position. 'Miss Gina?' The Chinese girl hesitated on the threshold. 'You sick? You want I call doctor?'

Gina dragged in an anguish-riven breath, rebuked herself for leaving the door open, though, she guessed gratefully, from May Ling's attitude it was apparent she hadn't seen the destruction in the office. She swiftly swaled her palms across her wet cheeks, stood and answered, 'No, of course not.' She knew her voice was too sharp but had no wish to prolong the girl's presence. 'Thank you. That will be all. Goodnight.'

May Ling stared at her a second before replying, 'Goodnight, Miss Gina,' and retreating.

Gina waited until she heard May Ling's shower running then she returned to the office and carefully began to gather her scattered possessions. She set the telephone and adding machine in their places, squared and stacked her papers, repositioned her ledgers and notebooks. When she was finished all was as before save the cookbook lying on the floor in its shredded jacket. Gina lifted it. After removing the jacket, crumpling it and dropping it in the wastebasket, she laid the book on the desk.

Stepping back, she surveyed the scene. Nothing had happened here. She was once more in control.

But the nightmare was back.

Gina's own cry woke her. She sat bolt upright, fingers taloned into the sheets, shaking uncontrollably, sweat drenching her nightdress, soaking the bed around her. On that brink between sleep and consciousness she stared into the blackness still seeing the demons of dream. Ugo Balbo's features were as real as if he were standing in the room, yet they were hugely distorted, gross to the point of obscenity, leering over the mutilated corpse of Alfredo Rossi which was lying in the aisle of a packed restaurant where Robert Fallon was talking heatedly to a group of men without faces. Gina called out to Fallon, but no sound came from her throat; she knew she must scream, must make him hear, but she could not, she was helpless, paralysed in the centre of the room where Balbo was gathering money from the customers as they filed out over her father's body.

Gina blew out her breath, sucked deeply, concentrated on stilling the terrible trembling.

It was moments before she gathered some semblance of composure and was able to switch on the light. The room was normal; no phantoms; no smell of putrefaction which a second ago had been acrid in her nostrils. She swung her feet to the floor, sat on the edge of the bed and pulled on her négligé. She was shivering, but not now from the nightmare; her sweat had chilled, was clinging clammily to her body. Standing, she crossed to the wardrobe, unhooked her camel-hair overcoat, hung it around her shoulders, went barefoot into the sitting-room switching on all the lights. The remnants of her dinner with Fallon were on the table.

She walked through to her office, found the unfinished tumbler of soave on her desk, emptied it in one long swallow. Had May Ling heard her cry? No sound came from the girl's room.

Gina sat at her desk. Gripping the oak arms of her chair she drew reassurance from the hard familiarity of them. Relief came slowly. She was all right now – so she told herself. But there, in that chill time of dead silence between night and morning, the metamorphosis that had begun to overtake Gina Rossi that day she returned with Max from their first trip to Las Vegas, caught up with her now. Simultaneously, the desire to exact retribution for all her pains – real and imaginary, justified and self-inflicted – hardened within her, calcified to the irrepressible physical need to strike at something. At someone.

She realized that Fallon hadn't returned. But wasn't surprised. Nor was she surprised when he came into The Lady at noon the next day to say he'd collected his suitcase from the apartment and was flying to Washington, didn't know when he'd be back. Gina told him, 'Fine, have a good trip, I'm busy right now,' and she left him saying his farewells to Max.

The following evening Gina threw a party at the Park Lane apartment. It was a tinselled affair where everyone laughed a lot and drank a lot and toasted Gina a lot and told her she was wonderful and talented and beautiful. She swanned amid the revellers and the freeloaders and the gate-crashers in white silk and diamonds, returning their glib charm, their bland intimacy, their synthetic flattery. It was the sort of party where a paragon from City Hall thought it great fun to spill ice down the front of a blonde starlet's dress; where a matinée idol told dirty jokes all night; where a football hero punched his boyfriend in the eye; where a leading lady of the theatre was sick on the kitchen floor; where somebody smashed a Venetian crystal vase and hid the remains behind the lavatory; where someone else left a burning cigar on the antique English lace bedspread; where a racing driver slid his hands over Gina's bottom and told her he liked to live dangerously. It was the sort of party which Harry and Max, had they been invited, would have left after fifteen minutes. It was the sort of party which Gina had never held before and would never hold again. It was the party from which she woke the following day beside a man she scarcely knew, cold and empty and haggard, neither wiser nor better, but with a reborn resolve which had been seeded within her eleven years ago, had swelled momentarily one nightmare night in Rome, and had lain dormant, but waiting, ever since. It was the party after which she devised her plan of revenge against Ugo Balbo.

33

That September was a crowded month for New York. Follow-the Feast of San Gennaro in Little Italy came the Hungarian Grape Festival in Queens' Bohemian Park. The Aqueduct

Race Meet opened, and the National Radio Exposition was held. There were record throngs at the Coney Island Mardi Gras, the highest-ever number of entries for the Washington Square Art Exhibition. Also jammed into the calendar were the Dahlia Show, the N.Y. Athletic Club Games, the American Ballads Contest, the Model Yacht Regatta, the Roosevelt Raceway Auto Event, and the Ice Follies extravaganza at Madison Square Garden.

None of these attracted the same amount of publicity as the grand opening of the country's first Rossi Tavern.

At seven p.m. on 1st October the sky above the city was a darkening blue, shot with gold in the west, touched by stars in the east. It was breezeless and warm. Someone remarked that Gina Rossi had paid for it to be this way.

She'd certainly pumped enough money into every other aspect of the event to ensure success. There'd been full-page advertisements in all the local daily papers as well as many of the out-of-town weeklies. There'd been a series of sponsored radio shows, billboards, movie-house commercials. Ten thousand balloons tagged with vouchers for a free bottle of wine had been released in Central Park. Five hundred young men dressed as gondoliers had distributed one million leaflets. And signed pre-publication copies of *The Lady's Cookbook* had been promised to twenty lucky diners every night for the tavern's first thirty nights.

All this, of course, was utterly out of proportion to the required response. This was more than sufficient to cause chaos in Columbus Circle. Which it did.

Beneath the darkening blue sky, police – reinforced from ten other precincts – strained to hold back a multitude which not only jammed the sidewalk in front of the restaurant, but also packed the street and the island around Columbus's column. 'But why,' asked a bemused Max watching from an upper floor window, 'did they come? What did they expect to see?' Gina answered flatly, 'They don't know. They're like sheep; they'll congregate wherever they're told, so long as you shout at them loudly enough.' She turned and walked away, oblivious to the shock and hurt in Max's eyes.

But, then, for the past month she'd been oblivious to everything save her mission. While Ethel Ponti, the Rossi Taverns staff, and the company's promotional consultants concentrated their efforts on spending the massive publicity budget in

New York, Gina personally made sure that it bought an equal amount of press coverage on the other side of the Atlantic Ocean. Every move she made, every cent she invested, she reported to the Italian news agencies. She was Contessa Ginessa Rossi di Savoia. She was the most successful female businesswoman in America. She airmailed copies of thousands of her press clippings to prove it. She sent photographs of herself. She sent a life story that was half-fiction, half-fact. She telephoned every major publication in Italy and gave them a personal interview. She told them about her fame, about franchises, about Rossi Taverns. She told them she intended to extent her empire into Europe, commencing with her homeland. She told them she would arrive in Rome next month.

At seven-thirty p.m. on 1st October, the mayor of New York cut a gold ribbon across the threshold of the Columbus Circle Rossi Tavern, went in with Gina Rossi, Ethel Ponti and half-a-dozen VIPs to the lobby which was a Venetian quay, across an arching footbridge above a canal, through the applauding celebrity guests in the restaurant which was a beamed and tapestried trattoria, to the table of honour on a terrace where live birds hung in real trees beneath a ceiling which was a star-studded Italian sky.

Gina said, 'Please excuse me for a few moments.'

She returned to the lobby.

She spoke with the Chief of Police, who had stopped to receive a crowd-control report before taking his place at the top table. He told her the throng was beginning to disperse; it had been estimated at six thousand; over a hundred people had fainted in the crush, none had been hurt seriously; traffic had been at a standstill for two hours; several store windows had been smashed; ten automobile roofs had caved in under the weight of overzealous spectators; one of the bronze ships' prows on the Columbus column had been severely damaged.

Gina thanked the Chief for the wonderful support of his men, assured him her company's insurances would meet the cost of all private and civil repair. She then went to the tavern's small office, used the telephone to ensure that the overseas wire services had all this information.

When she returned toward the celebrations she saw that Mrs Ponti was being toasted by the VIPs. She paused in her approach to the table. This was Ethel's moment, Gina would not diminish it. The impersonal determination which had gripped her these past weeks temporarily relaxed as she affectionately watched her old friend, landlady and first tavern-keeper enjoy her much-deserved place in the spotlight.

Only later, in the solitude of her bed, did she rekindle the cold flame of her intolerance.

There wasn't a news reporter in Italy who didn't liken Contessa Rossi di Savoia's arrival in Rome to the entry of Cleopatra into the city two thousand years earlier. The event had been anticipated by every citizen for thirty days – since Gina had commenced her unremitting transmission of Rossi Corporation propaganda across the Atlantic. No one was disappointed.

That ninety-nine per cent of what was written was fiction was a vindication of Gina's faith in the power of her self-promotion. As she'd averred to Max in the earliest days of publicizing the Lady, 'Shout something loudly enough and often enough, and not only will the majority of listeners believe it, they also will embellish it with their own wishful thinking.' Thus, while Rome's populace's imagination saw her procession from the airport to Via Veneto as a train of white and mauve Cadillac limousines laden with mountains of baggage and a vast entourage, in reality, having pre-arranged for four burly bodyguards to hurry her through the press army encamped beyond the customs hall, she arrived alone at the hotel in a shiningly new but inconspicuous black Fiat.

She wore an oyster silk coat with matching full-veiled hat which, though unostentatious, was sufficiently chic to draw gasps in the lobby from an audience starved of elegance and glamour through two decades of Fascist starkness plus two years of post-war austerity.

'Contessa. Welcome, welcome,' effused the director-general of the Palazzo d'Oro, bowing with copious courtesy as Gina approached him across the marbled and pillared grandeur, between the crowds of displaced royalty, forgotten movie stars, self-proclaimed literati, all those jostling to be seen as much as to see as this favourite of the gods whose American legend had been told during the past month by every magazine and newspaper in the country, was pursued by a barrage of camera flashes and bombardment of questions.

'Thank you, Signor Piranesi,' responded Gina, striding

beside the man as he led the way to the bronze doors of an elevator all the time emphasizing his great honour at receiving such a guest and assuring her of his personal attention twenty-four hours a day.

The silver speech continued all the way to the suite with its gilt and brocaded furnishings, frescoed walls, crystal chandeliers and balconied windows overlooking Via Veneto. It went on while the luggage was stowed, a champagne bottle was uncorked and set in an ice bucket, and it was relayed that the press reporters had retreated to file their stories for the evening editions. At last the director-general backed out of the suite.

Gina was alone.

She removed her coat, gloves and hat, went and sat in a chair. She had firmly instructed that she was not to be disturbed. She now needed this time to prepare herself for the confrontation ahead, the meeting which was the true purpose of this visit.

'Rome?' Max had queried. 'A vacation?'

'And an exploration,' Gina had replied. 'Into the prospects for Rossi Taverns in Italy.' She'd known this difficult question would arise, that for the first time in her life she would lie to her friends. Part-lie, that is, for, as she'd explained at the board meeting, appraisal of Europe's potential was essential to counter any expansion plans of competitor companies. And, she'd decided, she would take the opportunity to make such preliminary investigations of the Italian catering industry. That, however, would be after she had pursued her prime objective.

From the moment she had woken from the nightmare following her break with Fallon, Gina had tracked with unswerving single-mindedness her route toward revenge on Ugo Balbo, had held steadfastly to the conviction that his downfall would excise the cancerous core that years ago he had planted in her life. All her efforts of the past weeks to publicize the Rossi Corporation in the Italian press had been aimed exclusively at this end. Of the millions who read the stories of her huge financial success and her intended investment in this country, she was interested in only one. Balbo was the sole target for the tales of riches. He alone was marked for her web.

In the Palazzo d'Oro suite she waited. She didn't touch the champagne. Later she requested a simple meal to be served in her room. The night passed slowly. Her doubts had risen during the dark hours. Would he have delved into the semi-fictional autobiography she'd fed to the press? Would he have investigated her lineage to the House of Savoy? Would he have baulked at the name Rossi?

Gina concentrated on remaining calm, resolved not to lose her nerve, reminded herself of the answers she'd given to those questions when first she'd asked them. Balbo could not have pried into her American background without her knowledge. It would be virtually impossible to disprove her bogus ancestry – tens of thousands of families claimed kinship to the myriad nobility who once ruled the scores of city states which had been welded to form modern Italy. The name Rossi, though not as common as Smith in England and America, certainly filled several columns of telephone directories. There was scant reason for Balbo to connect a New York businesswoman with a Rome man – one of scores of his victims – whose restaurant he had pirated.

Gina clung to these assurances as she waited through the morning of her second day in the city.

It was mid-afternoon, the November sun's warmth concentrated through the hotel's windows, when Gina sat on the gilt and satin chair in the suite's sitting-room. The daylight was at her back. Her shadowed face was further concealed by the veiled ivory pillbox hat which matched her diagonally-draped afternoon dress.

To the rap on the door she called, 'Enter.'

She held her emotions together as the gross man lumbered across the room toward her. He was even fatter than when she'd last seen him, at least two-hundred-and-fifty pounds. But although the shirt collar buried beneath the layers of his neck was as sweat-stained as it had ever been, these days it was made of silk; and the crumpled linen suit of his early history had been succeeded by hand-stitched mohair. The war and its aftermath – as Gina's investigations had already proved – had been good for Ugo Balbo.

She remained seated when he halted before her mopping a garish handkerchief around his red jowls, panting as if he'd run all the way here. Gina peered at him, knitting a frown across her brow, questioning, 'Mister . . . ?' and though she regarded him with all the poise and anonymity of a marble statue, her assertion was trembling as she probed his face for the remotest sign of recognition.

'Balbo,' he said. 'Ugo Balbo, Contessa.' An unctuous smile ill-concealed his appraisal of her dress and jewellery. But that was all there was in his searching. When his gaze moved to Gina's face, she knew that he was looking at a stranger.

A small shudder of relief ran through her. Briefly consulting the open diary on the table beside her she said, 'Ah, yes. Balbo. You telephoned . . .'

'Several times since your arrival yesterday,' he interrupted. He glanced toward a nearby sofa, but receiving no invitation, continued, 'When I couldn't bypass your instructions for privacy, I called your American office. They were most abrupt. Yes, Contessa, I must say they were somewhat dismissive. Of course,' he added oilily, 'I do appreciate how busy you must be. I understand what it is to have a pressing schedule. And we in business, we captains of commerce, must protect ourselves from trivial interruptions, from lesser mortals who seek to waste our time. However, if you will permit me to say so, Contessa, perhaps your staff should make themselves more conversant with the names and importance of those who might call. Had they realized who I was, I am certain they would have ensured I was put in touch with you immediately.'

Gina's stare remained unmoved.

The gross man prompted, 'Balbo. I am Ugo Balbo. I am known throughout Italy. Surely . . .'

'Balbo?' frowned Gina. Then: 'Ah, yes, I recall. Signor Balbo. The . . . hotelier.' Though she was striving to maintain the façade, she was unable to keep the edge of sarcasm from her voice. She had known this confrontation would be difficult, had gathered her strength for the moment, but nothing could have prepared her for the way she now felt. All the hate, all the rage, all the blinding desire to kill, towered within her like a living beast, as monstrous now as it had been that night in 1945 when only the hand of fate had prevented her from plunging the dagger into Balbo's chest. She dragged in a ragged breath, held it; and on the brink of the chasm of ferocity, a thin thread of sanity held her from self-destruction.

Balbo said, 'Contessa, are you all right?'

His voice and his unexpected concern dragged Gina back to the moment. She answered assertively, 'Of course. I was pausing for a moment's thought. Signor Balbo, the hotelier.

Yes, my staff have appraised me of your local,' she paused after stressing the word, 'reputation. You own a number of establishments.' Back in control she flipped over the pages of her notebook. 'You cater mainly to the dinner trade, to what we may euphemistically term the middle class.'

Balbo's beady eyes struggled between incomprehension and indignation. Holding on to his bombast he returned, 'We serve only the finest cuisine. Our Italian chefs are the best in the city. Our wines are from the country's leading vineyards. My company has been at the forefront of Rome's catering trade for many years. We were respected by all those who appreciate excellent food and hospitality even during those terrible times – those shaming times – when our beloved homeland suffered beneath Mussolini and his Fascist barbarians. At great personal risk,' he clasped his pudgy hands as if praying for belief, 'I ceaselessly struggled against the tyranny, fought against all those who sought to level us to a nation of mediocrity. Americans, Contessa – if I may be permitted to say – will never know how much citizens like myself had to endure to maintain decency and honour.' Self-righteousness crawled across his features as he awaited Gina's response.

When he realized none was forthcoming, he hurried on, 'Yes, well, however, we must not dwell on the past. The future. That is where we must set our sights. We have to rebuild our country. Restore our people's pride. Also their prosperity. And it is through business we will do it. Through consolidating and expanding our commercial strength. I am sure I speak for all Italians when I say we understand that the route to that success is via co-operation with a great nation like the United States, and, on a personal level,' he oozed obsequiousness, 'with a renowned expert such as yourself.'

Regarding the sweating fat man, Gina swallowed her revulsion. She forced a smile, nodded in acknowledgment of the flattery. 'Am I to take it, Signor Balbo,' she asked, 'that this is the purpose of your interview? You are here to ask me to purchase your business?'

'What? No! You misunderstand. I do not . . .'

'You must appreciate, Signor Balbo, I receive a hundred such offers every day, and I really do not have time at the present,' she glanced at her watch, 'to engage in protracted discussions . . .'

'But I am not here to sell!' blurted Balbo, his jowls quivering with suppressed annoyance. 'Contessa, I have explained my importance. I came here believing I would be treated with courtesy. I am accustomed to respect.'

Unflinching, Gina set her jaw in a hard line. She held Balbo with undisguised disdain. This was the testing moment. If the fat man turned on his heel now she would lose him. She thought fleetingly of Max, wondered what odds he'd lay on this battle of human emotions. Greed versus arrogance was the contest behind Balbo's sweating face. It turmoiled there for several moments before collapsing into a contrite grin as he conceded:

'Of course, Contessa, I realize how you might have misconstrued my intentions. Please forgive my brief sharpness. This heat.' He mopped around his chins.

Gina knew it was the sweat of anticipation.

Balbo went on, 'If I may swiftly explain the purpose of my visit. I do not wish to sell my company. Rather, I wish to discuss a proposition. A partnership. Between yourself, your organization, and my own corporation. Please,' his voice shot up an octave as he saw the dismissal rising in Gina's face. 'Please hear me out. I am sure such a business arrangement could be most beneficial. To us both. Most profitable. And that, after all, is the prime importance, is it not? Our task, our duty – yours and mine – is to run our companies with the greatest efficiency, in order to ensure the greatest profit.'

Gina leaned forward a fraction, toned her response with cautious interest. 'It would seem, Signor Balbo, that you are one of the few people in this city who grasp the economic realities of modern commerce. Money is the only root of success. Money won the war. And it is money which will be the foundation of the future.'

'Quite. Definitely,' agreed the fat man.

'So,' said Gina, 'I am always interested in listening to anyone who is not merely concerned with lining their own pockets, but who also can suggest credible means of increasing the fortunes of the Rossi empire.' She came down heavily on the last word, gave Balbo plenty of opportunity to visualize the riches it suggested. 'A partnership, you said? Between our organizations? Please explain further.'

Balbo seized the opportunity. 'As you know, Contessa, I own the largest chain of restaurants and hotels in Rome. Through my personal skill I have not only opened a score of establishments, but also have taken over fourteen of my competitors' businesses. No one can now stand against me. The only concerns which are not in my control are a few rambling old hotels such as this.' He waved a dismissive arm around the Palazzo d'Oro suite. And they do not trouble me. One day, if I am inclined, I might buy them, modernize them.' He shrugged. 'But until then I have much more important projects to take care of.'

'Like allying yourself to Rossi International.'

'Certainly,' replied Balbo. 'I can assure you you will find no better local partner.'

'Why should I take in a partner at all?'

'For my expertise, of course. There is nothing I do not know about the Italian catering industry. I have investigated the financial strengths, and weaknesses, of the leading concerns in all our major cities. Many are ripe for plucking. Others will fall with little more than a nudge. I had appraised myself of the situation because, even before your arrival in Rome, I was on the verge of a considerable expansion programme. I intended, within six months, to treble my turnover. After which, sweeping up the lesser fry would have been a formality. Then I would have been without equal. And I would have had power. Power over all my suppliers. Those merchants who once dictated price to me would either agree to my terms or go to the wall. Or,' he licked his lips at the mental fantasy, 'I could trawl them into my net. That way I would have total control.' His eyes glinted. 'And that, is it not, is our mutual goal? Aren't you and I on the same road, Contessa? Don't we have the same ambitions?'

Looking into the gloating features, Gina felt sick. Whether this pig could ever make such a dream come true, she wasn't sure. In America he would have stood little chance. But Italy, a country bemused and weakened by war, was still easy prey for him and his kind. Just as it had been eleven years ago, when Alfredo Rossi died because of Balbo's greed.

Her fingernails digging into her palms as she restrained her loathing, Gina said, 'You are requesting a partnership – some form of financial involvement with my company – in return for your expertise.'

Balbo responded, 'I assure you, it would be worth your while. I could guarantee the smooth and successful progress of your operation. I understand not only the vagaries of our

464

country's corporate laws and financial systems, but also the peasant mentality of my countrymen. Many of them are as ignorant and as stubborn as hogs. You and your executives could spend – waste – months in negotiation with them. I, on the other hand, know what will break them down.'

'How to break them down.'

Balbo sneered, 'That too.'

'Then you and I would share the spoils.'

'There is no point in fighting over a pigeon that is big enough for two to pluck.'

'I have never been afraid of a fight.'

'Neither have I,' countered Balbo, adding boastfully, 'Nor have I ever lost one.' He reined his aggression however to say, 'But would a conflict between ourselves be sensible? Worth the effort? Or expense?'

Gina steepled her fingers beneath her chin, said carefully, 'So far, Signor Balbo, I have not divulged to the newspapers the extent of my proposed investment in Italy. As you have raised the subject of expense, and before you commit yourself to involvement with matters which are beyond your means, I think you should understand the financial outlay Rossi International will be making here. The initial amount – and I stress initial – which we have budgeted is one million dollars.' As she watched the words strike home, Balbo shifted from one foot to the other. The sweat was now running in streams down his face. Gina knew the strain of standing was torturing him. She understood too that she had him. The money she had quoted had hit Balbo like a physical blow. He was now prepared to do anything, would remain here on his paining legs all night in order to get his fat hands onto a slice of the gravy-dripping pie she controlled.

He cleared his throat. 'Yes. Of course. A substantial sum. But, I assure you, not one which intimidates me. It is,' he lied, 'no more than I expected. Indeed, I would not have considered involving myself in any lesser project.'

'So you are prepared to match my investment?'

'Pardon?'

'A partnership. Isn't that what we're discussing?'

'Yes. But . . .'

'I see,' shot Gina. 'You had no wish to be an equal share-holder. Then just what did you have in mind, Signor Balbo?' She put a cutting edge on her voice. 'I have given you a considerable amount of my valuable attention. In good faith. You assured me of your commercial standing. Am I now to assume this has all been some sort of hoax on your part? Or I should say, a confidence trick? Did you come here not as an investor, rather as someone looking for a means of quick riches at the expense of an international corporation? No,' she rose abruptly as Balbo began to protest, 'do not bother me further. I have neither the time nor the inclination . . . '

'Certainly I'll match your investment,' he bleated.

She had him. 'In property.'

'Pardon?'

'Our contract will stipulate that your organization is the master franchisee for Rossi Taverns throughout Italy. You will administer and collect the royalties from all sub-franchises. Your organization would thus receive a percentage of all initial franchise fees, plus a share from the annual royalties.' As Gina delivered her pre-prepared speech, Balbo's tormented expression churned amidst shock and uncertainty. He wasn't sure what was happening, yet his greed was blinding him to the abruptness of Gina's declaration. He was nodding though scarcely listening as she fired facts and figures. What did bounce him back to reality was her eventual statment:

'We estimate the master franchisee's annual income will be in excess of two million dollars.'

Balbo audibly hissed.

Gina continued, 'However, any master franchisee will be expected to own all the properties in which Rossi Taverns are located. That will be the purpose of your investment. To secure, with down payments, five hundred properties throughout Italy, so that, when the time comes, all those taverns will open simultaneously. Do you understand, Signor Balbo? Do you appreciate the need for speed, and for utmost secrecy, in this matter?'

Balbo muttered, 'Five hundred properties.'

Gina shrugged. 'Give or take a couple. Can you finance such an operation, Signor Balbo? Do you wish to head Italy's most powerful catering operation?'

The gross man wiped his palms on the sides of his jacket. 'There will be a contract?'

Gina hadn't expected him to be a fool. 'Of course. And as a sign of my good faith a substantial sum will be placed on long-term deposit at the Bank of Rome. Will that be satisfactory? I trust so. If, however, you require time to consider the propo-sals,' she again glanced with overt impatience at her watch, 'then I am prepared to postpone my meetings with the other potential master franchisees.'

'Other . . .'

'You surely won't pretend you thought you would be our only suitor. Since my arrival here I have received at least a hundred proposals of commercial marriage.' (This part, at least, of Gina's story was true. While no one had been able to contact her by phone, written propositions, letters of introduc-tion and engraved invitations had been delivered in a constant stream.) 'You, however, were the first to beat a path to my door.' She manufactured a smile for the fat man who by now was swaying under the massive strain of his own weight. Gina surged with a cruel pleasure which was almost a sexual thrill. If she wished she could hold him here until he actually collapsed. Don't lose sight of your ultimate goal, her sagacity warned. You don't merely want Balbo on his knees. You want him broken, destitute. You want him begging for mercy. She said crisply, 'Shall we say two days? For you to reach your decision, to determine whether you can raise the necessary finance.'

'I can,' Balbo replied promptly. Confidently.

Somewhat surprised, Gina responded, 'Forty-eight hours, then.' She rose, taking from the table a bulky folder – a dossier of facts and figures, photographs and drawings culled from the prospectus which had launched Rossi Taverns in America; none of it spurious, it was genuine enough, more than dramatic enough to impress and convince the most professional of Balbo's advisers. As the sweating man received the folder, Gina said, 'Good day.'

Whatever response he might have made to the abrupt dismissal was obviated by the relief at being released from his tortured stance. 'Thank you, Contessa,' he gasped and took a faltering backward step, wincing against his cramping muscles. 'I look forward to returning. I assure you, you will not be disappointed in our running of your Italian operation. You will see that we are partners to be reckoned with.' He lumbered to the door, made a brief obeisance of his huge shoulders. 'Until we meet again, Contessa.'

Gina watched the door close.

She resat in the gilt and satin chair. Strange, her bitterness in the moments of Balbo's leaving had rapidly evaporated.

Now she felt only a cold emptiness, an engulfing loneliness. She told herself it was an automatic response to the trauma of the meeting. She would not falter. The wheel was in spin, and she would not halt it. Soon she would go to the Bank of Rome and deposit fifty thousand dollars. A small price to pay to ensure justice.

'Two hundred thousand,' said the bank's vice-president. 'That is the law. New regulations govern foreign investment in our national economy. A necessity, you understand, following the financial corruption of the Fascist regime which left our country bankrupt. I am sure the measures are only a temporary expediency. However . . . ' He shrugged apologetically.

Gina ground her teeth, strove to maintain her façade of calm while conducting a rapid mental review of her chances of personally raising the money.

Banks. Damn all banks! Why were they the only institutions she feared?

I do not fear them, she asserted angrily. The man across the desk was watching her from beneath expectant eyebrows. She must not reveal her hesitation. There must be no cause for doubts to be voiced around Italy's banking circles, no queries raised which might reach back to New York. So far everyone there still believed Gina's visit to Rome was merely exploratory. There was no reason why they shouldn't continue to think so. Balbo understood the need for secrecy – the last thing he wanted was public knowledge of his deal pushing up the price of property. And this banker would respect Gina's insistence on confidentiality – she had explained that no communication whatsoever must be made with her, or her fellow directors, once the documentation had been signed and sealed. The only good thing about bankers, she thought with some irony, is their ability to keep secrets.

Two hundred thousand dollars.

The figure repeated in her head. She had known the post-war monetary regulations which stated that all foreign corporations wishing to establish a base in Italy must take on a local partner. It had been the crux of her scheme. She also had expected to show financial bona fides. What she had not known wat that this must be a statutory one-fifth of the local partner's initial investment. In this ignorance she had already mentioned to this banker Balbo's commitment of one million dollars. She unwittingly had placed herself in the position of having to find four times the sum she had originally anticipated.

Could she afford it? Could she tie up that amount of personal cash for almost a year – the length of time she expected Balbo to take to mortgage himself beyond redemption? Or was this the omen that her vendetta must end here?

The man across the desk coughed politely.

Gina said, 'I trust you will accept my cheque.'

34

Christmas glittered in the windows of Fifth Avenue and the adjacent streets. Platoons of jovial Santas distributed festive spirit along with invitations to imbibe it in the bedecked emporiums. The music of the season was carols, sleigh bells and cash registers.

In Burr's Book Cellar the onslaught of the past two hours had abated and Gina took a second to flex her shoulders and ease her creaking neck as the woman whose volume she'd just signed went happily away to have her purchase wrapped. The small desk at which she sat, surrounded by gleaming stacks of *The Lady's Cookbook*, before a giant photograph of herself, had been, since she first sat at it, a besieged island from which she could neither escape nor receive sustenance from the outside world. Not until five minutes ago had the store manager been able to reach her with a refilled water carafe.

Dorothy Hamm hurried forward, beaming delightedly as Gina stitched on a smile for yet another customer, numbly wrote whatever message had been requested, scribbled her name and intoned, 'Thank you. Merry Christmas.' Dorothy Hamm flustered, 'Isn't it marvellous? Just marvellous! More copies than your first signing session here last month. And you've beaten the record you set at First Editions in Philadelphia. Isn't it wonderful?'

Gina again pushed her pen across a presented page, said, 'Thank you. Merry Christmas.' She didn't remember Philadelphia, only vaguely recalled the hoopla that had followed her unparalleled sales there. The past five promotion-packed weeks, since the cookbook's launch party on November 4th, had retreated into a blur of bookstores, customers' faces, train journeys, bookstores, airplane flights, customers' faces, hotel rooms, bookstores and customers' faces while her publisher's presses consumed whole forests to meet the wildfire of demand whipped up by the gales of publicity from Columbus Circle and the subsequent mushrooming of Rossi Taverns across the country.

Gina Rossi, they said was beloved by the gods; her life was charmed; truly, whatever she touched became gold.

She pushed out from behind the desk, clipped, 'I need a break.' She strode toward the rear of the store, with Dorothy Hamm hurrying behind.

In the manager's office she picked up the phone, dialling, asked Dorothy Hamm, 'Do you have the latest national sales figures?' When the editor apologized, said it hadn't been possible, Gina's mouth tightened in a hard line. 'Put me through to Prentiss,' she snapped the instant her call was connected. After a moment the chief accountant at the Rossi Building was on the line. Gina demanded, 'Did the cheques from the new franchisees clear?' At the man's reply a glint of satisfaction crossed her eyes. She fired several more financial questions, followed by a series of curt orders. Cutting the connection she flipped open her notebook, rapidly scribbled a series of dollar figures. She nodded to herself. Everything was going fine. Excellent. She'd draw a personal cheque this afternoon, cover the instalments to the moneylenders.

The day after her meeting with the Rome banker, Gina had been back in New York, had abandoned further investigation of the potential of Italy's restaurant trade. After a further day she had secured a score of minor loans to cover the deposit of two hundred thousand dollars. That is, Prentiss had secured them.

Prentiss had been in Gina's employ for four months. He'd been bought in from Le Brun & Roth, one of the most successful and respected brokers on Wall Street. All Gina's executives and consultants were the best. 'The best money can buy,' she'd said. 'Anything, or anyone, less than the best isn't worth the time of day.' Prentiss was now receiving one-and-a-half times the salary he'd been making at Le Brun & Roth. For that Gina got first-class financial advice, gold-plated efficiency, unswerving loyalty, and blind obedience. When she'd ordered Prentiss to arrange, confidentially the clutch of small loans from whatever sources would waive the laws of collateral, the assignment had been completed inside twenty-four hours. That the interest was treble the norm was to be expected. Gina would cope. No need to rush the repayments. Besides, the two hundred thousand in Rome was merely on deposit; she could reclaim it at her own whim, whenever she decided to spring the trap on Ugo Balbo.

Everything was going to be fine.

Leaving the office, she said without looking around at Dorothy Hamm, 'Please be sure I have those sales figures by tomorrow morning.' She strode into the store.

An hour later she stalked into the Lady, up the stairs to the club, pulling off her gloves with angry tugs.

Harry glanced around from the six dancers on stage, starting to throw a greeting, then, seeing the red light in Gina's eyes, said over his shoulder, 'Okay, girls, take ten.' Producing a hopeful smile he welcomed, 'Hi, Gina! Come to watch the rehearsal?'

'Harry, I don't like picking up customer complaints off the street,' Gina fired sharply. 'I don't expect it either. This is Manhattan's premier nightspot, not a dollar-dinner joint in the Village. Why did the show start late last night?'

Harry's long face had flushed and he nervously fumbled with his unfastened bowtie. 'Just one of those things, I guess. Schedules run haywire once in a while. I lost the reins, is all. You know how it goes.'

'No, I don't know how it goes. Nor do I believe a word. You never lost the reins in your life. What happened last night? Who showed up late?' Gina raised a warning hand. 'Please don't cover for the culprit. If you don't tell me someone else eventually will. Loyalty is very laudable, but get your priorities right. Remember where your loyalty lies.' She was aware of the harshness in her voice, momentarily considered easing the taut atmosphere. But they had to learn, all of them, this was no longer some small-time operation. They were striding into the big league now. Slap-happy attitudes had to stop. The Rossi Corporation would command respect. Gina had angrily affirmed that to herself fifteen minutes ago when a blue-rinsed Park Avenue matron had descended on her outside Burr's

Book Cellar to say what a wonderful time she and her friends had had in the club last night but had added with smug relish, 'Such a pity, my dear, our little celebration was marred by having to wait so long for the show to start.'

As the woman's sanctimonious features reflamed in Gina's head, she demanded sharply, 'Well?'

Harry sighed, his features lengthening. He shrugged. 'It happens all the time. Fellers, and girls, once they see their names in lights, they let things slide a mite. Start feeling their feet. It's natural. I've seen it a thousand . . . .'

'So, Tony Nevada!'

After a pause, Harry reluctantly nodded affirmation. 'I guess it's that movie bit part he shot. Giving him a taste of stardom. He's flexing his muscles some.' He shifted uneasily. 'It wasn't so serious last night. He was just a little late.'

'Don't snow me, Harry. The show wasn't a little late. Not five minutes. Not ten. I know, it was forty. The customers – my customers – were forced to sit twiddling their thumbs for almost three-quarters of an hour. That isn't a starlet flexing his muscles, it's a prima donna acting bloody irresponsibly. At my expense.' Ignoring the colour her fierceness had slapped across Harry's face, Gina added unforgivingly, 'And I won't stand for it. Has this happened before? Don't bother to fabricate an answer.' She swung away. 'I'll find out for myself.'

Her anger pursued her to the street.

She'd known about Tony Nevada's movie role – a one-song appearance in a low-budget musical due for release next year – but had largely ignored it. She rarely saw the singer these days. She hadn't been in the restaurant for weeks. Even before the whirlwind promotion tour for her cookbook, she had been spending increasingly less time at the Lady, more of her days – and nights – alone in the Park Avenue apartment, scribbling memos, making phone calls, transmitting orders, gathering information. She had more important tasks than everyday chores. She didn't need aggravation; certainly had no intention of yielding to any from a narcissistic singer.

She stabbed the bellpush in the lushly-carpeted top-floor hallway of the building overlooking the East River.

The apartment door was opened by a black girl in maid's uniform. To Gina's enquiry she answered, 'I'm sorry, Ma'am, Mister Nevada isn't at home.'

Gina mentally swore. She'd been driven here, unthinking,

by her anger, hadn't paused to check whether the trip might be futile. 'When will he be back?' she asked calmly.

Cassie's voice said, 'When he's good and ready.'

Gina stared beyond the maid, to the apartment lobby where Cassie was standing with a large liquor glass in her hand. Before Gina could recover from the surprise of her friend's unexpected entrance, the redhead had walked forward saying:

'Okay, Lela, I'll take care of this.' She halted, surveyed Gina as the maid retreated. 'What's up, Hon? Cat got your tongue?' Her voice was threaded on barbed wire. 'Here to see why I'm not slaving again? Forgotten we lesser mortals get a day off occasionally.'

'No . . . .' The anger Gina had brought here was gone. Her emotions now felt as fragile as the tension in this doorway. She hadn't anticipated finding Cassie here; even less was she prepared for the way the redhead looked. Cassie's lips were pale, her face morose, and dark shadows etched tiredness beneath her eyes. She was wearing a pale green chiffon blouse, obviously no brassière, and hip-hugging emerald pants.

Cassie said, 'Don't you like it? Tony likes it. Likes me to dress this way. A woman should dress to please her guy. Or wouldn't you know anything about that?' The smile was cruel. 'Drink?' she asked abruptly and walked back toward double doors.

Uncertainly, Gina followed – into a sitting-room that was straight from a movie set. The room was big, with cream walls, cream velvet sofa and chairs, a deep cream carpet, and a cream grand piano in front of the vast window above the East River. Glossy photographs of Tony Nevada covered the walls, along with framed press clippings and his headliner showcards from The Lady.

Cassie was at a corner bar sloshing out a tall measure of gin. She lifted the liquor, swallowed half of it. As she began to fill a second glass, Gina said quickly:

'No thanks.'

'Too good to drink with the workers?'

'Don't be foolish. Isn't it a bit early . . . '

'What do you care?'

'I care a lot,' Gina returned, not really sure whether she meant it, but reaching for some sort of contact. 'I care that you're living in this place.'

'What do you mean?' shot back Cassie, her face reddening.

'Don't you think I belong in these surroundings? Are you the only one who's permitted to play Queen of the May?'

'That isn't at all what I meant. I was referring to the expensiveness. The luxury here. Tony can't afford this lifestyle.'

'But I can. And what's that to you? I can do as I please with my money. I can lend what I like. Anyhow, this isn't Tony's apartment, or mine. It's ours. Sure it is.' She looked around the cavalcade of photographs, went on, 'And Tony needs to keep up appearances. He – we – have important visitors. Record company executives. Guys from radio. A movie producer was here last week. They got to be entertained right. You know that. Isn't that why you've got your fancy nest on Park?' Cassie swigged the remainder of her liquor and recharged her glass.

Gina was struggling with the situation. She was now worried, very worried, about her friend. She understood that Cassie's infatuation with Tony Nevada went deeper than normal. The redhead was obsessed. The thought chilled Gina as it crept into her head. Yet she knew it was not an over-dramatization. From the reaction she'd seen in Tony Nevada's female audiences, as well as, most positively, the surging desire she'd experienced in herself the evening of her return from Las Vegas, she understood what the singer's sexuality could do to a woman's senses. At one time she'd never have believed it possible, thought it was always the other way around – men, older, desperate men, going crazy over some seductive, young starlet. Today she knew differently.

She said gently, 'Cass, we really can't talk here. How about we take a stroll? I could use the fresh air, and the exercise. Come on. It's an age since you and I had a good old chinwag, girl to girl.' She summoned up a cheery grin, 'Well, old dame to old dame. Hey, what say?'

Cassie peered at her. She seemed to hesitate, biting her lower lip. But the instant died and she snapped, 'Forget the old pals act, Gina. It won't wash. You and me quit being bosom buddies months, maybe years, ago.'

'That isn't so.'

'Of course it is. Who're you trying to kid? Don't tell me you reckon we're still equal, you sitting up on your throne, dictating, while I – yes, and everybody else – run around doing your royal bidding. How the hell you gonna figure we're like the old days?' Cassie swallowed more gin, before Gina could oppose her went on, 'Anyhow, we got nothin' . . . nothing, to talk about.' Her voice was becoming slightly slurred and she had regressed to the hard Brooklyn accent she hadn't used in years. 'So,' she tossed the word with a jerk of her head, 'don't waste any more of your precious time. Or any breath.' The last shot was sharp from behind brittle eyes.

Gina was floundering. She was treading a path which it seemed she'd been down before. Her exchange with Fallon loomed in her head, a pit into which she must not fall. At the same time, her annoyance was rising. Cassie was just being plainly damn stupid. What she really needed was a short, sharp slap to bring her to her senses. Gina said levelly, 'I never realized you felt that way, Cass.'

'You didn't realize a lot of things.'

Ignoring that, Gina continued, 'Maybe I have been over-busy sometimes. But that shouldn't have put a gulf between us. If it did, I'm sorry. Truly. If I'd realized . . .'

'Why don't you just leave?'

Gina caught her breath. There was now a harshness in Cassie she'd never seen before. Warning voices were sounding, but she was sure that if she left now she would blame herself for ever for what she imagined – knew – would happen to her friend. In a tone she hoped would give Cassie the jolt she needed, she demanded, 'And why don't you just come to your senses?' With some satisfaction she saw Cassie's shoulders jerk. 'All right, I've no objection to your rolling in the hay with Tony, or any other young, handsome feller for that matter, but for goodness' sake don't take it seriously. Don't call it love. You know as well as I, you only want what he can give you in bed. Fine. I don't blame you. But keep it in proportion. Realize what it means to your future. Where on earth can it end? You know . . .'

'You don't blame me! You've no objection!' Cassie shuddered with anger. Gina almost recoiled from what she saw in her friend, and she knew she'd made a fatal mistake. Cassie's hand shook and liquor spilled on the bartop. 'How bloody dare you? Who do you think you're talking to? What right do you think you've got, waltzing in here, telling me what I should or shouldn't feel? I told you, I love Tony. Yes, love. I'm not afraid of saying it out loud. I don't have any neuroses. I'm not abnormal. I'm not some sexual freak who doesn't know what she feels.' As Gina gasped, Cassie lashed out, 'Yes, you I'm

475

talking about. Lady High and Mighty who can't keep her own guy so she goes for somebody else's, and when he gives her the short goodbye she tries to foul up her so-called best buddy's life.' She bashed the glass down causing gin to slosh out and across the front of her blouse.

Gina was stricken. She was incapable of speech. Her only thought now was that she had to get out of here.

Cassie came around the bar, staggered, halted. 'What's the matter? Truth hurts, does it? Well, tough, pal. If you can't take it you shouldn't'a come hoity-toitying around here.'

'Cass,' Gina offered hoarsely. 'I'm sorry. We'll talk tomorrow. I'm leaving now.' She began to turn.

'Sure. Go on. Run back to your mountaintop. That's where you've always wanted to be, isn't it? And it's where you belong. Up amongst the ice and snow. Suits you, Hon. Where there's no warmth, there's no feeling. But don't expect anybody to want to join you. Because normal folks, like me and Tony, we don't want that kinda life. You're welcome to it. So clear off back to it.' Cassie took a couple of paces forward, swayed there, her upper body braced aggressively forward, her fist waving widely. 'And,' the word was a shout, 'keep away from Tony! Keep your hands off him. Yes, I know all about it. Think he wouldn't tell me? For somebody who's supposed to be so damn smart you're pretty dumb, lady. Of course he told me. He's my lover, you silly bitch. He tells me everything.'

A deadly sickness engulfed Gina. Words struggled to her lips but they died there.

Cassie's reddened features were filled with a mixture of anger and triumph. 'Certainly he told me how you threw yourself on him after getting him up to your bedroom.' Her lips twisted with disgust. 'You're pathetic, Gina. You're warped. Pawing Tony, slobbering over him, begging him to make love to you. And why? Because you wanted him? Or because you simply couldn't bear the thought of me having him? Isn't that why you came around here? A last effort to try and ruin my happiness? Revenge for Tony's wanting me?'

Gina was drowning in horror. She understood now. She saw vividly the icy spite in Tony Nevada's eyes the night she had rejected him. Taking a halting step toward the woman who had shared so much of her life, she whispered brokenly, 'Cass, you don't realize . . . . ' But what more could she say? How could she explain? And, in any case, she knew it was useless. The look on Cassie's face was enough to tell her this was the end of their story. Tony Nevada had torn apart the chapters of their friendship and flung them into the wind. She raised a faltering hand, a final, desperate attempt to reach the Cassie she once had known.

In an agony of time they faced each other; two girls in shapeless smocks amid the cacophony of the locker room of the Howard West. And for that second it was how it had been with them. Cassie's fingers moved an infinitesimal distance toward Gina. The moment hung suspended. Then it was carried inexorably into the past.

Gina turned and walked away, through the lobby to the door. She twisted the handle, hesitated on the threshold. In the apartment across the hall a piano was playing; voices, someone laughing. Behind her from the sitting-room came a small sound. She went out of the door.

The following morning, alone at her desk above Park Avenue she received a call from Harry reporting that Tony Nevada was reneging on his contract with The Lady. Harry asked if the attorneys should sue for compensation. Gina said no.

The earth moved across its arc in the heavens. The first issue of the multi-lingual European magazine *World Wide* ran its cover story: The New Golden Age. Between the lumberyards and abandoned tenements of New York's Cherry Street, Italians paraded for their Madonna delle Grazie Festival. Nearby, the home of Captain Samuel Reid, hero of the Britain-US 1812 war, was torn down to make way for a parking lot. The state of Israel was proclaimed in Tel Aviv. General Sir Hugh Lorwin of the Normandy campaign was given a ticker-tape welcome to Manhattan; at a civil reception he said he believed the children of the world would know peace for the next thousand years. The B.B.C. transmitted a documentary titled, 'Germany Under Control'. In a Las Vegas casino a Seattle shoe-store clerk won two hundred thousand dollars. The Arab states of Lebanon, Syria, Jordan, Egypt and Iraq invaded Israel. Britain introduced the National Health Service; a headline declared, 'Sickness, a Thing of the Past'. A fourteen-year-old boy battered to death a liquor-store owner in the Bronx. Outside a glue factory in London's Stepney, eight female workers staged a sit-down on the pavement for wages parity with their male fellow employees; after five hours the eight were arrested and later sentenced to thirty days' imprisonment for 'obstruction of police officers'. At a pacification meeting in New Delhi a man stepped from the crowd and fired a fatal bullet into Mohandas Karamchand Gandhi. When it was announced that the number of juke boxes throughout the U.S.A. had reached a million, a musicians' union spokesman said, 'This will spell the end of the night-club business within two years.' The Trattoria San Rocco, Rome's oldest Jewish restaurant, was burned to the ground; ex-Fascists were suspected. A petition with ten thousand signatories was presented to 10 Downing Street demanding delegalization of the sale of contraceptives. D.W. Griffith, who gave the world *Birth of a Nation*, died, all but forgotten, in a rundown Hollywood hotel. In the movie *June Bride*, Robert Montgomery said to Bette Davis, 'Even when I was making love to you, I felt you were wondering what time it was.'

It was at that point that Gina walked out of the theatre.

She hadn't been to the movies in years, had only visited the Globe on Forty-Second Street this drizzling late August afternoon of 1948 because the second feature was the low-budget quickie with the Tony Nevada spot. Eight months ago, following her row with Cassie and Nevada's breaking of his contract, she'd told Harry she hadn't the slightest interest in what either her ex-friend or her ex-crooner did next. Today she'd told herself she was going to the Globe out of morbid curiosity. Maybe it was something like that. The movie had been panned by the couple of critics who'd bothered to give it lineage. On the other hand, Tony Nevada's small role had received favourable mention by both writers; one had gone as far as saying, 'Move over, you old heart-throbs, a new breed of soul stirrer has arrived.' Gina wondered briefly about Cassie's soul. As far as she knew the redhead was still with the singer. To what depths had she sunk for him? How, after all this time, could she still want him?

Gina obliterated the questions – and the image of Tony Nevada – from her mind. On the rain-slick sidewalk she pulled down the brim of her hat. One thing was for sure, she didn't want, didn't need any male, hadn't so much as shared a cup of coffee with one, alone, since Fallon's departure. Nor had she even thought of the Englishman; had sliced him from her mind, cauterized the wound with work, work, work.

Robert Montgomery's words echoed in her head. She retorted aloud. 'To hell with you!' and started back to the Rossi Building.

She hadn't yet bought the office block where the first franchises had been vetted, but such had been the intensity of the publicity surrounding the proliferating taverns, the record-breaking sales of the cookbook, and the breakneck construction of the Silver Lady, that Forty-Seventh Street had been dubbed by one newspaper wit, 'Rossi Boulevard'. Inevitably, the family name was then tagged to the office building – much to the chagrin of the real owners.

Gina wasn't concerned for their feelings. Gina didn't care about anything but the advancement of her business; and the ruination of Ugo Balbo.

Following her meeting with the Rome hotelier she had spoken with him several times on the telephone, but never had put anything in writing. Still no one knew the true reason for her earlier trip to Italy. Each time she listened to Balbo she was filled with a loathing verging on sickness, nevertheless she complimented him on his acumen, encouraged him as he reported his progress.

She could hear the greed in his voice whenever he reported his latest acquisition. He had made down payments on buildings throughout the country. Premises, he'd scoffed, were cheap and easy to come by in the wake of the war; those made destitute by the conflict were willing to accept any deal. This had spurred him to plunge deeper into debt than even Gina had anticipated. He scarcely needed her prompting to pledge ever more personal security against the purchase of ancient stores, abandoned villas, disused hotels. The more he bought, the greater became his belief in his future. During his phone conversations, and in the letters he sent, with increasing frequency, he likened himself to the commercial barons of the world – Hearst, Guggenheim, Morgan, Krupp – bandying their names with indiscriminate intimacy as if he already was their equal. He stoked the furnace of his delusion with his own boastfulness; fuelled the reality with towering indebtedness. He had exceeded by far the original proposed sum of one million dollars; had, one way or another, run up the staggering total of two million in down payments alone. He, apparently, was in a pit of debt.

During the early months of Gina's vendetta she had burned with unholy joy at the success of her scheme. Each time she calculated Balbo's financial commitment, she counted another nail in the coffin of his existing business empire. Her desire for vengeance was absolute.

As time had passed, however, the passion had faltered. A vague unease had beset her. The pinpricks of guilt? No. She would not accept that. Balbo was the guilty one, and for him there could be no leniency, no mercy. In the dark of night, to strengthen her will, Gina conjured the gross man's image, willed herself to recall in minute detail every second from the hour of her father's arrest, through the torturing months of his imprisonment, the agony of his sham trial, the despair of his exile, to the moment she learned of his execution.

Balbo will suffer, she repeated over and over. My father, our family, will be avenged, in full.

Hate had become the only emotion Gina Rossi now indulged. A core of insentience had formed within her. She these days rarely slept more than four hours; ate little, drank not at all; relaxed never. She travelled around the rapidly multiplying chain of taverns, attended conventions of franchisees, spoke to chambers of commerce, appeared at charity galas, continued signing sessions at bookstores, addressed business women's rallies, was interviewed by the media whenever she touched ground. 'Where does she actually live?' asked one magazine profile, and answered itself, 'Gina Rossi doesn't live any place. She's always en route.'

As she entered her presidential suite in the Rossi Building, through her secretary's office, the chic woman behind the efficiently ranged typewriter, telephones and intercom handed her the afternoon's red-flagged messages and said, 'There was another call a moment ago. Long-distance. A very bad line. I didn't catch the name.'

'Give them the Las Vegas number when they call back,' instructed Gina striding into her own office, across the deep-pile brown carpet, between suede sofas, around the vast mahogany desk to sit in the baronial hide armchair.

Swiftly scanning the score of message sheets, she scribbled notations on each, set them aside. She turned to the three short transcripts of radio news reports. As she read them, she scarcely paused for thought as she drew her conclusions, formulated the plans of action. One: a strike at the Port of Los

Angeles was expected to spread along the west coast; imported wine shipments would be affected; extra provisional supplies must be arranged immediately to circumvent any shortage or rise in prices. Two: a landslip following heavy rains in Bismarck, North Dakota, had destroyed a popular local restaurant; residents would be dining out at alternative locations; special promotions must be mounted at the Bismarck Rossi Tavern. Three: renowned chef Josef Morande, who during the past twenty years had catered to almost every head of state in the world at the Commodore-Plaza in Washington D.C., had died at the hotel; international as well as U.S. press would report the funeral; a director of the Rossi Corporation must be seen to attend.

Her intercom buzzed. Flicking the switch she said crisply, 'Yes.' Irving Prentiss's voice said, 'I have the new transportation costings.' Gina answered, 'Bring them in.'

She drummed her fingernails on the desktop for the one minute of waiting for her chief financial adviser. She hadn't liked the forty-six-year-old accountant since she hired him; but would never admit that the sole reason for her animosity was that he was as commercially efficient – maybe more so – than she.

Prentiss entered. His grey suit, white shirt, blue tie and black hair were as immaculate as the balance sheets, profit forecasts and expense budgets he prepared. He sat opposite Gina, opened the folder he had carried in and set it before her. The straight lines and planes of his face moved into the half-smile that was neither friendly nor obsequious, was simply one of the precisely measured expressions he used as emotionlessly as the slim gold pen with which he wrote his perfect figures.

Gina surveyed the report. A new warehousing facility in Atlanta was proposed as a distribution point for supplies to all Rossi Taverns across the southern states. In the long term the saving against long-distance haulage costs would result in an extra one per cent profit on turnover; the initial capital expense, however, would be in excess of half a million dollars.

For five minutes the only sound was Gina's turning of the pages. When she looked up she said, 'The scheme is excellent. How soon can it be implemented?'

'Within three months,' Prentiss replied without hesitation, but added, 'So long as we can find the finance.'

Gina clipped, 'Should there be a problem?'

'Perhaps. Our existing loan facilities are all but drained. Tax and utility bills, which must be met by the end of next month, will consume present accumulating tavern royalties as well as all the franchise fees for the scheduled restaurants.'

'Yes, yes,' snapped Gina. 'I know all that. I realize our current liabilities exceed our assets. But it is only a temporary trough in our cash flow. We can't permit it to impede our expansion programme. This new warehousing,' she tapped the report, 'will keep us one step ahead of the competition. I want it instigated without delay. Further credit can be raised against half the acreage of the Las Vegas site. That land is better than cash in the bank. The extra half-million we paid for it will be returned tenfold inside four years.' She fixed Prentiss with immovable determination. 'I want the contract for the Atlanta facility finalized by this time next week.'

The accountant said, 'I'll see to it.'

After he'd left Gina swiftly penned her comments on the radio news transcripts. She took these and the notated messages out to her secretary.

The woman speared them on her URGENT spike, handed Gina an airline ticket wallet.

Tucking this in her purse Gina said, 'I'll be back for the board meeting Monday afternoon.' She strode to the door, turned there and added, 'By the way, please see Filipo. Tell him I'm sorry I can't keep our date this weekend. He'll understand. Give him a cheque for . . . twenty dollars. Scribble my love and kisses on the back.' She didn't wait for a response. Along the corridor she was calculating the loan interest on the capital to set up a warehousing facility in Oregon to handle supplies distribution across the north-west states.

Five years ago, a blazing wilderness; a desert cut by a rarely-used highway, with sagebrush, cactus and creosote bushes the only vegetation clinging to the sun-scorched rock and sand stretching to the ragged crags of the Spring Mountains, with coyotes, lizards and snakes the only creatures venturing amid this desolation four miles from the city of Las Vegas.

Today, the foundations of skeletons of casinos, motels and diners scattered across the burned landscape like fresh ruins. Surveyors, architects and real estate agents wandering the vastness like latter day prospectors. Cars, trucks and pick-ups dust-trailing along the two lanes of cracked concrete like a modern wagon train heading for the new frontier.

Inside the vast steel and chrome trailer, Gina bent over the blueprints spread along the bench beneath the window. As perspiration ran down between her breasts she tugged at the shoulders of her white cotton blouse, easing the soaking material from her skin. If Ed Solano, the construction engineer, wasn't standing at her side she'd have done the same to her beige pants which were sticking uncomfortably wherever they touched. Despite the four labouring electric fans, the temperature of the trailer's interior was little less than the ninety-eight degrees which shimmered in liquid waves beyond the window.

Gina said, 'Can you do it? Bring it in three weeks ahead of schedule? Double bonus for every man on site if you do. And five thousand dollars, cash, in your pocket.'

The stump of cigar which smouldered perpetually between Ed Solano's teeth shifted to the corner of his mouth. He straightened from bending beside Gina and his head almost touched the six-foot-six ceiling of the trailer. His khaki sweatshirt and jeans were moulded to muscles as solid as the buildings he'd raised during thirty years in the construction industry. His greying black hair was close-cropped, his skin the colour of whiskey-soaked leather. He was as efficient at his trade as Irving Prentiss was in his. Gina liked him as much as she disliked the accountant.

He said, 'Tall order.'

'I need the extra days, Ed.'

'Sounds like the wolves are at the door.'

Gina looked at his crinkle-cornered eyes. Ed Solano didn't mince words. Nor would he have worked for anybody who did. She said, 'They'll be under it and having pups if this heap of glass and concrete doesn't start paying its keep come October.'

Ed turned and faced a chart on the opposite wall. Horizontal bands of colour denoted scheduled work periods and completion dates for Excavation, Foundation, Steel, Carpentry, Electrics, Plumbing, the one hundred and eighty-six different trades that had to mesh like perfect gears in the twenty-four-hours-a-day unflagging machine which was the five hundred men erecting a building the like of which had never been seen before.

Ed chewed on his cigar butt, surveyed the chart for a long

minute. When he looked around at Gina he said, grinning, 'Don't think you'll get the five thousand bucks back at Max's tables. Every cent will be spent on something useful – like wine and women.'

Gina smiled gratefully. 'You know, Mister Solano, if ever I get to thinking I deserve you, I'll ask you to marry me.'

The construction engineer laughed. 'Then we could get famous as the couple putting up the weirdest buildings in the world.'

'My building isn't weird. Just different. Anyhow it will pull in the customers. That's all that matters.' She put on a straw cowboy hat, moved to the door. As she stepped down into the platinum glare she asked, 'Did you ever, seriously, think of getting married, Ed?'

He followed her, stood at her side. 'Sure. A couple of times.' He started across the dusty, compacted earth. 'But never in daylight.'

Gina went with him. 'Yes. Me neither.'

In the blazing afternoon, a battlefield of rutted rock, criss-crossing ditches, mountains of blocks and sand. Dump trucks trundling by, a bulldozer heaving into a drift of gravel, cement mixers turning, turning. Banging. Shouting. The incessant roar of compressors, the thump of a steam shovel, the ragged coughing of engines. Men hurrying, hauling, struggling across this ruptured landscape.

And ahead, the pyramid.

Not a concrete pyramid. Not a tiered, gargantuan wedding cake which could be seen in every high-rise city across the North American continent. But a dazzling, true pyramid. Weird, Ed Solano had said. A glass mountain, most of the press had said. The place I'll make my home, Gina Rossi had avowed.

She didn't love it – not the way she had once loved the Lady – but it had become her abiding obsession. Money wasn't the cause of her passion – the casino's income could never equal that of the multiplying Rossi Taverns – it was, simply, the existence of the massive monolith. Here was tangible proof of all her accomplishments. 'This is Gina Rossi,' they would say when they came in their thousands to stare in wonder and envy. And, she asked herself, why shouldn't I be envied? I deserve the accolades, and the respect, don't I? Why should pride be a sin?

While Ed Solano gave instructions to a trio of sun-blackened men unloading a timber truck, Gina surveyed the object of her ruling fixation, the monument to her success.

The pyramid was fifteen storeys high – the tallest structure in Las Vegas. The sides were clad in polished steel and mirrored glass. Travellers on the highway could see it from the horizon. From the air it was visible at fifty miles, a dazzling jewel on the endless panorama of sandstone and shale. Architectural associations had lauded it, conservation organizations had censored it, politicians had praised it, and religious extremists had condemned it as the temple of the damned. Gamblers, Gina knew, couldn't wait to come and spill their dollars in it. Beyond the luxurious lobby would be the biggest casino in the world; on the floor above would be a showroom to rival the best night-clubs in Manhattan; the next layer would comprise restaurants and bars; then would come eleven dimishing floors of hotel rooms and suites; finally at the summit of the crystal mountain, Gina's personal eyrie, the zenith from which she could survey the world below, the point which no one could surmount.

She bridged her hand over her eyes, watched the endless march of men in and out of the wide, black maw at the base of the tower. She glanced toward Ed Solano, impatient for him to be through with the timber truck so that he could accompany her into that entrance, to the anthill of activity where dunes of sawdust covered the floor, vines of cables festooned the ceilings, and branching pipework latticed the unclad walls.

'A further quarter of a million.' Wheldon J. Hoyt, president of the Eastern Commercial Bank & Trust Company, had shaken a cautionary head. 'Costs are escalating considerably, Miss Rossi. My directors and I are somewhat concerned at the extent of the investment. I must insist . . . '

Gina had listened, given her assurance, instructed Ed Solano to install the solid glass dance floor.

The construction engineer turned toward her now. She was about to go with him into the tower when the phone in the trailer began to ring. She strode back and up the steps.

Lifting the receiver she concentrated to hear the long-distance operator through the humming and hissing inter-ference. When she at last understood what was being said she experienced a tremor of pleasure which temporarily cracked the hard shell formed around her during the past months. The broken voice crackled through the waves of static. Gina gathered it piecemeal. She shouted her reply. Caught the question. Could she? She looked out through the window to the glass and steel tower. Could she leave it? For just a few days? Ed Solano didn't really need her. He'd get the job done. 'When?' she shouted into the mouthpiece. 'I could leave after the board meeting Monday, be with you midday Tuesday. Of course. I'd love to. It's been far too long.' A series of beeps and howls cut into the reception. She yelled, 'Can't hear you. Hope you can hear me. I'll be there. Tuesday.' The connection was cut. The operator came on with apologies. Gina said it didn't matter, dropped the receiver in its cradle.

She went out to spend the remainder of the day in her tower. But a corner of her mind was far away.

35

'Look at you!' enthused Sybil. 'How do you keep that figure? Me, the same shape as ever. It didn't matter when we all were allowed to go as nature intended, but now, in any fashionable crowd I stand out like a pumpkin on a plate of string beans. Confounded New Look. Pinched-in waists, coat-hanger hips. If I ever meet C. Dior I'll crown him. But here I am, prattling on. You must be utterly flaked. How was the flight? Dreadful, I know. Aeroplanes are jolly convenient, I'll grant, though why anyone would ever prefer them to the *Queen Mary* I can't imagine. Come on, old thing, I'll take those.' Before Gina could protest, Sybil had hoisted both suitcases and was striding toward the exit of the B.O.A.C. air terminal on Buckingham Palace Road.

As they came out into the sunlight, Gina briefly halted. She'd forgotten how low London's buildings were. Nothing on this street above six storeys. And everything so old. In Manhattan since the war skyscrapers had been shooting up like mushrooms in ever more innovative designs. Here Gina couldn't see even a sign of new development, let alone any examples of modern architecture.

'Hasn't changed a lot, has it?' Sybil remarked. 'Government restrictions on commercial buildings. Perhaps I should have warned you, in some ways the old place isn't half as cheery as it was in our Rainbow days. We still have rationing – you knew that – rising inflation, strikes all over the place. Some newspaper recently asked grimly, Who won the war? The motor's around the corner.' She set off.

Gina followed, pursued by a vague unease.

'I said to David,' Sybil continued, 'what we need is more women in Parliament. Women get things done. Isn't that always the case? In any organization, from a political party to a tennis club, the men form the committee, sit on the committee, spend endless hours discussing what the committee ought to do. But when it comes to the practicalities – writing out mailing lists, sticking on stamps, making sure the envelopes actually get posted to the correct addresses – who's responsible? The women, of course.'

A huge, sag-ended, ex-Army shooting brake, its uniform still visible beneath a brush-streaked dark green overcoat, waited at the kerb. Four small children were conducting an earthquake in the back. They yelled, almost in unison, 'Did you get the comics, Mrs Lowell?' as Sybil opened the rear doors, hefted in Gina's suitcases. 'Yes,' she answered, extracting a fat sheaf of papers from beneath her lovat raglan cloak. 'Don't fight over them. And don't tear them. Take them directly to the playroom and share them when we get home. This, by the way,' she added, 'is Miss Rossi.'

Four jaws sank.

Sybil said, 'Don't stare. It's rude.' Having sealed the children inside, she climbed into the driving seat while Gina entered the other side and turned to say, 'Hello,' to the gawping youngsters. Starting the motor, Sybil said, 'Don't mind them. They've heard a lot about you. You're a bit of a living legend among the smaller residents of the Grange. Maybe with their mums too. I'm afraid you're going to have to spend your time here recounting how you built their home brick by brick with your bare hands, then went on to win the war and become Queen of America.' She pushed a lock of hair up under her tweed trilby, swung the shooting brake out into the traffic. 'David does tend to exaggerate.'

Gina faced the front. Her sense of disquiet strengthened. That first moment's careless pleasure at Sybil's call to Las Vegas had been fading ever since. She felt there was a fracturing inside her, yet she wasn't sure what it was that was breaking. Certainly her self-assurance had slipped. In all the times she had travelled, voluntarily and otherwise, she had never experienced such . . . premonition? Of what? I don't believe in such nonsense, she told herself, as she had when the warning had first whispered to her on her way to the airport in New York. This is a short break, with old friends, before I return to the real business of my life.

She thought of The Lady, her presidential office suite, a glass mountain in the desert. But she couldn't hold the images. She turned from them, looked out at London trundling by. Red double-decker buses; clanking trams on rails; so many people on bicycles; posters plastered to old brick buildings advertising Persil, *Picture Post*, Lipton's teas. Familiarity. This was a part of my life. For a while we belonged to each other. Yet it seems so unreal. Like a twenty-year-old movie. And I don't want to be pulled back to it. I don't want to retreat into the past. I shouldn't have come here.

David was waiting on the steps of the Grange.

Gina hardly recognized him. He'd been plump when she last saw him; now he was positively stout inside his Fair Isle cardigan. The warmth in his blue eyes, however, was unmistakable as he strode forward to halt half-a-dozen paces from Gina, appraise her exquisitely tailored salmon and navy suit with genuine admiration, survey her face with true fondness and declare, 'Sybil, tonight we have to dine in style. I hope you haven't given my tails to the jumble.'

Then he was laughing, gathering Gina to him, kissing both her cheeks, telling her she looked wonderful. She returned his affection, told him he looked pretty good himself. They shared their reunion for several moments until Gina, glancing around, realized they were semi-circled by thirty or more silently staring children. The youngest was wobbly on infant legs, hanging on to the hand of a taller boy; the eldest was a girl of about ten with blonde pigtails over the front of her shoulders, tied with green ribbons. These were the only details Gina absorbed. All she really saw were their faces, their intent expressions, their eyes – all fixed directly on her – deep with wonder.

She shuddered involuntarily. Too much emotion here. Too much love waiting to be unleashed. She said breezily to David, 'What a handsome crew! I hope we'll be having a party later.'

'Tomorrow afternoon. We thought you'd want a bit of a rest

today.' He turned to the audience. 'Now, children, isn't it about time for lunch? In you go. And later, a special treat, you can all help with decorating the hall for Miss Rossi's party.'

A great, 'Hooray!' went up and the tension broke as abruptly as the semi-circle, and the youngsters charged off around the rear of the house. Sybil, who had hauled the suitcases out of the shooting brake, carried them toward the entrance saying, 'Come on, old girl. I imagine you're dying for a bath. And I'm gasping for a sherry. After I've shown you up, I'll make sure the feeding of the five thousand is under way, then we'll meet in the snug. Just the three of us.' Without turning: 'Those shoes are gorgeous. I hope you've brought lots more so that I can try them on. The styles here haven't improved one jot. Really, how this government expects to hold on to the women's vote when we're still clumping around in . . . ' She disappeared along the hall.

Gina and David exchanged a smile, followed.

The Grange had changed little, except now it seemed to be bursting at the seams with children (who were still on school holiday) and their mothers. Gina had bathed hurriedly, changed into a plain, beige wool dress and taken a quick tour of the familiar old building before meeting Sybil and David for drinks followed by oxtail soup and bread, cheese and pickle. There was so much news to exchange, coffee lasted well into the afternoon.

As the conversation went on, Gina's equilibrium began to tilt. The musketeer spirit of camaraderie she had once shared with these two, came flowing back. At the same time the differences in their lifestyles strengthened their apparentness. The English couple's commitment to the Grange was evident in all they said; while Gina for her part did her best to play down the huge success of her American ventures. And as she did so, as the intimate sounds and smells of the home closed in on her, the sense that some hard core within her was beginning to crack became increasingly unsettling. After the initial happy involvement with their gossip, she was beginning to lose her concentration, and it was with a sort of relief that her interest pricked up when she realized Sybil, beside David on the sofa in the small sitting-room, had said:

'We want to sell the Grange.'

Gina exclaimed, 'Give up all you've done here?'

489

'Here, yes, but continue elsewhere.'

'London,' put in David, 'has become quite unviable. It's as bad, almost, as it was during the war. Not only are we saddled with punitive rates and unreliable public services, but there's a clampdown on building. No development is permitted without a licence. And obtaining one of those for commercial purposes is nigh impossible. I don't recommend you drive through the East End. It's as depressing as it was when you were at St Maud's. The Government believes every acre of bombed land should be covered with council dwellings and something it calls Social Amenities. A noble conception, but utterly impractical. Not only isn't there the wherewithal for such schemes, but also, while M.P.s pontificate and argue about the subject, the city is rapidly dying for want of a massive transfusion of fresh industry and commerce. You know, twelve million square feet of office space was blitzed. Scarcely any has been rebuilt. Moreover . . . ' David halted, as if suddenly aware of the tension in his voice. He smiled, 'No, I'm not thinking of entering Parliament – I'll leave that to Sybil – it's just that I get so damned annoyed when I see what's happening.'

Gina thought, Sybil? Parliament? Hadn't she mentioned something about that at the air terminal?

'What I am getting at,' David continued, 'was that the present political policies are preventing us from expanding the Grange. We're strangled by red tape.'

Sybil said, 'We made ourselves into a limited company to satisfy the bank, and to put the home on a proper business footing. Fat lot of good it's done us. We're a privately financed operation. On the files of bureaucracy the Grange isn't classed as a residence for unmarried mothers but as a commercial hotel. We're having the devil's own job obtaining a licence to build an extension.'

Gina had been diverted from pondering Sybil's political aspirations. She queried, 'Extension?'

'To cope with more applicants,' explained Sybil. 'The problem, and the social stigma, Peggy Atkins and thousands of other girls faced in 1943 didn't end with the war. In fact, the situation is getting worse. So many factors are to blame. Primarily, lack of sex education. The ignorance of some youngsters is heart-breaking. We've had eighteen-year-old mothers here who only vaguely understood how their child had been conceived; others who wouldn't even use the word contraception because their parents had said it was dirty. Can you believe that?'

Gina, recalling her own embarrassed confusion over the subject less than six years ago, was glad the question was rhetorical. Also, though she espoused her friend's cause, she hoped they weren't in for an intense moral discussion. I'm no longer a crusader, Sybil. Besides, I have my own battles to fight.

Sybil forged on, 'What we need are fundamental changes in public attitudes. And that's where the Government should give the lead. But as long as the Commons is made up largely of Victorian Conservatives and naïve Socialists – the vast majority of whom are men – the situation will never improve. There has to be . . .'

'I think,' David interjected, 'we're forgetting Gina has been travelling for over seventeen hours. And that she's lost almost half a day. Perhaps, Gina, you'd like to rest awhile. We can tell you all our plans later.'

Gina looked at David, recognized in him more understanding than she'd seen in anyone for a long time. She smiled. 'No, I'm fine, thanks. It's just that European politics are somewhat confusing these days.' She hoped she didn't sound too dismissive; nevertheless wanted to be off that route.

Sybil stared at her, a long, probing gaze, before shrugging and apologizing, 'Sorry old girl. Getting carried away again. Riding my hobby horse.' She patted David's knee. 'What a good thing I've got someone to tug the reins now and then, prevent me from leaping too high fences and breaking my neck! Where were we? The extension. Yes, well, as the authorities seem determined to sink all our planning applications, we've decided the sensible thing to do is move. To larger premises. Outside London. We've already found the perfect place in deepest Wilts. A tottering pile. Used to be the seat of Lord Something-or-other before he died intestate. More rooms than you can count. Going for a song. Nobody wants ancestral homes these days. We'll easily cover the price, plus the cost of repairs, with what we make from selling the Grange – even after you've taken your share.'

Gina frowned. 'My share? No, we agreed, last year, I'd be a non-profit-sharing director.'

David said, 'Yes, in the business. But you're still part-owner

491

of the building. Remember, you and Sybil each took twenty-five per cent when we started the venture. That was one of the reasons for asking you over. There are one or two papers needing your signature before we can put the place up for sale.' He raised a hand. 'Please, no arguments. I gave you a quarter because I sincerely wanted to. And you more than deserve it. Without your determination, and sheer bravado, the Grange Home would never have got off the ground, hundreds of young mothers would never have been helped, plus, the most important fact of all, I might never have married Sybil.' He grinned at his wife, added, 'And would still be the lithe fellow who ate roast potatoes only at Christmas.'

Sybil fixed him with a steely eye. 'Right, my lad, grated carrot and beef tea tonight. And every night henceforth until you regain your greyhound flanks.'

David laughed. 'Seriously, Gina, Sybil and I have discussed the matter. We very much want you to have your share of the sale. Mind you,' he warned, 'don't expect it to be a fortune. London property values are a far cry from New York real estate. Also, it might be some time before we find a buyer. England isn't exactly swarming with investors eager to sink their cash in a rambling one-time hotel.'

Gina, moments ago, had been about to reiterate her protest against acceptance of the twenty-five per cent. However, the chumminess and obvious rapport between Sybil and David had struck a spark from her flinty impatience. Jealousy? They're my good friends. I'm happy for them. She suggested, 'But if you don't make a sale, will you be able to afford the place in Wiltshire?'

Sybil answered, 'I have a little cash, and a few gilts I could sell. The balance will have to be a bank loan.'

'Very costly if the Grange sticks.'

David said, 'We're prepared to take the risk. Nothing ventured, nothing gained. You understand that better than most.'

Yes, but I'm not a starry-eyed altruist.

Perhaps they saw that in her face. Sybil exchanged a glance with David before saying quickly, 'Anyhow, I never was a business brain. David will talk over the details with you later. Well . . . Look at the time . . . There's a drop more coffee in this pot. Do let's finish it.' She poured, added abruptly, 'By the way. Wasn't it great news? Fallon's book.'

Gina's senses reeled. Her hand, reaching for the coffee cup, froze in mid-air.

Sybil exclaimed, 'Oh! Hadn't you heard? About his novel?' She searched for a smile along with something more to say. 'No, I don't suppose there's any reason why you should. It only came out last week. I don't suppose it's been published in America. Of course it hasn't, what a stupid suggestion! I don't suppose . . . '

Gina had stiffened not so much at the announcement of the book, but primarily at the mention of Fallon's name. She'd known since she accepted Sybil's invitation that inevitably he would come up in the conversation during her visit. She'd assured herself she could handle it. 'That's wonderful,' she said, hoping her casual attitude would close the subject. 'I'm sure he'll be a success.'

'Certainly he will,' accorded Sybil, visibly relieved that her dropped brick hadn't, apparently, broken any toes. 'The reviews were super. And when he was on the wireless his interviewer waxed quite lyrical. Listening, we could well imagine Fallon's red face.'

'We also,' put in David, 'could almost hear him growl. Any sort of publicity ballyhoo always did get under his skin. I know he's already had a bit of an up-and-a-downer with his publishers. Told them his book is for reading, not for flogging like a packet of cornflakes.'

'Typical,' Gina retorted sharply. 'Always pig-headed about modern marketing.' And in that instant it was as if she had replied directly to Fallon. The fire that used to spark in her flared brightly, and she mentally flinched as her inner vision bounced back at her from the screen of the past. Shaken, she said brusquely, 'He'll very likely be playing a different tune when he starts receiving his royalty cheques.'

Sybil arose. 'We have a copy. You must see.' She went out quickly. While she was gone David recounted some of the plaudits of Fallon's reviews. Gina murmured response, nodded, raised a moderate eyebrow. She told herself she was pleased for Fallon but not overly interested, that when she saw the book she would remain impassive.

'Complete,' said Sybil re-entering, 'with author's signature. That's two signed volumes we have now. Fallon's and yours.' She presented the red-jacketed book.

Gina took it in both hands. *The Last Summer*. The silhouettes of a soldier and a girl facing each other. *A novel by Robert Fallon.* She stared at his name, felt her pulse increase. Unthinkingly, she ran her fingers over it. His presence was in the room. She slowly opened the cover, leafed through the pages. So many words. Fallon's words, battered out on his old Remington. The clatter of it filled her head. She paused, reading a sentence, heard him speaking it. She closed the book, turned it over. Her mind hazed as she faced his picture. Loosened tie, check shirt, cord jacket; one arm leaning on that typewriter; in his other fist, the pipe; hair more combed than usual, his mouth wide and straight, his eyes unfathomable - looking into her very soul.

She thrust the book back at Sybil. 'Yes, he must be very pleased,' she said, thinking her voice sounded strained and high. She wanted to say more, but everything tumbling through her head was inane. That is, he'd have thought so. He always went black at the cocktail-party prattle of characters who bandied their dips into the latest *de rigueur* bestseller in the same breaths as what colour they were decorating the bathroom and who was having an affair with whom.

Sybil began, 'There's a bookshop in Richmond . . . '

'What a good idea!' Gina interjected, rising quickly. 'The same one as the old days? Good. I'll take a brisk walk down there. I could use the fresh air. I'm not used to all this sherry and lunch. No, that's all right, David, no need to come with me. I'm sure you've heaps to do here. I'll see you later. Okay?' She was out of the room before Sybil and David could protest.

Within minutes she had snatched her jacket from the bedroom, had almost run out into the sunlight and was striding down the drive, along the pavement, onto the path beside the river. She was only partially aware of where she was, of the high shaggy hawthorn hedge at her left, the sloping grass bank to the slow-flowing water at her right.

Gradually, however, the turmoil subsided and she slowed her pace, concentrated on restoring her composure. Would Sybil and David be thinking she'd had a bit of a turn? They were so caring. She glanced around. They weren't following. So, maybe they'd merely thought she was getting eccentric in her old age. A smile came.

She walked beside the river for almost fifteen minutes. When she halted she had reached a small inlet with a worn, stone quay and a few wooden boats swaying gently. An old man in a green woollen cap was painting the mast of one of the boats; he nodded and smiled at Gina. She returned the gesture, surveyed the scene. England at peace. Regardless of any economic and social upheavals which might be taking place, there was a vast achievement here. Fallon had once said in one of his magazine articles, if a people had the will they could achieve anything. Wasn't that true also for individuals? Wasn't Gina Rossi proof of it? Hadn't she always told Paola and Filipo, nothing is impossible until you've tried? Shouldn't she now try, make a concerted effort to put her life on a less hellbent course?

Here, beside this tiny, peaceful harbour, that thought came unbidden. It was, Gina understood, an emotional response to the events of the day, accentuated by the comparison between this somewhat unreal spot and her usual turbulent existence. She neither rejected it nor welcomed it. She turned and walked back along the path.

She bought *The Last Summer* at the old shop where he and she used to browse; took it back to the Grange.

She assured Sybil and David she was feeling fine, said the fresh air had done her good but also had made her tired. On this excuse she went up to her room, unwrapped the book and sat on the edge of the bed staring at Fallon's photograph. Eventually she turned it around, thought about opening it. No, that would be too much, too soon; too like having him beside me. But isn't he here already?

She set the book on the bedside cabinet and lay back. Sounds of children. She hadn't meant to sleep, merely wanted to recollate her thoughts, but after a few moments she drifted, and the reminder of the afternoon passed her by. She had no dreams.

'You're going to a hotel in London?' said Sybil with surprise. 'But why? You're so welcome here.'

'I know I am,' replied Gina. 'And I've had a wonderful three days. But you don't need me under your feet any longer. Besides, I do have a business to take care of, and there are one or two contacts – hoteliers, restaurateurs – I'd like to see while I'm here. Then I must get back to Manhattan. And Las Vegas. You know, there is that little place called the Silver Lady which I ought to take a peek at, make sure there'll be water in the taps when you come over for the opening next month.'

David said, 'That's one event we wouldn't miss for the world. Sybil certainly needs the break.' As his wife turned to protest he insisted, 'Yes, you do. You haven't been away from the Grange for more than a few hours since the first mums arrived in your Red Cross truck over four years ago. The place won't collapse without your presence. The mothers who are your assistants are more than capable of coping. You know when we move to the new, bigger home, you'll have to learn to delegate more. That's what being in charge is all about, isn't it, Gina?'

She nodded. 'Certainly. And that brings me to the point I have to mention before I leave. The sale of the Grange. The purchase of Lord Whatsit's place. You need to clinch the deal right away, before someone else beats you to it. Also, you can't saddle yourselves with the impossible finance of having both places on your hands if – as you say is likely – the Grange proves difficult to sell.'

'It's a situation beyond our control,' said David. 'Perhaps we'll have to draw our horns in somewhat, nevertheless . . . '

'I'll buy the Grange,' said Gina.

The statement was so unexpected, Sybil and David merely stared. Gina, seizing advantage of the stunned silence, went on, 'But me no buts. You haven't any excuse for not selling to me. I'm as good as any other purchaser. What will I do with it? I don't know. Maybe reconvert it into a hotel. Then, in a few years' time, turn it into the training centre for British Rossi Tavern-keepers. We'll be planting our flag here as soon as there are signs of a breeze in the country's economy. You can't stay stuck in the doldrums for ever. Anyhow,' she had taken pen and pad from her purse, now scribbled Irving Prentiss's name and phone number, handed it to a dumbfounded David, 'I'll talk with that man from my hotel tonight. He'll contact you, our attorneys, everybody involved, and will have the entire deal signed, notorized, whatever is necessary, within a week.'

Sybil at last found her voice. 'Gina, this is marvellous of you, but shouldn't you take a while to consider?'

'I have taken a while. Two days. Since my first evening here. And, I promise you, I'm not doing you any special favour, I've given a great deal of thought to the economics. I'm sure the Grange will be a sound investment for the Rossi Corporation's future. So, don't let's spend any more of our last afternoon together on it. I want to say goodbye to all the mums, as well as all the children, to thank them again for the super

496

party they gave me.' She added, more quietly, 'For a lot more too.' She held out her hand to Sybil and David. 'Won't you come with me?'

In the hotel suite overlooking Hyde Park Gina settled in unhurriedly. She was feeling happily relaxed. Her one small regret was the white lie to Sybil and David. She hadn't come here to pursue her business interests but to be alone. Although she'd loved her children-filled days amid the hurly-burly of the Grange, she hadn't had a moment to gather the scattered threads of her thoughts which had been struggling to weave into coherence since the afternoon of her walk by the river.

Having unpacked, she changed into a simple blouse and skirt, sat at the sitting-room's small, antique desk. A slight lightheadedness touched her. A combination of satisfaction and hunger. I haven't eaten so much in my life as I have over the past few days. She'd go down to the restaurant and eat later; just as she'd telephone Fallon's office later. He wouldn't be there, of course, but they'd tell her where he was. Probably he was off on a book promoting tour. Growling all the way, no doubt. Wouldn't that be wonderful – they could compare notes on how many autographs they could manage in an hour!

Gina smiled to herself.

She reached for the copy of *The Last Summer* which had remained unopened since she'd bought it. She hadn't attempted to read it, had not wished to peck at it during her few short moments alone at the Grange. She wanted to read it properly. To do it justice. To savour Fallon's words.

Resisting the temptation to turn the novel over and see his photograph she stared at the cover awhile before slowly opening it. She carefully read the synopsis on the inner flap of the jacket. Moving on to the title page she read that too, including the name and address of the publisher. She turned again, to an expanse of white paper, and the message printed across its centre:

'This book, with affection, is dedicated to Jill.'

The words leapt off the page like physical blows. Yet, for all their force, Gina did not understand them. Her mind refused to translate them. She slowly re-read them. And again. So many times until they become a mere string of unrelated letters. Only after she had closed the book and carefully set it on the table at her side did the dedication repeat itself in her head with cohesion and meaning. Gina comprehended precisely what the words meant.

She arose and walked to the bathroom, stood at the wash basin and stared down at the white porcelain. 'I don't feel anything,' she said aloud. She ran cold water into the bowl, dipped her hands and doused her face. The chill penetrated her cheeks and eyelids, took her breath, but it didn't reach her brain. Still there was no emotion. Patting herself dry with a towel she returned to the sitting-room. All she felt was a strengthening rationality. Why hadn't Sybil or David mentioned Jill? Perhaps they didn't want to risk her reaction. Perhaps they thought she already knew. Did it matter anyhow?

Of course it didn't. Because it was all part of a dream. Everything that had happened since she arrived in this land had been fantasy. There was reality here, for Sybil and David. But not for Gina Rossi. She should have known it, should have heeded her instincts when the first apprehensions whispered. Instead, she had permitted herself to be bewitched, had entertained the most impossible of illusions. Life is not like that, she mentally rapped. It is not romantic fiction. And I am nobody's heroine.

She raised her hand, tensed her arm, then slapped her open palm down on the desktop with all her force.

The pain flamed up her arm directly into her skull. She gritted her teeth until it subsided. The hand still burned. But now her brain was icily clear. She lifted *The Last Summer* and without glancing at it dropped it into the waste basket. Taking the telephone receiver from its cradle she dialled the appropriate number from the hotel register. When a male voice politely answered, she said, 'Please book me the earliest available flight to Rome.' She set the phone to rest.

Gina Rossi was once more in control. She was back on the course of her destiny.

36

Camera flashes were non-stop lightning as reporters hurling questions surged around Gina in the lobby of the Palazzo d'Oro like baying hounds. She strode toward the exit, the path ahead being shouldered clear by six of the hotel's burliest porters. The barrage continued across the pavement to the limousine where the chauffeur struggled to hold the door open against the crush of bodies as Gina ducked into the rear and caught a relieved breath when she at last was sealed in.

Looking out she confronted a mass of strident faces. She wound down the window, held up a gloved hand against the din. Some semblance of quiet eventually percolated the newsmen and Gina said loudly and clearly, 'Thank you all for your interest. However, I have nothing to add to the press release which I issued this morning. After finalizing my business in Rome I shall be flying back to America tonight. I love your city and your country. I look forward to returning to you. Goodbye.'

Questions burst forth anew. Heads and hands thrust into the open window. Gina leaned quickly forward, rapped on the glass dividing panel, and the chauffeur, oblivious to the surrounding throng, accelerated away. Gina leaned back. As the breeze plucked at her hair she wound up the window. She didn't look out at the passing streets; sat facing ahead, her hands folded calmly on the purse in her lap. Inside the purse, a copy of the press release read:

'All media. Immediate publication and transmission.

'Following intensive investigations into the Italian catering trade and its long-term potential, the American Rossi Corporation had announced its intention to establish a chain of restaurant franchises throughout the country.

'In view of the economic expansion under way within the new Republic, and the progressive plans of President Einaudi's government, the Rossi Corporation has scheduled the opening of its Italian subsidiary's first tavern at two years hence. (Detailed costings, tavern specifications and proposed national distribution in attached report.)

'To ensure maximum local involvement in both the financial and administrative base of the subsidiary, the Rossi Corporation will be in contractual partnership with an Italian master franchisee. However, in keeping with the Corporation's policy of encouragement to all individual tavern-keepers, the master contract will be held by a separate Italian company in which all franchisees will be equal shareholders. Thus Rossi Italy will be a truly co-operative venture. No individual will profit more than any other except from his, or her, own tavern. Under the constitution of the Rossi Corporation no one person or organization will be permitted to hold the master franchise.

'Contessa Rossi di Savoia, president of the American Corporation, said she was delighted to be . . .'

In the rear of the limousine, Gina's face was stone.

She snapped at the baker, 'Bureaucratic nonsense!'

The man shrugged, spread expressive hands. 'The Italian law, Contessa. You signed an agreement. It cannot be broken. The money you deposited as security must remain here for a further six months. I am sorry. There is nothing I can do. I too am bound by red tape.' He smiled lamely.

Gina inwardly fumed. Damned herself for not reading the documentation small print that day she'd hurriedly signed her personal cheque for two hundred thousand dollars. Her plan, now that the trap had been sprung on Ugo Balbo, had been to withdraw the money and restore the balance of her finances. She gnawed her lip as she made rapid mental calculations, reviewed her tangled web of loans, pledged bonds and interest repayments. Though her anger at her own oversight still simmered, the temperature of her anxiety diminished when she calculated that no crisis was imminent. The most immediate need was settlement to Sybil and David for the Grange. But they wouldn't need her cheque for, say, three weeks, when the casino was due to open. She nodded confidently to herself; she was sure the launch of the Silver Lady would renew her borrowing capacity, at least sufficiently to cover the payment to Sybil and David.

The banker ventured, 'Perhaps, in view of the delay of your intended investment in our country's economy, I might be able to make some approaches to our Treasury authorities . . .'

'Don't bother,' retorted Gina, rising. 'You may keep the money. I have no need of it. Good day.'

In the suite of the Palazzo d'Oro she packed rapidly, her nerves still on edge. All she wanted now was to be away from here. Away from Rome. To be home.

She impatiently snapped shut her suitcases, leaving them on the bed went through to the sitting room to collect her purse. The sudden banging on the door caused her to pull up sharply. So loud. An over-eager, or ill-trained, porter. Insistent.

Impudent. Annoyed, Gina strode across the room, turned the handle. Before she could speak the door burst open, narrowly missed her head. She recoiled, stumbled backward as Ugo Balbo barged across the threshold. Gina instinctively turned to dash toward the telephone, yet knowing she couldn't reach it before he was on her. She swung to face him, to scream against his assault.

The cry died in her throat. What she saw in the gross man's features was not fury, but fear. Balbo's bulging eyes were terrified as he stammered:

'Contessa. Contessa. Your announcement to the press? Completely contrary to our arrangement. My company was to be your master franchisee. Why did you not warn me of your change of mind? Surely there is a mistake. No? Then what is happening? What of my financial investment? I have committed everything to our deal. You must believe me. Is there some further matter you wish to discuss? Just tell me. I can iron out all problems. Anything you wish, Contessa. Please, I have to know. You must give me the opportunity to understand the situation, to complete our transaction.' He took a further lumbering pace into the room, his sausage fingers meshing before him in supplication.

Gina was driven back by confusion. This was wrong. Something was out of place here. This was too much like her fantasy: the obese hotelier pleading for mercy, being broken by Gina's indifference, crushed by her triumph. She had reached the desk. Without removing her gaze from the fat man, her hand found the telephone. 'Signor Balbo,' she said, maintaining an hauteur she did not feel. 'This is an unwarranted intrusion. How dare you force your way into my suite! I shall call hotel security.' She raised the receiver.

'No,' Balbo cried. 'Please, permit me to explain. I intend you no harm. Forgive my abruptness. But, the situation . . . I had to . . . You were unavailable whenever I called. It was imperative I speak with you. To find out. They . . .'

'I am not in the habit of conducting business discussions under such untoward circumstances,' Gina retaliated icily. 'Besides which, all matters relating to the Rossi Corporation's Italian proposals are in the hands of my attorneys. Decisions have been made. Steps have been taken. I am no longer personally involved.'

'But you have to be,' Balbo insisted desperately.

'I seem to recall,' shot Gina, 'you once saying that executives such as we should not be concerned with trivia.'

'Trivia!' he bleated. 'This involves millions of lire. Don't you understand? I have taken mortgages and loans to purchase scores of properties to lease to Rossi Tavern-keepers. I have even raised finance against my own home, my antiques, works of art. It will all be for nothing if I am not the master franchisee. The properties will be useless. I will lose everything. I acted in good faith. On your word.'

'I made you no promises, Signor Balbo. Any actions you have taken have not been at my behest. You professed to be Italy's leading businessman. As such you knew the difference between investment and risk. You understood also that the latter does not involve only winning.' Gina's voice rose contemptuously. 'If you could not afford to lose, you should not have been in the game.' Her confidence was reflowing. This was what she had wanted, what she had schemed for for months, dreamed of throughout half her life. This was the closing of her personal vendetta. Her father had been avenged. Her family's score had been settled. And yet . . . It had all happened so swiftly. The victory had been so momentary, she scarcely had felt it. There was no surging of the blood, no sense of climax at the expelling of a passion which had been the driving force of all her ambitions. Facing the ogre of her nightmares, Gina experienced only a rising emptiness.

Balbo croaked, 'Help me!'

She stared into those gross features, at that overwhelming fear. And, fleetingly, her innermost susceptibility responded to the plea. She quashed the weakness. I loathe this creature, she avowed. I'll break his life as surely as he smashed mine.

Two porters stood in the doorway with a trolley.

Gina called, 'The luggage in the bedroom. Promptly, please.' She stepped to the sofa, gathered her gloves and purse as the men swiftly obeyed. She started for the door, thought to pass Balbo without a glance. Yet her eyes were drawn to him, as if, at this final instant she must imprint his image on her memory for ever.

There, in a bright hotel room, as her luggage was loaded onto the trolley, and beyond the window the city clamoured, they stood, locked together across the gulf of time. And now, in the recesses of Balbo's gaze Gina saw the struggle for understanding, the effort to remember. And that brought the emotion she had been seeking. The lacerating triumph she had seen in his eyes across a teeming courthouse corridor she at last felt in herself. So powerful was the surge, Gina swayed. She reached at nothing for support, and the obese man automatically responded. For a full two seconds he held Gina's hand as his mouth formed the silent question: Why?

She jerked away, a physical sickness assaulting her brain. She strode for the door, went out of there, along the hallway, could not wait for the elevator, was unable to stop, to look right or left as she ran down the stairs, across the lobby, out to the oncoming night, to slam herself into the dark recesses of the limousine. To shiver there in her last spasm of revenge.

It's over, her inner voice said. All over now.

37

SPECTACULAR OPENING . . . OCTOBER 10TH . . . THE ROSSI CORPORATION, IN ASSOCIATION WITH RKO RADIO PICTURES, PROUDLY PRESENTS . . . A NIGHT OF ONE HUNDRED STARS . . . FEATURING . . .

The glass and steel revolving sign, four storeys high, threw flashing sunbeams toward the Nevada horizon like a desert-locked lighthouse. It stood on the spot where Gina, six weeks ago, had asked Ed Solano to accelerate his completion schedule.

The engineer had succeeded. Beside the monstrous sign a wide, white walkway, flanked on both sides by young palms, stretched from the highway to the towering pyramid. Beyond the trees lay miraculously green lawns and vistas of freshly-planted blooms. At the head of the walkway, in front of the twelve glass double doors beneath the entrance canopy of the Silver Lady, six fountains at the centre of the forecourt spouted thirty feet into the air, their fine mist drifting and settling to glisten like diamond dust on the emerald turf and scarlet flower beds.

Inside those double doors, the lobby. Half an acre of brilliant blue carpet. Chrome and glass vines climbing mirrored walls. A marble pool, sparkling with silver fish beneath a galaxy of crystal chandeliers. An air of luxury as coolly, sharply expensive as champagne poured over cracked ice.

Beyond the lobby, the casino. A vast expanse of dice tables, roulette tables, blackjack tables; to the left a parade of archways to bars and lounges, each entrance flanked by a Big Six wheel; to the right rank upon rank of shining fruit machines, at the far end of the room a sweeping curve of staircase ascending beside the scripted wall sign – SHOWROOM.

No rattle of play here yet, no music, but the bright banter and punctuating laughter of the hundred coveralled men who were polishing woodwork, adjusting light switches, testing equipment, fixing the perimeter of the carpet.

Between Max Barzini and Ed Solano, Gina studied the papers on the clipboard she was holding. 'It's looking good, Ed. Three days to go. No problems?'

The construction engineer watched his working men. 'If there were I wouldn't tell you. Because these guys would have them ironed out come hell fire or high water. Not just because of their big bonus either. There's more to it than that. They know they're working on something very special here, that when they're through they'll be sort of special too. It's a matter of pride with them now. If the earth suddenly opened and swallowed this place, they'd still get it rebuilt by the tenth.' He grinned around at Gina. 'Don't worry, boss. You'll get your night to remember. Count on it.'

Gina nodded. She smiled briefly, but it didn't reach her eyes. The warmth that had once lit Gina Rossi's face had died. So had her youth. As recently as two months ago her radiance still might have caused her to be taken for five or more years younger. Today, in the cruel interrogation of electric light there could be no hiding the truth.

Her cheeks had become hollowed, shadows darkened her eyes, and the beginnings of creases beside her mouth accentuated the hardened line of her jaw. All Gina's bitterness had drained the day she had destroyed Ugo Balbo, leaving her satiated but empty, and the scars of her revenge carved into her features for all time.

She flipped over the pages on the clipboard, sharply ticked off several items before turning to the commotion which was approaching from the lobby. A score of men lugging microphones, drums of cable, klieg lamps and two huge cameras inscribed 'Movietone' entered the casino. Gina quickly checked her watch. 'Max, I don't have time to handle that. I must make the flight to New York. Please take care of them, will you?'

Max responded, '*Si*, Principessa.'

'Any other news people who turn up early too. Keep them happy. Make sure they all have a press kit. Plus fifty dollars apiece in chips. I want the best coverage there's ever been for any event bar none. The day following the opening I don't want there to be a single human being in the country who doesn't know what has happened here, who doesn't believe, implicitly, that the Rossi name is going to be branded on American history.'

Max repeated, '*Si*, Principessa.' As Gina returned to her clipboard he caught Ed Solano's troubled glance. He replied with a look of gentle understanding. Later he would say to the construction engineer, 'It's simply that sometimes she loses the best part of herself. But, then, who amongst us can claim never to have been less than whole?'

The Movietone crew was approaching. Gina said to Max, 'I'll be back in two days.' She turned to Ed Solano. 'I'll check out the showroom before I leave.' She strode toward the staircase.

She slept for two of the twenty-four hours she was in New York. Since returning to the city she'd divided the time between her offices at the Lady, the Rossi Building and the Park Avenue apartment. Harry had assured, 'There's no need to be rushing back and forth across the country. Everything's under control. We can cope.' Gina didn't doubt it; she knew she could trust all her people to keep the wheels spinning smoothly. In the midst of her activity she had paused briefly on that thought. So many people, she had pondered. Such a family. The Rossi family. All working, caring, sharing just as a family. Trusting too. Trusting me to hold them together. How many? She wasn't sure, for not only were there the hundreds of men and women who were a direct part of the Rossi Corporation, there were also those in the Rossi Taverns – from the franchisees to the lowliest kitchen trainees – who were reliant on her continuing energy and expertise. Did they, she wondered, ever pause this way to think about her? Did they ever consider how much of her life was consumed by theirs? Maybe not. But that's how it should be. That's what it means to be the head of the family. To be the *madrina*.

Gina had shrugged off these thoughts, returned to her accountant's and attorney's and consultants' reports. As Harry had affirmed, everything was under control. And inside another forty-eight hours, after the Silver Lady had been brought to life, she could draw a steadying breath, and, for a short while, sit aside and let time pursue its own course.

She looked up from her desk.

Filipo stuck his head around the jamb, grinned lopsidedly, entered, shrugging his rangy shoulders. Hands stuck in his pants' pockets he crossed to the desk, scuffing his toes at the carpet, peering down there as if he expected to find the words which Gina could see on his silently-working lips. For an instant she saw him as a boy again, eleven years old, coming in that night at Broome Street after she'd learned he had a part-time job as a gofer in a local fleapit movie house. The image retreated and he was once more six feet tall in a campus football jersey, black curls tumbling across his forehead, looking cautiously at her and saying, 'Gina, we have to talk.'

She glanced at her watch. Only two hours before her flight was due out. Can't it wait? She held back the question, said amiably, 'So, don't just stand there like a flagpole. Sit.' As an afterthought she offered, 'Coffee? Something stronger?'

Filipo shook his head, went and sat on the sofa by the wall, hunched forward, feet apart, hands clenched down between his knees like a player on the bench working himself up for the big match. He stared at his sister.

And a tremor of unease ran through her as she caught the unfamiliar light in his eyes. She asked briskly, 'Are you all packed? Ready for Vegas?'

He said abruptly, 'I want to go to California.'

Gina blinked. 'Pardon?'

'San Francisco. I want to go there.'

Is that all. For a moment, though she couldn't explain why, her nerves had been on a wire. Now the tension retreated – but not too far. She put some brightness into her voice, kept a check on her impatience. 'Fine. That's a fine idea. They say it's the most beautiful city in the world. All the time I was on the west coast I never had time to go there. Maybe . . . ' What was the matter here? Gina didn't know but she couldn't shake off her sense of premonition. 'Maybe we could go together. How about that? Your next vacation. Don't look at me like

506

that. I'm not such a dire travelling companion, am I? I'd like for us to spend some time together. It's been too long. I promise I wouldn't mention business. I wouldn't visit a single franchisee. We could . . . '

'Not a vacation,' interrupted Filipo.

Gina's winning smile evaporated.

Filipo went on, 'That isn't what I meant. What I want . . . ' He searched his sister's face before taking a deep breath and declaring, 'I want to go to live in San Francisco. To study. But . . . But not law, Gina.'

'What?' The muscles of her face tightened.

He held up defensive palms against the rising fire in her cheeks. 'Please, hear me out. Don't shout me down. I've thought about this. Believe me. This isn't some spur-of-the-moment decision. I've hauled my brain over it and over it until I thought I might go screwy. But I come up with the same answer every time. I have to go.'

Gina challenged, 'To study what?'

'Movie-making.'

She should have known. 'Don't be preposterous.'

'I'm not. There's a new school. It's good. Excellent. They have some of the industry's finest people as guest lecturers. Directors. Technicians. Writers. Weidermeyer from Germany. Hudson from England. Next semester Lafosse is coming from France to run a course on lighting techniques.'

'Lighting techniques! What on earth are you talking about? If you want to discuss lighting techniques I'll call an electrician.' That wasn't funny, Gina. And it wasn't worthy of you. Nor was the acid in your tone. She'd been about to snap, I'm not listening to any more of this, but faced by the continued hardness in his features she said with controlled calm, 'Very well, if you must discuss it we shall. But not now. I have the plane to catch. We'll talk about it in Las Vegas. After the opening of The Silver Lady.'

'No.' Filipo's tone was as rigid as his set shoulders. 'I want it settled now. Not after you've had time to work out how you can finagle your own way.'

Gina clenched the arms of her chair.

Filipo apologized. 'I'm sorry. I didn't mean that as an insult. But that's what you do, isn't it? You never really parley a subject. Yes, you're brilliant at making it appear as if you do. But, in fact, you always go into any debate with your mind irreversibly made up, and the avowed intent of having everybody come out on your side – whether they like it or not. Well, this time, Gina, I'm not being talked into or out of anything.' He stood. 'I think I will have that drink after all.' At the cabinet he set out two glasses, uncapped a bottle.

Gina watched his back, her mind a seething mass. Damn it, Filipo. I don't need this now! This is the last thing I want at this moment. She held his gaze with unshakable resolve as he walked toward her, set a glass on the desk, carried his own drink back to the sofa. She noted the physical distance he had placed between them, also the total absence of trepidation in his eyes. Her brother, she suddenly realized, was as determined as she.

He said, 'I came here to state my case. Not to discuss. Not to argue. Not to row. I love you, and it hurts me to defy you. But, despite what you might think to the contrary, I do know my own mind. At least at this moment. That's what's important. Can you understand? I want you to understand. At this moment I am one hundred per cent sure of what I want. I don't deny that in a couple of years' time I might feel differently. But won't you accept that that would be natural? People do change, should be allowed to alter their direction.'

Gina was gripping the edges of her patience as it began to fracture like a sheet of ice under unrelenting pressure.

Filipo continued, 'The San Francisco school has agreed to accept me at the beginning of next year.'

'You've talked with them?'

'Of course. I told you, this isn't some half-baked idea. I read their prospectus nine months ago. I've spent most of the time I've been living at college studying their courses. I visited when I was out west with Max at Easter. No, don't blame him, he didn't know where I was at, thought I was pottering around the wharf while he was meeting dice manufacturers.' Filipo sighed. 'Like I said, since then I've looked at the situation till my head ached.'

Gina countered, 'But didn't bother to tell me.'

Ignoring this her brother stated, 'I intend to take the opportunity. There isn't any more I can say.'

The air throbbed.

Gina laced her fingers in her lap, tensed them until her knuckles cracked. She asked tightly, 'And what about your present studies? What about all the time you've put in on your

508

law books? You're going to let that all fly out of the window, are you?'

'Gina, none of that was for me. Don't you realize? It was for you. All my work at high school, at college, has been for you. It was never what I wanted. I tried to make it so, I truly did. I figured if I applied myself, I might see it differently. But I didn't. I can't. I've given it my best shot and still I . . . I hate it.'

'Don't be so melodramatic.'

'I want to be an actor.'

'A childish fantasy.'

'Don't be so insulting.'

'And don't you answer me back. Can't you have a mature discussion without snapping? Or are you just acting? Practising for when you're offered lead billing by Darryl Zanuck?' Gina saw her brother's face burn. Her warning bells were ringing. She knew she must stop here, end this now, before it was too late. But I am right, she insisted. I do know what is best for him. She felt the situation was being swept along on a river of no return. They'd both drown if she couldn't pull them out. For swirling seconds that stretched like minutes there was apparently no escape. She was on the very brink of tumbling into the quarrelsome current when at the edge of her rushing thoughts she glimpsed a straw. She mentally frowned, straining to see into the recesses of her mind where that frail hope lay, struggling to construct the idea in these rapidly draining moments.

She stood abruptly, said, 'Excuse me a moment,' and before Filipo could respond strode from the room. She went into the bathroom, closed the door, stood staring unseeing at herself in the mirror. She remained there for five minutes.

When she returned she threw her brother a brief smile and declared with an air of tremendous calm, 'Very well. If you want experience of acting you may try it.'

Filipo stared. At last: 'You mean it?'

'I do. But I can't condone your attending a new, unproven school in San Francisco. If you're going to do something, you should do it right, with proper people, or not at all. Will you agree? Please? I'm going to suggest you take twelve months off from college and go work with a real movie company. I'll arrange it. I'll get you a spot at RKO. You already met one of their producers, Mister Felix Gilbert, who's helping us stage The

Silver Lady show. I'm sure he'll take you on. You can do the screen test, walk-ons, the works. Then it will be up to Mister Gilbert. He's the expert. If he figures you're a natural, if he wants to make you a star, so be it. I won't stand in your way.'

Filipo began to smile.

'But,' added Gina, 'if, after a full twelve months at the studio he says you don't have what it takes, then you'll agree to quit and go back to law school, no arguments.' She raised questioning brows. 'Is that fair?'

Filipo was on his feet. 'Of course it is. That's all I wanted. To have the chance. And I promise you I'll make it. I know I can.' He came across to the desk, around it to Gina, taking her hands, pulling her to her feet, gathering her into his arms. After a moment of hugging her he stepped back, holding her shoulders, reading her expression. 'You're really not angry? You aren't going to send me to bed without supper?'

Gina smiled. Her nerves smoothed themselves and she answered, 'I don't think that will be necessary.'

Filipo grinned. 'I love you, Sis.'

She answered, 'I love you too, Filipo. Very much.'

Beyond the towering revolving sign, the pyramid was a gigantic diamond, light blazing from all its facets against the black velvet backdrop of the Nevada night. In the forecourt, floodlamps transformed the spouting fountains into columns of liquid platinum. Still more lamps bathed the trees, the grass, the blooms in lambent blue. But outshining all this, across the fascia of the pyramid's entrance, in shimmering white letters twelve feet high – THE SILVER LADY.

Beneath this, a laughing, milling mass. Guests and pressmen and photographers and Rossi personnel ebbing and flowing as if caught in eddies of slow-motion water, many being drawn to this side or that to stare and stare up the face of the opalescent mountain to its crystal summit, their awestruck, tilted features glistening as if with silver rain. At last they would flow back into the main current to be swept through the high doorways.

Within the lobby, an explosion of light and noise, the people pouring through to the casino, gasping, shouting, pointing as they streamed beween the unmanned tables to the staircase, thence upward, looking back, looking forward, and into the showroom.

Here, tier after tier of white-linened tables and blue-upholstered banquettes descending to the wide curve of curtained stage. A dance band from a dozen hidden speakers provided a musical background to the percussion of conversation. Silver-jacketed waiters moved swiftly and attentively, constantly recharging glasses with champagne. The guests, dazzlingly elegant in evening dress, drifted, moved from table to table seeking their place names, paused in groups, chatting, sharing casual intimacy. Occasionally a pocket of gossip would cease as heads turned, smiles were switched on with practised ease, and cameras flashed on jewels.

Gina walked up the stepped central aisle of the showroom, fluttering her fingers here and there, laughing lightly, exchanging greetings as if she knew each guest personally. Sometimes she would pause to kiss or be kissed, to deliver a joke, to gather news and compliments and congratulations.

A man with a granite-hewn face beneath a shock of white hair beamed around from his group, surveyed Gina from head to toe with unconcealed appreciation. Gina's hair was upswept and pinned with diamond-encrusted butterflies. Her Lucien Lelong gown was silver-threaded white silk, single-shouldered, cut low above her right breast, plunging to below her waist at the back. It clung to her lines and curves like a second skin, flowed to the floor as if it was melting. The man said, 'You're the most beautiful woman in the world tonight.' Gina acknowledged, 'Thank you, Governor.'

She went on up to the topmost aisle which ran around the rear of the showroom, negotiated more clusters of well-wishers, then on an empty spot in the furthest corner turned to stare down and around, surveying the scene.

Everyone had come. Not one of the eighteen hundred invitees had turned down this night. The list read like a roll-call from the pages of *Life*, *Newsweek* and *Screenland*. And amidst the celebrities, somewhere, was Gina's family. She searched the faces.

Over there, Ethel Ponti in an elegant floor-length, cream and navy dress with a sequinned evening jacket, chatting nineteen to the dozen to a trio of hunky young World Series heroes. Nearby, Irving Prentiss, as immaculate as one of his perfect balance sheets, in close conference with a ravishing scarlet-sheathed blonde from the chorus of tonight's forthcoming show. Ed Solano, standing at his table, laughing around a cigar as he shared some joke with the sixteen inches shorter but no less distinguished Chang, and beside them May Ling, beautiful in an emerald and gold cheongsam. By the archway to the bar, Harry, no doubt in deep reminiscence with those four musicians from the orchestra. In a niche on the far wall, arousing more interest, eliciting more greetings than any of the movie stars present, Twickenham, gazing back at Gina with a private gleam in his eye. There too, Dorothy Hamm, probably trying to talk a book of folk songs out of that operatic diva. Wheldon J. Hoyt, certainly wheeling some sort of a deal with that automobile king. André de Sath offering the boxing champion advice on interior design. Felix Gilbert, extolling to everyone within earshot the fantastic prospects of RKO.

Gina smiled to herself. All the inhabitants of my life. The close ones, and the not-so-close. The loved, and the less loved. But each one, in his or her way, an essential part of my life, the movers of the jigsaw pieces that make me what I am to-night.

Not all here, of course. A wisp of sadness touched Gina as she thought of Fallon and Cassie. She held their image for only a moment though. No sad dreams; not this desert-scented night. Besides, life is too short for long regrets.

Speaking of missing faces: Paola and Johnny. They ought to have arrived by now. How typical of my thrifty sister to insist on driving all the way from Phoenix instead of flying! Serve her right if they've had a flat in the middle of the Arizona badlands. Actually, they're most likely downstairs in the casino, Johnny checking out the design of the fruit machines, a line he's planning on adding to his Vendomats. A shrewd man is Mister J. Sabato. Well, he married my sister, didn't he?

And what about my brother? Gina re-scanned the crowd. I told him he should take yesterday's flight with me. But no, he has to insist on staying in Manhattan till the last minute just to catch the first showing of some new movie. If he missed that plane, I'll . . . What? What will you do? 'I'll box his ears,' she exclaimed out loud.

Several nearby guests glanced around. Gina threw them a dazzling smile. Beyond them she saw Max towering through the throng. As he strode up to her, resplendent in his tuxedo, silver hair gleaming, moustachios positively twirling with importance, Gina smiled admiringly. 'Mister Barzini, you look like the grand vizier of some very important place – as well as the president of America's most fabulous casino. You make me so happy.'

The Tuscan giant beamed. Then his smile became more gentle. He reached out his huge palms, gathered Gina's hands and held them. 'And you, Principessa, make me so proud. The proudest man in the world. You make all your family proud. And, above all, you would have made your Poppa proud.'

Gina swallowed hard. Though she wanted to hold the thought of her father, she would not. This was not the time. Tonight was not for sad memories. Extricating her hands from Max's fists, she reached up, cupped his time-etched face, tiptoed and kissed his lips. She said, 'Thank you, old friend, for everything.' Then, quickly stepping back, before the big man could respond she asked briskly, 'Have you seen Filipo?'

Max frowned, pondered. 'No, Principessa. Now that you mention it, I have not.' Seeing the two small spots of colour spring to Gina's cheeks, he added placatingly, 'Don't worry. Filipo may sometimes be, how do you say . . . *capriccioso* . . . wayward, but he would never let you down. He'll be here in time. Besides, he told me, wild horses couldn't keep him from seeing you dance on the stage with Mister Danny Kaye after your speech.'

Gina muttered, 'Harumph! Goodness knows why I let myself be talked into that. And,' she shot, 'you can put that grin away. Don't think I don't know you and Harry bribed the producer to come up with the idea. If I fall on my butt in front of two thousand people, woe betide the pair of you.' She fixed him with a flinty eye.

Max didn't flinch. 'Principessa, you can't fool me. I know very well you've been rehearsing like a demon, and that you just can't wait to get up there and guarantee a photograph that will make the front pages from one end of the country to the other. Furthermore . . . ' he placed the end of his forefinger on the tip of her nose, gave a small press, 'the day you fall on your butt, I'll give up playing pinocle.' He turned and strode away.

Gina watched him with all her affection.

Sybil's voice said, 'There you are, old thing.'

Gina smiled around at the approaching English couple. David's carefully-tailored, double-breasted evening suit did much to camouflage his portly shape; while Sybil, in a high-necked, lace and chiffon, rust-coloured Victorian gown, her auburn tresses piled and gold-pinned, looked, unquestionably, every inch a duchess. Gina asked warmly, 'Settled in?'

'That suite!' exclaimed Sybil. 'Really, are you sure it wasn't meant for Prince Rupert of Hentzau?'

'If you're staying a whole week,' returned Gina, 'I felt you ought to have something slightly more comfortable than our old room at the Rainbow. David, I'm delighted you persuaded this dynamo to switch off for a while.'

'Actually,' he said with an askance but fond tilt at his wife, 'we've set up appointments to spend some of our time talking with several welfare organizations out here. Nevada, and a couple of the neighbouring states – California and Oregon – have some very progressive social ideas.' To Gina's exaggerated frown of exasperation, he added, 'But, I promise, I'll insist that Sybil spends at least half of our visit at Lake Mead, the Grand Canyon, and any other spot I can have her all to myself for a change.' He slipped his arm around Sybil's waist.

Gina suppressed the small twinge of envy which nudged her. 'By the way . . .' she said, delving her silver purse and extracting a cheque. 'The moment you cash this, I shall become the official owner of the Grange.'

Sybil acknowledged, 'Thanks, old girl. That will keep the roof over our heads. David, you hold on to it. Very firmly. And don't let Max persuade you to convert it to chips.'

David, grinning, took the cheque. 'Don't worry, this won't see the light of day for another week, until it's being handed over our bank counter. Gina,' he patted his inside pocket where the slip of currency now lay, 'that's heaven-sent. In the nick of time.'

Gina's smile faltered. 'I didn't think you were that desperate for cash. When I visited you in London, before I suggested buying the Grange, you said you had some finance to fall back on in the event of not being able to sell before you bought the new premises.'

'That was true,' said Sybil. 'But after we received your signed contracts, we decided our investments were no longer needed. What good were they doing? The new home was more important. So we cashed in the lot and used it for refurbishing. The job is almost complete. We took a leaf out of your book, got the plumbers, electricians, carpenters working round the clock. Well, almost – the craftsmen in Nettling Pastures, Wilts, couldn't quite be persuaded to work the same twenty-four hour schedule as their counterparts in Las Vegas, Nevada. Nevertheless, they did put in double shifts – eighteen hours a day – and have done us proud. We're quite the best-looking, best-equipped home for unmarried mums in Britain – Europe, probably.'

'So,' added David, 'we may be slightly boracic lint – skint – flat bust, as you'd say around here – but it's worth it, just to see the blissful smiles of the tinies when they park on their new, streamlined, jet-age, plastic potties.'

Sybil laughed out loud, exclaimed, 'David, really!'

Gina smiled. She searched for something to say to these two caring people, but could find nothing worthy enough. She declared, 'Well, less than thirty minutes to take-off. I'd better go check I can remember my speech. Sybil, no making faces at me from the front row. See you later.'

She negotiated her way back down through the congratulations to the lowest tier, across to a PRIVATE-stencilled side door, along a corridor, and into the cavernous backstage area. A kaleidoscope of colour and activity: high lamps flashing on and off; technicians climbing gantries, moving along overhead walkways; a gang hauling cables and a massive camera on a trolley; a score of girls running past, glittering in silver and white; a middle-aged woman in denim coveralls brandishing a clipboard; a man in a gold tuxedo perched on top of a twenty-foot high mirrored replica of the casino waving his arms; people hurrying and gesticulating and shouting silent orders, carrying musical instruments, wheeling rails loaded with costumes, raising a huge board lettered RUNNING ORDER followed by the sequence of show spots numbered 1 through 210, amongst which Gina could see, 7 – G. Rossi – SPEECH.

Her nerves had begun to jangle. Stop that, she told herself. You've been through all this before – openings, receptions, press conferences, public appearances – none of them threw you. Okay, so this is the daddy of them all, tonight's the night of all nights, but there's no cause to work yourself into a funk. You can carry it off, of course you can. Like always, you take a deep breath, you give 'em your dazzlingest smile, and you do it. A quarter-hour later it's all over. Easy. A piece of cake.

A vast clock mounted on a scaffold frame was counting the minutes. Ten to go.

Gina walked out across the expanse of stage. At the centre, where the curtains overlapped, after some searching she found the small hole in the material made specially so that the director, the master of ceremonies, or anybody else for that matter, G. Rossi included, could peep through to observe how the other participants of the evening – the audience – were shaping up.

Most of them were at their tables, chattering, chinking glasses, exclaiming over the silver-covered presentation programmed each had received. Anticipation crackled around the sumptuous, semi-circular amphitheatre like summer-night lightning. Gina felt it tingle through her blood. The trepidation of a moment ago retreated before the onrush of her excitement. Headiness swayed her as she saw the whole scene, saw separate pieces of it, saw particular incidents, saw individual faces. Didn't see Filipo. Did she? Was that him, coming in through the high rear entrance? She braced forward against the curtains, peering intently.

'Miss Rossi.'

Gina almost jumped out of her shoes, jerked around to the woman in coveralls who said, 'Five minutes. We're all set.' Gina stared, momentarily abstracted before realizing the stage was filling rapidly with plumed and spangled showgirls. 'Yes. Right,' she said. 'I'll make myself scarce.' She headed back toward the wide area beyond the stage which was now swarming like a fractured ant nest. Everyone who hurried by said, 'Good luck.' 'Break a leg.' 'Knock 'em dead.' The producer, in mid-stride, caught her arm. 'Are you all right, Gina? Got your cue? Remember your speech? Sorry, of course you do. It's going to be fantastic. Stupendous. Ziegfeld? Who the heck was he?'

Gina said she was fine, made her way to a spot by a fire hose on the wall. She regulated her breathing concentrated on getting her pulse rate to something near normal. The activity was dying down, like a movie decreasing to slow motion. Suddenly everybody was motionless. Dead silence. All eyes were riveted on the stage where the hundred showgirls poised in the glass and silver landscape around the mirrored pyramid. A man in a white tuxedo was similarly frozen at the centre-stage microphone. Gina thought the moment would last for ever. Then she heard a man's voice say, 'Let's do it.'

Lights blazed. The orchestra blared. The curtains swept

open. The audience erupted. The man in the white tuxedo bawled, 'Welcome. Welcome to the Silver Lady.' Music. Applause. Cheering. The showgirls sweeping into their routine.

An old boy of a stagehand beside Gina declared, 'That's it. Off and running. Excitement over for another day.' He wandered off to sit on a box and read his newspaper. Others too now drifted away from watching the action. Gina wasn't surprised. She'd seen all this before at the club. Yes, tonight was special, very special; but like any other show, once it was under way, much of the tension went out of the atmosphere. From here on it was a job of work for each individual who would concentrate on his or her own role.

For a few moments longer Gina observed the extravaganza. Then she also put her mind to her forthcoming performance. As the first number ended to fresh applause and the compère reappeared, she went over the words of her speech. The laughter out there retreated. She silently practised her intonation. Someone else was running out into the spotlight. She carefully considered her phrasing. More showgirls and male dancers made their entrance. She mentally pictured the steps she would take with Danny Kaye. She saw herself taking a bow. Several bows. On stage a singing group was belting out a recent hit. Again she reviewed the beginning of her speech. The compère was making an announcement. Her name. Cheering.

A man stepping up to her. 'Telephone, Miss Rossi.'

'What? Not now. I'm on in four minutes.'

'He said it wouldn't wait.'

'Who said?'

'He wouldn't give a name.'

'A nut?'

'Didn't sound like a nut. Sounded very serious. Said I should say you had to come to the phone no matter what.'

Gina looked from the man's face, to the stage, to the huge clock. 'Very well. Where?' The man pointed to a wall phone amidst scaffold and cables. She strode swiftly there, lifted the receiver to one ear, held her hand over the other. 'Yes,' she said impatiently.

A deep, flat male voice: 'Miss Gina Rossi?'

'This is she.'

'Listen to me, Miss Rossi. Listen carefully and do not

517

interrupt. I will not repeat myself.' A pause. 'You owe us one million dollars, Miss Rossi. One million. The amount we had invested . . . to be accurate, I should say our Italian cousins had invested . . . in Ugo Balbo. The late Ugo Balbo. Yes, Signor Balbo recently met with an unfortunate accident. The penalty of carelessness. A salutary lesson for others. However, that should not be your concern, Miss Rossi. What you must give all your attention to is the restitution of the investment we . . . our cousins . . . had in Signor Balbo. One million dollars, Miss Rossi. A not inconsiderable sum. One we are not prepared to overlook. We require payment. In full. Do you understand? I'm sure you do. Please do not call out to anyone. I assure you that would be most unwise. Just continue to listen. We are not unrealistic. We realize you may require some time to raise the money. You have seven days. Also, as a further gesture of our understanding, if you are unable to raise the one million we will gladly accept property in lieu of cash. By property we mean, of course, the Rossi Corporation, including the splendid building in which you are presently standing. The choice is entirely yours, Miss Rossi. I will contact you at this number in seven days' time with instruction on how payment – whichever method you have chosen – should be made. In the meantime, please dismiss all thoughts of contacting the police. If you do, I assure you we will know. I also assure you that if you do, you will never see the boy again.'

The connection was cut.

Gina was frozen. But her mind was being consumed by fire. All sound from the theatre had been cut off. Yet her brain was being hammered by a terrible roaring. She swayed forward, dropping the telephone, groping at the wall for support. In a paralysis of shock she slumped there, until the man's final words slammed again in her ears – 'You will never see the boy again.'

Reality gouged her. She gasped loud, 'Filipo!'

She swung left and right, her eyes desperately searching the surrounding faces, irrationally half-expecting to see her brother there. Then all at once she was running forward. Over cables. Past people. Slamming unheeding into shoulders. Stumbling in her headlong rush and almost falling onto the stage where she was caught, held back by concerned hands. She heard voices, 'Miss Rossi? What's wrong? Are you all right?' but scarcely understood them as she strove forward in the restraining grip to stare out to where Filipo should be. The lights and the dancers whirled before her. Where was he? Where? There, with that group.

An empty chair.

Gina cried out, wrenched herself free and staggered back. He must be here. Her mind refused to believe otherwise. The telephone voice re-echoed in her head against the background cacophony of music and applause. Clamping her hands over her ears she turned and fled across the backstage cavern, out to a long, naked, white-lit corridor. She raced toward the far door, the showroom noise diminishing behind, through beneath the SERVICE STAIRS sign and down the bare concrete flight, abandoning all caution on her skidding, clattering high heels.

She burst into the casino.

Three distant security guards jerked around reaching for their holsters. Recognizing her they started forward. Gina hardly saw them; they were not whom she was seeking. But there was no one else here. A sob caught in her throat as she frantically scanned the vast room. Helplessness enveloped her like a fog, a miasma at once saturating her with dread while sapping her reason. With a great inpull of breath she held her splintering senses together.

Ignoring the calls and the advance of the security men, again she ran. She ran between the dice tables and the roulette tables and the Big Six wheels, her hair tumbling, her arm banging against a wall, her gown snatching at her ankles. She ran out into the deserted lobby.

The ice-glitter of the crystal and steel and chrome was as piercing as the Arctic blizzard of her emotions. Gina didn't know which way to turn. There was nowhere else to go. Unthinking, she dashed through the open doors . . .

. . . to the blinding white night. Stumbling to a halt she threw up an arm against the assault of the bombarding light of the tower. She was drenched by the brilliance, felt she would drown in the incandescence pouring from the massive neon name sign, THE SILVER LADY. Her reason began to melt in the glaring emptiness. Had the past minutes actually happened? Had she really received the devastating phone call? Gina jammed her knuckles to her teeth, bit down, driving pain and rationality into her brain. She peered along the paved walkway, between the luminous trees, toward the wall of blackness which was the highway. A sound there? She strained to penetrate the dark. Something? Someone?

A figure advanced from the void.

Fear was a scrape of claws on Gina's flesh. The figure evolved. Became a man. Gina stifled a cry. Through desperate eyes she watched the rapidly oncoming features taking shape, achieving a semblance of familiarity. Gina stared, and reality knifed her, its pain sharply tangible in her chest. Her brain reeled as she recognized the approaching man. Johnny Sabato. Reason eluded her, yet with Johnny still twenty yards distant she called automatically, urgently, 'Filipo?'

Continuing forward Johnny answered, 'He's okay. His flight was delayed. He rerouted to Phoenix. He's stayed to take care of Paola.'

Paola? Gina's senses trembled in the balance. Then Johnny was less than twelve paces away, his heels cracking on the cold, white concrete, and in the harsh glare of the casino lights Gina saw the agony in his eyes. In that raging moment of shock she strove for understanding. The telephone voice flayed – 'You will never see the boy again.'

And her mind screamed, Little Frankie!

38

Gina felt as if she was existing at the bottom of an ocean. Her senses seemed crushed by an unrelenting pressure, and she had to raise a huge effort of will to make her muscles function. At the same time her nerves were stretched to screaming point. One minute she was sweating profusely, the next she was bitterly cold. She seesawed between raging anger and devastating grief. Above everything, crippling her like a terrible sickness, was her impotence. Throughout all her life, against the fiercest odds, in the darkest hours, she always had been able to reinforce her determination with some iota of hope. Now, there was no sight of even the flimsiest straw.

She was drowning in these helpless depths.

It was six days since the nightmare in Las Vegas, and the

events immediately following the terrible phone call had become slivers of fractured memory – Johnny confirming the dreadful truth in the pool of light before the casino; his broken explanation of discovering Frankie was missing, receiving a telephone warning not to contact the police, plus instructions to go directly to Gina; their subsequent distraught hours in Gina's office while below them the inaugural festivities of the Silver Lady roistered on.

Facing that continuing celebration had been impossible. Gina had sent word that she'd been overtaken by tiredness. Fortunately, the untruth wasn't questioned. In fact everyone remarked it was only to be expected; they sent their messages of love and concern, and Max even went so far as to post a guard at Gina's door to ensure she wasn't disturbed. Gina was deeply grateful to him for that; and the knowledge that he, and the rest of the family, cared for her so much was what had held her together during those devastating hours.

Johnny too had been a rock. Despite the cataclysm which had struck his life, he had rallied Gina with his strength and reason. He had accepted that for now they would tell no one, not even Max, what had happened, had agreed with Gina that the burden would not lessen with sharing and that there was no point in inflicting distress on anyone else. By the time dawn approached from beyond the far mountains, while Gina had felt physically haggard, her mind was back in control. Seven days the man on the telephone had given. Rationality therefore said that the people he represented understood the difficulties of raising a million dollars; though they were cold-blooded criminals, they were not deranged kidnappers. Gina clung to this grim thread of consolation, asserted to herself, and Johnny, that it was a guarantee of little Frankie's safety.

The morning following the phone call, Gina summoned the courage to face Max and Harry. She told them Johnny had brought news of Filipo's detour to the Sabato home where he had remained with Paola, who had been stricken with flu. She assured them the illness was mild but that she was flying with Johnny to visit her sister. This, at least, was true.

After hurried goodbyes to Sybil, David and several others, they left via a rear entrance, avoiding the news reporters still on the scene, and before noon were at St Mary's Convent Hospital in Phoenix.

'You may go in,' the young, dark-haired doctor advised,

'but no talking, please. Mrs Sabato is sleeping under sedation. The longer she does so, the better.'

Filipo arose from a chair as they entered the small, yellow-painted room. Gina had never seen her brother look so ashen and unshaven. Her paramount concern however was for Paola, and she went swiftly to the bed to stare down at the deeply breathing figure there. Her throat filled and it took all her self-restraint not to reach out to touch the pale cheeks, to brush the tumbled hair from her sister's brow.

Last night at the Silver Lady Johnny had recounted Paola's anguished reaction to Frankie's disappearance, her initial violent distress which later had collapsed into silent paralysis. He had had no alternative but to call the doctor, explaining away his wife's condition as the result of grievous family news. The doctor had insisted on Paola's admission to St Mary's. Filipo had agreed with Johnny to stand vigil, and, in the event of his sister's waking, to do all he could to reassure her, also, for Frankie's sake, to keep her from revealing the truth to anyone at the hospital. Apparently, the latter had not been necessary, Paola having been sedated since her arrival.

Gina stood at the bedside a long time. At last, beckoning her brother, she went out to the sunlit corridor. 'Are you all right?' she asked as Filipo joined her.

'I'm fine,' he answered. 'Are you?' When Gina nodded he stood mutely awhile, then he gathered her into his arms, held her very tightly. After several seconds he stepped back. 'Sis,' he said strongly. 'Please, tell me why they've taken Frankie.'

Gina regarded him. Her little brother. Eight years old, wasn't he, that morning, the other side of a lifetime, when she had left Ristorante Rossi to accompany their father into exile, not daring to look in on Paola and Filipo lest she had to share with them the pain of the stake that had been driven through her own heart? She now reached out her hand to him, felt his uncertainty but his strength too as his fingers closed about hers. She said quietly, 'Let's go and talk.'

Twenty-four hours later she was in Manhattan.

She had dearly wanted to remain in Phoenix for Paola's waking, but Paola had Johnny and Filipo to support her with the bedrock of their love, and Gina needed every precious moment to raise the million. That the task was hopeless was a possibility she had refused to accept ever since the demand had been made. She could do it. She had told Johnny so. With relentless insistence she clung to the belief, on the flight from Phoenix deafened herself to the voices of contradiction as she covered page upon page of her notebook with calculations.

By the time she reached the Park Avenue apartment she was nauseous from the prolonged concentration combined with lack of sleep and food. At the bedroom door the sickness swayed her and she clutched the jamb, squeezing shut her eyes then forcing them open to stare across the creamy sea of carpet to where it lapped the lace valance of the bed. She could go there. Lie down. For just a minute, for a few seconds relief. Gina banged her knuckles against the doorframe. 'Move,' she commanded herself aloud, and willed her body toward the bathroom. There she remained beneath an icy shower until the coldness reached the point of pain. She dressed in a fresh blouse and skirt, vigorously brushed her hair, made and drank two cups of strong, black coffee. For the next ten hours she worked at her ledgers.

It was not until the third night following Frankie's kidnap that the truth began to drive the nails of incontrovertibility into her brain. Yet still she refused to believe. There had to be an answer. She was sure it was here, in the welter of figures swimming before her eyes. But it eluded her, and her ability to find it was draining with her strength – as were the hours which were now tumbling toward the deadline.

On the fourth morning she called Irving Prentiss.

The accountant, returned from Las Vegas, came immediately to her bidding. Coolly immaculate, his balance sheets before him on the desk, he sat facing Gina and listened while she told him that it was necessary to raise one million dollars by the end of the week. As usual he didn't question her reasons. As usual his answer was unequivocal.

'Not the remotest chance,' he said impassively. 'Perhaps a few thousand dollars. But a million? I'm sorry. All our collateral is committed. We are, frankly, massively in debt. Even the two hundred thousand on deposit in Rome is spoken for. The amount you personally can raise against future royalties on the cookbook is negligible, but will just about cover the cheque you made out to Sybil and David Lowell. Your million-dollar project – whatever it is – will, I'm afraid, have to wait. Perhaps in three or four months' time, when we have more taverns under way and the Silver Lady is showing a profit, we might be able to raise the quantity of cash you're talking about. At the moment however . . . . ' He gave a small, negative shrug.

It was then that Gina had begun to drown. For she knew that Prentiss's assertion was irrefutable. In truth she had known it all along, but only now did the dark curtain she had raised against it disintegrate to leave her, in the cold light of reality, staring at the gallows of her own making.

Prentiss was saying, ' . . . would be possible. Perhaps three hundred thousand if you were to pledge your sister's and brother's shares. Also Max Barzini's and Harry Dix's shares are uncommitted. They would go some way toward . . . '

Shortly afterward Gina bade the accountant goodbye. Fatigue was a black cloud in her head. Still she refused to surrender to sleep. She remained at her desk, her hands taloned to the arms of her chair like bone hooks holding her above the pit of defeat. The hope that Prentiss had held out – the pledging of individuals' percentages of the Rossi Corporation – added to her torture. Her calculations had already shown that the amount she could thus realize, plus the cash Johnny had insisted he would raise against his own company, would more than cover the ransom demand. Between them, all the family could buy Frankie's freedom; and, if asked, they gladly, unhesitatingly would do so. Gina knew this as surely as she knew the sun would rise tomorrow. Yet how could she permit it? How could she allow them to give so much, to mortgage all they owned? How could she let anyone accept one shred of the responsibility which was wholly hers? For it was her actions, hers alone, her vendetta against Ugo Balbo which had wrought this horror, which, in three days time, whatever course of action she took, would shatter irreparably the familiar existence of all those whom she held most dear. Gina Rossi had been the sole author of her own family's jeopardy.

This was the guilt which was crushing her.

On the fifth morning she phoned Phoenix. Johnny said Paola was going to be okay. Gina prayed that it was the truth. In return she said everything was under control, that little Frankie soon would be home safe and sound. She lacked the courage to speak to Filipo, because it was his voice which most haunted her, the words he had spoken to his sister the first night they shared their room above Mrs Ponti's grocery store on Broome Street; in reply to Paola's whispered 'Are you frightened, Filipo?' his answer 'Of course not, Gina's with us.'

524

The hours bled remorselessly away.

Haggard with grief Gina wandered the apartment. She couldn't remain still, yet there was nowhere to go. She ached for activity, but there was nothing left to do. Never, never in all her years had she felt so useless, so defenceless, so stripped of every vestige of her capabilities.

In her office she stood before the wall of floor-to-ceiling bookshelves staring at the rank of her journals. Twenty-four volumes, from the first, faded, cracked-spined notebook she had kept beneath her sacking pillow in the hut in Baremo, to the latest morocco-covered volume, hand-made by a London bookbinder. So much of her life there: a sepia postcard of Ellis Island, a 1938 street plan of Manhattan, a work card from the Madison Employment Bureau, a pink dance ticket from the Starlight Room, the Lady's first menu, a duty roster from the Rainbow Corner Club, a photograph of a group of mothers and their children in front of the Grange's entrance, a Red Cross travel permit to Rome, a royalty statement for *The Lady's Cookbook*, a Rossi Taverns' franchise application, the interior decorator's sketches for this apartment, an English newspaper advertisement for Robert Fallon's novel *The Last Summer*, a $10 gambling chip scripted 'the Silver Lady'. All this, and more. Gina's hopes, dreams, plans. Her past and her present, all the foundations of her future.

She reached up, took down that final volume. The effort seemed to sap her strength and a wave of dizziness swayed her. The journal opened in her hands. Dazed, she stared at the blank pages, a field of white, a nothingness into which she was falling. You need sleep, her inner voice warned. You must sleep. I don't have time, she retaliated. I have to phone the family. I need them so much. Only they can save little Frankie now.

Gina peered at the journal. What was it? Where had it come from? She bit her lip, hard, striving to drive clarity to her brain. She gripped the book, clung to it as if to the edge of a precipice, her legs dangling above a bottomless pit. But the solidity beneath her fingers was crumbling, breaking away; her hands were slipping, slipping. She cried aloud, 'Help me!' And then the pent-up pressure of the past days burst through the dam of her self-command. Nausea rushed upon her, the sickness of exhaustion saturating her blood, drowning her stamina. She hung suspended in space for one moment more.

The book fell from her grasp, went slow-motion spinning into the void.

It was the final thing Gina saw before she collapsed unconscious on the floor.

There was a striding ringing, an insistent clamouring which threatened to split open her head. She didn't know at first if she really heard it or if it was a dream. When she opened her eyes all she saw was a thick, cloudy mass. Concentrating to focus it was moments before she realized the mass was less than an inch from her face, and it was a full minute before she identified it as the carpet.

With a supreme effort Gina sat upright. The room was bathed in twilight. The ringing had stopped. Reaching out to the bookshelves she pulled herself to her unsteady feet. This brought a flood of blood to her brain and she briefly feared she was going to be sick. The surge passed however and her senses began to return. Thirst was the first need to assail her. On legs as weak as jelly she made her way to the bathroom. The glass of water she gulped tasted like lead, but its chill sharpened her grip on reality. What time was it? How long had she been unconscious? She looked into the mirror. And almost recoiled. Deep hollows shadowed her eyes, accentuated the whiteness of the tight-drawn skin of her cheekbones. Cracks scored her lips which were pale to the point of translucence, taut to the hard lines of her jaw. Her hair was dull and tangled and where it grew from her temple there was the sickly discolouration of a bruise which, she guessed, had been caused when she collapsed against the bookshelves. 'God, what a mess,' she whispered.

Swiftly filling the washbasin with hot water she soaped and doused her face several times, dried it, then pulled a comb through her locks. She didn't really look any better, but felt less like death, a fraction more capable of facing the decision she had to make. She started for the sitting-room.

Someone was knocking, banging, on the door.

The sound startled her, its urgency causing her heart to jump. Gathering her still-tattered nerves she went quickly through the apartment to the lobby where the heavy-fisted knocking continued. Gina opened the door, and recognized the hall porter in his purple and gold uniform. 'Charles,' she said. 'What on earth . . .'

'Miss Rossi. Are you all right?'

'Of course. You . . .'

'I called you a few minutes ago. Your phone rang and rang. I was sure you were home as I hadn't seen you leave. Forgive me intruding but I thought you might be indisposed. Ill. Are you?' He peered concernedly at Gina's face.

'No, I said so.' Her tone was sharp, an echo of her discordant emotions. 'Actually, you're partly right,' she added more calmly, 'I did have a severe headache. I was lying down in the rear bedroom. It's cool and quiet in there. I suppose that's why I didn't hear the phone. I'm fine now though. Thank you for your concern. Now, I have some important calls to make.'

'There's someone to see you.'

Gina already had the door half-closed, wasn't sure she'd heard correctly. 'Here?' she queried.

'That's why I rang. Your visitor was most insistent. Ordered me to come up. Refused to take no for an answer.'

A small dart of fear pierced Gina and her thoughts raced. Again the question, 'What time is it? And what day is it? Had the deadline for Frankie's ransom passed?

'Shall I show her up, Miss Rossi?'

'What?' Too much was happening in her head. Panic was rising from the debris of her decimated reasoning. 'Her?'

'Mrs Alicia Cornell.'

That couldn't have been what he said. He hadn't really spoken, had he? Gina stared at his face, and though it remained waxenly inanimate she imagined she saw the lips move and repeat the name. A chill knifed her. She was caught in a blizzard of memories. No, her inner voice cried, this can't be happening. And then she heard the sound of the elevator doors. The porter glanced around, his features breaking into surprise. He looked quickly back to Gina. 'Miss Rossi. I'm sorry. I asked the lady to wait.'

The chill which had gripped Gina deepened. Like a child believing there is something dark approaching through the night, she sensed rather than heard the person in the hall. She said hoarsely, 'That's all right, Charles. Please, show her in.' Then she was retreating into the sitting-room, to stand at its centre, her chest full of drums, her mind incapable of coherent thought.

She was frozen there in suspended time.

The woman was small, little more than five feet, yet her

sudden presence seemed to dominate the wide room. Her severe black coat, almost to her ankles, was buttoned to the throat. The cane upon which she leaned, the purse hanging from her wrist, and her half-veiled hat also were black. Her face, with broad, Slavonic cheekbones and wide mouth, was darkly fissured by the years, yet it held no sign of weakening antiquity; rather it was carved with a timeless strength, a determination which was reflected in the penetrating gaze of the eyes.

Gina felt that gaze reached into her very soul. Before this tiny woman she shrank. In an instant she had been thrown back across an age to stand, wearing a shapeless brown smock and mobcap, rag pads tied to her knees, amid the opulence of the Cornell apartment where she glimpsed this woman beyond massive, mahogany doors.

The woman moved forward, the dry rustle of her petticoats like the stirring of dead leaves. She halted some ten feet from Gina, placed both her leather-gloved hands on the top of the cane, and, settling her stance, said, 'Good evening, Miss Rossi.' Her voice was deep and gravelly, but with no trace of the foreignness that was in her features. 'As your porter has already informed you, I am Alicia Cornell.'

So stunned was Gina she almost said reflexively, 'Pleased to meet you.' For nothing else came to mind. Her brain had been shocked into blackness.

Alicia glanced briefly about the apartment. Her expression registered no opinion, but when she again looked at Gina her eyes seemed less hard than a moment ago, so that a fraction of Gina's anxiety retreated and she even wondered if she should invite the woman to a chair. Alicia, however, forestalled the decision. 'I shall take up no more of your time than is absolutely necessary,' she said. 'There are only two days left until the end of the week.'

Gina's pulse once more jumped. She thought simultaneously, So the ransom deadline hasn't passed, and, Why should she mention the date? Her reason was now in tatters. It was torn asunder when Alicia said:

'You need one million dollars by Saturday.'

Gina took an involuntary step backward.

'I fail to see why you should be so surprised,' rasped Alicia. 'You know as well as I that in our business, in this town there are no secrets. Information is sold, bartered, stolen. How else would we survive?' She gave a small, matter-of-fact shrug.

For a swirling moment of abstraction Gina glimpsed an iota of fellowship in the words 'our business'. But the thought fled as swiftly as it had appeared, and in the brief vacuity that followed she mentally shook herself. At last she found her voice, said stiffly, 'Mrs Cornell, I have no idea why you are here, nor do I understand what you are talking about. I . . .'

'Ah,' interposed Alicia, 'you do have the power of speech. I was beginning to think this was going to be an entirely one-sided discussion.' The comment was flat, not sarcastic, merely a statement of fact. Before Gina could muster a response, the black-clad woman went on, 'As I was saying, it is impossible for anyone to attempt to raise a million dollars in this city without sending loud whispers around our walls. You should not, therefore, blame Mister Prentiss. He has done his utmost to be discreet.'

Prentiss! He'd been trawling for Gina's million. Her heart lurched with gratitude; and self-recrimination. She'd underestimated his loyalty and persistence. Should she have trusted him with the truth? If he'd known why she needed the money might he have made that crucial extra effort to succeed?

As if reading her mind Alicia remarked, 'Given a few more days I'm sure he would have done it. However, the end of this week is an impossible deadline.'

A repeated denial sprang to Gina's lips. But it remained unvoiced. Facing this small, dark woman she finally began to tighten a grasp on rationality. Control, she ordered herself. Get your nerves and your reason under control. Remember, your only concern is Frankie. She said calmly, 'Mrs Cornell, I'd be grateful if you'd come to the point.'

The tone of the remark apparently took Alicia by surprise, but then her features seemed to relax minutely with approbation of Gina's show of strength. As if settling herself, she leaned her weight further onto the cane and said, 'Why you need such a sum, so urgently, I'm not sure. However, since Mister Prentiss began his quest I have been making enquiries. At first, you see, I thought you were planning some swift and important coup. A takeover perhaps of some hotel or restaurant chain which I might have my own sights upon. It would not have surprised me. I have, of course, watched your rise with interest, particularly in recent years. You were the first competitor to cause me concern for as long as I can remember.' A ghost of a smile moved behind her eyes and she paused for several moments so that Gina was prompted to wonder if she was rambling. That thought was dispelled however when Alicia spoke again.

The smile had gone, and now her voice was deeply serious. 'But you are not seeking a million for some sudden business move. Of that I am certain. You have a darker, personal motive. Please,' she raised a black-gloved hand when she saw the anxiety pale Gina's face, 'don't be alarmed. I do not know your secret, whatever it is. But my investigators have picked up shadowy reports, a tenuous thread leading to the organization which has been extending its influence into our industry for many years. Yes, you understand who I mean. And the rumour is, you owe a debt to those people. A debt which must be paid by the end of this week.'

Gina's mouth now was so dry she felt she wouldn't be able to speak even if she could find something to say. Could this woman really have discovered that information? The answer, Gina knew, was yes. All Alicia had said about there being no secrets was true. Every company in the city, the Rossi Corporation included, had its means of gathering hearsay, innuendo, covert gossip, from paying a hotel chef for a coded recipe to bribing a City Hall official for a confidential planning report; and from all the furtive reaping and winnowing it was inevitable that some grains of personal as well as commercial revelation should come to light. How much of Gina Rossi's present bane had been gleaned?

'I assure you,' Alicia said, 'that's all I know. Nevertheless, it doesn't take a great deal of imagination to link the rumour of your debt with Mister Prentiss's quest for one million dollars. Nor is it necessary to speculate on why you should be willing to accede to the demand. Obviously, the people to whom you are indebted have some very definite means of ensuring your financial co-operation – as well as your silence. And for that I sympathize with you. On the other hand,' she shifted her stance, braced herself and her tone, 'I have no personal interest whatsoever in how you have brought about your predicament. My only concern, my reason for being here, is professional:'

Gina was confused, not sure whether she was afraid or indignant. She said crisply, 'You still haven't come to the point.'

'Do you, or do you not, owe one million dollars?'

The abrupt demand took Gina aback, so that she couldn't

answer immediately. Then without any inflection she said, 'You seem to have made up your own mind.'

Alicia gave a small sigh which might have been satisfaction, though when she spoke her voice was briskly unemotional. 'I will have the money, in cash, delivered here tomorrow morning.'

Gina gasped, 'You can't be serious!'

'Miss Rossi, please stop these foolish outbursts. Frankly, they're a waste of time. Precious time.'

Gina felt her face flush, the authoritative rebuke again jolting her back toward being a chambermaid. Fighting the disconcertion, she laid firm control on her response. 'Very well, supposing I do need the sum you have mentioned, why on earth should you be be prepared to pay it?' But even as she voiced the question, the answer sprang into her head, and before the old woman could speak she exclaimed, 'The Rossi Corporation! That's why you're here. To snatch my company for a million dollars.' Her anger reared. 'And if I don't accept your offer, what will happen? What will you do? Abandon me to what you suppose will be my fate, the retribution of whoever it is you think might have some hold over me? Well thank you, Mrs Cornell, but no thank you. You weren't invited here, now I'd be pleased if you'd leave. I'd sooner . . .'

'On the contrary.'

Gina's retaliation faltered.

Alicia said, 'I have no wish to acquire your company. Rather, I intend you to take over the running of mine.'

Nothing happened inside Gina's head. It was as if all ability to form thought, let alone words, had fled. She couldn't even move, was riveted to the spot facing a small, black-garbed woman leaning two-handed on a cane. All she could do was listen as the woman went on:

'Miss Rossi, you are aware of my history, that my father was a penniless immigrant who opened his first canvas-built saloon in California during the gold rush. I won't bore you by recounting the years, almost half a century, I have spent in building on the foundation my father laid down. Suffice to say, I have permitted nothing and no one to stand in my way. What it is important that you do understand is that all my efforts, all my sacrifices, have been dedicated not only to the survival of my business, but also, imperatively, to its remaining in my family's control.' Having stressed this statement Alicia took several deep breaths as if at last succumbing to fatigue. Nevertheless, she did not look toward any chair and after a moment continued:

'When my son, Howard, was born I assumed that upon my death he would ensure the continuance. But, as he advanced into his teens, I realized it would not be so. As you are probably aware, there is a . . . ' she hesitated before saying the word ' . . . deficiency in Howard. Perhaps it was in him at birth, inherited from my husband who was similarly . . . juvenile. Or perhaps it developed as he grew. But, for sure, he has never had the determination or the ambition to take over the responsibility of the West Corporation. I know that when I am gone, should Howard assume control, it would be only a matter of time before he, at best, sold the company, or, at worst, had it taken from him. Miss Rossi, I intend neither of those possibilities to come to pass.'

If Gina had entertained any doubts about Alicia Cornell's stoicism they were now laid thoroughly to rest. The resolve in the old woman's face was hewn from granite. During the speech Gina had heard all the words, yet her mind had still been locked on Alicia's prime declaration: 'I have no wish to acquire your company. Rather I intend you to take over the running of mine.' And though there were myriad questions tumbling in her head, what she asked was, 'Why me?'

Alicia replied, 'Because there is no other.'

'You expect me to administer your company in return for one million dollars? The idea is preposterous.'

'If you believed that,' rejoined Alicia, 'you wouldn't still be listening to me.'

Stung by this, Gina clipped, 'I really can't see any point in prolonging this conversation. You were right, my time is precious. So, if you'll excuse me . . . ' She began to move.

'The contract has been drawn up,' Alicia said in her flat, harsh voice, at last shifting her grip from the cane to open the purse on her wrist and extract a folded, grey document. Gina had been halted by the blunt statement and she automatically reached out to accept the contract as it was proffered.

Alicia went on, 'It is brief. Basically it states that upon receipt of one million dollars you will assume the role of chief executive of the combined West-Rossi Corporations.' To Gina's incredulous stare she continued, 'Yes, you will have complete control, immediately. I shall not stand in your way.

That is the price – apart from the money – which will be my side of our bargain. Additionally the agreement stipulates that your family will retain their existing percentages of the new corporation. Howard's one-tenth will remain in trust – a necessity, I realized years ago – and be administered by my attorneys. You and I will hold one-third each. You will assume full control of my shares upon my death. The latter event, I am assured by my physicians, will occur within the next two years.'

Two years?

Gina would become the head of the combined corporations in two years? Or less?

She stared unbelievingly at Alicia Cornell, mentally rerunning all that had been said. The words formed, a tide-race shot through with recall of the ransom deadline, little Frankie's safety, the Rossis' future. And amidst the swirling current Gina felt herself rising on a surge of triumph. This woman needs me, she thought. That is why she's here. Once she used her omnipotence to banish me from her son's life. Now only I can ensure the survival of that which she holds most dear – her family business.

A lightheadedness of unholy joy dizzied her. Full circle, she exulted. The ultimate irony.

And yet?

She faced Alicia; looked into those dark, hard eyes. And saw? Defeat, yes. But something more. Something which made her celebration falter. A reflection. At first far off, but advancing, becoming clearer. Until it flamed, bright and unmistakable. A mirror-image of Gina's own victory. She didn't understand. Now she stared uncomprehendingly at the woman before her. The question rose again: Why me? And why should she give me so much? How will that ensure the continuance of . . . West? Cornell?

Gina bit her lip, striving to see the total image, to find the one answer which would fuse the fractured picture. It was there. She could almost see it. Then it reared. She gasped aloud, and her mind recoiled.

Alicia said, 'There is a final clause to the contract. It states, irrevocably, that the entire agreement becomes null and void, that total control of the company – regardless of the consequences – will revert instantly to my attorneys should you and my son, Howard, ever be divorced.'

39

Gina sat on a bench in Bryant Park. It was five-thirty a.m., the morning following Alicia Cornell's visit. The first faint grey smudge of dawn was touching the sky. Dew was heavy on the grass and on the trees rusting toward winter. A veil of mist hung across the street so that the surrounding city was invisible. Nothing moved. No one was to be seen. It was as if Gina was utterly alone at the end of the world. Yet soon they would come, people, from near and far: the pretty girl from West Virginia, the hit of her high-school play, knowing she will soon be a Broadway star; the young man from England, coming to the Village where he is sure he will write a fine novel; the truck driver from Oklahoma, convinced that this is where he will build his taxi company; the family from Germany, thinking hard work and their pastry recipes will secure their future; the spinster school teacher from Ohio, determined to snatch a piece of life; the petty thief, escaping from across the river, swearing he'll never be caught again. They will all come, with their hopes and dreams. Some will stay. Some will succeed. Many will return to whence they came.

It's the believing that's important, thought Gina. You have to believe that what you're doing is right, is for the best. You have to know it as surely as you know day follows night. For it isn't the brave who win; it is those who have faith.

Her collar was up and her hands were in her pockets. She sat this way for a long time. Then, far off in the river narrows, a steamer lowed. Footsteps echoed distantly. A water wagon trundled by. The mist was lifting. The city slowly began to fill with light.

Gina stood and walked away.

White-hot noon desert. The dirt track to the Nevada ghost town lying like an endless ribbon across the wilderness beneath the furnace sky. Nothing breaking the merciless landscape except the scant Joshua trees and skeletal patches of mesquite shimmering like a mirage behind the curtain of heat.

Gina halted the limousine, switched off the motor and climbed out into the blistering air. Within seconds sweat was plastering her hair to her neck and brow, coursing inside her blouse. Shielding her eyes she scanned the horizon.

At first the car seemed unreal, a silent black blur projected onto the liquid screen where the track flowed into the sky. Then it grew larger, taking shape, its windshield blinding in the sun. It drummed across the compacted rock and sand, swaying and jolting, laying a smoke trail of dust. As it came closer, its engine hum growing louder, it slowed until Gina could see the two men inside. When it was within fifty feet it pulled to the side and swayed to a halt.

Gina walked forward.

The black car's passenger door opened and a tall man in charcoal grey business suit, white shirt and spotted maroon silk tie, his pearl Homburg level and straight, ducked out, straightened and strode toward Gina carrying Frank John Alfred Sabato. As he approached Gina the man said, 'Good afternoon, Miss Rossi.'

Gina replied, 'Good afternoon.'

Frankie called, 'Auntie Gina! Wanna walk!'

Gina held out the pigskin case.

The man took it, set Frank on his feet.

Frank ran a couple of paces to Gina, who swept him into her arms, held him, held him very close, her cheek pressed to his, her heartbeat thumping against his heartbeat.

The man had opened and closed the case. 'I won't bother to count it, Miss Rossi. I'm sure it's all here.'

'It is,' she said. She held back from Frankie, looked into his cheery face. 'Are you okay?'

'I watched television,' he enthused.

The man said, 'He's a cute kid. And bright.'

Gina turned and walked away.

Frankie swung around, shouted, ''Bye!'

The man chuckled, 'So long, son.'

Gina put Frankie in the limousine at her side.

Soon there was only settling dust on the desert.

PART FIVE

The time after

1950

40

The day was very still: not a breath of breeze stirred the tangled, head-high maquis flanking the rocky track beneath the noon-white Corsican sun. No sound, save the incessant drone of insects. No movement, save the infinitesimal drift of a lone shred of cloud across the cobalt sky.

Suddenly a cry. A crashing amidst the undergrowth and half-a-dozen swarthy men burst onto the track. They wore battered boots, rough trousers, dusty shirts open over sweating chests. Two had bandoliers of bullets on their shoulders; all carried pistols. They paused, glancing about, listening. The man in the lead waved his gun toward the far side of the track and as swiftly as they had appeared they ran and plunged from sight.

A voice shouted, 'Cut!' and a score of people broke from their frozen stances to check cameras, exchange remarks, swat flies, gulp soft drinks and do all the other things they had already done six times while the bandit gang returned to the track to take instructions from the assistant director.

'As I was asking,' continued the young, male English magazine reporter who'd arrived from the French mainland this morning, 'what brings you to the island?'

Gina reached up and adjusted the sunshade above the canvas chair on which she was sitting. 'Just a brief vacation,' she answered. 'Mister Felix Gilbert of RKO – his company produced the show which launched the Silver Lady a year ago – knew I was in Rome and kindly invited me over to watch the filming for a few days.'

The reporter scribbled. 'And might you be taking the opportunity to investigate the local restaurant trade?'

Gina smiled. 'At the moment my priority is Italy. I've spent the past three months there finalizing our plans for what will be our first European subsidiary. Your publication will soon be receiving a detailed press release from the office of Mister John Sabato, whose vending-machine company recently joined our organization and who is to be our vice-president in charge of overseas development.' Gina watched as the young man wrote, added, 'You may say that Mister Sabato's appointment is part of a continuing policy of expansion and a further strengthening of family commitment to our company.' To the reporter's quizzically raised eyebrow she explained, 'Mister Sabato is the husband of my sister, Paola, to whom I'm writing this letter.' She tapped the pad resting on a book on her knees.

The reporter nodded. 'As I said, commerce isn't at all my field – I'm only here for a story on the re-shooting of these scene for the movie – however, I'm sure our business editor will be most interested in all you've said. I hope you'll enjoy . . . ' He broke off, seeing someone exit from a trailer. 'There's the producer I have to interview. Please, excuse me . . . ' He hurried away.

For a while Gina watched the technicians and actors waiting for another take, then she returned to her letter.

'The photograph of little Frankie was gorgeous. Not so little though! My, hasn't he grown in a few months? I'm so looking forward to seeing him – and, of course, everyone else – at Christmas. I'd love to have come home sooner, but Sybil and David's one-year anniversary party for the new mums' home is going to be such an affair, I really couldn't refuse their invitation.

'Speaking of S. Lowell née De Belvere, the 'old girl' has joined the English Liberal Party (apparently a bit like the old pre-1946 Progressive Party in the States – everybody's heard of them but nobody has met anyone who ever voted for them. Trust Sybil to choose a bandwagon which far from bowling along requires shoving every inch of the way). Naturally, her intention is to stand for Parliament. She's certainly 'a bit of a face' – as she herself says – in Britain, but I'm sure her views are just too advanced to win many votes. Fighting on behalf of birth control and women's rights is controversial enough, but favouring legalized abortion is political suicide. (Though I love her dearly, I don't think I'll ever be able to agree with her on that issue. On the other hand, I'll never again read the newspaper that recently branded her 'Satan's Sister'. How hateful people can be!)

'Still, David is always wonderfully supportive, and I dare say come the next General Election he'll be pasting VOTE FOR posters with his wife's picture all over the countryside.'

Gina looked up as someone shouted, 'Quiet!' another voice called, 'Action,' and the bandits again dashed through their routine. Five minutes and she resumed writing.

'It's quite interesting here seeing some of the technicalities of movie-making, but the actual filming really is rather boring. I am enjoying the break, though. The days are delightfully lazy, and in the evenings I go into Ajaccio with Felix Gilbert and one or two others for a quiet dinner. Last night we were joined by Faith Domergue (the new "discovery" of Mister Hughes), who's playing the lead. She's a very pleasant person – and looks a lot like you now your hair is longer.

'Max mentioned H. Hughes in his recent letter; rumour has it he's bought more land in Las Vegas. Max thinks we should increase the hotel accommodation of the Silver Lady. He says the Desert Inn, which opened four months ago with 310 rooms (everyone said so many was crazy), hasn't yet had an empty bed. Looks like we'll have to find the money from somewhere. And Harry will have to get used to paying our showroom headliners much higher salaries.

'As you probably know, Harry was in Rome last week – he's looking into setting up offices for the talent agency in all the capital cities over here. He'd been in London for a few days and brought me a copy of Fallon's new book. It's non-fiction, an account of his experiences in Europe during the last year of the war. He's made it into a story about the scout car he travelled in and virtually lived in the whole of the time from D-Day to the fall of Berlin. It really is a fine book. It's been nominated for the Hawthorn Prize.'

Gina moved her writing pad to look down at the volume upon which it had been resting. A brown cover with white lettering. *The Long Road Home* by Robert Fallon. Beneath this title, the reproduction of a cracked, ragged-edged, black and white snapshot: the author in uniform, leaning against the door of a scout car whose battered flank bore the faintly discernible stencilled registration Z 9174 JILL.

She covered it again with her pad.

'Harry also saw Tony Nevada in London – topping the bill at the Palladium. He made it his business to "accidentally" bump into one of Nevada's entourage so that he could ask about Cassie. Reportedly, nothing's changed. She still never leaves the Beverly Hills house, is, apparently, uncaring of all Nevada's much-publicized affairs, even accepts his girlfriends at the house while she stays in the staff quarters. That can't be love. It's more a terrible sort of sickness. But I'm sure no one can cure Cass except herself. She's in my prayers every night.

'On a more cheerful note, remember Sergeant Roscoe Tucker, who helped so much to get the Grange under way? Sybil heard via one of her old officer chums that he was running a small hotel near Loch Lomond. She phoned him right away. He was delighted to hear from her. He'd spent the remainder of his entire army career in exile at the depot on the north Scottish coast, wasn't discharged until last year. But while he'd been up there he'd met a local girl. The day he became a civilian they were married, and a short while later they bought the hotel – plus a hundred acres of woodland and the fishing rights to a mile of river. (I dread to imagine how many crates of U.S. Army nylons, suspender clips and soft toilet tissue provided the wherewithal.) Anyhow, Roscoe and his wife will be at Sybil and David's celebration next month, and I'm looking forward enormously to our reunion. And who knows where the re-acquaintance might lead? You know, once the Italian subsidiary is off and running, I think Britain will be next to the starting line.

'Well, it looks as if these bandits are going to dash through the brush one more time before everyone breaks for lunch. I think this afternoon I'll go back to the hotel and work on my accounts – far more exciting than movie-making.

'Take care of yourselves. Lots of hugs and kisses to Frankie. See you in a couple of weeks.'

Gina signed with love; closed her pad. As she slipped her pen into her purse, there came the familiar shouted instructions, a hushed pause, followed by the half-dozen men bursting out of the now somewhat battered-looking undergrowth, miming their looking and listening routine, then running and crashing from sight. 'Cut! Much better. Print it.'

Thank goodness for that, thought Gina, her relief echoed by the sudden relaxation of the entire crew who now began to gossip and head for the mobile toilets and catering truck.

The bandits reappeared, laughing and batting thorns and burrs from their clothes. After a brief, good-natured banter with the assistant director one of the six broke away to walk toward Gina. His black curls were plastered to his deeply sun-burned brow; sweat rivuleted his strong throat, soaked his dusty shirt. His dark forearms were bloodily raked from the constant charges through the maquis. Striding forward he stuck his pistol in his waistband. 'Hey, Sis. What do you think?'

'I think you could use a bath,' replied Gina.

Filipo sniffed his shirt, grinned. 'Authenticity.' Nodding toward the queue forming at the lunch counter he asked, 'Shall I bring you something over?'

Gina flinched. 'No thanks. I sampled chuck wagon fish stew yesterday. I'd rather drive all the way back to the hotel. Their menu isn't a lot better, but at least the ingredients are dead.'

Filipo laughed. 'Well, shooting's over tomorrow. How about we meet for dinner at Rome's ritziest spot? I promise I'll change my shirt, maybe even my socks. Date?'

Smiling, Gina answered, 'My pleasure.'

Filipo planted his hands on her chair's arms, bent and kissed her forehead. Straightening he said, 'More mine.' He stepped back, winked, turned and walked away.

Gina watched him with great affection.

Felix Gilbert's voice said, 'Still leaving tonight?'

Gina glanced around. 'Yes, for Rome.'

'Then immediately to England?'

'No. I'll wait for Filipo. The decision you give him tomorrow isn't going to mortally wound him, but he'll be nursing his hurt for a while. I'll be around to share it, if needs be.'

Felix Gilbert reflectively rubbed his jaw. 'Are you sure you won't reconsider? As I've already said, he's worked hard this past year. And he shows a lot of promise. Maybe he'll never be a great actor, but I'm sure, given a couple of breaks, plus the influence you could wield in the industry, he could be a star.'

Gina rejoined, 'A handsome head, you mean. With nobody interested in what's inside it. His picture on the cover of fan magazines, his name in lights on movie-house marquees. But for how long? Until the fashion for Latinos passes. Or until he requires plastic surgery to keep his youth? No, Felix, I will not reconsider. Our family does not need a shooting star, no matter how bright. What it needs is the strong, steady light of endurance. Filipo, eventually, will see that. You will please tell him his term of employment with you is at an end, and will not be extended.' Gathering her purse, book and writing pad, she stood. 'And then you may make a deal, on your own terms, with Harry Dix for a two-picture contract with the young female singer whom Mister Howard Hughes has been pressuring you to sign for the past six months.' The RKO producer remained mute. Gina said, 'Thanks for inviting me here. It's been most relaxing, and interesting. Look, someone over there is beckoning you. I'll see you again, Felix.' She swung away along the track.

Up ahead the maquis gave way to sparser scrub, then to almost barren, sun-scorched earth. Gina paused, shielded her eyes and looked across the wilderness. Far, far off a lone figure moved in the shimmering landscape. Gina felt the sun's heat penetrating her cotton dress. She watched a raven circling; imagined she heard a wild dog cry. Memories tugged her.

She pushed them aside as laughter came from the cluster of trucks and trailers where Filipo was standing with his fellow bandits. She studied him. He'll make a fine lawyer, she thought. And, one day, a fine head of our company. And his son after him. And all the following sons. All of Poppa's blood. All Rossis.

She continued her walk toward a small, dusty blue car. Reaching it she was turned around by the hurrying footfalls of the young magazine reporter. As he came up to her he said, catching his breath, 'I couldn't let you leave without thanking you for answering my questions.'

Gina responded, 'You're welcome.'

He opened the car's door for her and she climbed in, found the key in her purse and pushed it into its slot in the dashboard. The young man said, 'Have a good trip.'

Gina smiled. 'I'll try.' She switched on the motor, pushed the gear lever into position. Glancing up she said, 'Goodbye, for now.'

The young man stepped back. 'Goodbye, Mrs Cornell.'